THE SHIMMERING THING SHAPED ITSELF
into a hazy form, indistinct at first, and then, slowly, into
a great white owl.

"By the Fates!" Luciana dropped to her knees on the
floor. She pressed her hand to her heart, fearing news
of another death. But then reason seeped in. Owls bringing news of death were mortal, and visitations came
through normal means of flight. What could this mean?
She paused. "Can it be?"

She stretched out her hand. The owl's beak opened
and snapped shut. There was no sound, but an unnatural
wind rose up and swirled around the room. The owl
stepped closer, its eyes piercing, mesmerizing.

Longing filled her heart. Luciana reached out.

The bird grabbed Luciana's finger.

Luciana bit back a cry and tried to pull away. The
ring on her left forefinger slid down, as though the owl
pulled it.

"No!" Luciana cried and grabbed at it. The bird
hopped away, dropping the ring on the carpet between
them, then did nothing as Luciana slowly reached out
and retrieved the ring. It was the crest of her position
as *Araunya di Cayesmengro*—Alessandra's title.

"Alessa? Is it you? Are you really Alessandra? Speak
if you can!"

The wraith bird clacked its beak, but made no sound.

Luciana leaned closer. "Alessandra, I will end your
suffering, but you must help! Speak to me. Try!"

MAGIC'S SILKEN SNARE

SNARE

Silken Magic #1

ElizaBeth Gilligan

DAW BOOKS, INC.

DONALD A. WOLLHEIM, FOUNDER

375 Hudson Street, New York, NY 10014

ELIZABETH R. WOLLHEIM
SHEILA E. GILBERT
PUBLISHERS

http://www.dawbooks.com

First Printing, April 2003
1 2 3 4 5 6 7 8 9

DAW TRADEMARK REGISTERED
U.S. PAT. OFF. AND FOREIGN COUNTRIES
—MARCA REGISTRADA
HECHO EN U.S.A.

PRINTED IN THE U.S.A.

To my brother, Dana, and the siblings everywhere who share our lives from cradle into the adventures of life—our partners, cohorts, the "evil menaces" and pranksters who sustain us through our joys and sorrows—you are remembered daily in our hearts, our dreams, our lives.

I cannot allow four sisters of the heart to also go unnoted—Phyllis Karr, Wanda Haight, Lisa Hawkins, and Lucia Fitzmorris Woods.

INTRODUCTION

I'M one of those writers who hate the old axiom "Write what you know." First, because when you're dedicated to writing speculative fiction there has to be some point where you take a leap into the infinite unknown and, second, I've always had these rather odd interests. Ultimately, however, it was those odd interests that got me writing this book.

I grew up a multigenerational military brat and, according to my last count, have attended more than twenty schools. It's not easy fitting in . . . especially when you're the kind of kid who likes reading. I developed an affinity for the "Gypsies" for they, too, moved, seemingly aimlessly, around the world, never exactly fitting in but determined to be who and what they were. There was an honor in that that resonated deeply with me.

There is a wealth of rumor and imaginings about the Rromani, starting with the name outsiders called them: "Gypsies." (I use the double "r" here because it is a modern use to keep themselves from being mistaken as Romanian, but in the book I use only the single "r" as is proper at the time the story takes place.) I was once told by a respected Rom on an Internet list that no "Tatcho Rom (no *real* Rom) would have anything to do with fantasy, elves and dragons" . . . because they were stuff and nonsense just as is much of what is rumored to be so about their people. I wanted to write something that would make him change his mind.

Another of my fascinations is herbalism, which I backed into through the door of studying poison and poisoning techniques. As you might have guessed, I was mightily fascinated by the Borgias and the various court poisoners over the earlier centuries. With my studies in herbalism came early medicine, midwifery, folkways, and magic.

This book began as a challenge to roll a number of interests into one project and has become a passion.

Tyrrhia is purely mythical and, as the map shows, is actually a geographically and, thus politically, much larger and stronger Sicily. I took my timeline for this seventeenth century novel back to approximately 400 AD with the death of the great Visigoth King, Alaric. Legend says that his bereaved crew stopped in Sicily, after sacking Rome once again, diverted the course of a river, and buried the King with his plunder. My fictional kingdom is funded by the discovery of that plunder some generations later.

As in reality, Tyrrhia (Sicily) was the melting pot of the Old World. The diasporas and witch-hunts sent Jews, Romani, Huguenots, and other folk to her shores in search of tolerance. As Tyrrhia now had the resources and geographical bounty to allow settlement, the religion and philosophy also changed and found favor.

In researching this book, I have found a way to tie in my tangible pleasures of painting silk by building upon the silk trade which actually existed in Sicily. As a student philosopher, I have enjoyed developing a viable political and theological system nestled in the bosom of the Roman Catholic Church—which, with all of its great gifts and faults, has figured significantly in the development of mankind.

To capture the ambience of Tyrrhia, the book is written in three languages: English (for the vast part), Romani, and Italian. I have relied heavily upon my personal library on the Romani and their language. I have learned much more than I can ever thank the Romani and non-Rom participants for at The Patrin Web Journal (http://www.geocities.com/Paris/5121/glossary.htm).

My husband of twenty years, Douglas, has lived in this world and agonized over it with me, supporting me at every step, as I developed Tyrrhia and this book. Without him, I don't know that I could ever have finished. My daughter, Brianna, learned to be a first reader and has become my office assistant so that I can focus more time on my writing. My son, Patrick, has provided the distractions which kept me from ever getting "too serious" or too lost in what I am doing.

Irene Radford has been a dear friend and valued critical reader who has gladly shared resources and endless quantities of patience. Raymond "Buzz" Nelson has been inordinately helpful in all matters of military history—from insignia, classic battles, and strategy to the various wild and woolly wars being fought during the period of my novel. Frank Lurz, Maestro di Scherma, Assistant Director of the Fencing Masters Training Program at San Jose State University, generously demonstrated many fencing techniques and advised me in the fight scenes. Adrienne Martine-Barnes and eluki bes shahar were invaluable in developing my concept. Mary Stella Flynn took copious notes during her vacation and helped research Sicily for me. I must also thank the Dream Weavers, my on-line writers' group—Brook and Julia West, Lois Gresh, Sverna Park, Catherine Asaro, Juleen Brantingham, and the late Jo Clayton—and the Word Spinners group, particularly Teresa Edgerton, Joy Oestreicher, Carolyn Hill, Christy Marx, Francesca Flynn, Jennifer Carson, and Kevin A. Murphy for their comments and guidance. A special thanks to Stephanie Pui-Min Law (*www.shadowscapes.com*) whose artistry gives images to the design of the Gypsy Silk Tarot Deck still in progress.

My thanks go to the good people at DAW Books who have brought my efforts to you and my agent, Carol McCleary. Sheila Gilbert helped me to realize so much more of my vision with her insightful editing and patience. Carol believed in me just as I started to wonder if I could ever make this happen and brought this book and Sheila together.

Finally, thank you, gentle reader, for making all these efforts worthwhile. Enjoy!

"A brave world, Sir, full of religion, knavery, and change: we shall shortly see better days."
—Aphra Behn

I

"Cloth'd in her virgin white integrity."
—John Donne

16 d'Aprile 1684

THE owl called. Despite the midnight hour, Luciana sat up, awake and restless. Owls did not often find their way so close to the main house of the Drago estates. The turmoil of fear and premonition tore at her gut.

She listened. Silence. It gave her no comfort. She cast aside layers of embroidered coverlets, drew back the heavy green velvet bed-curtains, and stepped out onto the cold oak floor. Her toes curled against the wood, and she shivered in the chill of the evening. She did not pause to put on the slippers placed beside her bed, nor to draw on the robe laid at arm's length over the back of a rose chaise.

When an owl first spoke to her, Luciana had been barely five. They found her father's body just beyond the encampment the next day. The owl came for her mother eight years later, but by that time Luciana had a *gadjé* stepfather with no time for silly young women and their premonitions.

Luciana had had a sense that something was very wrong all this day. She had enough to fret about with her estranged husband, the Duca di Drago, fighting the war against the Turks at the Morean front. She took no comfort in the luxuries of his estate, or the wealth from his properties and businesses during his absence. More still to worry over since her younger sister was spending the season at the White King's court looking for a husband.

The owl called again. With a growing sense of dread, Luciana ran to the doors of her balcony and pushed them open wide. She gulped against the sudden frigid breeze and stared out over the orchards. The gibbous moon made everything stark and colorless.

Seemingly from nowhere, an owl settled on the marble ledge and stared, unblinking, at her. It, like the moon, was a ghostly white.

The owl hooted.

Three cries. The warning of death.

The press of fear in her chest made it painful even to breathe. Luciana held out her right hand to the bird and watched it hop from the parapet to her wrist. Its talons cut deeply into her skin, but its pale yellow eyes held her.

"Who has died?" she asked.

The owl turned its head, blinking, as Luciana's dark hair blew into its face. It started to rise, beating its wings against the wind, but its talons never loosened on her wrist. It turned back, clicking its sharp beak, then grew still on her arm again.

She swallowed hard, struggling to keep her voice steady. "My husband? My sister? Or my grandmother?"

The bird blinked twice and rose to the wind, leaving tracks of blood on her arm as legacy of its visit.

Please! she prayed. She had lost so many dear to her already. She ran inside to her altar and knelt before it. Rubbing tears out of her eyes, Luciana lit the candle stubs from the flame of an oil lamp. Her hands shook. She took a box of gilt-inlaid cherrywood from the cupboard beneath the altar, unwound the protective silk, and spread her cards carefully.

Mingled with the all-consuming fear which made her heart thump painfully in her chest, she felt the draw of the familiar, the thrill of magic, the gentle sapping of her strength as she ran her fingers along the soft edges of the cards. Thinking of her messenger, Luciana selected one card. Only one. She held her breath as she turned the card. The *Pen of Ditale*—Sister of Thimbles. Alessandra!

A moan escaped her lips. How could Alessa be dead? It couldn't be true! But how could she ignore the signs? The owl never lied. Perhaps she misread the signs. She gathered her cards.

Another card fell from the mix, and, as it landed, glanced off a seam in the floorboards and fell faceup. *Pandlomengro*. The Tollgate. The Tower. Disaster. As though a sister's death were not enough! But disaster for whom? Was her sister not the only victim of some desperate intrigue?

Luciana hugged her arms to her stomach, overwhelmed with grief, fear, and the frustration of not knowing.

II

"If I had more time, I would write a shorter letter."
—Blaise Pascal

21 d'Aprile 1684

STEFANO, Duca di Drago, stared at Idala's words, too numb to react. His first thought, his only thought, was for Luciana and how she would receive the news of Alessandra's death. He was sick at heart, knowing the depth of her feelings for the sister who had been almost a daughter to her. News such as this could kill Luciana . . . or worse, knowing her temperament, get her killed. He let the letter fall to the desk and rose to pace.

Water dripped from the canvas seams of his tent as the rain continued to fall. While it gave cold comfort and made for damp housekeeping, at least the storm washed away the stink of gunpowder and blood. Stefano had had his fill of it for the past four years with his constant goings to and from the front.

At his king's command, Stefano lent his skills as a diplomat and occasional strategist to the allied armies of Poland, Austria, Venice, and Tyrrhia. His service had been honorable—and lengthy—beginning before these kingdoms with a common enemy considered an alliance. It had been a torment to leave his bride with their marriage still so new.

His call to replace a suddenly deceased ambassador

to Austria had strained their courtship and delayed their marriage. His father had drilled into him a strict sense of obligation and duty that served him well as one of the youngest members of the *Palantini*—the King's High Council.

That he was elder brother to the queen and had spent two years at the Palermo university with the king, earned him particular notice and high prestige, which in turn served the king well when there was need for a special envoy.

Stefano stalked irritably from one end of the tent to the other. In six years of marriage, he had never lived with Luciana for more than six months at a time, and they spent far greater stretches apart. Were their marriage intended to merely unite two noble families or some other arrangement, it would have been much easier on them both. But no, truth to tell, at least at one time, they had been very much in love.

The small chest sitting next to the scroll casings on his desk caught his eye. He reached out and fingered the clasp. This box seemed such a small thing to hold his love for Luciana. He dabbed at the splatters of rain on the maps scattered across his desk, then rolled each up and put it into its casing.

He sat, taking paper and quill. With deliberation, he did as he had done for the past year. He wrote the words of his heart, expressing his deep sorrow for Luciana's pain, how he longed to hold her, comfort her, and take care of all the troubling matters at hand.

Once done, Stefano reviewed the letter before him. In this correspondence, no poetry graced the pages, but the love was there, the tenderness was there. Its fate, however, was consignment to the chest with the other love letters written over the months since he had betrayed her. He was not worthy to send these epistles. It was not nobility of spirit that stopped him, though. He was afraid to send this letter and its companions. He feared she would reject them. She had reason enough.

The White King, Alban, had summoned the Palantini and other noble families to the capital for the birth of his heir, Dario Gian. A happy occasion, Stefano remembered, made all the more sweet by his reunion with Luciana. Alessandra, just sixteen, made her debut at court under her sister's watchful eye. They had played the devil to find time alone.

He remembered the long coach ride to the palazzo. Alessandra spent most of the trip peering out the curtained window and exclaiming on the wonders of the countryside, all the while oblivious to the suppressed passions of her traveling companions.

Word from the front dashed his hopes to remain in Tyrrhia with Luciana. The alliance of the kingdoms against the Turks was crumbling under the battle of egos among the generals. He was not long at the front before he received news from Luciana that she expected a child.

Over the years of their marriage, Luciana had formed a deep friendship with his sister and had been witness to the queen's succession of miscarriages. Two years before she delivered a child. Luciana spent weeks at the palazzo when the ague devastated the capital city. In her arms, little Princess Ortensia Marie took her last breath. With news of her own child to come, Luciana begged him to return home.

How many letters had he sent her, during her time of confinement, telling her that he must stay but another few days, not more than a week? It seemed duty to the crown and destiny plotted against them. Then came the day—he shuddered, remembering—when the messenger brought news. The child—his child, Luciana's child—arrived before the father. The child came too soon and the father . . . not at all.

Luciana's letter contained but four words. "Our son is dead." His cousin, Prunella, whom he had sent to be with Luciana until he arrived, said more. Alessandra's letter had been kindest of all, assuring him that the reports of Luciana's curses were, according to her grandmother, quite common when the pains came and a natural part of grief.

Stefano sighed. Memories did not ease his thoughts. How was he to keep Luciana at the estates and, hopefully, out of harm's way? Since he failed her by neither being with her when the boy was born nor returning to help her grieve—a bit of cowardice for which he could never forgive himself—by what right could he command her to stay or go, or even ask her to trust him to investigate the very curious circumstances of Alessandra's death?

He closed the lid of the box and turned the lock. He took another sheet of paper. Luciana's safety came before all else and that meant she must stay at the estate. Later, after he had settled this matter, *then* perhaps he could offer his apologies for this and his other crimes. With a deep breath, he picked up the pen to write the letter he must. He took the tone of an officer to his men, hoping that in the midst of Luciana's grief, she would respond to direction and strength.

After he was done with the writing, he folded the papers, sealed them, and packed them into the royal courier's pouch. He shrugged into his coat, clapped on the plumed hat and medal-bedecked sash that distinguished him as an officer, and went in search of the courier in the mess tent.

The rain came down heavily, drenching his coat through and through before he reached his destination, just a stone's throw from his own tent. He paused in the entryway to shake off the bulk of the mud sucking at his feet. At the first table, men rose, saluting. He waved them back to their meals. Their fellows at other tables took their cue from them and, likewise, sat.

The tent smelled more of wet clothes, mud, and unbathed men than it did of food. Telling the men apart by the color of their uniforms was impossible, but if one listened carefully, long enough, then accents and native languages gave them away as they bellowed and laughed among their comrades. Row upon row of tables with nary an empty seat occupied the majority of the tent. The only warmth came from the press of men and the cook fires at the rear.

Stefano found the courier seated alone, near the cook, taking what warmth he could from the nearby fire. Stefano hooked the leg of a chair and pulled it up to the table, frowning as mud came with it. He sat, but did not speak as he waited for his chair to settle as it would in the dirt floor. Sighing, he placed the courier's pouch next to the other man's hand and nodded his thanks to the cook's boy, who set a tankard of mulled wine and a platter of some sort of lumpy Austrian stew before him. Over the years, he had learned better than to hazard a guess at what the cooks served.

"Is your reply prepared, Your Grace?" the courier asked, pulling the pouch closer.

"Yes, there is the letter to my wife, which I bid you take straightaway to my estate, Dragorione."

"And a reply to the queen?"

"This is," Stefano said, tapping the pouch. "Report to the queen that I will be returning home, but I must insist that you deliver the letter herein to Dragorione first."

The courier nodded. "The queen said you would probably make such a request. It will be done."

"How long will it take you?"

"Five days . . . perhaps less." The courier swallowed the last of his mulled wine.

Stefano's brow raised. "You make good time, then. The normal post is considerably longer." But he relaxed on Luciana's behalf. This would reach her long before the end of the mourning period. She would still be at the estate and, thereby, safe. He would return before she could do anything that might bring her into harm's way.

The courier rose with a bow and put on his hat. "If you will excuse me, Your Grace, I'll be off now."

"Now? I thought you would at least spend the night. I have arranged quarters for you."

"For which I am grateful, Your Grace, but there is still a goodly amount of riding time, and if I can make Ziknaro by morning's light, then I'll have saved myself a day waiting for another ship to take me to Calabria."

"I will be but a day or two more finishing my affairs here and then I will be on the road home by way of Ziknaro myself," Stefano said, rising from his half-eaten, cold, and tasteless meal. The grayish, lumpy stew looked even less appetizing as fat congealed upon what some might call the surface. Normally, he would have eaten his food no matter how unappetizing since a soldier never knew when the next meal might be, but tonight he simply could not manage it.

"I am minded, then, Your Grace, to recommend Capitano Krosseus. He is thoroughly trustworthy. He runs a clean ship, knows the waters, and rarely suffers delays of *any* kind. All royal couriers seek him out."

"I will remember the name," Stefano said.

The courier bowed again and set off into the storm.

Stefano dragged his sodden body from his chair and trudged back to his tent. Removing his wet things, he draped them over the back of a chair. His man would come later to lay out his clothes, dry them before morning, and polish the mud from his boots. Unlike many of the other officers, he kept a minimal staff, just sufficient to complete the necessary work.

Climbing into his cot, the sheets and blanket clung to him, damp and mildewy. The feather mattress smelled of things he did not want to even consider. As he lay on his back, listening to the rhythmic beat of rain falling and the occasional roll of thunder, Stefano's thoughts turned to Luciana. He could not help but hope she would be pleased to see him, despite his failings. He would not let her grieve alone again, not if she would allow him the privilege. If nothing else, perhaps he might succeed in keeping her out of trouble.

His conscience twinged. Whatever reason he might tell himself brought him home; only Luciana drew him there. She would need someone to comfort her, and he wanted that someone to be no one but himself.

III

"If you strike down a Gypsy and cut him into ten pieces, you have not killed a Gypsy, but made ten!"
—Old Romani Proverb

25 d'Aprile 1684

A SPRY old woman with sun-baked skin and wind-tousled graying hair partially bound with a scarlet scarf swung down from the driver's seat of a gaily painted *vardo* with experienced ease. The profusion of golden bangles lining the woman's wrists jangled and glinted as she embraced Luciana.

Luciana allowed her grandmother to engulf her. She smelled reassuringly of woodsmoke, the road, and horses. She smelled safe. Laying her head on the other woman's shoulder, Luciana sighed. Even now she could not release her pent-up grief. She felt hollow.

After a time, she broke away. She longed to let loose her tears, more than the faltering trickle. Luciana noted that the *Daiya* shed no tears either. They stared long and hard into one another's eyes and then embraced once more.

Standing on the marble portico, Prunella cleared her throat.

Luciana stepped away from her grandmother, meeting Prunella's disapproving gaze evenly before she curtsied.

"*Beluni-Daiya*, I welcome you to my home. May I

present Prunella Allegra Carafa, my husband's cousin?" Luciana said, motioning to the young woman. "The duca sent her to help me in my time of . . ." She shrugged, unable to speak of her stillborn son.

The Romani Queen nodded knowingly, grasping Luciana's hands with her own leathery fingers. "You are . . . recovered, then?"

"I—" Luciana shook her head again. There were no words.

Prunella's face pinched into its normal frown, but she curtsied respectfully and stepped back so the Romani Queen could enter the ducal residence.

Luciana followed the older woman into the hall. Anxious to begin their discussion of Alessandra, she took care of her obligations first. "Will you be staying here?"

"Brother Tobbar set aside a most suitable site between the orchards and the little river. The *vitsa* prepares camp as we speak. I've come to collect . . . *her*."

Luciana winced. Hearing her grandmother avoid Alessa's name, as was the custom, gave a sense of finality. She did not look forward to telling the *Beluni* all of the news. "She is not here, *Daiya*. We must talk—" She guided her grandmother toward the stairs.

The old woman turned, no longer distracted by the polished surroundings and expensive decor. "What is there to talk of? I trusted the cards and your vision in the news you sent. Were you wrong?"

"No, *Daiya*," Luciana said, "but—"

"Have you misled me in this matter, *Chavi?*"

"There are no lies among the Wandering Folk, Grandmother," Luciana said. She reached out and took the old woman's hand. "Come to my rooms. We will have chocolate while we talk." She paused at the staircase, turning back. "Prunella, send up refreshments."

"As you wish, Your Grace," Prunella murmured. She gave a curt nod and disappeared down the hall toward the kitchens, her shoes echoing on the dark-green-and-black checkerboard marble floor.

The *Beluni* watched the young woman leave. Her mouth quirked. She looked up suddenly, catching Luciana watching her, and winked. "Considering the duke's kinswoman, I can only wonder at how, eight years ago, word of his marriage to you was received."

Luciana flinched. She refrained from confiding in the *Beluni* that the marriage had been a mistake. Like his family, he, too, regretted their union—enough that he could not be troubled with the expectations of an heir, probably because it was she who would have given him his firstborn. In fairness, though, not all of his family despised her. The White Queen was kind and generous.

Lately, too much pain filled her days. Luciana clamped down on her distractibility. She did not need reminders of the other great trials in her life.

The *Beluni* climbed the stairs so that she stood even with her granddaughter. She took Luciana's chin in her hand and leaned comfortingly close. "When you suffer, *Chavi,* you must take action on your own behalf. You won your man once, win him again. As to her," the old woman nodded in the direction Prunella had gone, "were this a more appropriate time, perhaps I would enjoy the lady's company more. There are so many . . ." She shrugged eloquently, a spark of the devil in her eyes. "That chit offers so many temptations for a good *dukkerin'* woman to explore. She's the sort who'd have her fortunes told and lie about it afterward."

Luciana started up the steps again. "Come, *Daiya,* there are things we must discuss."

"What is it you're not telling me?"

"Let us have privacy for this discussion," Luciana said.

"Tell me," the *Beluni* commanded. She took hold of Luciana's hand. Her rings bit like cold dark teeth into Luciana's flesh.

With an insistent tug, Luciana escorted her grandmother up the stairs and through the long upper gallery filled with its family portraits and pastoral watercolors painted for and by Stefano's predecessors. She closed the door behind them as they entered her sitting room and ushered her grandmother to the most comfortable chair.

"*Now,* will you tell me?" the *Beluni* demanded.

"I—I cannot even think where to begin."

"Your visitation, your reading of the cards are correct, are they not? My granddaughter is—the *Araunya-minoré* is dead." the *Beluni's* voice cracked with deep emotion. "I've confirmed your reading myself. What more could there possibly be?"

Luciana sat in her favorite wing chair, pulling her feet up beside her. She reached for a rosewood box atop the desk, her lacy sleeve catching on the corner of it as she placed the box in her lap. From the tiny chest, she withdrew a letter and gave it to her grandmother. "The queen sent me this."

The *Beluni* accepted the paper, pressing it open with curiosity. She left her chair and crossed to the balcony where she had better light.

As her grandmother read, Luciana closed her eyes. She had memorized every word of the *gadjé* queen's letter, which contained every essence of propriety, and still managed to convey her sincerity. She recalled everything, from the date to the text.

17 d'Aprile 1684

My Dear Friend and Sister,
It is with heavy heart that I inform you of the
death of your sister . . . There are too many
questions involving her death for me to give you
any satisfactory explanation.
At the time of her death, Alessandra grieved
the loss of her beloved Capitano di Montago.
She suffered the most vicious rumors that she
murdered di Montago over a lovers' quarrel.
In spite of my efforts, she was young and in love
and in no temper to be comforted.
She was found lying in her bed. Because of
the circumstances of her death—she being so
young and, otherwise healthy— inquiries are
being made. The entire affair is suspicious. We
have not been able to resolve questions regarding
the possible motive for her murder. I cannot
say if it is my own wishful thinking or truth, but

*I believe Alessandra took comfort from me in
her final days.*

*At my order, your sister's remains were placed
in a royal crypt. I pass on her ring and seal
to you.*

*As queen and sister by marriage, I extend my
deepest sympathies over your loss, which is
Our loss as well.*

*With deepest regards,
Idala*

"Then she was murdered," the old woman said.

Even though the *gadjé* queen could not possibly know of the filthy sacrilege it was for a Romani to die in her home, and certainly never in her bed, the entire circumstances made Luciana suspicious. It went without saying that if she were suspicious, the Romani Queen would be even more so.

The *Beluni* sat in the window seat staring off toward the orchards. "The queen's letter raises more questions than it answers."

Luciana's words choked out through silent tears. "There is more, *Beluni-Daiya*." She gave her grandmother the second letter bearing the White Queen's broken seal upon it.

The handwriting upon the parchment, Luciana knew, was unsteady, and the ink smeared with tears—hers and the *gadjé* queen's.

21 d' Aprile, 1684

Luciana,

*I have failed every trust you placed in me. I am
horrified to relay this final news regarding your
sister. During the night, someone broke into the
crypt and made away with Alessandra's body.*

*My conscience does not let me rest easy. I am
deeply grieved for you and wish there were
some comfort I could offer you. Do not hesitate
to call upon me if I can serve you in any way.
Idala*

The *Beluni* folded the paper in that absentminded way one had when deep in thought. It was a stunning blow from which Luciana still reeled.

When, after several long moments, her grandmother did not speak, Luciana rose and went to her side. "It is all so very hard to believe. How could . . . someone that alive be dead? She was always involved in something— dancing, the lute, and those ghastly perfumes! She had a lover even! A capitano in the Escalade. Her father, Conte Baiamonte, says they had begun marriage negotiations." Luciana wiped furiously at her eyes as they misted up. She laughed in spite of herself. Then her jaw jutted angrily. "And some dared insult her, accused her of murder, *Daiya!* How could anyone say that about Alessa?"

With a warning glare, the old woman covered Luciana's mouth and spat upon the carpet. "Have care, *Chavi!* Do not invoke the dead by calling their names!" After a moment, she removed her hand and moved away. Her face had grown stony and stoic with anger. "The *gadjé* court killed my granddaughter. I demand satisfaction."

"The *gadjé* court killed her only if she took her own life, which we know she did not. Even if her belief would permit such a thing, she would not have committed the act indoors, away from the lasa and the earth that gave her comfort. She would not have dishonored her host by dying in their *keir* nor risk separating herself from her lover in the hereafter!"

"What about this lover of hers?"

"What about him, *Daiya?* He was already dead. Even driven to distraction by her love for this man, she would not have ended it so. She would want vengeance. Vendetta would come before all else," Luciana said.

The *Beluni* stilled, her face growing even more expressionless. "My granddaughter was at court under the protection of your *gadjé* 'sister,' the queen. How could this happen? How could it have been allowed?"

"It wasn't *allowed,* of that much I am certain," Luciana said. "I don't know how this injury came to pass, but I plan to learn. The queen is no errant mentor. She must have believed Alessa would ultimately suffer no harm beyond the inevitable pain of having lost her lover."

"Then how did she come to her violent end, Luciana? If she had the protection of the queen, how could she be murdered?"

Luciana shook her head. "I cannot help but blame myself. Court is no simple place to be. I should have made her stay with me instead of letting her return after . . . the child was lost."

The *Beluni* took Luciana into her arms, almost cradling her as she had when Luciana was a motherless child, and kissed both of her cheeks. "You could no more have caged the wind than kept her away from court."

"But, still, she was my sister. I should have protected her. It was my duty!" Luciana cried.

"How would you have done that? From here?" the *Beluni* asked. "Listen, my *chavi*, you cannot ask the living to stop. It is unnatural. That was true for your sister when your son came and is true for you now."

A long silence fell between them, and Luciana retreated to her seat. After a time, the Romani Queen asked gently, "What does your husband have to say?"

"About what?" Luciana snapped. She took a deep breath. "Between my husband and me, there is only the briefest of correspondence. I sent word a day or two ago . . ." She waved vaguely. "I can't be sure."

"Only then? Is it so bad between you?" the *Beluni* murmured.

"He has not been here—I have not seen him since I conceived . . . more than a year now. He denied every appeal I made of him to return home. He returned to Tyrrhia for the celebration of the White Prince's first Natal Day, but he did not come here . . . to me," Luciana said. "I have nothing from him but a second cousin and his estate to comfort me."

The *Beluni* perused the room as though it were that of a stranger. She moved about slowly, touching the heavy brocade on the table, bending to smell the arrangement of flowers, taking in all of the details. "You have many nice things, *Chavi*."

Luciana leaned against the spinet, ignoring the discordant complaint of the keys. "I have many nice things, but they do not fill my life, nor content my heart. The open road offers more comfort than these . . . things."

"The *gadjé* life brings you so little pleasure then?"

"Nothing can replace family, *Beluni-Daiya*. These are cold substitutes for my husband's arms, and I do not see what the life ever gave Alesssan—my sister. Oh, that Mother never married a *gadjé!*"

The *Beluni* looked pained at the mention of her daughter. "And then we would never have had your sister. Would you wish that?"

Struck aback, Luciana shook her head. "No, of course not." She sighed and, for the first time, felt completely free to express her grief. "Why couldn't it have been me?"

"You would wish this pain on your sister?"

Luciana exhaled loudly. "No. I would never wish this on anyone, but—how could this have happened?"

The *Beluni* stroked Luciana's hair. "I don't know, *Chavi*."

Luciana let out a small cry. "And of all things to happen, her body is stolen! She'll be damned to become *mulló!*"

"The curse is upon the whole *kumpania, Chavi*."

Luciana clutched her chest. The tightness of her corsets felt like nothing compared to the constriction in her heart.

"There must've been a mistake. This cannot be true," the *Beluni* said. Her voice sounded ragged, as if she had aged in the moments since reading the letter.

"There is no mistake," Luciana said. The reality of never seeing Alessandra again struck her anew and the horror of her sister's missing body washed over her like icy water. "No. Not about this."

"Could there have been *patrins* at the cemetery? One of the other Romani *vitsi* might have seen to it that she was tended to properly," the *Beluni* said. She sounded as though she might wish and reality would turn on its ear.

"No. If that were true, we would have heard by now . . . and they wouldn't have stolen the body," Luciana said. There could be no hope of Romani rescue. Her grandmother handled the news no better than she had. Luciana steeled herself and forced the quaver from her voice. "What do we do now, *Daiya?*"

The *Beluni* squeezed Luciana's hands. "Knowing she was not taken by one of the tributary *vitsi,* we can only assume whoever *did* take her has mischief in mind. The remaining question is: mischief for whom—and why?"

"We *must* get her back. We must release her soul so that it will move on."

"Of that, there is no question," the *Beluni* said, handing the White Queen's letters back to her. "Did the *gadjé* have nothing more to say about this?" While her tone was casual, the very absence of inflection conveyed the depths of her displeasure.

"*Beluni-Daiya,* the *gadjé* king would not tolerate this sort of skulduggery and the queen, no matter what passes between her brother and me, is also family," Luciana said.

"You place such faith in them?" the older woman asked. Her eyes were eagle-bright as she assessed her granddaughter.

"They're not fools, *Beluni.* They know what their Romani subjects bring to Tyrrhia through the trade in Gypsy Silk."

The *Beluni* smiled ironically. "That has never stopped a *gadjé* before."

"Some are not like others, *Beluni,*" Luciana whispered. "These *gadjé* welcomed me fully as a member of the family."

"Is that so? What of her? The duke's cousin?" The Romani Queen asked, nodding toward the downstairs where they last saw Prunella.

Luciana sighed. "The queen herself took my sister in."

"And yet your sister died, was buried, and then stolen?"

Luciana sighed. "Even with that, *Beluni-Daiya,* as much as I loved my sister, I believe in the White Queen."

The *Beluni* gave a sharp nod. "We will observe the funeral rituals tonight as planned and then you and I, Luciana-*Chavi,* we will decide what we must do next. Have Brother Tobbar bring the *Araunya-minoré's vardo* to the camp."

From her window, Luciana watched the *vardos* pull out from the carriageway, Alessandra's behind the *Beluni*'s. She turned, surprised by a scratching at the door.

The door opened. Prunella stood on the threshold.

"What is it, Prunella?" Luciana asked.

The young girl blushed, dropping her gaze to the floor. "I–I was just wondering, Your Grace, what should I do?"

"Do?" Luciana shook her head, confused.

"About your plans. I thought your father, Conte Baiamonte, might want to know. Shall I send word to him for you?"

Luciana swallowed hard. She had quite forgotten Baiamonte, Alessandra's *gadjé* father. She suddenly felt tired. There could be none of that, however. She had responsibilities. Luciana took a deep breath. "The conte is my stepfather, Prunella, and what word would you send?"

Prunella frowned and, eventually, shrugged. "I thought you might have news for him, perhaps of your plans—or the—the old woman." She sighed. Her slim shoulders lifted in another shrug.

Luciana patted Prunella absently as she passed her. "There is nothing to tell the conte which has not already been said. His daughter was *Araunya* and her first debt was to our mother's people. It is we who claim her for funeral rites."

"But there is no body," Prunella blurted.

The truth, however obvious, cut deep. Luciana masked the pain that seemed destined to consume her. "I have not forgotten, nor will this be the Romani's first funeral without the honored guest." She took no comfort in that knowledge either.

"Forgive me, Your Grace, but how can you accept this dastardly work so calmly?" Prunella's look expressed her confusion.

Luciana looked up, knowing that her eyes could not hide her pain or the deep, burning anger. "Whoever told you I accepted the theft of my sister's life and then her body, Prunella?"

IV

"Is it nothing to you, all ye that pass by? behold, and see if there be any sorrow like unto my sorrow."

—Bible, Lamentations

LUCIANA lingered in her *vardo,* touching the crafted fixtures; the carved rosewood cabinets, the embroidered coverlet folded at the end of the pallet that served as settee during the day and bed at night, a wrought-iron kettle and a stewpot hung from pegs near the rear door. She heard the skewbald mares snort and stamp their feet as her Romani-born maid, Kisaiya, unhitched them. Beyond that was the noise from members of her *vitsa* setting up camp. The *boshmengros* tuned their fiddles. Somewhere a child sang a song of luck and a dog whined for scraps. All hands, save hers, were duly occupied.

Without the road or the *vitsa,* living on the ducal estates was a pampered prison. Removed from work and family, she lacked recourse or motivation. Woe haunted the Romani, but none save she and her sister had been cursed with a loneliness such as this . . . living in the *gadjé* world.

She sat on the pallet, rubbing her arms. The gold bangles beneath her sleeves jangled. It had been so long since she visited her traveling home. While she sometimes enjoyed the spacious opulence of Villa d'Drago-rione, there was something comforting, reassuring, about the close quarters of the *vardo* with all of its dark wood and tiny cabinets and drawers built into every nook and cranny.

How many afternoons had she stolen away with Alessandra to rejoice in their shared heritage? Not nearly enough, now that Luciana considered it.

She shivered, recalling memories long left buried. She barely remembered her father. He had smelled of *sigaros,* plum wine, and the silver forge. His dark shape loomed over her pallet at bedtime to brush whiskery kisses upon her cheeks and Mama sang in the background. After the owl came for him, she and Mama had been alone. More than Papa's whiskers, Luciana remembered Mama's tears.

Luciana tried to remember Conte Baiamonte entering their lives, but it was a blank. One day, Mama came to the *vitsa.* There had been words between Mama and the *Beluni*. Then Mama climbed onto the ledge of her *vardo,* pulling Luciana up beside her, and off they drove. It was springtime. The apples in the orchards burst forth their blooms and everywhere there was the sound of songbirds.

Luciana remembered the nightmares those first nights—closed up in a room of stone with the air blocked out by shuttered windows. In those days, Conte Baiamonte laughed. He brought her gifts and did not grow angry when she released the songbird from its tiny golden cage. She remembered the laughter as she adjusted to this new way of life with a roof between her and the stars. Some nights, she missed them, and Mama would take her onto the patio until she fell asleep.

And then, Luciana recalled, there came that magical morning. Baiamonte came for her, took her hand in his, and led her to Mama's bedroom. That morning was like the unfolding of a flower. The magic—which could not be named, only felt—blossomed. How clearly she remembered Baiamonte lifting her onto Mama's bed and her first look at her sister.

Alessandra's eyes were like blue violets. Luciana remembered how it felt staring into those wise, knowing eyes and how her chest swelled, filling with that nameless wonder. Because she had just turned eight, Mama placed Alessandra in her arms—and in that moment, life was complete.

Luciana savored the sweet moment. She counted the grasping fingers and each curling toe. Remembering, it seemed as though Alessandra never really left her arms. Not long after the birth, Mama fell ill and steadily spent more and more time in her darkened room. Baiamonte hired a wet nurse and grew quietly angry.

The village woman was content to nurse Alessandra along with her own babe though she ignored her other duties for the girls. Baiamonte did not notice. For Luciana, the village woman's negligence was a blessing; it meant she had Alessandra to herself.

Baiamonte protested when he discovered his infant daughter nestled in Luciana's bed instead of the heirloom cradle, but nothing changed. Mama grew more sickly and the conte grew tired of fighting with his increasingly determined stepdaughter.

Alessandra was two and already weaned when Mama moved on to the Neverworld—the *Praio Tem*. Baiamonte spent days in his cups, bartering the greater part of his wealth to the local priest for enough indulgences to get his heathen wife into heaven. Luciana, now ten, took full responsibility for her sister, and that meant teaching her the ways of Mama's people, their people.

Luciana saw to it that the *Beluni* and the clans knew of Mama's passing. With Alessandra in tow or riding on her back, she went on a trek to the forest road at the edge of her stepfather's estates. Little as she was when last she saw it, Luciana made the *patrin* for death—bits of stone, a broken branch and a white feather—so that the Romani would know what had come to pass. Alessandra was too young to understand and Luciana was sure the *patrin* was not quite right, but it was the best she knew.

The *Beluni* arrived within a fortnight and the fighting truly began. Luciana hid in a vestibule and where she was, so was her shadow, Alessandra. The younger girl trembled in her sister's arms, clutching her tighter and trying to shut out the sounds of her father's and grandmother's raised voices.

Baiamonte sent a maid scurrying to the nursery for his daughter and "the other one." Luciana did not wait

to be found. With Alessandra's hand grasped firmly in
her own, she pushed aside the tapestry and came out.

Their grandmother ran to them, falling to her knees
to embrace them both. Alessandra stayed frozen and
pale, having no memory of this woman who had been
yelling at her father. For Luciana, it was different. She
knew the *Beluni* well and went gratefully into her arms,
pulling Alessa with her.

"I'll take the girls tonight," the *Beluni* said firmly.
"Tomorrow, we will settle this matter of my daughter's
body."

"Take her first child, but the little one remains here.
She is my daughter and I'll not have her stolen with my
permission!" Conte Baiamonte retorted. Seizing Alessandra by the shoulders, he wrested her away from both
Luciana and the *Beluni.*

Where Alessa went, so did Luciana. She flung herself,
every ounce of her childish form, at her stepfather, grabbing for any handhold of Alessandra's nightgown or
slender ankle. Baiamonte grasped Luciana and pulled
her to his side.

"There! Even the child who knows you comes to me!"

Luciana knew then, even as a child, that she would
never forget the look in her grandmother's eyes . . .
bereft of family . . . daughter, then new granddaughter,
and now the first. Luciana could not bear to meet her
grandmother's gaze and buried her face in Alessa's
nightgown, clinging to her legs.

It took practically a summons from the recently widowed White King Orsino to sort out the family affairs.
The conte yielded his wife's remains for the funeral pyre.
The Romani Queen deferred her claims upon the conte's
blood daughter and bestowed upon Luciana, as her
mother's heir, the title of *Araunya di Cayesmengri,*
which gave her charge over all Romani silk holdings—
from orchards to sewing needles, from thread to looms,
every tool used by a Rom Guildswoman was under her
care. She also appointed Luciana guardian and protector
of her younger sister's heritage.

"*Daiya?*"

Luciana started. A shadowy shape stood at the base

of the stairs just outside her *vardo*. She raised her oil lamp to get a better view, surprised by how dark it had grown.

Nicobar stood on the lowest step and yet still his tall, strapping frame filled the doorway as he held up a wooden platter of food. "I thought you might be hungry."

"Already?" Luciana said. She had spent more time lost in thought than she realized.

"Do you prefer to eat alone?" Nicobar asked.

"No," Luciana murmured as she rose, "you are quite right. I will join the others." She accepted his proffered arm as she came down the steps, glad she had chosen to wear her Romani clothes since they made it much easier to get about. The idea of trying to navigate the interior of the *vardo* wearing anything more confining than a loose fitting Romani demicorset was preposterous. She paused only long enough to get her head scarf and draw the curtain across the entrance. She left the stairs down and the doors ajar.

Nicobar waited patiently while Luciana tied the small silk scarf over her hair, tucking the knot at the nape of her neck as was customary. "The *Beluni* is over here," he said.

As Luciana ducked her head beneath the awning that marked the boundary of her grandmother's campsite, the old woman twitched aside her skirts and indicated the tapestry-covered stool at her side. Once settled, Luciana accepted the cooled platter of food from Nicobar, who promptly faded into the shadows, leaving the two women effectively alone.

In the center of the encampment, a growing bonfire licked hungrily at the firewood, filling the air with the glorious scents of citrus and woodsmoke to mingle with the aroma of goat stew and crusty black bread baked in Dutch ovens. At least thirty *vardos* circled the area, with the wagons of the senior *Daiyas* closest to the fire. Families gathered near the brightly painted wagons of the mothers and grandmothers, settling down to share their evening meal and participate in the funeral rites.

The *Beluni* stood, bangles jingling, and moved to look

up at the stars, or what she could see of them through
the uneven canopy made by the apple grove.

Luciana put her food aside untouched.

"How long has it been since you've eaten properly,
Chavi?" her grandmother asked, without turning.

"I haven't been hungry," Luciana said.

"You'll need your strength for what lies ahead of
you," the *Beluni* said.

Luciana looked up. "Pardon?"

Her grandmother returned to sit beside her. "I think
our plans best not involve Baiamonte. Yes?"

"It will be as you wish," Luciana said.

Her grandmother nodded and settled back in her
chair, her eyes following the movements of the *vitsa*
around the encampment. She was silent a long moment
and when she spoke, her eyes never turned in Luciana's
direction. She seemed completely at rest, and yet she
spoke with strength and precision. "Whoever has taken
our *Araunya minore* must be punished. I am not satisfied
with the White Queen's inquiry into either her death or
the disappearance of her body."

"You are not suggesting the Queen of Tyrrhia is de-
ceiving us? *Me?* About something this important?" Luciana asked. "Just because she is *gadjé?*"

The *Beluni* shook her head. "Her heritage has nothing
and everything to do with this, but not as you think. To
lie, one must know the truth."

Luciana relaxed somewhat. "Do you propose, then,
that she has been misled as well?"

The *Beluni* shrugged. After a moment, she leaned forward and studied Luciana. Her eyes glittered by the light
of the bonfire. "You hold such account in these *gadjé,*
do you?"

"I do."

The old woman rested back in her chair with a sigh.
"Over many years, I have observed that one can tell the
heart of the *gadjé* royalty by how they treat the Wandering *vitsi*. There has been many a *gadjé* king who honored
the letter of the pact between us, but the heart . . . well,
such a thing they lacked themselves. You, *Chavi,* have
met these people and looked into their hearts. I taught

you the *dukkerin'*. You have an instinct for magic. It is in your heart, your very soul. If you tell me I can trust these *gadjé*, then I will trust them."

"I am honored by your confidence in me, Grandmother."

The *Beluni* laughed, her tone harsh. "My trust can be an awful burden, *Chavi*. Make no mistake in that."

"I will state it clearly, then, *Beluni*. These *gadjé* royals can be trusted."

"They were entrusted with the safety of your sister, before and after her death. How much further will I be asked to trust them?" the *Beluni* asked. Her tone was gentle, but her eyes, as she looked at Luciana, were piercing.

Luciana stared steadily back at her grandmother. "I believe the queen, *Beluni-Daiya*." She waited for a response that did not come. "You spoke of my future a moment ago."

"Did I?" her grandmother asked. She nodded. "I suppose I did." She sat forward again, rubbing the palms of her hands on her skirt. "Your sister's murder cannot go unanswered. But these other offenses compound the nature of the crime. It is a terrible thing to steal a body, even more so the body of a Romani, and if that Rom be in the family royal of all the Wandering *vitsi*, well . . ."

"You are confident then that this is murder and more?" Luciana asked.

"As you are," the *Beluni* retorted. "You've been the very soul of reason, but I, too, have played the cards out. Foul magic is behind this. Atop a murder, a further crime has been committed against your sister's soul."

"Only strong magic could defeat her fairy charms. I cannot understand how this *chovahano* defeated the fairies' gifts," Luciana said.

"The *gadjé* would not have known to leave the offering nor the signal and, undoubtedly, put her in a *gadjé* crypt, most certainly sealed with iron," the *Beluni* said. "You are in a position to give your sister her final rest. It is you who can safely go to the *gadjé* court. But be warned, *Chavi*, if the *gadjé* queen is to be believed, then the evil surely goes beyond murder and grave robbing.

I fear it goes even to the heart of Tyrrhia and all that makes this the one place where so many have found a home and sanctuary."

"I'll leave as soon as the mourning season has passed," Luciana said, but already she focused on the frustrations of waiting to do what she must at the *gadjé* court.

"We cannot wait. It seems like suitable justice to begin vendetta on a day the *gadjé* set aside to make peace with their own dead before the growing season. I would ask you to break trust with whatever demands your husband might have made in this regard and go to court on the day the *gadjé* celebrate their ancient rites of Lemuria. If you use this festival to your advantage, you may escape the scandalized gossip of the *gadjé* who do not understand the Romani way."

"There is wisdom in that, *Beluni-Daiya,*" Luciana agreed. While she had no idea how she would be ready in time, her thoughts raced ahead once more, wondering who could do this to her sister and why? What had been their motive? What could a young half Gypsy girl have done to be so ill-used . . . even after her death?

"There is one more thing, *Chavi.*"

Luciana looked up expectantly.

"By rights, the *Araunya's* estates and properties revert to me. It is my place to appoint the *Araunyas* when no daughter exists to inherit. Had either of my daughters lived to this day, or had I even another granddaughter, I might pass these properties to them, but there is no other." The *Beluni* paused as she spoke and turned to face Luciana. "The *gadje* place much importance on titles and such, which puts me in mind that placing the second title, properties, and responsibilities with you can only serve to your benefit. Will you take it?"

The offer astonished Luciana. It never occurred to her that she might inherit her sister's Romani estate—*Cayesmengro,* responsibility for all those living aspects of the Gypsy Silk trade from the worms to the trees in the mulberry orchards, the Weavers' to the Dressmakers' Guilds. She could not deny the *Beluni's* logic, the *gadjé* did place an unwholesome importance on such things, but the responsibilities that came with the inheritance were not to be accepted lightly. The fate of the entire Gypsy Silk trade and the wealth of the Wandering Folk would lie wholly in her hands alone as holder of both *Arauna* titles.

"Would that I could give you more time, *Chavi,* but I must have your answer." Even as her grandmother said the words, Luciana heard the *boshmengros* begin the burial song, calling the Romani to the fire for the rituals that began with the fading of the sun's last blush. The *Beluni* reached out and touched her wrist. "Luciana? Will you do it?"

She nodded wordlessly, though wishing fervently to bury herself in the Romani life and leave all the *gadjé,* and the pain they brought her, behind.

The *Beluni* let out a long sigh and rose. "Good! It is done, then." She crossed to the fire, leaving Luciana to her own resources.

Luciana watched, the familiar constriction in her chest returned as her grandmother let out the first mournful ululating cry. Around the camp, Romani rose from their dinners and *kumpania* to join their queen by the fire, answering her cry with wails of their own. The old men of the *Kris* came to the queen first, as was their place as the Guiding Council. The rest of the *vitsa* joined, even the smallest children still clinging to their mothers' brightly colored skirts. Babes in arms, be they frightened or aware, let loose with their own cries.

Feeling oddly detached, Luciana, too, left her chair by the *Beluni*'s *vardo.* Others respectfully made room for her to reach her grandmother's side. With the *vitsa* all about her, Luciana was a part of something greater, and yet there was a separation, too, because she was also part of the *gadjé*'s world.

Without Stefano and, now, without her beloved Alessandra, the desperate loneliness ravaged her, tearing at all she was and laying before her all that she would never be in the desolation that was now her life. All that might have been and should have been for Alessandra had come to an end. Were there no need to protect Alessa's soul, no call for justice, Luciana could not conceive of how she would withstand the all-consuming, grief-driven urge to end her own misery. The *Fata* did not forgive the mortals who cut their own thread, and nothing but damnation lay on that path, but now such an end seemed preferable to almost anything else— especially life—life with a future of solitude.

At the *Beluni's* side, Luciana gave voice to the deep, mourning lament of her sorrow.

---

6 d'Maggio, 1684

Stefano turned away from the *Sea Nymph,* having completed arrangements with Capitano Krosseus to leave in the morning. Mindful of his schedule, for a few liras more, the capitano offered him his own quarters aboard ship as an alternative to the inn where Stefano had stayed for the past day and a half.

He sent his valet to collect their belongings and pay their innkeeper, before taking advantage of Krosseus' recommendation of a local cantina where he might find a suitable meal.

The docks bustled with workers transferring goods from one ship to another or carts headed inland. He ducked and, when absolutely necessary, pushed his way through the crowd, keeping a tight hand on his rapier lest he cause affront.

He found the shop discreetly wedged between the Dock Master's office and a prosperous vendor of dry goods whose wares spilled out onto the cobbled street where the pier ended. The interior, however, was far more opulent than the outer appearance indicated. A young woman, neatly dressed, greeted him amiably in Greek.

"Dinner, My Lord?" she asked. Responding to his nod, she waved him toward a set of narrow steps and followed close behind. On the rooftop balcony, she seated him at a table overlooking the docks and poured a dry rosé into an exquisite glass goblet.

Stefano sipped at the wine. Crisp, excellent. He breathed a sigh of relaxation. The evening was warm and breezy. The sunset created a colorful panorama as it sank below the sea.

Luciana loved such evenings, especially if she had a vantage point from which to watch and comment on passersby. He used to tease her about telling the fortunes of unwitting clients. He smiled. She always wrinkled her nose at him, just so, then continued on. It was fascinating to sit and listen to what she was able to surmise about people as they went about their business.

By now, Luciana would have his letter advising her of his wishes that she remain at the estates. Another day or two and he would be in Messina and then mainland Tyrrhia once more. With Luciana safely tucked away in the country, he would be free to look into the questionable manner of Alessandra's death and seek redress. He sighed. It was a workable plan, and one that might win back Luciana's love while keeping her safe from harm.

Just thinking of Luciana filled him with an aching need to be beside her, so he turned his thoughts to other things, focusing on the products Capitano Krosseus received from other capitanos for shipment. The size and shape of the bags holding coffee and cocoa beans made them easily recognizable, as were the barrels of rum and molasses. Another ship's crew carried piles of pelts and packages of indigo.

As he ate his roasted songbird stuffed with prawns and served on a bed of *capalleni,* he watched the business of the docks gradually slow as the light grew dim. He noted his valet's arrival with his trunks and the crew of the *Sea Nymph* taking them aboard. As he finished his meal, he wondered what type of reception he would have from Luciana. He suspected it would not be the warm, loving one he wished for. How had they grown so far apart?

V

"There is no worse evil than a bad woman; and nothing has ever been produced better than a good one."

—Euripides

9 d'Maggio 1684

LUCIANA pulled aside the tapestry curtain of her carriage. Baldo, the driver, had stopped at the gates of the palazzo. She let the curtain fall into place as the Escalade duty officers approached. The carriage rocked as Baldo climbed down to present Luciana's papers and invitation.

Her companions were silent. Prunella sat brooding and Nicobar, her aide, looked as if he were resting—a mere ruse. She knew he paid perfect attention in these quiet moments. Seeming to feel her attention upon him, he sat up just as the carriage lurched forward again. The horses' hooves clattered on the cobblestone drive. No sooner had the carriage started than it jerked to another bone-jarring halt.

Nicobar was quick about the door, nimbly alighting and offering a steady hand to Luciana. His hand felt warm and strong, like the man himself. Luciana found it reassuring; she felt tired after the long, jolting trip and she faced an evening that would drain her even more. She was glad she had had the sense to stop, refresh herself, and change into her ball gown at one of the inns in the capital city. It saved time and permitted her to make the best of a difficult reentry into society.

The autumn wind that ruffled the fine black silk of Luciana's gown carried the smell of hot wax from the hundreds of candles glittering like jewels about the marble feet of the statue of Good King Alaric. She looked about the cobbled courtyard, awash with the radiance of torches and candlelight. The statue of the old Visigoth warrior king whose buried treasures financed Tyrrhia's bid for independence from its Italian and French oppressors centuries ago stood at the top of the fountain in the heart of the courtyard. The statue, draped in fluttering scarves of black and gray silk, looked appropriately wraithlike for the Lemuria celebration of the dead. Beyond, Escalade *vigilare* stood in attendance in shadowy alcoves.

The cold mantle of dispassion, which had cloaked her in recent days, slipped. Luciana swallowed the sudden surge of grief, longing for the return of the utter calm of ice-cold anger. She could afford no show of weakness. Not now. Not when she must face the courtiers and endure their whispers and avid curiosity.

Nicobar called up to the coachman, "Stable the horses."

Baldo touched his hat, then turned to deal with the quartet of hostlers led by a capitano whose mincing progress across the cobbles proclaimed his importance.

Nicobar growled under his breath and fussed with the lace shirt cuff beneath his new coat. Watching him, Luciana almost regretted bringing him. He did not belong here. But she needed his strength, his loyalty, and most of all his cleverness. Then again, she should not imagine she really had a choice in bringing him with her. No, Nicobar would have come no matter the obstacle.

Behind her, she heard Prunella cough delicately as one of the footmen helped her from the carriage. The young woman hurried to Luciana's side, her cheeks rosy from the wind. "Your Grace, I know you've bid me not speak of it again, but I must suggest one final time that it would be better to wait for the duca. I'm sure he would . . ." Prunella hesitated, worrying at her lower lip with her sharp little teeth.

"Her Grace is well aware of what she is doing, Signorina Carafa," Nicobar said sharply. "She owes no one an explanation."

"But what of the duca?" Prunella protested.

Luciana sighed. "I fail to see what my husband has to do with this."

"You fail . . . ?" Prunella gaped. "Consider His Grace's good name!"

Luciana turned pointedly away and motioned toward the palazzo. "I see lamps coming our way."

Prunella and Nicobar followed her gesture. Indeed, a full dozen servants approached with lanterns aloft to escort the new arrivals to the Queen's Masquerade Ball. A major domo dressed in white livery led the way.

Luciana stared up at the Palazzo Auroea, aglow with light gleaming from the doors and three stories of windows of the grand salon and banquet hall. The front gardens to her left offered a flowery refuge to the dancers within who might seek some privacy to woo or war. Like its name, the palace seemed golden, though not nearly so welcoming as her home in Dragorione. Already she missed her haven or, better still, wished for the anonymity of life on the open road, but her resolve to recover her sister's body and clear her name of the charge of murder held fast.

She adjusted her mask to avoid looking directly at her young charge while she schooled her own features into the implacable guise of calm she would need once within the palazzo where she would become the subject of the other courtiers' curiosity.

The major domo cleared his throat to draw attention to his arrival. He waited until Nicobar and Luciana turned to acknowledge him. He bowed deeply. "My Lord—"

"*This* is the *Araunya di Cayesmengri e Cayesmengro*, Duchessa di Drago," Nicobar interrupted.

The man's brows rose and he bowed once more, this time to Luciana alone. "The *Araunya? Araunya di Cay-*

esmengri? Forgive me! Her Majesty is receiving in the Grand *Sala da Ballo*."

Luciana nodded curtly.

"You may tell the Court Herald the *Araunya* will be detained a moment or two more," Nicobar said.

The servant bowed and backed away until he stood with the servants holding the lanterns.

Luciana turned to Prunella and spoke in that quiet, clear tone that brooked no further discussion. "Is everything in order now?" She touched the ebony beaded-and-feathered mask covering the upper features of her face.

The younger woman opened her mouth and snapped it shut, her lips thinning in disapproval. She brushed the back hem of Luciana's dress into place and nodded.

"Thank you. Are you sure that you do not want to change into your ball gown and join the party?" Luciana asked.

Prunella shook her head.

"If you insist upon waiting for the duca to arrive before you attend a party, Prunella, I fear you will be an old, tired woman," Luciana said.

Prunella shook her head again.

"So be it," Luciana said and turned resolutely to the wax-covered fountain. She approached slowly and knelt beside the rim, taking a small red candle from the velvet pouch that hung from her onyx-beaded bodice. She lit her candle with the flame of another. "For you, *Chavipen*. I will avenge you!" she whispered and carefully placed her candle among the others.

Luciana allowed herself a moment. Her grief was still sharp. How could the *Fata* take first her son and then her sister . . . almost a daughter to her? How could they choose so much pain for one woman to endure? She took a deep breath. No matter the "hows," this was to be her fate, her purpose in life.

She closed her eyes and opened herself up . . . to the *Fata,* the spirits. Surrounding her in the courtyard of Citteauroea, Luciana felt the presence of the *gadjé's* ancestors. Tonight was Lemuria, after all, the night when the dead walked. Somewhere, tonight, her sister's spirit must walk among them. She shuddered. Ghosts were *marimé*—unclean, impure just by their nature—and Alessandra was one of them now. One of them, indeed, in the most heinous way since her spirit and body had been defiled.

Luciana felt as though she had entered a crowded room with her eyes closed. She slowly opened her eyes. From the corners of her eyes, she caught glimpses of the waking spirits. She almost felt the brush of silk, heard the rustle of petticoats, smelled the powders and perfumes, and yet there was nothing. More aptly, there was nothingness—a sense of absolute absence that sucked at the soul like the undertow of the sea.

Though the spirit of her beloved sister seemed closer here, Luciana found no comfort. In the company of royalty and nobility, Alessandra's youthful innocence had proved fatal—in death, even worse than that.

"Before a year is out . . ." Luciana bit back the vow. Promises were too easily made. The truth came in the doing. She stroked the crested ring, which had so recently been Alessa's.

"Daiya?"

Luciana started out of her reverie and glanced up into Nicobar's solemn face. She rose, took a deep breath, and lifted the black silk damask hood onto her head. Conscious as she was now of the *gadjé* ghosts, Luciana could not avoid them, and the energy that awareness took sapped at her already exhausted reserves.

Nicobar bowed, proffering his arm.

Luciana steadied herself as she took his arm, savoring this final moment in the open air, a brief refuge before she faced the full onslaught of court and the intrigues surrounding Alessa's death. Her years of isolation were at an end. At this moment of her return to court and society, she missed Stefano dreadfully. She had not dared, after receiving his missive, to delay her trip to court for fear he would find some way to keep her at the estates. Now, when—if—he returned, her journey to find Alessa's murderer would already have begun.

She took another deep calming breath. While she had so many fond memories of court . . . of her days being wooed by Stefano, of celebrating the arrival of the White King's Heir, Dario Gian . . . there were also the sad memories, of the plague which struck the court and took little Princess Ortensia Marie four years gone. But this was not the court she once knew. She expected to find few friends here. Her last visit, for the birth of Dario Gian, had been spent mostly in the company of her husband. Her confinement had kept her from the celebration of his first birthday—it had not, she recalled bitterly, kept Stefano away, nor been cause for a visit.

As Prunella had said, the duca—Stefano—*should* be at her side on this occasion, but that was not to be. Luciana determined not to spare another second's thought on the matter.

———

Luciana paused on the threshold. She was resolved

An array of colors in the grand salon greeted her, from the banners and tapestries to the ornately dressed nobles in outlandish masks who danced or stood away from the dance floor laughing. Courtiers leaned over the balconies of the second and third floors, laughing and calling to one another. These could not be the same friends she knew when last she lived here. No, these were the aristocrats whose rumors and innuendos may very well have killed Alessandra.

Conscious of spectators, Luciana glided across the room and dropped into a deep, elegant curtsy before the King and Queen of Tyrrhia. She kept her expression calm as befitted one of her station.

"Your Majesties," said Estensi, the Court Herald. "Signora Luciana Mizella Elena Lendaro di Luna, *Araunya di Cayesmengri e Cayesmengro*, Duchessa di Drago."

King Alban inclined his head in acknowledgment. Barely a wrinkle formed on his fashionable, gold-encrusted white satin coat and pants, which suited his youthful, fit form. The king's dark eyes met Luciana's and held for a long moment. The queen, younger than her husband and dainty of figure, also dressed in gold and white, stepped down from the black marble dais.

"We are pleased to find our loyal subject returned to our court. We are pained by your loss."

"I am honored by your concern, Majesty," Luciana said, dropping into another well-practiced curtsy. Her heart warmed at the sight of her friend and sister.

Queen Idala turned to her husband and said, "I beg your indulgence . . ."

Alban rose, nodding, and motioned for her to proceed.

Together the queen and Luciana backed away from the dais and turned to stroll along the edges of the *sala*. The queen's attendants followed at a discreet distance, near enough to serve yet far enough to give the queen some privacy. Light cast by the chandeliers and ornate lamp stands flickered over the vast rectangular ballroom. Dancers whirled and spun on the wooden herringbone dance floor in the familiar steps of the Galliard. The sound of soft slippers scuffing and sliding on the floor accompanied the music as though part of the composer's creation.

"Oh, Luciana, I knew you would come, but I can't believe it is so soon!" Idala said.

"It was but a matter of time."

"For mourning, but I expected that to be so much longer, especially after your . . ."

"But, of course," Luciana replied curtly. She could not allow herself to be distracted with memories of her stillborn son. Annoyed with herself, she flicked her fan open and contrived to look past it at the long room and the bright figures eddying around it.

Idala glanced sideways at her while continuing to smile graciously at her guests. "You don't plan to . . . to make trouble, do you, Luciana?"

"Trouble, Majesty? I don't know what you mean."

"Don't play me for the fool, Luciana. I know you better than that. Couldn't you leave this matter to Stefano . . . or even Alban?"

Luciana stopped and turned to her friend. "I cannot rely upon my husband to handle this matter, not with him away. And I'm confident that His Majesty has more pressing matters to address than the death of a 'Gypsy,' be she *Araunya* or no."

Idala continued to walk, forcing Luciana to fall into step with her again. "If you insist upon staying, best you learn to guard your words. You should know how careful one must be at court. The higher your station, the more caution is required. A courtier willing to take advantage of an opportunity is never far away."

"Caution can become an affliction," Luciana muttered tightly.

"But it tends to be an affliction of the living," Idala retorted, turning a bright smile upon a masked couple who paused in their dance to bow to her. "Selfishly, I have no desire to compose another letter of condolence . . . least of all to my own brother!"

Luciana sighed and turned pointedly toward the dance floor. "And upon which courtier's whim does the court dance attendance these days?"

"The king's cousin, Bianca," Idala said softly, gesturing with her fan toward a cluster of women occupying what should have been a large part of the dance floor. Gentlemen hung about the fringes of the group, hoping either to woo away a young lady for a dance or to hear some of the apparently gay conversation. "There she is."

The princess was almost impossible to see until the crowd parted for her to make her way off the floor. Luciana studied the tall, slender, red-haired woman her sister had written so often and unkindly about. She frowned, trying to remember Alessa's exact words, and wondered why her sister distrusted the princess. She, herself, remembered the princess to be a rather fretful young woman, overly attached to her father and never fully recovered from her kidnapping by Turkish pirates.

"How long has it been since you heard from my brother . . . from Stefano?"

Luciana turned her fan to allow her a brief moment. She could not admit to receiving Stefano's last letter which had arrived a full week before she left the estate. Seeing Idala's knowing, sympathetic look, Luciana decided to simply pretend the letter had never arrived. She snapped the fan shut, her lips pinched. "I received a letter from him a month ago."

"Is there word about his return?" Idala asked hopefully.

Luciana shook her head. "None, Majesty."

Idala sighed. "I know it's too soon to hear word back about this business, but still I hoped . . ." She allowed her words to trail off.

A servant noting the queen's frown, stepped away from his station in a nearby alcove. Luciana touched Idala's arm, motioning to the servant with her fan. Idala waved the man away. She led Luciana into the next room where a splendid buffet had been set. All nature of treats filled tables decorated with spun sugar ornaments.

"This business between you and Stefano has gone on much too long, Luciana," she said.

"It was not I who volunteered to take a diplomatic post in the Morea," Luciana retorted tartly.

"You know he has his duties to the Crown and the Palantini," Idala sighed again, folding her hands together. "I hope you won't be offended, but I sent a letter to Stefano as well as the one to you."

Luciana kept her expression frozen in a front of calculated indifference. "Your kindness and thoughtfulness are much appreciated. I did not know what to say, so I said nothing. I'm confident you know your brother better than I."

Idala frowned. Her fingers plucked at the feathers in her fan, which would never be the same. "Perhaps we should sit?"

Together, they sat in a pair of chairs in the corner, arranging their skirts and taking in the sights of the courtiers dancing in the room beyond, while others tarried here, in the upper galleries, or wandered toward the gardens. At a motion from the queen, a liveried footman brought fragile Venetian glass goblets filled with an amber-colored wine.

"Now that I'm here, you must tell me what happened to my sister, Idala," Luciana said.

The queen took her hand and looked about nervously.

"Not here, not now. We will speak of this tomorrow at breakfast. Come to my suite."

Luciana nodded, wishing she could begin fulfilling her charge here and now. Across the room, the princess' gathering dispersed and she was lost in the crowd. Luciana's gaze fell upon a man in priest's robes who had just been with the princess but now watched her with the queen. Unlike the rest of the celebrants, this man wore no mask and, she suspected, his robes were not a disguise. His eyes were cold and penetrating even from a distance. Luciana shuddered and looked away. "Who is he?"

Idala frowned. "Cardinal della Torre. He's the ambassador for the Roman Catholic Church."

"But why does he stare?" Luciana asked.

The queen shrugged. "He is curious, I suppose. Pay him no mind."

Still conscious of being watched, Luciana turned her attentions back to the queen. "I was quite intrigued by the mention in your letter of the plots that put the kingdom in jeopardy. It gave me great pause. Was more involved in—in my sister's death than you were willing to say then?"

Idala opened her fan, trying to cover her look of surprise, but the mutilated accessory was inadequate at best. Annoyed, she closed the fan and dropped it onto her lap as she glanced around. "We will speak of these things in the morning, when we can be alone, but not now . . . not *here!*"

Estensi, the Court Herald, approached to beg the queen's attention to a matter at the thrones, which left Luciana alone again. The sound of laughter drew her gaze back to the princess, now surrounded by a cluster of women and a favored few gentlemen. No longer a frightened and silly young girl, it seemed the princess had grown into a woman all too aware of her own charms.

Luciana studied the other woman. Bianca was taller than most Tyrrhian women. Her flaming red hair and very fair skin made her look oddly out of place. Her gown of pale apple green was cut tantalizingly, and yet discreetly, low. Jewels covered her bodice and stomacher, enough that it looked as if she had robbed Great King Alaric's tomb herself. A large, jewel-encrusted crucifix dangled from her waist, adorning the front of her skirt.

"The princess is *so* beautiful! Is she not refined?" someone whispered nearby.

Luciana started. She had been so intent; she had failed to notice the very young woman who edged close. "Of course," Luciana agreed dryly.

The young woman breathed an enraptured sigh, nodding. Her fresh-faced innocence was all too reminiscent of the easily impressed Alessandra. The memory stung. The girl turned and smiled. She was young. Very young. Too young to be out in society in Luciana's opinion. "I am Letitia Amieri, daughter of the Conte and Contessa di Fuego."

Luciana nodded, but the girl seemed intent upon exchanging niceties, even if she were out of place. "I am the Duchessa di Drago, *Araunya di Cayes*—"

"Did you know the *Araunya* who was here? The one who killed herself? Did you hear that she poisoned her lover? Oh, it was very sad and tragic and—" the girl blurted.

"The other *Araunya* was my *sister*," Luciana said. She found it hard to keep from shouting that Alessandra had not killed herself, much less control her tone. She was glad the girl blushed and moved away.

Nicobar appeared at her side seemingly from nowhere. "I note you have spoken with the queen. Would you like to withdraw to your rooms now?"

His arrival surprised Luciana. Aware as she was of the undead tonight, it amazed her that she could so easily overlook the living. No doubt, he came from the very rooms he referred to. She smiled and nodded as she rose.

"Princess Bianca *is* a beautiful woman," Nicobar said.

"Indeed," Luciana agreed. She stopped, feeling a tug on her skirt. The ornate sofa frame had snagged the filmy silk. As she bent to free it, she sensed more than saw Nicobar's retreat and looked up to find Princess Bianca, followed by her associates, approaching with the speed of bloodthirsty wolves to a fresh kill.

Luciana curtsied. "Your Highness."

The princess acknowledged her with a nod and smiled knowingly at her companions. "Your Grace, I did not realize you had returned to court! It has been so long since we've seen one another and, now, upon this sad occasion . . ." She shook her head. It was a pretty gesture, if nothing else. The princess frowned. "Forgive me if my reminding you of your grief causes you any distress."

The press of the woman's devotees felt smothering and, truth to tell, she did not appreciate the young royal using her or Alessandra's memory to sharpen her claws. Luciana took a long deep breath and forced a pained smile to her lips. The princess' flock twittered and murmured, like great, puffing brainless birds.

Princess Bianca turned and scowled at her entourage. "Allow me to extend my condolences over the loss of your sister," she said, taking Luciana's hand. As she spoke, she drew Luciana apart from the courtiers.

Luciana accepted the statement with a stilted nod. The princess seemed greatly changed from the girl she had been and far friendlier than Alessandra had reported. Too friendly. Luciana glanced nervously at the flock of courtiers and noticed a foppish looking fellow standing behind one of the ladies, his gaze intent. When Luciana turned back, she saw the princess had been looking to him as well.

"I'm surprised you returned to court so soon after your loss with the mourning period barely begun," the princess continued.

"I am honored Her Highness has taken such interest in my grief," Luciana murmured. "I and . . , my sister were as close as two sisters could be. The mourning customs among my people, however, are . . . different."

"Of course." The princess nodded knowingly. "They *would* be, wouldn't they?" She pressed close again. "The entire affair between your sister and Capitano di Montago was most unfortunate."

Luciana flicked open her fan. "Was it? I understand they planned marriage, Your Highness."

"Really? Then that makes the events which followed most curious . . . unless the negotiations were not going well."

"To the contrary," Luciana replied stiffly.

"This conversation must be very difficult for you and I meant to be comforting," the princess murmured in a sweet falsetto.

"I am honored by your efforts," Luciana said, motioning to Nicobar. She curtsied. "Please excuse me, I find I'm tired after the long drive from Dragorione."

"Ah! And how has the duca taken the news, Your Grace?"

Luciana half-turned back. The princess designed her query to sting, of that there could be no doubt. Without the service of the royal couriers—which were not normally available even to the Palantini—Stefano could barely have received word of his young sister-in-law's death and certainly no exchange between them on the subject. It was no business of the princess' what nature their correspondence took. "I am confident His Grace shares in my grief. You will excuse me now, I hope. I am feeling decidedly unwell."

"But of course," the princess said.

Luciana departed quickly, thankful for Nicobar who cut through the crowd for her and led her to the palazzo's residential quarters.

VI

*"Gentle ladies, you will remember till old age
what we did together in our brilliant youth!"*
—Sappho

ANTICIPATION quickened Luciana's pulse. She
opened the door to the upper rooms where Prunella,
Nicobar, and her handmaid, Kisaiya, slept. She listened
carefully and looked for any glimmer of light to show
that a lamp still burned.

All was dark. All quiet.

She withdrew to her room and cast off her *vestaglia*.
Even as she wriggled into one of Kisaiya's black woolen
gowns as best she could unaided, Luciana felt guilty for
having taken it, for deliberately keeping her plans to
herself.

She did not want to think of reasons why she should
not make this midnight foray. There were too many reasons to do it. Nicobar would be angry in the morning
when he learned she had been out without him. He
meant well, but he would be a distraction. Kisaiya she
might have been able to use, but Prunella created disaster around spell work.

Luciana grabbed up her half-mask discarded earlier
that evening and tied it in place, then took the length
of black knitted lace hanging over the back of a chair
and wrapped it neatly around her neck and shoulders.
She took a decisive look around her bedchamber and
went quickly down the narrow stairs to the apartment
salon.

The queen had arranged for her to occupy the very
best suite the palazzo afforded for visiting dignitaries

and nobles. The rooms were resplendent with the most stylish furnishings from the crown-crested caned chairs to longcase clocks. Ornate candle branches hung from the ceiling, walnut gateleg tables lined the walls or accompanied a brocade-covered lounge. The room also contained a large assortment of utilitarian and decorative touches such as the pear-shaped teapot complete with tripod and spirit lamp. Nothing, no matter how small, seemed undone.

Amidst the splendor, a clutter of trunks and baggage filled the receiving room. Kisaiya had arrived later than planned and the unpacking had not yet been completed.

Luciana wound her way through the maze of baggage, pausing occasionally to poke into one container or another. Finally, her gaze settled on the object of her search, a particularly battered trunk large enough to hold a full-grown man without causing any undue lack of comfort.

The thought of a man in her trunk gave Luciana pause. The utter irony of packing someone away in her own luggage with her sister's body missing defeated even the most ghoulish twist of humor. She wondered if this were the method by which the villains secreted her sister away. Anger and grief roiled up, stealing the breath from her lungs. Determinedly, she pushed such thoughts away. There was work that *must* be done.

She tipped back the lid and burrowed through the trunk's depths. Hidden among the silken folds of her dresses, Luciana felt the distinctive texture of the tapestry bag containing her magical supplies. She breathed a sigh of relief. Just as requested, Kisaiya had tucked the bundle away from Prunella's prying eyes. The pocket hidden in the bag's lining contained the key to Alessandra's tomb. Satisfied with the results of her search, Luciana pushed herself up off the floor.

Through the paned doors, Luciana stepped outside onto the small patio reserved for her suite. In the moonlight, she hesitated. She still found it hard to breathe and her stomach knotted uncomfortably. Nothing but silly nerves . . . and anger mingled liberally with grief. Luciana dismissed the sensation as a weakness. It did not serve her purpose, and she would not allow it to influence the magic she intended to use this night.

Little natural light existed here to aid her on her way. The palazzo's towering walls and the close growth of the citrus orchard diminished what glimmer came from the heavens. The night smelled of sea, the vague tang of lemon and the sweetness of orange blossoms. She followed a roundabout cobbled path beyond her patio and, for a short way, along the length of the palazzo. She found her way to the rutted course through the orchards, ever so glad she'd participated in the Treasure Hunt all those years ago. Thanks to silly court games, she knew the palazzo grounds fairly well.

In a brief bit of open space between the palazzo and the first rows of the orchards, a cold sea wind blew off the Stretto d'Messina. The skirts of her borrowed gown flapped like a predatory bird and pressed close around her legs, almost knocking her off her feet. It was not the best of nights for intrigue. The winds threatened to turn foul, and she planned to disturb the already restless dead.

"Would tomorrow night be any better?" Luciana asked herself, straightening the lace shawl. She suppressed her shiver. The night was colder than she first thought and her heeled shoes were ill-suited for this midnight foray onto uneven ground and overgrown lawns.

Tonight was Lemuria. She hoped the *gadjé* had suitably honored their dead, lest she encounter their kinfolk wandering and vengeful. It seemed odd to find the *gadjé* so celebratory about their dead ancestors. Perhaps they had gained more from the Romani than she thought. Honor the dead and put them to rest before the planting season. Luciana shivered. If the planting went as well as the Queen's Ball, come fall there would be a healthy harvest. Being fully a part of neither the Romani nor the *gadjé* life, all of it seemed strange and, at times, improbable.

She raised her oil lamp higher and pressed on, bringing herself shortly to a path that was really little more than dirt-bare grooves worn into the lawn by gardeners' wagons over the years.

The night damp was not enough to make the path muddy and there were no puddles of note. Luciana hurried along, anxious to be about the business that kept her from her bed.

The orchard was an eerie place so late. The sounds of crickets and the wind whipping through the upper branches of the trees surrounded her. Luciana stumbled in a deep rut and cursed as she tramped on. The cemetery stood beyond the small grove of trees just ahead.

The rows of carefully cultivated trees ended abruptly, exposing her once more to the gusting wind. With the orchard between her and the Stretto, the wind battered her less. Luciana snugged the lace mantilla closer about her shoulders. Only a ditch and a gravel road separated her from the walls surrounding the cemetery.

She sat on the ground and worked her way into the ditch. With a little bit of luck and a couple of well-placed rocks, Luciana managed to avoid the little stream at its bottom. Using fistfuls of long, coarse grass, she pulled herself up the other side. It was a difficult climb made more complicated by her efforts to balance the oil lamp as she did so. The flame flickered crazily and she felt the oil slosh inside the lamp. Just as Luciana thought she would manage the feat, the spark of flame disappeared in a tiny puff of smoke. She cursed again, pushed the lamp up onto the road above and clambered, unlady-like, from the ditch.

She crossed the cobblestone drive in frustrated determination, useless lamp in hand. On the far side of the road stood two large wrought-iron gates easily twice her height. A stony wall, supported and accented by iron spikes reaching well above her head, surrounded the graveyard. A deep silence blanketed the area. The absence of sound seemed more portentous than anything Luciana imagined. Her skin crawled with goose bumps even more than it had done earlier in the courtyard at King Alaric's statue. The sense of nothingness spread its tendrils like the fog, absorbing all life in its path.

Shuddering, she forced herself to concentrate.

Despite the appearance of security, the graveyard gates were not locked. She pushed them open. The gates creaked at an ear-piercing pitch. Luciana flinched. She paused to look down the road to see if any of the Escalade *vigilare* roused. At last, confident she had drawn no attention, Luciana went on. For a long moment, the gentle crunching noise of her feet on the gravel filled the silence.

She rubbed her arms, hoping for a bit of warmth as she veered off the path and amongst the headstones, bearing for the section of the graveyard restricted to royalty. Luciana gathered her skirts, lifting them away from the gravestones as she passed along a narrow row, rather than risk brushing grave dust and inadvertently disturbing a *gadjé* ghost.

Alone in the graveyard, without a lamp to light her way, Luciana almost wished Nicobar had accompanied her, but that would have been as silly as it was useless. She wanted to see Alessa's grave for herself and, magic being a lonely art, she wanted the freedom to cast upon it without prying eyes, even Nicobar's. And since one never knew whom one would encounter during the day in a graveyard, the night seemed best for this task.

She spotted a small crypt, still new and not as weather-worn as those neighboring it on the outskirts of the royal section. Luciana headed directly for it, cutting her own path between the headstones and markers.

She dropped her tapestry bag and moved to the crypt. While modest in size, it had been no little expense to build. The entire structure, save the gated door, was made of whitish granite. Vines of ivy already climbed its walls as though the earth itself embraced the crypt. This had been built for at least a minor member of the royal family. A knot formed in her throat. Clearly, Idala intended every kindness.

Convincing herself of things she already believed, Luciana reminded herself, merely wasted time. All must come under scrutiny of one sort or another in the due course of her investigation. Vindicating Idala held no priority over her work here tonight. Luciana gathered her wits and closed her eyes, preparing for the physical and mental drain of the magic she must do. She touched the stone.

A shock wave of raw emotion erupted from the cool granite. Luciana let out a yelp of surprise and jumped back. She shook her head, closing out the rest of the world. The lump in her throat made it impossible to speak even the simplest words of magic. She felt cold, colder than she had been all night, perhaps colder than ever in her life.

And now she identified what had struck her. Anger and despair emanated from the walls of the crypt like a subvocal scream. Any lingering doubts about the nature of her sister's death faded. Alessandra did not pass from this world willingly.

Unbidden, an answering anger burst from the dark well of Luciana's soul where she had tried to contain it these past few days. She struggled to regain self-control, but her anger burned deep as she thought of the monster that had murdered, stolen, and defiled her sister. Luciana's heart beat like an angry echo to the tides of unchecked emotion flowing from the crypt.

All about her, the dead stirred. It was as though all dead things in this place turned their complete attention to her, fascinated and menacing. The *gadjé* ghosts—pale manifestations compared to the intrinsically magical, Romani accursed undead, the *mulló*—already awake for Lemuria, called out to her, recognizing her as one of the living who could still hear them.

Luciana heard the echoes of their passing, some peaceful, but most not. Could there truly be so many restless souls gone to their graves before they were ready? She shuddered at the thought. Could the *gadjé* not feel their ancestors' unrest?

At another time, Luciana would not have been able to resist these spirits' plight, but the sensations of Alessandra's torment left no room for kindly compulsions.

She steadied herself, took a deep breath, and focused upon the crypt before she touched it again. The wall felt smooth and unearthly cold beneath her fingertips. The sounds from the other graves drifted into the distance as she concentrated. At first, no sense of more than cursory identity distinguished itself behind the despair in the crypt, as though the soul forgot all that made it unique in the tragic moments of death.

Luciana pressed closer to the stone. The faint whisper of her sister's voice teased her. She pressed closer still, forcing words through her lips. A prayer in her native Romani, a promise to her sister. She waited.

Be it Alessandra's spirit, the *Fata,* or persistence, the *mulló's* voice came louder as it spoke again. Luciana's senses, augmented by the spell, confirmed what Idala's letters told her . . . Alessandra had been murdered and her body had not occupied this crypt for long.

With palms and face against the wall, Luciana slowly navigated the circumference of the crypt. She felt the vibrations of the stone as workmen cut it from the quarry, the touch of men's hands as they smoothed it and placed it piece by piece here. Beyond that, louder, clearer now came the voice of the *mulló,* the accursed living dead— Alessandra—who cried out to be free of her constraints . . . and, yet, these were only vague echoes.

At last, Luciana came to the door of the crypt. She opened her eyes and stared at it for a long moment. Solidly constructed of wrought iron, metal vines tempered into decorative swirls and adorned with bronze ivy leaves, already turned green. The leaves, artfully placed, covered the few holes left by the pattern of whorls. Someone had lovingly crafted it. She sensed the intense concentration mixed with pride. That emotion could only have been left by the artisan who constructed the door. She felt the echo of his hands even while cries of despair rang in her ears.

She trembled. Her eyes ached as though they were being used for the magic sight. She touched the door, her fingertips caressing the ivy leaves of bronze even while her eyes rose to the capstone over the door. A plaque resided there not so long ago proclaiming the occupant of the crypt to one and all. Luciana allowed her fingers to rise up, to touch the small holes where the screws once held the plaque in place. Fingers trailing, she felt the hinges. Strong, Guardians of a sort. Like great dogs set to protect their eternal ward.

At the top hinge, the granite ached from an imperfection, a dimple in its smooth surface. Made by a callous but deliberate hand. The guardian hinge had not yielded. No. The intruder moved on, to easier ground. Luciana followed the trace. His psychic scent left a scorching stain—his fear the only hamper to his determination. She smelled it. Greed on his mind encouraged him as he sought to break in. But his was not a casual greed, not the normal type, nor was this intruder the usual sort of grave robber. This looter had no interest in jewels and other valuables buried with the recently departed. No. His greed was for something else. For power.

Luciana dropped back, repulsed by the vileness that overwhelmed her as she sensed this man's purpose. His stink filled her nostrils and made her feel dirty, violated. Oh, how Alessandra must have felt! Even dead, with her spirit still lingering, to have been torn from its resting place by such a one as this!

For a moment the silent wails of despair became her own. Anger held her immobile until, at last, overcome by the sensations, Luciana fell away from the crypt. Bile burned in the back of her throat.

Panting at the exertion of her spell, Luciana picked herself up and wiped the psychic filth from her hands on the grass before going back to work. More determined than ever, she touched the door, letting her anger provide the energy she required to cast upon the crypt.

She stopped in surprise. Another had been here, examining the door, prodding about, intruding upon Alessandra's burial space, but his motives were unclear. Luciana frowned, trying to determine if this person came before or after the robber. At last she gave up the search. This secondary interloper had not violated Alessandra's burial place.

Luciana focused on the first intruder's trail and followed it to the lock. A trusty lock it had been. It spoke its own sorrow like a toothless hound. She felt the lock, still fresh and new; felt the touch of the groundskeeper who turned the key for, he thought, the first and last time; felt the distant traces of the key given to the queen and by her to Luciana herself. The key sang where it lay in the pocket of her woolen dress, longing to be returned to its mate, the lock.

Scrapes gouged the metal lock. A large chunk of the granite lay on the ground, fractured from the whole of the block. Rust, like blood, covered where the metal had been scraped. The beautiful crypt door was cruelly pried away from the granite where the locking mechanism should have been.

Luciana did not bother with the key. The breathless dread and unyielding anger grew inside her. Her head swam, making her feel even more faint. The lump in her throat seemed lodged like a permanent fixture. In spite of it all, she still grasped the door handle. She sensed the integrity of the crypt protesting this new violation, heard the wailing of Alessandra's *mulló* grow louder, deafening her to all around her.

The door clanged, banging in muted violence against its own jamb, but refused to open. She released the handle and took a deep breath, forcing herself to concentrate, to exert her will. She soothed the workings of the door, the walls of the vault, and even the echoes of the missing body with whispered words in Romani. The words rolled off her tongue, focusing her mind. Everything became acute. So crystal clear! She tugged on the handle again. This time, after a groan of protest, the door succumbed to her magic and relinquished its hold.

Sensations, one after another, rushed over Luciana as she stood in the doorway. The despair, the confusion, the anger, the fear, all eddied around her like a deadly whirlpool. All of it swept over her, tearing at her, leaving her shocked and emotionally bruised with the sure knowledge that Alessandra's suffering did not end with her untimely and unwilling death.

Luciana braced herself against the exhausting assault. For Alessa, she must be strong. She squared her shoulders and stood straighter. She forced her own presence to the fore, fighting for control of her senses. The change came quite suddenly. Something shifted within her, filling her with a greater strength of purpose.

She entered the vault and allowed the echoes of the *mulló* who once resided here to take her in its grip and batter her with its rage. Luciana took in every bit of emotion that came at her, assuming the raw power into herself; felt also the intruder and now his companions— four in all—all of this she accepted until she could take no more. There was nothing more for her to learn here. The body was well and truly gone. The evidence was clear even in the absolute blackness of the tomb. There were traces of others: the Royal Groundskeeper; others who came to see for themselves the violation done, including that second interloper. Was he friend or enemy? It made no difference. She should not count upon any friend at court now, not *any*. Someone took Alessandra's life and must be made to pay. She would not and could not allow any other relationship to infringe upon her loyalty to Alessandra and the Romani, their kindred people.

Luciana withdrew slowly, letting the sensations that enveloped her fade. Outside, the fresh air struck her as sweet—so very different from that within. She pushed the door closed with a shiver, resealing the tomb. Almost absentmindedly, she returned the key to its lock, giving the mates at least peace in their reunion.

Quivering with cold and exhaustion, she took a deep breath and sank to the grass, without particular care for the wet or the cold soaking through her woolen skirts.

From her bag, she took a small flask of wine and drank deeply. The wine, mulled with herbs, replenished her mangled nerves as it made a quick course down her gullet and into the pit of her stomach. She almost wished now that she had eaten earlier.

In the cold clarity of the moment, Luciana took note that, as feared, no fairy offering lay beside the crypt— yet another innocent mistake by Idala that potentially came at great cost to Alessandra. The lasa blessed Alessa's birth and proved a great resource to her over the years as she developed her own magical talents. In death, all knew to leave an offering of thanksgiving for the fairy-touched. Well, apparently, not *all* knew, Luciana thought. If the offerings had been left, perhaps the fairy folk would have—could have—guarded Alessa against the intruders, despite the iron door.

From her bag, Luciana took a bundled scrap of leather. She unfolded it and placed it and its contents, an oozing honeycomb, beside the door of the crypt. She also stacked cheese, bread, and the rest of her wine. Perhaps, if the fairy folk could be appeased, they might still aid Alessandra—perhaps even herself. Now, however, she could do little more than hope.

Reminding herself again that she did not want to risk calling a ghost because she had taken away its grave dust, Luciana rose and brushed herself off. She felt drained. Her work, though, was not yet done. She touched the crypt again, her hands moving over the door and broken lock, feeling for the slippery psychic vileness of the intruder. It was not difficult to find.

Intent upon the scent of the intruder, Luciana turned from the crypt and scanned the graveyard. It was as if a misty miasma rose from the earth where they had walked, their footsteps searing sacred ground.

By the wails and sobbing of the ghosts who still remained in their burial mounds, Luciana knew they had sensed the evil done to one of their own—however new Alessandra was among them—and protested. Either the intruder and his fellows could not, or would not, hear their voiceless pleas. So now, weeks later, it was to Luciana they cried their objections and thereby created a corroborating trail for her to follow.

As Luciana came once more to the gate, she was amazed that she had not sensed the trail left by the intruder and his minions before. The area fairly stank with his scent. She passed beyond the gate to the road and paused, refocusing. This was a back avenue from the palazzo. Judging by its condition, it was seldom used. It would be a relatively simple matter for someone to station a horse and cart here. Indeed, the trail was less clear here and, with no ghostly witnesses offering testament, she hesitated. Which way had they gone?

She knelt and touched the gravelly soil of the lane, concentrating. She could not find traces of the subjects of her hunt, but the horses . . . There had been many in recent days. Escalade officers come to investigate on the queen's behalf, and others on the same matter. She rose and moved farther down the lane, away from the gate. Ah! Here it was not so difficult!

It was the horse that gave the robbers away, and Luciana blessed her Romani stock for her affinity with the beasts. The horse was old and tired, taken from his stall after a day's work in the market. No grain for his troubles, just an ungrateful lout free with the whip. And the cart? Nothing like a Romani *vardo,* this cart was all plain and ramshackle, with a loose axle and uneven wheels which made it pull to the left. Luciana saw it and the horse clearly in her mind.

She pushed herself up off the ground, dusted her knees, and began walking down the lane. She was vaguely aware of sounds coming from the orchard, but she was intent upon her search.

When she heard the horses, she thought it only her vision coming clearer. Luciana stopped. The noises were coming from the wrong direction and there was—

The plummet seemed to go on endlessly, as though she were falling into a canyon. She landed in the bottom of the ditch with a groan and a sputter to rid her mouth of dewy, dusty grass.

Nicobar leaned close over her. "Are you all right, *Daiya?* Are you hurt?" he whispered.

Luciana nodded with a grimace. On top of the sore muscles from her carriage ride, she really did not need further bruising, never mind her embarrassment at an inglorious tumble. She shook free and struggled to sit up amidst the tangle of grasses and woolen skirts, angry.

Nicobar held her back and raised a finger to his lips. He pointed to the road just as a mounted officer called out.

"Ho, there, Citizen! Are you well?"

Someone shifted in the ditch nearby. Luciana turned and smothered an exclamation. Of all the people she might encounter on a lonely road behind the palazzo and beside a graveyard, she never expected to see her husband's young cousin.

Prunella moved forward, nodding briefly to her benefactress. "I'll go, you get Her Grace safely back to her rooms."

Nicobar nodded, and Prunella struggled up the embankment. "Good evening, officers," she said, and hurriedly made her way down the lane toward the *vigilare*.

"M'Lady, what brings you out at this hour?"

Prunella raised her hand, holding something out for the officers to see. "My mistress was riding today and lost this. She has been quite beside herself, so I thought to find it for her."

Luciana watched the exchange. Prunella was more resourceful than she gave the girl credit for. The officer talking to Prunella dismounted. His posture was stiff, but friendly as he motioned his companions to proceed down the road without him.

Nicobar pressed Luciana down into the grasses once more as the *vigilare* passed. Luciana's breath caught in her throat. They rode close to the ditch and were clearly looking to see if Prunella was alone. Luciana let out a sigh when the officers turned their mounts and rejoined the other who remained with Prunella.

"Well, M'Lady," the officer said, "it is not good for a young lady to be out and about by herself at these hours and I'll wager your mistress will not appreciate the risk you have taken on her behalf. Allow me and my brother officers to escort you back to the palazzo."

"Thank you, Capitano," Prunella said and permitted herself to be assisted onto the capitano's horse in front of him.

Nicobar touched his finger to his lips again and edged higher for a better vantage point. He dropped back down. "Prunella will be well. Undoubtedly they will reach the palazzo before us."

"Prunella will be quite scandalized by all of this," Luciana sighed.

"It was her idea." Nicobar shrugged. "I thought, *Daiya*, that you would not want to answer questions about your affairs here tonight."

Luciana grimaced. Her presence *would* be so much harder to explain.

"Come. We must get you back to your suite," Nicobar said, tugging on her arm.

She turned away from the guardsmen who were head-ing back and allowed her aide to help her from the ditch. It had already been a long night. She must rest. And think.

Luciana paused as they entered the orchard. "How did you find me?"

"Prunella noted that you left the suite and, feeling it was inappropriate for either of you to be out without an escort, she woke me. The rest was easy enough. There would be only one place you might go without announcing your intentions."

"There'll be the devil to pay in the morning," Luciana groaned.

Nicobar laughed. "I sometimes wonder who is the guardian and who is the ward."

"I'm glad *you* find all of this amusing, but I am expected to teach the girl what is expected of a young noblewoman. I'm no *gadjé,* and anything I do reflects upon my husband. This is no easy task and Prunella's nature makes it all the more difficult."

"I hope that the experience," Nicobar gestured toward the cemetery, "was worth the effort at least."

"It was," Luciana said, nodding thoughtfully. "It was."

VII

"Secret thoughts and open countenance . . ."
                                    —Scipione Alberti

10 d'Maggio 1684

LUCIANA lay restless beneath her coverlets. Nearly dawn, yet sleep evaded her. The cries of the ghosts still rang through her mind. Visions of her sister's torment troubled her. She silently cursed anyone who made a *mulló's* existence worse than death. There could be no mercy for one such as this.

But these acts had not been done by one. No, more were involved; she knew that much from the interloper's stink and the scent of his assistants. Were these latter men fellow conspirators or merely henchmen without the sense the Sisters *Fata* gave a mussel?

The leader's hunger for power still lingered as a bitter aftertaste. The corruption of power. Such a taint never grew without perverting those around it, and the afflicted sought the company of their kind for the breeding of plots and intrigue. How far had the degeneration taken this interloper? Was he at the center of whatever plot was brewing or did he hope to secure his own future by aiding and abetting the central player?

There were no answers to be found by putting the questions to herself. With a frustrated sigh, she pulled the blankets higher and snuggled into the depths of her pillows, determined to coax a little sleep out of the night.

She was exhausted. A two-day journey—even in the luxury of a carriage—was wearing, especially with their arrival timed to coincide with the Queen's Ball, never mind her late night adventures in the graveyard. She would be worth nothing to anyone without sleep.

It was not to be. Slumber had been a fickle lover these last weeks. Still wide awake almost an hour later, Luciana pulled back the bed-curtain and slid out of bed.

The moon shone through the high angular window, anointing the room with its light. The chill set in her bones from the night's adventure had not been vanquished by fresh, dry nightclothes, new bed linens, or a winter's worth of coverlets, or even by the bed warmer Kisaiya so thoughtfully provided. It should not be so cold, Luciana thought as she kicked her feet into her leather slippers, even in the middle of an early spring night. Her robe lay in a silky-frothy pool of gleaming white across the back of the bedside chair. Luciana reached for it. She froze, her hand hovering over the robe.

The robe moved. She blinked and stared. The frothy pool mistaken for her robe became iridescent, bubbling upward, outward, like a new spring breaking through an earthen crust. The shimmering thing puddled and shaped itself into a hazy form, indistinct at first, and then, slowly, into a great white owl.

"By the Fates!" Luciana dropped to her knees on the floor. She pressed her hand to her heart, fearing news of another death. But then reason seeped in. Owls bringing news of death were mortal and visitations came through normal means of flight. What could this owl mean? She paused. "Can it be?"

She stretched out her hand. The owl's beak opened and snapped shut. There was no sound, but an unnatural wind rose up and swirled around the room, stirring the heavy bed-curtains and her visitor's feathers. The owl stepped closer, its eyes piercing, mesmerizing. It stopped within a handbreadth of her and extended its neck.

Longing filled her heart. Luciana reached out.

The bird grabbed Luciana's finger.

Luciana bit back a cry and tried to pull away. The

ring on her left forefinger slid down, as though the owl pulled it.

"No!" Luciana cried and grabbed at it. The bird hopped away, dropped the ring on the carpet between them, then did nothing as Luciana slowly reached out and retrieved the ring. It was the crest of her position as *Araunya di Cayesmengro*—Alessandra's title. Luciana looked up breathlessly. "Alessa?"

Having said her sister's name, Luciana bit her tongue. But, if Alessandra were already *mulló*, did breaking the taboo of calling her by name mean anything? To use the name of the dead—the Romani dead—one risked pulling the spirit from the grave, risked the impurities found in such an association. Would name-saying invoke the *mulló* and make it easier for her to contact Alessandra? Or would name-saying only further defile her, further anger and hurt her? In the end, it did not much matter. She had spoken the name. Luciana took a deep breath. "Is it you? Are you really Alessandra? Speak if you can!"

The wraith bird clacked its beak, but made no sound.

Luciana leaned closer. "Alessandra, I will end your suffering, but you must help! Speak to me. Try!"

The *mulló* Alessandra had become withdrew still more, puffing its feathers and sinking into itself. In a few breaths, the iridescence grew faint, then murky, and faded backward, into the tapestry-covered wall beside the bed.

Luciana cursed and pulled aside the covering, looking for any signs of the spirit. She found nothing more than a cool stone wall. She beat her fist against it in frustration, then cursed again at the pain. It was Alessa. It must be. Atropos, blessed be, have mercy! Let it be Alessa! Despite her desperate desire to see her sister if even a moment longer in whatever shape she took, Alessandra was gone perhaps never to return, even as a *mulló*.

The terrible loneliness consumed Luciana once again. What was life to be like without her sister? Or anyone else she loved? Without even community? Why had *Fata* Clotho chosen this solitary path for her? What would become of Alessa if she could not free her sister . . . if she could not free herself from her grief and allowed it to finish her? Luciana sank to the floor and wept. Somehow she must find the strength.

How long she sat, chilled and frustrated, Luciana did not know, but she had much food for thought. Had Alessa's visitation been the gift of this special night, Lemuria, when the *gadjé* ghosts once more walked? Or had she somehow drawn Alessandra by her presence at court? Or invoking her name? Or her activities in the graveyard? Was Alessandra trying to reach her? Was this visitation but a mere dabbling by the *chovahano* grave robber? A demonstration of his power? Or, and she could not rule out this possibility, was this nothing more than a malicious court game of magic—a bit of audacious illusion or further torment of an already tortured spirit? Were it the latter, those foolish enough to participate in the ruse to toy with her would come to regret it.

Luciana shuddered. Did these men have any idea of the magic they wielded? Could the interloper comprehend the balances of black and white magic? Of his state of utter impurity—that he would be *marimé*, unclean, for the rest of his life by using this magic? Did he even care? She shook her head. He could not understand the debasement of *marimé;* the *gadjé* did not even have a word for it.

This much she knew, the violator of Alessandra's grave was a man and he dabbled in magic. But she also felt certain that this *chovahano* was *gadjé*. The magic she sensed in the graveyard was Romani, but it did not have the clean, biting taste one expected from a spell cast by a witch of the Wandering Folk. No, there had been the imprecision common with many white *gadjé* casters and an absolute disrespect for the defiling nature of dealing with the dead.

But what if she were wrong? What if this man was simply inept—and more stupid than a hedge post for getting involved with something he could not comprehend? Luciana could not decide which was worse, if the sorcerer knew what he was doing, then the possibilities of his threat to those around her were too unbearable to consider. The only thing worse was if the *chovahano* had no comprehension of the power he attempted to manipulate.

In any event, her questions would not be answered without some investigation. Luciana resolved that in the morning, she would send for Alessandra's books, then go through her sister's belongings. At least this *gadjé* custom of preserving the dead's things could serve her, unlike the others to date.

Kisaiya padded down the narrow stairs from the small apartment she shared with Prunella, shoes in hand to silence her movements. She paused before the mirror at the base of the steps and inspected her appearance. Her hair was neatly done up, her face clean, and her dress a circumspect brown.

Ruefully, Kisaiya pulled at her sleeves to make sure they covered the bracelets about her wrists, and checked that her earrings were discreet. Lady Prunella seemed offended that a servant might even possess such things, no doubt because her own fortunes were so meager. The *gadjé,* as a whole, did not understand the Romani custom of wearing their wealth, and Lady Prunella seemed less tolerant than most.

All in all, she was pleased with her lot in life. She glanced up the stairway fretfully at the sound of someone moving about. Was she up? She listened for a long moment and heard nothing more. Lady Prunella was noisy about her morning rituals, so she must simply have turned over. Kisaiya smiled at her own reflection. Everything was so much easier when Prunella slept, which is why Kisaiya liked the mornings. At the moment, she felt fresh and ready to start her day.

The hour was particularly early. Kisaiya planned to put some order to the *Daiya's* things before she woke. The *Daiya* would no doubt be pleased with her efforts. Her appreciativeness almost made up for the lost life of roving. Kisaiya frowned at herself. No sense in mourning over that life. Mama and Da were determined she get into one of the Silk Guilds and what better way, they reasoned, than serving one of the *Araunyas* since they owned the associated properties? Kisaiya chose not to think of leaving Luciana's direct service. She lived a good life here and the mistress was as good as they came, even with her *gadjé* upbringing. The mistress was a woman of two worlds, the Romani and the *gadjé,* but sadly, she seemed also to be of neither. This caused the *Daiya* great pain and confusion at times. If Kisaiya could ease that burden with service, then so be it.

Kisaiya smoothed a wisp of hair into place. She frowned at herself. Here she was up early and she had done nothing but gaze at her own reflection. Crimson touched her cheeks as she stared at herself further. At times like these she rued the conservative attire appropriate to her current station. With a particolored gown of silk and her wealth worn in a proper display, Nicobar could not help but notice her.

Enough of this! she thought to herself. With great determination, she picked up her shoes from the little end table but turned so sharply toward the lower rooms that the toe of one shoe pinged against a porcelain vase, causing it to tip.

Kisaiya lunged for the vase and fell with it against Luciana's door. Her hands shook as she surveyed the piece. Completely unharmed. She made a face at it. Since the queen had furnished the apartments, Kisaiya would take no chances.

She eased away from her mistress' door, wincing as it creaked when relieved of her weight. Kisaiya rose up on her knees and placed the vase back on the table then grabbed up her shoes before standing. She hesitated outside the door, listening to see if she had woken the *Daiya* with all of her noise. No. There was nothing. She breathed a sigh of relief and turned once more toward the parlor. She stopped at the sound of the latch lifting behind her.

The *Daiya* appeared in the open door, her face shadowed by the poor light in the tiny hallway. "Kisaiya? Is that you? It's not even dawn yet, *Chavi*. What are you doing?"

Kisaiya turned, dropping her shoes. "I didn't mean to

wake you. I was just going to start my day . . ." She hesitated as the door swung wide, revealing several lit candles about the room. She turned to Luciana, a question half-formed.

Her mistress seemed to read her expression. She stepped back from the door, waving her hand vaguely at the branch of lit candles on the table by the door. "There is no need to concern yourself on my behalf, Kisaiya, I was already awake."

The lighting improved in Luciana's chamber, what with the candles and the first rays of dawn stealing across the high sill of the bedroom's only window. The *Daiya* wore a simple shift, her dark brunette hair falling in a long, single braid down her back. She sat—or rather sank—tiredly onto the chaise lounge near her bed, pulling a shawl about her. Dark circles shadowed her eyes and intensified her pallor. She had not fully regained her health since the birth of her stillborn son nine months ago.

Kisaiya sat on the chaise, tucking the shawl around her mistress' feet. "Did you not sleep well, *Daiya?*"

Luciana shook her head vaguely, closing her eyes.

"I should have prepared a sleeping draught for you last night. I feared your visit to the *Araunya's gadjé* grave would be too much for you." Kisaiya spoke softly, hoping that Luciana had slipped into a doze.

Luciana pressed her fingers to her temples. "Even your potion would not have helped last night, I think."

"The morning is still young, and no one is yet about. I'm sure Lady Prunella and I could—"

Groaning, her mistress sat up. "There is too much to do, *Chavi,* and now that I am at court, my time is not completely my own. I am to breakfast with the queen."

Kisaiya rose resolutely and went to the bureau where her mistress' brushes lay. She paused as she saw the cards laid out in an arrangement unique to the *Daiya*. The cards revealed portents of complications and danger. She frowned and glanced back at Luciana, who watched her. Kisaiya picked up the brushes and left the cards.

Wordlessly, Luciana turned in her chaise as Kisaiya

drew up a chair and began to unbind her hair. Kisaiya was careful about her work, the *Daiya's* hair was particularly long and thick. If she allowed herself to become distracted, the *Daiya's* hair inevitably turned into a tangle. In only a few short moments, she began parting and arranging. She focused hard on her work. Luciana's hair must be just right, appropriate to appear in court, in a style both fashionable and yet simple out of respect for the period of mourning. She settled upon one and set about creating it.

"I like that," Luciana said after a moment.

"Pardon?"

"That song. The one you're humming."

"I didn't realize," Kisaiya murmured.

"And now you've stopped," Luciana said. She turned, reaching up to capture Kisaiya's hand. "Do you know that you only do that when you're worried?"

Kisaiya smiled slightly and shook her head.

"And that leaves me to wonder why you might be worried," Luciana continued. She looked pointedly at the cards on her bureau and eased back against the chaise again.

Kisaiya began again with her work, her fingers flying through the braiding of various strands.

"Have you spoken with Nicobar? About last night?"

"No, *Daiya,* I was sleeping when you returned." Kisaiya saw her smile and smothered a sigh of relief. The *Daiya* knew her well, recognized the lie, but was unoffended by it.

"There is no mistaking the signs I found in the graveyard, *Chavi.* My sister's body was stolen by a *chovahano* who is unhampered by conscience."

Kisaiya dropped her handful of braids and moved around to see Luciana's face. *"Marimé!* But a *chovahano?* Among the *gadjé?* And the magics one would commit using a body . . ." She shivered and forced down the bile which rose in her throat. "Could you be mistaken?"

"I spent the night considering just that, but I know what I saw, what I sensed." Luciana shook her head sadly. "And should I still be troubled by doubts, I am now even more convinced than I was in the graveyard. Last night, I was visited by—my sister's *mulló*."

Kisaiya jumped to her feet. "The *mulló* was here? And you did not call me?" She glanced about the room and knelt beside the chaise. "This is no simple magic, and no man of the Rom would meddle with powers this potent or impure."

"There are few enough *chovahani* who would try such a thing," Luciana replied. "But no, this is not even a *gadjé* witch. The evil was done by a man, a *gadjé* who probably doesn't know, much less understand, the depth of the powers he has invoked just by stealing her body."

"A *gadjé* sorcerer? Does such a thing truly exist?"

"It would seem so."

"And he sent the *mulló* of your own sister against you?"

"No, I had not meant that," Luciana said hastily. "I think—I hope she came to me of her own will. Her spirit has been invoked, her body most assuredly stolen, but I think this *gadjé* does not control her as well he might— be this through a certain laxity or immature talent, I cannot say."

Kisaiya rocked back onto her heels, sighing loudly. "I take no ease in either condition, *Chavi*," Luciana said, leaning back as Kisaiya picked up the brushes again. "If this sorcerer has been careless, then he raises a twofold threat to me and those around him. Possessing the power to cause much pain, he can hurt others through accident as well as design. If he has merely immature talent, then he does not understand what he meddles with. The power he plays with can consume him, and no one knows where the havoc will end."

"There is a third option you have not considered, *Daiya*. What if he knows what he is doing and merely toys with you?" Kisaiya asked.

Luciana turned, her eyes glimmering with fear, "I fear that possibility even more and pray that it is not the case . . . for my sister's sake, for . . . well, for all our sakes. Even so, I think it best that I send word to the *Beluni*."

As Nicobar opened the gate, he flashed Luciana a reassuring smile. The gate creaked heavily on its wrought
iron hinges, announcing her arrival. She stepped into the
sheltered inner courtyard of the queen's garden to be
greeted by the trills of gaily-colored birds flitting among
the lemon trees. The morning sun filtered through the
branches and dappled the tiles of the walkway surrounding the garden.

Luciana paused briefly. The queen had insisted upon
privacy the previous night, Luciana felt sure of it. Why,
then, did she hold court? A page waved a kerchief at
the bees hovering over the food. Tucked up against the
wall, one of the queen's ladies fingered a lute in an unin-
spired way, her gaze directed demurely at the instrument
in her lap. More importantly, however, Princess Bianca
sat at the edge of the walk, like a sleek cat sunning
herself. A small round man—bedecked in more bro-
cades, ribbons and laces than either member of the royal
house—held forth, waving his arms expressively as he
spoke.

The queen turned, pearls glinting in her dark hair, and
acknowledged Luciana with a smile. Luciana dropped
into a deep curtsy, sweeping back the folds of her heavy
indigo silk gown to expose the artistry of her embroider-
ers on the rose-colored petticoat. She hid a satisfied
smirk at the sound of the man's envious gasp. She
thought she recognized him from last night, a conte, one
of the Princess' hangers-on who had stared at her so
curiously.

The lute player stood and made a nervous curtsy. Luciana acknowledged her and turned back to the breakfast table. The conte bowed. His courtesy was so
extravagant that Luciana thought she saw him teeter in
his shoes. Bianca moved her skirts aside for Luciana to
sit as the queen indicated.

"Good morning, my dear *Araunya*," the queen murmured. She darted a glance at the princess. Idala's
smooth dark countenance barely reflected her irritation.
"You know our cousin, Bianca, but have you met . . . ?"

Here the queen paused prettily as though she had trouble remembering her guest's name. Just as he was about to speak, she laughed and waved him silent. "Have you met Conte Urbano?"

From long years of close friendship and frequent visits, Luciana read the queen's mood in a moment. These meddlesome two came to the queen's private breakfast uninvited. Luciana turned to the conte. "I don't believe I've had that . . . experience."

The conte turned to her with a flourish and reached for her hand, his demeanor that of a man with a purpose.

Luciana accepted a cup brimming with chocolate from an attendant at just that moment, leaving the conte to check the gesture and bend in a deep bow.

"Conte Urbano di Vega, at your service, Your Grace."

"My guest is the *Araunya di Cayesmengri e Cayesmengro,* Conte Urbano," Idala said. She spoke softly, but there was steel in her tone.

"But of course!" the conte murmured, bowing again and preening over the festive silk brocade jacket he wore. "As you can see, I am quite the ardent admirer of Gypsy Silk. Your people have collected a small fortune from clothing me."

"Not so small a fortune, I think," Bianca laughed.

The conte appeared perturbed at Luciana's mild response to his introduction.

Luciana looked at Princess Bianca, wondering how well she knew the queen's moods. Just how perceptive was this woman? Was she here because of coincidence or cleverness?

"You seem distracted this morning, Your Grace," the princess observed with a smile.

"I do?" Luciana took a bit of honeyed lemon and stirred it into her chocolate.

"As early as you left my cousin's ball, one should think you would be well rested," the princess said.

"Or could it be that Her Grace had an assignation with an admirer?" the conte asked with a knowing look.

Luciana set down her cup and accepted a pastry filled with minced veal sweetbreads and slices of prosciutto

from the server. She exchanged looks with the queen,
but remained studiously composed. "Perhaps the conte
is not aware that I am a married woman and so was
tucked safely into bed at an early hour."

"A most proper wife," the conte said silkily. "Your
husband is fortunate to have such a loyal, dutiful and
obedient spouse."

"I didn't see your husband when he arrived," the princess said.

"His Grace will not be joining me," Luciana said
tartly, then regretted it when she saw the princess' expression. Perhaps she read more into the princess' observation than was intended. She almost bit her tongue in
frustration. Unable to leave things as they were, she
added in a more conciliatory tone, "At least not right
away."

Conte Urbano arched one of his painted blond brows.
"Has he returned from the front in Peloponnesus,
then?"

Luciana turned to the round little man. "No, not yet."

"I would have thought you paid more attention to
other matters than the battle with the Turks," the queen
said. She watched him carefully now. "In fact, I was
unaware you took any interest in politics at all."

Conte Urbano laughed gaily and drew a lace kerchief
from his sleeve to dab at his lips. "There is frequently
more to a man than is revealed by his tailor or the pretty
poetry he writes. As married women, surely you know
that?"

Idala did not resist a sudden devilish grin at Luciana.
"His Majesty, for all his good qualities, is not much of
a poet."

"I seem to recall that your husband, the duca, was
fond of poetry, *Araunya*," the princess said.

Luciana nodded and attempted a smile. Was the reminder an innocent remark or a catty reminder of how
long her husband had avoided her company? She hid
behind an inspection of the nearest platter of marzipan
and pear tarts offered by an attendant. She could not
think of anything to say that would neither be a lie nor
reveal her own pain over Stefano's extended absence

and even more telling silence. As it was, too much of her private affairs were apparent to the princess, but such was the cost of having the queen's own brother for a husband.

"A man, inspired by beauty, cannot help but worship with words, so I can testify," the conte said, producing a sheaf of folded papers from inside his coat with a flourish. His ink-blackened tongue wetted his lips. Luciana noted that last bit with a shudder of revulsion.

"My Lord, wouldn't a private audience with Her Highness be more appropriate? For this first offering?" the queen said brightly. "I know I would be jealous if such expositions were made public before I was given time to relish them during those few quiet moments I am allowed. Can it be that my cousin feels so very differently in this matter than I?"

The princess smiled placatingly as she turned to the downcast nobleman. "Pray, good friend, save your dedications for another time. Besides, we were discussing my cousin's brother. We would not want these good ladies to think we were not sufficiently admiring of his noteworthy qualities."

"But, of course, how thoughtless of me! Perhaps you might share some news of the front and some of the metaphoric delights your husband has bestowed upon you?" The conte's tone was insinuating, as though he almost dared her.

Having lost her appetite before this, Luciana was saved the embarrassment of dropping her cutlery in surprise.

"It is possible, Conte Urbano, that the *Araunya* wishes to keep her letters to herself. What husband could fail to be impassioned by so lovely a wife as she?" a deep, masculine voice said from behind. "Indeed, my dear lady, your beauty is only overshadowed by my very own Queen of Love and Beauty."

"Indeed. I speak for both of us when I say that we prefer intimacy in all of our exchanges. Is that not so, Your Grace?" another male voice proclaimed.

As one, all at the table turned, rising as they found the king standing just behind them. Beside him, looking the worse for wear—the dusty signs of the road still upon him—stood Stefano.

Luciana saw his fury in an instant. *Fata,* above and below, she knew every aspect of his countenance. Even with her own mixed emotions at seeing him and his mood, she could not help but tremble from deep within—from love, most desperate, rather than fear or anger on her own part. He had given her his cue. They would speak later . . . in a more intimate setting.

The king waved them back into their chairs. "Forgive me, my dear, for the interruption, but I have just returned from my morning ride with Lord Strozzini where I happened upon your brother and thought, despite his wearing the greater part of the road from Peloponnesus to Citteauroea, you would welcome your brother and I to your table."

"But of course!" the queen ran to the men, pausing briefly to kiss her husband's cheek before engulfing her brother in a hearty embrace, completely disregarding the ruination it would cause to her gown.

Luciana came more slowly. She curtsied to the king and then stood a long, awkward moment before her husband after the queen stepped back. She could feel the gazes of the princess and the conte boring into her back. The court gossip mill would have fodder for days, and every moment that stretched out only gave them more grist.

Stefano, at last, broke the moment. His arm dropped away from his sister's side. He stepped forward and bowed low, taking Luciana's hands in his, he kissed them both and then stood, staring at her a moment longer. "Your Grace, you are as stunning as ever before." He turned to his sister. "Majesty, we interrupted your breakfast and I am fresh from the road, I—"

"You will sit and take something to eat. You will have time enough with your wife later," Idala said firmly. To Luciana, she said, "You *will* forgive my appropriating you and your husband for just a little longer?"

While the queen phrased it as a question, there was no mistaking the command ever so gently expressed in her tone.

"We are most gratified, Your Majesty," Luciana murmured. Her left hand, still in Stefano's possession, had begun to hurt from his grip.

While they had been speaking, pages stepped from their shaded alcoves and scurried to seat King Alban to the right of Idala and Stefano to the right of the king and to Luciana's left.

For a time, they sat in relative silence, watching the king as he ate. Fat bees danced in attendance. Alban ate with relish, mindful in a careless way of his frothy cuffs and cream-colored brocade coat. Stefano, Luciana noted, made a point of eating but without much vigor and he, clearly, had to remind himself to smile. Furthermore, he did not make eye contact with her. It was just as well that Luciana had already lost her appetite. It left her free to make the pretense of smiling and excitement at seeing her husband after so long.

After a time, Alban sat back, replete, and considered each of his wife's guests. "Had I known the company my wife kept at her breakfast table, my morning rides would always have ended thus."

"I'm not always as fortunate as I've been this morning," the queen said, bestowing a happy smile upon her brother. "Though I am most pleased whenever you have a spare moment in your day to share with me . . . and most fortunate when you arrive with such gifts as my brother returned safely home."

Alban took his wife's hand, turned it over in his own and placed a gentle kiss in her palm. It pleased Luciana to see such tenderness expressed by the royal couple, and yet the moment was bittersweet sitting here beside her own husband—returned and yet so very far from reach. She smiled, though. At least the royal couple found happiness. She knew from experience what a toll the drama of court life took on a marriage.

Bianca coughed delicately and observed to no one in particular. "One would think these two lovers rather than husband and wife."

"Oh, quite," Conte Urbano said with an indulgent little chuckle. "Indeed, Your Highness, such devotion takes much of a man's time and leaves him with little energy for his other . . . affairs." As soon as he had finished the words, he looked as though he wished he could bite off his own ink-blackened tongue.

Retaining his wife's hand, Alban turned a beneficent look upon the conte. "Forgive me, Conte Urbano, I had not realized I so presumed upon your time. Please, do not allow my presence here to further detain you from your business."

The conte blushed a deep crimson and blustered, "But, Your Majesty . . ." He bit off his protest with a strangled sound. The king remained serene and expectant. "Forgive me, Your Majesty," Urbano said as he rose. "I did not mean to speak out of turn."

"Not at all, Conte Urbano, I am duly reminded that there are more than the affairs of state to address. It would be most discourteous of me to interfere with the smooth management of my subjects' concerns."

"Of course," the conte said. He bowed deeply to the king and then to his hostess. "With your permission?"

"But, of course," Idala replied.

Conte Urbano backed from the table. At an appropriate distance, he wheeled and left the queen's garden. Luciana watched him leave, her eyes narrowing. Something about the man troubled her, but try as she might, she could not quite place what it was about him she found so disturbing.

At a signal from the queen, servants quietly whisked breakfast platters away and left the five nobles in relative privacy. The lute player stopped her fingering, looking relieved at her dismissal. She fled through the queen's solar in a flurry of skirts and discordant protests from her instrument as it banged against some unseen table or chair in her flight.

As though taking her cue, Bianca also rose. "If it pleases you, I will—"

"No, Cousin, please stay," the king said.

Idala looked across the table at Luciana and Stefano and then back to the king. "Perhaps Your Majesty would prefer privacy?"

"I would have you remain," the king said. To Stefano, he said, "Won't you stay as well?" He included Luciana with a smile. "I would have the counsel of you both in this important matter at hand. I had not hoped to find such an opportune time with a member of the Palantini also available."

"I am intrigued. What matter could this be that requires the attentions of we four *and* the Palantini?" the princess asked, leaning forward.

The King took his embroidered riding gloves from his knee and tossed them onto the cleared table. "Bianca, it is time we thought of making a suitable marriage for you."

The princess gaped, then pinched her lips shut. "You surprise me with this sudden familial interest."

"Not so sudden," the king said with an elegantly expressive shrug. "It is a matter I've been giving considerable thought."

"I would not want to trouble you so, when there are other, more pressing matters requiring your attention."

Alban laughed, loud enough to make the birds in the lemon trees take flight.

Stefano remained silent and attentive. Not returned an hour and he already knew what was afoot!

Luciana chewed her lip and watched the princess fidget with her rings, clench her fingers, and then tuck her hands into her lap. All the while, the princess' expression reflected only regal composure. Idala gazed down at the table; there was no telling just where her sentiments lay.

"His Majesty is most thoughtful in his consideration," Stefano said quietly. With the briefest of glances at his wife, he continued. "In some royal families, marriages wait until the women are quite late in their years so that they are set in their ways and disinclined to greet matrimonial prospects with pleasure."

Stung, Luciana felt a blush creep into her cheeks. "In other families, the royals aren't much more than children unable to comprehend marriage, much less find joy in such a union. I compliment His Majesty on his wisdom. The princess is young enough to appreciate a husband and old enough to enjoy . . . matrimonial pleasures. You are to be congratulated in your good fortune, Your Highness."

Bianca's absent smile was wan at best. Her hand reached for a fan in her lap. Finding none, her expression faltered.

Luciana wondered what exactly discomfited the princess. She had been raised knowing her marriage would be arranged.

Alban nodded appreciatively at Luciana, seemingly unaware of the princess' discomfort. "Thank you. Indeed, I would not wish my cousin to find me remiss, for all that we are not blooded brother and sister and she is the only child of our late sovereign lord. I wish to honor her father who reigned before me by seeking my cousin's comfort, if not pleasure in this matter of marriage, which is a cautious affair at best, especially a royal marriage.

"I know you were greatly affected by being kidnapped by the Turks when you were at such a vulnerable age. Who would not be? But I hope that you can put this in the past and look toward the future," Alban said gently. "You have probably not considered marriage yet, but I hope you will consider it now. Believe me when I say I have your best interests in mind and I hope that you will allow the good counsel of my wife and our sister-in-law to influence you."

"As it happens, Cousin, marriage has not been so very far from my mind these last few weeks," Bianca said. She reached for her cup of chocolate, then tipped it aimlessly when she found it empty. She appeared to stare down at her hands but stole quick veiled looks at the king as she continued. "I did not believe you would have much interest being as how I am not your sister, so I asked His Eminence, Cardinal delle Torre, to find me a suitable Catholic husband."

Stunned silence greeted the princess' words. She had admitted to making a grievously improper political step. Stefano's expression looked frozen as he stared at Bianca. Idala quickly averted her gaze to her lap again, but not before Luciana saw the look of horror in her expression. The queen quietly rested her hand on the king's arm, a wifely reminder of restraint, and Luciana could see what the queen had sensed. Despite the soothing attempt, the king's expression was thunderous. When he finally spoke, breaking the painful silence, his voice was stony.

"Marriage within the royal family is the prerogative of the king," Alban said. He sat up straight, towering over them all even in his chair. His furious expression spoke volumes.

"Indeed, Cousin, my life is subject to your whim. I have not married, although . . ." She fidgeted with her hands, finally spreading the fingers of her right hand out on the white linen tablecloth, displaying a large collection of rings. An ornate gold-and-ruby ring adorned the marriage finger. "I have accepted tokens of affection and, this may be presumptuous, but I consider us ring bound."

"When did you intend to discuss this with me, Bianca?"

"The cardinal, if I am not mistaken, planned to speak with you this very evening . . . after Vespers," Bianca said.

"My guards will relay my request to see the cardinal this morning, before the noon hour—"

"Have you forgotten morning Mass?" Bianca protested.

"It is not I who have forgotten, Bianca. Another priest can oversee Mass, the cardinal will be unavoidably detained!"

"But the cardinal's duties—" Bianca began soothingly, as one might speak to a recalcitrant child.

Luciana bent her head lest her own surprise show, watching the tableau unfold out of the corner of her eyes. Idala touched her husband's arm as if to check his reaction, but he would have none of it.

Alban rose from his chair and leaned across the table. "The cardinal's Heavenly Lord has promised him mercy. I, on the other hand, have not!"

VIII

"A woman seldom asks advice until she has bought her wedding clothes."

—Joseph Addison

"AT least Stefano has finally returned," Idala murmured as though to herself.

Another awkward silence had followed the king's pronouncement and the departure of the princess and the king and Stefano. Even the birds in the trees stilled, leaving a quiet that palled.

"Well, it seems the excitement is over for the moment," Idala observed wryly.

"And, yet, it seems that it has only just begun," Luciana said.

"Indeed," Idala agreed. She looked worriedly in the direction the king and Stefano had taken. "And here Stefano has finally arrived, but the two of you don't get a single moment together before the duties of the Palantini take him away!"

Luciana managed a rueful smile. "It has always been thus. If you recall, duty delayed our wedding as well. It is the way with your own marriage. Duty comes first."

"But duty does not keep us apart. The Palantini has kept Stefano away most of the years since your marriage," Idala said softly.

"It was Stefano's sense of honor and duty that drew me to him in the first place. It is not fair to complain when those obligations take him away." Luciana voiced the words, wishing with all her heart she could have the peace of believing that, of feeling that . . . instead of forsaken.

The queen leaned close. "But he is here, *now,* because of you."

"He is here now because duty brings him back. Honor demands satisfaction. Short of her father, Stefano is the closest male relative to . . ." Luciana choked back Alessandra's name.

Idala sighed and sat back in her chair. "You give him little credit."

Luciana gazed down at her lap, past her once more flattened stomach, to the knee upon which no child of her own had ever sat. She changed the subject. "The king was quite controlled with Bianca under the circumstances."

The queen sighed and rose to her feet. She led the way to her salon, motioning for Luciana to close the door to the patio. She looked about the room and, at last, sat upon her chaise lounge.

The decor, in delicate shades of champagne and rose complemented by gilt edgings everywhere, suited feminine tastes. Luciana chose the closest chair as she glanced around the queen's salon.

"We heard whispers weeks ago that Bianca contemplated marriage. Alban wanted to give her every opportunity to speak openly with him about her desires for a marriage. When she did not, he . . ."

"He broached the conversation himself," Luciana concluded. "Will he have them arrested? Bianca and the cardinal, I mean."

Idala shook her head. "In truth, he doesn't dare. Even though we, too, are Catholics, we play a delicate game of balances with the Church. Most Tyrrhian Catholics are conservative. They would rather see blood inherit the throne. Alban was a cousin and deemed more suitable than Bianca by the Palantini, but still there was talk. Further, Alban prosecutes anyone who brings witch-hunters and the madness of the Spanish Inquisition to our shores. While politically the Church stands with us—they have, after all, condemned the Inquisition—the local priests . . . well, they think and preach differently.

"So much of our wealth rides upon the heads of people who escaped previous persecutions. Tyrrhian bankers and merchants have funded Austria and Poland in this war with the Turks. Your people bring us the Gypsy Silk. The Inquisition could kill Tyrrhia and bring us back under Spain's rule." Idala shook her head. "It is a delicate thing this. I just hope Alban can keep his temper long enough to think before he does anything to the cardinal!"

Luciana nodded and settled back in her own chair, her mind in turmoil over what she had seen and heard this morning. There were many revelations, but none of the sort she sought.

As though reading her mind, Idala turned to face Luciana fully. "Enough of this! I promised a quiet talk this morning and we shall have it!" The queen hesitated a moment, looking around her rooms again. She stretched around to lean over the back of her chaise so that her face was mere inches from Luciana's. "I cannot tell you how upset I've been since . . ." The queen captured Luciana's hand in hers. ". . . since Alessandra died and now, to have her—well, to have her stolen! Oh, Luciana, what can I say?"

"There are few words that could help her now, but, perhaps if I knew what happened, if I could understand *why* she died?"

Idala shook her head. "Even I don't know why she died. It doesn't make any sense."

"You told me my sister had a lover," Luciana prompted. "And, in your letter, you said there were machinations at court. What did you mean?"

"I spoke of Capitano di Montago. He spent time in Peloponnesus fighting the Turks. He served particularly well and, when he returned, I invited him to court . . . where he met Alessandra," the queen said. She shook her head again. "I'm afraid I encouraged them. Though, upon reflection, they did not seem to need much—encouragement, I mean. You could see it in their eyes. When the capitano first met Alessandra, he was smitten, like a youth. It really was quite charming." She sighed. "And Alessandra, well, she seemed just as taken. Since she was here to find a husband and had refused to seriously entertain other overtures, I thought a half Gypsy war hero would not be such a bad match. You see my thinking?"

"Yes, and I cannot fault you," Luciana said quietly. "With her holdings and position, she did not need to marry for fortune or prestige. A war hero would please our father, and the Romani blood would please our grandmother."

Idala nodded and looked up sharply. "How has the Romani Queen—the *Beluni*—taken this news?"

"She grieves," Luciana said.

"Of course, but . . . does *she* blame Alban and me?" The queen pinched the bridge of her nose. "I have not asked you if *you* forgive us."

"We spoke of it last night, Idala. I come to court as your friend, your sister, but know as well that I am the only *Araunya* now and I must serve my grandmother and my people as well, so I must have answers. I must know more about this capitano. I must know what machinations there are at court to see if it has anything at all to do with my sister's death and until I know that . . ."

Idala nodded and took a deep breath. "I see, and if you decide that I did not do all that I might have?"

Luciana's stomach fluttered. "I do not expect I will, but should I . . . well, we must deal with that when the time comes. You are family to me—just as my sister was, Idala. So, don't let us dwell on this. Tell me all of what happened."

"There's not much I can say. Alessandra sought my counsel regarding the capitano, and I advised her that he was an admirable man and, in my opinion, worthy of her." The queen paused and looked up at Luciana again. "I still believe that. He is—was a good man. He served in my Escalade for more than ten years. His record was impeccable and his service noteworthy throughout his career."

"So the capitano was a good man who served you long and well. What else can you tell me about him?"

The queen twisted her fingers, frowning. "I do not know if he was Romani from his father or his mother's side. Perhaps that would be in his records. I'll arrange for them to be sent to your suite, if you like."

The thought of reviewing a man's military records did not sound as though it would help her find her sister's killer, but she could not afford to overlook anything. She must act quickly now that Stefano was here, for surely he intended to send her back to the estates. She must learn as much as she could while forestalling his efforts to relegate her beyond the reach of easy vengeance. "I would appreciate that, Majesty. You say that the capitano proposed marriage, that a marriage contract was being drawn up. Did you see it?"

The queen nodded. "Hasn't your father told you any of this?"

Luciana sighed. "Conte Baiamonte is my sister's father. He adopted me when he married our mother. We were never . . . close, and he is not inclined to take me into his confidence."

"Oh, I see," Idala said. "I'm not sure what I can tell you. Since I never did see the marriage contract, of course, but both the capitano and Alessandra seemed happy with the progress. Your sister spoke of a wedding before summer's end."

Luciana bowed her head, focusing for a long moment on her hands. Apparently, Alessandra had been so smitten she had not found time to relate all of these details to her. Luciana reminded herself that Conte Baiamonte only knew more of this because, as Alessandra's father, he must agree to the marriage contract. But still, it stung, hearing how happy her sister had been and knowing she had heard little of it directly from Alessa.

"Are you well?" Idala asked softly.

Blinking away the easy tears, Luciana nodded. She took a deep shuddering breath. "How did the capitano come to his end?"

The queen frowned, resting her chin upon her interlaced fingers along the back of the chaise. "Toward the end—what I know now was the end—the capitano appeared oddly distracted. I thought, perhaps, the details of the marriage might be the cause, but thinking on it now, he looked hunted in those final days.

"Once, I saw Alessandra alone—an unusual sight, by then. She was very quiet, which seemed most against her nature. She was always laughing, singing, talking. I was concerned so I sought her out. Even between the most devoted lovers, there come disagreements." Idala stopped, but her eyes had dropped to Luciana's wedding ring. She sighed. "I thought that perhaps I might comfort her. If there were a difficulty between them, I thought it might be in my power to smooth matters over between her and her capitano. It turned out there were no hard feelings at all, only that the capitano was being called away by duty."

Luciana rubbed her temple. Alessandra was all too familiar with the difficulties between her and the duca. No doubt, she feared similar complications in her own love life. Luciana longed to reach out and comfort her sister.

The queen continued speaking, drawing Luciana's attention back. "Everything became *very* complicated very quickly. Suddenly Alessandra was accused of murdering the capitano and then everything changed."

Luciana looked quickly up. "Excuse me, Majesty, but how did he . . . when did he die?"

Idala rested back against the chaise. "As I said, on the ferry to Calabria."

"And why was Alessandra with him . . . alone?"

The queen shook her head, sighing. "No. She did not go with him—"

"Then how could she have murdered him? Who would say such a ridiculous thing?"

Idala frowned briefly, perplexed. "It was not one but three who accused her and there was confirmation here at court."

"Three?"

"Indeed," the queen said. "Were you listening to me at all, Luciana?"

Luciana nodded, sighing in turn. "There is just so much to learn, to understand, to make some sense of. I get lost in the details."

"I was witness and I am confused," the queen acknowledged. She captured Luciana's hand again. "Now that Stefano is here—this business is man's work. Let—"

Luciana stiffened, pulling away. "Your brother is a

good and noble man, Your Majesty, but he was not blood kin to my sister. No matter his affection for her, as *Araunya,* for my people, *I* must do this." Seeing the queen's expression, she knew she had offended her. This time, Luciana risked the impertinence and took the queen's hand in her own. "Do you not see? The Escalade . . . it is your duty. It is your right to lead, by law and custom. This matter is the same with me for my people."

"But I may appoint an agent to act in my stead."

"When have you availed yourself of that? Even when . . . even four years ago, when you were ill and little Ortensia was dying, even *then* you did not appoint a successor or agent."

"I–I had appointed a successor," the queen replied quietly.

"But not an agent."

"There is little enough expected of me that I seem able to accomplish. After all these years, Dario Gian is my only . . ." The queen straightened but did not withdraw her hand.

"If ever there were a time you might appoint an agent—"

"Yes, yes, Luciana. If you do not want to rely upon my brother, then I must understand." She breathed deeply. "We were speaking of your sister and of her lover, Capitano di Montago.

"On the ferry, three sailors testified that the capitano came on deck, leaving his men in the cabin belowdecks. The Stretto is never calm, but that night the seas were rougher. The men reported that at first, they took his staggering for a man unaccustomed to the water, but then they realized something was wrong. They say that the capitano sweated heavily and complained of feeling unwell, and then suddenly, great spasms overtook him. In his final moments, they say the capitano suddenly cried out that he had been poisoned and that he named his poisoner as the Lady *Araunya* Alessandra Davissi."

"Poison? My sister?" Luciana shook her head firmly. "No, this could not be. You had only the word of these three sailors? May I question them?"

"There *was* more," the queen said quietly. "Even the

capitano's men testified that the capitano ate mushroom foccacio made by his lady. The capitano's men were devoted to him and, therefore, to his lady, your sister. They did not report this news lightly." Idala sighed heavily. "Your sister made herself invaluable in the court, preparing simples and tisanes for some of the courtiers, so there could be no doubt of her familiarity with herbs and suchlike."

"Tssa!" Luciana said, unable to hide her disgust. "Of course she knew the herbs and their ilk! She is Romani and I, myself, taught her most of what she knew."

"Yes, that is what many said. *Vigilare* were sent to one of Lady Alessandra's favorite spots for collecting herbs and there found mushrooms which the court surgeon identified as poisonous."

"This is impossible!" Luciana exclaimed. "Where was the capitano buried? I must see him myself. Or did his family collect him and have him properly burned?"

"Neither, I'm afraid. As I said before, the seas were not calm that night and, in his death spasms, the capitano was swept from the ship into the waters of the Stretto. His body was not recovered."

"Then it is, finally, the word of these sailors and ill fortune that convicted my sister? Only the word of these men tell the fatal effects of the mushrooms. If my sister loved her capitano so, why would she murder him?"

The queen withdrew and waved a hand vaguely. "Some of the courtiers hinted at jealousy. Reasons could be found by those who wanted them."

Luciana nodded. Such was the way of court life. Vindictiveness was like a spice used liberally here.

Idala frowned and spoke quietly again. "Everything that could go against your sister did. I was not alone in finding the circumstances too perfect. It was as though someone orchestrated all that happened, even to the point that we cannot be absolutely sure Alessandra took her own life—"

Luciana looked up sharply. "What do *you* believe?"

The queen appeared discomfited by the question and avoided Luciana's eyes. "I don't know. I–I can't be sure of anything anymore."

Idala's reluctance disturbed Luciana. Why did the queen avoid giving a direct answer? Did she have something to hide? Did she know more than she said? Examining her now, her face looked shadowed and drawn and she possessed an unusual pallor.

"What troubles you, Idala?"

"You are right, of course, I could not help but wonder if your sister's death did not suit some other purpose."

The queen did not answer the question Luciana had intended, though her answer gave Luciana pause. If even the *gadjé* questioned the circumstances of Alessandra's death—if the queen believed this herself, it still came as a blow to hear someone else, someone other than her grandmother, give voice to such doubts. Luciana struggled to remain composed, her expression a mask of control. "Such as?"

"If the capitano knew something he shouldn't—perhaps about the intrigues here at court—it might be assumed he told Alessandra, and that would make her as much a threat as the capitano. Someone could have killed them both and the accusations that Alessandra murdered the capitano were a part of their plan to protect themselves."

Luciana's stomach churned. "What could he have known? Or Alessandra, for that matter, that would put their lives in jeopardy?"

"If I knew that . . ." The queen shook her head. "This is the strange part. He wasn't assigned to any duty in particular. This is why Alban thinks Capitano di Montago discovered something he shouldn't have about the intrigues."

Luciana smothered an impatient sigh. "And yet my sister was accused of his murder?"

"There were accusations, that is true, but neither the king nor I believed the charges. In her final days, she was advised to keep to her rooms, not that she was inclined toward the frivolities of court life then anyway. She was not under arrest, you understand, but for her safety and the appearance of things."

"But *what* could he have known?"

"I have asked myself that a thousand times," Idala said. "He took the ship to Salerno on this 'matter of duty,' but his superiors have confirmed that they did not assign him either."

"Then this was a personal obligation he didn't want her to know about or these machinations at court you have referred to." *Perhaps both?* Luciana wondered to herself.

Idala's frown seemed ready to be etched into her dainty, olive-complexioned face. "The machinations . . . they were more my concern—distractions really. Mostly the sort you witnessed this morning. Bianca has been troublesome, acting more the spoiled child than a member of the Royal House. She seems overly influenced by the cardinal and that odious Conte Urbano. She has many followers and manipulates the court so . . . it is all very dreary, you understand, but I do not see how the capitano could have become involved with any of that. The plotting, for the most part, has been silly things—like usurping my breakfast plans this morning."

"But this business of the princess' marriage isn't such a silly matter," Luciana said.

"No, you have the right of it there," Idala agreed thoughtfully. She rubbed the bridge of her nose again. "This last is quite serious, I fear. The only saving grace is that Alban made no confirmation with any of the families he approached before he got wind of her schemes. If the marriage the cardinal has arranged is suitable, he will probably allow it, but it angers His Majesty to be manipulated. You see what I mean? The cardinal is one of the princess' closest companions. This is definitely more of her troublemaking."

Luciana nodded, but her mind was already elsewhere. "Can it be arranged for me to speak to the capitano's men? The sailors as well."

"Stefano will not countenance that. You will not want to meet with these sailors. They are rough and—"

"And perhaps hold the key to two deaths," Luciana said. "Besides, Stefano cannot protest what he does not know about."

"You would have me keep it secret from him?" Idala asked, her brows rising. She shook her head. "I do not like this, Luciana, not at all."

"But will you do it?"

Reluctantly, the queen nodded. "His Majesty told the sailors to stay in the city."

"They can be found, then? I would speak with them as soon as you can have someone arrange it," Luciana said.

"I'll see to it." Clearly, the queen was no happy conspirator in this matter.

"And the capitano's men?"

"That will not be so easy. The *ordineri*, the senior officers, gave them leave of the city. They have returned to their homes and will not be back for weeks yet," the queen said. She seemed to read the expression on Luciana's face and changed her mind. "I'll send word that you wish to speak to them."

"Thank you," Luciana said.

The queen plucked at the brocade of her chaise. "After his death, Alessandra kept to her rooms. I saw to it that she was not alone. I, myself, visited her on both days before her . . ."

"She was grieving?"

The queen nodded. "And angry, but not about being kept to her rooms, she wanted justice for her capitano."

"Which courtiers could have claimed was a ruse—" Luciana responded stonily.

"It wasn't," Idala said. She took Luciana's hand again. "Don't you see? She was angry, grieving, yes, but angry and not at herself."

"Then she may well have known something."

The queen nodded. "I–I took the liberty of looking through her things as her servant packed, but I found nothing out of order. Perhaps you will see something I did not. I've already arranged for Alessandra's trunks to be delivered to your rooms."

"It has already been done. I thank you for that," Luciana said. She chewed her lip, thinking. She had seen nothing of Grasni, her sister's maid. She came neither for wages nor to mourn with their people. "Do you know what happened to her maid?"

"Maid? Alessandra's?" the queen asked. She shook her head. "No. I know nothing, but I will have one of the girls who serve me ask after her."

There were few questions left to ask. Though she recoiled from even thinking about it, Luciana forced the words from her lips. "How did she come to be found?"

The queen shuddered again. "There came a general alarm from her maid early that morning . . . We—Alban and I, and everyone else for that matter—came at once. We found her as the maid did, in her bedroom. There was a tiny bottle in her hand. She did not die peacefully."

"There was a struggle then?"

"No," Idala said quietly, her gaze dropping away. "I did not mean that . . . the poison which she took . . . it must have been very painful."

"Oh!" Luciana felt horse-kicked.

"I'm sorry! I should not have told you . . . but I wanted you to know everything." The queen left her chaise and came to sit upon the edge of Luciana's chair, her arm around Luciana. Quietly, gently, she continued. "If a woman knows enough to poison herself, why would she not make the going an easy one? That is the question that has troubled me."

"You make a fine point," Luciana breathed, allowing herself to lean, however briefly, into the circle of the queen's arms. "Yet it was still decided that she killed herself?"

"Men do not seem inclined to think we women are capable of such practicality," the queen said, pressing Luciana close.

The stain of suicide in the family was a hard one to remove, especially among the Romani. Luciana knew, deep in her heart, even without her adventures in the graveyard, that Alessandra had not committed the foul act. There could be no proving it, however, until she recovered Alessandra's body.

Already, Luciana's thoughts were on the inquiries to come. Hopefully, there would be answers to at least some of her questions and, the Sisters *Fata* willing, proof available to clear Alessandra's name.

"Is there anything else you might tell me?" Luciana
asked.

The queen rose and paced away. "There is a possibility about her death that I have not told you."

Luciana looked up, but held her tongue.

The quiet stretched out for a long moment until, at
last, the queen turned and came back to sit beside her.
"There is at least one reason to believe murder, not
suicide, claimed your sister."

Luciana waited. The queen looked even more disturbed than she had before.

"You must understand, I do not believe this is what
happened, but I *must* tell you.

"There is an unwritten Escalade code, a matter of
honor among the men who serve together. They call it
Coda Condanna a Morte. The capitano's men may have
fulfilled it. We can prove nothing you understand, but
when an officer is murdered and there is no cause of
honor involved in the matter, the other men will judge
and condemn the murderer."

"You mean the *vigilare* might actually murder
someone?"

"We condemn it, you understand, but it happens—
especially when an officer like di Montago is killed. He
was very popular."

"But my sister? The capitano loved her!"

The queen nodded. "If she killed the capitano, who
loved her so dearly, all the more reason to exact vengeance. I, however, do not believe it. They would wait
until her guilt could be proved, if only for the capitano's
sake. But it is possible that their own grief was so
desperate . . ."

"I see," Luciana said. She tried to make sense of what
the queen told her. To all appearances, the capitano's
men suddenly seemed the most likely of murderers.
Their vengeance would have been made all the more
sweet by making it appear to be suicide so that Alessandra's death would be without honor. But then who stole
Alessa's body? And why?

"Is there anything else you might tell me?" Luciana
asked.

Idala shook her head.

"Perhaps I should speak with His Majesty as well?"

Idala nodded, then looked up. "He should be in the Throne Room."

"Of course. I will see Estensi about an appointment," Luciana said, standing.

"Tell him I've sent you," the queen said, following Luciana through the spacious salon to the door. She captured Luciana's hand as she was about to leave. "I am so very sorry all this happened."

"Of that I have no doubt," Luciana said. She kissed the queen's cheek. "I understand, Idala."

Luciana did not look back, but she knew the queen lingered by the door. She felt moved to comfort the queen, but if she did that, she could not speak with Alban and learn more while her mind was still so full of questions. Right now, for this time, Alessandra's need must be dominant.

She rounded the corner and paused at the edge of the Clock Walk, as the corridor outside the Throne Room was called. Lining the melon-colored walls on both sides were clocks of all sizes and shapes. The Palazzo Auroea was known throughout the courts of the continent for this collection. A spidery little troll of a man, who looked to be a bit of clockwork himself, sat in a tiny alcove at the head of the Walk. The Clock Keeper. He was a slave to time, always on duty, always tending to his charges with a ring of keys the envy of any jailer. Which reminded Luciana why she had come.

Luciana bowed her head for a moment, allowing the soft rhythmic echo of ticking clocks to wash over her. She concentrated upon Alessandra who had no doubt walked these halls not so very long before. Alessandra, for whom time no longer had meaning, had brought her here, to the palazzo, to the Walk. She took a deep breath, feeling her heart pounding in echo to the ticking of the clocks.

Luciana scratched at the Court Herald's door and waited. The door opened and Estensi appeared.

"Ah! *Araunya!* How may I be of service to you?" he asked, beckoning her into his office.

She expected to find something small and out of the way, but found instead a spacious room, neatly appointed with the requirements of the older man's duties. Shelves filled with books lined one wall and a large painting with the names of the highborn families of Tyrrhia and their coats of arms covered the wall opposite. A desk—large, polished, and filled to overflowing with papers of one sort or another—sat at the far end of the room near the window. A visitor's chair stood beside the desk.

Estensi waved her to it, adjusting the collar of his brocade coat over a long vest. His neat attire hid the middle-aged paunch that the vest alone would not completely disguise. His hair, curled in the latest fashion—complete with lovelocks—did not overwhelm his appearance, unlike the styles assumed by some members of court.

"Araunya?"

Luciana took the seat and ordered her thoughts before she spoke. "I have come for an appointment with the king. The queen bid me come."

"I see," Estensi said as he took his chair. He frowned and moved a stack from one side of the desk to the other so that they had a clear line of vision. "The king is in council at the moment. Perhaps this afternoon or tomorrow—"

"I would prefer an audience sooner, if possible," Luciana said. "I wish to speak to him about my—"

"Your sister, of course."

"Yes." Luciana stroked her finger along the edge of the rosewood desk.

Estensi sighed. "You are the *Araunya*. I know you must see him, but he has appointments—"

In a room beyond the office, men's voices suddenly raised, their words muted by heavy doors and wood paneling. The Court Herald rose from his chair, scowling. "You will excuse me?"

Luciana nodded, though curiosity gnawed at her and she preferred to follow him rather than stay put.

He left the room through a door hidden by the heraldic wall paintings, but reappeared momentarily, sealing the door behind him. "Pardon, *Araunya,* but I, of course, needed to—"

Luciana waved off his explanation. "Is the king well?"

Estensi hesitated as he rounded the desk to reclaim his seat. He looked at her, considering, chewing the corner of his full lower lip. "I am sure, *Araunya.* Lord Strozzini is there to see to his personal safety."

Luciana's brows rose at the thought that the king's chief bodyguard might be especially necessary. "Strozzini is needed for an appointment with Cardinal delle Torre?"

Estensi frowned. "Did I . . . ?" He shook his head, confident he had not. "There is little that I may say, *Araunya,* but I think it would be safe—considering all you have been witness to—to say His Majesty is not in the best of tempers."

"Then the marriage negotiations for the princess were further along than Her Highness led the king to believe," Luciana concluded.

The Court Herald looked at her with narrowed eyes. "You are quite well-informed, Your Grace, about matters only now developing."

Luciana smiled slightly and waved her hand dismissively. "I was—fortunate is not quite the word—to be present when the negotiations were revealed to His Majesty."

"Ah, but of course, and you have spent this morning with Her Majesty," the Court Herald murmured. He rubbed his brow and frowned down at the papers on his desk. "Since the king will not be available soon, is there anything *I* might do for you?"

"What do you know of my sister's death?" Luciana asked baldly.

Estensi sat back in his chair, his hazel-eyed gaze once more assessing. "I confess, *Araunya,* that I know too little to be of any help."

"Perhaps," Luciana said. "What do you know of Capitano di Montago?"

Estensi smiled broadly, but it was quickly shadowed. "I knew the capitano little personally, but I know his family." The Court Herald rose and strode over to the wall. With painstaking detail, he traced di Montago's lineage, pointing to pertinent coats of arms as he paced before the painting.

Luciana remained patient as she learned the long way about di Montago's family, impressed by the herald's ready knowledge.

". . . His father purchased him a commission in the Escalade some ten years ago. He served ably until his death," Estensi concluded.

Somewhat bemused by the onslaught of information, Luciana nodded her thanks and started to speak.

"You will want to know about your sister and the charges against her now, I suspect," Estensi said, returning to his desk. "It was a most unfortunate thing, those charges. His Majesty and the queen were quite beside themselves, but there was nothing to be done, what with witnesses against her."

"These witnesses, who were they? Specifically, I mean."

Estensi shook his head. "Sailors . . ." He shrugged. "They had no family claims that I'm aware of."

Cautiously, Luciana said, "The word of these sailors carried more weight than my sister's? She was condemned by sailors?"

"Condemn is too harsh a word, Your Grace," Estensi said, fidgeting with his vest. "You must remember that there were *three* sailors who witnessed against her.

"The word of a peasant must be held as good as a noble's—or so it must be if the king's egalitarian laws are to be enforced."

"At the moment, I care little about the king's dreams," Luciana said.

The Court Herald loosened his neckcloth, but nothing could ease his sudden blush. "*Araunya,* I understand your grief, but . . ." He stopped speaking and sat back. "Your people have freedom in Tyrrhia like nowhere else in the world because of these laws. These are the culmination of two reigns—more actually, but Orsinio was the first to press them this far. Surely, you do not so lightly dismiss them?"

Luciana shook her head. "No. Of course not."

"You are grief-stricken over your sister, I understand. She was a lovely young woman, or so I always thought. The misfortunes, well, I will not trouble you with such worries."

Luciana turned to more fully face the older man, placing her hand upon his desk. "You misunderstand me, Lord Herald. I am already troubled, and secrets about my sister are the source."

"Of course," he said, nodding. "I was most relieved to see your husband has returned— not just to serve the king, but also in this family matter."

"The *Araunya minore* was my sister, my family. I would know what you know about her final days," Luciana said bluntly.

Estensi stared at her long and hard, judging her seriousness. Could she be put off? Distracted?

Luciana stared pointedly at him, hardening her features with determination.

The Court Herald straightened his neckcloth. "The *Araunya* had some disagreement with Capitano di Montago the day before his departure—or so it was said by some of the courtiers—and Lady Alessandra became upset. If, afterward, she would have said what this disagreement was about, it might have helped, but she would not. This only raised more questions."

"I see. So the desire to keep a lovers' quarrel to oneself, followed by one of them gone missing and the word of three unknown, unavowed for sailors is enough to condemn a young woman *known* to the Crown?"

"You must understand, your sister was not condemned or convicted, not even officially charged. Considering that she was, well, who she was . . ."

"Romani, you mean?" Luciana asked softly, her tone steely. She was not pleased when the herald averted his eyes. "Our people have served the Crown of Tyrrhia faithfully for more than one hundred years! As a leader of her people, did this count for nothing?"

"Yes, but Conte Obizzi stood for the sailors—one of the men once worked for him. You must understand how difficult things became for His Majesty. With the conte's word, they seemed so much more credible."

"I find that I am being asked to 'understand' and to 'forgive' much in this matter." Her voice was cool. "This is not what I expect of Tyrrhian justice. For all that has happened, we might as well *be* part of Italy or Spain."

"You are too harsh, Your Grace," Estensi said, squirming uncomfortably. "This matter has not been handled as neatly as anyone would have liked but—"

"No one thought about this besmirching a lady's honor? Or what might be thought of her?"

"I understand His Majesty believed the capitano's body would be found, that she would be vindicated. We did not consider the *Araunya* so fragile that she might commit suicide."

"She did not!" Luciana said sharply. She bit her tongue. Souring any relationship with the Court Herald was just foolish and did nothing more than give the men proof that women were not suited to handle such matters. She took a deep breath, bowing her head slightly. "It is just such an awful thing. My sister was too young, by far. But if I must prove it, I'll see that all know she did not take her own life."

She was not comforted with waiting to find the capitano's body—and she had serious doubts that the Stretto would volunteer his corpse. Weeks had passed since charges were made against Alessandra and now her name was further besmirched with accusations of suicide. Did no one care about the honor of her name? It appeared that no one actually acted to defend Alessa.

Estensi remained silent, sitting in his chair. After a moment's contemplation, he leaned across the desk. "All has not been forgotten. Lord Strozzini has pursued this matter privately with their Majesties' blessing. He is frustrated but determined even though there seems nowhere to turn for answers."

"As simple as that, then," Luciana muttered.

Estensi nodded. "Perhaps, now that the duca has returned, matters will move more quickly."

IX

"He that seeks trouble never misses."
—Tyrrhian Proverb

STEFANO watched the king drum his fingers on the
curved oak arm of the throne. His Majesty did not
like waiting and the privileges of his office only catered
to the weakness. When pressed, however, Stefano knew
from their days at the university in Palermo that the
king was quite capable of patience, especially in the face
of intrigue. But, here, now, the situation troubled him.

Waiting was not something Stefano enjoyed either. He
looked to the Ducas di Candido and Sebastiani. Sebastiani was new to the Palantini and, thankfully, had the
good sense to learn and accept the guidance of his more
experienced peers. Di Candido, on the other hand, had
been welcomed to the Palantini by the senior Duca di
Drago, Stefano's late father, who then guided di Candido during those turbulent years while Orsinio was king
and his two daughters—Ortensia and Bianca, the only
blooded heirs to Tyrrhia's throne—were kidnapped by
Turks.

Di Candido had returned the attentions of the senior
di Drago by mentoring his heir, Stefano, when he joined
the Palantini nine and a half years ago. Di Candido was
no old man, but his fighting days were gone and he held
only a titular authority in the Escalade. That left him,
Stefano discovered, a great deal of time to be a more
political animal than he had been in his youth, and that
meant di Candido was not an easy man to judge.

So it was that Stefano sat in an echoing silence between the only two other members of the Palantini who

could be found on short notice. While minor members of the peerage—the contes and dons—would have gladly partaken in the day's events, discretion weighed more in this matter than a quorum. It could be argued, furthermore, that with the king—a member of the Palantini in his own right—a full quorum did exist.

"What did Her Highness say of the candidates we suggested?" di Candido repeated. He spoke quietly, with a gentleness of soul one might not expect considering his irascible demeanor. It looked as though one or more of the pronounced blood vessels in his neck or face might explode at any moment.

The king, familiar over long years with the elder statesman, sighed and waved his hand vaguely. "There were no suggestions put before her, Your Grace. It made no sense to discuss potential suitors until we know more."

"The cardinal is a good man, a man of faith. Surely it was out of order for him to act as he has," Sebastiani said, "but it may work out for the best. As her counselor—"

"You forget, Your Grace," Stefano interrupted, "that the princess has no right to counselors before the king. She is *la famiglia reale* and, thus, answers to the Crown—and the Palantini—before all else."

"But he is a religious adviser—"

"All the more reason for caution," di Candido snapped. He hobbled on a painfully gouty leg to a chair beneath one of the stained glass windows along the outer wall of the Throne Room, huffing with effort. "Tyrrhia is like the fly—already in the spider's web—but with luck and a great deal of vigilance we might yet escape the fate laid before us."

Sebastiani looked horrified. "Tyrrhia is a great nation—"

"Indeed," Stefano said, "as you say, like any other loyal citizen, but there is truth to what His Grace has said. Our great country sits as the foot of a continent of nations who do not share our enlightenment and, thus, our wealth. Money, however, cannot assure safety. It must be bought with other things, strategic alliances, and there is no better way to seal an alliance than a prominent marriage."

"Well put!" di Candido pronounced. "And the princess has made no secret that she would have the throne, Palantini or no. She cannot accept that the spokesmen for her country would choose anyone over the bloodline of the last king, nor does she keep her tongue about where her religious loyalties lie. She loves the Roman Church as much as she hates the Turks who stole her, and the Church holds too much sway over the rest of the continent. It helps none of us that Tyrrhia lies at its very breast."

"And that leaves us with the very interesting question, Your Majesty," Stefano said, turning to Alban. Lord Strozzini, the king's lifelong bodyguard, watched every movement before the throne, watched Stefano who stood closest to the king though he knew of the close ties between Stefano and Alban, and his guard never wavered. Out of respect for the man, Stefano did not close the distance between himself and the king.

"What would that be?" Alban asked, looking directly at him now.

"What will you do with the princess?" Stefano replied. "You showed remarkable control, for I fear I might have summoned the *vigilare* immediately and had her hauled off to—at the very least—her rooms."

"I haven't yet decided," Alban said. He leaned back in the throne, gripping the arms until his knuckles were white.

"*Sì*, and the princess is not alone in this. There will be the cardinal to deal with as well," Duca Sebastiani said.

"Not the best of situations," Stefano murmured.

"No," the king agreed. "It is a careful game of strategy we play with Rome and its Church. As has been said, one misstep and Tyrrhia is lost in a single generation, which makes the cardinal's play all the more surprising."

"Perhaps he hopes his treason is allayed by his dual citizenship with Rome," Stefano said.

"That is why," the king admitted through gritted teeth, "he has no fear of me."

"Us," Stefano said. "There is another option, Majesty. Perhaps the cardinal intended to make you angry."

"Then it would be part of a greater plan," Duca di Candido said. He did not look happy at that thought.

Before any more could be said, there came a clamor at the doors followed immediately by a flurry of purple-and-gray robes as His Eminence, Ambassador of Rome, Cardinal delle Torre made his entrance. He wrestled free of his escorts' grip and marched angrily across the marble floor, past the three ducas, his footsteps echoing in the near empty room.

"Your Majesty, I protest this treatment! Most assuredly these men have failed to comprehend your orders and seized me as I prepared for morning Mass. As a good Catholic, you yourself must understand the egregious—"

Stefano fell back, catching Sebastiani by the cuff as he did so, to stand near di Candido.

The King raised his hand, silencing the cardinal, then waved to dismiss the escorting officers. Cardinal delle Torre obediently fell silent, approached the throne, and adjusted his robes as he attempted to gather himself.

Stefano studied the cardinal carefully. He was a tall, imposing man, his dark hair graying at the temples. His clothes were fashionable, flowing clerical robes, mantle, and skullcap made from the finest Gypsy Silk and heavily embellished.

Satisfied that his robes were in order, the cardinal glanced around. His expression darkened only a little at the sight of members of the Palantini present. He looked then to the king who stared ominously down from his throne. The cardinal fidgeted and made another, more formal bow to the king. He took a deep breath and began, "Majesty, I beg your indulgence for my entrance. I was overcome with emotion, taken aback by the rudeness of the guards. You must understand that I was preparing for religious duty and . . . well, of course you understand."

"It seems, my dear Cardinal, that today we have both been taken unawares while in the service of our duties," Alban said quietly.

The cardinal made a pretense of confusion and then

comprehension dawning on an expression very near fear. "I take you to mean . . . no, no, pray tell me what you mean lest I misunderstand."

Alban smiled tightly. "I think we have no misunderstanding between us, Your Eminence. Indeed, for the sake of Tyrrhia, I hope there could be only one concern that would involve the duties and obligations of both the king and his ambassador from the Holy Roman Catholic Church. I hope that you will reassure me in this matter. Please, do." He sketched a wave and settled back in the throne, adopting an air of supreme patience.

The cardinal bowed nervously. "I cannot imagine, Your Majesty, what exactly it is that I have done to offend. Perhaps you might spare this poor servant further torment by explaining what it is that I may have done to cause you distress—for which, of course, I offer my deepest apologies?"

"You deny having done anything and yet offer deepest apologies," the king said with a laugh.

"We are all sinners before the Lord, Majesty, and I have not attained my rank without learning that I must atone for the sins of not only myself but my people. Considering the number of ranking Roman Catholics who might have somehow trespassed upon the king's good will, I can do nothing less than humbly apologize."

"How would you counsel a parishioner who made such a vague confession, Your Eminence?"

The cardinal looked pained. "But the confessional is a duty all good Catholics are expected to fulfill and they come prepared, knowing their sins, and ready to accept their penance. It is most difficult in my position now, Your Majesty, as I do not know what it is that I may have done to offend."

"Ah, well, there is progress, then," the king growled. "You at least admit that you are the transgressor." He raised his hand when the cardinal started to speak. "Please, Eminence, let us not go back to overtraveled discussions. Let us instead make progress on our pilgrimage in search of truth."

"Were I of the mind, I think I should be offended at such a remark, Your Majesty," the cardinal said.

"Take offense if you will. I most certainly have at your usurping my prerogatives."

"Usurping your prerogatives?" the cardinal said. He relaxed suddenly, his expression grew charitable. "May I take this sudden audience to mean that Her Highness has anticipated my appointment with you later this day?"

Alban remained silent. Stefano suspected that it was the only thing he trusted himself to do at this moment.

"Ah, yes, I see. This then is the source of your . . . outrage, if I may be so bold as to name it."

"I cannot see why you would not give name to it since you have committed further outrages *and* have shown no reluctance for boldness to date," the king said in strangled tones.

The cardinal bowed. He clasped his hands together in a prayerful manner and tapped his fingers to his pinched, thin lips. "Pray, My Liege, before I give my explanation, may I know the full charges against me?"

"How would you not know the full charges against you if you already know the circumstances?" Alban snapped. His voice rang resoundingly through the room. He thrust himself back in his chair. "I grow tired of these games. I am neither instrument, toy, nor fool to be played with."

"It is my thinking, perhaps, Majesty, that Her Highness—in her excitement, of course—presented you with news that the negotiations were further along than they were."

"And there is a difference between the treason of making an introduction for marriage and closing negotiations?" Alban demanded.

"I can see now, Majesty, that either is an affront to your dignity and authority. I pray you believe me when I tell you I meant no harm. I thought my presumption a small one since the princess—for all of being King Orsinio's full-blooded daughter—is, after all, only your cousin. I thought that, when seen in a certain light, this would please Your Majesty."

"Please me?" Alban repeated, as he came to his feet.

"You thought I would find pleasure in having my authority over *la famiglia reale*, over this realm, of my kingship, flaunted?"

"No, no, Majesty. There was no intent to flaunt anything. Were the princess any other woman and I any other spiritual counselor, her coming to me for help in making a match would not be such a bad thing."

"But the princess is *not* any other woman, and you are a cardinal of the Holy Roman Catholic Church and an ambassador to my court."

"I am also her Father Confessor, Majesty, and had only the best intentions. I planned to speak with you about this immediately, tonight," the cardinal said. "The timing—"

"Has nothing to do with it, Your Eminence," Alban said. "Why did you not come to me immediately with a suggestion?"

The cardinal jumped slightly at the sharpness of the king's tone, but it seemed nothing more than stage work to Stefano.

"Majesty, I must plead that your royal cousin and I became carried away with our ideas and thought to please you with a surprise—"

"An accomplished negotiation awaiting merely the delivery of the bridal goods."

"You wound me, Majesty, and do your cousin a grave injustice!" the cardinal protested with a hand over his heart and the other on the golden crucifix hanging from his cummerbund.

"The only injustice has been to Tyrrhia, Your Eminence. A royal marriage is meant to strengthen the kingdom and, if one is fortunate, it will do more."

"Ah, but, Majesty, a marriage into the deMedici line would strengthen Tyrrhia," Cardinal delle Torre said.

"DeMedici?" Sebastiani exclaimed. "Majesty, what better alliance? They are a rich merchant family, noted for their investments and fine works!"

The cardinal nodded in agreement, but frowned when di Candido stamped his cane on the marble floor and leaned his impressive bulk to the fore of his chair.

"Their line dies out," he said. He glowered at Sebastiani. "Who do they have to offer in marriage that is not too old, married, or spoken for by the Church?"

"Pierro deMedici is the very best of the family," the cardinal replied confidently.

Alban let out a short laugh. "My recollection is that the man you recommend so highly is a bastard, but we can always call upon the Court Herald—"

The cardinal grimaced. "No need, Majesty. There are some unpleasantries about his birth, that is true, but he is the son of the most notable Duca Cosimo deMedici, and I am assured that just as the young man has the father's name so he shall inherit the father's wealth. Does that not please Your Majesty?"

The king rapped his knuckles thoughtfully on the arm of the throne. "How far have these negotiations gone?"

"A date could be settled on the morrow . . . or we could negotiate a year or two more, as Your Majesty sees fit," the cardinal replied.

Stefano watched the king. His feet itched to pace the floor. He did his best thinking on the move. According to Alban, he had only meant to broach the subject of marriage to Bianca this morning. If she grew hysterical, as she had before, then, he would let the matter drop for another year or so, but now he was presented with a marriage all but sealed. The deMedici clan would be a good family to align the country with, and yet they would tie the country inexorably closer to the Roman Church. It would please the more conservative nobles, though.

Before King Orsinio's death, he and the Palantini had chosen Alban as heir. Alban understood the precious balance of freedoms of religion and politics within Tyrrhia. Alban, himself, was a compromise—a forward-thinking noble, but also Catholic. Both sides loved him and disliked him with equal vigor. Should any one force gain greater influence or control, Tyrrhia would be destroyed by civil war, mass emigrations, persecution, financial ruin, and would suffer the tyrannies of whichever force finally took her. Tyrrhian peace was a fragile thing, more delicate than a house of cards.

And now came this marriage. While tying the country closer to the Roman Church was unappealing, Stefano thought, it remained an absolute necessity—at least to Bianca—that she marry a Roman Catholic. Whomever she married, this compromise would be forced. The cardinal's proposal of the deMedici bastard, if acceptable to Bianca's discriminating tastes, was not such a bad bargain in all. Better, in many ways, than the unproposed list of candidates. However, just because this ultimately served the Palantini's purpose, they could not allow the cardinal or the King's cousin to go unscathed.

Alban, it seemed, reached the same conclusion. "If it will make my cousin happy, then I will do this thing, Your Eminence, but *I* will approve the negotiations and the bridal price. Whatever you have promised him as coming from the coffers of the royal family will come now instead from your own pockets." He held up his hand to silence the cardinal's protest. "Your Eminence, you are being let off lightly. By rights, I could have your head served to my cousin for supper! And do not whine to me of vows of poverty. If you have enough to afford vestments specially tailored in Gypsy Silk, then you have the wherewithal to cover your commitments.

"As to her dowry, the Princess Bianca comes with her birthright of titles, lands, and other properties which she inherited from her parents, but she takes nothing from the Crown. There will be no lands or properties gifted to the couple and there will be no titles granted. If the deMedicis are still interested in marrying my cousin, then, perhaps, I am well-advised to accept them."

"But, surely, the deMedici family will not accept so little from—"

"They offer me a bastard son with a gifted title in trade for a king's daughter. I am exceedingly generous, and you, Your Eminence, should know that more than any other. Arrange your marriage, if you can, but it is I who sign the papers."

"As you say, Majesty," the cardinal replied with a quick bow. "Does Your Majesty have a preference for the timing of a marriage?"

Alban's brow raised. The king seemed as taken aback

as Stefano felt. Was it possible they were really so far along as to consider dates?

The king regained his composure quickly. "The wedding will be when the princess can arrange it, but know this, Your Eminence, my cousin will be cloistered in her chambers until the arrival of her potential in-laws and will have to make her wedding plans from there. It seems only appropriate that she learn the importance of obedience *before* she marries."

"But how will—"

King Alban rose. The interview was over. "You are the masterful negotiator, Your Eminence. I leave it to you."

The cardinal bowed and backed away from the throne. He reached the back of the great hall and turned sharply on his heel, reaching for the tall doors.

"And, delle Torre," the king called, "I will also send word that I wish a new ambassador from the Roman Church."

"You were most just, Majesty," Sebastiani said, flourishing an elegant bow.

Di Candido made a rude noise as he got to his feet. "I am glad there were three of us here to give witness to this . . ." He made another rude noise and motioned toward the door. "You are being maneuvered, Majesty."

Alban nodded grimly. "I know it." He stared for a long moment at the end of the hall, then turned in his chair. "Strozzini?"

The ever-vigilant bodyguard appeared from the shaded depths of the hangings behind the throne, moving quickly to stand before his king. "Majesty?"

"See to it that my cousin is 'cloistered' in her chambers for the time being," Alban said. He paused, studying his advisers thoughtfully. "I will speak with her when I am of a mind to."

X

"Attention to health is life's greatest hindrance."
—Aristotle

"**D**AIYA?" Kisaiya came down from the upper rooms to the parlor as Luciana returned. "I have found your sister's things, though I cannot say they were packed with any care."

"Of course not! She was an accused—" Prunella began from her chair by the window. She swallowed hard and appeared to reconsider her words as she set aside her needlework. "Our cousin was accused of some horrible things, Kisaiya. What staff would care?"

"But Grasni would care," Kisaiya said. She turned in appeal to Luciana. "She was young and sometimes silly, but still—"

"Who is this?" Prunella asked.

"Grasni? My sister's maid," Luciana said. Turning back to Kisaiya, she asked, "Are you sure? The queen said she personally watched Grasni pack."

Kisaiya shook her head. "Then someone else has been through her things. The queen would not have excused such sloppiness, *even*," she said with a glower at Prunella, "if she believed what they said of the *Araunya minore*."

"Where are her things?" Luciana asked.

"Upstairs, in your rooms—"

"Your Grace."

Luciana stopped, her foot hovering on the steps to the upper rooms. She slowly turned to face Prunella, who stood, framed by the glass-paned doors to the patio, looking extremely pleased with herself.

"Perhaps, Your Grace, is unaware of this, but His Grace—that is my cousin—your husband has returned from the Morea," Prunella announced. She sounded almost like a child, giddy with excitement on Market Day.

"Yes, Prunella, I am aware of this. I had the pleasure of his company at breakfast," Luciana said. She gave Kisaiya a nudge, but couldn't get up the stairs quickly enough to avoid Prunella.

"But I understood you to have had breakfast with Her Majesty, and he could only have just arrived. I know because I directed his man to His Grace's rooms less than an hour ago!"

If she were not aching to see her sister's belongings, Luciana might have managed some sympathy for Prunella who was taking it hard that she had not borne the great news. "Perhaps my husband saw fit to come ahead of his servant," Luciana suggested. This time Kisaiya moved up the stairs a little more quickly, allowing her to gain a few steps.

"But why would he do such a thing?" Prunella asked.

Luciana sighed, gripping the rail hard. She took a breath and turned back to her husband's cousin. "I would not know, Lady Prunella, why my husband did this. You will have to ask him."

"I have a message, Your Grace!"

Luciana turned back down the steps again. "Yes?"

"From His Grace, your husband. He bid you make your way home straightaway. He said that he would be with you before you actually left." Prunella shot a spiteful glare up at Kisaiya. "I told Kisaiya we must pack at once, but she refused."

Gritting her teeth, Luciana descended a couple of stairs so that she might look down at Prunella. "You did not mention that you actually spoke with my husband."

"Well, no," Prunella admitted, looking confused. "I didn't, of course, because he has not been here—"

"Then it is possible that the message is not exactly as you thought. Kisaiya was right in waiting for me to consult my husband before taking on such a task, especially as I had given her directions to air my wardrobe," Luciana said.

"But—"

Luciana held up a hand. "Cousin Prunella, I am very pleased by the diligence you show, but please, I have obligations I must attend to as well." Before Prunella could think of another reason to waylay her, Luciana all but shoved Kisaiya up the stairs and into her chambers. She closed the door with a snap.

As Kisaiya had indicated, Alessandra's trunks were waiting, the lids already folded back for her attention.

"Did Grasni leave any notes, or a *patrin*, among my sister's things?"

"Not that I saw but I only made a quick search. You may find differently," Kisaiya said.

"No, she would have left *patrins* easy to find."

The contents of her sister's trunks were a shambles. "Have you spoken to the other ladies' maids? Do any of them know where Grasni may have gone?"

"She apparently kept to herself and, judging by the treatment I got from some of them, I can well understand why!" Kisaiya said, her tone scornful. "They said Grasni disappeared even before her mistress' burial. There was even some talk among the maids that Grasni's sudden departure was suspect."

"Suspect? How?" Luciana asked, tearing her attention away from the trunks. Alessandra's maid had always impressed her as honest; young, possibly foolhardy, but honest nonetheless.

Someone scratched at the door and then, without further notice, it was swung wide. "I am here to help, Your Grace, even if you will act against your husband's counsel—"

Luciana clapped her hands angrily. "You may stay, Prunella, but, *please*, allow my husband to speak for himself!" She turned pointedly back to Kisaiya. "You were saying?"

Kisaiya shrugged. "It sounded like more of the usual things said about us." She caught herself, looking from Luciana to Prunella and back again. "The usual things said about the Romani, I mean."

Luciana dismissed the self-correction. "We must know what has become of her." Luciana sat down, shaking her head. "The girl might be in danger for all I know. We must find her, at once."

"You cannot be expected to worry over every detail, Your Grace. The period of mourning is for reflection and grief," Prunella said in her most solicitous tone. "Undoubtedly, she has gone back to her people and you have nothing further to concern yourself about."

"Perhaps, Prunella, but I *would* be remiss in my duties to the girl if I followed your counsel," Luciana said. "We must know that Grasni is well and her future assured. We must be confident she hasn't suffered because of her service to my family.

"She may be in danger or she may know something of my sister's murder. If nothing else, she is owed a certain obligation on my part to make sure she has got herself another situation where she will at least come to no harm and, better still, where she will prosper." Luciana turned to the other girl. "Kisaiya?"

"At once!" Kisaiya bobbed her raven-haired head. She stopped and turned back. "Should I send Baldo?"

Luciana shook her head, sweeping loose hairs back behind her ears. "He's His Grace's man, a good coachman, but most certainly not of the blood. He would never find her family if they think they have reason to protect her."

"Then Nicobar will have to be sent," Prunella said, "and what will we do without him, Your Grace? Especially as we return home—"

Luciana did not even look up to acknowledge Prunella's assumptions. "He is my assistant. We will simply have to be more resourceful for a time. Invaluable as he is to me, he has to be the one to go. I daresay he will appreciate the escape from court, however temporary."

"Indeed, *Daiya,*" Kisaiya said.

"You *must* stop doing that, Kisaiya!" Prunella snapped. "We're at court now and we must not embarrass Her Grace by appearing to be disrespectful and nothing more than country bumpkins or ill-mannered Gypsy girls!"

Kisaiya looked stricken. "Forgive me, *Dai—Araunya—* Your Grace, I meant no harm! I I didn't think!"

Luciana smothered her impatience with Prunella and forced to herself to speak slowly. "You did not know, *Chavi,* because I did not see fit to tell you otherwise and I still do not. You have addressed me with nothing but courtesy and, because Prunella does not know our ways, she has corrected you." She scowled at Prunella. "As for Kisaiya, her honorific is appropriate to my position in the family, and as either *Araunya di Cayesmengri* or *di Cayesmengro,* and since I am both, it is doubly appropriate."

Prunella curtsied deeply. "As you say, Your Grace. Forgive my temper." She turned to Kisaiya, "I offer apologies for my correction. I hope you will accept?"

"Of course." Kisaiya nodded.

Prunella turned with a sniff just as the cathedral bells began to chime. Like any good Catholic woman of breeding, Luciana noted, Prunella immediately reached for the prayer book, bound with a ribbon, hanging from its golden chain at her waist. "Your Grace, perhaps I may be excused from my duties to attend morning Mass?"

Luciana nodded, relieved. "All good Catholics are allowed certain indulgences in their schedules with late morning Masses here at court."

"Thank you, Your Grace, you are most generous," Prunella said. She took one last look around the room, sniffed and reached for the door. She brightened. "If I should happen by His Grace, I will be sure to let him know where he can find you. I'm sure you don't want to have Kisaiya troubled with unpacking too much of the luggage."

There could be no escape, Luciana realized. Prunella must be dealt with, she must be made to understand. She looked longingly at the trunks and sighed. "I will walk with you, Pru, and we will have ourselves a chat."

"But I normally prepare myself for contemplation and—!"

Luciana fixed the younger woman with a pointed stare.

"As you wish, Your Grace."

Prunella was not so very resistant to her education in
the proper comportment of a young lady at court as
Luciana feared, though she still thought Prunella's quar-
relsome nature and' her predisposition toward intoler-
ance did not speak well of the girl. Luciana sighed. She
was going to have to dance for the devil to get Prunella
out from between her and Stefano. The girl was dedicated; she could appreciate that. She had her many good
qualities, but the one thing she and Stefano did not need
was yet one more person trying to help them along with
their marriage. As it was, everyone—from the White
Queen to the *Beluni*—seemed determined to meddle!

So, Luciana continued her internal dialogue, the duty
to teach Prunella more appropriate behavior fell to her,
as the duca's wife, as one of the senior women in this
gadjé family.

Lord Carafa, Prunella's father, apparently relied upon
Luciana's own *gadjé* upbringing. No doubt, sending her
to Dragorione required far less investment than sending
her to court and the queen. Torn as she was between the
gadjé and Romani worlds, Luciana found the business of
being a mentor to this woman bewildering. Having failed
in so many other ways as Stefano's wife—his continuous
absences testified to that fact—she felt duty bound to
help his unfortunate young cousin.

The rest of Prunella's education would not be so easy.
There would be trouble when the girl discovered that, at
least in Tyrrhia, except perhaps in the farthest provinces
where Prunella came from, there were more open-
minded attitudes, especially in the king's court. That presented a predicament. Prunella would naturally be drawn
to the princess' circle because of their comparable ages
and the charm of their prestige combined with their
shared Catholic faith. Considering the princess' impu-
dence of late and Alessandra's reports of the royal's behavior, it did not seem right to encourage such a
relationship.

As they walked, Luciana considered her surroundings.
Attached to the outermost of the palazzo walls, the ca-

thedral lay inland, away from the sea and potential invaders, particularly the Turks, who made a living terrorizing churches in the European coastal areas. Palazzo Auroea's very name beckoned greedy pirates to her shores.

The city's golden sandstone walls shone across the waters of the Tyrrhian and Mediterranean Seas in the heat of the sun, and gleamed like a beacon by the light of the moon. It spoke well of the craftiness of the king's *Corpo d'Armata* and the queen's Escalade that no pirating party had successfully invaded Citteauroea for the reigns of two kings. Though skirmishes with civilians in other religious ghettos of Tyrrhia and the taking of the princesses' ship years before had been more successful for the pirates, the military forces did what they could about that as well.

The sprawling, multisteepled Roman Catholic *Cattedrale d'Alaric*—ironically dedicated to the Visigoth king whose most timely discovered fortunes led to the founding of Tyrrhia as a nation independent of Spain and the Holy Roman Empire—was not so very far from the Ashkenazic Jews' towering Temple Beth Torah, and overshadowed the much smaller Moslem Mosque of Muhammad. Members of the court flowed to and from the holy edifices on their way to various observances each day. Their religious leaders greeted one and all on the doorsteps. The rabbi occasionally hailed a young man as he made his way up the steps toward the homely little priest greeting the courtiers in the line into the church. At other times, the priest would wave at a youthful lord or lady tarrying near the synagogue doors. The imam strolled up the walk leading from the mosque and greeted the courtiers as they made their way toward their pious studies. And so was their business of religious procurement accomplished.

Luciana lingered with Prunella, chatting while she surveyed the crowds. At last, she spied a young lady whose sister Luciana had known when she last attended court. Like Prunella, this other woman wore a most becoming, simple black gown embroidered, however, with red roses that complemented her complexion to perfection. She was about Kisaiya's age, Luciana thought, and thanks to the priest's greeting, Luciana had her name. She dove to intercept her.

Turning at Luciana's call, the young woman curtsied before cautiously approaching. "*Araunya*? May I be of service to you? Perhaps you wish to join me at Mass?"

"Lady Ursinia, this is my cousin, Signorina Prunella Allegra Carafa," Luciana said, gesturing to her young lady-in-waiting. Thankfully Prunella was cooperative for a change and bobbed a curtsy while offering her hand.

Lady Ursinia murmured appropriate pleasantries and exchanged handclasps, then turned expectantly to Luciana.

"My cousin is a Catholic new to the parish, perhaps she might join you in your prayers this morning?"

"Of course, Your Grace, I would be honored. Would you wish me to make introductions for you as well?"

"No, no, I–I do not observe Catholicism."

Lady Ursinia nodded sagely and took Prunella's hand. "Come, Lady Prunella, I suspect we will become good friends! I see we already have so much in common! Is this your first time to court, too? Oh, and here is Padre Gasparino! Padre!"

Luciana smiled as the two women moved away. If nothing else, she served Stefano's cousin well by finding someone who might bring a little gaiety into her life. Turning, she forced her smile to remain in place as she encountered Conte Urbano. She did not know how she'd missed hearing his approach.

"Your Grace!" He bowed deeply before her, snagging her hand to kiss before she could avoid him.

A shock jolted through Luciana's body like a thunderbolt. What little she had eaten at breakfast threatened a reappearance. She recoiled, snatching her hand away. Was that the scent of ill-used magic about him? It seemed so vile—no doubt, she suddenly realized, because she had been seeking him and putting so much of herself into the spells she cast. She reached out impulsively and caught his hand again, as though trying to maintain her balance. How did she miss this earlier? It explained so much, especially her instant dislike of him. Conte Urbano was the grave robber!

"*Araunya*? I do say, Your Grace!"

Luciana came out of her reverie with a start. A courtier and her escort stood by her side. Conte Urbano stepped back, allowing the newcomers access, but there was something about him—suspiciousness, nervousness showed on his face, at once swiftly covered with quite the show of concern. Luciana took all this in. She coughed and composed herself.

"Are you unwell?" the lady asked.

Luciana shook her head and regretted it. "I am perhaps more tired from my journey than I thought."

"May I escort you to your apartment?" the lady's companion asked.

Conte Urbano's gaze grew more assessing by the moment. Luciana gave a deprecatory laugh, allowing her eyes to leave his and to concentrate upon the two courtiers before her. "I will be quite all right, I assure you. The sun blinded me as I turned and the heat—"

"As you say, then," the woman said with a curtsy, then hurriedly joined her husband. Conte Urbano, however, was nowhere to be seen. Thinking of the man made Luciana ill again.

Of course, she was foolish to be so overcome by the sensations she felt when the conte took her hand, Luciana thought. She as much as admitted that she, too, knew the ways of magic. More than foolish, it was dangerous. Nothing could be done about it now, however, except perhaps to prepare.

After her encounter, she felt drained. Although she had little energy, she still wanted to look through Alessandra's things. With luck, something might be learned from her sister's personal effects. Prunella might disapprove; certainly she would if magic were used, but there was nothing for that. Better to avoid disagreement altogether and do the work now.

Kisaiya had arranged the two trunks at the foot of Luciana's bed. Luciana approached them tentatively. Contained within these trunks were her sister's most intimate belongings. It felt like an invasion of her privacy.

In normal circumstances Alessa's things would be examined as family packed them away immediately after her death. Luciana wondered if she should sort through her sister's favorite belongings and send them on to relatives who might want them. All of the *vitsi* felt the devastation of losing an *Araunya* so young, more so from among their own clan. Would the need to follow tradition, the ritual of keeping "a piece of the dead" better serve their *vitsa* than putting off such decisions, to a time when she no longer sought Alessandra's murderers? She might, after all, be able to draw upon some personal item to summon her sister.

The thought of turning over her sister's things to someone else's care, however, still seemed too horrible to think about. Besides, she did not want to risk having any among the *kumpania* deciding to commit Alessa's belongings to a funeral pyre, not when she might have need of them. But would they? Without the body? The *Beluni* had not yet burned the *vardo,* having chosen to wait until they had possession of Alessandra so that her *mulló* could be released to the heavens.

She decided once more not to risk misunderstanding between herself and the others, while secretly acknowledging that she could not bring herself to part with anything that had once been her sister's. That left one final decision for now, until a *real* resolution could be reached. Should she take on the taboo? The *Beluni* had not yet invoked the custom of honoring their loved one by assuming a taboo. It was the tradition for family and *kumpania* to take some token activity or pleasure the dead had been particularly fond of and make it a personal forbidden act, never to be repeated by them again so that the *mulló* would not be invoked—even accidentally—by its longing to rejoin the living.

But Alessandra was not at rest and, for now, Luciana decided, any pleasure her sister might derive from the living while in her spiritual slavery must be available to her. No doubt, the *Beluni* had reached the same conclusion.

Standing over Alessa's open trunks returned Luciana to her childhood. The fragrance from a sweet bag filled with clove, lavender, and rose wafted up at her, smelling so much like their mother that she was whisked to the past. Luciana sighed wistfully.

She straightened, arranging her skirts under her knees. Concentrating, Luciana lifted the covering sheet of un-dyed silk and set it, and the sweet bag of herbs, to one side. As Kisaiya warned her, the disorder that lay before her was the work of someone searching through things that they had no respect for.

Alessandra's lute lay atop the clutter. Luciana ran her fingers over the wood, horribly cracked. The veneer of the lute's delicate sound box was well polished, clearly a once cherished possession. Luciana had given it to Alessandra on her tenth birthday. She, herself, taught Alessa to play, though it was not long before the younger sister was much more accomplished than her instructor. Luciana smiled sadly as her fingers lovingly touched the frayed ligature.

Luciana took the lute into her arms, examining the instrument. It was not so completely beyond repair as she first thought. The ribs of the sound box's bowl had not cracked. The ligature and strings were easily re-placed and a good instrument maker might find the chal-lenge of making a new face for the sound box interesting. As she held the lute close to her, Luciana felt the sudden pull of Alessa's spirit. Beneath her breath, she prayed to the Sisters *Fata* for aid, focusing her energies and thoughts upon her sister. She strummed the chords.

The hair on the back of Luciana's neck rose as the air charged with a strange energy. A milky froth began to gather on the floor, near where the bird had stood the night before. A chill came over the room, but excite-ment made Luciana feverish. She stroked the instru-ment, as though to play it. The pool on the floor continued to grow and slowly take form, hazy, in the streams of sunlight filtering between the shutters.

Luciana focused her energies, drawing her sister to her with every ability she possessed. She felt the pull of death, the languid desire to rest wrenching at Alessandra as she formed. Guilt clawed at Luciana's heart. To her very core, she knew it was wrong, knew calling upon the dead was evil. But if Alessandra could help, if she could—

A scratch on the door jarred her concentration. Luciana jumped and wailed in frustration as the gathering figure of the *mulló* evaporated. Nicobar burst through the door. Stefano pushed past him.

"What's wrong?" Nicobar demanded, his eyes searching the room.

"Why did you cry out?" Stefano asked, reaching for her.

The weight of shattered magic crushed down on Luciana. Lack of nourishment and sleep took their toll as the broken magic consumed her.

Nicobar ran to her side. Stefano gathered her up in his arms. She started to speak, but words failed her. And suddenly everything was gone, enveloped by a soothing black blanket.

"Stefano?" Luciana opened her eyes, then closed them quickly. Why would she expect him to be there? He was never there.

"*Daiya*?" said a deep voice, laced with concern.

Luciana opened her eyes again. The bed-curtains were closed except for a small opening where a man sat to her right. Luciana blinked at the light that streamed in, making the man nothing more than a silhouette.

"*Daiya*? Can you hear me?"

Lacking the wherewithal to speak, Luciana nodded and winced.

"Praise be," Nicobar said.

"It's because she wouldn't sleep!"

Prunella. The thought exhausted Luciana.

"Perhaps you might fetch Her Grace a drink of water?" Nicobar suggested.

The sniff. Always the sniff.

Patting her hand, Nicobar drew the curtain closed behind him. "Her Majesty called upon you earlier. She has sent her physician. Afterward, Her Majesty is quite determined that you see her as well. Can you sit up?"

Luciana did not know which was the more tiring, sitting up or the very idea of facing a barber.

With moonlight gleaming through the window, bed-curtains tied back, and the oil lamps burning low, Luciana crept back to her bed dressed in a fresh silk *vestaglia*. The physician had come and gone, leaving her to rest. Prunella surveyed her, tucking the coverlet, flicking loose strands of Luciana's dark brown hair away from her face. Luciana suffered her attentions, too tired to thank her or do it herself. She sank back into the pillows and motioned for Kisaiya to open the door.

Nicobar loomed in the doorway, ever ready, ever alert. Seeing she was comfortable, he turned and left, returning after a moment with the queen and her barber.

Luciana forced a smile onto her lips and held out her hands to the queen, then patted the bed.

"Your Majesty, I am honored you would call upon me and that you would send your very own physician, but I assure you, as I assured your physician, my blood is *not* fermenting, and as for my animal spirits, far from being *shattered* as has been suggested, I can assure you they have never been more perfectly intact."

The queen laughed and sat on Luciana's bed. "I know you too well, friend. You've always been an abominable patient. Let the barber balance your humors with a good bleeding as the doctor advised and be done with it so we can have a nice chat before you sleep." The queen beckoned the wizened old man toward the bed.

He was reed thin, almost dainty, and hunched over from age, but his eyes were as sharp as his blade undoubtedly was. His gnarled fingers patted the pockets of his well-worn brocade coat absently. His grin was kindly and as crooked as he. He finally produced a rather largish bundle from the bag Prunella handed him. She sniffed with impatience, but remained beyond Luciana's line of sight, behind the bed-curtain at the foot of the bed.

Luciana reached out and touched the old fellow's hand. "Please, I am much better now. Majesty, I've taken my grandmother's remedy. Truly, all I need now is rest."

"But, *Araunya*, your humors must be in balance for you to fully return to good health and, begging your pardon, Your Grace, nothing but only a good blood-letting will correct that," the little old man said.

A bloodletting was in order, Luciana thought as Conte Urbano's unpleasant image passed through her mind. "I'm sure you mean well—" Luciana began.

"Your Grace, what can it hurt to cooperate? You've been out of sorts for months now. A bleeding will do you good," Prunella urged.

"You have every reason to be 'out of sorts' as our young cousin has pointed out," Idala said. "Do please let Girardo do the bleeding. I promise, even your little nephew, Dario, does not protest his gentle ministrations."

"I am confident that all you say is right, Majesty, but, really, I haven't the energy for a bloodletting," Luciana said.

"Precisely why a bleeding is prescribed. Balance your humors and you'll be back to yourself before morning," Girardo said.

Idala looked at Luciana's expression and sighed. She turned to the barber. "Girardo, thank you for coming. Clearly our patient will not cooperate."

"I am forever at your disposal, Your Majesty, *Araunya*. You have but to call for me—" the old man rumbled. His voice was amazingly deep for such a little man and conveyed the full measure of his disappointment with an uncooperative patient. As he turned, he paused and studied Prunella. "How long have you had that sniff, M'Lady? Have you consulted anyone? Come, let us see that *your* humors are in order."

Prunella was whisked away by the barber before she spoke another word. Nicobar closed the door behind them, leaving the queen and Luciana alone.

Idala shook her head, Luciana could not help but chuckle a little. "You didn't plan this—the barber, I mean?"

Idala only shook her head as she leaned back against the foot post.

Someone scratched impatiently on the door. "Your Grace? Your Majesty? Is all well?"

"Yes, Prunella," Luciana called.

"Your Grace, may I be excused from further duties this evening?"

"Yes, Prunella."

The sniff, a little cough.

"Pru?"

"Yes, Your Grace?"

"Have you seen the physician yet?"

"No, Your Grace. I will accompany the barber, if I may?"

"Be well, Prunella, and I will see you in the morning," Luciana called back.

They heard her steps distinctly as they receded down the tiled stairway to the salon where, undoubtedly, the eagle-eyed little barber waited.

Luciana burrowed back into the pile of pillows. The queen watched her.

"My dear, if you had not eaten at my table, if you had been anywhere else this morning, before this spell of yours, I would have feared Bianca's hand in this. I did not realize you were so ill. You shouldn't have come to court just now."

Bianca? Luciana frowned. It made no sense to her. The Queen, as she knew her, had never been one to have flights of fancy. Now, with treachery afoot, Idala could scarcely afford a fanciful imagination. "Why suspect Bianca of making me ill? There is a great deal of difference between being troublesome and— Do you really mean to imply Princess Bianca is capable of—of what? Poisoning? Me?"

"I do not know what she is capable of, but I do not exclude anything and even still she surprises me with her boldness," Idala said quietly.

Luciana's brows rose sharply in surprise, which made her wince. How her head ached! "But the king's cousin, Idala? It's true she flouted the king, and seems to be tiresome and uncooperative, but *really* do you think Bianca capable of such—such nefarious acts?"

"Perhaps you are right, but—" Idala said, her voice soft. Fear flashed in the queen's eyes, like a soul-consuming shadow. "She has grown uncommonly bold under the wing of the cardinal."

Luciana considered this. Her own brief experience with Bianca had been disappointingly inadequate. There was no doubt the young woman was impudent and Alessandra had intensely disliked the princess—that much was clear from her letters—but beyond that Bianca seemed to have grown into a decent sort. Perhaps Idala could be like Alessandra, unreasonable in her passions. "But do you really think Bianca so bold, so accomplished, that she might have some ability to cause me to take ill?"

The queen sighed and shook her head.

"For all of his ill-considered interference, the cardinal is a man of God. Would he truly lead her down a path of murder and poison? Bianca is, after all, your in-law. For that matter, so am I. Do you fear me?"

"No. Of course not!" Idala protested. Her laugh, however, did not sound quite as sincere as it might have. The queen seated herself on the bed and fussed over the arrangement of her skirt.

Luciana watched her for a long moment. "What is it, Idala? You can speak plainly with me."

"Sometimes I think I must be mad. It's true that Bianca is—" Idala struggled for the right word. "—unpleasant, but she is my husband's cousin. With both her parents dead and because she is the daughter of Alban's predecessor, it falls upon me to see to her interests, and yet I cannot bear to be around her.

"Do not mistake me, Luciana, this is more than a childish disdain. I distrust her—more even than I have already said." Idala rose and paced away from the bed. She stopped by the window and gazed up at the sky for a long moment before turning. "I find myself silenced by my position, and yet I fear that I'm endangered by my silence."

"Do you truly believe you're in danger?"

Idala nodded. "I have no doubt. Someone is going to a great deal of trouble to—well, I will not speak of it."

"What is it that really troubles you, Idala," Luciana asked.

Idala hesitated, looking torn and discomfited. "You will tell me it is nothing more than my imagination."

"I promise I won't."

"I have these dreams—nightmares really. Alessandra's ghost comes to me in the night," Idala said.

Luciana leaned back into her pillows and considered the queen thoughtfully. Could it be that Alessandra's spirit was being used to trouble the queen? To what end?

"Say something, Luciana, or I shall go mad. I should never have said anything."

"No, no, Idala. I find this quite informative."

"But do you believe me?"

"Of course. What does my sister's spirit do?"

Idala shuddered. "She watches me."

"Does she ever speak?"

"No. Not really. Sometimes she weeps, but there is no sound."

"Has anyone else ever seen her?"

Idala sighed heavily. "I *knew* you wouldn't believe me."

"But I do! I've seen her myself since coming to Palazzo Auroea."

Idala eyed her suspiciously. "You're not mocking me?"

"Never," Luciana promised. She waited for the queen to regain her composure before asking, "Are there wizards in your court, Idala?"

"Wizards?" Idala looked confused. "Wizards? No." She studied Luciana long and hard. "Do you make sport of me?"

"No. I would not. Not ever."

Idala rubbed the back of her neck. "Aren't wizards the stuff of stories for children and old wives?"

Luciana studied her hands plucking at the coverlet. "You know better than to ask me that. You know magic exists. The Church acknowledges it with its Inquisition. Even Tyrrhian law accepts that magic exists. Besides, you know what I am capable of, you've seen. If *I* can cast spells—"

"Sometimes I think magic may exist—certainly, it is something I want to believe in, except—" Idala shrugged. "I'm so confused, Luciana. I don't know anymore. I think not—that is to say, I do not believe there are wizards at court. Doesn't it take a great evil to become a wizard?"

"But you yourself believe that someone killed the capitano, then my sister, and is capable of harming me. What greater evil could there be?"

The queen rubbed the bridge of her nose and pushed back her hair. "Why do you ask such a thing?"

"Because I believe someone uses magic to force my sister to haunt you and it would take a wizard to do it."

"Forcing—you *are* mocking me!" Idala said. She rose and spun toward the door.

"I promise you, I'm not making a jest at your expense!"

The queen stopped and, after a moment, came back. "Then you really think a wizard is at work in our court?"

"I do," Luciana said.

"But who could it be?"

"I'd intended to ask you that."

"Oh," Idala said. She looked pained. "I fear I can't help you. Have you any suspicions?"

"I've only just begun, you understand, but I was thinking Conte Urbano—"

Idala erupted with laughter. "Don't be silly! The man has no rhyme, no reason, and certainly not the aptitude for such a thing! Even if he were capable of the magic, how could he possibly manage the intrigue?"

Luciana leaned back into her pillows, wriggling down

for more comfort. "But I already know he was involved in stealing my sister's body."

"No!" the queen exclaimed, aghast. "How do you know? Do you have proof?"

"I know only by the scent lingering on him from the grave."

Idala shuddered again. "He's a hateful little man, so full of himself and his poetry, but really, Luciana, that doesn't make him a grave robber and most certainly *not* a wizard of any sort!"

"I thought, perhaps—" Luciana sighed. "A grave robber does not a wizard make."

"You say you know this by his 'scent.' Is this magic you have cast?" When Luciana nodded, the queen's voice grew hushed. "You know Tyrrhian law forbids evidence of a magical nature. It is too easily toyed with and there are too few experienced in its ways. We cannot act against him officially, but, well, if you have sworn *vendetta*—"

"I'll do nothing until I'm sure. I must see where he leads me," Luciana said.

"I do not envy your task, my friend," Idala said. "You must be up and about tomorrow." She grinned, relishing something. "Bianca has been cloistered—restricted to her rooms until the deMedicis arrive. She has promised herself to Pierro deMedici, Conte de Solario. He is the illegitimate son of Cosimo deMedici, Grand Duca of Gascony. Even now, the duca, his son, and their retinue are traveling to Citteauroea to receive Alban's permission and be blessed by the cardinal."

"Alban could still refuse."

"I suspect Bianca is more concerned with the cardinal's blessing. And while Alban could refuse, it would be most awkward," Idala said.

"But he *is* within his rights," Luciana protested.

"Of course, but if he objects, he must deal with Rome. Since his marriage, Cosimo deMedici has become very devout. Do we dare offend Rome *and* the deMedici family? Alban would prefer not. Besides, he has met with the Palantini—at least some of them—and it is agreed, even by them."

Luciana wondered, briefly, if Idala were not now playing games with her. Stefano was here. He would have been part of the meeting of the Palantini. How could he ever have agreed to such a preposterous thing as bringing the Roman Church closer to Tyrrhia's throne?

"It irritates him, though," Idala said thoughtfully, "that there is more than a certain logic and convenience to allowing the deMedici marriage proposal to go forward."

Luciana stroked the coverlets thoughtfully. "So, Alban has been maneuvered by the princess and the cardinal. This marriage ties Tyrrhia closer to Rome and the Catholic Church with their impositions and Inquisitions. What would Bianca hope to gain?"

Idala said nothing, merely gazed at her hands as she toyed with her delicately embroidered hem. She looked up slyly. "Have you seen Stefano yet? Privately, I mean."

"No," Luciana said, shaking her head. She swallowed a moan and pressed her aching temples. She remembered now, in the flashing ache, that she had seen Stefano. Right here in her very rooms! "Yes, yes, I've seen him, but . . ." She sighed and laid her head back against the pillow. "I saw him briefly, but we have not spoken. Prunella did deliver a message—by way of his manservant—he wants me to return to Dragorione."

"You expected that, did you not?"

Luciana nodded slightly, grimacing. "It is almost as if he were still in Peloponnesus."

Idala looked confused. "How do you mean?"

"He sends word from on far and expects me to do it. All duties come before our vows to one another." Luciana hid as much of her bitterness as possible.

Idala was not fooled. "Stefano is a proud man, Luciana, but he loves you."

Luciana waved her hand dismissively. "He may have loved me once. But we have been married eight years and have spent less than a year together in all that time. He has *chosen* to be away from me."

"He has his duties—" Idala held up her hands to stave off Luciana's protest. She reached out then, and took

Luciana's hands in hers. "Can you not take heart in knowing that he loves you? Look at Bianca. She marries a man she's never met and there is no pretense of love. Not like Alban and I know . . . not like you and Stefano—"

"We may have known a love like that once, Idala, but, I fear, no more. He chooses to be away and even from a distance he would have me turn over my holdings to his chancellor . . ." She sighed bitterly. "It is beyond hope!"

"He is not Romani, friend, and will not bend to the bidding of his wife," Idala whispered.

"Nor will I blindly obey him like some silly, unthinking cow," Luciana retorted, the old wounds resurfacing. "He is a good man, I know, but he does not understand me or the heart of my people and—"

Idala raised her hands. "You do not have to refight your old wars with me, Luciana. Besides, you should be resting. I shouldn't have troubled you with so much." Idala rose from the bed and held out her hand. "Forgive me?"

Luciana took her hand and pressed it to her cheek. "Stefano is a reasonable topic considering he is your brother."

Idala nodded and turned to go. She paused. "Your sister was precious to me *because* she was cherished by you. I don't know what I would do were I to lose you as well. Be careful."

"As you say," Luciana agreed as Idala raised her hand in silent good night, the door closing softly behind the queen. Luciana leaned back into the covers and glanced toward her robe lying on the chair, remembering.

XI

"To have begun is half the job: be bold and be sensible."

—Horace

11 d'Maggio 1684

LUCIANA leaned back in her chair, sighing as the spring breeze brought the scent of the sea mingled with the tang of green citrus from the orchards. Her suite opened upon a tiny, private patio surrounded on three sides by a gated, ivy-covered wall of latticed iron rungs. The quiet solitude it afforded worked like a balm to her mind. The *Beluni's* remedy had served its purpose the night before but left her with a resulting sensitivity. Just now, her thoughts settled upon Nicobar whom she had sent in search of young Grasni. She could not be fully at ease until she knew Alessandra's maid had secured herself a position somewhere. She reasoned that had the girl been able to shed light upon Alessandra's death, she would have found some way to do so, but Nicobar would make sure of that. And then, of course, there was Stefano whom she had avoided thinking about as much as possible. Despite the early hour, he was nowhere in the suite.

"Shall I bring you your embroidery, Your Grace?"

Luciana twisted in her seat to look up. Prunella leaned out over the tiny balcony of the third story room she shared with Kisaiya.

"It would really be no bother. I could collect it from your room on the way down. I will be off to Mass, if that is acceptable?" the girl continued.

Luciana felt absolutely no desire to occupy her hands or her thoughts with stitchery. As she opened her mouth to speak, Kisaiya appeared through the paned-glass doors carrying a small bundle.

"Thank you, Prunella, but I see my package has arrived."

Kisaiya's dark brow rose in surprise as she looked from Luciana to the package. Without further guidance, she placed her item on the table before Luciana and turned to squint up into the morning sun as she tried to make out Prunella's form.

"And what of my attending Mass this morning?"

"But of course!" Luciana said as she tugged at the string. In a quieter voice, she continued, "This rather looks like one of Nicobar's bundles. He didn't leave it, did he?"

Kisaiya laughed outright as she slid into the chair beside her. "No, Nicobar would never forgive himself for such a lapse."

Luciana unwrapped the bundle of papers, but paused to motion to the pot of chocolate. "Would you like some?"

A characteristic sniff from the sitting room where she lingered heralded Prunella's eminent arrival on the terrace. Kisaiya quietly set down her just filled cup and pushed it away. Luciana noted the gesture with a frown, but held her tongue, turning as her husband's cousin joined them.

Prunella set Luciana's tapestry needlework bag on a nearby chair. "I thought perhaps you might change your mind, Your Grace." Prunella looked pointedly at Kisaiya sitting at the table and plucked a grape from the platter in the center of the table.

Luciana looked up from the papers—mostly reports from the various Guildmistresses of both *Cayesmengri e Cayesmengro* holdings—she was sorting. The cathedral bells began to ring. "You do not want to be late for Mass, Prunella," Luciana said.

Prunella curtsied. "I will return immediately after," she promised and quickly departed.

As the gate closed, Luciana sighed. "That girl can be so frustrating in her eagerness to help!" She motioned to the carpetbag Prunella brought down in spite of Luciana's refusal.

Kisaiya kept her eyes lowered, focused apparently on the swirling depths of her cup.

Watching her, Luciana sighed. "I'm too impatient with her, I know."

"Perhaps it is unfair that you hold your cousin to your standards, *Daiya*," Kisaiya said with a secretive smile.

Luciana nodded thoughtfully, considering the problem of Prunella and her education in a lady's conduct. It was all a means to an end as far as Prunella and her father were concerned. An advantageous marriage, preferably to a sensible farmer or to a man with money to infuse the Carafa family holdings, would save their meager inheritance so Prunella's sisters might have some hope of marriage. Tyrrhian nobles did not often see a dowry lacking sufficient funds to support the land that came with her bride price. Certainly few of them would consider such a marriage portion proper on any social level of distinction and most definitely not at the levels aspired to by Lord Carafa.

A sudden gust of wind from the sea blew through the patio, threatening to tear away the sheets of paper from the bundle. Luciana grabbed at one page, as it was caught up by the gust, and gathered the rest to her.

"Let us take this inside," Luciana said. She took the bundle into the sitting room and sat at the low secretary desk abutting the back of the settee. She spread everything before her, acknowledging the cup of chocolate Kisaiya placed near her right hand with a nod. "These came from the estate?"

"Yes, a rider brought it from Seneschal Tobbar. I sent the boy to the servants' kitchens to be fed."

Luciana barely noted Kisaiya's words, already preoccupied. In Stefano's absence, Tobbar Baccolo—Nicobar's father—ran the estate and managed her husband's various properties. Whatever Stefano's intent when he assigned the work to Tobbar, the old seneschal felt obliged to report frequently on his decisions and plans. She presumed he did as much for Stefano as well, but she made a point of setting those papers aside for him anyway before dealing with news from her own holdings, which now included Alessandra's.

Sorting through the bundle, Luciana paused. Atop the receipts and ledgers lay a thin vellum packet. Across it, written in the bold pen strokes of Stefano's striking handwriting, only the word "Lucia."

She contemplated whether to read it or not. She had received by special courier his directions to stay at Dragorione. This must be a letter already in transit, only now, some weeks since it was sent, newly arrived. Luciana glanced around the salon. She felt, oddly, like a thief. Perhaps, in contemplation of returning home, the letter finally bore more than a cursory acknowledgement of the baby, of . . . of other things. She pressed the letter flat.

8 d'Marzo 1684

> *Lucia,*
> *I have word from Cousin Carafa that he wishes*
> *Prunella to be sent on to court. Once you are*
> *recovered from your malady . . .*

Luciana stared at the letter a long moment. Was there faintness in the line? Had he paused as he wrote this? Silly, foolish hopes. The rest of the letter was nothing more than a blur of words. Such had been the nature of her husband's letters for approaching three years now.

Lest her shame be discovered by prying spies, she purposefully cast Stefano's letter into the fireplace and watched until she was sure the entirety would be caught by the hungry embers of the previous night's fire. Watching the letter burn, she struggled to maintain stoic control over her heartache. Where were the loving words he used to woo her? What happened to his feelings for her? She knew her own heart was forever lost, forever

Stefano's, but, oh, how she ached for him to return her affections!

She turned away from the pain and focused her attention on the reports on the smooth running of the *Cayesmengri* properties. Most of the mulberry trees had weathered the winter and the Weavers' Guild reported the purchase of three new looms in Ispica and the condition of the warehouses and the ships used to export the finished product. The Guildmistresses had been kind enough to provide lengthy and detailed reports. The *Cayesmengro* reports on the moths, the gardeners, the weavers and the storehouse keepers were considerably shorter as they had reported previously to Luciana. There was a separate note from the Chief Gardener who wrote that he would be in Citteauroea by the 12th *d'Maggio* in order to receive the yearly blessed waters which would be used to anoint each of the trees as the silkworms fed and from whence some of the magic of the Gypsy Silk came. Luciana gave that a moment's pause. It would be the first time she and Alessandra had not done this together in some years. She rose from her chair and stared pensively at the garden.

Behind her, she heard the latch of the door. She made a silent list. Nicobar was gone, Prunella prayed in the church, and Kisaiya would not use that door. The time had come, then. She took a deep breath and turned.

Stefano closed the door slowly behind him.

A rush of emotion flooded forth, making it hard to think. She looked at him now, as she had been unable to yesterday. As in the old days, he dressed with an understanding of the fine line between fashion and practicality—golden-brown quilted riding coat, ivory neckcloth, brown leather breeches. He looked leaner than he had so many months ago—it felt like a lifetime. He wore his brown hair tied back with a jaunty knot. Despite common practice, he wore only two short curls of hair from his temples to his jaw and, thankfully, forbore the bows normally worn with the lovelocks.

As she watched him, he swept off his green plumed hat and dropped it into a chair. Shadows haunted the edges of his eyes. His smooth-shaven jaw was set. His expression was not . . . not what she had hoped.

"Stefan."

"I am returned, lady wife," he said and bowed. "That is, I believe, how we should have greeted one another yesterday."

Stung by the edge of sarcasm in his voice, Luciana said, "Or perhaps in a few months from now?" She dropped to a low curtsy, glad to look away, however briefly, from his consuming golden gaze.

"Yes," Stefano murmured with a nod. "I do seem to recall writing a letter to you, my wife, instructing you to stay at the estates. This reunion should be taking place then in the near distant future." He closed the space between them, his movements fluid and sure, speaking of a quiet athleticism that his slim form belied.

"Distant future, did you say?" Luciana asked. Better to speak than stand here, silent as a dolt, absorbing him with her eyes.

Stefano chuckled as he reached her. The rich timbre of his voice made her ache. His long fingers cupped her chin and tilted her head back. "You are a woman gifted with many charms, but the ability to be demure is not among them." He took her hand and drew her up. "What court intrigues are you involved in up to your pretty little neck, Lucia?"

"Separated so long, Stefan, and you greet me with suspicions," she said, motioning him to a chair. She glanced about her and settled on the couch. She watched him out of the corner of her eye, noting his dark expression. His eyes met hers and, immediately, he grew guarded. An awkward silence spread like a veil between them.

"Her Majesty sent word of your loss," he said.

Luciana nodded silently.

"I sent a letter. I thought yesterday morning that perhaps you did not receive it, but Cousin Prunella has assured me you did."

Damn the girl's tongue! Luciana thought. She somehow managed a small noncommittal smile, but said nothing.

"You did receive my letter?" Stefano asked.

Luciana refused to look at him. There was nothing to be said.

He sighed and leaned back in his chair. Far from relaxed, he looked ready to spring up into action. "This silence from you is unexpected."

"A respite?" Luciana replied softly and then wished she had held her tongue.

"Is that what you think?" Stefano asked.

Luciana toyed with her sister's signet ring on her right forefinger. "It seems, from your letter, that you do not much care what I think."

Stefano laughed. There was no derision, but neither was there joy in his laughter.

Luciana bridled at his laughter at her expense. "And so you have returned to comfort me?" Luciana asked, her tone tart. "At last?"

His laughter died. Stefano looked as though struck. "I assumed, that as your husband, my solicitations would be welcome, but I appear to be mistaken." He rose and stalked to the open patio.

"And I was to wait at the estate for these solicitations?"

Stefano stared at her long and hard. "I suppose that a woman of your beauty would not be without gentlemen eager to ease your distress here at court. Fidelity is, of course, out of fashion."

"In some matters of fashion, perhaps I am less fashionable than my long-absent spouse." Luciana leaned her head back. She felt tired. She had longed for her husband's return ever since he left, yet she could not stop her bitterness at his abandonment from seeping into her voice or stiffening her spine. Were they to be forever doomed to these interminable arguments?

She felt Stefano's immediate presence, the weight of his shadow looming over her. Lest he think her afraid, Luciana opened her eyes and looked up at him. She found surprise and, perhaps, a bit of wonder in his eyes.

Stefano took her hand and bowed to her, in the manner he had used when courting her—intense and flirtatious. "When one has been so fortunate as to sample the finest wine in all Christendom, all others are as vinegar."

Luciana let herself laugh, remembering why she had so enjoyed the barbs between them at one time. "Your tongue, Your Grace, has lost none of its sweetness."

"And yours, my dear, has lost none of its bite!" He sat beside her. He reached out and touched her throat, his fingers curving around. His touch, though vaguely threatening, distracted her, leaving her breathless and feeling very alive. How could she have forgotten what it felt like to have a man's touch on her. *His* touch?

"There was a time . . ." Stefano's fingers stroked downward, tracing her collarbone with the tips.

Luciana could not hide the shivers his touch aroused. Her breath caught in her throat as she watched him, held his gaze.

Stefano looked down, watching his fingers trace patterns across her exposed skin. "I have always liked the cut of these gowns." He folded the fabric back, watching her now, then back to his fingertips. "You have delectable shoulders, Luciana. They beckon to a man, making him want to touch those little clefts, the soft flow of bosom, perhaps even to taste . . ." He leaned forward, cocking his head as he came close to her neck. She held her breath. Stefano paused, then pulled back. She saw him swallow hard. "Indeed," he whispered, "a most ruinous gown, for a man bent on withstanding your charms."

In spite of herself, Luciana succumbed to the warmth of his intimacy. "But you're my husband, Stefano, there's no reason for you to withstand my charms." Had it truly been so long? Yet she still ached for him, as though the anger between them did not exist.

"So delicately put," Stefano muttered, pulling away. He took her hand and kissed it. "I *have* missed you, Lucia."

The distance placed between them, however small, felt like a cold bath. Resentment replaced Luciana's ardor quickly enough. Stefano could not act on his passion. No, he must forever be in control. "Oh?" Luciana responded. "I should have known this from the letter you sent offering me your sympathies? Yes, it was a great comfort."

Stefano sighed and stood up. "I could not get away immediately. I came as quickly as I could. As it was, I did not expect to find you here. I had hoped to bring you word about . . . about your sister."

"I already know all there is to readily know about her," Luciana said.

"That is why you came to court?" Stefano asked.

"It is."

He shook his head angrily. "You'll get yourself killed, woman! This is man's business. You are to return home at once!"

Luciana lunged to her feet. "I will not!"

"Nothing can comfort your loss over Alessandra, Lucia. I know that," Stefano said with a growl, "but give me a chance to—"

"To do what?"

"It is my duty to protect the honor of my wife and her family," Stefano said.

"You think this is mere vendetta, then?" Luciana staved off the pain of being yet another of his duties and obligations. "This is about more than family honor, Stefano, it is about my people, my clan. It is our lives, Tyrrhia, and our work here."

"These matters which concern you are my concern as well. Let me—"

Luciana looked away. "You cannot answer to my people. The *Beluni* and the Guildmistresses, only the *Araunya* may do that."

"It comes to your holdings again, does it?" Stefano asked. He made an angry hissing sound as he moved away from her. "We have traveled this road a thousand times—"

"And our conclusion is always the same. I cannot give you what is not mine to give. I am trustee for my holdings as *Araunya di Cayesmengri* and now as *di Cayesmengro*. I am as much a servant to my people as Alban and your sister are to the people of Tyrrhia," Luciana said.

Stefano turned, poised to speak, then turned away again. He contemplated the vaulted ceilings for several moments before finally facing her. "You have been here a day. You say that you know all that there is to know about Ale—"

"Don't!" Luciana cried. "Don't speak her name. Please." Seeing him torn between confusion and insult, she touched his lace-cuffed wrist. "My people do not use the name of the dead. It is . . . it is *marimé* . . . unclean, evil almost. Please, do not say her name."

Stefano nodded. "As you wish, then." He paused for a breath. "I may speak of her, mayn't I?"

"When you must. You may refer to her by her title, if you wish, *la Araunya minore*."

He took a deep breath. "You say you know what there is easily to know about your . . . your sister's death. You have been here at court a day. If ever there was a woman who could get herself into trouble, Luciana, it is you."

Behind them, a man cleared his throat. "Your Grace?"

They turned together. Stefano's man, Bernardo, stood beside the open door of the suite. "Forgive me, Your Grace, but the king has sent for you."

Luciana shook her head and turned away, stopping when Stefano caught her by the arm.

"You may tell His Majesty that I am on my way," he said. After the door shut behind Bernardo, Stefano stepped close so that the warmth of his breath fanned across her cheek. "Think whatever you may of me, Luciana, but I do not want you to end up like your sister." He leaned closer, stealing a sweet taste of her lips.

Before she could stop him, he was on his way out of the suite. Luciana touched her lips thoughtfully. Whenever she thought she knew Stefano, he became someone different. He was as easy to understand as magic, which meant that he made least sense when she thought she knew him best.

Luciana breathed a deep sigh and sank back into the straight-backed chair at the desk. She closed her eyes. All around her was still and quiet, except for the ticking of the clock on the wall. It felt as though her mind spun in circles, moving in step with the timepiece. She did not understand her husband. When she prepared herself for the worst, that he might not love her, that he could never truly be hers . . . it was a confusion, a puzzlement.

She had too many puzzles before her. Had Alessandra ever felt this way, or—by the Fates—had she been lucky enough to be sure of her capitano? Alessandra. If she had meant to moon over Stefano, Luciana decided, she could have just as easily stayed at the estate and at least her husband would be happy!

The clock's noise echoed in the room, almost mocking her. The clock seemed to chant "Sissssssssss-ter. Sissssssssss-ter. Where are you?" It made Luciana shiver. Was it her heart pounding over Alessandra or did her *mulló* call to her? At this moment, there seemed nothing lonelier than the sitting room, except, perhaps, Alessa's fate. The clock continued its chant. "Sissssssssss–ter. Sissssssssss–ter."

She had no time. Luciana blinked. She had no time to wallow in despair for Alessandra nor to daydream about Stefano. With a growing sense of purpose, Luciana rose to her feet. Now was the perfect time to do a little work, to see what her own magicks might accomplish on Alessandra's behalf. She climbed the stairs to her bedroom, closing and locking the door behind her.

Luciana pulled the mottled blue Gypsy Silk away from the little table beneath the window to expose her altar and used the silk to cover her hair, as was the custom among the Romani *ababina* before they worked magic. She lit a dozen candles, whispering prayers to the *Fata* as she did so.

The sweet scent of burning beeswax tickled her nose. She removed her sister's signet ring and placed it beside the candles, then placed a strip of Gypsy Silk in the brazier, setting it ablaze with candle flame. Still murmuring prayers, Luciana stood and crossed to the largest of Alessa's trunks. She opened it and withdrew her sister's damaged lute.

Luciana recalled the Romani folk song her sister loved best and began to sing it beneath her breath, strumming the instrument's mangled strings with a loving hand. Alessa always lingered over the words, drawing out the sweetness of the ballad with her husky voice—and so it was for Luciana now. She prayed in that separate part of her mind conscious about such things as she called upon her sister's spirit in her heart.

As before, a pool formed in the center of the rug. At first, the figure of the ghost was like a swirl of dust motes in the streams of morning sunlight, light and inconsequential, colorless. As Luciana sang and prayed, the ghostly shape grew taller, thicker, more substantial. It cast a lengthening shadow across the floor. The *mulló's* burial weeds flowed about her like liquid. The burning Gypsy Silk seemed to renew her and draw her to the altar, to strengthen the *mulló's* form and Luciana's magic of Calling which summoned her.

"Alessa?" Luciana rose, setting aside the lute. She reached out tentatively.

The spirit also reached out, their fingers touched, passing through one another. It felt like the crisp ice that formed on the puddles in the winter rains, almost tangible, almost substantial enough to withstand touch.

Alessa moaned.

The sound ran like trickles of melting snow through Luciana's veins. She could not resist her own responding cry, dropping to her knees before the *mulló,* teeth chattering as much from cold as frustration. Through tears of grief and anger, Luciana said, "I'm sorry. I should have protected you!"

The ghost's hand stroked Luciana's head with a feather touch. Luciana watched as her sister's pale head shook from side to side.

"Can you speak, Alessa?"

Alessandra's mouth opened. "I loved you, Lucia." The sound of her voice was a soft, creaking sort of moan. It came not from wind in the lungs in the natural way, but from the core of the younger woman's ghost, as if her very desire to speak, to comfort her sister, overwhelmed the boundaries of the grave and nature itself.

"Alessa!" Luciana could not hold back her sob of relief. She reached to embrace the spirit, but stopped, recognizing the futility of such an effort. "What has happened to you, Alessa? How did you die?"

"The compulsion of magic in the air . . ." The specter's words choked off and her hand rose to her throat.

"Was it one of the Escalade officers?"

The tension in Luciana, created by working magic, broke suddenly as if by a blow, leaving her feeling hollow and surreal. Her hold on Alessa's spirit began to unravel. She grasped with her magic, singing its song in her mind. There was little time left. Luciana tried to regain control of the chords of power within her, to recapture her hold, if just for a little longer. She needed to learn so much! What did she ask?

Panicking, Luciana said, "How do I set you free?"

The spirit's mouth opened as though she spoke, but no sound came forth. At last, the creaking moan sounded again. "I cannot find my Mandero . . . find Mandero, Luciana! Find him. He is not safe." And with those words the spirit began to fade.

"Alessa, *please* don't leave me yet!"

The spirit stopped fading, but the dust motes continued to swirl within her essence. The voice was fainter still. "Evil is afoot. . . ."

Luciana rose from the floor, crossing to her sister's form. Alessandra's death-silk flowed, rippled by the winds of the spirit realm, billowing out to caress her. Gypsy Silk to Gypsy Silk. Sunlight sparked where the fabrics touched. "I vow to you, Alessa, I will find and end the evil."

"I fight . . . the magician needs my essence . . ." The creaking moan was a mere whisper now. "I am tainted—"

"I will seek out the one who did this to you," Luciana vowed.

"Find Mandero." The ghost's shape fell in on itself, absorbing the light of the day. The room grew abruptly dark. The spirit was gone and the light returned, stark, clear, empty.

XII

"It is much safer to obey than to rule."
— Thomas à Kempis

"*DAIYA? Daiya,* are you unwell?"

Luciana became conscious of the speaker at the same time the odor of burning feathers wafted through her senses. She opened her eyes, pulling away from the unpleasant smell.

"Fetch the barber! She should have been bled yesterday, but she refused to be sensible. Clearer heads will prevail today!" Prunella said, then sniffed, setting aside the smoldering feathers.

Luciana opened her eyes wide. "No barber! No! I was merely taking a nap, I grew suddenly tired."

"The barber, Kisaiya."

Luciana sat up quickly, ignoring the rushing waves in her head and forced a mask of complete composure. "Do you think I am some chit to be countermanded, Prunella?"

"No, Your Grace, but—"

The still smoldering feathers made Luciana's stomach lurch, but she stayed sitting up as a show of strength. Her vision blurred briefly and she put out a hand to catch herself, encountering Prunella's steadying arm.

Opening her eyes, Luciana saw the feathers in Prunella's hands drifting dangerously near. She swung her feet over the edge of the bed and directed a stern gaze at her husband's young cousin as she pushed the feathers away. "I sat up too quickly, that is all. I am fine."

"Then why couldn't I wake you? It was frightening, and you so recently risen from bed!" Prunella exclaimed.

"You are mistaken, Prunella. You are so recently risen from bed, whereas, I was awake and away from my bed well before dawn."

Prunella looked as if she were going to say something, then closed her mouth with a little sniff. She folded her hands demurely in front of her so that she did not distress a line of her austere, Spanish-cut gown. Luciana could not count how often she was disrupted by sniffs and sullen demands to obey all of those social conventions that came as soon as Prunella presented herself each morning.

"I am duly chastised, Your Grace."

Luciana sighed again, taking Prunella's hands. "I didn't mean to chastise you, Pru. I meant only to point out that I didn't sleep as well as you last night by way of explaining my . . . my nap."

Prunella nodded, but it was clear she did not accept Luciana's explanation which, in turn, irritated Luciana all the more. "You haven't needed a nap like this previously, Your Grace, not . . . not for some time and it really was quite distressing when you would not wake. I feared for your life." Prunella glanced to the snuffed candles on the tiny altar, leaving no doubt that she also feared for Luciana's immortal soul.

Kisaiya seemed to sense the change in the conversation—or perhaps she recalled that Luciana slept this deeply only when she worked magic—and turned quickly to cover the altar.

Despite her frustration, Luciana was touched by Prunella's concern. She softened her tone. "I assure you that a little deep sleep has done me a world of good. I cannot say how long it has been since I felt quite this well! Indeed, Kisaiya, Prunella, I think a light luncheon would serve us all. We will eat in the salon, or better yet on the patio so that we may survey the orchards."

"Yes, Your Grace," Prunella said with a curtsy, leaving Kisaiya to follow her.

With the door to the upper rooms closed, Luciana sagged against the bed. She still felt so very tired. Her mind continued to reel as she thought of what Alessa had told her. An odd thought occurred to her then. It was only natural that Alessa would search the beyond for her lover. His passing had been no more peaceful than hers, according to Luciana's information. But would his ghost have been able to rest without Alessa? She thought not. From all she had heard, their affection seemed mutual and Alessa had always been a good judge of character, albeit she lacked a certain ability to sense danger. If that was so, why did Alessa want *her* to find the capitano?

Still shaking, Luciana crossed to the altar, drew back the cloth, covered her hair, and knelt. Her scrying dish, fired black with embedded flecks of gold nugget, received the basin water she poured. She lit the candles again, glancing back to make sure the door to the upper rooms, where lunch was being made, remained closed.

Luciana stared into the dish, seeing it but not seeing it, reciting prayers and focusing on the water. Her vision blurred, but she stared determinedly at the black water, thinking of the Stretto d'Messina and of the capitano, Mandero, who met his end in those treacherous, godforsaken waters. At first she saw nothing, felt nothing. Suddenly, inexplicably, she felt soaked to the skin. She *was* soaked and the water dragged at her. Her vision clouded with the sting of salt water in her eyes.

The black waters of the strait battered her—battered *him*, lifting him to the surface and then sloshing over his head again. The salt stung the deep wound in his back. Something spiny and scaled brushed against his leg, then crested through the waves beyond.

"Sisters Three, protect me!" he cursed. His sea-frozen fingers grabbed instinctively for the handheld crossbow at his side and found the hilt of his dagger instead. He felt the big fish's current before it bumped him again, this time harder. He was too weak and clumsy to strike well, nearly losing his dagger to the numbness in his fingers. He kicked vainly to avoid the next bump and felt rows of jagged teeth graze the layers of his sleeve. He struck as hard as he was able, taking a battering from the tail as the monster of the sea twisted away.

He waited, cold and shivering, for the fish to return, but nothing. The water lapped at him, dunking him in its briny depths, gagging him. Breathing was so very hard, yet he struggled on. Though he could hear the shouting of his men in the night, the ship was gone. He called out, but his words were swallowed by the waves and left him gasping for air. He rolled onto his back and attempted to stroke toward the heartland, but seized up in pain from the wound in his back. Swimming was impossible. His energy was depleted; nothingness began to creep into his vision. He tried to shake it off, but did not even have energy for that. At some point, the dagger slipped from his nerveless fingers. He did not concern himself with the loss, he needed both hands to keep afloat. He thought desperately of Alessa and the danger she was in. His last conscious thought was of her, the woman he loved. Then the nothingness took him . . . leaving Luciana tired and spent as she fell back from the scrying bowl.

Kisaiya came through the door and let out an exclamation as she hurried to Luciana's side. She helped Luciana to her feet and onto the settee. "*Daiya,* you'll be the death of yourself!"

"Just let me rest here a moment," Luciana gasped and sank back. She plucked the handkerchief from her bodice and dabbed at the salty water on her face. She wrinkled her nose. "I'll have to change."

Kisaiya glanced over her shoulder. "Prunella sent me to set the table on the patio. She'll be down before long."

Luciana rubbed her head. Kisaiya had already snuffed the candles and covered the altar again. It was becoming a trial having Prunella so near her personal spiritual work space. There was no tolerance in the girl for her beliefs, but what did Luciana expect? Raised in rural Reggio di Calabria, Prunella's father apparently taught her one was either a "good Catholic"—which had too much of the austere Spanish influence to Luciana's mind—or a thieving sinner suited for eternal damnation. At least this was the opinion she exhibited most often. Luciana rubbed her temples. She rose and chose to ignore the throbbing and reeling in her head as she made her way determinedly to her dressing table.

Kisaiya stopped, meeting her mistress' gaze in the dressing table mirror. She waited a moment more. When Luciana did not move, she left the room, her leather-soled slippers scuffing on the granite steps to the upper rooms.

While Kisaiya was gone, Luciana selected a gown of Gypsy Silk, a black dress with flounces and a dramatic undergown of gray. It was a simple dress made stunning by the fabric and cut to expose a modestly suggestive amount of bosom by the scooped neckline. She and Kisaiya had spent hours working the dove-gray embroidery and lace along the edges of the black outer gown and blackwork on the loose gray sleeves. The gown was among her favorites and remained appropriate—as far as the *gadjé* courtiers were concerned—for her state of mourning.

Luciana wondered briefly at the response she would get if she wore true Romani mourning: scarlets, crimsons, vermilions, and russets, the color of spilled blood. She might never get a reaction from the courtiers. Prunella probably would bar her in her rooms first!

She rummaged through her assortment of jewels, brooches, and other adornments and completed the ensemble with a large cameo at the breast, between the flounces of gray. She chose jet earrings with a silver setting, to match the hairpins already styled in her hair.

Kisaiya returned as Luciana set out the last of her things. Changing was a tiresome matter slowed by Luciana's attempts to speed the process. At last, done, they proceeded down to their waiting lunch.

───────────

Surrounded by her sister's things and engrossed in Mandero's and Alessandra's love letters, Luciana was barely aware of the scratch at the parlor door.

"Your Grace?"

Luciana looked up absently to find Prunella flanked by a liveried servant. His introduction secured, the servant bowed and proffered a piece of cream-colored paper.

Intrigued, Luciana accepted the letter, waiting until

the servant and, finally, Prunella stepped aside. She broke the king's seal and quickly read the letter within, a formal request to attend the king in the Throne Room at two. She glanced at the ornate mantle clock perched over the hearth. Its golden hands indicated fifteen minutes before the appointed hour.

"Does Her Grace have a response for His Majesty?"

"I will respond to His Majesty's request in person," Luciana said.

"As you wish, Your Grace." The servant bowed again before departing.

Luciana rose thoughtfully from the divan and motioned to Kisaiya. "His Majesty has summoned me. I must be sure my appearance is acceptable."

Prunella's face brightened. "It is well, then, that you changed earlier, Your Grace." She moved quickly to open the door to the upper rooms for Luciana.

It was clear from Prunella's expression that she anticipated being presented to the king. Luciana caught her hand gently. "Pru, I am requested for a *private* audience with His Majesty. You will not be able to stay."

Immediately crestfallen, Prunella composed herself quickly. "But, of course, Your Grace," she said. "I will escort you as appropriate."

Luciana nodded. Her cousin was accepting this better than she might have thought. She could not help but feel sorry for her though, especially since this was the first time the girl showed any excitement. She would have to make up for it.

Kisaiya was quick about her work, hiding the telltale signs left by the strains of magic. Powder covered the clamminess of Luciana's skin and she used a delicate hand with the rouge to brighten her cheeks.

The filigreed clock on the dressing table revealed they had a moment or two more. Ignoring Prunella's squeak of disapproval, Kisaiya plucked the combs and pins from Luciana's hair, letting it fall in deep brown cascades over her shoulders. With quick, expert hands, she brushed out the locks and styled them into a deceptively simple arrangement of curls and braids. She replaced the combs and pins as she went and was done, leaving more than enough time for Luciana to make her appointment with the King—if she hurried.

Suitably freshened, Luciana surveyed the result, ignoring Prunella's fretting. She frowned at the powders and rouge, but it looked as natural as such things ever could. She gave her thanks to Kisaiya then glanced back at Prunella. "If you're coming, then?"

Prunella fell in behind Luciana as she made her way down the stairs to the salon again. Hastening, they passed through the various twists in the hallways, and the Clock Walk, at last reaching the Throne Room as the multitude of clocks began to strike two. Two officers of the Corpo d'Armata, in dress uniforms of tan, completely polished from head to toe, snapped salutes and with flourishes of their golden-colored capes, they opened the doors for Luciana, and after a quick peek, Prunella turned away and began to retrace her steps.

The Throne Room was a vast hall. A series of two-story arching windows occupied the east wall, stained with depictions of Tyrrhia's birth as an independent kingdom. Notched along the edges of each window were carefully crafted tiles bearing the crest of each Tyrrhian king. White columns reached from cream-colored marble floors to the vaulted ceiling painted with designs of the heavens.

The king sat on his throne atop its white marble dais, unaccompanied by either the queen or Bianca, though the Court Herald stood to the king's left. Strangely, Lord Strozzini, the chief bodyguard, was missing. Another man in the King's Detail stood resolutely behind the monarch. From brown knee-high boots to the carefully gold-buttoned coat and neatly tied back hair, the man was well polished. His head never moved, but his eyes followed Luciana as she made her way up the hall.

Farther behind the thrones, draped from the ceiling, was the king's coat of arms cast in the whitest satin tapestry. On the coat of arms, stitched with threads of gold, rose the royal griffin rampant sinister. As always, Luciana was struck by the sheer grandeur of the hall and felt almost insignificant by comparison.

Estensi stamped his staff twice as Luciana approached.

"Her Grace, Signora Luciana Mizella Elena Lendaro e di Luna, *Araunya di Cayesmengri e Cayesmengro,* Duchessa di Drago." He stamped his staff again when he concluded.

Alban, in all of his regal finery, rose to receive her. He kissed Luciana's hand as he drew her up from her curtsy, turning expectantly to Estensi.

"You may lock the doors. There will be no further audiences with the king today," Estensi told the guards.

With her hand still held by Alban, Luciana watched the guards bow and exit the Throne Room.

"We will retire to my study," the king said as he led her through the open doors.

Luciana nodded, surprised but curious.

They entered a small, stuffy antechamber, which contained little more than a small settee, another door, and a stairwell. Emblems of Estensi's office as Court Herald hung above the vestibule. Alban motioned for Luciana to precede him up the stairs, stepping around her as they reached the landing to unlock the door and let them in.

Luciana surveyed the luxurious room with its dark polished wooden paneling and ornate furniture. It had changed little in the past few years, still a comfortable room designed as a haven for a man with great responsibilities. As in the Throne Room below, arched windows of stained glass lined the east wall. The glass portrayed Tyrrhian life—farmers in their fields, merchants in their stalls in village squares, bankers in their money houses, glassmakers at their art and Gypsies in the mulberry groves and at the loom, making their silk—all scenes a conscientious king such as Alban and his uncle-predecessor thought important enough to influence them in their daily business. There was no real decor to speak of, what with the furniture placed rather haphazardly about, as though drawn from one place to the next during the course of conversation with a restless companion. The king clearly sought sanctuary here.

At his invitation, as on previous occasions, Luciana chose the comfortably stuffed high-backed divan near the oversized desk. She carefully shifted the stack of books from the seat to a small table already piled perilously high with reading material.

Inexplicably, the king hesitated by the door and seemed unable to decide whether to leave it open or to close it. At last, he left the door ajar and crossed the room to sit on the edge of his desk, his eyes straying toward the door and stairwell beyond.

Luciana watched him, alert to his unease so incongruous with what she knew of his nature. His mood was contagious, she realized, as she too began to feel wary. But of what? She wondered at the king's behavior, his hesitation, and this private audience. He shifted restlessly, as though at a loss for words.

"How may I serve you, Your Majesty?"

He gave her an appreciative smile and visibly relaxed. Alban stroked his mustache thoughtfully. "I know you are good and dear friends with my wife beyond the fact of your marriage to her brother." He hesitated and shifted about on his seat on the edge of the desk. At last, he spoke in a rush, "I need to know exactly how candid my wife has been with you."

"I am confused, Majesty. What would you have me tell you that Her Majesty has not told you herself?" Luciana's stomach lurched with the trepidation that she might be called upon to betray a confidence. Using every skill her grandmother ever taught her in *dukkerin'*— never betray your own sentiments, concentrate on the subject—she fought the urge to take flight, and made herself meet Alban's eyes steadily.

"Don't insult my intelligence with pretty deprecations, Luciana," the king said with a grim smile.

She held her peace, growing as curious as she was anxious.

"Do not mistake me. I have absolute faith in Idala's loyalty, but she has been troubled of late, by more, even, than Alessandra's death. She has expressed fears for the young prince. I know that she does not sleep well, though she takes pains to hide the fact. There is more, I'm sure, though she does not confess it all. Has she, perhaps, spoken of it with you?"

Luciana drew back. So there it was. The invitation—
no, the royal request—to break Idala's confidence. She
chose her words carefully. "I thought she kept few secrets, but you know her better than I."

"Which tells me precisely nothing."

Luciana looked up, her expression pained. "Would
you truly ask me to break a confidence, Majesty? A
royal confidence?"

"No. Of course not," Alban said. "Your loyalty is
commendable and I think, perhaps, that you have told
me what I needed to know on that score." He rose and
opened the door to his office, peering down the stairwell.
"I never trust that I am completely alone. I don't question the loyalty of Lord Strozzini or his staff. He fought
at my side when I was with Stefano in the Escalade.
And yet, he is Roman Catholic and I sometimes
wonder . . ." The king paused and shrugged. "I do not
know if I am being unfair to this man who vowed to lay
his life down for mine, but one can never be sure if a
promise of life means that he is willing to risk his *soul*.
In that, the cardinal is his shepherd."

"Do you have reason to doubt him? Strozzini, I
mean?"

"No, at least, not directly. It is the cardinal I am more
concerned with."

"The cardinal? But you are influenced by the cardinal
in the same way he is. If you trust the man, then he
must be a gentleman of discernment. Strozzini must see
the flaws of the cardinal's leadership as well as you do."

The king nodded. "Let me come more to the point.
What have you learned since you arrived at the palazzo?
I know that you must be looking into the matter of Ales-
sandra's death. Is this not so?"

Unprepared for his bluntness, Luciana tried not to
stare. "I would be a deplorable sister if I were not at
least curious."

Alban took a long moment, studying his words. "I ask
you to share your opinions, which is no slight request."
He sketched a wave in the air, motioning toward the
Throne Room. "You know from the queen that we have

troubles here at court. You saw just yesterday morning some of our travails. You also have the trust of my wife, I believe, an objectivity which comes from your . . . well, you are not, exactly, one of us."

"You mean, because I come from the black-blooded people," Luciana suggested.

"I would not have put it in such a way as that. You are a loyal subject, like anyone else, but you . . . you were raised differently than most of the courtiers. Your perspective, therefore, is different, more removed."

Luciana nodded, suddenly awkwardly aware of the darkness of her complexion compared to the king's . . . and to the court . . . and to Stefano.

"You are the wife of a member of the Palantini, there-fore, you are as obliged as your husband is," the king said.

"I would not withhold my counsel, especially if I thought it welcome," Luciana said, smiling. "Why have you not spoken to Stefano? He corresponded regularly with Her Majesty, I understand, and he *is* already in your undoubted confidence, isn't he?"

"Yes, yes, of course," Alban said, "but some confi-dences are not easily or wisely put to paper—and women, I believe, talk more freely amongst themselves."

"Yes, Majesty, perhaps we do, but that is because it is just between ourselves. We need not worry that our bosom friends will consider us frivolous or overwrought. Husbands—even the best of them—do not always understand."

The king considered this a moment. "Her Majesty as-sures me that you are a woman of discretion and that is most evident here, but she also values you for your perception. It is not for mere flattery that she says such things and, knowing Stefano as I do, I know that he values your intelligence. As an intelligent, perceptive woman, Luciana, I would value your opinion of matters at court."

"I'm honored, Majesty."

Alban let out a bark of laughter. "It is no easy honor, *Araunya,* and you have wit enough to know it."

"I do not see what fresh perspective I might offer. Surely you have resources of your own throughout the court better informed than I who has only just arrived?"

"Of course I have my sources, but they are in the middle of it all and I seek an outsider's view, especially one with good reason to peer into the shadows and behind the masks. So, tell me, what have you learned?"

Luciana unfolded her fan and refolded it. A royal request, a demand for information. Yet, she *knew* nothing. She began nervously. "I have been here but a day . . ."

"Stefano tells me that you are already acquainted with details concerning your sister. I would like to know what you know."

Luciana toyed with her fan some more. She was not ready to share how much she did not know with anyone else, especially not with someone she had not chosen to confide in. Sighing, she said, "I searched the graveyard. Four men stole my sister's body."

"And you know this how, precisely?" Alban asked.

Again, Luciana hesitated. "I have availed myself of certain . . . gifts."

"Magic, you mean."

Luciana nodded.

"You know that evidence of a purely magical sort is not considered sufficient proof in Tyrrhian court?" Alban said softly.

"I know."

Alban leaned forward in his chair. "What else have you learned?"

"My knowledge is almost purely through magical resources," Luciana protested.

"And we are not in a Tyrrhian Judicial Court," the king retorted. "What *aren't* you telling me?"

"I've discovered, through magical means, that Conte Urbano was one of the grave robbers, that it was he who stole my sister's body."

"Conte Urbano? Are you serious?" Alban laughed.

Luciana stared at him, no evidence of a smile upon her face.

"You *are* serious!"

"I am."

"Who would have thought the conte possessed the animus to commit such a crime? Until now, his greatest crime has been an offense to all things poetical and a frequent violation of fashion."

"There is also a wizard at court, someone who now possesses the body of my sister and uses it to torment the queen, troubling her in the night with the ghost." Luciana watched the king's expression. At the moment, he looked . . . doubtful? "I, too, have seen the apparition," she said.

Alban shuddered. "As have I," he admitted. "She troubles my sleep and my conscience. I wish that there had been more I could have done to protect her, at least to ease her pain so that she did not—"

"My sister did not commit suicide, and I believe strongly that she did not kill the capitano either," Luciana said brusquely.

The king sat back. He looked surprised and thoughtful. "How much of this do you know and how much do you believe?"

"I believe all of it, I can prove none of it, but just as I know that Ale—" Luciana paused, suddenly mindful that she had nearly spoken Alessandra's name. It was one thing to use her sister's name in her thoughts, such a thing could not be prevented, and the *gadjé* neither had the custom of avoiding the deceased's name nor the power to invoke a *mulló,* but she must not allow herself to be lulled into such dangerous liberties as the unwitting *gadjé* took. "My sister's body was stolen by the conte. I also know that she did not take her own life."

The king sighed heavily. "So it is confirmed, then. She, too, fell by a murderer's hand. Do you know who did it?"

"She, too?" Luciana repeated.

"There is the capitano who, by all accounts, was murdered."

Luciana nodded. "I do not yet know who is responsible for my sister's death. There are possibilities. It has been suggested that the capitano's men may have fulfilled the *Coda Condanna a Morte.*"

Alban's brows rose. "You think the Escalade would do that?"

"Why not? I understand the capitano was very much loved by his men."

"Hmm, that is so," the king said with a worried nod. "What else?"

"My sister was a political innocent. Through the capitano, she was drawn into a court game she wasn't experienced enough to play."

"Do you think *you* are 'experienced enough'?"

Luciana shrugged, "I intend to learn, if the path to the truth takes me in that direction."

"Stefano would prefer that you did not," Alban said. "He fears for your safety."

"As I have feared for his during all of his tenure at the Morean front. My fear could not bring him home, and his fear will not send me to the estates."

"I would not argue the issue with you. I leave it to your husband." The king winced. "I do not know what comfort it may bring you, but I, too, believe your sister was murdered because of her association with the capitano. Perhaps these conspirators we have in court—whoever they are—thought she knew something. Perhaps she did and, in her own way, sought to serve and protect the Crown."

Intrigued, Luciana said, "You think my sister 'sought to serve the Crown,' you say? How do you mean? I've heard nothing of this."

"I learned from some of the officers in the Royal Escalade Garrison that the capitano had suspicions about the cardinal. I've thought from the beginning that your sister and her capitano died because he asked too many questions." Alban stroked his dark mustache. "The cardinal is skilled enough politically to know that arranging Bianca's marriage without the consent of the king would create trouble—other regents would imprison him, at the very least, for such an offense. During his audience with me, he did not seem impressed with my anger over his presumption."

"But if you think him guilty of arranging Alessandra's and the capitano's deaths, why do you do nothing?"

"I have no proof, merely suspicions."

"He counts on his position and reputation to protect him," Luciana said bitterly.

"Of course he does. Direct action against him will only anger the Tyrrhian Roman Catholics, not to mention the Holy See, and cause the other Ecclesiasts—not to mention the Palantini—to wonder if I might possibly act against them as well."

Luciana's mind whirled as she contemplated all that the king had told her. Suddenly, it occurred to her that she was not his most likely confidante. "What purpose does telling me all this serve?" She had grown cold to the point of shivering as the king spoke of these bold conspirators. Brave, free Tyrrhia, the new homeland of her people, was threatened. It made sense that Alessandra might get herself killed protecting that. No bordering lands would shelter the Wandering Folk the way Tyrrhia did, especially not now, not with the latest Inquisition. "Who are these conspirators you suspect?"

"I suspect everyone and no one. It is easy to believe, however, that the cardinal has involved himself in politics beyond making the arranged marriage of my only cousin."

"But you have no proof," Luciana said.

Alban shook his head. "The capitano might have given me the evidence I need, but now he is gone."

"And what would you have me do?"

The king stared at her a long moment then rose and closed the door. "I ask for a divination. I must know who I can trust."

"Divination?" Luciana gasped and rocked back in her seat. "Surely you jest?"

"I was never more serious," Alban said.

"But if the Palantini ever found out . . . ruling by divination . . . Majesty, you are Roman Catholic yourself," Luciana protested.

"For the sake of my family, I must know who I can trust."

Luciana shook her head. "It doesn't work that way, Majesty. Even if I were to use the cards, they would only give vague representations which might be mistaken. I do not even use them to uncover this *chovahano,* this wizard I seek myself."

Alban frowned. "What wizard?"

"The wizard who uses my sister's body to control her spirit. Only a wizard could do that," Luciana said.

"You seriously believe that there is a wizard in my court?" Alban shook his head. "It seems so improbable. Do you have any idea who this might be?"

Luciana hesitated. "As I said before, I thought perhaps Conte Urbano, but—"

Alban laughed again. "It is hard enough to imagine the man a grave robber, much less a master of mystic arts."

"Then my only hope is that he can lead me to such a man."

"You know that it is a man? Couldn't it be a woman?"

Luciana shook her head. "No, this is a man's work."

"For all the uncertainty you claim of divination, you are remarkably firm in your opinions," the king said.

"Forgive me, Majesty, but these are things that I can know from something I've touched and it deals with the surety of past actions. What you ask of me is nebulous at best, and there is no known element for me to interact with."

"Then you must keep me apprised of your investigation. If you learn anything, I would know of it. Am I understood?"

"Yes, Majesty."

XIII

"If a man will begin with certainties, he will end in doubts; but if he will be content to begin with doubts, he shall end with certainties."
— Francis Bacon

12 d'Maggio 1684

SUCH little things, the decisions that made one a villain or a pawn. Luciana's conversation with the king still ran through her mind. Who was the villain here? How was she to find the *chovahano?* She doubted he would volunteer his presence and, now that Conte Urbano suspected something was amiss, the black wizard would take steps. With Nicobar gone, her options were limited. He was with the *Beluni* to find Grasni and whatever else he might learn, but what she needed now was information from a local. Did she dare take Stefano into her confidence? Perhaps, but she had not seen him since yesterday afternoon.

Luciana calculated what her next move should be. She would be going to the city for her duties to the mulberry overseers, perhaps the Guild Mistress would know more. Considering her obligations to the Guilds, she decided not to tell Stefano. She did not want to fight with him again.

No longer able to stand the thought of eating, Luciana tossed her sugared plum to the birds. The birds came out of hiding and squabbled as they fed greedily. She had accomplished little—less than nothing since her arrival.

She comforted herself with the realization that that self-assessment was not exactly true. She had visited the cemetery, learned something of the one who invaded Alessandra's tomb and, Luciana was sure, identified the interloper as Conte Urbano. Of course, what help this would be to the king, she had no idea. Perhaps, if she concentrated upon one intrigue at a time—

"Your Grace?"

Luciana looked up. Prunella hovered just out of her line of vision, forcing her to turn and squint into the sun. "Yes, Pru?"

"It is time for Mass. May I be excused?"

Lost in thought, Luciana waved her on. "Of course, of course."

"I will pray for you as well, Cousin," Prunella said.

Luciana smiled. Prunella was nothing if not determined. "Thank you."

As Prunella turned toward the patio gate, it occurred to Luciana that the conte and his master probably could not keep Alessandra's body on the grounds of the palazzo—or, at least, not on the immediate grounds. So where might he hide the body of a noblewoman close by?

Luciana lifted her hand, catching Prunella's attention. "As you pass the stables, tell Baldo I intend to ride this morning."

Prunella looked surprised and hurried back to the table. "But, Your Grace, Nicobar is not here. Who will accompany you?"

"I do not need Nicobar to take a ride," Luciana replied.

"But it isn't seemly, Your Grace, and Baldo is only a coachman. *I* will stay and accompany you," she said. Her expression suddenly brightened, "Unless, of course, His Grace is escorting you?"

Luciana bit her tongue and fussed with the napkin in her lap to distract Prunella's gaze while she composed herself. "My husband has other obligations this morning," she said, having no other answer to that suggestion.

"I am reluctant to interfere with your prayers. Besides, I fear that we did not bring riding horses of a temperament suitable to your skills." She held up her hand to forestall any further protests from the girl. "I will take Kisaiya."

Prunella hesitated but seemed to think better of whatever she was about to say. She acquiesced with a sniff and a nod. "I will tell Baldo to prepare two horses, then."

When the girl did not leave immediately, Luciana forced a smile. "Thank you, Cousin."

"Is there perhaps something else I might do for you?"

Luciana frowned. "Something else?" She shook her head. "No, I think not. Go along to Mass, and I will see you later."

Still the girl hesitated. "Are you *sure* you will not want my services?"

"I think not. We will take in the fresh air and perhaps see the markets in the city. I'm sure Kisaiya can assist me with anything I might need."

Prunella's lips twisted into a frown of doubt. Luciana realized the girl felt torn between her duty to attend Mass and the prospect of an adventure in the city. With a pang of guilt, it dawned on Luciana that this was the first time her husband's young cousin had shown interest in anything that did not involve duty and obligation. Were her plans less vital, she might relent, but Prunella would be torn between her Catholic faith and outrage at the magic that must be done.

Luciana reached out and touched the girl's arm. "Please, Pru, I'm confident that all will go well. His Grace and I have no plans to leave Citteauroea soon, so there will be other trips to the city. I promise. We'll take the carriage then and be quite silly, take lunch in the marketplace and buy ourselves something new."

"There is the mourning period after all," Prunella murmured.

"Yes," Luciana said with a nod and a sigh. "I will be out for the air. I am sure the day will be dismal."

"As you say, Your Grace." Prunella, looking much relieved, finally departed.

Luciana left the patio and the remnants of her breakfast. She found Kisaiya in the lower bedroom, airing out dresses.

"I have an appointment in the city. I've decided upon a ride to clear my head."

Kisaiya promptly set aside the dress she held and plucked the black riding habit from the back of another chair. "Will this be acceptable, *Daiya?* With the green petticoats?"

Considering all the ties, hooks and buttons involved, changing gowns went quickly. While Kisaiya changed, Luciana adjusted her neckline and lingered over the accessories. She selected the green-tinged white pendant on a thin golden chain, and the black velvet mask that any lady of consequence wore when joining the press of the market crowds. She tucked a finely embroidered kerchief into the cuff of her gusseted sleeve. Luciana completed the outfit with a pair of black gloves made from supple kid leather.

The day was fine, sunny with a breeze off the sea to keep it cool and comfortable and not a sign of rain in the spring sky. Luciana and Kisaiya left by the patio to stroll through the apple and pear orchards along the length of the outer palazzo on their way to the stables. They passed the queen's outer, iron-grated courtyard, and the Throne Room. The white stucco Escalade barracks began, pressed near the side of the palazzo. Streams of the elite guard could rush to the queen's assistance at a moment's notice.

Like most of the palazzo, the barracks were three stories high. The first floor was open to the stables, and held an office or two. Beyond that was a wide open side where the soldiers, sweaty and exuberant about their work, could be seen practicing their fencing. The barracks did not smell so very different from the stables what with the aroma of sweat, liniment, and polished leather. In the gymnasium, a cacophony of men's voices rose in shouted orders, conversation, and the sort of thing one said in the heat of battle. Sabers clashed raucously, booted feet scuffed the wooden floor, and men groaned as they wrestled with one another.

The soldiers closest to the open doors of the gymnasium spotted Luciana with Kisaiya. They paused and greeted her over the distance, foil guard to nose, in the fashion of fencers honoring one another before their fray. These salutes created a ripple effect as other soldiers beyond also paused to salute. Luciana bowed her head in acknowledgment of the greetings and continued on her way.

The stables were just visible through the trees. A small courtyard held the carriages of the palazzo residents just as the assorted paddocks and stalls contained their mounts and driving teams. To the Romani, raised around horses, the smell of horse sweat and dung rose as a welcome fragrance. Liveried stable boys walked horses, some saddled, some not. The steeds passed sleepily, tails swishing and hides twitching at the flies. Older men in shirtsleeves, their livery coats hung on pegs close by, moved with practiced ease among the animals, their hands buckled into brushes which stroked their charges in quick, sure movements.

It was easy enough to spot Dragorione's grays among the chestnuts and bays which populated the stables. Even now, the plump Baldo was huffing and fussing over two of the dappled horses. He polished a saddle buckle with his cuff then turned with a winning smile and bowed. "Lady Prunella said you wished to ride this morning, Your Grace. I prepared your mount and a second for your companion." He dabbed at his sweaty pate with a large, plain kerchief and winked at Kisaiya.

"Thank you, Baldo. As usual, you have done well." Luciana reached out to stroke the velvety nose of her favorite mount. She pulled bits of sugar from a pocket and fed them to the horses, then turned to greet the dogs—wire-haired, gray-brown, Gypsy mongrels—which served as carriage dogs. The two yipped and bounced up, struggling to displace one another as they vied for her attention.

"I have taken the liberty of borrowing a mule so that I may accompany you."

Luciana hesitated. Reluctant as she was to be encumbered by an escort, she was not at her estates, after all.

She permitted common sense to reign. "We do not travel far, merely to the city and back." She motioned. Both dogs sat promptly, their shaggy tails thumping in the musty straw. She scratched the dogs' ears as they whined excitedly.

"Thank you, Your Grace. We're ready and at your disposal," the coachman said.

Baldo consulted with Kisaiya as he helped her mount, but was silent as he assisted Luciana onto her mare. As soon as she was securely seated, he hurried to the bay mule and mounted. He smiled broadly as he turned his trusty steed and bowed awkwardly from the back of the mule.

Luciana paused in the arrangement of her skirts, considering the sun. She shifted about on the sidesaddle. The leather and wood construct creaked ominously. The whole thing was preposterous, Luciana thought to herself. The *Beluni* had spoiled her for such *gadjé* traditions as the sidesaddle when the old woman allowed her five year-old granddaughter to straddle the sleek, fat horses which pulled the Romani *vardos*. Since then, most conveyances seemed absurd to Luciana. As was to be expected, Conte Baiamonte Davizzi did not appreciate his stepdaughter being taught such scandalous things and warned Luciana against teaching Alessandra. She ignored him, of course, but, by then, he seemed to expect that.

Luciana shook off the memories and resolved to at least *appear* comfortable. She met Kisaiya's knowing grin with a secretive smile of her own and then urged her patient mare onward.

They skirted the end of the orchard and the Escalade barracks, encountering a corner of the smaller vineyards before they entered the cobbled courtyard featuring King Alaric's statue and the fountain. The waxy remains from hundreds of candles and various offerings from Lemuria and Alaric's Day were now cleared away from the base of the statue, the shroud gone.

From the courtyard, they gained the road, passing the gardens on either side, and at the end of the palazzo. The "ghetto" where the church bells of the cathedral maintained a respectful silence during Mass, occupied the southernmost outer wall, and on the opposite side of the road were the vineyards proper.

The Escalade Duty Detail greeted Luciana with salutes. They were dapper men in their blue-and-gold uniforms with shiny boots and polished golden buttons, as they stood all in a row before the grand gate.

"*Araunya,* can we be of service?" one of the officers asked. Behind him, others scurried to open the gate that led to the road to Citteauroea. "Is there any way I or my men might be of service? Perhaps you would like a guide? I can provide you with a full accompaniment of a dozen men." The officer snapped his fingers at the *vigilare.* "It will take but a moment—"

"No, no, please!" Luciana protested. "A single man will suffice, sir."

The officer frowned. "Is Your Grace certain? Would not at least three be more suitable?"

Luciana shook her head firmly. "I am not interested in creating a presence. One man will be sufficient."

"I would escort you myself, but I have duties which keep me here. Would you accept the services, then, of my lieutenant, Pias de Mari?"

The indicated man sprang into the saddle of a chestnut gelding, a fine animal to any but a Romani's standards. The officer doffed his plumed hat, bowing as the constraints of the saddle permitted. With a nod to the gallant lieutenant and his superior, Luciana guided her horse through the gate followed by Kisaiya and Baldo, who slowed his mule to pace with the lieutenant's gelding. The lieutenant followed close behind, but at a discreet distance. He clearly had practice at this or had been well-trained—probably both.

The dust rose from the narrow road, churned up by the horses' hooves. Unlike most roads, this one lay straight and free of potholes and deep furrows. Beyond the gates of the palazzo stood more orchards. A mile farther and the orchards became wild wood cut back from the road. Glancing back, Luciana saw that the lieutenant sat up straighter, watching the forest closely, one hand on his scorpinini. There could be no doubt that he rode with bolt loaded in the small crossbow. Baldo looked attentive as well.

Despite its prominence and location by the sea, Citteauroea could not be confined by the artificial boundaries of walls. People said that once barriers surrounded Citteauroea, but God merely laughed and sent a quake to tear down the man-made impediments. City walls, if they still existed, now served as retaining walls or parts of townsfolk's homes well within the sprawl of the capital.

Luciana urged her mare onto the first cobbled street branching off the road. Almost immediately, she doubted her decision as she ducked beneath low-slung balconies and wet clothes hung out to air. Noise echoed off closely built walls—children laughed and played, mothers called out, a man and woman argued, pewter plates clattered to a tiled floor, and animals barked, bayed, bleated, and crowed. As the street twisted, every type of avenue, from cobbled walks to muddy alleys— some barely more than passageways wide enough for one thin man to walk naturally—to create a rat's warren of networking byways. She followed the turns, keeping to the cobbled streets until finally she came to a point that was almost impassable. Confused, she pulled her mare up short and twisted in her saddle.

The second-story shutters of a nearby house banged open and a smiling blonde woman leaned out waving her fan flirtatiously. She wore her gown provocatively low. Another woman came to her side and edged into the window beside the first. Neither woman left much to the imagination and their signals with their fans could be described as nothing less than brazen. Thankfully, they seemed content to make their solicitations with the language of the fan and suggestive looks and saved Luciana and Kisaiya the embarrassment of having their escorts called up.

Luciana looked pointedly away, back to the lieutenant, who moved to her side.

"Pardon, Your Grace. You seemed familiar with the roads and I presumed my services were not needed."

"Thank you, Lieutenant—?"

"De Mari, Your Grace. If you will permit me?" He dismounted as he spoke and reached toward her mare's bridle.

Luciana felt so relieved she only nodded.

The lieutenant bowed with a smile, handing his horse's reins to Baldo, and took the bridle of Kisaiya's horse as well. It was no small feat to back the horses out of the narrow alley, but the lieutenant seemed quite adept. After turning the horses, de Mari leaped onto his own mount and, with a slight bow, took the lead.

So it seemed that Citteauroea, unencumbered by city gates, protected itself with mazes. De Mari explained that there were two well-guarded ways into the city where one did not encounter the maze of homes and, as de Mari called them with a slight cough, "domestic establishments." Luciana smothered a rueful chuckle. Her amusement would only embarrass the lieutenant and only the three *Fata* knew what Kisaiya's reaction would be since she was capable of incredible naïveté and cynicism in rapid order.

"What are your needs, Your Grace, here in the marketplace, I mean?" de Mari asked. "Where would you like me to take you?"

Kisaiya looked at Luciana nervously.

"It has been so long since I have been here. Perhaps we might visit the square and proceed from there? I will need to visit the local Gypsy Silk Guildmistress," Luciana said. She was glad of the mask she wore as a wet dress flapped in the wind and caught her across the cheek.

The lieutenant nodded and preceded them again, glancing back periodically to see that they were well. Baldo followed close behind.

"Is the Guildhouse your only visit today, *Daiya?*" Kisaiya asked quietly, leaning precariously out of her side-saddle so that she might be heard by only her intended audience.

Luciana put out a cautioning hand and smiled at the lieutenant who chose that moment to look back. "Careful, *Chavi,* I would not want you to hurt yourself."

"My curiosity will always get the better of me," Kisaiya admitted. She looked at her mistress expectantly.

"I've learned that the *Araunya-minore's* body was stolen and her soul has been subjected to . . ." Luciana shuddered.

"And that a sorcerer has taken her, of course," Kisaiya said. She turned and smiled at de Mari, who pulled his horse up.

The lieutenant dismounted and came back to them. "The market square is just beyond," he said, motioning. "It is easier going on foot. We can leave our horses with the local vigilare so that I may be at your complete disposal." As he finished speaking, he held out his arms to assist Luciana down.

It would be easier to dismount without assistance, between the cumbersomeness of her skirts and the side-saddle, but Luciana brought a practiced smile to her lips and accepted his assistance, hiding her wince when she turned her ankle as she landed on the irregular cobbled street. When Kisaiya was safely on the ground, de Mari gathered the reins of the four mounts and hurried off.

Luciana's party followed at a slower pace. Faced with the cobweb of streets, Luciana realized she still would have been hopelessly lost.

Ahead, the lieutenant selected a street like any of the others she had already seen in Citteauroea, alternately cobbled and clear or little more than a muddy rut. Given that it had not rained in some time, Luciana chose not to consider what made the streets wet enough to become mired, though she held her skirt a little higher and wished she had chosen to wear a perfume. Kisaiya, on the other hand, seemed quite at ease ducking beneath laundry flapping in a lackluster breeze and sidestepping the occasional occupant or hazard—laundry baskets, refuse buckets, chamber pots, and suchlike.

The alley took another curve up and over a cobbled hillock and, as they reached the rise, all the riches of Citteauroea's marketplace lay before them. Luciana paused to catch her breath and take in the fresh breeze blowing over the market. The scent of baked sweets and breads, the perfumery, the fruit sellers, even the fishmongers offered an almost refreshing change from what had preceded.

Kisaiya let out a gasp, drawing Luciana's smile.

"Have you never been to Citteauroea?" Luciana asked, looking back to the market spread out before them.

Kisaiya shook her head. "Mama promised, but . . ." She shrugged and continued to stare down onto the bazaar of mercantile activity.

The market occupied a large quarter of the city in a series of cobbled plazas. The first plaza lay before them, with the second barely visible just beyond the corner of the perfumer's shop and the bakery across from it. Booths, if the ramshackle tables and awnings could be called that, were built in clusters with vendors of every type—smithies' boys with silver, brass and pewter; glassmakers with all nature of glassware, imported and domestic; young girls waving colorful plumes; cobblers; medicine wagons; and so much more for the eye to feast upon— all hawking their wares.

Wealthier merchants and the Guilds maintained shops edging the plazas. The watchmakers, the jewelers, the perfumeries, the purveyors of cloth and even one of the Gypsy Silk Guildhouses resided here. The patrons came from all walks of life. A lady, dressed in her new Egyptian cotton gown, wearing a hood and mask even on this hot day, pressed in next to the washerwoman at the fishmonger's stall. A tradesman haggled with the fruit seller. Everywhere there was noise and color and scents. It was a sensual kaleidoscope.

"Shall we, then?" Luciana said, glancing back at Baldo. The lieutenant went ahead to tether her grays, Baldo's mule, and his red gelding under the watchful eye of a uniformed vigilare. The Escalade's post, she noted, sat between storefronts facing the mercantile plaza. She waited for the lieutenant, who had completed his task and was hurrying toward her.

Upon reaching them, the lieutenant bowed deeply, doffing his cavalier's hat. The yellow plume pinned to it danced saucily as he placed it back on his head. "I am at your disposal, Your Grace."

Luciana grinned and squinted up at the sun, shielding her eyes with her fan. The sun was high and her empty stomach rumbled. She had neglected her breakfast this morning. "Perhaps we might find some shade and take lunch."

"May I take the liberty of making a suggestion?" de Mari asked. "At your pleasure, Your Grace, I will recommend an inn in the plaza just beyond this, or we can take advantage of the various booths below."

Luciana looked at Kisaiya. "What would you like to do?"

Kisaiya grinned like a child. "You have no preference?"

Luciana shrugged.

Kisaiya danced forward and whirled back. "I— Should we return to the city, Prunella would most likely join us, wouldn't she?"

Luciana nodded.

"Prunella would surely prefer the inn."

"Then we will visit the booths," Luciana said, motioning de Mari to lead on. Baldo kept to the rear.

Lunch was a simple affair: *pane di segale* from the baker's, spiced plums and apricots from a farmer's booth, spit-roasted songbirds marinated in rosemary and red wine from one of the market stalls, the smiling shopkeeper at the *confetteria* provided them with sweets— macaroons and sugary confections—and red wine from one of the dozen or so *tavernas* bordering the plazas.

As Luciana finished her apricot, de Mari reappeared at her elbow and offered her a dampened towel. Where or when he had gone, Luciana could not tell, for she thought him to be at her side only the moment before. This lieutenant was an enterprising fellow, she thought, as she wiped the sticky juice from her fingers.

De Mari accepted the damp towel from Luciana and Kisaiya and looked at them expectantly. "There is a sausage maker just beyond. I can recommend—"

"I think we've eaten quite enough, thank you!" Luciana said quickly. Already she wished her corset was not so snug. The thought of further indulgences only made her ache.

"As you say, then," de Mari agreed amiably with a

bow. "Did you bring a list of items you wished to purchase, or perhaps you would like to dally? Whatever you
wish, I am at your command."

Kisaiya smiled at Luciana, apparently pleased by the
lieutenant's attentiveness. Luciana had noticed the officer's winks and the special care he took to include Kisaiya as though the girl were a station above her own.
It pleased Luciana to see Kisaiya happy, and she was
sure the officer offered a distinct difference from Nicobar's gruff, businesslike manner. It would probably do
her assistant good to be set upon his ear. Perhaps another suitor might draw his attention to Kisaiya.

With an indulgent smile, Luciana turned to de Mari.
"I have obligations at the Guildhouse. We shall go
there first."

"As you say then," de Mari replied with a bow. "It
so happens that the Guildhouse is in this plaza. If you'll
just follow me." He turned on his heel and was off,
cutting a swathe through the crowd.

The Guildhouse sprawled over a good section of the
street. A banner with the Gypsy Silk emblem and bearing the crests of the *Araunyas* hung above the door. At
the doorstep, Luciana paused.

"Gentlemen, I have business indoors which I must
carry out. Kisaiya can stay, but I'm afraid that I—"

Baldo held up his hand. "Your Grace, I have been
intending to replace some fittings on the carriage. The
lieutenant can show me to an appropriate shop. It would
take at most an hour?" He paused as the lieutenant
concurred with his plan. Baldo watched Luciana's face
and with a smile said, "Perhaps, it would be better to
take, say, two hours? The fittings must be just perfect."

Luciana nodded her approval. "Then we will find you
gentlemen just returned when we conclude our business within."

The lieutenant and Baldo bowed and waited until Luciana had raised the heavy horse-head knocker before
they took their leave. The door was opened in short
order by a very young girl in a work smock worn over
a practical black dress.

"Madam, may I help you?" the young girl asked.

Luciana held out her hands to show her signet rings. The girl immediately fell into a deep curtsy.

"Forgive me for not knowing you, *Araunya!* Let me fetch the mistress!" Without further word, the girl turned and ran down a dark hallway, leaving Luciana and Kisaiya on the doorstep.

Kisaiya giggled.

Moments later, the girl returned with a middle-aged woman, finely dressed, though her gown was pierced with dozens of threaded needles. The older woman held the door wide, beckoning them in as she dropped into a low curtsy and offered her hand.

Luciana took it, feeling the fine calluses on her fingertips from years of work with the needle, and raised her up, offering, in turn, both of her own hands bearing the rings of her positions. The woman kissed the rings as she rose.

"I am most honored that you would attend my house, *Araunya-Daiya,*" the woman said. She smoothed her graying hair unconsciously. "I am your hand and invite you to use my house at your will. How may I be of service to you?"

"Are you of the blood?" Luciana asked quietly, removing the mask covering her face.

"I am *pushrat*—half-Romani, *Daiya,*" the woman said.

"And your name?"

"I am Eleni di Beshli, Mistress of this Guild Chapter. I am completely loyal to my brothers and sisters in the Growers' and Spinners' Guilds," she said. "The Guildmaster of the Growers' Guild is resting upstairs. Shall I fetch him?"

"Peace, Mistress Eleni," Luciana murmured as she laid a placating hand on the woman's shoulder. "I come to bless the silks as is my duty, but first I would appeal to you, as a Roma local to Citteauroea, for information."

"Whatever I can do for you, *Daiya.*" She shooed the girl up the stairs with a quiet order to fetch the Guildmaster and slid open a paneled door to a small salon. She closed the door snugly after Luciana and Kisaiya, then rushed to move bolts of silk from the chairs so that they might sit down. "Forgive me, *Daiya,* we have been quite busy of late and . . ." She sighed heavily. "Forgive me," she repeated.

"There is nothing quite so comfortable as a woman's workroom," Luciana said, surveying her surroundings. A bulging bag of remnants leaned against the couch next to the Guildmistress and three dressmakers' dummies with measuring strings and bits of fabric pinned to them huddled in a corner. Needles were absently stuck into everything, including the arm of the couch and the curtain behind the Guildmistress' desk.

"The Guildmaster arrived only this morning, before the morning post which bore his letter warning me of his arrival. I *really* was not prepared—we've been so busy of late—"

"Your dedication serves the Wandering Folk well, Mistress Eleni," Luciana said soothingly.

"I was most horrified to learn of—" The Guildmistress stopped and continued more carefully. "To learn of the *Araunya-minore's* death. We are still in mourning as you see," the Guildmistress said, motioning to her own black gown beneath her gray work smock. She again rushed to explain when she apparently felt her explanation was not suitable. "We observe the *gadjé's* use of black because of—"

Luciana raised her hand and motioned to her own dark gown. "As do I, Mistress Eleni. Our ways are different and your customers would not understand. I thank you for your kindness." She leaned forward on the couch. "Perhaps you can help me, in the matter of my sister's death—"

There was a rough rap on the doors, which then slid wide. A middle-aged, middle-sized man with nondescript coloring entered the room, bowing. Across his swelling middle, he wore a mulberry-colored baldric neatly embroidered all the way around with a forest of the trees he tended. The baldric was the sort worn only by the Guildmaster of the Trees. Beneath the baldric, he wore an old-fashioned leather jerkin, red shirt, and black pants. He coughed loudly and rubbed his bristling brownish mustache.

"*Araunya!* You received my message?" the fellow asked in a booming voice—seemingly unaware of the Guildmistress and Kisaiya wincing at his volume.

"Indeed, Master Geralamo," Luciana responded, rising from her chair. "Where are the waters that must be blessed?"

"In the stables, on the flatcart. Seemed the best place to keep them. I have some lads keeping watch," he said.

"This way, *Araunya-Daiya,*" Mistress Eleni said, gesturing down the long dark hall from which she had originally come.

They skirted the stairs to the upper floors and ignored the ornately set up fitting room suitable enough to receive a queen. Doors to several rooms were cracked open and curious young girls watched them, giggling and whispering among themselves. The Guildmistress clapped her hands. "Back to work, *chavis!*" The doors shut obediently as the mistress continued on her way. At the end of the long hallway, they reached a door, which Mistress Eleni flung open.

The back lot was alive with drying silk hung on lines from the windows of each story of the Guildhouse to the three-story stable. The stable was not more than a stone's throw away. Tall fences hemmed in the Guildhouse from its neighbors on either side.

"I have a storeroom, *Araunya,* just on the second floor that you might be able to use, but I don't know if it will suit your needs," the Guildmistress said.

" 'Twere better done at the groves just 'afore feeding the trees, but seein' it ain't possible and there be observers outside, the room'll do," Geralamo said gruffly. He shouldered open the heavy wooden stable door and barked orders at two youths sitting on the steps of a *vardo* stationed beside a flatcart. A woman came out the back of the *vardo,* hands on hips. "*Araunya,* me wife."

The Guildmaster's wife curtsied after coming down from her *vardo.* She motioned the lads toward the flatcart. They obeyed her without hesitation, momentarily disappearing behind the flatcart and then reappearing, each carrying a keg beneath each arm.

The Guildmistress led them up the stairs in the back

of the stable, past a storeroom to another room just like it, except that it contained no cloth or other stuffs. The boys set the kegs in the center of the room and joined with the others hovering at the door. The guildmaster pried open the lid of the first keg, then turned to scowl at the waiting group. "Leave us be. 'Tis a job for the *Araunya* and me."

The door closed with a snap behind Luciana. It narrowly missed catching her hem in the process.

Geralamo continued prying the kegs open until all four lids rested against the wall. He looked at Luciana standing near the door, watching and not speaking. He ducked his head a bit, as he stood. "The wife says she's a saint to put up with me this time a year 'cepting she doesn't believe in saints any more'n me or any other Rom. I'm worse for bein' away from the groves."

Luciana nodded, accepting his gruff apology as she lifted her lace shawl to cover her head. "You brought our supplies?"

Geralamo motioned to a small *putsi* pouch dropped by the door.

"How long will it take you to return to Terranova and the orchards?" Luciana asked.

"A week, maybe a ten-day," the Guildmaster replied.

"Then I will provide for that in the blessing. Are you sure there's enough water?" Luciana asked.

"One and a half kegs are spare, *Araunya-Daiya.* There's enough for each of the trees to receive the blessed waters and then some."

Luciana nodded again. "Then we will begin." She took a bit of chalk from the bag at the door and drew a large circle in the center of the room, around the barrels.

As the circle was completed, Geralamo moved the kegs to the four points of the compass star Luciana drew. Within the star, she drew the figures of the three Sisters *Fata,* scraping her knuckles on the wooden floor as the last of the chalk disintegrated in her hand. She dusted her hands across her knees and dug out the kerchief she had tucked into her sleeve flounces. Within the kerchief awaited two spiced plums. She carefully split the plums, placing a half beside each of the kegs.

"For the *lasa,*" she murmured, hoping that the fairies had not deserted the Rom because of the circumstances of Alessa's death and burial. They could be easily offended, and winning them back would be difficult.

Answer to her worry came quickly. She heard their silent song rise up and felt the glimmer of the fairy folk's presence in her palms as she whispered her prayers. It seemed, then, all was not lost.

She knelt in the center of the starred-circle and bent forward, pressing her face to the floor and the northern-most point of the star. She positioned herself so that her arms and legs took the places of the four-pointed star. The drawing of the *Fata* lay beneath her belly. Luciana called upon the Sisters, invoking the Fates from the very center of her being.

Geralamo placed a wand of mulberry at each point of the star, whispering his own words of prayer. Luciana sat up, cross-legged, and accepted the brazier Geralamo presented her. In years past, she would have continued drawing the magic into the circle while Alessandra played the next part. She placed the brazier in front of her and broke mulberry bark into it before setting the contents ablaze.

Into the brazier, Luciana poured oils of cinnamon, vanilla, rosemary, and carnation. Vapors of scented smoke filled the room. The magic sang through her, conforming to her own internal rhythms.

With a small ladle, Geralamo placed a bit of water from each of the kegs into the brazier, dousing the fire and sending up showers of multicolored sparks. The sparks danced upon the wind, toys of the *lasa* as her prayers went heavenward.

Luciana reached in, mindless of the hot contents, and dropped equal portions into the four barrels as she hummed words of prayer. Geralamo followed her on the outside of the circle, sealing each keg after she placed the contents of the brazier inside. Luciana stepped outside the circle. Moving with the magic song, she touched each of the lids, whispering a sealing prayer. She felt the energy siphon through her fingertips with each utterance.

By the time she was done, she was spent and all but collapsed into Geralamo's arms.

Luciana sipped her tea, conscious of everyone watching her and how little time she had left before Baldo and Lieutenant de Mari returned. After she fainted, Geralamo had carried her back to the Guildhouse and the Guildmistress' office. While the Romani had little time for hartshorn or burning feathers, they believed a good pinch would revive all but the dead. Luciana would have some pretty bruises to show for this afternoon's escapade.

"I didn't realize you were ill, *Araunya*," Geralamo said apologetically.

"I am not ill, Master Geralamo. I've been using much of my magic of late, and this leaves me vulnerable. In either case, we could not have put off the blessing until another time, so it would not—could not have changed matters any," Luciana retorted, setting her cup of tea aside. She swung her legs to the ground despite the protests of everyone else in the room. With her feet firmly planted beneath her, Luciana leaned forward. "There is another matter we must discuss and this is the death of my sister, the *Araunya de Cayesmengro*."

"Perhaps, *Araunya,* now is not the best time? You are stressed and—" Mistress Eleni began.

"There is no better time than now," Luciana replied. "You have all, no doubt, heard the various rumors surrounding her death—that she murdered her lover, that she killed herself out of sorrow. I want you all to know that none of this is true. If you could have any doubts, know then that she was found in her bed!"

The Romani looked at each other meaningfully. They understood the crime in this, greater even than suicide. They understood *marimé* in a way that the *gadjé* never could, and so this was proof to them. Satisfied that she had their attention, she continued, "There is a *chovahano* at work in the palazzo."

"*Chovahano?*" Mistress Eleni said with a squeak. "But they are so rare! Is he of the blood or *gadjé?*"

"*Gadjé,* I'm sure," Luciana said. "I cannot be everywhere and know everyone. I must find where he has taken my sister's body. I must free her from the enslavement of the damned. To do this, I must take steps to learn who the *chovahano* is. I must learn where he went for his supplies to cast his vile spells, but I do not know Citteauroea. Can you help me?"

All eyes turned to Mistress Eleni who looked very pale. "I will help you as best I can. I'll ask among the other tailors to see if anyone has had robes made, or anything else this man would have used."

"What about his source of supplies?" Kisaiya asked.

Mistress Eleni nodded. "There would be only one shop that I know of in all the city which could supply everything a black wizard could need." She picked up a scrap of paper and jotted down a name and address, which she handed to Luciana. "I know these shops well and only this one would sell what a *chovahano* would need for such black work."

XIV

"The long habit of living indisposeth us for dying."
— Sir Thomas Browne

BALDO and de Mari waited at the foot of the stairs to the Guildhouse as Luciana and Kisaiya bid their farewells.

"Where would Your Grace like to be taken now?" de Mari asked with a flourish of his cape.

Luciana handed the lieutenant the paper Mistress Eleni had given her and waited. The young lieutenant's eyebrows rose, but he nodded and motioned down the street without further comment.

Baldo caught his mistress' sleeve as they turned to follow the lieutenant. "Are you well, Your Grace?"

"I am merely tired, Baldo," Luciana said softly and continued on her way.

"Your Grace, if you wish it, you could return with the lieutenant—or both of us. We can come again another day . . . or I could come for what you lack," Baldo suggested.

"No, no, all will be well enough in time," Luciana said reassuringly, but in her mind she could only imagine Prunella's reaction to being taken to a shop of this nature on the next, promised visit to the city.

Luciana sighted the store to which de Mari was leading them. She gathered her skirts and thrust herself into the midst of the crowd, leaving Kisaiya and Baldo to make their own way.

A shingle above the door proclaimed the store to be "The Dragon's Hearth." The shop was a tiny one, set so far back from the other, grander establishments on

either side that it almost disappeared from view. While
the store's neighbors displayed products prettily arranged along the walk—under the watchful eye of a
clerk—there were none here. The door was one of those
split affairs, and only the upper portion was open. The
windows in the front were comprised of small, heavily
paned glass and afforded little to draw the eye of a potential patron. Only the curious or the purposeful would
venture inside.

Luciana gave the bell pull a tug before reaching inside
and fumbling for the latch. The door swung wide with a
slight push, its hinges well oiled. She stood a moment,
surveying the inventory and could not help but be impressed.

Shelves lined the back walls, from floor to ceiling, behind the long counter that occupied the better portion
of the store. Upon all these shelves was every nature of
vessel in a range of sizes. As Luciana approached the
counter, she saw that some of the containers were so
large they sat on the floor at the end of the shelves. The
shop was poorly lit, but clean, as far as one could see.
There was a musty odor about the place, though not an
unpleasant one.

Luciana glanced back to see if Kisaiya, Baldo, and de
Mari had joined her. Kisaiya stood well within the shop
and seemed equally curious, but the lieutenant positioned himself in the doorway. His right hand crossed to
his sword and the other to the scorpinini in his belt.
Judging from his expression, he did not find the smell
of the shop as charming as she or Kisaiya did. Baldo
stood beside him, looking just as displeased.

"I appear to be in error, for surely this isn't the right
location," de Mari said. He pushed the door wide behind
him and stepped back, silently inviting Luciana to leave
the store.

"The name is the same," Luciana said with confidence. She wandered closer to the counter, peering this
way and that. Neatly tucked in what she had taken for
an alcove was a door which led undoubtedly to the back
of the shop, further wares, and, if she were particularly
lucky, the proprietor.

"But this place hardly seems—"

"Watch your tongue, there," a voice said.

Luciana turned about, looking for the source of the voice, but the half dark of the store revealed nothing.

A gnomelike crone doddered out from the back of the store, her hand resting on the crook of an equally gnarled cane. Luciana could not help but wonder if she were part fairy. As she came into the improved light cast through her windows, the old woman appeared quite different from the image Luciana had begun to form. She was bent, surely, and her eyes were keen and sharp, as expected, but where Luciana had supposed a perhaps less than attentive eye toward the mirror, she found that the old shopkeeper was quite well turned out. Her white hair was neatly combed and arranged, her dress elegant and clean though perhaps not so fashionable as it might have been a dozen years before. The dress, while perfectly practical, was not the sort usually assumed by merchants, nor by the Romani, for that matter.

The crone crossed, with a painfully awkward gait, to a stool in the corner behind the counter. She plumped a worn red-and-gold velvet cushion and squirmed into a comfortable position, then beckoned Luciana to her with one of her crooked little fingers. "Not you," she said when Baldo moved to Luciana's side. "Just you, My Lady."

Luciana sidled closer. She glanced back and saw Kisaiya catch de Mari's sleeve to draw him aside. Baldo had gained some sense in her employ and waited watchfully by the door. Luciana looked expectantly at the shopkeeper.

"You take no offense at my manner?" the old woman asked. She inspected Luciana with a careful eye, missing nothing.

"I take no offense," Luciana replied. "Nor do I question my elder's practices."

The old woman gave a soft grunt. "What pretty manners, my dear. They shall take you far—if you let them." After a moment, she scratched her chin and motioned for Luciana to sit opposite her on a small, dusty, lopsided chair on the customers' side of the counter. Without hesitation, Luciana sat.

The old woman smiled slyly. "You will, of course, pardon my humble accommodations."

Luciana glanced around the store with its overly full shelves and odd containers, then looked pointedly back at the shopkeeper. "There is nothing so humbling as to be in the presence of a woman who knows her business and is surrounded by her wealth."

"It's the Romani in you, then," the shopkeeper retorted, "for no lady of consequence I've ever met would say such a thing. Who are you, child? Which of the clans do you hail from?"

"I am Lendaro-born and now the Duchessa di Drago."

A spark of recognition lit the crone's eyes. "There was talk of a Roma at court who died . . . one of the *Araunyas?*" Thoughtfully, she laid her finger along the edge of her nose.

Luciana met her steady gaze, schooling her own features into the expressionless mask of a fortune-teller. "Have you also heard that her body was stolen from its grave?"

The old woman frowned, nodding. "But I didn't believe it. The Rom burn their dead to ease the spirit's passing into the next world. Isn't this true?"

"It is the way of my people," Luciana agreed. "But the Rom . . . the girl was my sister and she was away from her people. The Royal House did what they thought best."

The old woman grimaced. "And before you could reclaim the body, it was stolen?" She paused, looking thoughtful. "So you believe someone ill-uses her body? Is that what you fear?"

Luciana could only manage to hide her distress with a noncommittal shrug. "I am not sure what their purpose in taking her was."

"Whatever their intent, they would need to preserve the body. Yes?"

Again, Luciana nodded.

The old woman slid down off her stool and limped in her ungainly way to the far side of her counter, disappearing for a long moment behind it. When she reappeared, she bore a large dusty book, which seemed nearly as big as she was. She hefted the book onto the uneven surface of the countertop. A faint cloud of dust erupted from the book. With her gnarled fingers rubbing the worn binding, she looked up at de Mari, Baldo, and Kisaiya still hovering at the front of her store.

"Lieutenant?" Luciana called as she, too, stood.

De Mari was at her side with surprising speed. With a wary eye still on the proprietor, the lieutenant bowed before Luciana. "May I be of service, Your Grace?"

"I have been quite absentminded, Lieutenant. I brought nothing to carry my parcels in. Would you be so kind?"

"I will be most happy to carry any purchases you make," de Mari said.

Luciana smiled and looked pointedly at the shopkeeper. "But some of my purchases will be small, and it will be too easy to lose track of them, especially once we are on the way back."

"I am sure that the Duty Officers from the station would be glad to—" de Mari began. He swallowed the rest of what he had meant to say as her meaning finally dawned upon him.

"I saw a lovely stand not far from here with all manner of baskets. Perhaps *Daiya* would not mind if I were to take the lieutenant with me?" Kisaiya said. She caught the lieutenant's sleeve. Baldo followed willingly enough, though he remained outside, leaning absently against the building, as the others went on their errand.

The old woman gave a snort as the three left, banging the half door closed behind them. She crooked a finger at Luciana. "Your lieutenant is very . . . protective," she observed. "Or perhaps he was asked to spy upon you." She shrugged.

Luciana chuckled, glancing toward the door. "No, My Lady, I believe him to be very much the queen's man, and the queen, I doubt, would have him spy upon me when I already give her my confidence."

The crone humphed, then waved her hands over the

book. There seemed to be a momentary gleam, as though jewels flashed on unseen rings. Faintly, Luciana heard magic-song.

The storekeeper opened the cover of the book to reveal surprisingly crisp, clean white pages. She looked up at Luciana then. "What am I looking for, Your Grace?" She spoke casually, but this was clearly a test.

"There are few variations of the spell for such dark magic."

"And?" the old woman prompted.

Luciana concentrated, racking her mind for all the *Beluni* had ever taught her of such things. There had been little of this in her education on magic, just enough so that she would recognize the evil if she encountered it. "The components are mostly the same, but the rituals vary."

"What determines which of the rituals the conjurer chooses?"

Luciana shook her head.

The old woman nodded. "Who taught you?"

"The *Beluni* . . . the Queen of the Romani," Luciana replied.

"She has given you an almost adequate education of foul magicks," the crone said. "But when you meddle in the affairs of a dark conjurer . . ." The old woman patted the book in front of her with an open palm. "You will need to learn more."

"I haven't the time."

"Then you will have to prepare yourself, and the price could be high. You will not be able to delay the inevitable." The shopkeeper gave a matter-of-fact nod and turned back to her book. "First, the spell."

The old woman leaned down over her grimoire and spoke to it in a soft voice, using a language Luciana had never heard. Done, the crone blew on the pages as if she breathed life into smoldering embers, then stepped back. Pages rifled, blown by an invisible breeze, and suddenly fell still.

With a grin of pure pleasure, the old woman smoothed the pages flat. She licked her index finger and ran it down the right-hand page. She paid no attention to Luciana craning her neck across the countertop, trying to see what she read.

Despite having acquired the skill of reading upside down, the print seemed to Luciana to ripple across the pages. She rubbed her eyes and adjusted the lamp on the old woman's table so that the flame burned steadily upon the pages. Even so, the words in the book would not hold still. Or, at least, they did not for her. The proprietress did not appear to have any problems with the text. The book was protected, Luciana concluded, just as the *Beluni*'s had been, as was her own.

"Such a spell as we have discussed would call for a considerable amount of wine and equal portions of vinegar and salt water." She looked up at Luciana, frowning. "These ingredients are all too easy to come by in Tyrrhia."

"Of course."

The crone looked at her. "Large shipments of wine and vinegar to Palazzo Auroea would go unnoticed."

Feeling somewhat defeated, Luciana nodded. The amount of wine needed would not even serve the staff at a meager meal. Then it occurred to her that not everyone could gain access to the cellars where such supplies were stored. This also meant—for the conjurer to have access to all he wanted or needed—that Alessa's body was probably not so far away as she originally feared.

Turning back to her book, the shopkeeper sighed over further ingredients of sea salt, dirt of the grave, and the miscellany of basic tools such as candles, an appropriate receptacle, and thus and such ordinary tools. She smiled suddenly. "Here we are." She stabbed the page with a twisted finger and waved at a stack of worn books piled at the other end of the counter against the wall. "Get me the ledger." She paused. "The green one."

Luciana considered the stack dubiously. There seemed no way to tell the books' colors. She approached the stack and peered close. The second book was almost imperceptibly a faded green. When the shopkeeper snapped her fingers impatiently, Luciana grabbed the book and handed it to her.

The old woman paused, frowning at the book and Luciana. With a shrug, she folded the ledger open, flipped several pages, then let out a satisfied sigh. "Here we are!"

"What have you found?"

The crone smiled sadly. "Devil's Fugue, Devil's String, Dittany of Crete, aniseed, cankerwort, Lady's Thistle—all the items I expected."

Luciana released her breath, barely aware she had been holding it. She sank onto the stool. Now, there was no denying her fears. Somewhere her sister's body was being preserved, and her soul pressed into some form of vile service. There could be no other interpretation of Alessa's words now.

"It's what you expected," the old woman said matter-of-factly.

Unable to speak, Luciana could only nod. After a moment, she choked out, "Who made these purchases?"

The shopkeeper dragged the green ledger closer. "My clients expect a certain privacy, Your Grace. You'd not be wantin' everyone to know your business, now would you?"

Luciana sighed. "If it's a matter of money—"

The crone laughed harshly. "If 'twere a matter of money, I know more'n a handful of prosperity charms. Don't insult me."

"Then what do you want?"

The old woman leaned back and looked at her with an assessing eye. " 'Twould be easy to ask for a bolt of silk, or some finery."

"I'd gladly give you ten bolts or a dozen dresses," Luciana said.

The crone grinned, sucking on her teeth. "That is too easy and, thus, the price too cheap, *Araunya*. You must pay dearly for this information, or the confidence I give you will mean nothing."

"Then what do you want?" Luciana asked.

"A lock of your hair and a clipping of your nails," she said.

Luciana stared at the old woman appraisingly. Such personal items could eventually give this crone almost as much power over her as the *chovahano* held over

Alessandra. But here, she was alive and this choice was freely made; Alessandra had no choice, and there might be no end to her torment. "So be it," Luciana said.

The ancient crone cackled with glee and produced shears from her apron pocket. She handed them to Luciana and watched as she pulled one of the tiny braids from behind her ear out of the arrangement. Luciana snipped the hair and placed it on the counter, then carefully and precisely trimmed each of her fingernails.

The crone produced a small bag and scraped her new treasures into them. She pocketed bag and shears, then drew the ledger back in front of her. She flipped open the book and peered at the entry. "The sale was made in two parts on the same day. One part was made to a Signor Rufio Lando and the other to one Signor Nofri."

A flicker of hope sprang up in Luciana's breast. "There was more than one sale?"

"Do not allow yourself to be misled here," the old woman said. "These sales were made on the same afternoon." She grinned. "He tried to disguise himself—twice—which gave me all the more to study. Had he not bothered, I might not have taken such notice of him."

"Do you know who he was?"

The old woman shook her head. "He did not quibble over the cost, so money was no object. He had the money to have two sets of clothes and to hire a place where he might change. There was some business he did with his face—one was mustachioed and the other was not, but instead he had a warty face. Nonetheless, I know they were the same man."

"How can you be sure?"

The shopkeeper laughed again. "For all his fancy clothes and business with the troubadours' makeup, both men were remarkably the same in one very particular way—besides, I know my business, Your Grace. I sell little enough of Dittany of Crete in a year and less of Devil's String. Then, to sell such a quantity of both so close? In one day?"

"I see," Luciana murmured. The secret bud of hope died. There was no room for false hopes anymore. Alessandra was being ill-used. She glanced at the ledger.

"And you place no confidence in the record of these names either?"

"None."

"But you mentioned there was one thing remarkably the same. What was that?" Luciana asked.

"The lips," the crone said with another cackle.

Luciana was puzzled. What could be so distinctive about a man's lips? But even as her mind latched upon the answer, the crone continued. "His lips were black-stained, as though from ink."

Luciana closed her eyes. Conte Urbano again. He was well and truly mixed up with this *chovahano,* then. "What must I do to break the spell?"

"This is no slight task, Your Grace, and not generally something I would advise a lady to take on. What about your man or the other?" The shopkeeper waved vaguely in the direction of the door where Baldo remained.

"Baldo is not family and the other is the queen's man. The *Araunya-minore* was *my* sister. There is the matter of vendetta for my people, for the sake of an *Araunya's* honor. For the Wandering Folk's honor."

"But vendettas are not normally considered a woman's affair," the crone observed to no one in particular as she closed the ledger and replaced it. "They can be a bloody business at the best of times, and they're rarely that."

Luciana stood. "This vendetta is *mine* to fulfill. No one else will do it."

"Your sister had no husband? No lover? What of *your* husband. What of your father?"

"No. They cannot help me," Luciana said fiercely

The crone nodded. "Then you must be prepared."

"I intend to be."

"Do you have everything you will need?" the shopkeeper asked. She looked up at Luciana. Her expression seemed almost sympathetic, yet there remained a certain hardness of intent.

"I'm not sure," Luciana admitted. "Tell me what I must do to break this spell."

The proprietress shook her head and turned back to her book. "You're a brave one, I'll give you that. As

Araunya, you must have some sense, but I see none of
it here. If you insist, then let us make sure you do it
right." After a moment's reading, she said, "You must
not only find and reclaim the body, but there is a vessel
as well wherein her living spirit is held. Her body will
be bound hand and foot with the Devil's String. You
must break these bindings with a knife made of Obeah
and Elderwood. The body must be cleansed in a bath of
seawater to purify and wash away the vestiges of this
conjurer's magic."

Luciana listened intently. "Wouldn't fire cleanse her?"

"Yes, but not enough, and you cannot burn the body
until you find the vessel. If you burn the body before
you have found the vessel and broken all of its ties to
your sister, then you have doomed her soul to a ghostly
existence for the rest of eternity. If you free the vessel,
but not the body, then her spirit can be compelled into
another vessel."

"So, if I do not free my sister—body and spirit—this
conjurer still has command of her?"

"Yes, but without either component, he must use
greater magic to exercise his influence. He cannot control her manifestations as reliably, so he will seek to
undo any advantage you have."

They worked over the spell book for nearly an hour
more before de Mari and Kisaiya returned. In addition
to the large beribboned basket, Kisaiya had purchased
a length of sheer silk lace for Prunella. De Mari and
Baldo fetched the horses while Kisaiya helped pack the
basket until it was overflowing. Luciana carefully reviewed each parcel loaded into the basket to be sure she
had forgotten nothing.

The road to the palazzo seemed even dustier than in
the morning. Orchards of orange and lemon bordered
the right side of the road between the city and the palazzo walls, to the left, the copse of trees at the edge of
the wildwood. After the crowded marketplace, the scent
of the orchards and open air—even mingled with dust—
was cleansing.

Preoccupied with her thoughts, Luciana was caught
unawares when a fox scurried across the road, causing

her horse to shy. She barely managed to keep her seat
as she reined in the mare and tried to soothe it. The
dapple danced about and pulled at the bit, seeming to
confuse whatever direction Luciana gave it.

"Would you rather my horse, Your Grace?" the lieutenant asked as he pulled his own mild-mannered gelding alongside.

Baldo was already reaching for the reins, talking
soothingly to the mare. Luciana merely shook her head
but when the horse would not stop its nervous starts,
she dismounted and came around to its head. The mare
fidgeted, wild-eyed and trembling. Using the bridle strap
to pull her head down, Luciana stroked the horse's fore-
head, whispering to the beast in the way Romani
horsemen had for centuries. Baldo watched and seemed
to be having a difficult time resisting the urge to take
his charge in hand.

Nickering, the mare dropped her head and swiveled
her ears toward her mistress. Luciana continued to
soothe her as she gathered up the reins and prepared to
remount, but just as her foot reached the stirrup, the
lieutenant let out a shout and leaped from his own
saddle.

Luciana's mare reared and jerked away, knocking her
to the ground in the process. She grabbed at the trailing
reins but lost sight of them in the cloud of dust kicked
up. She coughed and gasped her way out of the haze.
She ached from the tumble and felt cross for having her
efforts disrupted, never mind that the prize mare had
escaped and would probably be a devil to catch. As she
left the envelopment of the dusty road, Luciana saw a
half dozen ruffians facing off with the lieutenant.

Kisaiya jumped from her saddle and tossed Luciana
the reins of her mount. "Ride, *Daiya,* I'll return with
Lieutenant de Mari and Baldo." She ran to place herself
between Luciana and the intruders.

Baldo had dismounted as well and pulled a pistola
from inside his vest. The pistola went off with a crack
and one of the men fell as Baldo pulled a second pistola
from his vest.

Luciana could not leave her maid, her coachman, or the lieutenant in such a predicament.

Kisaiya tugged a pistol-sized scorpinini from the pouch she wore at her waist. She loaded and cocked a bolt with one quick, firm movement.

A competence with weapons was not one of the skills Luciana expected from either servant, but her maid's easy familiarity with a weapon was the more surprising. Women knowledgeable about weapons usually ranked among the nobility who took them up as sport—or the family members of highwaymen. Kisaiya was neither. Even as she thought that, Luciana realized she possessed only a small dagger tucked into the cuff of her dress. She turned toward the battle.

De Mari lunged, knocking aside two of the ruffians' rapiers and, with a quick riposte thrust, dispatched one of them. The fellow howled, flinging his arms wide as he fell. His rapier landed a dozen feet from Luciana.

Acting on the thrill of fear, she ran forward and seized the rapier's hilt. Behind her, Kisaiya shouted for her to stay back. Something whizzed by Luciana's ear even as she turned toward the younger woman. Kisaiya had shot her scorpinini!

Excitement blazed through Luciana as, turning back to the battle, she saw one of the men clutch at his throat and fall. Kisaiya closed in and dispatched the man with a quick thrust of a dagger between his ribs.

The lieutenant waved for Luciana to stay away. Not wanting to get in his way, she backed up but kept the rapier at the ready.

One of the seedy men turned toward Luciana with a grin. He sidestepped de Mari and closed with her. Baldo struggled to draw his sword, leaving her to meet this man in battle.

Luciana deflected the man's first tentative thrust. This was no classroom—and years since she had been in one. She also did not have the advantage of having chosen her dress to suit the activity. The lengths of fabric that made the petticoats so pretty now hampered her movements as she tried to take a firm stance. She kept her eyes on the man, from his smudged face to his shifting position and the way he held his blade.

With quicksilver excitement running through her veins, everything moved slowly. The man feinted toward her low line and thrust up. Luciana stepped back and warded off another blow. She lunged, driving toward the *spadaccino* and his open high line.

Kisaiya cursed from close behind. "*Daiya*, this is no sport! Move away so I can shoot him!"

Luciana's focus did not waver from her opponent's eyes. She watched him, ready and waiting for his next move.

A call sounded from the copse. The lookout, apparently. Her opponent glanced toward the road and yelled to his surviving companion, "The Escalade! Run for it!"

Both men turned on their heels and ran for the trees with the lieutenant just behind them. Seemingly out of nowhere, a flurry of Escalade officers on horseback joined the pursuit. Luciana watched the chase with a mixture of breathless excitement and frustration.

"Luciana! *Dios!*"

Luciana looked up and, to her surprise, saw Idala reining a big white gelding closer. What a relief to see a friendly face! Just beyond her, however, was Stefano. He jumped down from his blood-bay mount's back. He did not look nearly so friendly as his sister.

"Have you been hurt?" Stefano demanded as he reached her side. He took her arm roughly and spun her around, examining her from head to dusty toe.

"Are you well?" Idala asked.

Only now, with a friend and Stefano at her side, did Luciana realize the full danger she had been in. She cast aside the rapier and pulled back from Stefano. He did not immediately release her arm and when he did, he scooped her into his arms and practically threw her onto the saddle of his horse.

Not quite sure how she managed it, Luciana caught her balance and grabbed a handful of black mane.

"What in the devil were you thinking?" Stefano asked her sharply. He accepted a flask from the queen and thrust it into her hands.

"I didn't think," Luciana replied quietly. Hysteria threatened to bubble up. A reaction to battle, she told herself and concentrated on regaining her equilibrium, which only faltered again when Stefano mounted the horse and adjusted her weight so that she sat on his lap. "I–I had to do something."

"Why couldn't you have waited for me?" Stefano asked in her ear.

"I had business in the city. I did not plan to be accosted," Luciana said.

"Someone get this young woman onto her horse," the queen commanded, waving at Kisaiya who now stood at the roadside staring at the carnage left by the battle.

Baldo hastily left the field of battle and helped Kisaiya onto the only remaining gray horse.

"You did well, Kisaiya, thank you," Luciana said.

"Yes, you served your mistress well today," Stefano said. "I would never have suspected that my wife needed a maid so conversant with weaponry."

"I am as surprised as you," Luciana said. She wriggled to look up at Stefano angrily.

The Romani girl managed a dazed smile. "Blame Nicobar. He wanted me to be prepared and to know how to use the scorpinini."

"Nicobar?" the queen asked, reminding all of her presence.

"My assistant," Luciana said.

"He apparently knows you well enough to provide for incidents like this," Stefano whispered. Louder, he said, "Then I will have to thank him myself when we return to the palazzo."

"I have sent him away—to the *Beluni*—on an errand," Luciana replied loud enough for all to hear her. Irritated as she was with her husband, she did not want to think what it might have cost her if Kisaiya and Baldo had not been armed.

"I am only thankful you're safe," Idala said.

A dozen officers rode out of the copse just then. One horse bore a second rider. Luciana breathed a sigh of relief when she saw the second rider was de Mari. One of the men broke from the cluster of horses and approached the queen. He dismounted as he reached them, bowing in turn to Idala, Stefano, and Luciana.

"The bandits have escaped, Your Majesty. They had horses waiting for them," he said. "If Your Majesty gives me leave, I and some of my men will follow, but we must first be sure of your safety."

Idala nodded.

Stefano turned his horse in a tight circle so that he could more easily face the vigilare. "We will return directly to the palazzo. Leave me three men, the gates are less than a mile away."

The officer glanced briefly at the queen to see if she would countermand the duca. When she did not, he saluted. "As you say, Your Grace." The officer doffed his plumed blue hat as he bowed once more.

The last leg of their excursion was, thankfully, spent in silence. Luciana waited for Stefano to say something more, to criticize her for leaving the palazzo grounds. She had a number of ready answers for him, but he gave her no opportunity. The sun was hot overhead and, now that the excitement was over, Luciana began to feel decidedly tired. With the rhythm of the horse beneath them, it was difficult not to lean back into Stefano's arms. She fought the languor, the urge to take comfort, but, finally, she gave in and slowly relaxed. By the *Fata,* she had forgotten his smell, how reassuring it was to leave the world and its frustrations to someone else . . . even if only for the brevity of a ride.

The vigilare on duty greeted them with shouts. By the time they reached the stables, grooms were on hand to take the horses.

Stefano dismounted, ignoring the stable boy who had reached up to take Luciana from him. Once on the ground, he held out his hands to assist her himself. He was very quiet, which never boded well.

"Stefano," Idala said, catching his sleeve. "Do not be angry—it could just as easily have happened to me."

"Except that you had a proper escort with you," he replied.

"Only because I have no choice."

Luciana remained quiet, too bone-weary to protest.

Idala frowned at her brother and took Luciana's arm, guiding her toward the palazzo with Stefano trailing behind them. "So, Luciana. What happened? Who were those men?" the queen asked.

"I don't know who they were, thieves probably," Luciana said.

"But that is so odd. We haven't had highwaymen on the Palazzo Road since . . . well, it's been years and years."

"Then I am as confused as you, Majesty," Luciana said. She looked back at her husband, still close behind them.

"Perhaps you were followed from the city," Stefano suggested.

Luciana shook her head. "The lieutenant seemed quite capable. I doubt anyone could have followed us that he did not see."

"Well, never mind, then. Let us think of other things," Idala said with a shrug. "What do you plan to wear tomorrow night?"

Luciana blinked, surprised. "Tomorrow night?"

Idala considered her with a mock-scandalized look. "Yes! How could you forget the event in honor of Bianca's fiancé? He arrives tomorrow."

Luciana stopped so suddenly that Stefano bumped into her. "I didn't realize it would be so soon . . . *could* be so soon," she said.

"Yes," Idala said. "Apparently, the cardinal, during his earlier interview, forgot to mention their impending arrival. He came back with the news this morning. A messenger came ahead to announce the Duca deMedici and his son."

"The Duca deMedici?" Luciana gasped.

Idala turned a stern gaze on Stefano. "Haven't you told her?"

"I counsel the king. It isn't my place to make announcements for Her Highness," Stefano retorted darkly.

The queen shook her head and turned back to Luciana, "Yes. The cardinal has arranged for the princess to marry deMedici's son." She pulled Luciana's arm and continued walking. She lowered her voice as they entered the palazzo and its long, echoing halls so that their words could not be heard over their footsteps. "His name is Pierro and he holds a court title of something silly—what was it, Stefano?"

"Conte de Solario," he said with a sigh. He watched the corridors. "He's a *bastarde*."

"Stefano!"

"Oh, he means *really*," Idala laughed. "The duca's child from an illicit *affair d'amore*."

"Perhaps we should not discuss this here in the halls," Luciana murmured anxiously. She scanned the passage before her and turned around, trying to get her bearings.

"But, of course, you are quite correct," Idala said, "though you seem to be the last to know." She paused to frown pointedly at her brother again, then turned back to Luciana. "You now look most decidedly the worse for your experience. Do you feel unwell?"

"No," Luciana said. Though she did feel decidedly light-headed, she was not about to admit to any such thing with Stefano hovering over her, looking for any excuse to send her back to the estates.

"You should get some rest, my dear, and then plan what you will wear to the wedding. I anticipate this will be a short courtship," Idala said.

XV

"It is certain that to most men the preparation for death has been a greater torment than the suffering of it."

—Michel de Montaigne

"I WANT you safely home at Dragorione. Your obligations to your people are done here, or so you said," Stefano declared, opening the door to their suite and ushering her in.

Luciana swept past him and sank gratefully onto the dainty gateleg couch. She was not about to let him have his own way. He knew it, too, which was why he spoke with so much determination now, hoping to sweep aside any arguments that she might begin to form before she could utter them.

"Stefano, don't be ridiculous. It is simply impossible for me to return to Dragorione, as well you know. It would be ungracious to refuse Bianca's invitation to her Betrothal Ball, which, apparently, you had not yet told me about. A temporary lapse, I'm sure."

"I am capable of making excuses," Stefano said. He leaned against the marble mantle opposite her and stripped off his riding gloves.

"Yes, but it would be seen as a ruse. You are, after all, a member of the Palantini and it is my duty, as your wife, to attend. I have no reason to leave just before the ball, not when I am already here, not when I have already received an invitation, not when I have nothing that demands my immediate attention elsewhere," Luciana replied. She worked hard at sounding quiet and reasonable. He would not know how to respond to that, she thought, but then, perhaps, that was because she was so rarely quiet or reasonable.

Stefano shook his head. "Luciana . . ." He stared up at the ceiling. His jaw hardened. She could see the muscle twitch along his jawline.

She sat forward, primly attentive. He could not refuse her now. She looked up at him, waiting.

He shook his head again. "You'll be the damnation of us both yet, Lucia." He dropped his gloves onto a nearby table, removed a crisp bit of folded vellum from his inside coat pocket, and handed it to her.

Luciana barely glanced at it, recognizing the purple waxen seal of Her Highness. The invitation. She rose. "No matter what my feelings or ambitions, Stefano, I would never see you damned. It is trial enough that my sister is in a veritable hell of magical damnation, I'd not have you there as well."

"For Al—for her sake," Stefano said.

He would have turned away, but Luciana caught his arm. "For your own sake, Stefano."

"For times past?"

Luciana felt struck. She swallowed her pride and met his eyes. "The future is yet unmade."

Stefano stared at her, as though her steady gaze had somehow captured him. He reached out, his hands cupping her face, his thumbs caressing the curves of her face.

Their kiss was sweet, and as timid as a first kiss. He seemed as unsure as she. Luciana leaned closer, sighing against his lips as his hands fell to her waist.

They broke apart like guilty lovers at the sound of hard pounding on the suite door. Stefano cleared his throat and excused himself, setting her back more steadily on her own feet as he moved away to answer the door.

Luciana dabbed at her lips and watched Stefano at the door with the courier. At last, he nodded and sent the liveried servant away. He stared after the lad a moment or two more before actually closing the door and turning to face her.

"I am summoned by His Majesty," he said. Stefano looked confused, frowning. "I am to come immediately."

"Of course," Luciana said. She worked hard to keep her voice steady, but failed.

Stefano came to her side, the movement of his lithe body quick and sure. He took her once more into his arms with a possessiveness that made her ache. "If you think I am happy about this, you're wrong." He kissed her, pulling her against him. "The full court is to gather on the hour."

"I am to come as well?" Luciana's voice came out as a breathy squeak.

"Especially you, I am told," Stefano said. He kissed her again. "I do not know what this is about, but . . ." He pushed her gently back, away from him again. "I do not know what this is about, Luciana, but the king specifically wants you present." He smiled and touched her cheek, slowly turning her to face the mirror above the mantel.

Her cheeks were rosy bright even on her dusky skin. Her hair had come unbound and a thick layer of dust covered every inch of her. She looked to the clock. She had barely enough time. Gathering her skirts, she hurried up to her room, calling to Kisaiya.

Prunella appeared, shutting the door behind her. "Your Grace, I took the liberty of giving Kisaiya a brandy and having her lie down," she explained, watching in dismay as Luciana unpinned her hair. She did not sound happy as she asked, "How can I assist you?"

"I've an appointment with the king. He has summoned the court—"

Prunella bit her knuckle. Finally, seeing a way to help, she brushed Luciana's hands aside and unbound her corset.

"I'll wear—"

"The gray," Prunella announced, pulling it from over the back of the dressing screen.

If nothing else, Kisaiya had steadier hands and was, by far, more adept in the dressing process, but Prunella could not be faulted for her determination. Luciana

turned this way and that to check Prunella's work in
the mirror. She wanted to be especially careful of her
appearance. One did not attend the king looking anything other than her best, even when summoned with
nary a moment to prepare.

With a displeased expression, Prunella tucked the last
bodice lace out of sight. "It looks better when Kisaiya
does it, Your Grace."

"You've done just fine, Prunella." Luciana looked
from her own reflection to the younger woman. "What
is it?"

"Kisaiya said that you were accosted on the road. I
cannot help but think that, perhaps if I had—"

Luciana sighed. No matter how carefully she spoke,
Prunella invariably misunderstood. With her nerves all
on edge, it would be far too easy to insult the girl. She
caught Prunella's hand and drew her around. "There is
nothing you could have said or done to change what
happened today. I had an appointment with my people
and, therefore, could not have been dissuaded. If you
had been with us, Prunella, there would have been no
better outcome. There was nothing you could do, and
don't fret so, Nicobar—even absent—has demonstrated
wonderful skills in anticipation."

Luciana inspected herself in the mirror one last time.
With all of the excitement—no doubt, as much from
Stefan's kisses as the men who accosted her—a blush
had replaced the pallor of recent weeks and her eyes
sparkled.

Prunella arranged her dark brown hair into a simple
twist with dainty curls framing her face, doing an excellent job despite the cutting of her hair and everything
that followed. She bit her lips to heighten their color
and turned away from the mirror. Nothing more could
be done but to wonder why the king called for a general
audience on such short notice.

A masculine voice called from the salon below.
"*Daiya?* Are you here?"

"Nicobar?" Luciana hurried down the stairs.

Standing in the salon, packages nearby, dusty from his
travels, stood the irrepressible Nicobar. Luciana slowed

to a more sedate pace. "Thank the *lasa,* you're safely returned!"

"But of course, Your Grace," he said with a courteous bow.

"You look exhausted."

"Not overly so. I bring you news. We must be on the road within the hour. I'm told that—" He fell silent when Prunella entered the room.

"Your timing, Nicobar, is impeccable as always," Prunella said. "You've arrived just in time to escort Her Grace to the Throne Room. She has been commanded to attend the king, and His Grace appears to have gone ahead."

Nicobar looked to Luciana, his eyes curious, but he recovered with a smile and stroked his unshaven chin. "I hope there is perhaps a moment or two for me to change from this coat into something more acceptable?"

"That will be fine. I will wait for you here," Luciana said, settling onto a divan covered in wine-colored brocade. After Nicobar departed for his room, she considered Prunella. "I would have thought you would be disappointed to miss court again."

Prunella shrugged. "There is time enough."

Such patience! Intrigued, Luciana studied her cousin more carefully. "I am still surprised. I thought you would be quite anxious to accompany me."

"I do not know your plans, Your Grace," Prunella hesitated, "but I, too, have received an invitation to the Betrothal Ball for the princess. I was hoping that you would . . . that since I *am* the queen's cousin that I . . ." Prunella faltered to a halt, looking pained.

"I see," Luciana said. She evaluated Prunella sitting anxiously at the edge of the sofa. "I'm sure your father will be pleased that you will be presented at court on such an occasion."

"Then you don't mind?"

"You must go, of course. We're supposed to be finding you a suitable match, after all."

Prunella blushed again. "Cousin . . . Your Grace . . . there is another matter that I should bring to your attention." She stopped to clear her throat, darting apprehensive glances toward Luciana as she did so.

"What is it?" Luciana asked, growing wary.

"I have not much of a dowry, and hoped that you and the duca might be persuaded to pursue a good match . . . beyond just the introductions, you see. But I have not been able to state my case to the duca. I was hoping that, perhaps, you might be willing to help me."

"Your father's hopes, as expressed to me, were not so different than your own," Luciana said. "While I have not discussed this with His Grace yet, I fully intend to see you advantageously wed."

"Thank you!" Prunella gave a relieved sigh. "I should have known you would understand. After all, you made a good marriage for yourself, and you would recognize a similar need on my part."

Luciana snapped her mouth shut and swallowed back the first and second choice of words that came to her. She took a deep, calming breath and turned to look at her husband's cousin once more. "Prunella, while I made a good match, you don't seem to appreciate my status as *Araunya*. Now that my sister is gone, I am inheritor of *all* the Gypsy Silk trade, which, as one of Tyrrhia's largest exports, is a great financial resource for the entire kingdom. My husband did not receive my gypsy properties as part of my dowry, but his wealth was greatly increased nonetheless due to the influence it gave him."

Luciana raised one hand, cupped. "I am *Araunya di Cayesmengri,* inherited from my mother who is in the line of the Queen of the Romani, and this title refers to my properties of land and mulberry trees, and of all those tools which the crafts people use to make the silk. Without *Cayesmengri,* there would be neither worm fed nor cocoon harvested nor silk woven, none would be done without the properties I own."

Luciana hesitated, looking at Prunella to make sure she understood. When the girl remained silent, Luciana cupped her other hand and placed it next to the first. "I am also *Araunya di Cayesmengro,* inherited from my sister who inherited from an aunt in the line of the queen, and this title confers to me properties of the silk-worms and the efforts of the crafts people and the magic they use to create the silk. Without *Cayesmengro,* there would be neither raw silk nor fabric made."

She closed her hands in a sealing motion. "Without *Cayesmengro* or *Cayesmengri* there would be no Gypsy Silk and Tyrrhia would lose even more of its silk trade to France. Do you understand?"

Prunella frowned. "But, you say, my cousin does not own these by right of marriage?"

Luciana shook her head. "Tyrrhian Romani inheritance is only through the women. Men share the benefit of their lady's wealth, but do not take her property when she concedes to marriage."

"A most strange affair, indeed! I do not understand how my cousin could be satisfied by such an arrangement!" Prunella said with a gasp.

Luciana bit her lip to control her response. Prunella's thoughtless remark cut deep. Stefano had also not fully realized the depths of her responsibilities to the Romani and her Gypsy Silk holdings. He had made it clear—certainly in times past—that he did not care for his wife being called away to attend the business of the silk trade. "I am trying to show you that I'm aware of your father's desires and that, perhaps, if you would speak freely with me, I might be in a better position than you thought to assist you."

"Oh! But I don't want to marry a Gypsy! I want a husband with some wealth and position of his own and if, as you say—"

"Basta!" Luciana snapped. She rose so quickly that the little divan almost tipped over. "I did not mean for you to marry a Rom."

Prunella, looking affronted by Luciana's sharpness, sighed. "Actually, Your Grace . . . Cousin, I meant to ask you if you would be willing to consult with Cardinal delle Torre to arrange a marriage for me. It's unusual, I understand, but after Her Highness, Lady Ursinia says—"

Luciana turned away from the younger woman, cutting her off, rather than speak or let her expression say what she chose not to. She had no intention—and hazarded that Stefano would feel likewise—of inviting the cardinal into their family affairs, especially after his treasonous interference with the marriage of Princess Bianca. While she had been absorbed in pursuing Alessa's murderers, she had not completely forgotten Prunella. She stole a glance in the mirror above the mantel. Prunella looked pensive, but still hopeful.

"We will not discuss this just now," Luciana said finally and very firmly. A little time and she could regain perspective. The stinging reminder of the differences she and Stefano shared would be blunted. She saw Prunella's crestfallen expression and almost changed her mind, but before she could, Nicobar returned.

He paused in the doorway, apparently sensing the tension. He gave a polite cough. "*Daiya,* didn't you have an appointment?"

"Of course," Luciana replied. "Are you ready now?"

He stepped back, straightening his brown coat with its black-and-gold trim, patting the front slightly. "Is this acceptable?"

Luciana grinned. "You are always acceptable. And I? Prunella?" She stepped back and peered, on tiptoe, at the mantel mirror.

Prunella fussed with the back hem, then sniffed her approval.

Once in the outside corridor, Nicobar slowed their pace. "Forgive me, I know you must hurry to attend the king, but you have an engagement to see the *Beluni.* We must leave tonight—sooner, if possible. She has a camp not far from Citteauroea."

Luciana silently winced. Stefano would not be happy about this. She resolved not to tell him until after, if she could get away without speaking about it. For once, she would be glad of Palantini business. "Did you find my sister's maid? Grasni?"

"I'm told that Grasni is studying the trade of wisewoman. I have asked that she find some way to see you so that you may learn what she knows. The message will be sent through her people, but I'm told she was—*is*— very frightened."

"Interesting," Luciana said. "But she is safe now?"

"Indeed, or so the *Beluni* told me. She will be reluctant to return to this place if she's frightened."

"She has cause," Luciana said. "I was attacked today. I thought nothing of it at first, merely highwaymen, but . . ."

Nicobar stopped. "You were attacked?"

Luciana waved dismissively. "You protected me quite capably without even being there. Kisaiya and Baldo are excellent shots."

"Kisaiya was with you?" Nicobar relaxed, then suddenly tensed again. "I did not see Kisaiya. Is she well?"

Luciana smiled ironically. "You think that I would fail to mention if she were hurt? She *is* precious to me. Prunella gave her brandy and sent her to bed.

"I must thank you for planning so far in advance. Baldo made sure Kisaiya had the scorpinini with her when we left, again at your direction." She squeezed his wrist where her hand lay. "I don't know what I would do without you . . . here we are!"

They turned the corner into the Clock Walk. Luciana lingered, watching the press of nobles filter into the Throne Room. The walls of the Walk were painted a golden melon with decorative white plasterwork at the floor, ceiling, and in a band along the wall, waist high. The floor was white with pink-and-green-flecked marble. Clocks of all sorts sat upon cherrywood tables. Hundreds of others hung on the walls all the way to the ceiling. Creases low in the wall indicated sections where the wall pulled away. The drawer inside contained the ladders the Clock Keeper used to climb to the highest of his charges. The ticking seemed an almost constant sound emitted from both sides of the long hall from the hundreds of clocks. If one stopped and concentrated, the ticking seemed to blend into a single sound, like a giant clock, and its sound came with the thumping of one's own heart.

Nobles of every rank and station, dressed in their daytime finery, edged their way into the Throne Room. All were, undoubtedly, as curious as Luciana regarding this call from the king.

"Your Grace! You are looking well."

Luciana turned to see the princess standing at her left.

"Thank you, Your Highness." She hoped that the princess did not notice her reserve. She had not expected to see the princess out of her rooms, but, of course, she must have been summoned as well.

"I have just heard about your . . . your misadventures. I am pleased you were unharmed."

Luciana raised a brow. "I am honored that in this time of excitement over your own betrothal you would take the time to notice."

"And there is the Betrothal Ball tomorrow night," the princess added. "You will be attending, won't you?"

"I would not dream of missing such an important occasion," Luciana said. How quickly it all moved! Was it only a day ago that the princess first mentioned this marriage? It seemed impossibly quick and now there could be no doubt that the princess, the cardinal and the deMedicis had been a long time planning this.

As they spoke, Conte Urbano rounded the corner looking quite intent. Spying them, a silky smirk touched his lips. He came forward, bowing, and kissed the princess' hands. "I wanted to wish you congratulations again, Your Highness, though my heart is aching that it is not I who has won you."

"My lord, how you flirt! And I soon shall be a married woman—like the duchessa here. It isn't suitable to accept the attentions of such admirers, is it?" the princess asked no one in particular with a laugh.

Luciana smiled thinly, uncomfortable in the insinuating presence of the conte. "It is done, Your Highness, though I prefer the attentions of my husband to any other."

"How lonely you must be then for the duca when he is away so often," the princess murmured. Her voice sounded sincere, but her eyes flashed with speculation.

Luciana smiled, unable to think of any response.

"Perhaps we should go inside?" Nicobar said in Luciana's ear, but loudly enough for the others to hear.

Grateful for the escape, Luciana made her way into the Throne Room, leaving the others behind. Luciana took her place in the front of the room, near the thrones, as was her right. Nicobar, confident that she was established, faded back.

Almost immediately, the princess and Conte Urbano arrived. As the princess passed, Luciana curtsied ever so slightly, as it was her place to do. The princess seated herself on the lowest dais beside the throne while the conte stopped farther away, among the press of lower nobility. Another conte and his lady stepped aside to make room for him.

The door behind the thrones opened, and the king and queen entered with Court Herald Estensi and the Royal Bodyguard, Lord Strozzini. Several members of the Palantini followed, Stefano included. The courtiers sank as one into a deep bow while the royal couple mounted the dais. The Palantini faded into the crowd, Stefano moving to Luciana's side. Estensi stamped his staff. The court rose.

Alban smoothed his white coat as he stood. He wore delicate shades of white in some of the finest Gypsy Silk Luciana had seen in some time. As was its magical nature, the silk gleamed and enhanced the king's regal bearing. "Today should be a most fortunate day. Our beloved cousin Princess Bianca's affianced, Conte Pierro of the esteemed deMedici family, will be arriving. Unfortunately, the evil which has haunted this court once more rears its ugly head."

The room erupted as the nobles responded. Ladies gasped. Everyone talked in excited whispers. Luciana hid her own surprise and stole a quick look at Stefano, then around the room. She saw the princess glance toward the cardinal and then to Conte Urbano, who seemed equally intent upon the reactions of the princess and the cardinal. The cardinal's attention, however, remained focused upon the king.

"It is evil brought on by refusing the word of God!" the cardinal pronounced.

The imam in his flowing robes of white and the rabbi, twisting his beard nervously, leaned forward, intent upon making timely protests should the cardinal utter something they considered blasphemous.

"This is a matter of man's evil, Cardinal. I leave their souls to you and your colleagues." Alban signaled to Strozzini, who immediately left the king's side. "Today, men attacked the Duchessa di Drago on the road. Imagine my surprise when the bodies of two of the attackers were brought before me. Strozzini!"

The king's guard returned, followed by four Escalade officers. They carried the bodies of the two fallen attackers between them.

Luciana swallowed hard and folded her hands in front of her to hide their trembling as the vigilare dumped the corpses on the floor in front of the thrones. With the rush of danger gone, she found her nerve was nothing but a memory. Her stomach twisted in knots. Stefano reached out a reassuring hand, gently taking her arm in his. The queen's fan covered the lower half of her face as she turned away. The courtiers milled forward in a crush of horrified fascination.

The dead men lay where they had been dropped. Death did nothing to help their appearance. One man's face was twisted into a gruesome mask of pain, apparently having died more slowly than his companion who seemed to be sleeping except for the unpleasant way his body had stiffened in the grip of fleeting mortality.

The king seemed disinterested. "My apologies if anyone here is offended, but I must ask you, members of my court, to look at these men and tell me if they look familiar to you."

After a moment's pause, the king motioned to a nobleman in the middle of the room. "You, Lord Obizzi, do you recognize these men? Either of them? No?" Alban turned his attention to the cardinal. "What of you, Cardinal delle Torre? You confirmed Lord Obizzi's vow for these men. Conte Urbano? Or even you, Cousin?"

Bianca's face paled. "What are you saying, Majesty?"

The king smiled tightly. "I merely asked my dear cousin if she recognized either of these men."

"Why should I? They look to be commoners . . ." Bianca's nose wrinkled. "Why would I have anything to do with cutthroats and thieves?"

"Indeed! I would not expect you to, but you took such an interest in the accusations against Lady Alessandra and, later, in her death, I thought that might make these men more familiar to you. Do you not recognize them now? No?" He turned to the court at large. "Any of you? No? Strozzini."

The king stepped back while Strozzini leaned over the bodies with a wet rag. He roughly wiped their faces, clearing some of the blood and mud, and then stood back.

"What say you now?" the king asked.

A lesser nobleman frowned and pointed to the body on the left, farthest from Luciana. "Isn't that one of the seamen who testified about the death of the Escalade officer?"

"Yes, yes, it is!" another agreed, coming to examine him.

Conte Urbano shook his head, and then paused as he looked at the body. He bent closer. "Your Majesty, your eyes are better than mine to recognize such a man through all that dirt!"

"You are most kind," the king said. "Indeed, this man is dead by the hand of an Escalade officer this afternoon. The vigilare acted to protect the Duchessa di Drago. Odd, considering barely a month ago this man testified against the duchessa's own sister. This man who, before that fateful night, had no connection to the *Araunya* or her capitano."

"Most curious indeed," the cardinal said.

"Nothing more?" the king asked.

"What do you expect, Majesty?" the princess asked, her tone unpleasant. "A confession? But what is there to confess? These men were the attackers—at least some of them—and they are dead!"

"Verita," the king said. He turned to Luciana. "Your Grace, I fear a great injustice was done to your sister. I say this, publicly, because I fear these men were involved in something greater." He turned back to the cardinal. "I am surprised, Your Eminence, that you, who supported Lord Obizzi's testimony for these men, did not recognize them. At least this one here."

"There are many people who accept the protection of Our Lord at the *cattedrale*," the cardinal said. "I do not know all of the Lord's sheep. A most unfortunate affair this."

"Indeed. Most unfortunate," the king said.

Luciana looked across the coach at Nicobar. He sat quietly, his chin resting on his chest as though asleep. She was confident, however, that he sat wide awake, aware of every creak in the coach and the snapping of every branch, as the vehicle careened down the irregular country road.

It had taken strong words, using the full weight of her position as *Araunya* and Duchessa di Drago, wife of a member of the Palantini, for them to leave the palazzo unescorted by vigilare intent on protecting her should she be attacked again. While Luciana understood Stefano's concerns and fully anticipated his outrage, she must defer to another for she answered to the black-blooded Gypsy Queen and that woman of the Romani would be most offended should Luciana arrive with an escort of *gadjé* guard. For now, all trust in Luciana's safety lay with the driver of her coach, who proved to be a remarkable shot with the pistola, and Nicobar, who never failed her—even in his absence.

Anxious to arrive, she leaned forward and pulled the leather strap of the window covering to peer into the chilly night. The moon glistened in shades of gray-green off the trees. The horses kept up a dizzying pace. The road was bare of landmarks. Luciana dropped the shade and settled back into the upholstered seat.

"We will be there soon," Nicobar said. He sat up. "Maybe you should try to rest?"

"How could anyone rest?" Luciana replied.

The coach pitched to the left suddenly, jarring them out of their seats. Luciana landed in a tangle of skirts and bruised nerves on the narrow carriage floor.

With an unsteady lurch, the coach rumbled forward

again. Nicobar muttered something impatiently and
shoved the window open to shout a warning to Baldo.

Luciana regained her seat, feeling considerably the
worse for wear. The creaks and groans of the carriage
lessened, enough so she heard the wind in the treetops
and the sounds of the surrounding forest. Finally, the
carriage rocked to a stop and Baldo called out.

Nicobar stayed his mistress' hand as she reached for
the door. "I will be back, *Daiya.*" Squeezing his lanky
frame through the door, he snapped it shut behind him.

Luciana waited, listening as the driver scrambled from
his seat. Rattling the chains on their harnesses, the
horses snorted and stamped restlessly. She resisted the
temptation to leave the coach.

After a time, the door opened and Nicobar leaned
inside. "We have found the first *patrin.* We should find
the camp soon. Until then, I will ride with Baldo."

The door snapped shut after him, and the carriage
started forward again much more sedately. She could
almost make out Baldo's and Nicobar's conversation as
they proceeded, stopping and starting while Nicobar dug
about in the underbrush for further signs and *patrins.*

Without company, Luciana was left to her thoughts.
Moments like this haunted her, she was so aware of
being caught between worlds—between the people of
her birth and the people she lived among. Rather than
linger on such thoughts, she considered the mysteries
around her. Idala and the king seemed convinced there
was more to the attack on the road than was apparent.

Considering Alban's revelation of their identities as
witnesses against Alessandra, she, too, felt convinced
there was more to this than met the eye. Now there was
the *Beluni* sending for her through Nicobar with nary a
word of explanation. Never particularly good at controlling her curiosity, Luciana could not help but feel vexed
with frustration.

At last, the door swung open again. Nicobar peered
in. "We are close. Do you wish Baldo to drive into the
campsite?"

"No, we'll walk. There's no telling if even Baldo could

get this *gadjé* carriage out of a camp once it was in," Luciana said.

Gathering her skirts, she accepted Nicobar's hand as she stepped out. He took her cloak from the coach and placed it about her shoulders. She fastened the neck clasp and squinted into the darkness. Not even a camp-fire glimmered and the trees grew so thick the moon failed to shine through them.

"Baldo will stay with the horses," Nicobar said at her side. Taking her elbow, he guided her into the thickets along the lane.

They found the Romani campsite with little difficulty despite the overgrowth. A dozen or more brightly dressed Rom moved about the circled wagons. The bon-fire in the center of camp burned like a beacon. Luciana looked in the direction of the carriage, surprised she had not been able to see the campsite from the road.

"Chavi!"

Luciana turned at the sound of her grandmother's voice.

Solaja Lendaro, aglitter with golden baubles and ban-gles, her gray hair loose and wild about her shoulders, greeted Luciana with a familiar embrace and bestowed a kiss on each cheek.

The Romani Queen stood back, eyeing her up and down, her expression growing distant. "You look like a fine and proper *gadjé,* Duchessa."

A pang of doubt struck Luciana as she looked down at herself. She wore demure black from head to toe. Even in mourning the Gypsies did not absent color from their daily wear, preferring reds and the favored colors of the deceased. All in black, she looked a proper *gadjé,* to be sure.

The *Beluni* laughed and patted Luciana's cheek. "Do not let the *gadjé's* ill humor infect you, *Chavi,* you have little enough to laugh at as it is."

Luciana embraced her grandmother, relief melting her mounting tension. Oh, how she wished for the liberty of the road! The *gadjé* life seemed so complicated in comparison.

"Beluni-Daiya, it is good to see you."

"To the fire, *Chavi.* Warm yourself," the *Beluni* said, pushing Luciana toward the center of camp. She paused and offered Nicobar her hands. "How is the fate of my cousin's grandson?"

"I fare well, *Puri-Daiya.*"

"To the fire with both of you." The old woman clapped her hands. "Divero, the *bosh!* Give us music!"

A middle-aged man disappeared into one of the painted wagons, returning with fiddle in hand. Staying beyond the flickering light of the flames, he sat upon a stump and started to pluck the strings. By the time Luciana and Nicobar settled, the *boshmengro* was drawing a soft melody from his instrument. A scruffy camp dog whined and curled at his feet.

The *Beluni* hooked a stool up to the fire with her foot and motioned to the younger women, who brought out carved eating utensils. One of the women squatting by the fire glanced surreptitiously at Nicobar from the corner of her dark eyes. She stoked the fire with a branch and dragged two clumps of clay from the flames. With quick, sure hands, she broke the clumps open on a rock and deposited the mass, cracked clay and all, onto a serving tray.

Luciana took a deep breath of the herb-scented air. Her mouth watered. At the White King's court, there was a definite lack of Romani delicacies in the well-laden larders; nothing, certainly, that Kisaiya had access to.

The *Beluni* peeled away the hedgehog's coat with shards of clay, exposing tender steaming meat stuffed with herbs and wild vegetables. Another woman tore a crusty polenta loaf and placed large chunks of it on another wooden platter, which she handed to the *Beluni,* who served up generous rations of the *hetchi-witchi.*

Luciana placed her platter on her knees, but watched a younger woman take one of the plates into a caravan before the rest of the meal was divided among the family members. The *boshmengro* set aside his fiddle as he accepted dinner. For a time the campsite was quiet, except for the sounds of nature around them and the crackle of the fire.

Something about dining in the open, beneath the

trees, moon, and stars affected the appetite. For the first time since Alessandra's death, Luciana found herself eating with pleasure. Shortly, the food was spiced by the song of the fiddle as the *boshmengro* picked it up again and began to play.

Sated, Luciana closed her eyes, listening to the music of her mother, the music of her early childhood, before her father died and her mother married the *gadjé* conte, before Alessandra was born . . . before her mother died. The music sang in her soul, loosening the fetters of a lifetime and the tensions of the past weeks. Only a Rom could play a fiddle so that it sang like this.

"So, *Chavi,* your heart still dances with the fiddle, does it? Then perhaps you are less *gadjé* than we feared!" her grandmother observed with a laugh. "You put the fear of the Inquisitors into me with your *gadjé* manners!"

Luciana smiled and sat up, opening her eyes. She relished this moment of belonging. A girl took her plate and gave her a hot, wet rag to clean her hands.

"So, what have you learned?" her grandmother asked.

The question brought everything flooding back, and now even the *bosh* could not reach Luciana. "I've learned much, and nothing at all."

The older woman gave her an appraising look and nodded. "Spoken like a fortune-teller." She picked up a twig and rolled it between her fingers. "So, have you been *dukkerin'* at court, then, my pet?"

Luciana shook her head. "I avoid fortune-telling and divination. They are too easy to be meddled with. I must proceed cautiously."

The *Beluni* snorted. "Caution is a *gadjé* word. Sometimes you must take risks."

"It is complicated, *Daiya.*"

Solaja Lendaro considered her granddaughter with an arched brow. "Should I appoint someone else, *Chavi?*"

"No, no, please don't," Luciana said hurriedly.

The older woman made a noise under her breath and stuck the end of the twig in her mouth as she contemplated the fire. "What have you to tell me, then?"

"All seems to be as we feared, and more."

"More?"

"Yes, *Daiya*." Luciana hunched over, narrowing her eyes. The woodsmoke smelled of pitch and pine, refreshing to the nose, but hard on the eyes when the wind whipped it in her direction. "She was taken by a *chovahano* who has asked no ransom. He has bespelled the body and forced her spirit into service."

"You are sure of this?"

"Yes, *Daiya*."

The *Beluni* grunted again. "You know that the conjurer is a man, then?" Her face twisted in displeasure when Luciana nodded. "Men make a hash of magic." She flung the twig into the fire. *"O beng te poggar il men!"*

Luciana turned and spat reflexively lest the devil's curse settle on her. She was quite content, however, for the devil to do his will upon Conte Urbano and anyone else in league with him.

"You must discover what spell he used."

"I found the *strega* who sold him his tools," Luciana replied. She smiled into the fire. "I know his spells."

"She was not Romani, then, this witch you found?"

"No." She lay a restraining hand on her grandmother's arm as the old woman began another curse. Luciana did not dare put a curse—or let someone else—on the woman who held so much over her. "The *strega* is no friend of the conjurer."

"Then why would she do such a foolish thing?"

Luciana shrugged. "She is a merchant." She dusted her hands figuratively. "It is done. *Basta!*"

"Done?" The *Beluni* shook her head at the sky. "This is not done until my granddaughter rests! Tell me, this *chovahano*, is he of the blood?"

"No," Luciana said. She hesitated, thinking on his fair complexion. "I do not think so, but some of his magic is Romani. He knows enough of our ways to use it in his spells."

"How do you know this?"

"The components that he uses . . ." Luciana shrugged again.

"Is that all? The *gadjé* can use the same tools we do, Luciana. You must do better."

She sat up straighter. The *Beluni* did not use her given name often, but when she did . . . "My sister's *gadjé* grave reeked of this *chovahano* and his spell work. What better way is there for me to determine the nature of his magic? Besides, when I chanced to touch his hand, it confirmed everything. *Daiya,* I could feel his stink." She shuddered. "But, alas, I've had no luck yet in finding the leader."

"Hmm!" the *Beluni* murmured with a nod. "The *chova* does not lie. And the *chova,* you are sure it is Romani magic, not *gadjé?*"

"Not completely one or the other and yet neither," Luciana said. Rather like herself, she thought, but sickened at the concept of being equated with this *chovahano*'s magic.

"And what does that tell you?"

For a moment, Luciana was confused by the question. She closed her eyes and quelled the nervous fluttering in her stomach. The answer would come. And then it did. "He experiments, and with things he does not fully understand."

"Which makes him more dangerous because not even *he* can predict what he will unleash."

The thought was unsettling. Then, to think of Alessandra's spirit tangled up with the games of the conte's collaborators, she felt even more unnerved.

"Do you have the tools *you* will need?" the *Beluni* asked.

Luciana nodded.

"Good. Has your man, Nicobar, told you that Grasni is with her clan, probably already in Ispica?"

Luciana nodded again. "He has, *Beluni-Daiya.*"

"I think the girl must know something. Word through the clans is that she's very frightened. I've sent word that she is to go back to Citteauroea and meet with you. I have told her to go to a Guildhouse. She must be protected, *Chavi.* She has *my* protection. You understand?"

"I do," Luciana said, but she was also acutely aware that the others in the camp watched them. Beside her, the *Beluni* stretched, her bangles jingled with the motion. Luciana looked at the old woman thoughtfully. "I've been at the palazzo for only a few days. It's not your nature to be so impatient, *Daiya*."

"You think me impatient?" the *Beluni* asked. She flicked a floating ember from the bonfire away from her face. "So my granddaughter reproves me."

"I mean no such thing, *Daiya,* but I am puzzled. I thought you would give me more time before demanding a report."

"*Demanding* a report?" The *Beluni's* eyebrows seemed to almost disappear in her mass of silvery white hair.

"What other reason have you for leaving Ispica so soon? You could only have just arrived," Luciana said.

"We did not reach the *cavas* before we turned back," the *Beluni* replied.

"You did not even reach them?" Luciana repeated. "Were you waylaid? Did you have trouble with the *gadjé?*"

"*Chavi,* you learn more when it is your ears that are open." The *Beluni* signaled to one of the girls hovering nearby. "We were waylaid, yes. But the fairies, fortune, and the *Fata* smiled upon us."

Mystified, Luciana watched the girl the *Beluni* had signaled disappear into the *vardo* she had noted earlier. Barely a moment later and the girl reappeared, speaking to someone and motioning toward her and the *Beluni*.

A man stepped out of the darkness of the *vardo* and paused at the foot of the stair. While not particularly tall, he possessed a sturdy and athletic-looking build. Clean-shaven, with his hair drawn back, he wore a tattered blue uniform coat draped over his shoulders. His left arm rested in a sling. Beyond the obvious wounding, he looked tired and sorely weathered.

Luciana knew, once she met his eyes, who he was. Through those eyes, she had *seen* what she presumed was his death.

He left the *vardo* and crossed the encampment, which had grown suddenly, unnaturally still. He stopped at the edge of the *Beluni*'s carpet and bowed deeply to Luciana and her grandmother. "I am Capitano Mandero di Montago."

Completely forgetting herself, Luciana stared at this man her sister loved. A flood of unidentifiable emotions swept through her. "Forgive me—I–I cannot believe you are alive. So many testified to your death."

"They were misinformed, Your Grace." The capitano's voice shook. He looked grim-faced from pain.

Luciana rose immediately, motioning for him to take her stool. "One doesn't survive a swim in the Stretto every day, Capitano. Please sit!"

The capitano turned to the *Beluni,* the request for permission to avail himself of her personal hospitality was little more than an exchange of looks. Instead of taking the stool, the capitano nodded to Nicobar who hovered nearby and sank to the rug with a heartfelt sigh. " 'Twas a blade between the ribs which nearly brought my ond. The swim in the Stretto was but a diversion."

"He is why we returned," the *Beluni* said, plucking a bit of grass from along the edge of the rug. She rolled it between her fingers, staring through it at the fire. After a moment, she cast the grass aside and considered her granddaughter with her fathomless eyes. "We found him along the coast, between Taormina and Catania. The sea brought him ashore, and he found shelter in one of the old temples."

"You must have been there for some time," Luciana said. How, she wondered, had he managed with his injury?

Mandero smiled grimly. "For that I must thank the *Fata.* The clans are ending their winter roaming and moving on to Ispica. I was given refuge by them."

"The capitano is my brother-in-law's second cousin twice removed. She married a *gadjé* farmer," the *Beluni* said. "Mandero *is* who he says he is, *Chavi.*"

Luciana looked at the capitano. "But you didn't return to the palazzo? To my sister?"

The capitano turned away so that the flames danced light and shadows across his face.

Solaja laid a hand on Luciana's arm. "He was deathly

sick when the clans found him. It is only by Atropos'
blessing that he lives. Until I told him, Mandero did not
know of his lady's death."

Of course, the *Beluni* was right. How could he have
known of Alessandra's troubles? And yet, he lived and
her sister did not.

"I loved my *pireni*—your sister. Every day I live,
knowing . . ." Mandero sighed heavily. "Would that I
died instead."

XVI

"Perfect courage is to do without witnesses what one would be capable of doing with the world looking on."

—Francois, Duc de La Rochefoucauld

THE capitano shifted in his seat beside Nicobar and readjusted his arm in its sling. The interior of the coach seemed smaller with two men in it. The combination of uneasy silence and close quarters was stultifying. Luciana wished Nicobar would speak, break the silence somehow. She had so many questions for Alessa's lover she did not know where to begin. But no, Nicobar would be silent and not intrude.

Luciana looked out the window, mulling over her thoughts and feelings. She was overwhelmed at finding the capitano alive, especially when the most likely murderers of her sister were his own men on vendetta. The forest passed by the window as a blur of trees.

"Forgive me, Your Grace, but . . ." the capitano began.

Luciana looked up, causing him to pause.

He began again. "Your sister—" The capitano seemed unable to give voice to whatever he had intended to say and fell silent again. Awkwardness spread between them.

Luciana muttered a silent prayer to the *Fata* and gathered her courage. "Please, I am told you loved her as much as I—well, differently, but . . ." Sensing some of the capitano's own anxiety, she licked her lips and searched for the right words. "This is so very difficult!"

The capitano smiled crookedly. "I had hoped to meet you under better circumstances."

"I cannot imagine worse at the moment." Luciana cleared her throat. The coach jarred and her words spilled out, almost as a consequence. "H–how did you meet my sister?"

The capitano smiled reminiscently, his face heavily shadowed in the flickering light of the coach lamp. "I was confused about court protocol, it being another sort of beast than military protocol. I am a soldier, after all." He waved his good hand expressively. "I did not know my place among the nobles when attending court. She always said I chose to stand on her foot."

Luciana laughed. Alessa's humor could be sharp. She missed that. "I was surprised to learn of you."

"Did she never write?" He sounded surprised. "She mentioned several times that she had been remiss in her letters to you, but she would write later. I suppose she took comfort in the knowledge that the queen no doubt told you of our affair."

"She wrote, but not until after . . ." Luciana shrugged. "Not until after my sister was accused of your murder."

"Who would accuse her of such a thing? *How* could she be accused?"

"Apparently, killing you by poison was considered a natural conclusion because she made herbal remedies for the courtiers."

"Poison? That is ridiculous, I was stabbed! I was lost in the Stretto. Surely my own men defended her?" the capitano protested.

"They testified against her," Luciana said, keeping her voice bland. It was not easy. Knowing his fellows condemned her grieving sister only made it worse, that they might have murdered her as well choked Luciana into silence.

"Della Guelfa wouldn't have permitted it! He knew I loved her!" The capitano hit the coach door with his fist.

"I recognize this della Guelfa's name from my sister's letter. He stood as the chief accuser."

"How can that be? Della Guelfa would not betray me, and to betray her is to betray me!"

"But if they thought you dead by her hand? They were men devoted to their capitano, were they not? And I've heard of this Escalade custom, the *Coda Condanna a Morte.* It seems only reasonable that—"

"Don't say it!" the capitano said in a strangled voice. "*Dea,* let it not be so! Let my men not have condemned her with more than words!"

Luciana accepted the capitano's protest with a quiet nod. "What really happened that night?"

"The night I was lost?"

The coach heaved perilously to one side, nearly dislodging its occupants and making the coach lamp sputter.

"I'll speak to Baldo," Nicobar growled, reaching for the door.

"No, the roads are bad. He is not to blame," Luciana said.

"There is no need for great speed now."

Luciana thought of Stefano at the palazzo. By now, most assuredly, he was no longer with the Palantini. Had he come to her bedroom? Did he know that she was gone? Was he angrier that she disobeyed him or that she was gone? She blinked, aware that she and Mandero stared at one another in the darkness as Nicobar called to the driver. The pitching eased as the carriage slowed.

"As to that night, I was in the galley with my men." The capitano frowned. "My memories are so unclear. I've been ill, and I'm not sure what was dream and what . . ." He shook his head. Shocks of dark brown hair escaped the tail he had made of its length. "I went up on deck to think, take in the air, and I felt this great pain in my back. Somehow—no—some*one* pushed me over the edge and I was left." He rubbed his eyes. "Please, Sisters *Fata,* don't let this be della Guelfa!"

Remembering Alessa's letter, Luciana was compelled to ease the capitano's torment. "It's possible someone misled della Guelfa. My sister's letter shows no animosity to your man even though he accused her. Indeed, as I recall, she spoke of his unfailing loyalty."

The capitano laughed softly, sadly. "She always thought of others, even when unhappy."

"Three mariners testified against her."

"Mariners? But— There was a man who spoke to me! One of the sailors, just before . . ." The capitano ran his hand back through his hair, further loosening the tail. "That must be it. It must have been them. What did they say?"

"That you grew violently ill, naming Alessa a poisoner."

"And the king was duped?" the capitano asked scornfully. "I would not have believed that of the White King!"

"He had no other explanation or witnesses. After all, why would someone kill you?"

The capitano grew still and his voice quiet. "My mission."

"Your mission? What *was* your mission?" As the words sank in, Luciana could envision the intrigue as it probably unfolded. Lovers shared confidences. The conspirators would have assumed Alessa knew what secrets the capitano protected. It was an assumption that probably proved fatal.

The capitano sat back and crossed his arms. "I vowed not to speak of it, even to . . . her—especially to her—" He hesitated over her name, his voice lingering on Alessa's unspeakable name. "I vowed not to speak of it unless I had proof. Having none, I will not put you in danger as well by voicing it."

"Truth be told, it doesn't matter whether you tell me what this mission of yours is or not," Luciana retorted. "Two of the three sailors attacked me this very day and attempted to murder me. My life is already marked. Apparently, your strategy failed my sister who died for what she did *not* know."

"But she was in the custody of the queen! I didn't believe anyone would be so bold as to harm her charge."

"Someone did not let that stop him."

"Who did this?" Mandero asked.

Luciana shook her head irritably. "My sister was found in her bed with a bottle of poison in her hand. Some say it was suicide. For the sake of an honorable burial, the king pronounced it murder, though we have no idea how the murderer got in or out of the room—"

"In the room? Then she was indoors? She would never have done that!" Mandero declared. "Her spirit could not rise freely to the heavens!"

"My conclusion as well. One theory which remains a possibility is the *Coda Condanna a Morte*."

"The *Coda?* It can't be! How have you come by your information?"

"Specifically? Letters, the queen . . ." Luciana shrugged. "So, will you tell me about this mysterious mission?"

"I've no proof of the accusations I would make. I hoped to get the evidence I needed before I went to the king."

"We could still get evidence."

"The evidence is gone," di Montago said. "The proof I sought anyway. It's too late."

"Too late? What were you after?" Luciana asked.

The capitano hesitated. "The princess' marriage contract."

Luciana sat back, nonplussed. "Why her marriage contract?"

"It was authored by the cardinal, not the king."

"Is that all?"

"Is that all? Isn't it enough? In the course of my duties, well, they were not my duties so much as habit. I often accompanied the Watch on their rounds and would sometimes take a different path around the palazzo. It was on just such an occasion that I overheard the princess, the cardinal, and another man in the gardens."

Luciana looked up, surprised. "Who was the other?"

"I did not get a clear enough look at him to know. They spoke treason, Your Grace. They spoke of a Catholic Tyrrhia where the princess would rule with the cardinal and this other man as her chief advisers. They said nothing I could prove until they spoke of the marriage with a faithful Catholic deMedici."

"A Catholic marriage is to be expected for the princess," Luciana replied.

"True, but this was a man of the cardinal's choosing. The princess' loyalty was to be proved by this marriage.

The cardinal could expect to influence the court through the consort's faith and obligation to the cardinal," di Montago said.

"But to do this . . ." Luciana stopped, unable to say the words.

"The entire royal family must be dead—every one of the royal family but the princess."

"All cousins and relations?" Luciana asked faintly. Thoughts of the king and queen, their innocent son, dead, choked her with outrage. But the thought, too, of the extended family—which included Stefano—dying filled her with a mind-numbing fear and anger.

"It would have to be so, Your Grace," the capitano said. "Perhaps this would include even a full rebellion to overthrow the Palantini before the council could elect anyone else."

"The other faiths would never stand for such a thing!" Nicobar protested.

"The Church has the power of the Inquisition behind it. Tyrrhia's history of religious tolerance would create a frenzy should the Church get its opportunity here," Luciana said with a shudder. "The Throne, backed by the armies of the Church and its followers, with the dead king and heir . . . it could be done."

"There is the matter of the Escalade and the Corpo d'Armata," di Montago countered.

"But with the royal family dead and the Church behind the princess, it would only be a matter of time before they fell in line, especially if the Palantini fell with the king or soon after," Luciana said. "How would the Marriage Contract provide proof if it is nothing more than a contract for marriage?"

"The contract was more than that. There were actually two contracts, one for all to see, and a second, which dictated that the deMedici and his children would be the only heirs to the Tyrrhian throne. That could only be true if the entire royal family was dead," the capitano said.

"A most vile plan," Luciana muttered.

"And one that cannot be proved. I have nothing I can

take to the king. If I spoke too soon, if I revealed what I knew, then the princess and her cohorts could protect themselves."

"It seems they've already protected themselves," Luciana said. "They've tried to kill you and thought they were successful. They killed my sister. Now they turn to me."

"They're edgy conspirators," di Montago observed.

"At best," Luciana said. What, she wondered, would these conspirators do if they learned the capitano lived? What were they willing to do to protect their plans? "It would be best if they didn't know you still live just yet. If you could remain hidden until I have something I can prove, we might still thwart them."

The capitano nodded.

"Where shall we hide him? He should be accessible to you, but far enough away so that he will not be noticed," Nicobar said.

"We can test della Guelfa," di Montago said. "If he remained true, then he will take me in. He has a farm near Citteauroea. He talked of retreating there when he finally took leave. With my death, he would probably have done that."

Nicobar peered out the window. "We near the capitol even now. I will have Baldo stop so the capitano can direct us."

Di Montago leaped from the carriage and paused long enough to assist Luciana. He raised a silencing hand and pointed to the light that glimmered on the second story of the farmhouse.

"Who goes there?" a man's voice called from the window.

Remaining in the shadow of the carriage, the capitano called up. "Another of the Escalade. I come with this noblewoman seeking shelter!"

"I will give it. Who among our number asks?" the man called.

"You know me, della Guelfa," the capitano called back.

"The voice is familiar, but I–I do not recognize it," the other man replied.

"You recognize it," di Montago said. His good hand twitched and, for the first time, Luciana saw the scorpinini ready to fire.

"Do you need that?" she whispered.

"I don't know," he said grimly, "but I will soon enough."

The light in the window faded. Soon they heard the door bars grating in their grooves. Their host swung the door wide and stood in the doorway hastily dressed in pants and a half-tucked nightshirt. He held a saber in his hand, but it was point down. "Pray, *Dios,* is it you, Capitano?"

Di Montago stepped away from the coach. "It is I."

Della Guelfa tossed aside the saber and came to embrace Mandero with a cry of welcome. Another light came on in the house above. Della Guelfa and Mandero greeted one another with hearty thumps on the back, despite the capitano's wound. At last, their host threw his door wider to reveal another two men thundering down the stairs who greeted Mandero much as their host had done.

Della Guelfa stepped aside and came to Luciana, bowing elegantly. "Forgive my appearance, My Lady, but may I offer you shelter for the night? It is late and a lady must have her rest."

"The duchessa is not sure she can take your hospitality and, I fear, that I am equally hesitant," the capitano said, suddenly serious.

Immediately, the mood changed. Della Guelfa stepped back as though struck. "Pray, Capitano, why would you deny my hospitality? How have I offended you?"

Di Montago motioned to Luciana. "This good woman is the Duchessa di Drago, the *Araunya di Cayesmengri e Cayesmengro,* but more importantly, she is the sister of my beloved."

The mood grew cooler. "Know you now, with me before you, that you were wrong to accuse my *adorata* of poisoning me? Would you see the wound in my back? Or does one of you know the wound well enough already?"

Della Guelfa and the men with him grew even quieter than before. The others looked to della Guelfa who had apparently become their spokesman. "None of us knows your wound, nor knew of it, Capitano. I swear on my love for Tyrrhia that none of us left the ship's cabin. None of us followed you topside until one of the sailors called out that you had fallen overboard. We can all testify to our presence in the cabin below. Do you not remember our game of draughts?"

"I remember," the capitano said.

"The sailors must have done the stabbing, Capitano, for none of us would. If we had a grievance with you, we took it to you, as was the custom. We are good men and true."

"Were you good men and true even after my supposed murder?"

Again the men grew silent. Again it was della Guelfa who spoke, and when he did he looked the capitano and Luciana in the eye evenly. "We were and are your good men; not even death keeps us from being true."

"Then who took the *Coda Condanna a Morte?*" the capitano asked.

Della Guelfa raised his chin and stepped forward. " 'Twas I, Capitano. I was senior man. It was my duty and my honor to avenge you who were, by testimony of us all, murdered by the woman you loved and swore your life to. We could not know that she was innocent."

Luciana felt ill and leaned back against the carriage. Somewhere within her, there was rage, but now only horror at the error overwhelmed her.

Della Guelfa reached out but stopped short when di Montago and Nicobar placed themselves between him and Luciana.

"Capitano, please, you must understand. We believed she murdered you, but even still we failed you in the *Coda*. She was condemned in an Escalade court by your men. As senior officer, I was chosen to carry out the

Coda, but she was dead the very night we made our judgment. None of us touched her. We had nothing to do with her death. We will swear it on our swords . . . on your sword if you wish," della Guelfa said. "The Lady Alessandra was condemned of murdering you, but justice by the *Coda* was not carried out."

Di Montago sighed, his whole body wilting.

"Do you believe them?" Luciana asked.

Di Montago could only nod. After a moment, he turned back to della Guelfa. "Who did murder her?"

"Most say she committed suicide," della Guelfa said.

As one, Luciana and Mandero declared, "She did not!"

Della Guelfa nodded. "As you say, then, but we don't know who did. The only other thing we know is that her maid disappeared the night of her death and no one has been able to find her."

"I'll deal with her," Luciana said softly. "She knows something, I'm sure, but she is afraid."

"Will you stay, then, Capitano? Or do you go on to Citteauroea?" della Guelfa asked.

"We need to hide him for a time. One option is the Guildhouse in—"

"No!" della Guelfa said sharply. His expression immediately turned apologetic. "The capitano should be protected by his own men. We failed him once. We will not do so again. No one would suspect him here, and soldiers are about often enough."

Luciana looked to di Montago.

Di Montago stared from one man to another and, after a long moment said, "I will be safer here than anywhere else, Your Grace."

"And what of you, Your Grace?" della Guelfa asked.

"No, I must return to the palazzo." Luciana motioned to the capitano's wounded shoulder. "He will need care, and I would have news of him, but bear in mind that no one beyond this farm must know of his survival."

"I will bring news myself," della Guelfa promised.

"Good. I will watch for you, then. Nicobar, Baldo, let us be on the road!"

Baldo sprang to the driver's seat and Nicobar helped Luciana into the carriage.

"What will you do now?" Nicobar asked Luciana as the carriage started moving again.

"I, like my intended brother-in-law, have no news for the king that I can prove; but unlike him, I am not presumed dead and *I* can attend the Betrothal Ball."

XVII

*"Between good sense and good taste there is the
same difference as between cause and effect."*
                                        —Jean de La Bruyere

13 d'Maggio 1684

GARLANDS of flowers and painted silk banners of
cornflower blue, saffron, and white decorated the
Grand Sala, bringing it to its festive best. Luciana
watched from her corner, waiting for the first sight of
the princess' intended. Beside her, Prunella beamed gid-
dily at everyone who passed.

"Prunella, child—" Luciana said, putting out a hand.

Prunella turned, apparently sensing correction, and
frowned. "I'm sorry, Your Grace, but I've never had a
dress of Gypsy Silk before. It tingles!" She wore a dusky
pink satin dress with cream-colored petticoats of the
finest Gypsy Silk, a gift from Luciana. It seemed so different from the girl's usual dark colors. Prunella insisted
upon changing the gay pink ribbons to somber black out
of respect for Alessandra's death and Luciana's mourning. Luciana preferred the pink but allowed the girl to
do as she saw fit.

"It's the magic, child, the enchantment of the fabric,"
Luciana said. It occurred to her that perhaps Prunella
made her so uneasy tonight because she so rarely saw
the girl happy. Instead of saying anything, Luciana

pointed across the room with her fan. "Isn't that your friend, Lady Ursinia, over there?"

Prunella smiled, her relief visible, but the frantic edge to her gaiety faded. She started to wave but caught herself and gave a restrained nod to Lady Ursinia who promptly appeared to be making excuses to her companions. Prunella hesitated, looking anxiously at Luciana.

"Cousin, Your Grace, may I be excused?"

"Enjoy yourself." As Luciana watched Prunella circle the dance floor to greet her friend, she smoothed her own skirts, which had been crushed by sharing the love seat with Prunella. Pearls, sewed into the sleeves and along the off-the-shoulder neckline, adorned her outer gown of black silk brocade. The undergown of watered silk, was of a deep color neither blue nor green. A large green-and-white cameo, inherited from her mother, held her collar of pearls snug to the width of her neck. Kisaiya had fashioned Luciana's dark hair into an intricate weave of loops and coils pinned with pearls and tiny bits of oriental jade. Kisaiya had outdone even herself.

Stefano appeared beside her, just behind her line of vision. Luciana shivered as his hand dropped to her bare shoulder and down to the back of the love seat. His thumb caressed her back as his fingers toyed with the dangling pearls, which fell from the catch. He bent down and placed a perfunctory kiss upon her cheek. He stopped as she was about to rise and whispered into her ear, "I am surprised to find you here, my darling."

She did not mistake the bitterness of his tone for anything but what it was. Luciana looked up at him nervously. Upon her return early this morning, she had found a single rose of the palest cream across her pillow, wilted from lack of attention. By the time she awoke, Stefano had left the suite some hours before without word of when he might be back.

"Didn't you think I would eventually get out of my room?" she asked.

Stefano drew a key from his coat pocket. "Eventually, yes."

Estensi, the Court Herald, entered the hall from behind the throne and stamped his staff. "Their Royal

Majesties, King Alban Mirandola e Novabianco and
Queen Idala di Luna e Novabianco. All hail Their
Majesties!"

Luciana rose and dropped into a deep curtsy. Around
her, everyone followed suit as was the custom for their
sex. Estensi stamped his staff again as the nobles rose.
"Her Royal Highness, Bianca Isabella Novabianco. All
hail Her Highness!"

Again, the curtsy, but not so low this time. Luciana
rose, waiting expectantly, watching as did the others
about her as the princess took her place. She glanced
sideways at Stefano. He watched the door intently. The
princess moved aside the skirt of her red dress to reveal
a second chair beside the thrones, a place of honor for
her fiancé.

Estensi stamped his staff again. "I present to you Signore Pierro deMedici, Conte di Solario."

Luciana acknowledged the general introduction with
an inclined head, his station being lower than her own.
She watched deMedici make his entrance. It seemed the
princess' choice of men was destined to be the likes of
the foppish Conte Urbano. The deMedici was short, but
on the lean side, so at least he did not combine diminu-
tive stature with portliness. He wore blue-and-gold-
brocade coat and pants, white lace neckcloth, lace at his
cuffs and collar. Gold ribbons and bows adorned his
cuffs, shoes, and the fashionable lovelocks in his hair.
He posed, hand on cane, as he acknowledged his audience with a condescending smile. He bowed with a
flourish to the king and queen, then took Bianca's hand
and kissed it before taking his seat.

Conte deMedici was a pompous little man, dark and
shifty. Luciana disliked him intensely, not that she had
been prepared to like the man chosen by Cardinal delle
Torre to replace the king and take the throne at Bianca's side.

Estensi signaled the musicians, and the king motioned
his cousin and fiancé to the dance floor. As the newly
betrothed couple danced, Luciana retired to her love
seat and flicked open her fan, noting for the first time
that Stefano had left her side. Prunella stood with Lady

Ursinia in a corner, blushing now at the attentions of a young man who seemed quite intent.

Luciana allowed her thoughts to wander as her gaze roamed the crowd. Idala nodded in quiet acknowledgment when their gazes met, then returned to her husband. Alban seemed impervious to everyone else, smiling blandly at the nobles.

Conte Urbano simpered in a corner, away from Prunella and thereby relieving Luciana of any sense of obligation to rescue Stefano's young kinswoman. The conte wore black-and-red velvet brocade, overdone as always, but amazingly not as exaggerated as his new rival for the princess' affections.

Luciana paused, studying the man to whom Urbano spoke. Another little man—thin, dark, and mysterious. His manner seemed quiet and plain, startling in comparison to Urbano. Her curiosity roused, she rose and, turning to straighten her dress, found herself face-to-face with Cardinal delle Torre.

"Good evening, Your Eminence," Luciana murmured.

"Your Grace," the cardinal said coldly. "You've been at the palazzo for a few days now, and have yet to visit the cattedrale. Don't you share Their Majesties' Neoplatonic persuasions?"

"I wholly support the individual's search for truth and his God," Luciana said. She darted a glance around, hoping to find Stefano or some other escape.

"Then, I am surprised you've not exercised your curiosity enough to venture into the Catholic faith," the cardinal said.

Luciana hid her discomfort behind a lighthearted laugh. "I, a woman of considerable years, have had a lifetime to sample the various religious teachings."

The cardinal laughed, though with an edge of mockery. "You are a young woman, Your Grace, too young to be led astray."

"I am sure that Rabbi Sanzio would say much the same thing, don't you agree?" Luciana asked, keeping her voice sweet.

The cardinal started to speak, but buried his protest

in a smile that did not light his serious eyes. He, too, was a dark man, his hair, shorn close, was free of the curls most men favored these days. He wore black ecclesiastical robes, austere except for the gold cross with its heavy chain and the rings, which denoted his station. Unlike the others, the cardinal was tall, thinly built, though his facial features were narrow and sharp. He was tall enough that he loomed over her.

"I was curious, Your Eminence, if you knew who that man was?" Luciana motioned with her fan to the man talking to Conte Urbano.

The cardinal's brows rose in apparent surprise. "One of Pierro deMedici's entourage, I'm sure. Why do you ask?"

Luciana shrugged. "He seemed interesting . . . and so intense."

"All the Gascons are intense, or hadn't you noticed, Your Grace?" the cardinal replied.

Luciana looked up at him in surprise. "Not having been introduced to any of them yet, I fear I would not know." She waited for him to offer an invitation, but he did not, staring off into the crowd instead.

She sighed in vexation when the cardinal bowed and moved away. His Eminence was in high form this evening. All things considered, she would have expected him to be more circumspect. She examined the room quickly, looking for sign of Stefano. He was, still, nowhere to be found. Still curious about the stranger, Luciana strolled nearer.

Urbano turned as she approached, bowing courteously, though his smile appeared somewhat forced. The little man also bowed, his expression remaining reserved.

"Are you enjoying yourself, Your Grace?" the conte asked.

Luciana spread her fan with an artful chuckle. "Pray, my good conte, how could I not?"

The conte flushed a little. "But of course, the queen has taken considerable steps to assure that we *all* enjoy ourselves."

"Yes," Luciana said with a sad gesture. "She has assured the pleasures of even those she is unacquainted with . . . just as this gentleman and I are similarly lacking in introductions."

The conte turned an ugly shade of crimson that did not suit his brocade at all. Flustered, he bowed repeatedly to them both. "Your Grace, the Duchessa di Drago, may I present Lord Exilli."

The little man took Luciana's hand and kissed it. "Gregorio Exilli, of Rome. And you, Your Grace, you are Tyrrhian, or is it only your husband?"

"No, I am as Tyrrhian as my husband, though my people are of Romani blood," Luciana said.

"And your husband would be the Duca di Drago, of course?"

"Yes," Luciana said. She grew even more curious. "Do you know my husband?"

Exilli glanced at the conte, then smiled reassuringly. "I met a Duca di Drago when I was at the Morean front. This would be the same man?"

Luciana considered him, wondering what this man's search for the most diplomatic words hid. "My husband was in Peloponnesus for some time. When were you there?"

"Some time ago," Exilli said, licking his lips. "I think nearly two years ago. Did you say he has returned? Is he well?"

"The duca is married to such a lovely woman, yet he remained at the front for ever so long—of course he's not well!" Conte Urbano said with a devilish chortle.

"It isn't so ill for a man to serve an ideal he holds dear," Luciana said stiffly.

"Indeed, a most noble man with noble ideals," Exilli said. He took Urbano by the elbow. "You were going to teach me that dance step which is so popular here. Perhaps Her Grace—?"

Luciana shook her head. "No, I–I think not. I am in no mood to dance just now. Won't you excuse me?"

Finding her love seat occupied, Luciana worked her way through the crowd. In a corner of the room, most distant from the mingling courtiers, she found a seat. She felt troubled. What was it that unsettled her? Besides the mention of Stefano by this stranger? What about the little man, Exilli, made her so uneasy? Why did her mind linger on the name as if it meant something? Perhaps Stefano mentioned it in a letter?

Luciana had lost her taste for court. It was no longer the refuge of gaiety and mystery it had once been. All the fun had gone out of it, leaving only sinister overtones and ominous intrigues.

Lost in thought, she gave a little jump as a wineglass suddenly appeared before her.

"What troubles you, my sweet?" Stefano asked as he sat on the couch beside her.

"Now I am your sweet, am I?" she asked, sipping the wine he had brought for her.

"As you have ever been," he replied. He lounged back in the small sofa, dusting nonexistent debris from his port-wine-colored Gypsy Silk noil coat.

Luciana shifted to appraise him. "You are free with pretty words, Your Grace." The clothes he wore appeared new, making him look sleek. Apparently, he had gone to one of the Guildhouses for fitting shortly after his arrival and had been there earlier today to retrieve his goods.

"And why not? Do you find them so offensive?" he asked.

Luciana looked away, to the dance floor and then to the goblet of glass in her hand. "No."

"They *do* bother you," Stefano murmured. He leaned forward. "Why?"

"Because they mock me."

"Mock *you?*" Stefano said.

"I am not without feelings," Luciana replied, stiffly.

"You are angry that I locked you into your rooms, is that it?" Stefano asked.

Luciana managed a strangled laugh. "Wasn't that the point? To make me angry, I mean?"

Stefano shook his head. "No, it was meant to keep you where I could find you, where I knew you would be safe."

Luciana sighed. "Alessandra was murdered in her bed. I would not guarantee that our private chambers offer any certainty of security."

"I'd intended to lock the world out as well, but perhaps I was being presumptuous," Stefano said, rising to his feet.

"And was the rose so that I might enjoy my cage a little more?"

"No. It was foolish sentiment on my part. I thought . . ." He shrugged.

"You thought what?" Luciana watched his every move. He looked tired and haunted. "What did you think, Stefano?"

Stefano sighed. "I thought you might . . . that you might welcome my . . . my attentions and then I found you gone, so soon after someone had tried to kill you. It was not until Prunella dragged poor Kisaiya from her bed that I learned you'd left of your own accord."

"My grandmother summoned me," Luciana said. Did she dare believe the pain she saw in his expression?

"Yes, of course. I understood, but still . . . you frightened me. I, at least, want to know where you are going, Luciana. This intrigue was the death of your sister, I would die myself if it took you as well."

"Are those just pretty words, or—"

Stefano suddenly tensed, his eyes focused beyond the dance floor. Luciana also stood. The princess and her new conte danced, quite apparently enjoying one another's competence on the dance floor. Near the wall, Prunella stood in the midst of Bianca's cluster of friends, watching the dancing and talking excitedly.

"I was not aware that Cousin Prunella moved in such high circles," he said, clearly unhappy.

"It is my fault," Luciana confessed.

"Your fault?"

Together, they rejoined the press of other courtiers closer to the thrones and dance floor.

"Yes. I introduced Prunella to Lady Ursinia. I thought they might become friends. I had not expected, however, that she would become such bosom companions with the lot of them, especially this quickly," Luciana said.

Stefano gave her a perturbed look. "Isn't my cousin, here under *my* protection?"

"I did not think it would be a problem, or I would not have made the introduction."

"But you have, quite effectively, sent her into the lion's den!" Stefano asked.

"I did not send her, she seems to have found her way there herself. Don't worry, though. Conte Urbano will pay her little attention—enough to make her blush and feel pretty. She has no dowry to speak of and is not royal," Luciana said.

Stefano nodded thoughtfully.

"Perhaps Your Grace would honor me with that dance now?" Conte Urbano's silky voice requested.

Luciana turned, feeling sick to her stomach, and found the conte at her elbow.

She was relieved to feel Stefano's arm encircle her waist.

"I believe, my lady wife promised *me* this dance," Stefano said firmly. Turning to her, he held out his hand, "Your Grace?"

Conte Urbano stepped back with a solicitous bow.

Stefano swept her onto the dance floor after they deposited their wineglasses with a steward. Luciana gladly welcomed the opportunity to dance with her husband. Stefano's poetry was wonderful, but no one danced with the lightness and flair he did. He was like a fairy spark dancing upon the wind. She tingled where his hands touched her, as they met, whirled, and parted again in the lively dance.

Luciana could not help but watch him as she danced, taken once more with his blondish-brown hair and fair good looks. He was dapper-slim, not particularly tall. He dressed with a flair and finesse all his own. He did not need the Gypsy Silk to enhance his grace and nature, but it conformed to him, and the embellishments served him well. He wore the port-wine quilted, short-sleeved coat with folds upon folds of shirtsleeve tied in place with ribbons; lace hung over the cuff of his knee-high boots at the bottom of his pantaloons; he also scorned the stylish fancy heels; and his hat, carefully pinned, brimmed with feathers. He carried the style with athleticism and poise.

She noticed for the first time a darkness, almost grimness, in his expression that had never been there before. Had their separation put that there or was it worry over her behavior? Or could it be remnants of the war with the Turks. Though these last few days had seemed a lifetime, Stefano was still only newly back. Luciana muttered a prayer of thankfulness for his return even as he pulled her into his arms and did another turn around the dance floor with a sudden relish. By Clotho's heart, how she had missed him!

The dance ended all too soon.

Stefano escorted her from the dance floor and said, "You will forgive me, Lucia. I will find our drinks."

Luciana waved her fan, catching her breath. She had forgotten how dizzying dancing with Stefano could be.

Stefano turned to leave, but stopped and tensed, his attention drawn elsewhere. She followed his gaze.

Gregorio Exilli leaned quietly against a chair. Their turn on the dance floor had brought them directly before him. Exilli bowed promptly, deeply, to both of them and turned to Stefano. "I had not expected to meet you again so soon, Your Grace."

Appearing suddenly, Urbano joined them again.

"You just mentioned wine?" Exilli said. He took two goblets by their rims from the table behind him. With another courtly, little bow, he presented Luciana and Stefano each with a goblet.

Something about Exilli's gesture made Luciana uneasy. The way his hand hovered over the cups as he took them from the table, perhaps. Without stopping to think, she dropped her goblet and watched it fall. The glass shattered loudly on the marble floor. The burgundy wine sprayed outward. She jumped back, one hand pulling her skirt aside, while quite deliberately knocking the other goblet from Stefano's hand.

Everyone stared at her, at the seeping debris, at the fortune in shattered glass. Luciana touched her hand to her throat and only half-pretended her dismay, startled as she was by her own behavior.

Stefano's eyes narrowed, but he immediately became solicitous and bent to flick droplets from the hem of her gown.

"I fear this will do ruinous things to your gown, my dear," Stefano declared, shaking his head as he stood.

"And it's one of my favorites!" Luciana said. "I must retire and do something about the damage."

"Let us both retire then, Your Grace. You will excuse us?"

There was little for Urbano or Exilli to do but bow and permit them their escape.

Outside the Grand Sala, people flowed between the ballroom and the Clock Walk. Not until they passed the Clock Keeper and entered the residential sections of the palazzo did they have any sense of privacy. Immediately, Stefano slowed their pace, nodding to a lord and lady lingering in the shadows of the hallway.

"Why didn't you tell me Antonio Exilli was here?" Stefano demanded. "He's the most notorious poisoner since the Borgias!"

Luciana gulped as she recognized the name she had tried to place earlier. "He said his name was *Gregorio* Exilli."

"A ruse and a poor one at that. If nothing else, he was introduced to *me* as Antonio Exilli in Morea, and I have every reason to believe he's *not* a pretender to the name."

"What happened?"

"One of our officers died. Poison was suspected," Stefano explained. "The most likely assassin was Exilli, and with his reputation . . ." Stefano shook his head.

"Why wasn't he arrested?" Luciana asked.

"He escaped in the confusion. There were a number of us willing to run him through, but he was away before anyone could act."

"We should tell Alban, then. Perhaps he can do something?"

"Other kings have jailed Exilli, but all eventually let him go, banishing him from their court and country. It's said that he holds some truth over nearly every king. Granting this is not so with Alban, he might still find

himself contending with a neighboring kingdom afraid
of Exilli spilling his secrets. The longer the man is here,
the more danger he is to all around him. Rumor has it
that he could make water into poison, which reminds
me, my dear, would you care to explain what happened
in the Sala? You saved me some quick thinking."

Luciana blushed. "I cannot say that anything happened, just that . . . well . . ." She hesitated, trying to
remember what, if anything, she had seen. "The Rom
are fine ones for sleight of hand . . ."

"Elegantly put. Go on."

Luciana laughed nervously. "It was something in his
gesture, in the way he took the glasses. Forgive me. I–I
didn't think, I just acted."

"You have a good eye for this business," Stefano said,
studying his wife thoughtfully. "If I didn't know better,
and I do, I'd think you were all too familiar with the
ways of poison."

"I *am* an herbalist. At times there isn't much difference between the two, I should think." It occurred to
her that such had been sufficient to condemn her sister.

"Perhaps not so very much as I would have thought
anyway. You were wise. Disturbed as I was to find Exilli
here, it did not occur to me that he could attempt something so impromptu."

"He may not have, though it would be easy enough
to explain—an illness brought from the front and I, in
close proximity, also taken ill. Another death or two
would explain it away."

"And whose death would it be, eh?" Stefano asked.

They were silent a long moment. Stefano pushed open
the door to their rooms, motioning her to precede him
and, then to her private bedchamber upstairs. He sank
onto the sofa by the bed.

"We *should* warn the king," Luciana said, pacing.
"We know he already suspects foul play, but this . . . he
must know."

Stefano nodded. "When did Exilli come to Tyrrhia?
Do you know who brought him here?"

"I have not seen him before this," Luciana said.

"Nor I."

"He must be part of Pierro deMedici's entourage, then."

"Fine mess that." Stefano sighed heavily. "If the king sends Exilli away, he risks insulting deMedici *and* the princess. Alone, the deMedicis are not to be offended, but the complication of Bianca . . ." He rubbed his mustache thoughtfully. "It's a fine mess indeed, and no doubt carefully planned."

"But did they expect to be found out so soon? Or at all? It's not as if everyone can recognize Exilli's face. His name is one thing, but . . ." Luciana shuddered.

"It's a wonder he used his own name," Stefano said, frowning. He lay back on the sofa, extending his feet, crossed at the ankle, on the floor.

Luciana recalled Urbano's confused introduction. "It was a mistake, I think." She ceased her pacing with Stefano's legs in the way. She realized, like a slow-witted fool, it had been months since he had been in her bedchambers. Well, not so very long, he had been here last night. But that was different as she had not been here as well. She was finding it increasingly difficult to concentrate with him here, in her bedchambers. She cleared her throat self-consciously. "I think they thought we would not know Exilli here."

"Overconfidence seems to be a recurring weakness in these conspirators' plans. Perhaps we can make this work in our favor."

Luciana felt unexpectedly warm and flipped her fan open as she sat on the straight-backed chair at her vanity table. "He seemed anxious to tell me that he met you at Morea." Had Stefano been toying with her earlier? Did he toy with her now?

"Did he?" Stefano murmured. He traced the line of his mustache, his hazel eyes half-closed in thought. "What was he thinking, I wonder?"

"I don't know," Luciana said. Her breath felt constricted in her throat. She waved the fan agitatedly.

Stefano sat up, as though suddenly aware of his surroundings. "I'll trouble you no further," he said, rising and moving to the door. "I wish you a good night."

Though reluctant to take a chance and have her heart

broken again, Luciana could not help but call him back. "You . . . you do not have to leave . . . if you do not wish it."

Stefano looked at her, surprise written in his startled smile, but something, some shadow of doubt, darkened his brown eyes. "I would not wish to . . ." He seemed at a loss for words and, at last, said "I would not wish to—to trouble you."

"You are, after all, my husband."

"Yes . . . after all," Stefano repeated quietly.

Luciana folded her fan and stared at her hands. "Much has passed between us."

"Yes," he said sadly, "some of which can never be undone."

His words were like daggers. Still he found fault with her?

"Your letters were few," Stefano said, as though to no one in particular.

"I could say the same," Luciana snapped back. She bit her tongue angrily. She glanced up slightly. His head was leaned against the door. He had not yet gone. Perhaps there was reason to hope? "After a time, I did not think mine would be welcome."

"You thought that?"

"I did."

Stefano shook his head once more. "Why ever would you think that?"

"You were gone to a war at your choosing, your letters were infrequent, businesslike," Luciana shrugged again and kept her face turned so that he could not see the tears forming in her eyes. "What was I to think?"

"War has a way of stealing the poetry from a man's soul, Luciana, and . . ." Though he had not moved, he sounded distant. "After all that happened . . ."

Luciana wrapped her arms around herself, bereft. The only grief that distracted her from Alessandra was that for her son . . . and her marriage. Stefano's hand took hers. She could not look at him.

"I do not mean to make your grief worse. You have more than enough of it now, with your sister."

"My sister?" Luciana stopped struggling to hold back

her tears. "My sister was more my child. She was all my own—even her father could not claim her as much as I."

Hesitantly, Stefano's arms encircled her. He gently pressed her head onto his shoulder. "And to lose her so soon after . . ." He stopped and drew a ragged breath. "I am sorry, Luciana. I would do anything to ease your pain. It is why I returned."

Luciana pulled away, wiping her eyes. "So that you could exact vengeance for me?"

"At least let me do this for you," Stefano said.

"So that you could 'protect me' and send me back to Dragorione? Do I embarrass you that much?"

Stefano looked stricken, pale. "You are no embarrassment to me."

"Mmmph!" Luciana pulled a kerchief from the cuff of her lace sleeve. "I could not even produce a child for you and now I flout your authority over me. It's a wonder you've tolerated me as long as you have." There! She had said it. She took a deep breath and looked up, meeting his gaze and willing her tears to subside.

He stood there, staring at her as though he had lost his wits. After a long pause, he snapped his mouth closed and shifted as though to approach her and, then, turned toward the door. "You think that?"

"What other reason is there? I have failed you on all scores and, now, as I said, I do not behave the way a proper *gadjé* wife would and timidly let you exercise vendetta. How I must shame you, a member of the highest nobility, a member of the King's Palantini, for the Sisters of Fate's sake!"

"I love you now as I loved you from the beginning," Stefano protested.

Luciana could not even look at him now, knowing that he thought she would believe pretty lies. It was beneath both of them. "I'll not leave for Dragorione until I am done here. When I return, if you want, I will—"

Stefano gazed at her and then turned silently on his heel, interrupting her with his silent departure. She stared after him. She put an unsteady hand to her bedpost and grasped at her heart, which felt as though the remnants of it were being torn apart. She sank to the bed and leaned against her arms, unable to stop the deep, racking sobs.

"Luciana?"

She gulped air and rubbed fiercely at her eyes. "It's late, Stefano. Must we continue this now?"

He placed a small wooden chest in front of her on the bed. He pulled a silken cord with a key from beneath his shirt and held it out to her. "If ever there were a way, I would make amends, Lucia. If it gives you comfort, take this, read the contents, and know the truth of my heart."

Luciana studied the key, warm from his body. She touched the beautiful veneer of the box. "What is it?"

"Letters . . . that I did not dare send you, that I had no right to send," Stefano said.

"No right?" Luciana studied him. He was sincere.

The key fit neatly into the lock. She heard the gentle rasp of the mechanism and then slowly lifted the lid. Stefano turned, as though to leave. She caught him by the wrist.

"Stay. Please."

Stefano nodded silently.

Luciana stirred and sighed. It seemed as though a dream that Stefano lay beside her. She rubbed her eyes. Her face felt puffy and swollen from her tears. Despite the deep satisfaction of having her husband here that she might, at her own will, touch or kiss him, something disturbed her contentment, had woken her, she realized.

Stefano groaned and reached for her as she sat up. It felt as though it were a cold winter's night. She pulled the robe of her negligee around her as she pushed aside the bed-curtains to see if the window remained open.

She stopped.

Alessa's filmy form hovered near the bed, beckoning.

Luciana glanced around the room. "Alessa? Can you speak?" she whispered. Slipping out of the bed, she pulled the bed-curtain closed behind her. At last her sister's *mulló* returned and the parcels from her visit to the city remained untouched in the salon below, thus leaving her without her yet-to-be-fashioned tools. She felt like a fool.

The ghost only wept soundlessly and floated backward. Luciana followed her sister's spirit, watching helplessly as Alessa evaporated through the narrow door on the far side of the bed.

Without hesitation, Luciana ran to the entrance of the servants' hallways, which connected the rooms of the palazzo's second floor. She saw tatters of white froth slip around a corner and pursued. Desperate as she was to find the source of her sister's *mulló*, she could not help but pray no one saw her.

On tiptoe, she traced the trail of ghostly wisps, which floated along the passageway and around the chilly, narrow corners like weeds in a river bottom.

The *mulló* moved swiftly, beckoning whenever Luciana got close enough to see a bit of hand or face. The hall seemed full of turns where someone might appear at any moment. As Luciana rounded each, she held her breath and prayed. Each time, she found the corridor empty save for the disappearing spirit.

At last, they rounded the final corner and Alessa seemed to struggle outside of a door, fighting whatever drew her in. She reached for Luciana, her mouth opening in another silent plea. The *mulló* collapsed into the door, insubstantial fingers clawing as if something sucked her into a void.

Luciana hesitated, breathing heavily. A miasma of rancorous magic filled the confined hall. The song of the foul magic flowed just below the level of hearing, taunting her. Someone on the other side of the door worked spells. This was a servants' entrance to a noble's room. Would they notice if she followed Alessa inside? Servants' comings and goings were frequently ignored. Did she dare? But even as she asked herself, Luciana turned the handle and pushed the door open a fraction.

Someone moved in the room beyond. There came the smell of candles and the distinctive scent of mecca bal-

sam burning. Had she any doubts before, she could be
sure now. Mecca balsam was burned to command the
manifestation of spirits.

She glanced around the corridor, trying to figure out
whose room she spied upon. Conte Urbano seemed the
most likely candidate and from what little she could hear
of the spell caster's voice, it seemed male. But even considering the conte's crimes Luciana knew of—robbing
the grave, most notably—she did not want to accuse him
falsely. She needed to be certain whether the conte was
the *chovahano*.

Luciana leaned against the gap, trying to see better.
When she could not, she eased the door a little wider.

The door creaked. Loudly.

She bit her lip and held very still, trying to breathe
softly and control the blinding urge to run as she listened
for a reaction in the room. It came quickly enough. A
man's voice, unmistakable now, called out softly. There
was the sound of scraping and of . . . what? Of wings
beating?

Luciana backed away. Footsteps, soft but steady, approached the door. Cursing her stupidity, she slipped
across the hall and edged around the corner. All of this
would be a waste if she could not identify the *chovahano*. She waited, pressed back against the wall, where
she could see who came from the room.

Conte Urbano pushed the door wide. He muttered his
own curse and made the gesture to break a ward. The
movement of his hands drew her attention. He held a
pistola and the hammer was cocked!

Luciana turned and ran. She did not dare look back
for fear even a brief hesitation would give the conte the
time he needed to spot her. Once in her own rooms, she
turned the key in its lock and fled back to her bed.

She slid beneath the covers and lay shivering for a
long while, listening for footsteps in the hallway beyond
her door. Just when she began to relax, to count herself
lucky, Luciana heard the scraping sound of the door handle being tested. She whispered a prayer to the *Fata* and
gently shook Stefano.

The door creaked as someone applied their weight.

Luciana held her breath and leaned over Stefano to open the bed-curtain nearest the door. A moment more and the handle eased into place. There were footsteps, soft, going away.

Luciana fell back in her bed. Curling into Stefano—as much for protection as warmth—she whispered a prayer of thanksgiving. Her mind raced. Did the conte know whose room this was? How sure was he that his intruder had come from here? Did this mean he was the *chovahano* or only that he worked with the wizard casting the spells as she originally thought? What was she to do?

These were not the sort of thoughts which made sleep come easily, so she spent the time making a list of all she had discovered, even the parts which were of a magical nature. Should the conte ever capture her, there would at least be some record of her discoveries, she thought as she tucked the papers containing her list into her own letter box.

XVIII

"O, that it were possible, we might but hold some two days' conference with the dead!"

—John Webster

14 d'Maggio 1684

LUCIANA watched Stefano as she ate her apricot *torta*. He was distracted and not particularly interested in eating, so different from mornings past when, at the very least, he made an attentive breakfast companion. She wondered what had transpired this morning on his ride with the king.

"You are distracted this morning," she observed quietly.

Stefano breathed heavily, leaning forward. He captured her left hand and kissed it. "Luciana, I know what we discussed last night, but . . ." He hesitated awkwardly, holding her hand to his cheek. "I know how you feel . . . about staying, about everything, but . . ."

Luciana studied him and then gently withdrew her hand. "You still want me to return to Dragorione."

He sighed and nodded, looking up. "You would be safe there."

She stabbed her sausage with her fork. "I'm sorry, Stefano, but I cannot."

"I'm thinking of your safety."

"I know, but perhaps I have gone too far for a retreat."

"What have you done that you cannot make a retreat?"

Luciana almost laughed at the sudden caution in his voice. "There's not much more that has happened than I have told you."

"Which tells me nothing," he said, frowning.

"Stefano, I am the *Araunya* and I am vowed to the *Beluni* to find my sister's murderers and avenge her." She shoved her plate away, no longer particularly hungry.

"Perhaps she will change her mind if—"

"She will *not*," Luciana said sharply. "Even if it were only the debt of honor, it is my responsibility and mine alone."

"If anything happened to you—"

"Retreating to Dragorione would be no guarantee of my safety. The enemy knows that I know them. They could not risk leaving me alive, knowing what I know."

Stefano stared up at the sky, finally nodding. "You probably have the right of it, but you don't have to do this alone."

Tucking her hands into her lap, Luciana looked down at her plate. "She was my sister, an *Araunya*. We owe our first allegiances to different queens."

He looked at her sharply. "Do you think my sister is involved somehow?"

Luciana rolled the fork on the table. "*I* do not believe so, but . . ." She licked her lips. "Idala is not confident of her own innocence."

He stared at Luciana and then looked away, rubbing his mouth thoughtfully. "You don't think she's involved. This does not say what you do believe."

Shaking her head, Luciana turned to meet his gaze. "I–I do not know. She is not well. Have you watched her? She frets and does not sleep. Even Alban is worried, and yet he knows nothing either. Were I to guess," she hesitated.

"Tell me."

"I know that my sister's body is being used most foully with a magic that . . . that should not be toyed with. I have seen my sister—"

"You've seen Alessandra?" Stefano immediately covered his mouth. "You've *seen* your sister?"

"I have, as late as last night," Luciana said.

"Last night?" he asked, shaking his head. "When?"

Luciana blushed and looked down at her hands. "After . . . I was woken." She stroked a nonexistent errant lock back behind her ear. "We were speaking of your sister, Idala. I suspect that she is being haunted, that the *chovahano* is sending my sister's spirit, waking her in the night so that she does not sleep, perhaps at other times as well."

"Can you—"

"I can prove nothing," Luciana said. She took a deep breath. "Your sister has not even taken me fully into her confidence and what little I do know comes from my observations and . . . from my own magic." She took a deep breath. "I know you do not like magic, that I use it, but—"

Stefano raised up his hand. "Do not defend yourself to me. There is no need." He captured her hand. "I cannot say that I like magic. I do not understand it and, even now, see how it can be misused."

"Magic, when it is right, it is a prayer, a song that beats in your heart, its music is another way of seeing or understanding. Do you follow me?" Luciana asked.

"I think I am beginning to see," Stefano nodded. "Is there . . . or will there be a way of proving what you know through magic?"

"I am more interested in justice than appearing before one," Luciana said.

"In truth, what members of the Palantini I have spoken with share the same sentiment. It seems that every which way I turn there is a conspiracy or a conspirator."

"It is a tangle."

"I'll speak with the king."

"Tell him of Exilli to be sure, but know that he is not willing to take bold actions against his cousin or her friends."

"Excuse me, Cousins?"

Luciana turned. Prunella! How long had she been standing at the patio door? "Yes?"

"I was wondering, Your Grace, if you had spoken to my cousin regarding my request?"

"Request?" Stefano looked up. He gestured for Prunella to take the chair opposite him. "We have not had much of a chance to speak of anything in particular."

Luciana leaned back in her chair, watching Prunella sit primly. The girl smiled apologetically at Luciana and turned back to Stefano. "I have asked Her Grace, your wife, to permit Cardinal delle Torre to arrange a marriage for me."

"You did what?" Stefano looked from Prunella to Luciana and back to Prunella again. "Why ever would such a thing be necessary? I suppose, then, with this presumptuous request, that you already have a candidate?"

Prunella sniffed nervously. "No, no, Cousin, I have no candidate, but . . ." She leaned forward. "I am no princess, this I know, but the cardinal is acquainted with families throughout Christendom. I hoped he could find me a suitable marriage."

"You would leave Tyrrhia for a marriage?" Stefano did not hide his surprise.

"I hardly think that will be necessary, but the cardinal leaves for Salerno today, and I wanted to take my case to him before he left."

"Oh?" Luciana edged her chair forward. "I saw the cardinal last night. He did not mention he would be traveling."

Prunella shrugged. "I learned of this after Mass yesterday. Had I known you would be interested . . . I'm sorry, I did not think you would care. I—" She shrugged and sniffed again.

"No criticism intended," Stefano said smoothly. "Just curiosity."

Prunella cheered. "May I speak to the cardinal then?"

Stefano shook his head. "No. Your father gave me this trust. The duchessa has acted in my stead, but now I mean to see to your marriage myself."

"But, Cousin—"

"There will be no need for you to trouble the cardinal." Stefano was decisive.

"Yes, Cousin," Prunella said, staring at her folded hands.

"Now, see here, there is no need to despair," Stefano said cheerily, tossing aside his napkin as he sat back with his cup of chocolate. "So, did you enjoy yourself at the ball?"

Prunella brightened slightly. "I relished every moment."

"You will forgive me for not dancing with you, I hope," he said glancing at Luciana. "There was the unfortunate affair with Her Grace's gown."

"Yes," Prunella said. "I saw. Most unfortunate. Conte Urbano was quite distressed on your account, Your Grace."

"To be sure," Luciana said.

"I have the impression, Your Grace, if I may be permitted?" Prunella asked, hesitating as she rethought.

Luciana nodded.

"It seems you do not particularly care for the conte."

Luciana considered her response, trying to forget the image of her sister's spirit being sucked unwillingly into Conte Urbano's rooms. She licked her lips.

"I'm sure that my wife only has feelings for the conte which are appropriate for a married woman," Stefano said, taking Luciana's hand and squeezing it while turning to Prunella.

"But of course!" Prunella exclaimed, blushing. "forgive me, Your Grace, I did not mean—"

"Yes, I know." Luciana contemplated the younger woman. "You, however, seem to be quite taken with him."

Prunella blushed again and sniffed. "He is quite . . . quite charming and so very handsome."

Luciana and Stefano exchanged glances and turned back to Prunella.

"Does my young cousin fancy the conte a suitable candidate?" Stefano asked.

Prunella fidgeted in her seat. "There are certain qualities which the conte offers that make him an excellent candidate for someone like myself, someone with no fortune, no hope of bettering herself *except* through marriage. I know that I am being particularly brazen bringing my case to you, but I have sisters at home who wish to marry as well and once my course is set, I see no reason to delay."

"Oh? And you think that the conte would be agreeable?" Luciana asked.

Apparently sensing disapproval, Prunella hesitated, sniffing nervously. "Well, you must understand that I am inexperienced in such matters, but it would seem to me to be an advantageous match for us both. The conte's title is a court title inherited from his father. He possesses some wealth but no real property yet, while I am inheritor of my father's rather poor estates. An infusion of wealth would make a considerable difference to the viability of my father's property. As a dowry, I bring land in an area the conte has considered settling in, and there will be more land upon Father's death."

"You sound as if you have given this considerable thought," Luciana said.

Prunella shrugged diffidently.

"Aren't you concerned that he is so much older than you?" Stefano asked.

Luciana glowered, but held her tongue.

"But you're older than Her Grace, Cousin," Prunella countered. "I think it suitable for a man to be older. A man is expected to be wiser and more experienced after all, isn't he?"

Luciana coughed and looked pointedly at her husband. "There is a certain truth to your observations, Prunella, but perhaps His Grace meant that with a marriage between two more close in age or experience, there are certain niceties that one might experience. My husband and I are a few years apart in age, but—"

"Yes," Stefanò said, leaning forward. "Marriage should not be entered into lightly."

"I have no heady aspirations," Prunella said. "I do not expect a love match. I cannot afford such a thing. No, I will be satisfied with a sensible match that will help my father."

"You are nothing, if not dutiful," Stefano said.

"Indeed," Luciana agreed heartily.

"Thank you," Prunella said, obviously pleased. "Will you be speaking to the conte, then?"

"Uh . . ." Stefano paused. "I will consider an appropriate match for you. I have not quite decided that the conte is as ideal a match as you think."

Sniffing, Prunella said quickly, "Forgive my presumption, Cousin. I meant no harm."

"No harm done," Stefano said.

"Then, if I may be excused?"

"Is there no other who draws your attention, Prunella Especially after the ball last night," Luciana asked.

"I think I will leave this matter in the capable hands of your husband, Your Grace, and meddle no further," Prunella said. She turned back to Stefano. "May I be excused?"

"Of course," Stefano said.

"Your Grace, may I attend Mass or will you need me?"

Neatly done, Luciana thought. *She's—at least in her mind—cut my influence from this decision.* Luciana could not work up the energy to be more infuriated than she already was due to the frustration and sense of insult. "Go to Mass," she said quietly. After Prunella had gone, she turned to Stefano. "What do you think?"

"I think I must find someone to distract my young cousin rather quickly. I have no intention of presenting the likes of the conte to her father, especially not after last night. I would rather know where his loyalties lie before I do any such thing with my uncle's trust."

"Her argument was well reasoned," Luciana pointed out ironically.

"Well reasoned or no, I wouldn't consider the man as I know him now," Stefano said, reclining. "The girl is nothing if not intent."

"Indeed. Only yesterday she told me she hoped I would be more helpful, having made such an advantageous marriage myself."

Stefano winced. "My young cousin has a way with words."

"Indeed," Luciana said. "So, what do you think of the news about the cardinal?"

"I find it interesting that he should decide to leave while his victory over devising such an advantageous match for Bianca is so fresh."

"As do I. Truth be told, my curiosity knows no bounds." Luciana wondered what the cardinal planned next, and how to discover it. Such curiosity had gotten Alessandra—and nearly Capitano di Montago—killed.

"Lucia, did you hear me?"

Luciana stirred from her thoughts and turned back to Stefano who watched her impatiently. "I'm sorry. What did you say?"

"I asked if, perhaps, you would forgive a brief absence so soon after we are reunited?"

She blinked, surprised. This *was* soon. Not even a week? Had he already grown tired of her? So soon? She kept her voice light so she would not betray the hurt. "What have you in mind?"

"I think a trip to Salerno to inspect my ventures there is in order. It would be surprising to learn that the cardinal was my companion on the ship, don't you think?"

"Surprising, yes, Stefan, but for whom? No matter the differences between us, I have no desire to become a widow."

"For your sake, then, I'll be careful," Stefano smiled wryly, kissing her hand again. "You have been a most forgiving wife with me always away and, now, here it is again."

"We each have duties which obligate us beyond the bounds of the usual marital expectations." Luciana tried to muster a smile, but could not.

"I promise to take every precaution to avoid inflicting you with such an onerous designation. We have struggled too long to . . ."

Luciana turned away. She did not want him to see her being weak. It made perfect sense. Another officer in the Escalade had no right to challenge or converse with the cardinal outside matters of his faith, but a member of the Palantini was the cardinal's equal. Of all Alban's counselors, Stefano could undoubtedly offer the best excuse to travel to Salerno now. He did, after all, have properties there that needed his inspection. But sense did little to stop her stomach from churning at the thought of Stefano taking such a risk.

"Ah, *cara mia,* do not do that." Stefano spoke softly, regretfully, as he captured her chin. He rose and kissed her on the cheek. "Do not fret, I will be fine."

At the door into the apartments, he turned back. "I will be leaving shortly. I must see the king regarding Exilli, before I go."

———————

Luciana strolled along the garden path, framed on either side by hedges well over her head. She felt no desire to hurry, nor to seek out the company of the courtiers gathering for the garden party and deMedici's presentation. Attendance was not a social necessity, but even still, she was not willing to miss it. No, the players in this little tableau were too much in the thick of things for her to ignore.

It was a gray day after such a sunny morning. Storm clouds gathered overhead. She wondered idly what would become of the princess' party should the heavens unfold, unleashing the threatened rain. She could hear laughter ahead, musicians playing a light ditty. She stopped. The thought of celebrating this union, this potentially fiendish match, made her ill, especially in light of all that had transpired between her and Stefano over the years . . . how they had struggled and sacrificed so much of themselves not just for one another, but for Tyrrhia. *Fata* help her if anything happened to him now that *he* was off again, in service of Tyrrhia!

Luciana lingered, listening to the well wishes of the courtiers. Alessandra had wandered these garden paths not so very long ago. Was this where the capitano overheard the cardinal and Bianca or was it in the deep maze beyond the pleasure gardens? She regretted now not having given more credit to the queen's worries earlier. But just how deep in these conspiracies was Bianca knowingly involved? Did she know of the wizard? Even more interesting, did the cardinal know? Such thoughts

brought no resolutions, so she set them aside and continued on. She paused at the edge of the patio, allowing
herself a final moment to assess the gathering.

Idala sat on a marble bench at the back of the party,
a dainty Venetian glass goblet of white wine in her hand.
She had apparently sent everyone away since even her
ladies in waiting were gathered on the far side of the
patio. Someone called for dancing. Servants scurried to
stay out of the revelers' way as the musicians began a
tune for the courtiers to dance the sarabande.

Luciana looked for, but did not see the imposingly
tall Alban amongst the princess' celebrants. Perhaps that
explained why the queen appeared so quietly forlorn?
In fact, upon closer consideration, she looked tired, and
her pallor proclaimed her uncharacteristic fragility. The
rouge applied to her cheeks in the hopes of hiding whatever ailed her only highlighted the queen's condition.

Quite content to keep Idala company, Luciana left the
hedges and approached. "Good morning, Majesty."

Idala smiled, straightening as she tapped the open
space on the marble bench beside her. She glanced
around expectantly. "Where is Stefano?"

"Stefano has gone to Salerno. He has business there."
Luciana accepted a goblet of wine from a steward.

The queen was quiet, momentarily lost in her own
reverie. "Bianca seems quite pleased."

Luciana glanced to where Bianca and Conte Pierro
led the sarabande. The conte was shorter than his wife-
to-be, despite the height of his heels, but what he lost
in stature, he made up for with a certain elegant flair.
She smiled ruefully. Conte Pierro danced almost as well
as Stefano.

"I'm sorry," Idala said quietly. Her face shadowed.

Luciana did not try to hide her surprise. "Whatever
for?"

Idala flicked an imaginary speck on her skirt. "That
Stefano has not remained. I so hoped—"

Luciana covered her friend's hand with her own. "He
will not be gone long, have no fear. I daresay he'll be
back in a day or two."

The queen nodded, squeezing Luciana's hand lightly.

"It's just that I had such hopes for the two of you. You deserve happiness . . . both of you."

"Stefano and I made our peace," Luciana said quietly, "but the parting was not of our choosing."

"I am heartened by this news, but I am minded that none of your separations have been at your choosing, at least, as I understand it." She sighed. "You deserve children of your own, and I pray that you will eventually fare better than Alban and I. Our fortunes on that score have been enough that over the years several members of the Palantini have suggested an annulment so that Alban might marry another who can give him viable heirs rather than risking the upheaval of the Palantini choosing the next to sit upon the Tyrrhian throne."

Luciana shook her head. "Treason, Majesty. The king loves you and such talk will never amount to more than that." At least, that was what she hoped. This business of conspiracies was dangerous, and the queen was vulnerable.

Idala nodded listlessly. "Isn't that Prunella over there?"

Luciana followed the queen's gesture. Prunella, obviously happy in her austere gray gown, stood with the more finely turned out Lady Ursinia. They had found a bower of early roses into which they tucked themselves and were deep in conversation.

"She seems to be enjoying herself," Idala observed.

Luciana said, "She has most definitely benefited from her social opportunities. It seems that she is quite taken with Conte Urbano."

"Oh, how dreadful!" Idala wrinkled her nose and shuddered.

"She considers herself very practical and even asked Stefano to open negotiations."

"No!" Idala exclaimed. She smiled apologetically at the nearby Escalade officer who turned at her cry. The queen lowered her voice to a whisper. "Tell me you aren't serious!"

"But I am!"

Idala shuddered again. "I've always wondered how Bianca could put up with him hovering about. He's an odious little man, so obtrusive and positively beastly!"

"Of this, I am painfully aware."

"Ohhh, and his poetry!" Idala swallowed hard, grimacing.

"And he finds his little jokes so amusing!"

"You missed this morning's performance," Idala said conspiratorially. "He promised Bianca a ball gown for the wedding reception. It will be of his own design and made of the finest Gypsy Silk! He also, very graciously, offered a matching outfit for Conte Pierro."

"Of course he did," Luciana muttered. "And he made them promise to wear them, too, didn't he?"

"You met him but a few days ago and yet you know him so well."

Luciana groaned. "That, Majesty, is a foul thing to say!"

They fell, once more, into a companionable silence, watching the courtiers dance. A stiff breeze buffeted the party, even protected as they were by the tall, surrounding hedges. Idala shivered. Beneath her pallor, she looked nearly as gray as the morning.

"Idala, are you ill?"

The queen only shook her head. "No, no, of course not. The wind caught me by surprise. I took a chill, that is all."

"Perhaps you should retire and call for the physician."

"But I cannot!" the queen said with a forced laugh. "It would be unseemly for me to leave, especially when Alban did not come. What would people say?"

Luciana made a dismissive noise. "Where *is* His Majesty, for that matter?"

"He thought his presence might be a distraction," Idala said.

"If you won't call the physician, at least let us go inside. You don't look at all well."

"I'm fine. I do *not* need the physician, and retreating indoors will serve no purpose," the queen insisted. She raised her wineglass in salute as the pavanne brought Bianca and her conte near, just on the other side of the overflowing bank of flower beds filled with the riotous colors of spring.

"Are you with child again?" Luciana asked.

The queen looked startled. She smiled slightly and shook her head. "I–I am not sure. But, with my history of miscarriages, we do not want to arouse attention until we can be sure."

"Does the king know?" Luciana asked.

The queen fell quiet. "No, not just yet."

Luciana's excitement stilled. "But surely, *he* has the right to know."

Idala nodded and then looked suddenly shocked. "Of course he has the right! I just do not wish to unduly excite him, not before I am sure."

"Are there problems . . . between you and the king?" Luciana asked.

"No, of course not," Idala said, her voice sharp. "There is nothing wrong."

After a painful silence, Luciana tentatively asked, "Have you been bothered by more visitations?"

The queen blanched. The expression on her face could be described not as surprise, shock, or outrage, but perhaps a bit of each. "What are you implying?"

Luciana watched her, attempting to read her, to understand the source of outrage, even going so far as to capture the queen's hand in an effort to gain some magical sense. Idala exuded an angry energy and, behind it, masked as fury, lay a well of guilt.

"I mean to imply nothing, Majesty. I only ask a simple question."

"Nothing about you is ever simple," the queen replied, but she slowly relaxed. A tear slid down her cheek. "Truly, Luciana, I did everything I could for her. I never believed she would take her own life—or that she was in immediate danger, not even from the Escalade's *Coda*. Not yet, anyway."

"But she had already been condemned by the *Coda*," Luciana said.

"No! Where would you hear such a thing? The results of a trial for the *Coda Condanna a Morte* are kept secret," the queen wept. "If this is so, then it was my fault! The Escalade answers to me. Oh, Luciana!"

Luciana could have bitten her own tongue. "You rush to condemn yourself, Idala."

"Then what is the explanation for my dreams?" Idala demanded. She splayed her fan and used it to hide her tears from the courtiers dancing closest.

"Tell me more about your dreams," Luciana requested.

The queen's head bowed in shame. "Your sister . . . she condemns me nightly. I–I cannot sleep without her coming to me." She shuddered.

"But she would not appear to me night after night if I'd done nothing wrong. I must have made some oversight, something I could have done which I left undone."

"My sister does not haunt you at her own will, Idala. Her spirit is controlled by a wizard," Luciana said firmly, keeping her tone as quiet as she could.

"A wizard like Conte Urbano? Forgive me if I cannot find that plausible," the queen said, her voice tight and dismissive.

"If you cannot believe that, then take greater care of yourself. There are poisoners about."

"My tasters are well, my family is well. I've been excessively careful on that score," Idala insisted.

"But these poisoners can be quite creative—"

"It is *not* poison which troubles me! Oh, that it were!"

"Don't say such things!" Luciana gasped.

Idala sighed and took Luciana's hand. "I'm sorry, I *shouldn't* say such things. You are a dear friend. It is just that . . ." She left off with a hopeless little shrug.

Unwilling to let the subject drop just yet, Luciana opened her mouth to speak, but before she could utter a word, a commotion broke out on the far side of the patio. The musicians brought their tune to a discordant end as they too turned to see what caused the disturbance.

A very young girl, who by all accounts should not have been out in society yet, stood at the center of it all looking frightened and embarrassed. The outrage in the

princess' expression made her temper abundantly clear
to one and all, so it came as no surprise when she bore
down on the girl with the Contes Pierro and Urbano in
her wake.

"Oh, dear! I must do something before this gets out of
hand," Idala said and jumped up, ignoring the wineglass
knocked to the slate-covered patio where it shattered.

Luciana thrust her own glass into the nearest servant's
hands and followed. Nobles gathering about the scene
made way for the queen and Luciana, but by the time
they reached the center of the mishap, the young girl
was in tears. Princess Bianca vented her anger, unchecked by an understanding nature or good graces.
Conte Pierro stood at his future wife's side and appeared
equally enraged. Conte Urbano, on the other hand,
seemed amused.

Behind the girl lay a wreckage of golden latticework,
the shambles of a large gilded cage. One peahen remained inside, trapped in a far corner by the bent bars.
A peacock and two more peahens took flight into the
maze.

Conte Urbano caught the princess' hand. "Pray, Highness, do not be angry with the child."

"She has destroyed it!" Bianca fumed. She looked
back at Conte Urbano. It seemed as if she read something in his eyes. Her mood changed swiftly as she withdrew her hand from his. "It's just that this was a prized
gift," she said to no one in particular.

"I think it's not permanently ruined, Your Highness,"
Luciana said, perusing the wreckage. She bent and freed
the girl's dress from the tangle of bars, drawing her to
one side, out of Bianca's reach. "It seems particularly
fine. Conte Pierro, you chose a skilled artisan to make
this, yes? It is so well-designed that almost any craftsman
might fix it. Isn't it so?" She looked at the conte expectantly, knowing that all eyes turned to him. Would he
dispute her assessment or take the compliment?

The deMedici flinched, but forced a tentative smile to
his   sullen   features.   "The   cage   *was*   specially
designed . . ."

"There, you see, Cousin? All is not lost," Idala said.

"What of the fowl?" Bianca asked sulkily.

Conte Urbano gave her an icy glare. "This serves as a diversion, does it not, Majesty? What a game can be made of bringing the peafowl out of the maze again unharmed!"

"Yes, do see to the hunt and find the birds!" Idala said. She sounded cheerful, but looked unconvinced.

Conte Urbano seized the linen folded over a servant's arm and shook it loose. "Come, there must be more of these! Let us find her Highness' presents!" He waved the cloth near the caged hen which cried out and darted to the other side of the wreckage.

One of the ladies laughed and, without further encouragement, the party broke into groups which disappeared down various corridors of the hedge maze.

Bianca viewed the departing courtiers and let out a sigh. "Do not let it be said that I cannot find my own gifts. If we are to make a contest of this–this—" She waved her hand at the mess before her. She turned to the contes, "Come. I will not lose my own contest!"

Idala let her pent-up breath loose. "That was well done."

Luciana nodded, drawing the unfortunate girl who precipitated the catastrophe before them. Without the confusion caused by royal tantrums, she recognized the girl as the admiring young lady from the ball on the night of her own arrival.

"I'm so dreadfully sorry, Your Majesty, Your Grace." The girl dropped into a deep curtsy.

"None of that," Idala said. "Where is your mother, child?"

Fretting and anxious, the girl rose, twisting her fingers nervously. "Mama stayed abed with a headache, Majesty."

"Perhaps it might be wiser if you were to attend her, then," Idala said.

The girl nodded and started away. "It really was an accident, Majesty. My foot caught on my hem and—"

"What is done is done," Idala said, waving the girl on. "See to your mother."

Luciana surveyed the shambles the patio had become.

Servants gathered dishes while others swept up broken fragments. The musicians scrambled after sheet music dispersed by the wind and trampled upon by their audience.

"It appears that the party is over," she said.

Idala nodded. "What say we take advantage of the moment and walk the gardens? The air would do me good."

"Perhaps, if we walked the perimeters, we might have some time alone. I am ill-fit for company today," Luciana said.

"Then we are of a mood." Idala looped her arm through Luciana's as they came to a secluded path, closer to the palazzo and one of the more uncomplicated tangles of the hedge maze. "I'm most astonished by Conte Urbano's performance just now. Who would have thought he would settle a crisis instead of encouraging one?"

"Conte Urbano seems to have a strong effect upon the princess for being such a minor noble," Luciana said quietly. She glanced about, remembering that Capitano Mandero had overheard much in the garden only a few short weeks ago. "This isn't the first time I've noticed it either."

"I'm prepared to forgive the man almost anything for handling this matter so masterfully—anything but his poetry, that is. I would never have been able to handle the situation so well."

"You underestimate yourself, Idala," Luciana said.

For a brief moment, the queen looked stricken, but she hid it behind a soft laugh. "No, Luciana, never that." She hugged Luciana's arm closer. "What a dreadful end to a garden party! While the party *was* made in haste, I've never had such an abysmal failure before."

"I suggest that perhaps it was not so much the hostess' failure as that of the guests of honor."

"As usual, you are kind," Idala said. She released Luciana's arm then and moved ahead. "I really don't deserve such a good friend as you."

"Don't be silly," Luciana laughed. When the queen did not join her, she frowned. The queen was not normally so self-contained, beyond even what good manners called for. Other clues also hinted something was amiss, her pallor, her mood. "Idala, is there more you're not telling me?"

The queen shook her head. "Perhaps I'm only imagining things. I've never been as clever as you, but I am no fool. Nonetheless, I still cannot concentrate. I think my head must be quite empty at times."

"It's your troubled sleep, Majesty. No one is in top form when they cannot sleep," Luciana said.

"No, it's more than that. It's—"

They turned the hedgerow corner only to stumble upon one of the missing peafowl which let out a cry so loud and so human sounding that both women jumped back. The queen screamed and fell backward into the hedges, hand clasped to her throat, looking even more frail than before.

Luciana gave a nervous little laugh as the peacock took flight. "It was only one of the birds! We probably frightened it more than it frightened us."

Looking decidedly on edge, the queen tried to manage a smile and failed. "I somehow doubt that." She sank to the ground and bowed her head to her knees.

Concerned, Luciana knelt beside her friend and took her hand. She waved a warning at the Escalade vigilare who came to the queen's aid.

"Are you well, Majesty?" the senior officer asked.

The queen nodded.

"Perhaps you should take her to her rooms," Luciana said, helping the queen to stand. "I'll fetch the physician myself and be with you—"

The queen clasped Luciana's hand and leaned heavily upon the guard. "No need for the physician—"

"I shall take as much heed as you took of me the other day," Luciana said.

"Let one of my ladies do that, then. Please, Luciana? Stay. Enjoy what is left of the sun before the rain comes. Find Bianca's damnable birds." When she hesitated, the queen squeezed her hand almost to the point of hurting. "As a favor? To me?"

Luciana bowed. "As you wish, Majesty." Frowning in

contemplation, she watched her sister-in-law be gently escorted away. Whatever distressed the queen, someone must get to the bottom of it. She thought again of the physician, wondering if he could help if the queen were being poisoned.

Still troubled by her thoughts, Luciana went in search of the peacock she and the queen had discovered only moments before. She returned to the end of the hedge-row, where the maze took several turns. Of all the paths, the cobblestone walk, with its mossy crevices, betrayed no evidence of having been disturbed by the truant birds. The hedges grew close together so that one could not see between them, their branches mingling and grown over, in places, by lazy vines of ivy. A bird might be able to squeeze beneath the hedges, but even a child most certainly could not.

A most irritating situation. Luciana sat on the marble bench in the tiny juncture yard trying to decide if she would even bother to look for the fowl. She only considered it now because Idala asked. It was not much more than a goose chase and better left to the capable hands of the gardeners who knew the maze well.

At a distance, she heard the cry of another peafowl and the laughter of courtiers. Apparently, someone had good luck. As the first drop of rain fell, Luciana resolved to return to her rooms. Accounts from the various silk houses needed review, and she had yet to make all the inquiries about Alessa she intended.

But as she rose from the bench, she heard the grating of metal on metal as though a heavy iron gate opened or closed. This seemed particularly odd, considering the walls of the maze were hedgerows and ivy. She had never seen gates or stone walls in the labyrinth. When she listened carefully, she heard whispering. Though the content was lost, the situation intrigued her.

Taking care to walk softly on the cobblestones, Luciana crept closer to the hedge. The voices were still indistinct, but she knew she had not misheard. Someone spoke conspiratorially to companions. Of course, it could merely be courtiers dallying, but considering the fruit born of previously overheard conversations in this garden, Luciana knew she must investigate.

She tried to peer through the bushes but found the effort futile. Intent upon easing her curiosity, she chose to damn the rain that had begun to fall. Luciana knelt on the cobblestones again, completely disregarding the disastrous effect the muddied water would have on her moss-green-and-black silk gown.

With her face pressed into the bush bed, she just made out the shoes of two men and a woman, though the woman stood back. They congregated before an open gate, covered in ivy for the most part. Even here, though, Luciana could not make out what they said. The surreptitious whispers, the hidden gate, the probable confreres seemed suspicious. Luciana tried to remember all of the turns of the maze, to figure where this gate must be.

There was a squeal and a laugh and the sound of running feet coming closer. Frustrated, Luciana scrambled off the ground. Better not be caught spying or in such an awkward position that would raise questions. She brushed the worst of the gravelly water off as she hurried along the path to keep just ahead of the other revelers returning to the palazzo.

Luciana paused on the patio. A throng of courtiers ran toward her to get out of the rain, but the princess and her contes were not among them. Their party was of the right size and makeup. Considering her suspicions of Conte Urbano, Luciana grew steadily more certain that it had been them in the maze.

She turned that concept over in her mind. So it seemed that the princess was truly involved in this matter of espionage. Luciana shook her head. While she did not like the young woman, she had hoped to disprove Capitano di Montago's suspicions. It did not seem particularly possible to prove the princess innocent at this point. And now, another facet had been added to the mystery. Where did this gate lead and why would the princess and her confederates use it?

XIX

"With foxes we must play the fox."
—Thomas Fuller

THE ship creaked and rolled. Stefano braced himself and watched the door to the cabin where the cardinal took his afternoon repose. Della Guelfa stirred at his elbow.

"Will he come out, do you think?" della Guelfa asked.

Stefano shrugged and looked over the dense blue waters of the Stretto d'Messina. "He will choose his time."

Della Guelfa nodded and turned away from the sea, shuddering. "I'd hoped to avoid this trip again for some time yet. The last time, I thought I had lost my dearest friend and senior officer."

"Mind yourself now. No one yet knows he lives. If not for the duchessa, even I would not have known," Stefano said, glancing at the others on shipboard. One of the other Escalade officers, seeing Stefano look in his direction, set his cards aside and, hand on saber, started to rise, but relaxed again when the duca shook his head.

"Do *you* believe that the cardinal is involved in this treason?" della Guelfa asked.

"What has di Montago told you?" Stefano asked, shifting anxiously. He leaned against the railing of the ship, but even as he did, della Guelfa tugged at his sleeve and motioned to the seats built into the capitano's cabin.

"Mandero told us nothing then, only that we made the trip to Salerno with the cardinal," della Guelfa said. He adjusted the gloves in his belt, straightening his coat, seemingly uncomfortable in civilian clothing.

"What has he told you since?"

Della Guelfa stirred uneasily. "I am sworn to secrecy, Your Grace."

"Of course, of course," Stefano said. "But keep in mind, della Guelfa, that you are now acting as his agent and there may come a time when that information should be offered."

His companion nodded, then his dark eyes narrowed and he motioned with his head to the cabin door.

Stefano followed his gaze and saw the cardinal bend his tall frame to exit the cabin. A young priest followed, looking worried and attentive. The senior ecclesiast straightened and adjusted his wine-colored robes, taking in long, gulping breaths of sea air. He looked ill. Stefano rose and approached.

"Good day, Your Eminence!"

The cardinal turned and looked even sicker. "Your Grace."

The younger priest bowed to Stefano and moved quietly behind the cardinal.

"You do not look well, Your Eminence. Did your dinner not settle?" Stefano asked.

The cardinal looked cornered and queasy. "I did not take a repast," he said slowly.

"Oh? Forgive me! I did not realize you were a poor traveler! The sea does not suit all and the Stretto, with its rough waters, even less."

"Truer words were never said," the cardinal agreed. "Aside from the Gospel of Our Lord."

"Of course," Stefano said, with a little bow. He nodded to the other priest who smiled tentatively, but remained silent.

The cardinal staggered to the hatch, waving off the attentions of the other priest, and sank down, adjusting his skullcap automatically as the wind ruffled through his thin, graying hair. "I'm surprised to see you, Your Grace. You've just returned from the Morean front, haven't you?"

Stefano bowed. "I'm honored, Your Eminence, that you've taken sufficient interest to notice the doings of a humble Protestant such as myself."

"I consider all within Palazzo Auroea my flock, for all

are potential Catholics if they will but consider the true
faith," the cardinal said, his hand falling to his stomach
as he shifted uncomfortably. He looked pitiful and miserable sitting there being buffeted by the winds of the
Stretto.

"I am, nonetheless, honored by your attention," Stefano said.

The cardinal looked discomfited. "Do you go to
Salerno?"

Stefano's brows rose, but he otherwise hid his surprise
behind a pleasant smile. "I've matters to attend to."
Since overboldness was to be so acceptable, he asked,
"And what takes you away from court on this abominable trip across the Stretto?"

"I go to . . ." The cardinal hesitated. "I join a Council
in Salerno."

"You'll return to preside over the princess' marriage,
of course?" Stefano said.

"That is my plan," the cardinal said. "You must forgive me, Your Grace, but I am feeling unwell and must
lie down." The cardinal rose unsteadily, accepting the
aid of the younger priest.

"But of course," Stefano said with a bow.

The two priests retired to the cardinal's cabin, leaving
the deck to Stefano and the other passengers. It was
entirely possible that the cardinal's trip was an innocent
one of duty to the Church, Stefano thought, but it came
so unexpectedly. He shrugged. Time enough to consider
such things later.

The streets of Salerno were busy, brimming with the
press of people going about their business, even here on
the docks. Stefano watched from shipboard as the
crowds fell back, making way for the holy men in clerical
black as they arrived to meet the ship berthed on the
eastern shores of the Stretto d'Messina. Here the influence of Rome was much stronger, as it had always been.

From the prow, Stefano and della Guelfa had an ea-
gle's view of the cardinal's slow departure from the ship.

He moved with the aid of his attendant down the gang-plank and was settled into a sedan chair. Passersby called out to the purple-robed figure for blessings, reaching toward him even as his entourage began to make its way down the street.

Della Guelfa shook his head. "They wouldn't do that in Citteauroea."

"No, I don't think they would," Stefano agreed. "They are probably going to the abbey, but follow them and be sure."

"As you say," della Guelfa said with a quick salute. "I'll take de Mari with me. We'll separate and take turns so that we won't be noticed."

"Of course," Stefano said.

Della Guelfa rose and gestured to the men as he left Stefano.

Stefano watched them leave before returning to his cabin and preparing for his own departure. Until he heard from the men from the Escalade, he would keep himself busy.

With the rain still beating upon the windows in an almost hypnotic rhythm, Luciana relaxed, finally feeling warm and dry. She had sent the girls away, assigning chores to Prunella in the hopes that keeping her busy would dissuade her from snooping. Nicobar was long since gone on the charitable errand of delivering a bottle of brandy to the gardeners. He would, of course, take the opportunity to make some subtle inquiries about the maze.

Content for the moment, she took a packet of letters from the ornate box on her dresser and untied the pale blue ribbon. The letters were already worn and fragile from many readings. She selected a letter at random. Smoothing the pages flat with loving hands, she read her sister's words.

. . . I never said the words of love, though I am confident he knew my feelings. That he should

*come to such a violent end without those words
grieves me, Luciana, and now you are the
only witness to my love. How foolish we lovers
are! We believe there is so much time—an
eternity—but who counts on such a short season?
I am robbed and afraid even while a part of
me yearns to join my Mandero in death as we
were unable to be in life. The Sisters Fata
know my heart, and I pray that they will help
me through this.*

Luciana turned the page and skimmed ahead.

*At court, I was accused of poisoning my
Mandero! I cannot believe they would say this
of me! While I consider steel plunged through
the back particularly toxic—and this is what
the cards tell me—I would not consider it a
poison, nor did I wield the knife.*

"Luciana."

At first, she thought it nothing more than an illusion
created by the gentle but steady sound of rain. She set
the letters on the bureau, only now aware of the cold-
ness in the room.

"Luciana." The voice was thready, but unmistakably
Alessa's. The candles on the altar bloomed mysteriously
to life, the flames dancing in the gentle gusts of cold cast
off like a cape by the spirit.

"My Mandero. Where is my Mandero?" The ghost
wrung its hands as the wisps of her burial cloth floated
around her. She was bathed in white with no color
about her.

Luciana rose from her chair, fingering the sachet of
lavender, selago, and burned mecca balsam around her
neck. The summoning charm worked!

"Luciana!" The *mulló* floated back, maintaining the
distance between them. "Where is my Mandero?"

"Mandero lives, Alessa."

The ghost let out a groan. "My Mandero is dead . . .
I surrendered to death to be with him."

"He lives, Alessa. I have seen him."

The ghost covered her face and her shoulders shook. She looked up, her face showing her torment. "Free me, Luciana. Free me from this slavery!"

"But . . ." Though she had not intentionally commanded this ghost into being, Luciana could feel the drain on her own energy as it wavered over the rug, between bed and altar, and slowly began to fade.

"My death was for naught, Luciana!"

Luciana reached to touch the *mulló,* troubled by her sister's pain even after death. That anyone could be so utterly depraved as to torment a soul sickened Luciana. They cast the foulest of magicks, meddling with the dead and involving themselves with the *marimé.* Even she was tainted by these visitations from Alessandra. How could the *chovahano* continue this? These conspirators, clearly, were not going to stop at even the most obscene acts to gain the throne.

"You must protect yourself!" the ghost bade her, fading toward the wall.

She followed the wraith, watching curiously as it seeped into a previously unnoticed crack between the stones. The *mulló* was gone. The candles on the altar flickered and died. Luciana touched the wall, running her fingers along the crevice where her sister disappeared, then paused as her fingers brushed against an irregularity in the cold stone. She leaned forward for a closer look, but the shadows hid the groove just so. She saw nothing unusual.

Luciana studied the wall, noting the odd stone situated beside the pawing left hoof of the unicorn featured in the wall tapestry. She took a candle from the altar and relit it, protecting its flame as she brought it to the wall. It took a moment, despite having marked the spot, to find the irregularity again. Leaning close, she pressed the candle to the wall, mindful of the tapestry, and watched as the candle flame blew away from the wall, then extinguished.

Luciana repeated the process, only to have it doused again—except this time she observed that the flame was put out by a breeze coming *from* the wall. She set the candle on her bed stand and poked at the fault in the stone with her fingers, feeling along the edges. She pressed on a lump barely detectable with her fingertips, only to leap back when the wall rumbled and began to move.

The wall did not shift far, creating only a recess. A shaft of darkness stabbed between the stones. It seemed to beckon her, inviting her into some unknown intrigue. Her curiosity could not be contained. Luciana pressed the wall and felt it swing away on unseen hinges to reveal only more blackness with the light cast from her bedchamber's candles making only the slightest impression. She took the lantern from beside her bed and lit the candle inside it. With lantern raised high, she peered once more into the dark.

The shadowy grotto turned into a corridor leading away from her chambers. Luciana entered, stepping gingerly on the dusty filth that covered the floor and muffled her footsteps. She shuddered, unwilling to look down for a closer inspection. She studied the door carefully and found that, on this side, a handle triggered the latch easily. Gathering her courage, she pushed the wall almost into place.

In the flickering light cast by her lantern, Luciana could see only one way to proceed. Two bare walls, the latched wall and an open, albeit narrow, corridor stretched before her. Cobwebs covered the low ceiling and every other surface. The corridor was silent except for the sound of Luciana's breath and the scuttles and squeaks of rats echoing off the stone.

Luciana raised the lantern higher and squinted ahead in the gloom, then behind. She took a deep breath and edged down the walkway, raising her skirt with her free hand as her foot splashed into a puddle. Seeing a mossy run of water along the walls collecting in little pools on the floor comforted her. The source of her soaking feet could have been something far more unpleasant and did not bear further consideration.

Puddles spread out tendrils like a watery cobweb on the floor. Luciana steadied herself. She found a set of stairs, shallow and slippery with moss. Without railings to secure her progress, she braced herself on the water-slick wall and forged ahead.

It seemed to take quite some time before she came to a corner. She held the lantern out into the passageway. Again, only one way to proceed, unless she wanted to turn back, but she had already come so far. She continued, around the corner and down the long corridor stretching before her. Not much farther, she came to a deep shadow on the right wall. Shining the lantern close, she found a wooden door, damp and crusted with moss.

Luciana's fingers felt cold and numb as she touched the stiletto tucked into her sleeve. She pressed her ear against the door and listened. She heard nothing, except for the dripping water in the corridor and the faint echo of her own breathing. She tried the latch, but the door did not budge. Automatically, she touched her hair and dress, making herself presentable before trying the door again. Locked! Her curiosity got the better of her so she knocked.

Footsteps, the shush of tapestries, the grating of a key and the creak of the door. Light from the room beyond silhouetted the man who now stood before her, a pistola aimed straight at her heart. Luciana gasped as he pushed the door wider so that in the improved light she saw the king.

She backed away. "Your Majesty, forgive me!"

Alban considered her with a certain fascination, then, looking over her shoulder, beckoned her into the room. He took her lantern and set it beside his pistola on a rather large bulky table. With his arms crossed over his chest, he leaned against the desk. "Would you care to explain how you found this passageway, Your Grace, and then how you came to use it?"

Luciana glanced around the room. It was smaller than the king's office and, undecorated, bore the touch of a man's hand. Maps papered the otherwise unadorned plaster walls. The smooth wooden floor, bare of rug or tile, was scuffed and scarred by pacing feet and haphazardly arranged furniture. Only a single narrow window, an archer's portal, opened to the elements.

"Your Grace?"

Luciana paused and then slowly sank into the indicated chair. "Forgive me, Majesty, I . . ." She shrugged, blushing under his stern gaze.

"Will you not tell me how you came to find the passageway?"

"I saw my sister's spirit—"

"Your sister's spirit? You mean her ghost?" Alban asked sharply.

"Y–yes, she disappeared into the wall. When I inspected it—the wall, I mean—I found a latch to a secret door and, well, I followed the passage here."

"Really?" Alban said. "Weren't you afraid?"

Luciana paused in dusting cobwebs from her skirt, feeling suddenly foolish. "Well, no, Majesty, it didn't occur to me to be afraid."

"I thought ghosts naturally disappeared into walls," the king said.

"Is there anything natural about a ghost?" Luciana asked. "No *mulló*—" She paused and smiled awkwardly. "No *ghost* walks of its own will. Something brings it back to the living and it's rarely a good cause."

"Ah, I see," the king said quietly.

"Does she still trouble you at night?"

"I must confess that, indeed, my rest is troubled by her visits," the king said. He frowned, considering her a long moment. "Is anyone else—besides you and me—likewise troubled? I blamed her visits upon my own guilt in failing to protect her here in my court, but why would she haunt you?"

Luciana chose to ignore the last question, it would be too difficult to explain. "What of the queen? Has she seen anything the past few nights?" She knew the answer, of course, but she wanted to know what the king knew.

"She hasn't mentioned it."

"No?" Luciana said. "She has spoken of it to me, but there's more. Did Stefano speak to you about the poisoner, Exilli?"

The king nodded. "But we have taken such precautions that we feel quite safe."

"You must never relax your guard around one such as he. It could literally be your death!" Luciana exclaimed.

"We have the matter well in hand, Your Grace," the king assured her.

Luciana sighed. The king seemed all too confident and that troubled her almost more than Exilli's presence. Confidence often led to a miserable end. It appeared that it would be left to her to make sure that the king's efforts were sufficient. "What about the queen, Majesty? She's out of sorts—not herself."

"Isn't that to be expected? What with the death of her charge? And someone so important to her personally and politically?" Alban asked. "If there is anything that can be done, then, by God, let us do it!"

"Something *is* being done, but against Her Majesty. I believe Conte Urbano uses magic to intensify her distress. She has told me of unsettling dreams, and there have been hints of other things to trouble her. In her weakened state, I am concerned for her well-being."

"Are you saying that Idala is mad?" Alban ground out.

"No, Majesty, but I fear that between the dreams and whatever else is being done to her, she is being toyed with and it is affecting her constitution. She has trouble concentrating, difficulty using her full faculties . . ."

The king nodded grimly. "What more have you learned about these conspiracies since we last spoke?"

"Very little, I'm afraid. I know Conte Urbano purchased certain goods in the city that would be needed to enslave my sister's soul. I confirmed that my sister was *not* killed because of the Escalade's *Coda Condanna a Morte* and heard testimony that Princess Bianca plans to lay claim to your throne. This deMedici marriage is but another step toward that goal."

"Another?" the king scoffed. "Bianca has made no secret since the day I was crowned that she should hold the throne. The Palantini would not hear of it then and will not hear of it in the future. She was deemed too unstable after her kidnapping by the Turks."

"But what if you and your heir are done away with?

Couldn't she lay claim, especially with a deMedici at her side?"

"DeMedici, for all his Italian blood, is a Gascon now, a Frenchman. I knew the Palantini would not stand for it. I knew that the cardinal thought differently. If anything, her marrying the deMedici only strengthens my hold on the throne. Their conspiracies are troublesome, but beyond this marriage matter, Bianca hasn't the nerve to try anything else. DeMedici and the cardinal may toy with the idea, but no, they cannot risk the Palantini's reaction."

"But if you are dead, what good will the Palantini be able to accomplish? You have no suitable heir—Dario, when he is older, and there will eventually be wards. What, until then, protects Tyrrhia from them?"

"There is always you, Your Grace." The king paused, studying her. "All these petty conspiracies are an annoyance, but I do not see any real threat to my kingdom. More troubling is that I must always consider that you have sworn vendetta against one of my courtiers." He paused again, rubbing the bridge of his nose. "You are the wife of my dearest friend and brother-in-law and, almost more importantly, your position with the Gypsies and the silk trade cannot be overlooked. You're well-situated to be forgiven, but there would be a hue and cry nonetheless. While you have my every sympathy and I can fully appreciate why you have sworn vendetta, I cannot be seen as showing too much favoritism on your behalf, and so the sword of justice cuts both ways."

Luciana kept still. She could offer no honest comfort to the king and had no intention of placating him with lies. The silence spread between them like a pall. "What of Conte Urbano and what he does with his magic to your queen?"

"If Conte Urbano is really a wizard, if he does the things you claim, tormenting my wife, then there will be a reckoning. It will be a simple matter of who gets to him first, you or I," Alban said. He sighed and nodded toward the door through which she had arrived. "Now, as to the passageway . . . you say you followed your sister? But surely she wouldn't use the secret door."

Luciana waved dismissively. "I found the catch to the door by happenstance. My curiosity brought me the rest of the way."

"Most respectable women would not have made such an exploration alone." A grin briefly lit the king's dark features.

"Respectability is a pretense. With my bloodline, I don't feel as obliged as most of my peers to observe pretty pretenses."

Alban laughed.

"Were my character stronger, perhaps I would not be so free with my speech. Certainly my husband counsels me against it."

"I've found, to be a good king, one chooses one's arguments carefully. I hope that you will not be offended by my reluctance to argue against your husband's counsel?"

Again, there was nothing to be said in response to the king. Luciana turned her focus to the room again, her curiosity continuing to get the better of her. "I do not know this place."

"It is a secret office, a war room, whatever the need be. For me it is a retreat."

Luciana rose. "I–I am terribly sorry for intruding."

The king waved her to her seat again. "No, you are here. Your entrance was a timely one, though it gave me a turn. I was not aware that others knew of the passages."

"It leads to my bedroom . . ." Luciana could not refrain from at least hinting at the question nagging at her.

"Your room has been traditionally kept for the king's mistress so that his visits to his *amante* could be discreet."

Luciana blushed, half-rising from her chair.

"Please, Your Grace!" The king laughed, motioning her back to her chair. "You were given the room because it is a particularly spacious one, a place of honor for a cherished friend. I would not presume on our friendship or forget our marriages. That corridor has long gone unused and I have every intention that it remain so."

"Thank you for setting my mind at ease. I did not mean to suggest that . . ."

"But even you have your standards of respectability, pretty pretenses or no," Alban finished for her.

"Quite right," Luciana agreed. She hesitated, reflecting over their discussion. "Majesty, you cannot take this poisoner too lightly. He is dangerous."

The king waved a dismissive hand. "All the families of the continent meddle with that particular cancer—especially the deMedicis and especially those from Gascony. Why *wouldn't* there be a poisoner in the lot?"

"The one they call 'Exilli' is the one. Be mindful of him, Majesty, he has a way about him that I would not trust. I would hesitate to let him touch my dog lest I die before midnight."

"Could it be that, with your sister's death and the intrigues you've already found, you overestimate this man's abilities?"

"I fear, that, if anything, I underestimate him. Stefano has encountered him at the Morean front and found him to be quite treacherous. I think he even attempted to poison us."

The king turned his full attention upon her. "Your husband was equally insistent. I will keep your counsel well in mind should I have anything to do with him." Alban sighed heavily, nodding. "I will do as you say. It means little change, but what have you told my wife?"

"As yet, I have told her nothing, but—"

"Let me address this matter with Idala. I'll take appropriate steps to protect her. As to this Exilli, I cannot act without the risk of offending my future cousin. Now is a particularly delicate time. Once Bianca is married to deMedici, as Catholics, it is not easily undone, especially with the Church arranging the marriage."

"I understand. Have no fear, Majesty," Luciana said. "I remain always at your service and Stefano shouldn't be away long, perhaps a fortnight at most. Business matters demand his attention on the mainland."

"Can you get word to him?"

Luciana nodded, frowning. "But you spoke with him only this morning, before he left, did you not?"

"I did," the king said, "however, I've since learned that Bianca and deMedici want to move up the wedding date. If Stefano is to be in attendance, he will need to return within a week."

"So soon?" Luciana murmured. "Did they give reason for this unnatural haste?"

"I do not doubt Bianca's virtue in this nuptial matter, but I rather suspect her fear of being confined has encouraged her to make this a speedy wedding rather than one with all the pomp and circumstance she would normally prefer."

"Confined? But she is hardly *confined* even though you ordered her to stay in quarters. She regularly attends court functions."

"Ah, but you are not Bianca, Your Grace, and you did not undergo the disaster of being kidnapped and kept in a seraglio while waiting to be ransomed."

"And she was at a most delicate age," Luciana agreed thoughtfully. She could almost feel sorry for the princess until she thought of Alessandra.

"In either regard, my wife will be much comforted to have her brother at the wedding."

"Of course," Luciana said. She rose and peered around her. Two doors, both of them hidden. She hesitated. "Which way should I leave?"

"You will forgive me, I hope, if I suggest you return the way you came?" Alban rose and swung the half-open door wide for her, following her into the corridor. His nose wrinkled. "I know the walk will not be pleasant, but I fear we could not explain how you came to pass the ever vigilant Estensi's office unnoticed."

Luciana pointed to the other door. "This leads to your office?"

"The public one, yes."

"And the rest of the corridor?"

The king grinned. "You are as inquisitive as a cat, my friend. See that it doesn't get you hurt."

"A warning?"

Alban chuckled, appearing as though he had not a care in the world. "I wouldn't make that mistake! It would be an enticement."

"You've been speaking to my husband again, I fear."

Alban laughed again. "These passages spread throughout the palazzo. I'm told that they even lead to catacombs beneath us, but I have never explored myself. Disuse has led to disrepair in some of these passages. I doubt any of it is safe."

"As you say, then," Luciana said. "I'll make my way to my room and hope that my absence has gone unnoticed."

The king frowned. "I fear the state of your dress will belie most explanations."

Luciana looked down. The natural sway of the fabric in her gown prevented her from making a proper inspection, but the cobwebs . . . She shuddered. "Yes, I see." She accepted her lantern from the king. "Forgive the intrusion."

Alban bowed with a flourish. "There is nothing to forgive." He paused, his hand on the door. "Do you wish an escort back?"

"It isn't necessary," Luciana assured him.

———————

Coming out of the hidden passage, Luciana startled Kisaiya who was laying out a dress. The girl took one look at her mistress and locked the outer door. "No need for Prunella to see you like this," she said, wrinkling her nose at the gown. "You are such a mess!"

Luciana smiled ruefully and turned her back to Kisaiya who immediately began to unlace her bodice.

Kisaiya clicked her tongue, "Oh, and your hair, *Daiya,* your hair! We will have a devil of a time getting you ready for the queen's dinner."

"Dinner?"

"Yes, your invitation arrived while you were . . . out."

XX

*"We have left undone those things which we ought
to have done; and we have done those things which
we ought not to have done."*
—Book of Common Prayer

STEFANO brooded over his *stufato,* pushing disinterestedly at the bits of dried bread floating in the vegetable-laden broth with his spoon. He had left his lonely residence and come to Salerno's main garrison, but della Guelfa and the others had not yet returned. He looked up at the sound of a bowl scraping across the tabletop.

A grizzled old fellow sat down and sighed while scratching his chin. He looked at his stufato and then up at Stefano.

Stefano squinted at the man then sat forward with a laugh, offering the man his hand. "Alberti! How long has it been?"

The old man grinned, showing several missing teeth. He took Stefano's hand with a strong grip. "I hear you've been at the wars." He pushed his bowl away and leaned forward intently. "It's been a long time since I've seen a battlefield, my boy. Too long. I'm too old for a soldier." He made a disgusted sound. "The colonel talks of retiring me from even teaching the saber to the young pups who imagine they could be the queen's men."

"You're still spry. Have no fear, Alberti, you'll yet die with a blade in your hands."

"Better through my ribs, make it quick. This old age is tiresome." He grunted and scratched his gray beard. "Take my advice and never grow old."

Stefano laughed. "I, unlike you, have a wife."

Alberti made another ugly noise. "I had one of those once. How do you suppose I came to be so old? The harridan . . ."

Stefano grinned and poured the old sword master a cup of wine. "I'm glad you found me. I'd intended to search you out. Let us talk of other things first. Do you remember saying that my classical education was wasted?"

Alberti scratched an old burn mark on his left cheek, testament of a cannon barrel and sparked powder. "To a soldier it is, I suppose."

Stefano grinned. "Not so." He sat back in his chair, relishing the moment. "In Morea, I was on a reconnaissance mission late one night—a little change from my diplomatic duties—and wandered near the old Argos. I bumped into some Turks."

Alberti hunkered down and grinned. "Tell me the story, boy," he urged, taking a quick drink from his cup.

"Well, I knew there was a ruin a short distance away, so I ordered my escort to ride for it."

"What of your horses? There's no battle another day if you can't retreat."

"True enough, but I knew there was a ramp under the gate, marked by headless lions, so we wouldn't lose the horses. I knew that from my reading, too," Stefano said with a grin. He paused to refresh their cups. "We lured the Turks into the walls, such as they were."

"And . . .?"

"We broke their first charge with our pistols, and when they gathered at the base of the hill, we took out our new muskatoons. We loaded them with tight ball and waited for the Turks' return.

"Soon enough they rushed, but our muskatoons discouraged them. All we had to do was wait. I knew Frandisburg's company of dragoons would arrive soon, but would it be soon enough?" Stefano took a swallow of his wine. "Twice more the Turks charged. We were in real trouble. Then the White Caps of the Jannisaries appeared, and the fire thickened. I thought we might not make it.

"I knew our muskatoons wouldn't be enough to stop them. They were good shots and, in from cover, they were hard to hit. They closed on us and the gate. We were pistol and sword to their scimitar and clubbed muskets. When we heard the trumpets of Frandisburg's dragoons, the White Caps ran to the base of the hill. The Turks covered their retreat, but we left six of the Jannisaries dead on the ramp."

"Well," said Alberti, taking a long draft, "you didn't read all your classics."

"What do you mean?"

"Just like Marcellus and Crispinus, you didn't take enough escort which, if you recall, got Marcellus killed and Crispinus a wound that finally did him dead."

"But had I not known my classics, I would not have known that I was near Golden Mycenae and used the old stones for a *modrun de fange*. I lived and they died, so all is well," Stefano said.

"A scout is an alert private soldier. Armies recruit them by the hundred," Alberti said with a shrug. "You don't think the Turks wouldn't like to do to you what they did to Birchario? Stuffed with hay like a horse? Besides, I said that a classical education would fill your head with idiot ideas like short swords, open pikes, like that overeducated Florentine, Machiavelli."

"We have much to learn from the ancients," Stefano said. He rubbed his nose. "I thought you didn't have time for reading the classics, Alberti."

"Strategy. The old war dog *has* to learn new tricks," the old man retorted, banging his cup on the table. "Now—"

"Your Grace!"

Stefano looked up to see della Guelfa and di Mari. Stefano waved them to the table. "Well? What did you learn?"

Della Guelfa hesitated, taking a chair beside Alberti and glancing meaningfully at the old man.

"My old sword master, Michele Alberti, sergeant at arms," Stefano said. "Alberti, these are Lieutenants della Guelfa and di Mari. They've been doing a little business for me. We are all Escalade."

Alberti raised an eyebrow in interest, considering the two men. "Are they scholars, too?"

Stefano laughed. "No."

Della Guelfa frowned and shrugged, pointing young di Mari into the opposite chair between the duca and the old man. "We are all Escalade, but are we all heathen?" della Guelfa asked.

Alberti laughed. "I was baptized Catholic, but I earned the everlasting fury of the priests so many years ago it doesn't count. A priest's anger I can live with, but the wife . . ." He shuddered. "Better the divorce."

"Honorary heathen, then," Stefano declared and turned back to della Guelfa. "What did you learn?"

Della Guelfa poured himself some wine rather nonchalantly, then glanced over either shoulder. "The cardinal has taken temporary residence in the abbey. The good friars have said that a cardinal from Rome also resides there but is scheduled to leave on the morrow."

Stefano rubbed his hands, contemplating the candle flame. "So, it begins, then."

Alberti edged his seat forward and looked quickly around the room. "*What* begins?"

"We have yet to find out. We need to know what the Cardinal of Auroea is up to," Stefano replied.

"The cardinal from Rome brought a full unit of armed guards," di Mari said.

Della Guelfa made a lowering gesture with his hands. "Have a care, Lieutenant."

"A *full* unit? Two hundred men?" Stefano asked.

"That is what the brothers told us and we saw plenty of men about the courtyard," di Mari said. "Easily two hundred."

"What does a cardinal need with that many armed men? Here? In Tyrrhia?" Alberti asked, looking from man to man.

"A good question. A good question, indeed," Stefano said thoughtfully.

"What can I do to help?" Alberti asked.

Stefano looked at him in surprise and struggled to think what he might say that would not offend.

"Now, none of that, boy," Alberti muttered darkly. "I know the abbot. Does that help?"

"I thought you weren't on friendly terms with the Church," della Guelfa said sharply.

"The Church I'm not, but . . ." Alberti shrugged. "The abbot is my brother. He is, shall we say, more tolerant of my human failings than his holy brethren."

"Do you think you could get us into the abbey?" Stefano asked.

Alberti nodded. "The chapel is always open, and I'm sure I could see my way to escorting a visitor or two farther inside. My brother has been encouraging me to retire to the abbey."

"From soldier to priest?" Stefano asked. "I can't say it would be a novel transformation."

"But it won't happen to me unless that's what it will take to get you into my brother's abbey."

"Let none of us be put to such drastic measures," Stefano muttered, tilting his head heavenward.

Prunella meandered through the garden, enjoying the flowers and feeling guilty that she lingered when she really should be returning to Her Grace. But these stolen moments in the garden served to keep her perspective when she constantly found herself besieged on all fronts by Gypsies. Keeping company with Gypsies really was one of the most nerve-racking experiences she'd ever encountered. Never mind their strange religion and heathen ways, it was the "Romani way" of doing things that often distressed her. Everyone seemed so casual, so disrespectful of Her Grace and, to further confuse matters, Her Grace actually *encouraged* this!

It really was unforgivable to waste this time, but she so needed it. She missed the workings of her father's farms, and being surrounded by the queen's garden with the gardeners moving about reminded her enough of home that it settled her nerves. She rounded a hedge and discovered Conte Urbano leaning against a tree, a handkerchief pressed to his heart.

Prunella let out a squeak of surprise which brought the conte abruptly to his feet.

"Conte Urbano!" Prunella gasped. "You surprised me! I did not expect to find you here!"

"Did you expect to find me somewhere else?" the conte asked with a pleased smile. He stepped forward, touching the kerchief to his lips. "But the gardens are open to all, are they not, dear lady?"

Prunella blushed.

The conte's smile deepened. "I found this and thought to return it to you," he said, handing the bit of plain linen to her. "Tell me please that I did not mistake the initials so lovingly embroidered there?"

Prunella accepted the square and examined it before pressing it to her own heart. It tingled in her hand, against her breast, like Gypsy Silk. "It *is* mine! I've been looking everywhere for it!"

"I found it in the chapel, by the candles. I must confess that it has taken me these three days to bring myself to part with it," the conte said dramatically and gave a flourishing bow.

Prunella's blush deepened. "You flatter me, Signore." She looked around nervously, like a frightened lamb. "We should not be alone together. Thank you—"

"Is this all the reward I shall get from you, lovely lady? At least give me back your kerchief so that I may once more carry it by my heart."

"Conte! Please!" Prunella murmured, clutching her kerchief closer. The tingling sensation from the fabric spread, making her feel warm and languid—in a way she had never experienced before. She found it unsettling. No doubt it was the attentions of this very important noble, for was he not a dear friend of Princess Bianca? "Surely, Signore, you tease me."

"Nay, 'tis I who claims to being teased. A beautiful woman such as yourself toying with a man's affections. Have you no regard for my feelings?"

"I would not hurt you, Signore Conte, but surely you have mistaken me for—"

"Is that your kerchief or not?" the conte demanded

silkily. "Of course it is, and therefore I am not mistaken. Come, let us sit here on the bench and talk a while. We are not completely alone. Anyone can see us."

Prunella nodded uncertainly and allowed herself to be drawn to the bench. She felt warm and breathless, knew her cheeks were heightened with color, but hoped he would not notice. She did her best not to sidle away when he sat beside her.

"I would have composed a poem for you—comparing your hair to the velvet of the night and your face round and bright like the moon, but, alas, I feared my attentions might be spurned."

"No one has ever spoken to me like this before," Prunella said, driven to distraction by his very direct and intent attentions.

"No one? Now you toy with me again, for a young lady such as yourself must be fighting off the suitors and I am only one in a hundred!" Conte Urbano said, leaping to his feet. "Would you truly be so discourteous to a man expressing his deepest admiration?"

"Well, no, of course not," Prunella murmured. She felt trapped, and yet the tingling of the kerchief against her skin was nothing beside the strange flames of excitement which held her in their sway like a song with an irresistible tempo which made your toe tap, eager to dance, almost against your own will. "Pray, Signore Conte, I really do not know what to say—what to do. I swear that I am not teasing you, but truly, Signore, I do not know how to receive your attentions!"

Conte Urbano stood back, his gaze assessing. "Then, my dear lady, you have been so modest that so many have recognized they are unworthy and I, in my rush of feeling overlooked this. Or perhaps, in your estimable innocence you did not recognize their attentions for surely a fine woman such as yourself does *not* go unnoticed."

"You flatter me, Signore. I am nothing but a country cousin come to court. I do not have the elegance and skills of the other ladies, nor do I share their charms, and they most certainly are far finer in their way of dress than someone like myself," Prunella replied.

"Who but the viewer is to tell which is finer, the peacock or the pheasant? There are particular charms in the refined restraint of your demure attire. One can see at a glance that you are a woman who does not need to declare her beauty with gaudy colors and a mockery of powders and rouge when already your skin is fair, your cheeks are rosy with health and, your lips, if you will pardon me, are like the pink buds of a newborn rose kissed by the dew—chaste, charming, and utterly, utterly refreshing," the conte said, dropping once more to the bench beside her. He gently reached out and took her hand. "Am I to be encouraged that you are willing to hear me out? Pray tell me if I have been too forward and I shall remove myself at once, forever, if you wish it, for your esteem of me is all that matters!"

Prunella touched her hand to her throat, tingling from head to toe with delight at the attention being lavished upon her. Breathlessly, she said, "Tell me, Signore, just so that I might hear the words, that you do not play with my feelings, that this is not some court game devised at my expense."

"My dear, sweet lady! May the good Lord strike me down if there be anything less than an absolute determination to win you with my courting!"

"Courting? Me?" Prunella squeaked. "And you've taken the Lord's name!"

"But not in vain, for the intentions are quite sincere!" Conte Urbano declared, leaning ardently nearer. His hand captured hers. "Tell me you won't reject me out of hand!"

Already overwhelmed, Prunella could not imagine refusing him for any reason! The tingling had become a heady sensation and with the words he spoke to her, Prunella was enraptured, enchanted.

In all her days, she had taken a practical view of marriage. Her parents had not loved one another, but Mother had spoken of the companionship, but, more importantly, the *duty* to marry well and improve the family's lot in some way. As a farmer's daughter, she had taken for granted certain duties and obligations a wife would have, but never, in all her practical years, had she considered love as an element of marriage. She thrilled at the thought, at the touch of his hands on hers.

"Do not tell me my protestations have so well served my case? Can this be true?" Urbano said wonderingly. He brought her hands to his stained lips.

Prunella could only stare at him, breathless and unable to concentrate. "I–I don't know what you mean."

Urbano leaned closer, his hand rose to caress her cheek. "No? Have you not come to court in search of a husband? Isn't this the custom? Can I state my case more clearly?"

"You— You would marry me?" Prunella squeaked again. She giggled, looked away and then back again to see if he, too, were smiling. "You would really marry me? But my dowry . . . it is—"

"Of no matter to me! I am a wealthy man. I understand that you will bring land—"

"I inherited my mother's ancestral home and one hundred acres—"

Urbano placed his fingers against her lips and then gently leaned forward to steal a kiss.

Prunella gasped and jumped to her feet. "Signore! Please, I am no—"

"You are a lady and I was forward. I beg your forgiveness, my ardor overtook me. Oh, that we could be married right away!"

Prunella sat again. She felt dizzy and light-headed. "Would you really have it so? Where would your protections of the marriage contract be?"

Urbano sketched a wave with his hand. "Nothing can protect me from the feelings in my heart. Tell me, would your father find fault in a suitor like myself?"

Prunella shook her head. "I think not. He is anxious that I marry and marry soon. I have four sisters, and already they have suitors pressing their cases. My family has become quite embittered at the delays."

"The delays . . . ah, yes," the conte said, suddenly looking saddened. "The Duca and Duchessa di Drago are your advisers in this matter. *They* would refuse me, I'm sure."

Sighing, Prunella could only nod. She had never understood Her Grace's casual manner about finding her a husband and now, Prunella had found one on her own—a most wonderfully suitable man—and Her Grace would most assuredly disapprove. Prunella had noted the suspicious way Her Grace watched the conte and, knowing the duchessa as she did, Her Grace would find every excuse. "Our love is damned."

"But, if your father would be happy, why should we be denied?" the conte said. "If only . . ."

"If only what?" Prunella asked. This time it was she who captured his hand and drew him around to face her.

The conte shook his head. "I was just thinking that if the cardinal were not away perhaps he could talk Padre Gasparino into marrying us, but even that is not fair to you, my dear one, for you must answer to Her Grace first."

"I must answer to my *father* first," Prunella said. She felt so light-headed; the tingle had become a warm glow, and everything seemed suddenly possible where there had been practicalities to consider before.

Conte Urbano squeezed her hands. "My dear, brave one, does that mean you would be willing to risk the wrath of Her Grace?"

"His Grace's as well, were he here," Prunella said.

"His Grace, yes, I'd forgotten . . . but you say he is gone now?" Conte Urbano asked.

Prunella nodded. "Gone to Salerno. He is far more understanding than Her Grace . . . at least, I think he could be."

The conte pulled her closer. "Come away with me and be my contessa! Let us marry in Citteauroea and surprise your father."

Prunella hesitated, trying to concentrate, which for some reason seemed exceedingly difficult. "But Her Grace—"

"We will send her word from Citteauroea. Come, my carriage is ready. I'd planned for a trip to the city anyway. Oh, do come! Think of the adventure, think of the fun, think of how pleased your family will be!" the conte urged. His hand took her chin, turning her so that she looked into his eyes. "You cannot refuse me."

From some far off distant place, Prunella heard her own voice say, "No. I cannot refuse you."

XXI

"A man must make his opportunity, as oft as find it."

—Francis Bacon

LUCIANA looked up from the Silk Guild reports and toward the patio. It was well into the afternoon. She set the papers aside and rose from her chair. In the servants' parlor, just beyond her own, she found Nicobar polishing a pair of boots and Kisaiya relaxing with a bit of lace tatting. They looked up expectantly.

"Yes, *Daiya*?" Nicobar asked, setting aside his boot.

"Have either of you seen Prunella? She should have returned from Mass by now," Luciana said.

"Sometimes she goes to the garden after Mass, to think she says." Setting her work aside, Kisaiya glanced at the mantel clock and frowned. "She should have returned. Indeed, I should have served *merenda* nearly an hour ago! I lost all track of time."

"It seems we all have. Nicobar, would you trouble yourself to check the gardens? Kisaiya, the upper rooms, in case we did not see her? Perhaps something is wrong."

Nicobar and Kisaiya moved quickly to their assigned tasks. Luciana returned to her sala and leaned back into her chaise. Prunella did not tend to be tardy or lax about her duties. A nagging worry began to take form. Something was wrong. Something was very wrong.

Kisaiya reappeared, her frown only deepened. "She's not upstairs, *Daiya,* and nothing seems out of place."

Nicobar returned as she spoke, Baldo on his heels.

"*Daiya*, I think you'll want to hear this," he announced, motioning Baldo forward.

The coachman turned his hat in his hands as he bowed nervously before Luciana. "I should have said something earlier. I beg your forgiveness, Your Grace. I'll understand if you send me on my way—"

"Baldo, please! What news do you have?" Luciana asked, rising.

"I saw Signorina Prunella get into a carriage not long after Mass. At least, I thought it was her and then figured I was mistook," Baldo said.

"She got into a carriage?" Luciana repeated, tossing aside her papers. "Did she go willingly? With whom?"

"She appeared happy . . . well, kind of happy, but distracted too. Bein' as she was so happy, I didn't figure it could've been Signorina Prunella," Baldo said. He ducked his head as a blush crept up. "Beggin' your pardon, Your Grace."

"Whose carriage did she take?" Luciana asked. She corrected herself promptly, "Whose carriage was she in? Was she alone?"

"Oh, no, Your Grace, she was with one of the gentlemen from court," Baldo said.

Luciana's stomach quaked. "Whose carriage was she in then?"

Baldo thought for a moment, twirling his hat in his hands. He raised a finger at last, a smile of satisfaction on his lips. " 'Twas one of the fancy new carriages of one of the contes . . . Conte di Vega, I believe. 'Twas his chestnut geldings pulling it. They're fast ones, they are."

The words washed over Luciana. She sank onto the couch. "Conte Urbano di Vega?"

Baldo shrugged. "I think so, Your Grace. I can ask in the stable yard if you like."

"Where were they going, do you know? How long have they been gone?"

The coachman shook his head. "I've no idea where the conte was going, but they've been gone well more'n an hour, I'd say."

Luciana sighed. She looked at Nicobar. "I fear something quite untoward has happened. Find her, Nicobar, and, whatever you do, bring her back unharmed."

"Aye, *Daiya*," Nicobar said with a bow. He took Baldo's arm, and the two of them departed.

Kisaiya watched Luciana carefully. "What will you do, *Daiya*?"

"We have to get her back, of course. Before that *benglo* can harm her." Luciana shook her head. "This is my fault! She didn't think I paid any attention to her need to marry and, in truth, I've been far more worried about my sister's murder. I just thought it could wait, that *she* could wait."

"I wouldn't have thought she'd do anything like this though," Kisaiya said. "She's so practical."

"I am as surprised as you. I've failed utterly," Luciana said, rubbing her head. "I must see the queen. She will help us. Prunella is her cousin, too."

With Nicobar and Baldo still gone and now the Escalade on the alert, Luciana dressed with care for the night's festivities, a dinner for the princess and her Conte deMedici. Kisaiya did the best she could to hide the worry lines with powders and rouge, but for all Luciana could tell, it seemed to only make matters worse.

Luciana peered into the smaller of the palazzo's banquet halls. A quartet played in the far corner, filling the room with melody. The table in the center of the room had been set so that the guests did not sit quite within arm's reach of one another.

This tactic of putting space between the celebrants might keep the guests from "flavoring" the food of their companions, she thought with a wry grimace.

She moved forward in line and returned her attention to the princess' fiancé, Conte Pierro deMedici, who stood but one guest away. He was shorter even than Luciana herself, which made him nearly a head shorter than his bride to be. He was dapper; neat in his choice of dress, a somber black matching coat and breeches, and a lace bow at his neck. Colorful embroidery covered his lapels and cuffs, thick as cloth appliqué. His left hand rested on a tall walking stick. His black hair was curled; his lovelocks were long, hanging in front and down his lapels with matching yellow ribbons. He trimmed his mustache thin.

At last Luciana took her turn to be presented. She curtsied, not deeply but sufficiently respectfully. Pierro took her hand and kissed it lightly.

"And you are the Duchessa di Drago, I believe?"

"You are correct, Conte deMedici."

"Your husband is the queen's brother, is he not? Where is *he* this evening?"

"I beg you forgive his absence, Conte Pierro, but my husband was called to business in Salerno. I anticipate his return within a week, perhaps two."

"Hopefully he'll return in time for our wedding," Conte Pierro said.

"I did not realize you intended to wed so soon," Luciana responded, deciding upon pretense rather than reveal she had the king's ear.

"Yes, we plan to marry well before the end of May," the princess said, taking Luciana's hand and drawing her along.

Luciana curtsied to the princess and forced a smile. "I wish to congratulate you, Your Highness."

The princess nodded, then leaned forward. "Your Grace, I am so grateful that you could attend even without your husband. It would have been so easy to beg off, especially with Signorina Prunella's strange absence. I hope that all ends well."

Luciana forced a smile. "Your Highness' wedding is an important event, and I would not wish to slight you in any way. Has your friend, Conte Urbano, said anything to you about Signorina Prunella?"

"I must confess that he has, but I beg your leave to discuss this later," the princess said, motioning to the line of guests, "when we will have more time to talk."

Luciana nodded her assent as she passed on to the king and queen. After greeting them, she moved into the banquet hall and hovered indecisively. She counted the place settings idly. Thirty. She glanced around the room and estimated that most of the guests were in attendance already.

Sick with worry, Luciana studied the other guests wondering which, if any, had assisted Conte Urbano in this afternoon's misadventure. Had Urbano left his ghostly charge to another sorcerer? Or was Alessandra's body unguarded . . . and how did young Prunella play into this intrigue? She turned when someone touched her elbow and found the queen at her side.

Idala motioned with her fan and turned to stroll. Luciana acquiesced and, together, the two of them wandered the length of the table toward the musicians.

"Has there been any news?" Luciana asked.

Idala shook her head, gesturing to the chair beside one head of the table. "Come."

"No word at all, then, not even from Nicobar." Luciana looked at the queen appraisingly. She still looked pale beneath the skillfully applied powder and rouge. She also seemed very tired. "I'm surprised, considering the great measures you've taken of late, that you're hosting this dinner," Luciana whispered.

Idala nodded and started to speak, but stopped as servants stepped forward to assist her into her chair. With the queen seated, other guests began to wander to their assigned places.

The queen waited a moment longer, nodding to a guest farther down the hall, then turned back to Luciana. "I've had my nurse supervising the cooks all day. I've taken every precaution. I couldn't very well avoid this evening, even with Prunella and Conte Urbano missing! A royal engagement *must* be celebrated and Bianca would take offense if we did not."

"Bianca be hanged," Luciana muttered crossly.

"Shh." Idala smiled at another guest as they hovered nearby. "Don't let anyone hear you say that!"

Luciana schooled her expression into one of benign patience, but her tone did not change. "If she bedevils you so, why placate her?"

Idala frowned. "Alban and I do not have your freedom, Lucia. We must rule judiciously and not give that one cause to move against us. You have the freedom your wealth and station give you, not to mention your Gypsy blood.''

''You really believe she would *openly* move against you?'' Luciana asked, glancing down to the middle of the table where Conte Pierro assisted Bianca into her chair. ''He makes it look as if it were a love match between them.''

''He *does* seem quite taken with her, doesn't he?'' Idala said. She turned toward Luciana, ''As to whether Bianca would rise against us . . . well, leave it said that I wouldn't put it past her. She has her forces. Now hush, here comes Rabbi Sanzio.''

The rabbi bowed graciously and took the seat to Idala's right, opposite Luciana.

Luciana surveyed the other guests and felt undeniably pleased Exilli had not been included in this event. Even so, she could not muster much appetite and watched Idala's every bite, tasters or no.

Stefano motioned to the door of his house. Alberti, di Mari, and della Guelfa who followed, waited while his key scraped inside the lock of the outer gate.

''Excuse me, my lord!''

The men turned to greet the interloper, hands to sabers in the thoughtless way soldiers have. A haggard-looking man approached, hands clasped as he bowed and squinted at them in the hazy light cast by the door lantern. He was a graying old man, small and hunched, carrying not so much as a pistola. The man met Stefano's eyes and gasped, dropping into a deep bow.

''Your Grace! So it *is* true! You *have* returned!''

Stefano frowned. It was impossible to make out the man's features clearly in this light, but the voice was vaguely familiar. ''How may I help you, good fellow? The night is growing cold and we should be abed."

"Indeed, Your Grace. If my cause were not important, I would not trouble you at this hour, nor would I have stood by this door for the last half day hoping I might have the good fortune to see you pass."

"He's a beggar, give him some coin," della Guelfa said, digging into his pouch.

"I'm no beggar, Your Grace. I keep your books . . . or I did until a week ago when the Master of Banco di Drago sent me on my way with nary a reason and hardly a *soldibianco* in severance after all these years of good service."

Stefano sighed. The night was clearly not over yet. "Come inside, man, and we'll discuss your severance."

Seated by the fire, Stefano thought the man looked familiar. This visitor, in better light, did not look so old as he had in the night. His hunch and demeanor had been misleading. He was passing middle age, but not old. Now, he held his cup of brandy but did not drink as the others did.

Stefano set aside his own glass and sat opposite his visitor, warming his hands by the fire.

"Brother Jacob is in the Escalade, a paymaster," the visitor said. "He saw you in the garrison this morning and sent word that you were here."

"I do not know what to say, Signore," Stefano said, watching the man intently.

The visitor took a gulp of the brandy, winced, and coughed. He rose, placing his cup on the little table beside the bottle. "Forgive me, Your Grace. I am a man of little consequence. I should not expect you to remember me after so many years. I am Davino Foscari, and I was hired to keep books when you opened Banco di Drago in Salerno nearly ten years ago."

"That was shortly after I inherited my father's estates. You have been in my service this long? What brought the end of your work under my roof, Foscari?" Stefano asked.

"The master of the banco said my services were no longer needed."

"Just like that? With no explanation?" Alberti asked with a disbelieving snort.

"He offered none, even when I asked," Foscari replied patiently. He looked back at Stefano. "Your Grace, I have been a good and loyal servant."

"I remember you, though slightly," Stefano admitted. "What redress do you seek?"

"I am a father with a family to feed. If I cannot work in the banco, perhaps you could find need of my services elsewhere?"

"You still have not said *why* you were sent away from your job at the banco," Alberti said, leaning back in his chair.

"I was *given* no reason, but I suspect because I am a Jew," Foscari said, his voice tinged with bitterness.

"A Jew? What difference would this make to the master if your service was good and honest?" Stefano demanded. "This is Tyrrhia, not Rome."

"I do not have this from the man's own lips, it is my suspicion only. The master converted two years ago and the clerks hired since then have all been of the faith. At first, I thought it charitable work he did, to hire these men and no matter for my concern, but gradually all of the clerks not of the faith have found themselves shut of the banco, sometimes without even references to see them to new employment," Foscari said diffidently.

"These are not petty allegations you make," Stefano said.

"No, Your Grace, I know this and it is not something I'm comfortable telling you for fear I'm wrong, but there are too many of the faith employed in the banco now and little of the 'heathen' left. Indeed, I think I was the last."

"Hmm. I will consult with the master of the banco in the morning and we will learn more of this. Leave word where you can be reached with my man," Stefano said, beginning to brood.

"As you say, Your Grace," Foscari said. He bowed his way out of the room.

"Do you believe him?" Alberti asked.

"I have no reason to doubt him at the moment," Stefano said with a shrug. "It's easy enough to learn whether there is truth in his claims."

The princess sank onto the couch beside Luciana.

Luciana moved aside her skirt and turned from the musicians. The quartet playing at dinner had now been joined in the library by other players and their music became more complicated as they were led by a visiting *maestro di cappella,* a very talented young Tyrrhian by the name of Alessandro Scarlatti, recently from the Queen of Sweden's court.

The princess, however, seemed intent upon the musicians, so Luciana decided to bide her time and turned to watch as Lady Ursinia stepped up to the small dais and motioned to the long-legged maestro. Lady Ursinia looked lovely in a gown of ivory satin with a lace shawl accenting her dark hair and skin. She held a red rose in her hand. The maestro tapped on his music stand for attention. All eyes turned to him, as though he cast a spell upon the assemblage of nobles.

Lady Ursinia began to sing the maestro's aria. Her voice was clear and pure and sweet to the ear. Those few who continued in conversation now fell silent. The maestro had promised them something exciting and new. It seemed, now, that he kept his promise. Luciana tried to remember exactly how the maestro had described this new presentation called opera, a form of liturgical drama and Greek tragedy. It had much to recommend it, Luciana thought, especially when one so talented as Lady Ursinia lent her strong, fine voice to the wide ranges of

the song about love and loss. Lady Ursinia moved
blithely into another melody, her voice taking on a lilt
with the gaiety of these new lyrics.

"Her talents are quite surprising, aren't they?"

Luciana glanced away from the performance to Princess Bianca and saw that Conte Pierro stood behind her.
She started to rise but the conte motioned her back into
her seat. "Forgive me, what did you say, Your Highness?"

The princess chuckled indulgently. "I was commenting
upon the quality of Lady Ursinia's voice."

"Oh! Yes, of course! Her voice is quite delightful,"
Luciana agreed, feeling flustered by her own distraction.
The music mesmerized. The peril of young Prunella tore
her attention from the music as she focused her attentions upon the princess who seemed more than ready to
be engaged in conversation now.

"Indeed," Princess Bianca agreed. She leaned closer,
conspiratorially. "She lacked the confidence to approach
the queen with her talent, so I spoke for her. I am
quite pleased."

"A most fortunate discovery," Luciana whispered,
wishing she could find a way to change the subject
delicately.

"Perhaps we can talk now while we are alone . . . so
to speak," Princess Bianca said, glancing up at Conte
Pierro and to the spellbound courtiers beyond. "I
learned of Urbano's and Prunella's wild escape a short
hour before dinner, otherwise I would have come to ease
your concerns sooner."

"Escape?" Luciana queried. The thought of her husband's cousin "escaping" with the likes of Conte Urbano—or anyone else, for that matter—bordered on
the absurd.

"Yes, Conte Urbano has been quite taken with your
young cousin, but has been afraid to address it with you
or the duca. He said only last evening that he hoped to
speak to her this afternoon and she must have received
him well, considering what they say followed."

"As romantic as this assignation may sound, His
Grace and I were not in favor of such a union."

The princess waved away the protest as if it were nothing. "The conte is quite wealthy. He is a man of letters, horsemanship, and the courtly graces, not to mention a good man of the faith. How can you argue against a union such as that when Signorina Prunella Carafa has nothing to offer save a bit of land he could easily purchase and a distant relationship to the queen?"

Luciana blinked. "The relationship is not so distant as all that though her dowry is not much to speak of."

"Was not," the princess chided. Seeing Luciana's expression, she continued hurriedly, "I'm sure he would not take advantage of her, but marry her as is proper."

"Most properly, he would have approached her guardians rather than the subject of his affections." Luciana did not intend to antagonize the princess regarding her friend if she could help it, but neither could she forget her concern for Prunella.

"True. But when one is in love—tell me, Your Grace, have you never allowed love to make you do something foolish?" the princess asked.

Luciana felt trapped, frustrated. Did the princess *really* not see how preposterously unforgivable this situation was or was she simply prepared to forgive her friend anything? Or perhaps, compared to the princess' marital arrangements, the *faux pas* committed by the conte seemed negligible?

Bianca touched Luciana's arm with her fan. "I know you and Her Majesty are worried over your young cousin and I can see where you might be, but really, truly, she *will* be kept quite safe in Conte Urbano's hands. He would let nothing harm her. When she returns married and a contessa, all this drama will be forgiven and forgotten."

Luciana bit down hard on her tongue and tasted the saltiness of blood, but at least it kept her from bursting out with the protests this situation merited. The princess, apparently satisfied with what she had relayed, rose. Conte Pierro followed in her wake, leaving Luciana without the comfort Her Highness possibly intended to give her.

No. Luciana felt no comfort in the knowledge that

Conte Urbano intended to marry Prunella now he had run away with her. Luciana sat back on the couch, fanning herself. This would make interesting news for Stefano. She wondered how he would receive it.

XXII

"Surely as the divine powers take note of the dutiful, surely as there is any justice anywhere and a mind recognizing itself what is right, may the gods bring you your earned rewards."

—Virgil

15 d'Maggio 1684

FOR a spring morning, it was remarkably chilly and gray as the rising sun broke through the fog. Stefano stretched and breathed deeply of the fresh air, watching his exhalation mist and be swept away by the cold, gentle wind. He turned as the bell hanging over the perimeter gate jangled. Di Mari and della Guelfa, bleary-eyed and yawning, joined him in the street. Alberti strode behind them, wide awake and purposeful now that morning had come.

"Are we off to the banco?" Alberti asked.

Di Mari cast Alberti a sour look and scratched his stomach.

"I thought we should address this matter of Foscari's employment early, and then learn what we can do about the cardinal. Let us stay together. We do not want to wonder where one of our number is when we could be about this business," Stefano said. "Are we agreed?"

The other men nodded and fell into step. They traveled but a quarter mile to a narrow little courtyard where the street disintegrated into a maze of stonework fences and alleyways. Two small cherubim fountains splashing water on the marble well occupied the middle of the courtyard. A pretty sight for the middle class residents of the houses crowded around.

A tall angular man dressed like a spadaccino shoved himself away from one of the gates and moved to block their path.

"And where would you be going?" he asked.

Stefano deliberately kept his hand from falling to the rapier or the scorpinini tucked into his belt in easy reach. He smiled pleasantly. "We are about our business. Why do you ask?"

The stranger grinned. "Because I am about mine." He drew his rapier in a lithe movement which spoke of much practice.

"Oh, please," Alberti said with a little cough. "There are four of us to your one. Your Grace, shall I teach this scoundrel a lesson?"

"Methinks the old man miscounts, Your Grace," the stranger rolled the title around in his mouth and made it sound anything but complimentary.

One of the perimeter gates rattled as it opened and a full dozen rowdies poured into the street with rapiers drawn.

However tired di Mari was, he looked suddenly wide awake. The four men fell back, placing their backs to one another, drawing their own blades.

Stefano remained calm. He took his money case from his breast pocket and held it aloft. "If it's money you're after, then there's no need to fight for it. I give it to you willingly." He tossed the case at the stranger's feet.

The man looked at it and sneered, advancing. "Were that all I were after, Your Grace, I'd accept, but, alas, I mean you to end your days here."

Stefano raised his blade. "I thought as much. Would you consider allowing my companions to leave?"

"Your Grace!" della Guelfa protested, turning to stare at Stefano. "We would not leave you!"

" 'Tis no matter, their days are at an end as well. Unfortunately, your company is not healthy," the stranger said.

"Perhaps we should have at it rather than discussing the issue?" Alberti snapped, feinting toward one of the men and leaving an invitation to advance upon his low line.

Stefano waited for the leader to move, centering his attention upon this one man rather than allowing himself to be distracted by the others circling like ravenous dogs. The leader stood tall and lanky, his reach half again more than Stefano's, but the duca knew he could, thankfully, count upon his own speed.

Out of the corner of his eye, Stefano noted a fellow edging forward. His left hand slipped to the scorpinini tucked into his belt. Without removing the pistol-sized crossbow from its frog, he aimed the cocked bow in the general direction of the man and shot off one of its two bolts. The fellow howled and grabbed his knee, falling to the ground. The leader lunged. Stefano parried and allowed his blade to glide down the other's. The leader was slightly out of position as he riposted and—snick-snack—Stefano left a blood trail on the *bravo*'s left cheek.

The leader cursed. Stefano grinned and remained in the easy stance of St. George's Guard, leaving an invitation in fifth.

The leader smirked and feinted toward Stefano's heart. Stefano parried, feinted, broke ranks, and lunged for the spadaccino's heart. His rapier hissed along the leader's as the other man made a quick parry and leaped out of the way.

Alberti and della Guelfa closed ranks, putting di Mari at their backs. The villains swarmed forward like angry bees to attack their breach.

Stefano spared no time on the other men. The leader and another two of his bravi joined in the battle, stepping over their fallen friend still clutching his knee. Stefano jumped to the edge of the fountain, caught his balance and jerked his dagger free in time to divert a thrust, and aimed a swift kick at the attacker's diaphragm. The man did not counter quickly enough and doubled over. Stefano punched the man squarely in the face using his dagger-braced fist. His opponent fell atop his injured comrade. Stefano parried two quick thrusts from the spadaccino and his bravo—easy enough with his position of height.

Stefano parried again and flipped his dagger so that he held it by the blade and threw it at the second man. The bravo howled and clutched his eye as the dagger glanced off. Not exactly what Stefano had hoped for, but he took the momentary advantage and lunged for the bravo's throat. The blade buried itself deep. The man looked surprised, then reached for the blade as he fell into the leader. While the leader tossed his fallen crony aside, Stefano took advantage again and thrust home, striking the man squarely in the heart as he leaped forward, off the fountain, adding to the impetus of his thrust. The leader quaked, but remained standing for half a moment. His blade dropped from nerveless fingers as he fell.

Stefano jerked his blade free and used it to catch up the spadaccino's rapier. Armed with two rapiers, Stefano turned to help his friends. He hit two men in the back of their heads with the hilts of the rapiers, glancing blows, but successful enough to knock one unconscious and to spin the other in his tracks only to find Stefano with a blade at his heart. The man dropped his weapon and put his hands to his head.

Alberti quickly turned and surprised his next assailant with a rapid feint to the low line. The hapless swordsman parried wildly, but his blade met only thin air as Alberti eluded the desperate parry with a tight disengagement to the high line, driving his weapon deep into the man's chest with a vigorous lunge. The remaining three bravi threw their blades to the ground and raised their hands.

"Di Mari, fetch the Escalade!" Stefano ordered, never taking his eyes off his captives.

"Aye, Your Grace!" di Mari jogged off down one of the alleys leading from the square.

Alberti and Stefano motioned the felons into a group while della Guelfa searched each man. The pile of weapons by the fountain—rapiers, pistolas, scorpininis, and daggers—grew steadily. When the collection was com-

plete, della Guelfa took the men's belts and used them
to tie their hands behind their backs. The felons sat back
to back in the middle of the square while Alberti hovered nearby, ready to address anyone who felt they
might have a chance for escape. Della Guelfa tied the
unconscious men, leaving Stefano to tend the man with
the scorpinini bolt through his knee.

The fellow had passed out, Stefano noted, but it did
not stop Stefano from disarming him. Reasonably assured the patient would not wake and attack, Stefano
tore open the man's breeches. The bolt ran solidly
through the man's leg. Clearly it would have to wait for
the surgeon. He tugged open the man's shirt so he could
breathe easier and paused as he discovered a crucifix.

He squinted in the harsh glare of the early morning
light and met the gaze of one of the men Alberti
watched over. "Where are you from?" he asked.

The man looked away, staring at his boots.

Alberti nudged him with his foot. "Answer His Grace
or answer the judge."

"Gascony," the man growled.

"What brings you to Salerno?"

Alberti nudged the recalcitrant man again. "Answer
'im."

The man jerked his legs away. "We followed our
lord."

"Your Lord? Do you mean you are on a pilgrimage?"

"I am in service to the Duca di Gascony."

"DeMedici?" Stefano asked, surprised.

The man grumbled at one of his friends who glared
at him.

"Does he know what you do in your off-hours, or is
he behind this?" Stefano asked.

The man's dark complexion tinged crimson and he
looked grim. "My lord is unaware of my activities."

"And your bravi," Stefano asked, "are they de-
Medici's, too?"

"Some, but not all," the man admitted.

"Haven't you said enough?" one of the others snarled,
jerking against his bindings.

"Oh, not nearly," Alberti said, prodding the complainer with his rapier. He motioned to the first man. "You were saying?"

The man looked pained. "There's nothing more to tell."

"Nothing more to tell?" Stefano repeated in surprise. He wiped his bloody hands on the wounded man's coat. "Part of a gentleman's contingent and yet you're looting like a petty thief?"

"It–it wasn't like that," the man said.

"Shut up, I say!" his comrade bellowed, using his entire body to slam against the other.

"None of that now," Alberti said, poking the man in his ribs.

"Ferenzi is dead. We have no hope of gaining protection, why shouldn't we talk?" the other man said.

"Ferenzi is this one?" Stefano asked, motioning to the leader.

The confessor nodded.

Stefano glanced over and saw the crucifix dangling from the man's neck. "Are you all Catholics?"

"We are."

"You'll get us killed for your troubles," the other man said.

"We can offer the protection of the Escalade," Stefano said.

"Ha! An Escalade prison, you mean!" the second man retorted.

"Of course. Attacking men on the street is against the law in Tyrrhia as well as in Rome or Gascony," Stefano said.

"We won't be safe anywhere you put us," the first man said.

"Why not?"

"Catholics are in the Escalade, aren't they?"

Stefano's brows rose. "Indeed, but why would your Catholic brethren in the Escalade be of interest to you? You don't mean to infer that *they* would harm you?" he said to the second man.

The men greeted his question with silence.

"Our officers will not break their oaths of office. You'll be safe. But tell me, what have you to fear from your fellow Catholics? One would think you could turn to them for comfort in your hour of need," Stefano said.

"One would think. But not us. Not now," the first man said.

"Why *not*?" della Guelfa asked.

The two captives exchanged looks; the first turned back and sat straighter in his ties. "It was the nature of our mission. We did not fall upon you by happenstance."

"No? Who set you upon me, then?" Stefano asked.

The second man shook his head, but the first went on. "Only Ferenzi knew for sure, but he told us that a priest bid us put you out of the way—that you were interfering with Church business."

Stefano sat on the edge of the fountain and considered both men. Was the cardinal really willing to be so brazen? Di Mari returned with a contingent of vigilare who made a quick business of the arrests and creating a pallet to carry the injured man.

Luciana pushed her breakfast away. She felt sick with worry over Prunella. Nicobar had returned late last night with news that the conte and Prunella had found a priest and made the last ferry to Reggio di Calabria before they could be caught.

What use did Conte Urbano or his patron have for poor Prunella, and did the girl have any idea what she had got herself into? Luciana doubted it, which is why she composed a very long letter to Lord Carafa about the dangers of his new son-in-law and the advisability of annulment if such a thing were possible. The Sisters Three only knew what good it would do!

Kisaiya quietly took away the plate and Nicobar edged into her line of sight. She looked up expectantly.

"I fear that I didn't make my report the other night when I visited the gardeners," Nicobar said.

"I thought you'd have said if there was anything to tell."

"You are quite right, of course, *Daiya*, but I thought I should tell you nonetheless."

Luciana shook her head, a smile came reluctantly to her lips. Nicobar knew her too well for their own good.

"So. What will you do?" he prodded.

"I lost the battle for Prunella before it began. There might be some hope that she can be regained, but my instincts tell me this is a diversion. Get your coat, Nic."

"Where do you send me?"

"To Salerno, after my husband. I will write a note, but you must impress upon him the urgency of the circumstances."

Nicobar bowed and disappeared up the stairs.

Luciana sighed. Much as she loved Stefano she still chaffed at the expectation to consult and report to him about these latest turns of event. How much easier would it have been to manage Prunella if she did not discount Luciana's advice because she was not the man. Roma women respected their men, but were not expected to await their pleasure before taking action. Even spending most of her youth in a *gadjé* home, she noted the difference—and fell in love with a *gadjé* anyway.

She sorted through the papers from the guilds on her writing desk until she found a blank sheet. Nicobar returned as she finished composing her note. She took a leather folder from the desk and handed him several lira notes.

"Take the next ship to Salerno. You will find my husband at our Salerno house. Return as soon as you are able," Luciana said.

"Of course, *Daiya,*" Nicobar said and tucked the bundle into his jacket. "Will there be anything else?"

"No, Nicobar. Go quickly and be safe," Luciana said.

"Always, *Daiya.*" Nicobar bowed and took his leave.

Alone, Luciana wandered up to her room. Her eyes strayed to the tapestry behind which lay the secret door. This had been Alessandra's room and, eventually, it became her jail. Someone intent upon doing Alessandra harm could have come through that door, she thought. The king seemed to think only he and perhaps Estensi knew of the secret passageway, but what if he were wrong? She gave no credence to the thought that the king might be the murderer. No, that was too silly. He had no need to kill with his own hands when he had executioners to do it for him. But then who had been able to get into these rooms and poison Alessa?

Luciana went to the bureau where she kept her sister's letters. She took the ribboned packet from the box and opened one, then another, until she settled on one dated after the capitano's death had been announced.

14 d'Aprile 1684

. . . The princess came to visit today. I don't know why. I found it impossible to feign tolerance of her presence. Were I more magnanimous, I might believe the princess is really concerned about me, but I know the woman's heart.

So, the princess did come to the suite, Luciana thought. It seemed odd, considering Alessandra's enmity. Her sister had never been good at hiding her feelings.

Luciana looked once more at the tapestry covering the secret door. Where else did the corridors lead? She resolved to explore them further, perhaps in the evening, when she was less likely to be disturbed or discovered.

XXIII

"Even victors are by victories undone."
　　　　　　　　　　　　　　—John Dryden

STEFANO paused outside the Banco di Drago, staring in dismay at the large crucifix by the name shingle. The others stood beside him, also staring.

"It seems Foscari had right on his side," della Guelfa said.

"Do we take it down?" Alberti asked.

Stefano nodded. "I'll be inside."

"Aye," Alberti said.

———————

A bell over the door heralded Stefano's entrance. A wiry man with flowing whiskers and a balding pate rose from his chair to greet him. "Greetings, m'lord," he said with a quick bow. He snapped his ledger shut. "Whom do you wish to see?"

Stefano glanced around, taking in the changes. Clerks worked at three polished tables, sitting at all four corners, doing their accounting in long ledger books. Most of them did not even look up from their books to see who entered and those who looked, turned back to their books quickly enough. He did not remember having so many clerks. He hoped at least this meant the bank flourished.

Distracted, Stefano told the clerk, "I'm here to see del Bene, the Banco Master."

"I see," the clerk said, wiping his hands on his coat. "Do you have an appointment?"

Stefano's eyebrows arched, the only sign of his displeasure. "No, I do not, but—"

"Then perhaps I can make an appointment for you," the clerk said, taking a small appointment book from his desk.

"I don't think that will be necessary, you see—"

"I'm sorry, m'lord, but the Banco Master will be busy all morning. The only way you can see him is if you make an appointment. *Now,* when would you like to come in?"

Stefano took his card from his pocket and handed it to the man. "If that means nothing to you, then perhaps you will ask the Banco Master who his employer is," Stefano said sternly.

The clerk looked at the card, turning three shades of red, and then at Stefano. "Excuse me, Your Grace, I didn't realize."

"You're new, aren't you?" Stefano asked.

"I—I've been here going on two years, Your Grace," he replied. "I'll just fetch del Bene."

Stefano watched as the clerk hurried—not into the old Banco Master's office but into Stefano's own office where he worked when in residence in Salerno.

Moments later the office door flew open, banged against a desk, and startled a bookkeeper about his work. Del Bene, a tall, slender man, rushed out, hastened through the work area, opened the swinging gate, and bowed deeply before Stefano.

"Your Grace! I hadn't realized you returned from Peloponnesus! I expected news. I—what are those men doing?"

Stefano followed del Bene's gaze out the window to see della Guelfa mounted on di Mari's shoulders. "They are correcting the shingle, I presume. You're not too busy to see me, I hope?"

Del Bene chewed his lip. "Your Grace, I beg your indulgence for just a few moments longer. I'm meeting with an important client. Perhaps we can speak when the appointment is over?"

"Over? No, I would not hear of it. After all, we *are*

dealing with my money, aren't we?" Stefano said agreeably.

"I have made a considerable profit for you over the last few years," del Bene said diffidently.

"I know that. I have a seneschal minding my business. Unfortunately, he was apparently unaware of some of your . . . improvements, shall we call them? But never mind that now, let us see this client," Stefano said. He took del Bene's elbow and guided him toward the door of the office, releasing the protesting bank officer only as the two of them entered. Stefano took in the changes in the office: the rearrangement of furnishings, the carpet from the Orient covering the floor, and the painting of the pope placed prominently over the desk. He noted this all without a word and then considered the elderly, well-dressed gentleman sitting in the chair opposite the desk.

"I hope this interruption of yours has been dealt with, del Bene, I am in a hurry this morning," the man said as he turned. He paused, staring at Stefano, then rose from his chair, looking to del Bene, who minced to stand between the two.

Stefano waited for the introduction, studying the man. Small, dark, aging, extremely wealthy, foreign by the cut of his dress, undoubtedly of noble birth.

Del Bene bowed to the two men. "Your Grace, Duca di Drago, may I introduce, His Grace, Duca di Gascony."

Stefano, in turn, bowed, smiling in a friendly fashion as he circled and took the chair behind the desk, leaving del Bene to stand uncertainly nearby as the noblemen sat, studying one another.

"I'm afraid, Your Grace, that I am unaware of the details which brought you here. Perhaps you might tell me?"

Duca deMedici's raven-black brows—flecked with wisps of white—furrowed as though in surprise, but he did not turn his beaky glare to del Bene who cringed as Stefano spoke.

"I'm in Tyrrhia for only a short time, Your Grace, long enough, however, to encounter some expenditures for my men . . . above and beyond the normal costs, of course. I came seeking funds to see me through until my own banks could repay this debt," deMedici said. He motioned to a sheaf of papers in front of Stefano. "You'll find my papers in order and, as one Catholic to another in this heathen land, you can trust my word of honor that the loan and suitable interest will be paid promptly."

"Would that we could take one another's word as one Catholic to another, Your Grace, but not being a Catholic, I will ask that I take your word as one gentleman to another," Stefano said with a ferocious smile.

DeMedici grimaced. "I was given to understand this was a Catholic organization."

"I'm sorry, you've been misled. I'm afraid this is *banking,* pure and simple, and any representation otherwise is a falsehood. I can't imagine who would tell you such a thing as my employees know well that I don't give preference to Catholics or anyone else."

Del Bene squirmed, his blush deepening. Stefano ignored him, concentrating upon deMedici who held his gaze, though apparently nonplussed.

"Does that mean that you will not advance me the money?" deMedici asked finally.

Stefano glanced down at the papers, noticing the sizable sum. "This figure is quite large, Your Grace. May I ask how many men you have in your employ here that this is to cover?"

"I have brought a unit of men to safeguard my household on the roads between Gascony and Salerno. I must supply for them as well as my rather large household," deMedici said.

Stefano sat back in his chair. A full unit of men? Not to mention the force the cardinal brought with him. Were their plans really so advanced that they could risk such an obvious show of force on Tyrrhian home soil?

"Yes," Stefano murmured pleasantly. "I had occasion to meet some of your men this morning, less than an hour ago, in fact."

"*My* men? At this hour of the day? You must be mistaken."

"No. I don't think so. They claimed to be of your household . . . and their paperwork backed their claims," Stefano said.

"Paperwork? Was there trouble?"

"No trouble—if you do not consider attempted assassination a problem," Stefano said.

"*My* men?" deMedici repeated, standing. "There must be a mistake! How could this be? Where are these men?" deMedici snatched his cloak from the back of his chair.

"The last I knew, your men were being taken to the Escalade stockade . . . those that still lived that is. They were not spectacularly successful," Stefano said.

"Whom did they attempt to assassinate?" deMedici asked.

Stefano bowed. "Alas, I fear, my humble self drew this attention."

"You will forgive me if I leave? I must verify these are my men and see what explanation they have to offer," deMedici said.

"Of course. I understand completely."

"But what about the loan?" del Bene asked.

DeMedici did not answer as he swept from the room.

Del Bene started to follow, paused and turned. "You will be wanting to speak with me, no doubt," he said. He closed the door behind the Duca deMedici and came to stand before the desk. "I have been trying to gain his business for nearly two days."

"Won't you sit?" Stefano asked, motioning to the chair deMedici had just vacated.

Del Bene hesitated but sat slowly.

Nicobar tossed his bag to the wharf and vaulted nimbly over the rail, anxious to be on land again and not willing to wait for the gangplank to be set in place. It was already late in the day, and he had no interest in wandering the streets of a strange town in the dark, not without a Romani or two at his back. He picked up his bag and stared at the busy pier. People crowded everywhere as if this were market day at the bazaar. Shouldering his pack, Nicobar waded into the mix, glad of his height which permitted him to see over the tops of most people's heads.

He found a tradesman and took the opportunity to get directions to the residential quarter of Salerno. Based upon the instructions, it would be easy enough to find his way, crowds and all, to the duca's Salerno estate, *Drago Maniero*.

Shoppers packed Nicobar's route through busy cobbled streets. Students mixed freely with patrons as they shuffled between classes at the university. The streets smelled of breads and cheeses, books and humanity, with the constant buzz of raised voices calling to one another. Nicobar resisted the urge to linger and pushed through the crowd.

He found his way to the residential quarter, as the tradesman directed, though Nicobar could see that he would not find *Drago Maniero* among these houses. Besides being barely more than tenements built one atop another on the steep sloping hills, the neighborhood echoed with the noise of children, animals, and adults busy about their daily affairs, open to the public for one and all to see and hear.

Children played in the courtyard and several women gathered round one of three fountains, alternately sitting, kneeling, or bending as they scrubbed laundry on old washboards or with paddles. For the most part, the younger *gadjé* women did the wash just as the Romani did, leaving the older women to other duties. Some in the Wandering Tribes contended older women were not up to the backbreaking work, but Nicobar knew better. He shouldered his pack a little higher and passed the women, who took no notice of him as they continued to laugh and gossip among themselves.

Half a league farther on, the Drago city house stood nestled in a hillside, complete with a perimeter fence bound on either side by the hedges of neighboring nobles' homes. It seemed even the wealthy were crowded in here, more so since the quake of fifteen years ago which left the city with little standing.

Shingles bearing the family name hung above each of the nobles' gates, but none so colorful as the Drago household which bore a dragon curled around the duca's surname, Novabianco.

Nicobar tugged on the bell cord by the solid wooden gate. Momentarily, he heard the sound of a door opening and someone hurrying down the path. He waited. A small door at face level—for someone shorter than himself—opened and a woman peered out.

"Yes, m'lord?"

"This is *Drago Maniero*?" Nicobar asked.

The woman glanced upward at the sign, looking peevish, but her voice remained pleasant. "Yes. How may I help you?"

"I come from the duchessa with a message for His Grace. I am her personal attendant, Nicobar Baccolo."

The small door closed and the larger swung wide. "His Grace is in the parlor with his friends. This way," she said.

Nicobar followed, admiring the gardens and then the house as the housekeeper ushered him in. The woman was portly and moved with a busy bustle common to working women of her size. She stopped almost immediately and rapped on the nearest door. "Your Grace? I bring a messenger from your wife."

The door opened. Nicobar recognized della Guelfa from the night at the man's farm. He hid his surprise and entered the room to find the duca sitting before the fire with two more men, one old, the other young. All the men wore swords.

"Your Grace," Nicobar said and bowed deeply.

Stefano rose from his chair. "Nicobar? What brings you here so soon?"

"Her Grace did not want to trust the post and bid me bring this to you directly," Nicobar replied, proffering the papers.

The duca nodded as he received it. "Come, come by the fire. It's been unseasonably chilly."

Nicobar did as he was bade, watching as the duca broke the seal and read the letter within. The duca's brows rose in surprise and then furrowed.

"I see," the duca said.

"Do you have a reply? Or perhaps you will be accompanying me back to Citteauroea?" He tried to keep the hope from his voice.

"I cannot return just yet," the duca said, glancing at his companions. "You must rest here for the night and take a message back to my wife. Against our better judgment, it appears that my young cousin has eloped with Conte di Vega."

"You'll do nothing, then?" Nicobar asked, startled.

"Prunella has gone to her father if she goes to Reggio di Calabria. I cannot see how I or my wife can do anything more," Stefano replied. He sighed and returned to his chair, motioning to the younger of the swordsmen. "Pour our traveler a bit of brandy to warm him. You will join us for dinner, Nicobar, and the servants will put you up in one of the rooms."

Nicobar bowed. "As you wish," he said.

XXIV

"Depart from your enemies, yea, and beware of your friends."

—Apocrypha

16 d'Maggio 1684

LUCIANA looked long and hard at her husband's words, aware of Nicobar waiting. She tucked the letter away, considering her words carefully. "He advises me to do nothing regarding Prunella. She is in her husband's hands now, and, if not him, then her father's. I think, however, the king should see this bit of correspondence. The duca advises me that we must make sure the king is aware of a buildup of troops in Salerno."

She smothered her frustration with herself. With Stefano barely back, she already leaned upon him as though helpless to make up her own mind. Sufficient reason kept Stefano in Salerno, despite her desires. She hated herself for the weakness, but could not resist wondering if Stefano would prefer a weaker woman. A *gadjé* woman. She shook her head. She could not afford this mental lapse to focus on such matters.

She handed Stefano's letter to Nicobar. "You'll take this to the king personally. Did the duca confess what he planned? He says nothing in his letter and I thought . . ." She shrugged but looked hopefully at Nicobar.

"I'm sorry, *Daiya,* but your husband made no confidences although—" He hesitated, frowning. He looked as though he debated with himself over whatever he might divulge. At last, he said gently, "There was talk of an attack on the streets."

"Attack?" Luciana leaned back in her chair, her hand to her throat. "You mean Stefano—the duca? Is he well? Was he—is he hiding a wound so that I won't worry?"

"I saw no evidence of injury. *Daiya,* I would tell you if I had seen something that concerned me." Nicobar kept his tone calm as he knelt before her and looked directly into her eyes. He hid nothing from her.

Luciana tapped his shoulder. "Yes, of course you would, but what of this attack? Do you have any details?"

"The Escalade officer, della Guelfa, let slip that there had been an attempt upon the duca's life. The duca was not forthcoming with further details and the old man— he seemed to be an old sword master of the duca's— changed the subject."

Torn between concern for her husband and aggravation with his secretive nature, Luciana chewed her lip. At last she nodded to Nicobar. "Thank you. You have served me well."

"Is there anything else that I can do for you, *Daiya*?"

"No, Nic, just deliver this message to the king." She hesitated. "Let me send a note of explanation." She took paper and quill and jotted a quick note, to which she added her seals.

Stefano hunched into his coat and adjusted his sleeves. He took a narrow-eyed look at his companions, similarly dressed in long, dark coats against spring gusts. He stuffed his hands into his pockets, feeling the scorpinini buried within, easily cocked, and nodded to Alberti.

Alberti glanced around, his gaze lingering on the encampment of soldiers sprawling out over Church grounds beyond the abbey walls, then pulled the golden chain hanging beside the doors.

A small window opened in the right door and a tonsured man peered out. "God be with you, brothers."

"And with you," Alberti replied, tipping his hat.

"How may we serve you?"

Alberti made a great show of hunching against the cold. "Abbot Alberti is my brother. I and my friends seek spiritual retreat."

The monk closed the small portal and opened the larger door. Wind whipped around the four men and fluttered the monk's long black robes. "I am afraid the abbot is detained by his superiors, but I bid you welcome in his name. I will show you to the chapel." He beckoned the men inside.

Stefano went last, turning back for one last look at the encampment. Inside, he made a quick study of the abbey buildings. The monks' cells appeared to be built into the outer walls, a church rose from the tiled, mosaic courtyard—a great edifice of stone and stained glass—and a second large building which seemed to squat beside it.

Stefano lingered behind as his party climbed the stone steps to the church, watching clerics hustling in and out of the second building. The monk noticed his interest.

"We keep offices, the refectory, and other such functions there." The monk caught Stefano's arm and gently tugged hm toward the church. "Come, brother, Vespers are about to begin."

Stefano followed the monk inside, slipping into a pew beside his comrades at the rear of the chapel. He observed the functions of prayer perfunctorily, dredging his memory for the appropriate responses, all the while surveying the attendants until, at last, he spied the cardinal and Duca deMedici. He watched them surreptitiously, ducking his head when the cardinal looked out over the audience.

At the conclusion of Vespers, their host appeared at the end of their pew. He placed a finger to his lips and motioned them to follow. Outside the chapel, he drew them to one side.

Stefano put his back to the door so that the exiting faithful could not see his face.

"We sup immediately after Vespers," the monk said. "While you are dining, I will make arrangements for a room. I'm afraid that our lodgings are already taxed with an abundance of visitors. I won't be able to get you private accommodations."

"I'm sure any arrangement will be satisfactory. We do not wish to be more of an imposition than necessary," Stefano said.

Della Guelfa and di Mari nodded.

"I am sure whatever hospitality my brother can offer will be appreciated, Father," Alberti added.

"Brother, please, I am Brother Ferrante," the monk said. "This way, please."

The refectory was a simple room in the back of the second building. Two long tables occupied the center of the room and a third, smaller, high table sat apart, near the windows at the head of the room. Brother Ferrante seated the four men at the far end of one of the long tables beside the priests. Another brother served them a simple fare of bread, *zuppa*, and wine.

At the high table, Duca deMedici joined the abbot, the cardinal, and another man Stefano recognized as another cardinal by his robes. He watched them as they ate and conversed. The abbot seemed somber, listening and nodding but rarely joining in the discussion with his guests. The others, however, spoke in an animated manner, though they kept their voices low.

Brother Ferrante appeared at Alberti's side as they finished dinner. Stefano made sure Alberti, della Guelfa, and di Mari surrounded him so that the cardinal or the duca would not see and possibly recognize him.

The brother led them into a hallway. It was all wooden floors and paneled walls ornamented with a prominent portrait of Benedetto Odescalchi, the pope, His Holiness Innocent XI, hanging at the opposite end, a golden crucifix just outside the refectory at eye level, small portraits of holy men, undoubtedly abbots of the Holy Brothers of Salerno. Brother Ferrante ushered them into a room with four cots. A desk and a small altar occupied the near wall. Clearly, three of the four cots were not original occupants.

"We can offer you nothing more than Brother Gregori's room, I'm afraid. All of the rooms have been taken. If we had known . . ." Brother Ferrante raised his hands eloquently. He went to the small desk and collected what appeared to be a manuscript and some books, though he left a prayer book. "Brother Gregori will want these. He's a tad absentminded, our librarian, always with his books and manuscripts."

"This will be satisfactory," Stefano said, surveying the room. "I hope that we have not discomfited Brother Gregori in any way—"

"Peace, brother," Ferrante said. "We are your hosts and give of ourselves willingly. We are only sorry our accommodations are so meager. The other guests, you understand?"

"Of course," Stefano said, following Brother Ferrante to the hall. Another door stood opposite theirs and another at the end of the hall. "The rooms of other brothers?"

"Ah! This is the library and that is Abbot Alberti's office, but you'll not be bothered. His office is being used by guests and the door is locked," the brother said.

"We would not wish to interrupt, of course."

"Since my brother is busy with his other duties, would you convey my appreciation for this hospitality?" Alberti asked.

"But of course," Brother Ferrante said. "And now, if there is nothing more, I hope you will excuse me to my other duties?"

"Yes, yes, of course," Stefano said.

The cleric closed the door behind him, leaving them alone.

Stefano shed his coat and scabbard and tossed them onto the closest cot. "This is too easy, far too easy."

Della Guelfa opened the door and peered out. He looked back with a grin. "I can open these locks. It'll take some time, but . . ." He shrugged as eloquently as the brother had just moments before.

"We should wait until later," Alberti said, rubbing his face.

"Indeed," Stefano agreed. He looked out through the narrowly opened door. Voices buzzed in the room at the far end of the hall and the light damped out oddly as though someone within paced. "We cannot get close enough to listen at the door without being seen should one of the brothers stumble upon us."

Della Guelfa opened the door wider and crossed the hall. Casually, he tried to open the library door. He shook his head and came back. "The door is locked. Even if there were a way to hear what goes on in the abbot's office from there, we couldn't get in without picking the lock and—"

"Then we shall have to be patient," Stefano said. "We will apparently need to get into the abbot's office later." He sighed. "We will be up late, gentlemen, I suggest we get some rest now."

"I'll keep watch," di Mari offered.

"So be it." Stefano dragged his cot to partially block the door and settled in. He dozed fitfully, always conscious on some level of di Mari sitting nearby, of the lamp being lit as darkness fell, of di Mari reading the prayer book . . .

XXV

"Good neighbors I have had, and I have met with bad: and in trust I have found treason."
—Elizabeth I of England

THE day's events replayed again and again, thoroughly defeating any hopes Luciana held for a good night's sleep. Worry, frustration, and indecision drove her from bed.

Luciana shrugged into a robe and paced, barefoot, around her room. Her toes curled when her feet encountered the cold tiles which lay beneath the scattered rugs. Haunted by concern for Stefano and Prunella, she doubted she would be able to sleep at all tonight. She rubbed the back of her neck, wishing she knew what to do. She faced a stalemate on all fronts and, even with the apparent reconciliation, her relationship with her husband seemed fated to suffer from diverse loyalties and repetitions of arguments already made and lost. Prunella, no matter how contrary, had been her charge, and now she was at the mercy of an evil, repulsive man—joined by law and who knew what unnatural acts? The thought of what she knew about Conte Urbano made Luciana physically ill. Considering what she suspected him of doing to Alessandra, she felt heartsick when she thought of Prunella's future.

Indecision gnawed at Luciana. She hated this inability to act, this confusion and her, so far, baseless suspicions. As she turned once more in her pacing, the cherrywood box sitting on her altar caught her eye. She felt the bud of unworked magic in her gut. With a growing sense of purpose, Luciana removed the silk scarf used to cover the altar and wrapped it around her hair, then removed her cards from the box.

She swept the cameo brooches on her dressing table aside and spread the cards. They told her nothing she did not already know. Luciana ground her teeth. Seeking distraction, she idly turned another card and stared at it thoughtfully. *Dinnelo*. The Fool.

Am I being played the fool or does it suggest I should act impulsively? Luciana wondered. Act impulsively? Here, at court? With so much at risk?

She stroked the card, tracing the pattern of the Rom playing the part of the village idiot, all the while collecting coins as the *gadjé* laughed. It was no simpleton's game to play the fool. It called for shrewd judgment and unflinching nerve.

She gathered the cards, wrapped them in their silk kerchief, and returned the box to its place. She knelt before the altar and folded her hands over her heart in prayer. The *Fata* were wise. Perhaps the Sisters would grant her insight.

"Please, Laechisis who weaves the thread, give me justice for my sister and strength to protect Prunella," Luciana whispered. But would it be better to pray for something else? She had already failed Prunella. Who knew what the girl's fate was—or, she thought, shivering—had been. She prayed for another opportunity to protect Prunella.

A gentle scratching sounded behind Luciana. She turned, seeing Kisaiya peer around the door.

"*Daiya,* I hope you will forgive the interruption. I've someone you must see."

"At this hour of the night?" Luciana motioned Kisaiya in.

Kisaiya came quickly to Luciana's side, touching her heart as she stood before the altar. "I've managed to convince the princess' maid to come to you."

Luciana blinked, searching about in her memory of Alessa's letters. "Dulcinea?"

"Yes, *Daiya.*"

"Is she here now?" Luciana asked.

"Yes. Shall I bring her? I would not wish to interrupt your prayers," Kisaiya said.

"No. Please bring the girl." Luciana removed the scarf from her hair and draped it back over the altar.

Kisaiya returned a moment later leading a reluctant young woman from the upper rooms.

Luciana eyed the girl as she curtsied low, noting the burn scar across her right cheek, almost hidden by the way the girl wore her black hair braided and coiled to the side instead of behind. She was a dainty thing, the size of a child almost. She looked like a miniature doll. Pretty but for the scar.

Taking the girl's hand, Luciana raised her up. The girl moved obediently. "I understand you knew my sister."

"*Sí,* Your Grace," Dulcinea said, bobbing her head, but she avoided eye contact and touched her cheek self-consciously. "Your sister kindly tended the burn."

Luciana reached out, cupping the girl's chin as she turned her face so that the scar shone in the light of the bedside lantern. "How did you come by it?"

Dulcinea blushed deeply, but did not pull away. "It was worse before your sister's salves. It came from an accident with a curling iron."

Luciana glanced over Dulcinea's head at Kisaiya who shook her head. "Your mistress is the Princess Bianca, no?" Luciana gently released Dulcinea's chin.

"Yes, Your Grace," Dulcinea said, pulling away. "It was an accident—she did not mean to—it was an accident."

"Of course," Luciana said agreeably. She folded her hands together, searching for something she could say that would make the girl trust her.

"Your Grace, may I tell you how sorry I am about your sister? Her death, I mean?" Dulcinea spoke quickly, as though she expected a reprimand for speaking out of turn.

"Thank you." Luciana sat on the chaise, patting the end of the couch beside her.

Dulcinea approached slowly to sink down beside Luciana.

Luciana studied her. "Does the scar—the wound—cause you any pain these days?"

Dulcinea shook her head.

The girl clearly would not volunteer any information, and it would not do for her to feel pressured. She must choose her words with great care. "How long have you been in the princess' service?" Not the best choice, Luciana thought, once the question had been given voice, but she could do nothing about it now.

"I—I don't think I should speak of Her Highness to you, Your Grace," Dulcinea whispered. "She would be displeased."

"She might," Luciana conceded, "but your mistress would have to be told first."

Dulcinea blinked and nodded.

"I would not divulge the subject of our conversation," Luciana said. "Am I mistaken in believing you would not feel obligated to tell her yourself?"

Dulcinea hesitated. She looked like a mouse cornered by a cat. "What—what would you have me tell you, Your Grace?"

"You saw my sister fairly often?" Luciana asked. She must go slowly, she reminded herself, all the while wanting to ask what the girl knew of Alessandra's death.

Dulcinea nodded, her gaze lowered demurely. "She was a kind lady, but you want to know more . . . like about her death . . . don't you?" She looked up then, searching Luciana's eyes. "Why would I know anything? I'm merely a servant."

"I have yet to meet a lady's maid who has served more than a month and does not know most—if not all—of the household affairs. It's clear to see that you're clever enough."

Dulcinea squirmed and bowed her head again. "I—I cannot say that the princess was involved with Lady Alessandra's death, Your Grace, but I know she took a keen interest in your sister and her doings . . . much as she is interested in you and your business, which is why I . . . You must understand my position, Your Grace. I cannot afford to lose my post or otherwise displease my mistress."

"If it comes to pass, Dulcinea, you may come to my service and have no further fear of Her Highness," Luciana said.

Dulcinea blinked up at her. "Your Grace, I am honor-bound to my mistress—"

Luciana took her hand. "Do not mistake me. I know you give first loyalty to your mistress and I would not have this any other way, but surely you can see that justice needs to be served?"

"My mistress has little enough to do with justice," Dulcinea said, clasping the crucifix dangling from her throat. "Justice and judgment is Our Lord Father's province, and for this reason I will help you . . ."

Luciana sat back, waiting. She did not want to pressure the girl any more than she already had. The girl was fragile of mind and spirit, and Luciana wished her no further harm.

"Her Highness took considerable interest in your sister's affair with the Escalade capitano . . ." She paused, thinking. "Mondavo was his name, I think."

"Di Montago," Luciana said quietly.

The girl nodded and almost smiled. "The capitano seemed to forever be turning up, sometimes with your sister on his arm. My mistress was frequently distressed by his presence. She spoke of it to the cardinal and Conte Urbano, and then there came the news that di Montago was dead.

"I don't know why she took such pleasure in the accusations against Lady Alessandra, but pleased she was. She spoke of keeping secrets buried, but I only heard this from the stairs. I don't know who she spoke to since she locked the door to the sala.

"My mistress made an effort to visit Lady Alessandra during her period of grief." Dulcinea glanced around the room and seemed to grow more distressed. Fear of ghostly hauntings, no doubt.

"Do you know why she took an interest in my sister?"

Dulcinea bit her lip. "Perhaps she—my mistress—thought Lady Alessandra knew something?"

"Have you any idea what this might have been?"

"Truly, I do not. I swear it!" Dulcinea said, looking

more frightened than before. She rose. "Forgive me, Your Grace, but I've already stayed longer than I should. I must be going."

Luciana rose, resolved not to upset the girl more by delaying her. "Come to me whenever you please and if you have any more . . . accidents, well, I'll make salves for you as my sister did."

Dulcinea curtsied low. "You are kind."

Luciana watched Dulcinea back away and disappear to the upper level where the servant quarters were. Kisaiya followed on the girl's heels, but returned a few moments later.

"She seemed very frightened," Luciana said thoughtfully. It was no secret that the princess had a temper and had been unstable ever since her kidnapping by the Turks. Considering this and the fact that both Alessandra *and* the queen disliked and distrusted the princess, Luciana wondered how shortsighted she had been in taking their concerns so lightly. It gave food for thought.

"Indeed, *Daiya*. She made me check the corridors to be sure no one saw her coming or going," Kisaiya said, folding back the coverlets on the bed. "I cannot imagine what it's like to serve someone I am that frightened of."

Luciana removed her robe and climbed into the bed. "Yes, *Chavi-pen*, it is at the very least revealing."

"Indeed, *Daiya*, indeed," Kisaiya said.

———

The utter silence of late night woke Stefano with a start.

Di Mari blinked owlishly at the sudden movement, his own hand falling to the scorpinini lying cocked on his lap.

Stefano put his finger to his lips and nudged Alberti who grunted and snorted into awareness. The older man prodded della Guelfa as he sat up, yawning and stretching.

"Have you heard anyone?" Stefano asked quietly.

Di Mari shook his head. "Not for some time."

Stefano pressed his ear against the door and beckoned

ElizaBeth Gilligan

to della Guelfa when he heard nothing. He moved aside
as della Guelfa joined him and pulled a small set of tools
from his vest pocket. Della Guelfa crept from the room
and down the hall. He listened carefully at the abbot's
office door. Stefano watched with increasing interest as
the other man worked at the lock, grinning as the tum-
blers clicked into place.

"I won't ask you how you came to be in possession
of such tools," Stefano whispered, joining him outside
the abbot's office.

Della Guelfa shrugged and stepped aside for Stefano
to listen at the door before he edged it open.

Pausing, Stefano looked back at Alberti who waited
by the librarian's door. The older man eased down the
hall, peering back toward the salon. Alberti gave the "all
clear" and Stefano eased the door open wider. Di Mari
handed della Guelfa the lamp and retreated to the librarian's room. Della Guelfa raised the lamp, shedding
light into the darkened office.

Stefano assessed the room quickly. The office was
small and functional. Tables lined the walls, books lay
stacked everywhere. Clearly, the abbot did not take full
advantage of his station to provide himself with the niceties Stefano had expected to find. It served as a clear
reminder that not all priests shared the cardinal's weak-
nesses and colonizing aspirations.

Stefano crossed the hardwood floor and set the lamp
on the table in the center of the room. Papers sat in
heaping mounds at the corners, and rolls of parchment
were braced against the stacks. He took the largest roll
and spread it open.

Della Guelfa helped smooth the parchment flat and
let out a low whistle. "The Church seems very interested
in the placement of the Corpo d'Armata forces."

"So it would seem . . . or at least the cardinal and his
friends. How accurate would you say this is?" Stefano
asked.

The other man studied the map for a long moment.
"Very. It would take information from within to be
this accurate."

"And there . . ." Stefano breathed. "Damnation! Look at this!"

Della Guelfa leaned closer, studying the spot where Stefano tapped the map. "The Escalade! They must have spies there, too."

"But see, the most detailed information is here, in Salerno and then Citteauroea," Stefano said, pointing at the offending spots on the map.

Della Guelfa nodded.

"That means that the spy—or spies—are probably local to Salerno," Stefano concluded.

"That makes sense. The Catholic influence is stronger here on the continent than in the heartland," della Guelfa agreed.

The pistola makes a distinctive noise when cocked. Stefano and della Guelfa froze at the all too familiar sound. They slowly looked up. The cardinal stood framed in the doorway, candle in one hand, pistola in the other.

"I thought I recognized you at Vespers, Your Grace." The cardinal smiled. "How disappointing to find you so predictable."

"How did you know we were in here?" della Guelfa asked, straightening.

The cardinal shrugged. "Let's say that the Lord is with me."

"You can't shoot us . . . not here . . . not both of us . . . the noise . . ." della Guelfa said, taking a step toward the cardinal.

The cardinal turned the gun toward della Guelfa. "Actually, I can. This is double chamber pistola and, as to shooting you, well, I will think of something to say to the brothers. My guards are already on the way and my conscience, at least, will be clear since you have revealed yourselves as enemies of the Church." He looked inquiringly at Stefano. "So silent, Your Grace?"

"There doesn't seem much to say at the moment," Stefano said. "Although, I was beginning to wonder about your head."

"My head? What—" The cardinal crumpled to the

floor. Alberti grabbed the candle as it rolled from the cardinal's senseless grasp and tucked his own pistola into his belt.

"Good timing, Alberti," Stefano said.

"What do I do with him?" Alberti asked, hand on dagger.

"No, not that," Stefano said. "That is the king's decision."

"But he'll be trouble," della Guelfa protested.

"And we'll have even more trouble if *we* kill a cardinal," Stefano said. "If the guards are truly on their way, then we'd best hurry. They'll know we were here, so we needn't cover our tracks. Get that satchel there. We'll take these papers and the map."

"I'll get di Mari," Alberti said, disappearing into the hall.

They made quick work of gathering the papers and their belongings before slipping out of the building. Darkness offered a welcoming cloak for them to escape to the outer gate. Della Guelfa eased back the lock and peered outside. With finger to lips, he pointed to the military encampment beyond the wall.

"There's a sentry post just outside," della Guelfa whispered.

"How close?" Alberti asked.

"Close enough for the scorpinini?" Stefano asked as he turned to look back at the abbey.

"A throat shot," Alberti said.

Della Guelfa nodded to Alberti and looked out the door again. He grimaced, "Tricky business this shot."

"We haven't much time. Would it be easier to sneak up on him?" Alberti asked.

Della Guelfa shook his head and pulled his scorpinini from his boot and two bolts from the cuff of his coat. He loaded and aimed with care. The scorpinini twanged audibly. Della Guelfa cursed and aimed again, shot and lunged from the confines of the abbey into the open. He finished the guard with a quick thrust of his knife and beckoned the others out.

Stefano caught Alberti's arm. "We should separate lest we're spotted. Take di Mari."

Alberti nodded. "Where and when do we meet?"

"The cardinal will have men watching my home and probably the Banco," Stefano said.

"And we can count on them watching the Escalade Quarters, not to mention the docks," Alberti added.

"Aye," Stefano said. "There is the tavern the Escalade frequents. No doubt the cardinal's men will be there as well, but we can meet in the back, behind the kitchens. The cardinal's men won't anticipate gentlemen going there."

"Away with you, then," Alberti said.

Stefano darted out, motioning della Guelfa to follow. They'd just reached the closest of the alleys when a shout of alarm came from the encampment. The two men never looked back, but continued with their precious ill-gotten evidence.

It did not take long for them to hear the sound of pursuit, booted feet clattering on cobblestone streets, gasping, and the crashing of body against the miscellany stored in these back ways—a barrel tipped here, a broom banging to the ground there, but always just behind.

Stefano rounded the corner of an enclosed courtyard and fell against the wall, seizing della Guelfa as the other man skittered behind him. Three men sped around the corner and past them, but one gave a shout and stumbled to a stop, rounding on them with saber in hand. Stefano charged the man, capturing the end of his blade in his left hand. He knocked the man low with an upper cut, then turned and headed in the opposite direction with della Guelfa fast on his heels.

Cutting around another corner, Stefano leaped over a low wall. He smothered curses when he landed on a thorny rosebush. Della Guelfa ducked just as the soldiers ran past.

The duca leaned his back against the whitewashed wall, brushed another branch free of his heavy outer coat and dabbed at his bloody cheek with the back of his hand. He let out a deep, shuddering breath and grinned at della Guelfa.

"We'll wait," he said and turned to survey the garden they had invaded.

Della Guelfa peeked out over the top of the fence. He bent down quickly and laid a finger to his lips.

On the other side of the wall, they heard running men. More than two. A shadow fell across them as one of their pursuers leaned against the low wall breathing hard.

Stefano and della Guelfa pressed themselves closer to the wall and waited.

"They must be around here! We saw them come this way!"

The responses were mumbled.

"We'll split up, then. I want them found! These are the men His Eminence called us for, so they *must* be found!"

After a moment, Stefano peered over the wall again. "They're gone, but I wouldn't trust our luck to manage avoiding them."

"But how long can we wait here?" della Guelfa muttered. "It will be morning soon and the servants will be about before long."

As if by cue, a light bloomed in a far window of the house.

"That will be someone in the kitchen to light the fires," Stefano said. He looked over the wall and surveyed the alley.

Della Guelfa tapped his shoulder and pointed across the way. "The stable, Your Grace."

Stefano frowned. "We'll have to take the roof."

Della Guelfa nodded.

Together, the two men slipped over the wall and crossed the alley. Using a water barrel for a ladder, they climbed up onto the roof just as two red-coated soldiers returned. From their vantage point, Stefano and della Guelfa spotted nearly two dozen men searching the nearby alleys.

"What now, Your Grace?"

Stefano sat on the dusty wooden roof and leaned against the extending wall. "We shall wait."

XXVI

"If ever I was foxed, it is now."

—Samuel Pepys

17 d'Maggio 1684

LUCIANA closed the garden gate and waved to Idala who sat beneath a lemon tree with Prince Dario Gian playing by her side. The boy looked up from his wrought-iron coach and team of horses, saw Luciana, and came toddling to her.

She knelt to greet her nephew, chucking the boy under his chin, and then lifted him into her arms. Luciana crossed the lawn to where Idala sat and joined the queen on her blanket as she indicated. Dario wrestled free to tumble across his mother's lap and back to his toys. In a corner on the patio, Dario's middle-aged *bambinaia* sat mending her charge's clothing.

"He is looking well, Majesty," Luciana said, grinning.

"Truth. It seems he grows bigger by the day," Idala said indulgently.

"You, however, look tired."

Idala waved her hand dismissively. "I do not sleep well, but I told you this already."

Luciana's brows raised. "Did my sister's spirit disturb you again last night?"

Idala smiled in a reassuring way. "No. Surprisingly, I was left on my own. Nonetheless, I simply couldn't sleep and when I finally drifted . . ." Her voice dropped off as she closed her eyes. "Luciana, do you forgive me for your sister's death?"

"There is nothing to forgive, Idala," Luciana said.

"Do you *really* mean that?" Idala asked. She sat up straight and reached out to fondle Dario's curling locks. "I know she was almost a daughter to you. I have lost my own children, but to fate, never by human hand. What I wouldn't do to someone who hurt . . ." She fell silent and gathered a squirming Dario Gian into her arms. "Are you taking care of yourself, Luciana? You look tired yourself this morning."

"I had trouble getting to bed," Luciana replied, pressing a lock of hair behind her ear.

"Ah," the queen said knowingly.

"What do you mean?"

"Politics trouble me, Lucia, and I think I see the symptoms in you."

Luciana waved her hand dismissively. "I care not a soldibianco for politics."

"Hah! You're in the thick of it. I watch you. To learn what you have . . ." the queen shook her head. "No, my dear, you are in the thick of it. You must be careful, though. It is an exhausting game of wits."

"Politics and intrigue wear on the best of us, but time will out and it will all be over," Luciana said.

Idala snorted. "It's never over. Just one more move in the chess game and then it begins again."

"Have you spoken to the king yet?"

"No," Idala said, her hand dropping to her midriff. "I am not sure, and if it be another child, this pregnancy is like none other I have had before."

Luciana frowned. "What do you mean?"

"Before, always I have known the child from its first budding in my womb and always I have felt a kinship with it." Idala shook her head, stroking her stomach. "Try as I might, I feel nothing for this one . . . and it frightens me."

" 'Tis early enough yet, Idala," Luciana said. She took her friend's hand and pressed it to her cheek, remembering her own recent pregnancy. "It will change when you are not so uncertain, when you feel it quickening inside you."

"Perhaps," the queen said. "But you see why I have not told Alban. He is troubled enough, I don't need to bother him further—especially what with poor Prunella running off with that ghastly Conte Urbano."

"I shall never forgive myself for allowing that to happen."

"Allowed? It is the game of politics and this one was hard to see coming. Urbano clearly angles for more than a landed bride. Now he has married into the royal family—in a sense—and has even gained a connection to the Gypsics' Guilds through his relation to Stefano and, thereby, to you."

Luciana was silenced by that perspective. She had never considered it this way before, thinking only of Prunella and what Prunella offered. The cold calculation of such a union turned her stomach. Prunella was all the more a means to an end. How safe was she in Urbano's hands, and what more could she do?

Silence passed between them as they dwelled on their own thoughts and watched the playful toddling prince caper about the queen's garden.

At last, Luciana pushed such thoughts away. She must consider all of this at another time, probably even consult Stefano about it. Until then, however, there was still the puzzle of her sister's last few days. "Were you aware that Bianca visited my sister when she was in mourning?"

Idala sat up, her brows raised high. "No, I was not. I wouldn't have supposed that she *would* visit. I mean, she seemed quite confident that your sister killed Capitano di Montago."

"I thought it strange myself," Luciana agreed.

"In retrospect, Bianca took far too much interest in the death of one of my Escalade officers. How did you discover this?"

Luciana shrugged.

"You'll not tell me?"

"It was a confidence I'd rather not break."

Idala's lips quirked. "That, itself, is interesting," she said. Her eyes sparkled with curiosity. "So tell me, friend, what *are* you up to these days? First you know of the ghost and now this. Are you communing with the dead here in the palace?"

Luciana's guilty silence caused the queen to turn and stare. A mixture of horror and fascination crossed Idala's face as she said, "*Dios mio!* You have! Oh, Luciana!"

Luciana looked away, self-conscious. She would not lie about what she did, but perhaps she should consider a better answer than silence. "I've called upon my sister's spirit, 'tis true, but I don't commune with the dead . . . exactly."

"I'll not press you further," Idala said, but immediately observed, "it's just that you're so secretive of late!"

"I mean it only for your good, Majesty. There are some things you will benefit from not knowing, I think, but I will share what I can. My sister and her capitano died for what someone thought they knew. I wouldn't put you at the same risk."

"I took my risks when I married Alban. Till death do you part means so much more when you marry a regent," Idala said softly. She plucked a bit of grass and twisted it between her fingers. "Do you truly mean to exact vendetta yourself?"

Luciana shrugged, but remained silent.

"So you *do* seek death for a death," Idala pressed. She shook her head. "And you wonder why I worry if you have forgiven me?"

"Do you chastise me for wanting vengeance?" Luciana asked.

Idala sighed heavily. "No, my friend, but vendetta— even a bloodless one—is men's work. It is a dangerous matter that I would prefer you not be involved in. I could not bear it if I were to lose you as well."

"I promise you, I'll be careful," Luciana said.

"Please, Luciana, please keep that promise."

Luciana squeezed the queen's hand. "I promise that as well."

The letter was written in a Guild cant and came as close to written Romani as there was. It came from Guildmistress Eleni in Citteauroea. Grasni had arrived but feared coming to the palazzo, even for the *Araunya*. Luciana handed the paper to Nicobar. "Prepare the horses. I'll be going for a ride."

"Will you bring Kisaiya as well?" Nicobar asked.

"As well?" Luciana asked.

"As well as myself, of course," he said with a winning smile.

"I hadn't thought that far," Luciana admitted, seeing Nicobar's look of determination.

"After your last trip beyond the palazzo gates, I'd think you would not hesitate to welcome company."

"Armed company, you mean," Luciana corrected. She sighed. "Of course, you're right, Nicobar. Yes, arrange to come as well, but I'll leave Kisaiya here."

"As you wish."

Luciana snorted. "As *you* wish," she said.

Nicobar grinned and bowed.

Luciana watched him leave, then went upstairs. She changed quickly with Kisaiya's help and wound her way to the stables where she found Nicobar waiting for her. At the gate, she learned there were standing orders from the queen and Colonello di Luna, the Duca di Drago, that she be accompanied by a full dozen officers whenever she left palazzo grounds. Somehow Luciana maintained a gracious front despite her unease at the attention so many guards inevitably drew.

For all of the careful preparations, which included Luciana arming herself with a scorpinini, the ride into town proved uneventful to the point of boredom. She felt silly climbing down from her horse, Nicobar in close attendance, with six Escalade vigilare dismounting on either side of her.

The Guildmistress came to the door, her eyes widening at the contingent of men. She glanced behind her, into the depths of her house, and came out onto the front step.

"Will the *Araunya* be bringing everyone inside?" she asked as Luciana mounted the steps.

Luciana looked back. It *was* an intimidating sight seeing all these men arrayed behind her.

"We will wait for you here, *Araunya*," Nicobar said in a staged voice as he looked back over the men.

The Guildmistress sighed in relief and opened her door. She whispered quietly, "The girl is quite skittish, *Araunya-Daiya*. I don't think she came even this far willingly."

The *Beluni* was not one to be denied, Luciana thought sympathetically, though her compassion did not go so far as to let the girl stay away. "Where is she?"

"I have her in the sewing room with the other girls. She's no seamstress, but it makes a good way to hide her while we waited," Mistress Eleni said.

"Hide her? Do you really think it necessary?"

"She seemed to think so and, had she seen your escort instead of me, she'd be gone like a hare to its warren."

"Then I am most certainly thankful that it was you who greeted me," Luciana said. She followed the Guildmistress down the central hall of the house as if to go to the stables once more, but her hostess paused halfway and pushed wide two sliding doors to reveal a large work-room with a dozen and a half girls all gathered around a cream-colored gown embroidering pearls into its train. Everyone looked up. Except one. She sat in the far corner, a bit of the dress' extensive train on her lap and several sewing needles between her lips.

Though some months separated her from her last sight of Grasni, Luciana still recognized the girl. Due to the confines of the workroom and the women crowded into it, with the dress spread between them all, no one could get to Grasni easily. Even so, she looked frightened and ready to run. Guildmistress Eleni had rightly assessed the girl's disposition, Luciana decided. She took a deep breath and folded her hands, trying to look as unimposing as possible.

"Grasni-*chavi*? Come. Let us talk," she said gently.

The dark-haired girl looked up, her eyes wild for a moment as she craned her neck to be sure Luciana was alone. The other girls inched their stools away from the wall for her to squeeze past. Grasni took off the Guild-gray work smock and laid it neatly on the cutting table, along with the needles and other paraphernalia she'd collected as part of her disguise.

"Where can we talk?" Luciana asked her hostess.

Mistress Eleni motioned back toward the front of the house, after closing the doors to the workroom. The girls inside could be heard chattering and giggling immediately. Ignoring the girls' noise, the Guildmistress led them to the room Luciana had seen on her first visit. She noted that not only were the windows drawn but they would be difficult to get to because of all the bolts of fabric stacked about. Better Grasni *not* see the guard which had been called on to protect Luciana.

The doors shut quietly behind them as Mistress Eleni returned to the workroom. The two women eyed one another.

Grasni was clearly frightened, her eyes wide like a horse's, her small nostrils flared as though she might catch the scent of an enemy. She wore traditional Romani clothing, colorful and accented with jewelry, her hair braided and coiled behind.

Luciana moved aside several bolts of Gypsy Silk, feeling the invigorating tingle of the fabric's magical hum as she did so. With space cleared, she motioned for Grasni to sit and then joined her.

The girl had sought out traditional associations when she left the palazzo. It seemed reasonable that the girl would find formality soothing enough to put her at ease. "I am the *Araunya di Cayesmengri e Cayesmengro,* and I am here to hear what you know about my sister's death. You *are* Grasni of the Calvino Clan?"

The girl let out a trembling breath. "I don't know what they told you, *Araunya,* but your sister did not kill herself!"

Luciana sat back, a little startled by the outburst. The confirmation of her own conclusion, however expressed, felt like a balm to her troubled soul. "How do you know?"

"Besides my finding her indoors?" Grasni asked. She

shook her head and knotted her fingers nervously. "The bottle. The one they found in her hand. That wasn't like anything she had."

"Is this the only—"

"No, there's more," the girl said. "I knew the *Araunya*. She was grief-stricken, it's true, but she talked of vendettas not of killing herself. Her faith in the *Fata*, in justice, was too strong."

"Then how did she die?" Luciana asked.

Grasni looked around the room, the air of the hunted about her. "I'm not sure, *Araunya*, but the last to see her was Princess Bianca. She came calling and the *Araunya* sent me away, so I went upstairs as she said, but I didn't feel good about it."

"The princess came and my sister sent you away?" Luciana asked, unable to hide her surprise.

"Aye. The princess gave me a slip of paper which I took to the *Araunya*. After she read it, she said she would see the princess and that I must go away." Grasni wiped sweaty hands down her thighs hidden beneath thick, scarlet skirts. "It was the princess who killed her, *Araunya*. That night, when I went up to my rooms I fell asleep straightaway. I never do that, *Araunya*, but since studying the herbs these last few weeks and what my *ababina* tells me, there could've been something on the paper that made me fail my mistress."

"Do you know that, or do you guess?" Luciana asked.

Grasni pointed with the fingertips of one hand at her stomach. "The *chova* tells me. The cards confirm it. There was something on the paper, some bit of magic, some bit of poison, or perhaps both. When I accepted it, I consented to the enchantment. The bewitchment was to sleep, I'm certain."

Considering what she knew herself from the *chova*, Luciana could not dismiss Grasni's reasoning—besides something inside her responded to the explanation. A magicked thing accepted, however innocently, was enough to accept the effects of certain enchantments or charms.

"So you fell asleep," Luciana said.

"*Sí, Araunya-Daiya,* and left my mistress with the princess." She broke into silent, inconsolable weeping.

"It isn't your fault, Grasni. You mustn't blame yourself. You were nothing more than a pawn, as, it seems, was my sister," Luciana said. So, she thought, the princess *was* involved in all of this. She had been a fool to take the queen's instincts so lightly. She was reminded now of the card she had drawn the night before—*Dinnelo,* the Fool. Now she must play it out.

"The *Araunya*—your sister—sat with the princess in the sala. My mistress seemed very interested in whatever the princess was going to tell her. Of course, because I fell asleep, I know nothing of their conversation. I woke near midnight and went in search of my mistress, to see if she needed me.

"I looked in her room and did not see her, so I went to the sala. When she was not there, I went back to her room and that is when I found her. She was lying on the floor wearing her *vestaglia.* But it was wrong, all wrong—more than just being indoors! She never wore that robe with that gown and her cards hadn't been laid out. She always did a reading before she went to bed, *always.* There was the smell of *chova* in the room—even though I am not, was not as talented as you or your sister with the magic, I know *chova* when I feel it. The air in the room reeked of it. Then there was the bottle. I'd never seen it before. You know how she liked perfumes, always there was a new bottle, but she showed me each as she collected them. I would have *known,* but I did not recognize it."

"Why did you leave?"

"I could do nothing more for the *Araunya.* She was dead, gone, and I knew the princess had so recently been to visit. I know that the *Araunya*'s capitano had learned something important about the princess before he died. It seemed too dangerous to stay. The *gadjé,* they owe me nothing and if they would kill an *Araunya* . . . Because I was a maid, who would ask questions if I, too, were found dead?" Grasni paused to catch her breath, gulping air between racking sobs. "I knew it was wrong to leave her like I did. Forgive me, *Araunya-Daiya,* but I did not want to die, and I knew there was no one I could turn to. Who would believe me? Can you understand? Can you forgive me?"

"There is nothing to forgive, *chavi,*" Luciana said gently. She gave the girl her kerchief. "If you had not run, I would probably never have known about the princess. Now I know."

"She had help, and I sensed no *chova* around her—the princess, I mean. She has another who does her magic."

"Do you know who the *chovahano* is who works with her?"

Grasni shook her head and dabbed at her eyes. "The princess keeps the company of the cardinal and Conte Urbano, but I know nothing more than that."

"Did Dulcinea perhaps give you some hint?" Luciana asked.

Again Grasni shook her head. "That one is too afraid to even think without the princess' permission. Dulcinea knows as little as she can and still serve her mistress. It's the way she protects herself. Were the princess my mistress, I fear, I would do the same." She took a deep shuddering breath and looked toward the curtained windows. "Even now, I'm afraid the princess will find me and have me put to death so I can't tell anyone what I know. If only I knew more, something that would damn her!"

"You know enough and now you aren't the only one with the information," Luciana said.

"Will it help you, *Araunya-Daiya*? Do you plan vendetta for my mistress?"

"I do."

"Then I shall pray for you. Blessed is the *Fata's* thread," Grasni said, folding her arms over her chest prayerfully.

Luciana repeated the gesture and sensed the tension in the other woman easing. "You're studying the *chova* now, I'm told."

Grasni nodded.

"Then I take your blessing and know that I'll be guided," Luciana said.

Grasni bowed her head. "Through service to the *Fata*, I atone for my part in my mistress' death. I'll walk the Sisters' path and will forever be at your call, *Araunya*. If there is any way I can undo the harm I've—"

"You've committed no harm, but I will remember your promise, Grasni, and, one day, I *will* call upon you."

"As it is said, so it shall be," Grasni whispered.

XXVII

"Where it concerns himself, who's angry at a slander makes it true."

—Ben Jonson

19 d'Maggio 1684

LUCIANA looked over her shoulder and carefully surveyed her surroundings. While no one could fault her for lingering in the garden, especially on a day like this, it would be best for all concerned if no one guessed her actual purpose. Prunella had been gone for nearly a week. She worried over the girl. As long as Prunella remained with Conte Urbano, Luciana would worry, and the distress over failing the girl would likely never fade even if, somehow, by the graces of the Sisters, Prunella managed to find happiness with the unscrupulous conte.

It occurred to Luciana, in these recent days, that in spite of Prunella's expressed interest in the conte, running away with him did not make sense in light of what Luciana knew of the girl's nature. Luciana could imagine no argument anyone might use to sway the ever practical Prunella to act impulsively—at least, Luciana could think of no argument short of magic. The more she thought about it, the more certain she became that someone employed foul means and evil magic to get Prunella's cooperation.

With magic involved, a chance existed that remnants of it might be found in the garden. This latest foray into sorcery, considering the magicks which must have been used, would be convincing proof—at least for Luciana—that the conte and the *chovahano* she sought were one and the same. Confirmation of the sorcerer's identity would resolve so many pieces of the puzzle and, with that knowledge, it would be safe enough to bring the capitano out of hiding.

Frustrated after wandering the gardens for nearly an hour and finding nothing, Luciana sagged down on one of the many marble benches, resolved to reevaluate her search. She very much doubted the practical-minded Prunella would seek the maze for her musings. No, she would wander through the traditional flower and herb beds where gardeners, bent over their work, turned the earth daily. It would feel more like home, Luciana thought.

With renewed determination, Luciana relaxed. If someone used magic in the garden, she would find signs of it more easily by being calm and open. Almost as soon as she finished the thought, she became aware of the growing tingle in her stomach she associated with magic. Though she felt only the fading drifts of *chova,* it sang up her spine and caused the world to tilt briefly.

She frowned and looked around. How many times had she passed this bench? More than once to be sure. Why had she not sensed the magic before? In truth, the *chova* felt very faint, but still she should have sensed the lingering magic. She turned sideways on the bench and examined her surroundings.

"Were you perhaps looking for this, Your Grace?"

Luciana looked up, startled, to find Lord Strozzini, the king's bodyguard, standing over her. He held a bit of linen.

"I—uh—thank you," Luciana said as she accepted it. She felt the magic upon the fabric immediately. She unfolded it and found Prunella's initials neatly embroidered in one corner. The *chova* carried the same scent as she had found in the graveyard, and when she encountered Conte Urbano outside the church. Luciana longed to be alone so she could concentrate upon the kerchief, but Lord Strozzini did not seem inclined to leave.

"Am I right, *Araunya*? Has a glamour been put on the cloth?"

Luciana looked up at Strozzini sharply, a hundred questions leaping to the fore. With so many questions begging answers, she shifted aside on the bench and motioned for him to join her. "Won't you sit, Lord Strozzini?"

Strozzini bowed and sat, carefully adjusting his coat so that his uniform did not rumple. He flicked a bit of mowed grass from the toe of one shiny boot and then turned to face her. "You will pardon my insistence, but you did not answer my question."

"Your question . . . yes, indeed," Luciana murmured. She lay the square of linen on her lap, in her hands the *chova* distracted her. "It seems a rather strange question to ask."

"It does? Pray tell me why, Your Grace."

"If one knows enough to ask if something has been enchanted, then one generally knows enough to answer his own question."

Strozzini nodded thoughtfully. "But what if one were say a good Roman Catholic and did not believe in the actual use of *most* magicks, finding them possibly against the tenets of his faith, but was experienced enough in the ways of the court to know that not all think as he does?"

"True, but why would he assume some bit of linen he found on the ground is enchanted rather than simply mislaid or discarded?"

Strozzini folded his arms over his chest. "Perhaps he has knowledge that the owner of the cloth was spirited away in what, he is told, was a very uncharacteristic fashion."

"But still why the question of magic?"

"Perhaps he knows that some members of the court like to dabble in the dark arts and wants to assure himself of the truth or falsity of such things?"

"But being a good Catholic who does not believe in magic, why would he seek a magical answer? And would all things magical necessarily be of the dark arts?"

"Let us speak plainly, shall we, Your Grace? I have

it in mind that neither of us is the sort for this style of exhaustive conversation," Strozzini said.

"Court isn't the safest place to speak plainly."

"Indeed," Strozzini agreed, "but I suspect that we are both working at the same purpose if not quite for the same reason."

"An intriguing thought," Luciana said. "Please continue."

Strozzini sighed. "We are both looking into the cause of your sister's death and the theft of her body, are we not?"

"I don't know if *we* are doing anything of the kind, Lord Strozzini, but I have every intention of learning who murdered my sister and stole her body," Luciana said.

"Vendetta?"

Luciana nodded.

"It's not often a woman takes on such a task. It's a dangerous affair at the best of times. I would be remiss if I did not ask you to leave such matters to the servants of justice."

"You have capably performed your obligation," Luciana said.

"Murder is murder, Your Grace, for whatever reason. You risk your neck to the executioner's ax," Strozzini said softly.

"I make note, my lord, that the executioner's ax has been kept silent too long for my tastes and, since the servants of justice have not made that blade sing, perhaps it's the time for others to serve a higher justice," Luciana said, her tone frosty.

"Justice comes in its own time. It cannot be rushed any more than the hatching of an egg or the boiling of water."

"It isn't the hatching of eggs which concerns me," Luciana retorted. "You asked me if there were magic on this cloth. If I told you there was, what, in turn, would you tell me?"

"I would tell you that I saw Conte Urbano with something like this just a few days before the young lady and he departed rather spectacularly. I would tell you that, in fact, I had seen the conte *steal* it from the young lady, but thought nothing of it at the time since this is the way of some court games."

Luciana sighed. Just as she feared. She looked at Strozzini thoughtfully. "Why you asked me if the cloth had been enchanted is easily understood, considering my heritage, but, if you thought it magicked, who did you think performed the magic?"

Strozzini frowned. "Conte Urbano, of course."

"He's too frivolous to study the dark arts," Luciana said, but she watched Strozzini carefully to see where his thoughts lay.

"That is what he would have people believe, but I've watched him for well over a year now. There is steel beneath the curls and lace. The man is not one to be toyed with. Even I, in all my persistence, haven't been able to take full measure of the conte."

Luciana paused to think. While she had no doubts that Conte Urbano practiced magic, it was still hard to believe him capable of casting such magic untutored. But then hadn't she suspected the conte almost from the beginning? The disguise as a bumbling fool was fiendishly clever. In contrast to what she knew already, was she still willing to believe the conte incapable of using such powerful *chova*? Considering Strozzini's suspicions, it seemed she may well just have underestimated the conte . . . as he intended.

"You're really quite serious, aren't you?"

Strozzini nodded.

"But why? Why would he steal my sister's body?"

"More of his magic, no doubt," Strozzini said.

The sense of intimacy she felt with Strozzini struck Luciana suddenly. Why would she be so at ease with this man? Without speaking, she took Strozzini's hand and turned it over, wrapping her hands around his. The touch of his hand seemed comfortable and familiar. She cast about in her memory, trying to place where her sense of recognition came from. Her eyes opened slowly. "You were at the crypt, too—at my sister's crypt. Why?"

Strozzini pulled his hand away and crossed his arms again. "I suspected he—Conte Urbano—might try something. I went there that night, as soon as I was able, but he'd already been and gone. I could find no trace of him and whoever helped him."

"But why would you suspect him of doing something to my sister's body?" Luciana asked. "If you do not practice magic yourself, whatever gave you such an idea?"

Strozzini sighed. "Part of an overheard conversation that I hoped I'd misunderstood."

"Apparently, you hadn't. Can you tell me what you heard?"

Strozzini looked deeply pained. He turned his face away. "I heard the conte and the cardinal speaking of not letting certain advantages pass them by."

"The *cardinal*?" Luciana repeated. She would not have thought the cleric would involve himself directly in magic.

"Until then, I didn't believe the cardinal could truly be involved."

"Involved?"

"Capitano di Montago approached me after *he* overheard a conversation in the garden. I know he followed the cardinal to Salerno during the marriage negotiations for the princess. He'd hoped to get proof that the cardinal was working with the princess to take the throne," Strozzini said, glancing this way and that to be sure *they* were not being spied upon.

"But you still thought the cardinal innocent?"

"I did. He is a man of God, after all; the worldly affairs of kings are not within his purview. It's one thing to counsel the king and quite another to conspire."

"The cardinal *is* an ambassador from Rome," Luciana pointed out. "That, in and of itself, is a political position."

"All the more reason for him *not* to involve himself in such things."

"To what end do they plot?" Luciana asked.

Strozzini gave her a look of annoyance, his dark mustache twitching. "To see the princess on the throne."

"If you didn't think the cardinal involved, then who did you think was plotting?" Luciana asked.

"I note," Strozzini said softly, "that none of this has seemed to strike you as surprising."

Luciana shrugged, but remained silent.

"You asked, I believe, who I thought was involved in the plotting. At first, I thought it only the conte, with the princess being the fortunate benefactress of his machinations."

"The man is devoted to the princess as all can see, but beyond that, what would the conte's motivation be?" Luciana asked.

"There again, I was fooled. I thought he hoped to win her hand, and yet, he accepted this plan with the cardinal without so much as an argument according to what I learned from the capitano, and I've seen no sign of problems between them since," Strozzini said.

"The princess and the conte, you mean?"

Strozzini nodded.

"When did you first suspect the princess?"

Strozzini looked at her, surprised, then glanced around the garden again. He nodded to the gardeners moving closer to them. Together they rose and she followed him onto the cobbled drive in front of the palazzo. He took his own large linen kerchief from his pocket and laid it across the rim of the fountain and motioned for her to take advantage of it.

"There seems very little you don't know or haven't figured out," Strozzini said. "The princess has been particularly frail since her kidnapping by the Turks. At first, her fears were excused. She was young and traumatized. Who could not sympathize? After her kidnapping? And losing her sister, Princess Ortensia? But as Bianca grew older, none of the trauma seemed to pass, always it was as if the pirates had just released her. The crimes against her were always fresh and new in her mind."

"And no one has been able to comfort her in all these years?" Luciana asked, her disbelief putting an edge to her tone.

"Not even her father seemingly could help her. King Orsinio was a good man who sheltered his remaining child as best he could. He never forgave himself for not having a stronger escort for the princesses and he devoted himself to comforting his remaining daughter. But no matter his sympathies, it was clear to Orsinio and the Palantini that Bianca could not inherit the throne, which is why King Alban was named *before* Orsinio died."

Luciana nodded. "That was near the time she was sequestered for her education, wasn't it?"

" 'Twas no matter of education, but one of temper. It seemed that Orsinio eventually convinced her this was the right decision, that even without the crown, she wouldn't lose her place in court. The White King kept his uncle's promise. He has cared for her throughout his reign. Over the years, there have been petty plots, challenges to his authority and he has weathered them all."

"Until?"

"The conte seems to have made a difference in her outlook. In many ways, the princess has become calmer. She has blossomed socially. You must understand that, except for this wedding, the princess has done nothing in the least questionable. She behaves better than ever before," Strozzini said.

"But I have been told she seemed to delight in agitating the king," Luciana said.

"The queen, you mean," Strozzini said. "It's never been an easy relationship between those two. The queen clearly strives to be peaceable, but not the princess." He shook his head. "In this way she makes the king's life difficult as well."

"But if, in every other way, the princess' behavior has improved, why do you doubt her? The princess is no longer a child, after all," Luciana said.

Strozzini smiled again. "Permit me to amend your statement. The princess is no longer a child *and chooses her own friends.* That, I think, is the source of her greatest failing. I've always watched the princess and her friends. The king thinks me overcautious, but it is my place to be."

"But that brings us back to this," Luciana said, touching the linen in her lap. "And to your guess that Conte Urbano might have something to do with my sister's body. What do you think is happening here?"

"I believe the conte and the cardinal are comrades. They both influence the princess and, so far, this has been good, as I've said. The cardinal has now proved with this marriage contract that he will act against King Alban. The conte . . ." Strozzini shrugged.

"What do you suspect him of?" Luciana urged.

"I suspect him capable of the blackest of arts. I've no proof and I'm not exactly sure why he does what he does, only that he intends it to bring him power—if nothing else, power from behind the throne. He'll not have it with the White King, of course, but with Bianca . . ."

"Then you knew all along about him?"

"Knew?" Strozzini repeated, sitting back. "No. I didn't *know*, but I suspected. I believe him as capable of the black arts as of espionage."

"And yet you let me enter the maelstrom?"

Strozzini rose, folding his hands behind his back. He stalked a dozen feet from her, then turned. "It's true. I confess it. But I'm no Gypsy who *knows* about such things."

"So you assumed, because I was Gypsy, because my sister was murdered and I was hungry for vengeance that I would go where you would not?" Luciana asked. "Not every Rom is well-acquainted with the magical arts, Signore, and the type of magic the conte dabbles in can forever lose my sister and surely get me killed and maybe even cost me my soul as well."

Strozzini stared, his mouth not quite agape. "But I thought all Gypsies . . . I thought, since you were a Gypsy that . . ."

Luciana raised her hand. "It's done. Now it is a simple matter that we agree about the type of man Conte Urbano is."

"I have misjudged again," Strozzini said. "I regret ever having discussed my own doubts with Capitano di Montago for I'm sure that's what got him and *Araunya* Alessandra murdered."

"The capitano was a man of action and would have investigated in any case," Luciana said. She muttered a quiet prayer hoping Lord Strozzini would forgive her when the time came to reveal that the capitano lived.

"Who would have orchestrated the murder of my sister and the attack upon me?"

"It could be any of the three. The cardinal surrounds himself with his office and, I daresay, does little of the dirty work that needs doing. The conte, well, we have been calculating the lengths to which he will go. And the princess, surrounded as she is, has developed a malingering evil all her own. To my eye, she's as capable of it as the other two, but, in my experience, the princess is a most careful woman," Strozzini said quietly.

"Is the circle complete with the princess, the cardinal, and Conte Urbano?" Luciana asked.

Strozzini shrugged. "I am fairly confident. The French ambassador is most pleased with this turn of affairs— the marriage to the deMedici—but I don't suspect anyone would trust the ambassador enough to include him in their plans."

"And you're sure of Conte Urbano working magic?" Luciana asked. She'd concluded this much herself, but to have confirmation . . . "Even though he is Catholic?"

"He practices the faith with the princess. He makes regular confession to Padre Gasparino," Lord Strozzini said.

"How would you know that?"

Lord Strozzini looked at her, eyes open wide with innocence. "I see him when I make *my* confession." He smiled wryly. "Had I the nerve, I might violate the confessional to hear what he admits, but I suspect they're all lies in any case."

"So you don't think Padre Gasparino is involved as well?"

Strozzini shook his head. "Not the padre, no."

"Because he is Catholic?"

He stared at her thoughtfully a moment. "Because he *is* God's man. With some contemplation, I can believe what I think to be the truth about the cardinal, but I cannot make sense of Gasparino being involved."

"I am curious why, if you know Conte Urbano is a practicing Catholic, that you suspect him of working magic," Luciana said.

"He works his spells for the princess. I know it because I've seen him do it."

"You've seen him?" Luciana repeated.

Lord Strozzini got to his feet and paced away from her. "What I have seen was a minor illusion, an entertainment, if you will, one that at a distance I might have mistaken. But I have a sympathetic ear and the princess' handmaiden, Dulcinea, is a troubled child. She deserves better than her current lot."

"And *she* told you? What has she seen, then?"

Lord Strozzini looked pained. At last he shrugged and came to sit beside her again. "She told me she has seen him do illusions. To entertain Her Highness, he has taken on the visage of others. He has committed other, darker, magicks that Dulcinea will not speak of—she's too frightened."

Luciana considered the king's bodyguard for a long moment. "What do you think the princess capable of?"

He sighed and jumped restlessly to his feet once more, but did not pace away this time. "I would put nothing past her now she has had the poisoner brought to court."

"The poisoner?" Luciana hoped Strozzini could not tell that she prevaricated. Had the king spoken to Strozzini about Exilli after all?

"You wouldn't pretend not to know this man for what he is? Not to me?" Lord Strozzini said. "I saw his attempt on you and your husband at the party, and I saw your very clever ruse to upset it. Nor, as I recall, was this the first attempt on your life. You, like the capitano—and perhaps even myself—are in danger. Once out of the way, it will be easier for the conspirators to strike at the royal family. This Exilli that Conte Pierro brought with him from Gascony is a known poisoner. He worries me." Lord Strozzini looked up attentively. "How did you know? When he made his try to poison you, I mean."

Luciana shrugged. "My Gypsy heritage saved us. The duca said he encountered Exilli at Peloponnesus, that he poisoned a *generale*."

"I note that neither you nor the duca saw need to bring this poisoner to my attention," Lord Strozzini said. "Or did your husband not trust me with this information?"

"No, no, nothing like that," Luciana said hurriedly. "My husband informed the king before he left for Salerno. I thought you were made aware of it as well."

"But the king did not tell me," Strozzini said quietly.

XXVIII

"I have often repented speaking, but never of holding my tongue."

—Xenocrates

"IT'S been three days, Your Grace. How much longer can we afford to wait?" della Guelfa asked. He paced the length of the shabby room the two men shared.

Stefano edged the shutter open for the hundredth time and peered out over the alley to the back of the tavern. From here, they had a perfect vantage point of the comings and goings of anyone doing business at the Escalade's favorite retreat.

"We have time on our side . . . for now. We stand a better chance of fighting our way through the cardinal's men if there are more of us. More of us to stand witness, as well." He turned grimly from the window, "Besides, I have no wish to lose any of my men, and if we're away before they reach us, their chances of survival are dismal."

"But the longer we wait, the longer the cardinal and his people have to create another plan," della Guelfa said.

Stefano moved away from the window with an irritated sigh. "The princess is the focal point of any attempt the cardinal might make to take Tyrrhia. The princess is at court preparing for her marriage. We have time, but not forever. The wedding will be the turning point, a binding of the princess to the Church by her marriage to a Roman Catholic of their choice."

"Captain di Montago said he learned of a marriage contract between the princess and the Church. The at-

tempt on his life was made when he followed that contract to Salerno."

"I was wondering when you would share his secret,"
Stefano said. He turned back to the window. "Come see
this." He motioned to something in the alley below.

Della Guelfa crossed to the window and peered out.

"Do you see that boy there?" Stefano asked.

"The boy with the blue vest? What of him, Your
Grace?"

"He has been back and forth to the back door half a
dozen times since last night. The tavern keeper sends
him away every time and yet the boy comes back.
Why?"

"An interesting observation, Your Grace. I think I
will ask him myself," della Guelfa said.

"Have a care. The cardinal's men have been in the
tavern and we don't know who all of them are," Stefano warned.

Della Guelfa nodded and pulled on his coat as he left.

Stefano watched from the window as della Guelfa
came from their inn and peered up and down the alley-
way. Della Guelfa looked up when he could not find the
boy. Stefano pointed toward the market area where the
boy had gone. Della Guelfa set off quickly, winding his
way through the narrow thoroughfare.

Several minutes later the door rattled and sprang open
to reveal della Guelfa with the boy in tow. The boy
bowed awkwardly to Stefano. He looked back and forth
at both men, fidgeting with his hat.

"Go on, boy," della Guelfa said gently.

"Please, m'lord, forgive me, but may I see your ring?"
the boy asked. He shied away from della Guelfa as he
spoke.

"There now. None of that. No one will hurt you,"
Stefano said. He approached the boy slowly and held
out his right hand, spreading his fingers for the boy to
see his signet ring.

The boy squinted and looked close, his lips moving as
he muttered to himself.

"What do you see there, boy?" Stefano asked softly.

"The winged dragon with the sword," he replied.

He looked up at Stefano, his dark eyes narrowing as he studied his face. "Are you *really* the Duca di Drago?"

"Would you believe me if I said yes?" Stefano asked, unable to suppress a grin.

"What if he said no?" della Guelfa asked.

The boy looked suddenly frightened and pulled away.

Stefano touched the boy's shoulder. "No fear, boy. I *am* the Duca di Drago." He bowed with a small flourish. "And whom do I have the pleasure of receiving in my parlor?"

The boy looked around the room and its dingy shades of gray. The single room contained only an uneven table, mismatched chairs, pallets for beds, rotting blankets, and scurrying mice. "I didn't expect to find a duca in a place like this."

"Yes, well, my choices are limited at the moment. Now, why have you been looking for me. You *were* looking for me, weren't you?" Stefano asked.

"Yes, Sir," the boy said. "I've come from Signore Alberti."

"Alberti? What of di Mari?" della Guelfa asked.

The boy shrugged and turned to Stefano. "Please, Sir, I only know about Signore Alberti, and he is not well. Can you please come right away?"

"Is Alberti injured?" Stefano asked.

"Yes, Sir. Mother's been tending him because he said he'd have none of the Escalade surgeons nor any other," the boy said.

"Then let us make haste," Stefano said. To della Guelfa, he said, "I don't think we will return." He pulled a leather folder from inside his coat and removed a number of *lira* notes which he left on the table.

Della Guelfa handed Stefano his overcoat and the satchel.

The boy proved quick of foot. He led them through back byways and into the marketplace, moving easily among the press of people. Stefano and della Guelfa were hard-pressed to keep up with him and it made watching for the cardinal's men difficult. They passed from the marketplace into the residential quarter—a cluster of small houses pressed together so that even the cobbled street was overshadowed. Laundry, strung up overhead between the houses, flapped in the stale air. Children raced from house to house, their voices echoing off plaster walls.

Their guide stopped at one of the houses—virtually indistinguishable from the others—and opened the door. The boy beckoned them inside, closing the door quickly after them.

"*Madrecita*?" the boy called. He ran up the stairs, leaving Stefano and della Guelfa to wait. Momentarily, he returned with an older woman, bent with years and hard work, at his side. "Signores, this is my mother."

Stefano bowed. "Signora, we are indebted to you for aiding our comrade."

The woman shrugged. "He's up here. You haven't much time."

She led them to a darkened room. Nonetheless, light streamed through the patched shutters and down on the pallet in the corner. The only sounds in the room came from the street and the soft rasping of a man struggling to breathe. The woman stood back against the wall, folding her hands in her apron.

Stefano crossed to the pallet. Alberti looked gray. Flecks of blood dotted his unshaven face and stained the shirt he wore. Stefano reached down and took his old sword master's hand. "Alberti? Alberti?"

The old man's head turned and his sightless eyes fluttered open. "Is that you, Your Grace?"

Della Guelfa pushed one of the shutters open partially so more light could shine through.

Alberti patted Stefano's hand. "I was beginning to think you wouldn't come . . . at least not in time."

"Don't talk like that. We'll get you to help," Stefano said.

"The proof is what you must attend to . . . getting it to the king . . . don't waste your time on this old war dog," Alberti said breathlessly. He winked before convulsing with a fit of coughing which brought up fresh blood and phlegm. "Besides, the one who did this to me felt *my* teeth as well—only I walked away."

Their hostess came forward and handed a much-washed rag to Stefano who gently wiped the ailing sword master's face.

Alberti pushed Stefano's hand away. "You must go on without me, Your Grace."

"Is there anything we can do to make you more comfortable? To ease your way? Surely you'll let us bring a chirurgeon?"

"No. I won't last much longer."

"What happened to di Mari?" Stefano asked.

"I saw him captured," Alberti said roughly. Pain swept over his expression. "He tried to escape and was killed."

"And your injuries?" della Guelfa asked.

"We were chased down in the streets, cornered. I made my escape when di Mari distracted them. There was nothing I could do for him." Alberti spasmed into a fit of coughing again.

Stefano waited patiently, motioning della Guelfa to be still. "I've been away these past years. I don't know the personnel stationed here in Salerno, Alberti. Who can I trust?"

"Yesterday I would have said everyone—even the Catholics—but today, with the information you have . . . trust no one, Your Grace."

"That does not speak well of our fellows in the Escalade," della Guelfa protested.

"Concern for the kingdom must take precedence even over the honor of the Escalade," Stefano said.

Alberti's hand tightened on Stefano's arm. "Your Grace, the port of Salerno is easily watched. It's like a noose. The Escalade has made an art of cinching that noose around ne'er-do-wells hoping to elude capture. You must go to the port in Reggio di Calabria, but do not take the main road, that will be watched, too." Alberti fell back into his pillow, gasping for air.

"Do not tire yourself, friend," Stefano urged.

Alberti shook his head weakly. "The boy . . . he can take you to a roadside hostel where you can hire horses. Use my name to Rudolfo, the owner. Go on. I'll be well-cared for." Alberti sagged even farther into his pillows, his eyes drooping shut.

Stefano rose and turned to the woman.

"He'll sleep now," she said and ushered them toward the door.

Stefano took some money from his coat and pressed it into the woman's hands. "This is for caring for him, for sending your son, please take it."

The woman considered the money for a moment and then slid it into her apron pocket. "I'll keep it for medicine . . . or for the boy. Rest your minds, Signores, he will go easily."

"We are indebted to your kindness," Stefano said.

The woman shrugged. "He's been kind to us over the years . . . even after I remarried. I'd not turn him away."

Stefano paused and turned. "You were Alberti's wife?"

The woman nodded. "But that was in our foolish youth, long long ago."

"If, in the future, there is anything that I might do, do not hesitate to call upon the Duca di Drago," Stefano said.

"Take the boy and be off with you, then. I'll not risk his enemies coming to my house," the woman said gruffly.

The boy was waiting expectantly by the door.

"To Reggio di Calabria, then," Stefano said, waving della Guelfa to the door.

———————

Luciana leaned back on her chaise, fingering Prunella's handkerchief. *Chova* permeated the cloth. She dwelled upon the sensations elicited by the magicked cloth, trying to identify its entire purpose. The magic sang out its most obvious intent, but she hoped to find traces of other spells cast on or near it. Unwilling to accept absolute defeat, she concluded that she must focus upon the dominant purpose and be satisfied with that.

The magic took the form of a glamour, a charm. Once accepted from its bearer, the *chovahano,* Prunella was bedazzled, under his complete control. But Luciana also caught the flavor of the *chova,* a cloying scent which reminded her of the crypt that night in the graveyard. What more proof did she need that the same sorcerer committed both magicks?

Her mind wandered to Lord Strozzini. The man's sudden confidence seemed odd to her. Why had he not approached her sooner, warning her of Urbano in a more timely manner? For a moment, she doubted her conclusion that there was only one wizard, one *chovahano.* She wondered if *he*—Strozzini—could be the other. But no, she thought, dismissing the idea, she caught no scent of magic about him. Except, perhaps if Strozzini were good enough, then he could remove his scent. The thought intrigued her. Luciana knew such a thing was possible though only a few *chovahani* reportedly mastered the technique. Could it be that she now faced a wizard of such prowess?

But if that were true, why not remove the *chova* from all the items magicked? Did he not care? No, she decided, Strozzini's only involvement with the magic came in detection, not in its use. She also dismissed further thought of a second *chovahano.* It made for a good theory, but the evidence showed only one wizard and he, capable of casting all magicks so far encountered.

There came a scratching at the door. She looked up as Nicobar peered in. "All is ready, *Daiya.*"

Luciana nodded firmly. "I should've done this some time ago. I was a fool not to."

"Won't you let me go in your stead? What will people say if you're discovered?"

"At this hour? We should encounter no one in the halls, and his rooms have been clear for days. Even his manservant has gone with him," Luciana said. "I must act before he sends for the rest of his things and any traces of his work are removed."

"You are quite determined?" Nicobar asked.

Luciana jutted her chin and glared. With a nod, he

opened the door to the servants' corridors and disappeared briefly.

"The hall is empty. Come. Let us be done with this," he said, holding the door for her.

Luciana crossed in front of him and entered the narrow corridor. She peered around the first corner as Nicobar came to her side. As reported, no one was about. Lamps burned low in their sconces, casting a dreary half-light suitable only for late night errands and the Watch, should they decide to patrol these halls.

"Let me," Nicobar said. He moved into the next passageway and stopped, listening, then motioned her forward. He led her around another corner and to the door Luciana had come to nights ago when she followed Alessandra's *mulló*. Nicobar tried the door and muttered beneath his breath. With a knife from his boot wedged into the lock, he applied some pressure and the door sprang open. He pushed it wide and stepped back.

She peered through the gloom of the unlit room, wondering where to begin. Nicobar brushed past her. She heard the sounds of wood scraping and hinges creaking in protest, then pale moonlight filtered into the room as Nicobar opened the shutters.

He stepped down from the window seat, dusting his hands. "I'll fetch a lamp."

As he left, she wandered to the window. A small writing table occupied the space beside the window seat. She opened drawers, poking through the assortment of used nibs and ink-stained quills.

Nicobar closed the door and lifted the lamp to cast more light. Illumination revealed nothing more of interest in the drawer. Luciana's gaze dropped to the floor. She caught her breath, kneeling. A single white feather lay on the carpet.

"What have you found?" Nicobar brought the lamp closer.

She held the feather up. "What does that tell you?"

He took the plume, staring at it. "Someone controls the *mulló*."

Luciana rose, laying a soothing hand over her heart.

"He has captured my sister's spirit in the form of a bird. This is how he invoked the *mulló*. This confirms absolutely that he *is* the *chovahano*. The room stinks of his *chova*!"

"But this is Romani magic, *Daiya*. How would he know it?"

Luciana shook her head as she took the feather back. "Pull back the carpet, Nic, and let us see if he cast his circle here."

Nicobar handed her the lamp and rolled the carpet back.

She gave the lamp back to her aide, her full attention on what she saw on the floor. With great care, she traced the faint lines made with chalk and salt. "You see it here?"

Nicobar touched the line with a finger and tasted. He wrinkled his nose. "It stinks of ill magic."

"It does indeed," Luciana said, stepping back. "What I want to know, however, is where Conte Urbano keeps the bird he used to capture my sister's spirit."

"Either he took it with him, or—" Nicobar said.

"Or has left it in trust with someone."

"The princess?" Nicobar asked.

Luciana considered this possibility and shook her head. "Her Highness strikes me as a woman with little patience for such a chore and it wouldn't be one she could entrust to poor Dulcinea."

"Nonetheless, I'll have Kisaiya speak to Dulcinea and see if a bird has taken up residence in the princess' suite."

"So be it," Luciana agreed. "Come, we've seen enough. Let's leave before I'm ill."

Once in the hallway, away from the markings of the conte's magic, she leaned against the wall to regain her equilibrium. She caught Nicobar's arm. "Now we can be sure who we deal with. We know that he stole Alessandra's body and that it was he who pressed her into service. He could not have taken her body with him to Reggio di Calabria, so he must have her nearby. We must find and set her free, and it seems to me that we have enough of interest for the king to consider that we might bring our capitano in, eh?" She pushed away from the wall and headed toward her rooms, no longer caring if anyone saw her and made note of it.

XXIX

"Of all I had, only honour and life have been spared."

—Francis I of France

20 d'Maggio 1684

NICOBAR pulled his horse to a halt and dismounted even before the dust settled around the skidding horse's hooves. Chickens squawked at being sent to flight by the horse. A spotted dog tethered in the shade set up a racket of barks and howls, lunging like a puppy to the end of his rope, tail wagging in welcome.

A young woman pushed open the door to the farmhouse and came out, wiping her hands on her apron. Flour smudged her smooth olive complexion and dusted her black hair. She waved for a young boy coming from the barn to take the horse.

"Good afternoon, Signore," the woman said.

Nicobar bowed.

"If you've come for my husband, he is away," she said.

"You are Signora della Guelfa?" Nicobar asked.

"Yes." The haunted look came over her. It was a look common to the wives and sweethearts of soldiers.

"Please, Signora, there is no cause for worry."

The boy, not old enough to be afraid, stared curiously at him as he took the horse's reins. Still watching, and obviously listening, he led the horse to the trough.

"Walk the horse first," Nicobar said absently. He turned back to della Guelfa's wife. "I've come for your . . . visitor."

Signora della Guelfa dropped her apron and raised her eyebrows. "My visitor, Signore? You must be mistaken—"

"Signora, I am sent by Her Grace, Duchessa di Drago, for Capitano di Montago," Nicobar said. "Forgive me, I should have said this before."

A shutter from the second story opened wider and di Montago leaned out. "Show yourself, Signore, and move slowly."

Nicobar lifted his hands away from his body and backed slowly from the house until he could see di Montago clearly sitting on the second-story windowsill. Di Montago held a pistola aimed at his head.

"You're the duchessa's man, Nicobar Baccolo, aren't you?" di Montago called down.

"Yes, Capitano," Nicobar confirmed.

Di Montago released the cock and set the gun aside. "So, the duchessa has finally sent for me, has she?"

"Yes, she bids you come quickly . . . tonight. Preferably under cover of darkness," Nicobar replied.

"Then you will have time for supper first. 'Tonio, feed the horse and saddle another for the capitano," Signora della Guelfa bade her son. She held the door to her house open and beckoned Nicobar inside.

After a fine meal at the della Guelfa farmhouse, Nicobar and Capitano di Montago began their journey back to the palazzo at dusk. Di Montago saw no reason for further delays and his escort saw no reason to disagree. They rode in a companionable silence, watchful of the road and averting their faces when passing fellow travelers. Di Montago wore a heavy coat and a mask such as the noblemen wore when they wished to travel anonymously. Nicobar and the capitano both hoped these precautions would serve.

"It will be hard not acknowledging my fellows when

we reach the gates," the capitano said as they approached the southwestern end of Citteauroea.

"As long as you're not recognized, we still have the option of returning you to della Guelfa's," Nicobar said.

"But I'm an officer in the Escalade," the capitano continued gruffly. "I've already forfeited my life for my country and there's little enough to live for now that my adorata is dead."

Nicobar felt a pang of sympathy. The thought of losing someone as dear to him . . . well, it just did not bear further consideration. "Your grief speaks well of you, Capitano, but if you're dead, you cannot testify against the conspirators."

"What is there to testify to other than suspicion and an overheard conversation which might mean nothing if granted another context?" Capitano di Montago asked. "Do not forget I never actually saw the marriage contracts."

"No. No one has forgotten, but the time has come when you must tell what you know to the king. The players are revealed, and now we must root them out," Nicobar said.

Amiable silence fell between them again for a time as they continued on their way, resting their horses between spates of mile-eating runs.

Just north of Citteauroea, the sharp-eyed capitano dismounted without warning. "Nicobar! Over here!"

Nicobar slid off his horse and grabbed the other steed's reins before following di Montago into the gully.

The capitano knelt and rolled over what appeared to be a huddled mass of cloth. A man's skin glistened in the moonlight.

"Is he dead?" Nicobar asked, kneeling beside di Montago.

The capitano shook his head, his fingers going to the man's throat. The stranger's lips moved silently.

Nicobar and di Montago leaned closer.

"We didn't hear you, friend, speak again," Nicobar said.

The man grasped weakly at Nicobar's coat. "Messenger . . ."

"You're a messenger?" di Montago asked.

The man's head shifted in slight nod. His eyes closed, but his hand freed itself of Nicobar's coat and reached down to his own side, fumbling until he found the edge of a leather satchel.

Nicobar pulled the bag from under the man and placed it on his chest. "Here. Is this what you want?"

The man's lids drooped heavily. He pushed the folder into Nicobar's hands and coughed.

"He's gone," the capitano said and brushed the man's eyes closed. "Victim of bandits, perhaps?"

Nicobar looked around the open space surrounding the road, the forest not far away. He shook his head. "Thrown, more likely. There's his horse over yonder," Nicobar said. He took the satchel and sighed. "We'll see to it his message is delivered later, but now we must get you to the palazzo."

"Yes, best we be off. You can send soldiers out to collect him when we reach the gate," di Montago said as he mounted.

Both men breathed a sigh of relief as they reached the turn in the road where the palazzo gate came into view. The horses, sensing respite, picked up their pace.

Nicobar dismounted and pulled the chain at the outer gate. A shutter opened.

"Who comes?" a voice called out.

"It is I, Nicobar Baccolo, servant to Duchessa di Drago in residence at the palazzo. I am accompanied by Malleco Pral, a visitor summoned from Dragorione," Nicobar replied smoothly.

"Gate curfew is sunset," the guard said.

"My business kept me away. This is the duchessa's card," Nicobar said, presenting the card he carried in his breast pocket.

The guard took the card and closed the shutter. The bar scraped against the gate which finally opened. Escalade guards waited on the other side. They considered the two men for a long moment, then motioned them inside the perimeter.

Nicobar remounted and called to the Officer in Charge. "There's a man thrown from his horse not more than a mile down the road. He's dead, but you'll be wanting to collect him."

As the vigilare sorted themselves out, some mounted horses while others stayed behind to man the gate, Nicobar led di Montago down the lane, past the queen's orchards and the Escalade barracks to the stable where Baldo waited, drowsing on a rain barrel.

Nicobar prodded the coachman's shoulder.

Baldo stirred himself and greeted Nicobar with a sleepy grin. He took the horses without a word.

"We can take the back way. We'll draw less attention," Nicobar said, motioning to the orchards.

Di Montago followed Nicobar along the walk. With a suitable distance between them and the Escalade barracks, the capitano said, "*Malleco Pral,* eh? What would you have done if the guard spoke Romani? False Brother, indeed!"

"It seemed fitting," Nicobar said with a shrug. "It worked. And here we are." He opened the patio doors and ushered di Montago in.

Luciana woke to persistent shoulder shaking. Kisaiya. The girl would not wake her on a whim, and they awaited an important arrival. Luciana brushed the clouds of sleep from her eyes, set aside her shawl, and swung her feet from the chaise. "Is he here, *Chavi?*" she asked.

"Yes, *Daiya.* He waits below in the salon with Nicobar," Kisaiya said. She smoothed Luciana's skirt into place.

"Then bring him up," Luciana said. While Kisaiya ran down the steps, she lit another lamp and checked her appearance in the mirror.

Kisaiya gave a warning scratch on the door as Luciana smoothed a final lock of hair into place.

"Come in. Come in," Luciana bade them. She greeted Nicobar with a smile and extended her hand to di Montago.

The capitano removed his mask and bent over her hand.

Luciana led the capitano to the chaise. She motioned for him to sit as she searched for the best place to begin her briefing. "I've arranged for you to speak to the king. You must tell him all you know."

"Of course," the capitano said. "Have you learned anything . . . about my amorata or . . . ?" He took a quick shuddering breath. "Have you learned anything more since we last spoke?"

"I know that the *chovahano* is Conte Urbano—"

Di Montago gave a snorting laugh. "You'll pardon me, I hope, *Araunya,* but the man is . . . he's a simpleton!"

"A ploy, I believe," Luciana said.

"It would take someone of immense capabilities to fool so many so completely," the capitano protested.

Luciana nodded, meeting the capitano's gaze evenly. Were she relying upon logic or reason alone, she would doubt the conte capable of such acts herself; indeed she would be confident to the point of surety that the conte was *in*capable. However, she knew what the conte was from a deeper place, a deeper truth. The *chova* never lied like this.

The derision in his expression faded. "You truly believe this?"

"I do."

"You have no room for doubt?"

Luciana shook her head.

Di Montago paused to digest this news, looking to see if perhaps she displayed even a hint of a jest. "How can it be possible?" he said, more to himself than to her.

"Think of that night in the garden. I know it was some time ago and so much has happened, but . . . could the other man's voice have been Conte Urbano's?"

Di Montago's face worked into a deep frown. "I suppose it's possible. I mean, I never considered it before and now, well, I might be convinced that it was anyone's voice I heard."

"Was there someone else you suspected?"

"Suspected?" Di Montago shook his head. "I wanted the contract and so paid little attention to anything else. I did give it some thought, but I could think of no one— at least not at the time."

"But now?" Luciana prompted.

"But now, as I said, I could believe it to be almost anybody. Considering all this, it makes sense that it could be the conte. He remains close to the princess and, no doubt, has aspirations of his own. Yes, it makes a twisted kind of sense."

"So you agree with me?"

"I cannot confirm your suspicions with any evidence or testimony available to me, but I can tell you that I could not and would not attempt to refute your theory."

"Then I must be satisfied with that," Luciana said. She could not deny her disappointment, not even to herself, but better the truth than false evidence, and there were other matters to discuss. This man had once loved her sister. He deserved to know about Alessa's *mulló*. She touched his arm. "Capitano—Mandero—" She hesitated, not sure how to begin. "I have seen—" Luciana paused before speaking Alessandra's name. The taboo was strong. "I've seen my sister."

Di Montago made a ward against the evil eye and spat, his expression dark with anger, but then there came a dawning of hope. "You've seen her? You've seen my . . ."

"I've seen her *spirit*," Luciana corrected, hating the sight of hope dying in his eyes. "I've seen her more than once. She asks for you."

"You drew her back by taking her name? How dare you?" di Montago seethed, rising to his feet angrily. He spat again and wiped his mouth. "How could you claim to love her and then curse her to a *mulló's* existence?"

"It was not I, Capitano, but Conte Urbano who summoned her. He has forced her into servitude—"

"Conte Urbano?" di Montago spat the name as though it were filth, *marimé*. "What would he want with a tormented spirit? And why our . . . our . . . loved one?"

"He uses her to torment the queen, for what else, I do not know."

The capitano shook his head. "That doesn't make sense. How would he do such a thing? And why? To what end?"

"What troubles the queen, troubles the king. She blames herself for Alessa's death. I suspect Urbano means to wear Idala and Alban down so that they are more easily maneuvered when his other intrigues come to fruition."

"He is *benglo!*" di Montago said, but restrained himself from spitting upon her carpet again. He paused and studied her thoughtfully. "You would not toy with my sentiments, *Araunya*—"

"Never that!" Luciana assured him quickly. "I have truly seen my sister. She lingers, seeking you on the other side. I think that is the only comfort she finds in her current existence and it is what draws her to me. I am her agent to reunite you."

Mandero sank onto the chaise beside Luciana again, but promptly jumped to his feet, making the warding sign to protect him against the *marimé* cast off by the *mulló* and its known associates. He could not, however, refuse his heart. Luciana saw that in his eyes. "She didn't forget me, then? But can she forgive me? For not being there? Waiting for her?"

Luciana smiled sadly. "She loved you. She begged me to tell you she would wait for you."

"I never deserved such a one as your sister, *Araunya-Daiya,*" he said. He shook his head once more. Looking up, his expression grew fierce. "And you believe Conte Urbano did this, that he is capable of doing such an evil thing to my adorata?"

"I'm confident this is his work."

"He must die for what he has done," Mandero said through gritted teeth.

"And his confederates. This deed, if not actually commissioned, was blessed by someone."

"This matter is vendetta for you?" he asked, his voice dangerously soft.

"I have sworn the blood oath. He cannot go unpunished for his foul work," Luciana said.

"Does he still control her?" Mandero asked.

Luciana hesitated, remembering the feather she'd found the night before in Urbano's room and her fruitless attempts to find the body. The capitano read in that pause all there was to know.

"What hold does he have?" he asked.

"All that he possessed before—except now I know that it is he we seek, that he has entrapped her spirit in the form of a bird . . . and I know what spells he uses to keep the body."

Mandero stared up at her aghast. "You have accomplished nothing, then?"

Stung more by her own guilt and frustration than his words, Luciana turned away. He had every right to be disappointed. It was a poor showing. "I'll offer no excuses. I'd be done with this sooner than later and so it will be when I can make my opportunity. But, before I can act, I must protect her—"

"Protect her? What more could he do that he hasn't already done?"

Luciana rolled her shoulders and rubbed the back of her neck. The weight on her shoulders, while proverbial, was stultifying. She *must* measure up. "If I act prematurely—should I exercise my vendetta against the conte and still not know where my sister's body is, I may never be able to discover her whereabouts and she will be forever trapped as a *mulló*."

"Then, by all means, we must find her!" Mandero said. "After you find her, then she will be free?"

"Almost," Luciana admitted, avoiding his eyes. "He possesses some little of what is left of her earthly spirit. Like an unmatched glove, it is useless, but a piece of her is with him nonetheless. I must reclaim that bit so that no one else will be able to press a claim against her soul."

"Were you anyone but the *Araunya,* I would take the claim to the vendetta away from you, do it myself," di Montago declared, rising to his feet. He paced away from her and spun back. "You *will* permit me to aid you in this matter?"

"If it is within my power. Have no doubt of that." She took up the lantern. "The king is waiting for us," she said. "We must tell all so that he can decide what he must do."

"Let us not hesitate a moment longer, then," Mandero said, reaching for the door.

"Not that way. We don't want you seen if we can avoid it," Luciana said.

"Surely no one would dare act against me here, in the palazzo, even if I were seen," Mandero protested.

"My sister was here in the palazzo, Capitano." Luciana shook her head. "If I'm right, we know who the conspirators are, but let us not take any chances, Capitano. We should take no risk that another conspirator, unrevealed to us, might do what his associates dare not. Come, there is another way, a way which will permit a discreet retreat if keeping you secret still serves the king's purposes." Luciana crossed to the tapestry and pulled it aside. Deftly, she pressed the door open.

"Your resourcefulness is amazing, *Araunya-Daiya.*"

"One merely takes advantage of what is at hand. Come, we should not keep the king waiting longer than necessary."

The capitano followed her into the hidden passage. She noted that he sniffed and wrinkled his nose. The corridor smelled no better than on her previous visit. Odors of wet fur and dank spaces were not to her liking either.

"The corridors here do not smell as fresh as the others, Capitano, but secrecy is more sure."

The walls seemed narrower this time. Moisture dripped from the ceiling, wetting her face. The rats squeaked nearby. The feel of her skirt being brushed by tiny bodies, the brief pressure on the toe, however, Luciana found unsettling. Relief swept through her when she found the door to the king's retreat. She tapped softly and waited.

The sharp glare of a lantern nearly blinded her when King Alban opened the door. "Your note was most mysterious. I must admit to being quite curious," he said, and then his gaze fell to Mandero and he stopped, speechless and staring. "Capitano di Montago? Can it be true?"

"Yes, Majesty," the capitano said and bowed deeply.

"Come in. Please." The king ushered them into the room to the chairs opposite his desk. He pushed aside papers and sat on the edge, continuing to stare at the capitano. He shook his head at last. "I am amazed. I most assuredly never expected to see you again . . . at least not alive."

"The *Fata* watched over me," Mandero said lightly. "I found haven with my mother's people, the Romani, and they, in turn, presented me to their representative to the White King."

"The duchessa," the king concluded. He looked at Luciana, his gaze speculative. "You are, perhaps, even more resourceful than I hoped, though I am surprised even you would keep such a secret, Your Grace."

"Majesty, this man's life was entrusted to me. Until I could reasonably expect he would not be jeopardized by being revealed, well, you must understand my dilemma?"

The king nodded and rose from the desk. He paced to the end of it and back, clearly calculating. "So, at least Lady Alessandra's name can be cleared."

"If you'll pardon, Majesty, but none should have believed it of her in the first place," di Montago said ardently. While he kept his words courteous, the capitano could not hide his anger over the injustice. Luciana liked him all the more for it.

"Of that, I was already confident," the king said. "So, tell me, Capitano, what *did* happen to you on the Stretto that night?"

"I was stabbed in the back and shoved overboard, most likely by the very same sailors who testified against my lady."

The king nodded. "Were any of them left living, I would summarily have them brought in and put to the gallows. And what of this mission you were reportedly on?"

The capitano shuffled his feet nervously. "I planned to steal the princess' marriage contracts from the cardinal who was taking them to Salerno."

"Contracts? More than one, you say?"

"Indeed, Majesty," Mandero said. He shifted forward. "I returned to the gardens hoping to find a fan my lady had mislaid. While I lingered in the maze, Cardinal delle

Torre and Her Highness passed nearby with another man—"

"I am confident this was Conte Urbano," Luciana said.

The capitano frowned, but nodded. "I did not intentionally listen to what they were saying, but they took no pains to be secretive. The cardinal wanted to arrange a marriage suitable to the Holy Roman Church's designs for Tyrrhia. In exchange, she was to have his backing when she made a claim to the throne. The other man said that he, too, would support her if she made this binding contract with the Church. To this, the princess very willingly agreed, stipulating certain conditions of her own about whom she would find suitable."

The king sank down on the desk again and rubbed his eyes wearily. "There was no mistaking who the parties were?"

"No, Majesty, at least not the cardinal or Her Highness. The other man must have gone another way, but they came around the corner and discovered me. I pretended to have heard nothing and excused myself, but they must have suspected and that was why the attempt was made on my life," the capitano said.

"You must see that this marriage the cardinal arranged would tie Her Highness more closely to the Church," the capitano continued, "and her loyalties to the cardinal? Duca deMedici is renowned for his piety, and his loyalty to his Church and the Vatican. His son could not have expected to make such a good marriage being born, as he was, out of wedlock, but with the Church arranging the match for him, he, too, would be obligated to the Church."

The king sighed heavily. "I take no pleasure or satisfaction in this marriage contract, but treason it is not. Not by itself."

"Which is why the second contract was so important," the capitano said.

"Yes, you mentioned contracts," the king said. He hooked the leg of a chair with his foot, drew it to him, and sat, motioning for Luciana and the capitano to also be seated.

"In the second contract, Bianca promises that de Medici's children—by her—will be heirs to the Tyrrhian throne," the capitano continued, "or so their discussion implied."

The king nodded. "So there has been no end to Bianca's scheming. She has merely improved her technique."

"And perhaps found more capable conspirators. Conte Urbano is a *chovahano*," Luciana said.

"A what?" the king asked.

"He is the wizard who stole my sister's body. It is he who has been sending the ghost to your queen to torment her sleep . . . and to you," Luciana continued.

The king shook his head. "It's preposterous. The man isn't capable of that much thought!"

"Ask Lord Strozzini. He knows it as well," Luciana said.

"Then who killed your sister?" the king demanded.

"Bianca."

"Princess Bianca?" both men said at once.

"There'll be no proving it. Magical forces were at work, so, of course, we know that the conte assisted her, but it is she who committed the act. She, according to my sister's maid, was the last to see . . ." Here Luciana paused automatically, but she forced herself to go on, using her sister's name for clarity's sake. ". . . Alessandra alive. By means natural or magical, she compelled my sister to drink the bottle of poison she was found with."

"Are you sure that in your desperation—justified, of course—to prove that Alessandra did not take her own life, that perhaps . . ." the king began.

"My lady did *not* kill herself," di Montago declared. "She wouldn't. It's as much against our faith as it is the Catholics'."

"Why Bianca? There was no love lost between the two, but it just doesn't make sense," the king said.

"It would if perhaps the cardinal and the conte thought Princess Bianca might betray them if the situation became difficult for her. It could have been their way of insuring her complete commitment to their plan," Luciana said.

"That makes sense," the capitano agreed.

The king smiled wryly. "But it is supposition based

upon secondhand testimony of a maid who ran away the very night her mistress was murdered. Tell me, when and where did you speak to this maid, Your Grace?"

Luciana sat back and took a deep breath. She needed to keep her wits about her. "Grasni met me in Citteauroea. She was too frightened to come here and had to be persuaded by the *Beluni* to come that far."

"You must see that I cannot convict Bianca of murder on such evidence? As to the conspirators, let them think they have won—for now. I have spoken with the Palantini, and it is agreed that after the marriage she and deMedici will be banished from Tyrrhia, as will the cardinal. The conte, he is another matter, and perhaps we can charge him—or banish him as well."

The thought of the princess eluding a more real justice was like a blow to Luciana. "You will do nothing about my sister's murder?"

The king shook his head sadly. "I cannot. To do so would be to draw a dividing line between the nobility. If the princess were tried, with so little evidence . . . Don't you see? She would become a martyr, and then their plans may well come to pass."

Luciana could see, could understand, but it gave her no comfort. She turned to di Montago. He looked no happier.

"If I can find a way—" Luciana began.

"If you can prove she murdered your sister, then there will be a trial," the king concluded. "You will come to me if you have more news? Something more tangible I might use?"

"Of course, Majesty," Luciana agreed reluctantly. She had pinned her hopes on the king taking greater action with the evidence she brought him. "Though it has already been said, a cautious eye upon the cardinal would not be amiss. Nor a closer eye upon Conte Urbano if he returns—as I think he will."

The king nodded. "That one will pay dearly for what he has done, that much I can promise you."

She felt a pang. In all of this discussion, Prunella seemed to have been forgotten. Prunella, by her marriage to the conte—if they at least did that—would be caught up in all of this, and there was still the matter of finding Alessandra. "Majesty, this may seem insanity to you, but I find that I must plead for some indulgence for the conte before charges are pressed."

The capitano turned to stare at her, his anger still seething just below the surface.

"Indeed, Your Grace? I cannot imagine why you would suggest any leniency for the man."

"It is not for him that I plead, but for our young cousin, and I need the conte to move about freely so that I might more easily follow him to where he keeps my sister's remains."

The capitano's gaze dropped to the floor, and he no longer seemed ready to erupt.

The king nodded, "A most sensible demand."

Luciana glanced sideways at Mandero. "What of Capitano di Montago? Does he return to the Escalade or to his shelter?"

"The plot has been foiled, and I have not acted against either Bianca or the cardinal. The capitano should be safe now . . . as long as he does not take any unnecessary risks."

"I will return to the barracks this evening then, with your indulgence, Majesty?" Capitano di Montago said, rising.

"Yes, of course, and make your presence known to Her Majesty. She was most grieved by your loss," the king said.

"Of course."

XXX

"Malice is of a low stature, but it hath very long arms."

—George Savile, Lord Halifax

21 d'Maggio 1684

LUCIANA dropped her napkin across her lap and sat back, taking in the overbright morning and the budding fruit trees in the queen's orchard. A feeling that something was wrong nagged at her. She had woken to that premonition and it had stayed with her until now. Anxiety swelled uncomfortably in the pit of her stomach. Fear threatened to overwhelm her as she remembered the last time she had such a feeling. *Not now,* she prayed.

Kisaiya poured more chocolate and pushed the honeyed lemon closer to Luciana's right hand.

Luciana forced a smile. "Thank you."

Kisaiya took Luciana's plate and set it atop her own. "Have another cup of chocolate and enjoy the morning. You seem troubled today."

Luciana rubbed her temples. "I'm concerned about the duca. It's been a week since Prunella ran away, and I last heard from him the day after."

"Daiya?"

Luciana twisted in her seat to greet Nicobar as he came onto the patio. "Join us." She indicated a chair to her left. As he sat, she saw his expression and ashen complexion. "What is it?"

Nicobar placed a leather satchel on the table. "*Daiya*, I have done something that I should not, but you must see this."

"You're frightening me," Luciana said. The knot in her stomach contorted.

Nicobar shoved the satchel closer. "I'd forgotten this until a moment ago. The capitano and I took it from the body of a messenger we discovered along the road from Citteauroea."

Luciana reluctantly drew the courier's pouch onto her lap. It contained a folded paper, its waxen seal carefully broken. "Did you open this?" She removed the document from the bag.

"I know it was wrong, but . . ." He pointed to the wax impression. "It's the cardinal's seal and the letter is addressed to the princess."

"Princess Bianca?" Luciana said, feeling numb as she stared at the seal. She folded the paper open and pressed it flat. The words scratched onto the page were from a scrawling hand. The words themselves were in an odd mix of French and Latin. Luciana frowned and began to decipher.

17 d'Maggio 1684

For the express attention of Her Most Royal Highness of Tyrrhia, Bianca Isabella Novabianco,
  I write this letter to inform you that the Duca di Drago, Stefano di Luna, and his confederates have discovered certain papers within our possession which might lead them to uncover particular plans best not made public at this time. I leave it to your discernment to which plans I refer.
  We have pursued the duca and his men. One was arrested and killed when he attempted escape, a second we are sure is fatally wounded, but we have been unable to locate him. The

*duca and one other have so far eluded us. I urge
caution. We will continue to pursue this matter
here in Salerno. My return to Tyrrhia's heartland
will coincide with the securing of the stolen
documents.
Pius Enrico delle Torre,
Cardinal of Citteauroea, Holy Roman Church*

The paper drifted from Luciana's fingers to the table.
Her dread took form. Why could she never be wrong
about such things? Her chest constricted painfully. She
felt ill and at a loss.

"Daiya?" Kisaiya whispered.

"No, no. I must think," Luciana said, pushing herself
to her feet. She crossed the patio on shaky legs to the
open doors of her suite. "I must tell the queen. I must
see Idala with this news." She sat in the nearest chair,
her hands shaking. "I–I must tell the king!"

"And what of the letter, *Daiya?*" Nicobar asked.

Luciana took a deep breath and gathered her
thoughts. She would do no one any good if she allowed
hysteria to take over. Stefano's life might depend upon
her ability to sort through this, and she was not about
to fail him, not in this. "I must show the letter to the
queen," Luciana said, taking it from him with a growing
sense of purpose, "but preserve the rest, Nic. We may
yet want to deliver it to the princess. Better she not
suspect anyone else ever saw it." She turned to leave,
but stopped. "And, Kisaiya, send for Capitano di Montago. Have him come to the queen's rooms."

Idala did not pretend to hide her anger, dismissing the
attendant who hovered helplessly nearby. "How did you
come by this letter, Luciana?"

"Nicobar and Capitano di Montago found a fallen
messenger by the roadside. Nicobar forgot about the
satchel until this morning and then, when he saw the
seal and who the letter was for . . ."

"I'll kill her if anything happens to Stefano!" Idala swore.

"We must keep our heads. She mustn't know we suspect her," Luciana said.

"But we must do something!"

Luciana had taken the time to collect herself, and now, with calm came reason. She sat on the sofa beside the queen. "If Stefano had gone to the Escalade in Salerno, we would most assuredly have heard from him. We would know what this entire matter is about by now."

"Unless he's dead," Idala murmured.

"No. If he were dead, then the cardinal would have sent that news to the princess. He would have contrived some way for Stefan's body to be found," Luciana said, taking what comfort she could in her own calculations.

The queen took a long breath, staring at the paper. "So, until we hear otherwise, we must presume Stefano and his companion are alive."

"It is our only hope," Luciana agreed.

"But why didn't he go to the Escalade? He has a commission. They're his fellows! Why didn't he go to them?"

"I have been giving this some thought," Luciana said. "The only thing I can think of is some of these plans that the cardinal referred to must have something to do with the Escalade. Why else wouldn't Stefano have gone to them?"

Idala shook her head again. "But how could it have involved *my* Escalade, the Queen's Guard? You're speaking of treason with*in* the Escalade."

"Perhaps," Luciana agreed. She did not want to consider such a possibility. It meant Tyrrhia's position was even more fragile than she had thought.

"We can't know for sure, but I think it would be advisable to follow my brother's lead in the matter. We can turn only to those we *know* we can trust absolutely."

"I agree, Majesty, which is why I have taken the liberty of sending for Capitano di Montago."

"Good!" Idala said, rising to her feet. She swayed for

the briefest of moments and then stalked thoughtfully away. "In the meantime, what do I do about Bianca?"

"We will keep this letter as evidence. When the time is right, we'll use it," Luciana said.

"But first, before all else, Alban must see it," Idala said.

Luciana nodded. "But will he agree?"

Idala sank upon the arm of a chair. "He will. I'll make him see that this plan is the best. Since it involves my Escalade, I have some power in this decision as well."

"If we expose this too soon—" Luciana began.

"It could all be excused with a little quick thinking by these conspirators," Idala said. "Better to let Bianca think all goes well."

"How will we get the message to the princess when the time is right?"

"Messengers are waylaid all the time," Idala said.

"Of course," Luciana agreed. "And she will think that if we knew of this correspondence, we would act against her."

"It is a plan, then," Idala said, "though I confess to not liking the odds. Let us see the capitano."

Stefano stroked the velvety nose of the horse. Marco della Guelfa paced nervously, kicking up straw with his dusty boots. The creaking barn door heralded the return of the stable boy and his master, the innkeeper.

The innkeeper was a ruddy man, fairly dressed for one of his station, devoid of the customary apron. "Who be you gentlemen?"

Stefano left the stall and approached the innkeeper, bowing before him. "I am the Duca di Drago. I presume you are the innkeeper, Rudolfo?"

The innkeeper nodded. "Are you the gentleman of whose coming I was advised?"

Stefano smiled to himself. The man's formality at this time of night spoke of his own discomfort. "Could you be so kind as to tell me in whose name I prevail upon you for aid?"

"We must be careful, mustn't we?" the innkeeper said with an ironic smile. He jerked his thumb toward the door and the stable boy skulked out. "You come in the name of my friend Alberti?"

"Yes, but I must bring you the sad news of his passing."

The innkeeper swore bitterly, turning away from Stefano and della Guelfa. He turned back a moment later, his expression composed, though the pain showed. "As his friends, I welcome you. Alberti came to my aid many times and, even after death, I am prepared to return his favors."

"We are honored to accept in his name," Stefano said.

"I began to fear you wouldn't arrive. The boy came with news of your impending arrival days ago."

"We are gladdened by your concern," Stefano replied. "We had the misfortune of finding it most difficult to leave Salerno."

"The Catholics?" the innkeeper asked. His voice said what his words did not.

Stefano's brows rose. "You feel strongly about the Catholics, I see."

"It's the witch-hunters who have my ire. My experience of them has been less than favorable. I am not Tyrrhian-born, you see," the innkeeper said. "My family was originally from Ancona. I am a Jew. The Church persecuted my family, burned our books, and arrested my parents. My *tantela* managed to escape with me and brought me to Tyrrhia and here I have stayed. There are not many places in this world where my people are accepted without persecution and contempt."

"We, unfortunately, live in oppressive times."

"There were worse times," Marco said.

"I do not forget the Inquisitions," Stefano said, shaking his head. "But, yes, Signore Rudolfo, there were complications in eluding the cardinal's men. The roads from Salerno were well guarded, so it wasn't easy to find a way out of the city."

"You will find the roads beyond not much improved, I fear," Rudolfo said. "I receive frequent visits from the cardinal's men on patrol. They fairly haunt the roads to Reggio di Calabria."

Della Guelfa sank down on a bale of hay. "At this rate, we'll be hard-pressed to reach Citteauroea before the princess' wedding."

"You will probably need to specially commission a boat from Reggio di Calabria. My tantela retired there and her son has taken to the seas as a fisherman. His name is Davino. Tell him I sent you and perhaps he will take you across the Stretto to the heartland," the innkeeper suggested.

"We are grateful for your generosity," Stefano said.

"Would you care to take advantage of the inn before you go on your way? It must be some time since you have bathed or rested properly."

Stefano glanced down at his own dust-caked clothes and considered the innkeeper's offer longingly.

"We must rest sometime," della Guelfa said. Exhaustion was etched upon his face. "Perhaps this will be our last opportunity. If nothing else, let us take advantage of a meal and the opportunity to nap."

"We could be on our way at the turn of night," Stefano said.

"You must stay in my own chambers, away from the common rooms where a patrol might discover you. Come, my wife will be pleased to make you something to eat," the innkeeper said. "My son will have the two fastest horses saddled and ready for you."

———

Mandero nodded his thanks to the maid who let him in. Curiosity lent him more speed than was usually decorous, but one did not waste time when receiving a royal summons to the queen's chambers. "Your Majesty, Your Grace," he said, bowing.

The queen looked pale, but determined. The duchessa looked much the same. He sat down as the queen indicated before she turned to Luciana. "We have news that my brother, the Duca di Drago is in danger. We want you to go to his aid at once."

Mandero blinked. Now he understood the worry in the expressions of both women. His life was the queen's, he had sworn oaths, but beyond even that he owed much to the duchessa as well. He felt compelled to spare these women any further losses if it was in his power to prevent them.

So, there was no mystery here, but danger and a chance at thwarting conspirators against Tyrrhia, for who else would threaten the duca? He took a deep breath, carefully controlling the thrill of anger and anticipation of action. "I would be honored to do whatever I'm able to in order to assist the duca, Majesty," he said, keeping his voice calm and measured.

"Thank you," the duchessa said. "We have reason to believe there are spies within the Escalade—"

The queen's protest permitted him the moment he needed to hide his own shock.

"Surely he must be warned?" the duchessa insisted. "If Stefano avoided the Escalade in Salerno for a reason, we could be committing a grievous error not to tell him."

"Perhaps you might enlighten me?" Mandero suggested, drawing the women's attention.

"Of course! You would know none of this!" The duchessa looked to the queen for permission before quickly explaining what had been discovered. "So you see," she concluded, "we need someone we can trust absolutely, someone who will also go to the aid of the duca."

Mandero let the full story wash over him as he considered the letter now in his hands. Self-irritation flamed. How could he have been so careless as to have not looked at the messenger's satchel himself? If this delay resulted in the duca's death, then he was as much at fault as the cardinal and the princess.

He became aware of the women watching him. He managed a confident smile in that perfunctory, efficient way that would best ease their concern. The matter was in his hands now and they would have the benefit of everything he could muster.

He returned the letter to the duchessa . . . the *Araunya.* "I presume the duca's companion is either Lieutenant di Mari or Lieutenant della Guelfa. They are both good men, to be sure," Mandero said. They had both served under him, trained under him. They were *his* men and Mandero owed them a debt of honor as well. The queen and *Araunya* were still waiting, watching him. "I am yours to command."

"You realize the risk?" the queen asked.

"Of course."

"You are barely recovered, barely returned from your misadventures, you have every right to decline—" the queen continued.

"I am your man, Majesty, of that there can be no doubt, surely?" he said and turned to the *Araunya*. "Where would your husband go?"

The duchessa shrugged. A hopeless gesture. "If he were being hunted, it makes sense that he would continue to try and evade the cardinal's men, but where he would go, I don't know."

"Does he have friends on the mainland?" Mandero asked.

"Yes, but they are all in Salerno," the duchessa said.

"What about Cousin Arturo?" the queen suggested.

The duchessa nodded excitedly. "That's true! He could turn to Lord Arturo for aid—unless he would hesitate because they are also Catholic?" A sudden look of horror crossed her features. "And Conte Urbano is there, with Prunella!"

"Then it would make sense for him to go to Reggio di Calabria," Mandero said, "but not necessarily to Lord Arturo." He tapped his chin thoughtfully, recalling the western coast of mainland Tyrrhia. "There is another Stretto crossing nearby. It makes sense that he try to escape the cardinal's men by going farther away from Salerno."

"Quite logical," the duchessa said. She leaned forward, her agile mind clearly reviewing the possibilities. "But wouldn't the cardinal consider that as well?"

"Such is our misfortune," he admitted, "but the lieutenants and the duca are intelligent men, too. They will account for this."

"You must find a way to intercept them and bring

them back to Citteauroea safely. If they cannot cross in
Reggio di Calabria, you must find a way!" the queen
said, her voice rising with worry.

"There's Gypsy Crossing," the *Araunya* said quietly.

"My thought as well," Mandero said. He tapped his
chin, thinking aloud. "If there are spies within the Escalade in Salerno, then there must be a danger of spies
here as well, both in the palazzo and also in Citteauroea.
I must proceed with caution, you understand?"

The women nodded, looking unhappy.

"If I am to take the duca over the Gypsy Crossing, it
makes sense to turn to the Romani. There are other
Rom within the Escalade, and there are sufficient men
within the Romani community to give further aid should
we need it. If I have your leave, Majesty, I will ask the
Gypsy Queen for aid."

The queen nodded. She would have agreed to anything at this moment, he thought. The *Araunya,* on the
other hand, had grown calm and calculating. She rose
and tapped his shoulder. "I will prepare a letter for the
Beluni, adding my name to your request. When can you
be ready to leave?"

"Within the hour, if not sooner," Mandero said, also
rising. "Shall I come to your rooms when I am ready?"

"Yes, please," she said. "Majesty, if we have your
leave?"

The queen rose, nodding. She captured Mandero's
cuff. "Capitano, you *must* bring my brother back safely!"

"I will give my very life in that endeavor, Majesty."

Stefano started awake at the sound of an opening
door. The innkeeper's wife put a finger to her lips and
crept into the room. Stefano nudged della Guelfa and
rose into a sitting position.

"Is it time?" della Guelfa asked tiredly.

"No. There is a patrol in the common room asking
after you. You were seen near here by one of the farmers," the woman said. "My husband suggests I take you
to the cellar."

"Would they really search your home?" della Guelfa asked, his voice betraying his surprise. "They take too many liberties! They aren't the king's men! They aren't even Tyrrhian!"

"They've invaded our living quarters in the past. We secure your safety, Your Grace. Please! Hurry!" she said. She opened the door and peered out, motioning them to follow her.

Stefano and della Guelfa scrambled from the bed, gathering their sabers and other belongings as they went. There was no time to do anything else but leave it to the innkeeper's explanations.

The cellar was cold and cramped, overflowing with foodstuffs and purchased blocks of ice. It was clean, and a slinking tabby cat kept it relatively free of rodents. The innkeeper's wife left them a candle and showed them how they might escape should the guards come down.

Stefano shifted aside sacks of carrots and sat on one of the wooden ale kegs. He shrugged into his coat.

Della Guelfa, however, paced. "I am outraged by the cardinal's liberties! It is as though he already ruled Tyrrhia!"

"Calm yourself, friend," Stefano said. "They're anxious to regain their plans. They have too much at risk."

"But don't they think they'll arouse suspicion with this behavior?" della Guelfa asked.

"It is different here on the mainland, as you, yourself, have noted. Here, the Church is closer. The people of continental Tyrrhia are accustomed to certain behaviors. If nothing else, would they dare complain when their neighbors might hear?"

"So you say the Church still holds sway?" della Guelfa muttered. "This is supposed to be a land free of religious restriction, where every man is free to find God in his own way. We fought to repel the Church from our borders, and now they filter among us like weeds in a garden!"

"The Church is not wholly bad, della Guelfa. It is the leaders who govern the mortal men, rather than show them how to lead their moral existence, with whom I have a problem," Stefano said. He leaned back against the cool brick wall. "The cardinal is among the worst, and *he* does have designs upon the throne."

"Spoken like the philosopher you are," della Guelfa said with a dissatisfied grunt. He sank onto the cellar steps and prepared to wait out the patrol.

"Try to rest. While the comforts of this cellar are poor in comparison to the feather bed we just left, it might be the last time we can sleep with any surety of our safety for some time."

The hours passed quickly in the cellar, marked by the chill and uncomfortable sleeping arrangements, but somehow both men managed to rest. They were eventually woken from their fitful slumber by Rudolfo who brought them a platter of fish and pasta and large mugs of warm, dark brown ale.

"They are gone now, well and truly gone," Rudolfo said as he watched the men eat. "I sent my boy—you saw him in my barns—on the pretense of an errand and I bade him keep an eye out for the patrol. He said they are gone, down the southerly inland road toward the Sala Consilina."

"Have you noticed a pattern to their patrols?" Stefano asked.

"They usually seem to follow the main roads, every once in a while taking one of the smaller avenues. They rely upon the faithful and easily intimidated, and I suspect they have even made confederates of the bandits," Rudolfo said.

"Would they go so far?" Stefano asked.

"Have they stopped at anything yet?" della Guelfa retorted.

"There is truth in that," Stefano agreed amiably. "Can you recommend a route we might take?"

"I recommend you take to the fields and follow the coast. The way is longer, but perhaps you will less likely be found out," Rudolfo suggested.

"A sensible plan," della Guelfa said.

"Then we'll be off, under the cover of dark," Stefano said.

"It is already dark, Your Grace," Rudolfo said. "My

son has saddled two horses and my wife has packed them with provisions."

"You are most generous," Stefano responded. He reached for his wallet, but Rudolfo waved him to a halt.

"Please, Your Grace. I do this for the good of Tyrrhia. As Tyrrhia is safe, so, too, is my home and family. If that is insufficient, then I do it in the name of our mutual friend, Alberti, to whom I owe a great deal."

"We will arrange to return your horses," Stefano said.

Rudolfo shrugged. "If they are returned, so much the better, but easily enough replaced."

"Will you at least take money for the horses?" Stefano asked.

Rudolfo shook his head. "Come, gentlemen, you will want to be on your way quickly while you can take advantage of a full night to travel."

XXXI

"In the pursuit of knowledge, one must take steps."
—Tyrrhian Proverb

26 d'Maggio 1684

LUCIANA dismounted and gave Baldo her horse's reins. On her walk back to the palazzo, she found Nicobar waiting for her at the edge of the stables.

"Did the ride do you good?" he asked as he fell into step.

She shrugged. To one who knew her, her mood was clearly unsettled. She dropped onto the edge of the fountain in the palazzo's front courtyard and, letting out a troubled sigh, trailed her fingers in the water. "I worry about the duca and now the capitano, as well. What if I have only made matters worse?"

"Then the ride didn't serve its purpose," Nicobar said.

"Oh, the airs were good for me, I cannot deny that, but how can I think of anything else?" She looked up at the sound of a carriage. Pulled by a team of four blood-bay horses, the vehicle's polished black sides dazzled in the sun. Luciana did not recognize the design and guessed it must be one of the newer models of carriage that were all the rage in England. Someone had gone to great expense to import it. "I wonder who comes?"

"Perhaps someone arriving for the princess' wedding?"

She frowned at Nicobar. "An early arrival?" Luciana

rose to avoid the stamping carriage horses, but craned her neck to see who the hostlers assisted from the coach. "But I suppose it isn't so very early with the wedding little more than a week away," she said, then paused, as her heart rose to her throat at the sound of Conte Urbano's ingratiating tones. She moved around the fountain, looking to see if Prunella disembarked with the conte. She found no pleasure in welcoming one of the conspirators back to the fold, but at least she could be reassured of Prunella's safety.

Nicobar followed.

"I don't see Prunella," Luciana whispered and immediately tried to hide her concern as the conte, apparently alone, turnd away from the hostlers.

Unable to hide his own surprise, the conte minced across the cobbles and bowed flamboyantly. "I'm most gratified that you come to meet me! A mere distant cousin by marriage! I cannot help but be surprised you knew *when* I would arrive, as well. You are most assuredly a clever woman, Your Grace."

Luciana felt no need to force a smile. Even Conte Urbano could not ignore the ill-mannered nature of his elopement. "I'm surprised to see you so soon. I thought you might stay in the country a little longer."

The conte affected a deprecating laugh. "I could not miss the wedding of Princess Bianca and Conte Pierro. I am, after all, fortunate to count myself one of Her Highness' friends," he said. "My wife graciously agreed that I should be at court."

Luciana glanced meaningfully toward the carriage. "And have you brought your wife?"

"The contessa?" Urbano asked sweetly. "No, not just yet. She wished to get our affairs in order and to spend time with her family. One of her younger sisters, Maria, I think, is getting married in a few weeks as well. Have no fear, though, my Prunella will be arriving within the next day or two for the festivities."

A chill coursed through Luciana. She knew she could not trust Urbano and, with Prunella tucked away somewhere, she had no way of ascertaining the girl's safety. She found security for the moment in pretty pleasantries.

Insincerity came all too easily when dealing with the likes of the conte. What *was* difficult was finding the appropriate words so that she sounded at least civil. Trying to force some semblance of a smile, she said, "I'm sure you'll be relieved not to be apart from your bride for very long."

"But, of course, what newlyweds are ever eager to be apart?" Conte Urbano smiled silkily. "Long separations are for those who've been married some years and have, perhaps, grown tired of one another, Your Grace."

Luciana flinched at his gibe, but made herself laugh it off. "My cousins should not be in such a rush, then, to appear the old married couple." She noted his ink-blackened lips and said, "I see you have taken advantage of the carriage ride to write. Perhaps your wife, Cousin Prunella, will be greeted with a sampling of your poetry?"

"The Tyrrhian roads are just horrid at this time of year," Conte Urbano simpered, licking his lips self-consciously. "Actually, I was writing something for Her Highness, a dedication for her wedding. Now, pray forgive me, but I must supervise the unpacking and call upon Her Highness so she knows I am returned for her wedding."

The conte turned to the servants unloading his bags. He caught hold of one man removing a cloth-covered box from the carriage and took it himself. Luciana took note. The package was large enough, could it be that she now stood close to the housing of Alessandra's soul? To the living bird he used as a mortal cage?

When she and Nicobar were within the palazzo, she released her pent-up breath. "Did you see that box the conte took?"

Nicobar nodded.

"I'll wager the bird he has been using to control my sister's spirit is in it," she said. "The thought of him having the bird, touching it and abusing it . . . I *must* free her. Oh, poor sister!" She shuddered, crossing her arms over her chest as though to find warmth against a sudden chill.

"What will you do?" he asked.

"I haven't decided, but I must free it. We haven't found my sister's body yet, and, until we do, he could force her into another bird. I'll end his fiendish hold over her or be damned myself!"

"Have care, *Araunya*," Nicobar said, peering around them in the long echoing hallways of the palazzo. "Perhaps this would be better handled by someone less prominent? Someone whose continued efforts are not imperative to save Tyrrhia from the princess and her cohorts?"

Luciana bit her lip, duly reminded by his caution. "We must not be overheard." She hurried along the hall, coming to an intersection of two corridors. She paused here, able to see anyone who might approach from any direction. "*I* must do this."

"As I knew you would say, but at least permit me to—"

"How can you help me with a plan I have not yet formed?" Luciana said crossly. She sighed. Nicobar did not deserve her anger. He was as faithful and true a man as could be found. She patted his wrist absently and motioned for them to continue toward her apartment. "You know I will turn to you, Nic. I note, however, that this is probably an occasion where it will be far easier to explain my presence alone than with you at my side."

"It sounds like you already have a plan," he said uneasily.

"I have the beginnings of one, but nothing complete. Come, I am due to have luncheon with the queen, and I must prepare."

Nicobar retraced his path again and tried another corridor. How many times had he searched the garden maze looking for the *Daiya's* mysterious alcove? So far his efforts had proved fruitless due—he was sure—to the meticulous nature of the Head Gardener. Usually, the *patrins*—no more than a rearrangement of the decorative rock and a bit of branch twisted just so—were small

enough to escape the attention of anyone who did not
know to look for them. These *patrins,* however, had
fallen victim to the Head Gardener's obsessive sense of
order and, as a result, he found himself forced to use
the imprecise directions of a map. It seemed useless, but
his sense of duty would not permit him to abandon the
search for the *Daiya's* one possible lead to finding her
sister's body.

He considered the reaction he might receive if he
brought one of the carriage dogs into the maze to see
what it might sniff out. He could not, of course. The
maze fell into that part of the palazzo and grounds intended for the nobility. The gardeners, he felt sure,
merely tolerated his presence since certain exceptions
could be made for a senior member of staff or one of
the queen's guests. The gardening staff, nonetheless,
watched him suspiciously as they went about their work.
Perhaps they left him to his work because of his station
relative to their own. In either instance, he did not care
so long as they continued to give him a wide berth.

He stopped, frustrated once more by a dead end. He
studied the map and could make little from it. Either
the *Daiya,* having little need of them, was poor at making maps or he, having less need, could not read them.

"Benglo la prestrare!" He spat to rinse the devil's
name from his lips. Nicobar regretted the gesture immediately seeing the spittle land before shabbily booted
feet. Wincing inwardly, he looked up, an apology already
on his lips.

"Peace, *pral.*"

Nicobar considered the gardener who called him
"brother" in his native Romani. By no means the Head
Gardener, this brother stood shy of what would eventually be his full height. The youth wore pants nearly as
shabby as his muddied boots, but the work smock he
wore over them appeared relatively new and an apprentice's cap perched at a rather jaunty angle upon his head.

The youth stepped closer, his voice lowered and full
of awe and excitement. The glint of mischief in his eyes,
however, drew Nicobar more. "Are you here on the
Araunya's behalf?"

"Sí, pral," Nicobar said. He winked at the boy. "I did not expect to find a Rom in the queen's gardens."

"No?" the boy grinned. "We are commonly forgotten, we *giv-engroes,* but were it not for us the mulberry trees would die and so the worm would follow, then where would our Romani *pralar* be?"

"Being a farmer is not the Wandering Folks' nature," Nicobar said. "But if your families work the silk orchards, why are you here?"

The boy pulled his cap from his head and stuffed it into his boot. "As you say, being *giv-engro* is not our normal way, so we must learn—those of us who will tend the trees for the sake of the worms. *Me mamie-dei* thought apprenticing me to the queen's Head Gardener might serve me well when I take my father's place overseeing the orchards."

"It's no small part you take then in the future of Gypsy Silk," Nicobar said. "How do you like being in service to the queen and her people?"

"They are no *Rom.* My master is *gadjé* true and through and has naught but a rough hand for any small mistake. I haven't ever seen again the last lad to make a big mistake." The boy winked. "I've christened many of the queen's gardens after speaking his name, such as you have just done."

Nicobar nodded, but already his mind wandered back to his problem. He wondered cautiously if he should take advantage of the Head Gardener's apprentice.

" 'Tis proof of his *gadjé* nature, the man cannot stand even a twig out of place . . . like so," the youth said. As he spoke he reached out a dirtied hand and twisted a bit of bush. His voice lowered conspiratorially, "Nor a mite of pebbles out of place. He being *gadjé* from his head to his toe, that mightn't look like overmuch to him, but, to another's eye, well, it could be almost anything. Couldn't it?"

The youth's meaning could not be mistaken, but whether Rom or no, Nicobar did not know him. "As you say then," he replied, "for I do not know the Head Gardener well."

"You're cautious, *pral,* but before I serve anyone else,

the *Araunya* has my allegiance. Why else would I work for the *beng*?" he paused to spit, "when I might have the road like the others?"

The Head Gardener's apprentice gave a grunt. " 'Tis I who have caused you these days of misery. I saw the *patrins* for what they were and took steps to cover them myself."

"And never mind the Gardener *Rye*?"

The apprentice grinned mischievously and shrugged. " 'Tis true he'd've had me straighten them as I did. But it would have caught his eye. Would mean nothing to him, mind you, but it would have gained his attention and what gains his attention oft as not finds its way to the princess' ear."

"A twig out of order would gain the princess' ear?"

"*Sí*. That day especially, for all knew that the princess and the *Araunya* had both been hereabouts. The Head Gardener, he doesn't know our ways, but he's heard enough that he would have reported it in the hopes such news might please Her Highness."

"So you hid the *patrins*?" Nicobar asked. He did not so much disbelieve the youth as wonder at his game. The boy showed no shyness about taking advantage of the moment, of course, it would be a rare Romani who did not seize upon an opportunity. It came as instinctively as breathing. "Why did you say nothing before?"

The youth shrugged. "Same as you, caution, but you've been here many a day. To the careful observer, you look for something. I thought a good *Rom* like yourself had better to do than wander these *gadjé* paths where nothing proper and wild is permitted—unless the *Araunya* sent you. And since the *patrins* were left the day of her last visit and you being the first who could read them since . . ." He shrugged again. " 'Tis always possible that I reckoned wrong."

"You didn't," Nicobar said.

The lad nodded, straightening. The look of mischief did not leave him, but he seemed suddenly more serious. He glanced this way and that, then gave Nicobar a shove down another of the paths. "The Head Gardener has gone to spend the day in the orchards. He promised to be back this afternoon to see after our work. There's time left, but little enough, so make haste, *pral*."

How the boy recognized one path from another, or even one bush from another, Nicobar could not say, but the boy seemed to know where he was and went straightaway as though they were on the palazzo road instead of this knotted place.

At last the youth stopped on a short cobbled thoroughfare, a break with a nexus of paths to either side. He laid a finger to his lips and went back to the path they had just left. Still with the finger to his lips, he looked down the other, then, oddly, he dropped to his belly and writhed about like a speared snake.

"I mean no offense, *pral,* but what are you doing there?" Nicobar asked, keeping his voice low as he crouched down.

The lad pointed to the gap below the shrubs and grinned as he hopped to his feet. "I didn't think they would follow us, but I had to be sure. They're good lads, the others, I mean, even though most of 'em are *gadjé*. The master can be hard on us, you know, so I don't take my chances with anyone."

"Most wise, I'm sure," Nicobar said.

"*Me mamie-die* raised no fools," the other said. He dusted his hands on his gardening smock, then reached into the shrubbery. There came the sound of grating metal, of hinges whining open. Branches of shrubbery, which appeared thoroughly interlocked, gave way for a narrow metal door. The boy wedged through the half-open gate, ducking beneath the chain intended to keep it closed.

While the boy squeezed through easily enough, Nicobar was a man, fully grown and strapping. He considered the lock on the chain, wondering how difficult it might be to pick.

"You haven't the time, *pral.* I've spent too many afternoons working at it. It's like none other I've ever seen," his guide told him. Nicobar accepted the boy's word as fact and suffered the indignity of jamming his frame through the gate. "You'll have bruises to show for this day's work, I'm sure," the apprentice gardener said.

Paying no mind to the bruises, Nicobar reviewed his clothes. Not even the kinder eye of young Kisaiya could miss the torn coat, or the rust rubbed onto his white shirt. What was done was done, however, so he turned his attention, instead, to his surroundings.

This neatly crafted bower barely allowed room for both men to stand without overfamiliarity. A tiny stone shed occupied the greatest portion of the space. Nicobar turned to the apprentice, waiting for an explanation.

"It seems a place of little import, doesn't it? A hidden place for the staff to keep their tools maybe," the boy said. "But none of the staff is permitted here. We aren't even supposed to know of it. And consider the chain and padlock. If this is but an area for tools, why the lock?"

"You've a good eye for details," Nicobar said. He opened the shed door to discover nothing more than one might expect of a garden shed: shovels, a pick, a handful of hoes, a bucket of seed, a spare smock, and other oddments. He looked expectantly at the youth, knowing he was waiting to reveal more.

"The tools are here, but the question of the lock remains. Unusual for a garden, I thought, so I looked about," he said.

Nicobar looked where he pointed. He found a gap the space of a man's shoulders between the shed and the shrubbery. "What do you see, *pral*?"

"A puzzlement, isn't it?" the boy said, grinning. "I always wondered what fascination this place held for the Gardener *Rye,* but more so when I began noting how often Her Highness came this way. Why is a princess, pray tell, interested in a garden shed?"

"Have you answered that one?" Nicobar asked.

The apprentice shook his head. "I've only given it a month of Sundays' consideration and found naught for my troubles."

"But you say you've seen the princess come here?"

"Aye, and her friend toady, as well! In fact, he more often than she," the apprentice said.

"Her toady friend? This would be Conte Urbano?"
Nicobar asked.

"I know him not, *pral*, but he dresses like a fair cox-
comb, most certainly he looks the part of the fool."

"That would be Conte Urbano. He's more dangerous
than he appears. Have a care around him, do you hear?"

"Sí, I will," the lad promised. He shifted from foot to
foot, clearly nervous.

Nicobar watched him with misgivings. He knew, beyond the shadow of a doubt, that the boy's curiosity was
going to get the better of him yet. He had been much
the same at a comparable age.

The boy thrust his hand out suddenly. "I am called
Inago. You will remember me to the *Araunya*?"

"I'm sure she will be pleased," Nicobar said, taking
his hand. He stepped around the boy to take a closer
look at the wall, running his fingers along the crevices
of cemented stone, searching but not sure what he expected to find.

"Is it true, what they say? That the other *Araunya*
haunts the palazzo?"

Nicobar looked at him sharply.

"I mean no offense, but the staff, they talk, and I
could not believe it . . . even though all know that her
body was stolen . . ."

"It's a cursed thing, more so that it is true," Nicobar
said. "It is something which pains the *Daiya*, she would
not look kindly upon gossip. Should such gossip reach
her—"

"Say no more. I wanted only to know," Inago said.
He leaned forward. "What have you there?"

As they talked, Nicobar had continued his search, prying the crevices, but now, suddenly his questing fingers
found a catch that at his touch sprang free. There
seemed to be an odd groan from the wall and then, with
the sighing sound of rushing wind, it eased open. There
came, immediately, the smell of the sea and with it a
dank mustiness.

"Let's go in!" Inago said excitedly, reaching for the
door.

Nicobar caught his arm and raised a finger to his lips.

"Have care, *pral*, we don't know who is just beyond."
His hand fell to the scorpinini in his belt. He pulled the
tiny crossbow free, loaded both bolts and eased into the
narrow stairwell beyond the door. Inago came just behind, quiet as a thief. That, at least, his father seemed
to have taught him well, Nicobar thought.

The stairs were narrow and spiraled downward. Like
the shed that concealed them, they were made of stone
and mortar. Slippery footing threatened an ugly spill into
the unknown so Nicobar proceeded with care. He could
not comfortably navigate the passageway. The nar-
rowness compelled him to turn sideways. Moisture filled
the air with smells of salt, sea, and the dankness of mold,
which accounted for the slippery steps.

Mounted sconces on the walls provided no light. Only
what light filtered down from the sky gave them any
sight. The rough-hewn walls below the shed were solid,
packed earth and basalt, stained with salty residue from
the sea. Nicobar held his hand to the first torch, then
touched its top. There was no warmth to it. It had not
been lit that day. He sniffed the resulting char on his
fingertips, then tasted it. No salt sediment on the torch
as on the walls, which meant the torch had been used
recently.

The stairwell turned on itself several times before it
ended abruptly in a space of darkness blacker than even
a starless night. The blackness seemed to yawn endlessly
before them. Nicobar stepped back, putting the last stair
just behind his heel.

"Shall I fetch the torch?" Inago offered. His hand
rested on Nicobar's shoulder.

"No. I'll come again and bring my own. I don't want
to alert anyone we were here."

"Then what will we do?"

Nicobar looked into the void ahead, wondering when
the lad became a partner in this adventure, but then he
could not fault him for the assumption either; he had
already proved useful. Mentally, Nicobar went through
his options. He carried a bit of flint in his pocket, but
the air felt too moist and the torches would give them

away. There was nothing for it. "We—I shall return another time, better prepared for exploring."

"But we're here now!" Inago's words echoed off distant walls.

Nicobar clapped a hand over the youth's mouth. "Have a care," he hissed through clenched teeth, "anyone might hear you!"

As if to prove his point, there came the sound of a man's voice calling out a cautious greeting. The voice was nearer than Nicobar expected. Turning to his left, he could see a flicker of light dancing upon a cavern wall. He gave the boy a shove up the stairs, but lingered a moment longer so he might catch a better view of what he had uncovered.

The light drew closer, casting long shadows which stretched up the path toward Nicobar. He was saved from view himself by the wall the stairwell afforded him. With the torch less than a hundred yards away, there was enough light to reveal a huge cavern with a honeycomb of apertures and bridges—natural as well as manmade—and what seemed a labyrinth at least as large as the palazzo and gardens above.

With the residents of the cavern all too near, Nicobar hurried up the steps, taking care to move silently. As he reached the door, he heard a man's voice bellowing orders in the garden. The Head Gardener? Where was Inago?

A small motion caught his eye and he saw the boy crouched low in the shrubbery, wedged between the bushes and the shed. It was a poor enough hiding place for Inago and certainly would give Nicobar no shelter. Even as he hesitated, he heard the Head Gardener rattling his keys on the path just beyond and the sound of men's voices coming up the stairwell. There was no retreat!

Be it whimsy or the grace of the *Fata*, Nicobar looked up. The shed was sturdy and the roof looked solid enough. He climbed the shed in swift, lithe movements and rolled onto the roof. It was thatch, but appeared strong enough that it could support his weight. He leaned over the edge and waved to Inago, seizing the boy's wrist when he reached up. Inago pulled his booted feet up as the garden gate opened for the Head Gardener, who looked irritated as he examined the gate pushed ajar to the full extent of the chain.

The Head Gardener was a thick, balding man with a greasy, trailing mustache. Otherwise he seemed too clean to be an honest laborer. As he lingered by the gate, clipping the padlock on the chain closed and examining the gate lock, the hidden door of the shed swung wide.

Two men came from the shed, one a tall, muscular lout and the other, shorter, rounder, with a hat bedecked with plumes. This second man let out a strangled cry as he came face-to-face with the equally surprised Head Gardener. "What are you doing here, you fool? Why didn't you answer me?"

Speak of the *benglo*! Conte Urbano. Nicobar eased farther back on the roof so that he was less likely to be seen.

"What have I done but just entered the bower?" the Head Gardener protested. "It was you who left the gate pushed wide!"

"I did no such thing!" the conte snapped. "Didn't you hear me calling you in the caverns? Why didn't you answer?"

"But it wasn't me! I've only just arrived! I came looking for my apprentice and . . ."

"Nonsense! I heard you in the passageways myself!"

The exchange between the two men grew even more heated and threatened to last some time. Nicobar felt the roof thatch beneath him shift as it started to give.

Slowly, carefully, Nicobar peered out over the edge of the shed. One side opened directly into the bower where the men stood arguing. On either side, a narrow, uncomfortable gap lay between hedge and shed. The back of the shed, however, offered an escape route if he was willing to risk life and limb.

He caught Inago's eye and gestured that he could lower the youth onto the garden path. Inago studied the drop and looked back at Nicobar as though he were mad, but even as he did so, the weave of the hatch sagged just a little more, thereby demonstrating the desperation of their circumstances. Inago looked heavenward, mouthed a prayer, then nodded his consent.

Nicobar took the lad's hands and helped him ease over the edge of the roof, over the spiked heads of the iron fence, then wrestle across the tops of prickly shrubs. He stretched across it all for a perilous moment, then Inago nodded again and released his hold.

The leather soles of Inago's boots slapped against the cobblestone walk—had it been heard? Nicobar peered over the edge into the bower to see.

The two men stopped their quarreling.

"What was that?" Conte Urbano demanded.

"How should I know?" The Head Gardener reached for the gate.

Nicobar glanced around desperately for some distraction. While it was one thing to risk his own life, Inago could not have known the trouble he would be in. Nicobar opened his mouth to speak.

"Master?" Inago called from the maze.

Nicobar had to sit up and look around to place where the youth's voice came from. Smart lad! he thought as he realized the boy had circled round by one of the other paths and approached the hidden bower from the opposite direction.

Relief wrote itself on the Head Gardener's face.

"Where are you, boy? I've been looking all over for you!" the master said, his voice an angry growl. He motioned to the conte to be silent and then left the bower.

Urbano pressed up against the fence so that he might see some of the excited exchange between master and apprentice. His henchman crossed his arms and yawned, only to receive the conte's scowl for making noise.

Nicobar eased himself over the spikes and the hedges and dropped to the path. The sound of his jacket tearing was hidden by Inago's loud protestations, his voice cracking as it grew shrill.

Yes, Nicobar thought, he would remember Inago to the *Araunya*. He was resourceful and would come in handy in the future, of that Nicobar could be sure.

XXXII

"One should always have one's boots on and be ready to leave."

—Michel de Montaigne

STEFANO led his horse along the ledge of a seaside cliff, urging the beast on with the sound of his voice. The horse whinnied and balked as the wind battered them. He pressed on until, at last, he found the shallow cavern again. Inside, he hobbled the horse and went back into the driving rain to help della Guelfa.

Mud spilled down the cliff face, narrowing the ledge even further. Stefano swore as he retraced his steps. He found della Guelfa working his way down.

"The cavern is not much farther," Stefano called out.

Della Guelfa waved in acknowledgment.

The wind welled up from the Stretto and tugged at them—Stefano, della Guelfa and the second horse—threatening to pull them into the churning black waters that dashed against the rocks below. It seemed a frigid eternity before they reached the cave.

Della Guelfa wiped his face with a soaked kerchief, gasping and shivering. "I think we're being followed."

Stefano gritted his teeth and peered out into the storm. Thunder rumbled like cannons as lightning flashed across the sky.

"We'll have to return the way we came," Stefano said. "The rest of the path doesn't go all the way to the top of the cliff. We're perfectly situated for an ambush."

"Either way, we'll have to wait out the storm. I don't think we could make our way back up that path just now."

Stefano dropped to the rough floor and leaned back against the uneven wall. "Well, there is a juncture in the ledge where one of us might work our way up to the road."

"A few strategically aimed bolts might negate the ambush," della Guelfa agreed as he sagged to the ground. "I'll go ahead when there is a break in the storm."

Stefano wrung out his kerchief and mopped at his face. "Perhaps we can both make our way up and—" He stood up, raising a silencing hand. "There's someone on the ledge."

Della Guelfa nodded and pulled both of his scorpininis from his belt, thankful he did not have to contend with a pistola and wet gunpowder. Stefano drew his sword and pressed himself up against the wall of the cavern.

"Your Grace?" a voice called just before a burly figure blocked the mouth of the cave, blotting out their only light.

"State your name and keep your hands where we can see them. I have a scorpinini aimed at your heart," della Guelfa growled.

"Della Guelfa? Is that you?" the man asked.

Stefano looked over his shoulder, into the blackness of the cavern, waiting for someone to slip behind them. Della Guelfa's voice betrayed his surprise. "Capitano?"

The man at the cavern mouth sighed. "Thank Laechisis' eyes! It is I, Capitano di Montago."

"Di Montago?" Stefano repeated in surprise.

"Kneel so that I may see you," della Guelfa ordered.

The man knelt so the feeble light caught his face. He removed his hat, shaking back his soaked hair.

Stefano heard the releasing of scorpinini cocks and relaxed. He rose, sheathing his sword, and offered his hand. "I am Stefano di Luna, Duca di Drago, colonello in the queen's Escalade."

The newcomer bowed, spattering the men inside the cavern with the water falling around the cavern mouth. He stepped in out of the rain and accepted Stefano's hand.

"I'm most pleased to meet you, Your Grace," Mandero said. "I was sent by your wife and Her Majesty to see if I could be of assistance."

"My wife? The queen? How did they know?" Stefano sputtered.

"There was a small matter of a message gone astray that Her Grace had opportunity to peruse," the capitano said. He unbuttoned his coat and shrugged out of it. With the casualness of someone completely at his ease, he looked around the cavern and found a stalagmite to hang his coat on.

"How did you find us?" della Guelfa asked.

"There are those who've noted your passage," di Montago said cryptically.

"How many of the Escalade did you bring?" Stefano asked, pretending a casualness he did not feel.

"There are three of us, all of Romani blood." The capitano stretched and surveyed their shelter. "Her Grace and the queen surmised there might be a reason you did not avail yourself of the Escalade in Salerno, and thus we trusted your judgment. I'm assisted by your wife's people, Your Grace."

"Gypsies?" della Guelfa said.

Stefano nodded. "And it was they who saw us on the road?"

"Yes, Your Grace."

"But we never saw any Gypsies," della Guelfa protested.

The capitano grinned. "There are times when it is convenient for a Rom to not be noticed."

"We are fortunate they noticed us then," Stefano said. "Where are your people now?"

"Making an encampment above on the ridge. The *Beluni* offers you her personal protection," the capitano said. He looked around the damp cavern and grimaced. "I think you'll find a *vardo* far more comfortable than this place, Your Grace."

"You know we're being sought by the cardinal's men?" Stefano asked.

"Aye, they've been spotted along the coast as well. You've been fortunate to avoid them so far," di Montago said. "Come, the clan is cooking a fine dinner. I should think it would be a welcome change to growing moldy in this cave."

He led them back up the ridge and from there to a sheltered grove not a stone's throw away. The wind battered at them, but ceased, eerily, as they passed into the shelter of the trees.

Brightly colored awnings spread between the *vardos* and bender tents. A large campfire burned in the center of the circle of wagons despite the rain. A young girl ducked under the edge of an awning and ran to them. Laughing, presumably at their appearance, she took their horses.

"This way," di Montago said and led them to one of the awning-covered campsites. He bowed before an elderly woman ensconced in a rocking chair with a quilt over her lap. She paused in her sewing and acknowledged their guide. Di Montago rose and spoke with respect, "*Beluni-Daiya,* I present the *Rom* of *Araunya di Cayesmengri e Cayesmengro,* Stefano, and my *churomengro-pal,* della Guelfa."

"What did he say?" della Guelfa whispered.

Stefano schooled his face into a pleasant expression. "He just introduced me as my wife's husband and you as . . ." He hesitated in his translation.

"He introduced you as his brother soldier," the old woman said. She pointed to the short footstools scattered about on the carpet. "You may sit."

Della Guelfa looked to Stefano who sat uncertainly.

The old woman eyed Stefano, her dark, birdlike eyes assessing and curious. "So, you are the husband of my *chavi-pen.* You have been away, but now you are returned. Will you stay with her now?"

Stefano rocked back, appalled by the woman's bluntness. "I do not plan to leave Tyrrhia again."

"No?" The old woman picked up her sewing. Without looking up, she continued. "I didn't want Luciana's mother to marry a *gadjé,* but he convinced me otherwise. When Baiamonte wanted his Romani daughter to marry a *gadjé* as well . . . this I did not like. No. But I prayed to the *Fata,* I read the cards, I threw the bones, and I listened to my *chavi* who said she loved you. So I gave my permission for you to marry."

"I didn't know," Stefano said softly.

The old woman smiled crookedly. "Of course not. You are *gadjé*. You do not understand the importance of the *Mamdie,* the grandmother to our people." She set her sewing down in her lap and clapped her hands.

Two girls came promptly. The old woman spoke to them in a soft, low voice and sent them on their way.

"The *pen* will bring you a change of clothes and find you a place to sleep. We'll take you to Gypsy Crossing come morning tide," the Gypsy Queen said. "Follow the girls."

Della Gueifa and Stefano rose uncertainly. Di Montago, who had not sat, motioned for them to come.

The *Beluni,* however, coughed and looked at Stefano pointedly. "*You* will join me for dinner and we will discuss my *chavi-pen.*"

"As you wish." Stefano bowed.

She snorted and leaned back in her chair, returning to her sewing.

Feeling dismissed, Stefano turned and joined della Guelfa and the capitano.

In one of the *vardos,* their host directed them in their change to drier Romani costume. The pantaloons were longer, fuller, and made of coarser stuff than Stefano was accustomed to. The shirts were made of a finer silk, gaily embroidered, and closed with multiple ties up the front. Stefano elected not to wear the broad, brightly colored sash.

"You do not care for our dress, Your Grace?" di Montago asked with a wry grin.

Stefano shrugged wordlessly.

"You must agree, Capitano, that your ways are different," della Guelfa said. "The old woman didn't defer to the duca at all."

The capitano's brow rose. "Why should she? She is the *Beluni,* Queen of the Wandering Folk. The only importance His Grace holds for her is that he married her granddaughter, the *Araunya.*"

Della Guelfa shook his head.

"You know of Gypsy Silk, don't you?" the capitano asked patiently.

"Well, yes, of course, it's one of Tyrrhia's main exports, but—"

"Did you think that Gypsy Silk had nothing to do with the Romani?" di Montago asked.

Della Guelfa raised his hands helplessly.

"The Tyrrhian Gypsies are craftsmen in peacetime. The *Araunya* is their emissary to the *gadjé*. She controls their trade," di Montago said.

"So, this *Araunya* is, essentially, a merchant prince?" della Guelfa asked.

The capitano shook his head. "You have spent too much time studying arms, Lieutenant. A good soldier must have an understanding of the economics of his country. The *Araunya* is a woman, *always*. Indeed, there are usually two *Araunyas* representing different aspects of the silk trade, but with the death of . . ." Here he paused as though great pain took away his breath ". . . the death of my *adamente,* all *Araunya* rights passed to Her Grace."

"Don't you mean, His Grace? She is, after all, his wife, and properties owned by a woman become a husband's possession," della Guelfa argued.

The capitano laughed. "It's just the opposite among the Romani and, in making peace with the Tyrrhian *gadjé,* certain concessions of Romani law and independence were guaranteed." His eyes narrowed as he looked at Stefano. "If I may be so impertinent, Your Grace, that must have caused considerable misunderstanding in your marriage."

Stefano remained tight-lipped.

"Ah!" di Montago murmured. "Please forgive me."

"How should I address the . . . the *Beluni?*" Stefano asked.

"You must call her *Daiya,*" Mandero said. "She is the grandmother of your wife and the senior matriarch present." He considered the two men and nodded. "Come, let's see about dinner. I hear the *boshmengro* tuning up, so he must have already eaten."

Their host led them outdoors again, moving naturally

between the awnings, skipping over puddles and avoiding the irregular spills of water off the overhead tarps.

The *Beluni* rose when Stefano returned to her. She studied him, a twinkle of humor lighting her eyes. She motioned him to sit in another rocking chair he had not noticed before.

Stefano murmured his thanks, but waited until she sat before sitting himself. As he leaned back, he surveyed the encampment. Lanterns hung from the tent poles holding up the awnings. With them, the camp was well-lit despite the rain and darkness of the night. A fiddler sat on a stool beneath an awning on the other side of the fire. The *boshmengro* played music that seemed vaguely familiar, but nothing Stefano was personally acquainted with.

One of the younger women came with two platters. She served the old woman first. The meal consisted of greens, risotto, and a spicy stew with a hunk of flat black bread. Another girl came by shortly after with mugs of hot, mulled wine. It did not take long for Stefano to feel the warmth returning to his bones.

"Our ways are strange to you, are they not, *chavopal?*" the old woman asked softly.

Stefano sighed. "I never knew there could be such luxury in a campsite."

The old woman let out a bell-like laugh that rippled richly over the encampment. It reminded him of Luciana. In fact, much about the woman reminded him of his wife. The strong, clear features, the dark, inquisitive eyes. The sharp tongue.

"You see Luciana in me, eh?"

"How did you know?"

The woman winked and set aside her plate. "So long married to my granddaughter and you do not know our ways?" She clucked her tongue, her expression turning serious. "But, then, you've spent much of that time away, no?"

Stefano nodded and fidgeted with his empty plate. He looked up when the woman reached over and took it from him.

"You knew she was Romani, didn't you? When you married her? Baiamonte did not keep this from you?"

"I knew . . . well, I thought she was his daughter and, therefore, only half-Romani. It was only afterward that I realized she was full-blooded Romani," Stefano said.

The *Beluni* laughed. "You did not read the marriage contract carefully, did you?"

"I did, but I didn't care, I thought it would all just work itself out," Stefano admitted.

"So. You were in love as well," the old woman said softly. She let the silence between them spread, scented by the crackling fire and punctuated with the fiddler's serenade. "You could have had the marriage annulled."

"No."

"No?" the Gypsy Queen repeated and chuckled softly. "You are as headstrong as she. I offered to have our *Kris* annul the marriage or give her a divorce over three years ago."

Stefano did not know how to respond. Luciana refused an annulment and did not tell him about it? Why? But these meditations were best made alone. Determined to change the subject, he sat forward in his chair. "Thank you for coming to the aid of della Guelfa and myself—"

The old woman waved her hand, her golden rings flashing in the firelight. "You are of the clan now, Your Grace. *Gadjé* or no, you're one of us." She studied him for a moment. "Will you leave my *chavi* again? Or will you stay and do your duty by her?"

"Pardon?" Stefano asked with a cough.

"No woman should be deserted by her man. A Rom would never have left his bride to fight someone else's war. A woman like Luciana should have a flock of children by now, someone to take her place as *Araunya* and to keep the clan strong. It's a bad thing being Romani with no children."

Stefano straightened in his chair. It seemed that among Luciana's people privacy did not exist. He was unaccustomed to discussing such matters with anyone, even his wife. But, perhaps, this was the heart of the problem and one son, even if he had lived, did not a flock of children make.

"You have nothing to say?"

"What is there to say, *Daiya?*"

The old woman's lips pursed. "Luciana would not appreciate the advice either. Rest, Your Grace, and tomorrow we will be on our way. You will be in Citteauroea within two days."

XXXIII

"The woman that deliberates is lost."
—Joseph Addison

"WON'T you reconsider?" Kisaiya asked anxiously. She twisted her hands, wringing a just-pressed kerchief. "Won't you at least wait until Nicobar returns from his errand?"

"Of course not, I created that diversion for the express purpose of having Nicobar away," Luciana said.

Kisaiya frowned. "There were advantages, I think, to keeping Lady Prunella about. You wouldn't have done this when she was here."

Luciana sighed, shaking her head. "Yes, I would have . . . it just wouldn't have been so easy."

"Then I shall be as determined as she! I'll come with you."

"No. It isn't safe, *chavi,*" Luciana said.

Kisaiya crossed her arms. "What if you're discovered?"

"Two are more likely to be discovered than one, and I know, thanks to your diligence with Dulcinea, that the princess invited the conte to supper. He should still be dining and I've waited *just* long enough so that the servants should be clear from the back hallways by now. I must be on my way quickly."

"What if you're discovered?" Kisaiya repeated, following Luciana to the door.

"I'll deal with that problem when it arises," Luciana said.

"But—"

Luciana held up her hand. "I *am*, after all, a duchessa. I won't permit questioning."

Kisaiya sighed, frustration clear in her expression. "Isn't there something I could do?"

"No, the risk is too great and no need for more than one of us to deal with the filth of his magic, the *marimé*."

Her maid's lip curled in disgust even as she nodded her reluctant acceptance. "How long will you be gone?"

"It should only take a matter of minutes."

"What if you're delayed?"

"Then I am delayed."

Kisaiya shook her head. Luciana could have no doubts that the girl had serious misgivings on her behalf. She caught her maid's sleeve. "I am honored by your loyalty. Thank you."

Kisaiya nodded unhappily.

Gathering her wits about her, Luciana edged into the servants' halls then carefully made her way to Conte Urbano's rooms. It seemed as though she retraced this path a thousand times. She had, in her way, of course, just today planning what she must do. Each trip—in her imagination or by foot—felt like a new journey into the devil's lair. Already, she felt the smothering blanket of *marimé* created by evil magic reaching out to engulf her. She steadied her resolve. Alessandra needed her!

The thought of Conte Urbano capturing another bird, of working his spells over it to trap Alessandra's soul once more made her nauseous. She took comfort, however, in the knowledge that for the conte to repeat his spells, he must go to the body.

She turned a corner and startled a maid carrying a high stack of linens. The girl let out a frightened squeak. "Forgive me, Your Grace. I–I didn't expect . . . are you lost?"

Luciana drew herself up and stared down her nose at the girl who immediately blushed.

"Forgive me, I did not intend impertinence," the girl said.

"You may go."

The girl curtsied and scurried away. Luciana watched her disappear around the corner then breathed a sigh of

relief. However had she managed that one? she wondered, but it seemed there was to be no respite. She
heard more footsteps. Rather than risk another encounter, she crossed the corridor and hurried down to the
next to Conte Urbano's rooms.

Luciana pressed her ear against the door. It was hard
to hear over the sound of her own heart's pounding, but
at last she felt certain. Silence. She scratched on the door
and waited for a response. Hearing none, she opened
the door and looked inside. A single oil lamp burned
low on the writing table near the window, casting the
only available light. She took a deep breath. Her heart
beat so quickly it almost pained her, making it hard to
concentrate, but she could not afford to indulge her
excitement.

Closing the door behind her, Luciana crossed to the
other door leading down to the salon. Silence there as
well. With great care, she shut the door and turned the
key then began to assess the stack of cases still waiting
to be unpacked. Her gaze fell to the large cloth-covered
box. The motive of her search.

She approached the crate carefully, examining it as
she did. An extensive length of heavy brocade enveloped
the box, held in a place by a pin. Luciana heard muffled
rustling. She knelt beside the package, pulled the fancy
pin free and tugged away the cloth.

A white dove huddled inside.

In spite of herself, outrage burned in her heart. To be
trapped inside a bird—not even an owl—the conte had
taken all possible steps to weaken Alessandra. Luciana
cursed the conte quietly. Feathers littered the bottom
of the cage as testimony to the dove's frustration and
impotence. Now it ruffled its feathers and emitted a
warning coo. A pitiful defense to be sure.

The window, like the others on this floor of the palazzo, was placed high, above the inset window seat. The
shutters were closed. Luciana clambered onto the seat
and struggled with the portal, prying at the pins Urbano
had wedged into the frame to keep it from being opened.

After a considerable struggle, Luciana freed the fetters
and flung open the window. Rather than risk the bird

flying desperately about the room, she dragged the cage
to the window seat and climbed back up with it balanced
precariously in her arms. She wrestled with the door to
the cage and swore beneath her breath when her hand
slipped and she cut herself on the metal filigree.

Somewhere below, Luciana thought she heard a man's
voice. She paused, listening. Standing on the tips of her
toes, she looked out through the window and below,
hoping the men she heard could be seen there, but no,
the path encircling the palazzo was free of courtiers or
servants.

Did that mean someone had come into the suite?

With growing desperation, Luciana returned to her
task. She placed the cage on the seat. It took time to
manage the cumbersome cage and, if it fell, anyone in
the salon below would come to investigate. No more
time for delicacy. Luciana pulled the stiletto from her
sleeve and pried the lock off the cage door. She *must*
free Alessandra's spirit. She *must!*

The cage door sprang open with a whine of cheap
hinges. Luciana cursed the noise again and reached
inside.

The bird fluttered against the bars, battering itself as
it tried to escape her hands. It pecked her as Luciana
grabbed it with ungentle fingers, doing her best to pin
its wings to its body. Blood already stained the bird's
neck and breast from previous grapplings with its perse-
cutor or, perhaps, ineffectual attempts to gain its freedom. The bird drew blood from her hands and wrists as
Luciana clamped hold of it and pulled it from the cage.
Ignoring the sound of her rending skirt, she staggered
to her feet on the seat cushions and flung the bird out
the window.

With her task completed, Luciana took a long, deep
breath and listened. She climbed carefully down off the
window seat and went to the salon door. Had she really
heard someone in the salon below? Or had it been only
her imagination? After a few moments, she felt certain
that whoever had been downstairs was either engrossed
in something or had gone off on an errand.

Luciana breathed a silent prayer of thanksgiving and

paused to review the room laid out before her. She wondered if she might find the evidence of Alessandra's murder here. How often could she expect to be in these rooms with such a golden opportunity? So far she had encountered no difficulties in making these little forays into Urbano's lair. If nothing else, however, she intended to never come here again. Now that her task was done, she could note such things as the stench of *marimé* which threatened to overwhelm her. The unholy miasma felt like putrid grease on her skin and sang a discordant song. She stood in the room, her safety at least momentarily confirmed and evaluated her circumstances, she would be a fool to not use such an advantage, Luciana reasoned. But where to begin?

First things first. She returned the cage to its previous location and wrapped the cloth around it again. Resolved on her new agenda, she began with the desk.

She shuffled through the papers she found, taking care to return everything to its previous place. Her search turned up nothing more than she expected: bad poetry, paperwork on Urbano's accounts with various merchants, but little else of interest or value.

In a bedside table, she uncovered several small dark blue bottles all in a row. Though the bottles did not conform in exact size and shape, the tags dangling from the necks were all labeled alike: *"Aqua Fina."* She sat back in surprise. Had Urbano truly discovered the recipe for the legendary Borgia family poison or had the little Italian, Exilli, concocted the malignant brew and christened it with a name worthy of its potency?

No matter which origin, the fluid would be toxic. She considered once more the number of bottles and her hands shook. She felt more angry than nervous. With this much poison, he could take out the entire royal family and the Palantini Council and still have a bottle or two to spare.

How tempting to have access to the conte's private rooms and his poison! For a moment she considered pouring a bit of it into the man's inkwell. The next time he sucked on his quill, it would bring new meaning to his "deathly prose," but such action would be an indulgence and compromise her plans of following Urbano to Alessandra's body.

She unstoppered a bottle and sniffed. Absolutely without scent. A poison such as this would be almost undetectable. She knew better than to taste it and reasoned that if there were a taste, by the time someone realized the flavor of their food was not quite right they had probably already ingested enough of the venom to kill them.

Poisoning was a nasty business. She wondered, with a mixture of sadness and anger, if this had been what did poor Alessandra in. But did the poison need to claim another victim? Could she substitute something else for the poison? While considering this, she put the vial back into the cabinet and looked around the room.

Below her came the distinct sound of someone entering the suite. Damnation! She could do nothing about the poison now, she would have to come back! She took one last look around the room. If there was anything to find, she had missed it. She cursed again and quickly slipped out the back door of Urbano's bedchamber into the servants' halls.

Making sure the door behind her closed with a satisfying click, Luciana craned her neck to see if any servants were about to spot her this time. No one. She breathed a sigh of relief and darted to the narrow hall leading to her own rooms, but drew still at the sound of footsteps approaching. Better to wait than draw attention with a suspicious retreat, she decided. She held her breath and leaned back against the wall trying to come up with some plausible excuse for being here, then stopped even that.

What had she heard? Or, more accurately, what hadn't she heard? Why did this servant move so slowly? His step did not have the accompanying sounds expected from someone with a cumbersome burden—no grunts and groans or gasps for breath, no sound of his bundle being set down or leaned against any of the walls or tables. No, Luciana thought, this man moved cautiously, carefully, and he stopped every few paces, not unlike the way she moved through these halls. She found the concept intriguing.

Exercising as much caution as she could muster, Luciana pressed closer to the wall and leaned out, ever so slightly, to see if she could spot the other occupant of the hall. At the first peek, she saw no one, but the second time she got a clear sight of Exilli creeping toward the conte's rooms.

With pounding heart, Luciana held absolutely still. She did not want that man finding her, especially not now. But what was he doing here? Then she remembered the bottles. The poisons in Conte Urbano's room, no doubt for safekeeping. Something—besides the little Italian—was afoot! She must send word immediately to Idala and Alban to take extra precautions.

XXXIV

"I sing the progress of a deathless soul."

—John Donne

27 d'Maggio 1684

IDALA pushed a bit of rare lamb across the plate with her fork. She had barely eaten.

"Really, Idala, one would think you were ill," the princess said, her expression sour as she spread more mint upon her lamb. "Does this perhaps herald the expansion of the Royal House?"

"Of course the Royal House will be expanding, Your Highness. By one. A mere week away, or have you already forgotten your own wedding?" Luciana asked lightly.

One of the servants poured Idala more chocolate.

"Don't be obtuse, my dear Duchessa!" Bianca retorted.

Luciana feigned confusion.

Idala spread and ate the morsel she had been chasing across her plate. "Were there announcements to be made, Cousin, family would be the first to know." She managed a forced smile as she chewed.

"Where is Conte Pierro this fine morning?" Luciana asked.

Princess Bianca's expression turned sweet. "The conte is riding with Alban . . . His Majesty."

Idala glance at Luciana before bending her head to

take great interest in the morsels on her plate. The queen was not pleased, and a shadow of fear touched her eyes.

Luciana reached under the table and touched Idala's left hand. This turn of events—Alban and Pierro riding together, alone—was exactly what Luciana had hoped could be avoided when she sent her note of warning more than a week ago now. She hoped that, if Stefano was not present, then at least other members of the Palantini were.

"I'm surprised that Conte Urbano is not with you, then," Luciana said. She tried to hide her nervousness. She had so far managed to restrain from prodding about the missing bird, to see what Bianca knew. All Luciana's plans waited upon the conte's next action, when he returned to Alessandra's body to renew his hold over her. Anxiety for the chase to begin gnawed at her like Cerberus. Her thoughts were awhirl. Had the princess been told about the bird? Was that the reason for her illtemperedness this morning?

"Indeed," said Princess Bianca. "I've begun to wonder about the conte myself. I invited him to join us." She turned apologetically to Idala. "I hope you do not mind my presumption?"

Idala gave the princess a stern look, but shook her head.

Princess Bianca sighed heavily. "I am so glad. I simply did not think, but since the conte is welcome, I will send for him immediately, if that is acceptable with Her Majesty?"

The queen did not respond immediately, which gave the princess pause. After several long moments, Idala sighed, "As you wish."

"Then you will excuse me while I attend to his summons," Princess Bianca murmured.

"But of course," Luciana said.

Princess Bianca rose and retreated to Idala's salon in search of one of the ladies in waiting.

Idala caught Luciana's hand. "I do not see how you are able to seem so casual, so serene? Have you heard news that I have not?"

"No, I've heard nothing either and it worries me greatly that I may be a widow so soon after our reconciliation. Truth, I hope to never be a widow and go before him, but I am also bound not to give *that* woman the satisfaction," Luciana said. "Besides, I have confidence in Stefano, and we more than balanced the odds with the capitano."

"I hope you're right."

"I must be. I cannot live with the thought of failure," Luciana replied. "Now smile and be gay, the princess returns."

Idala looked up with a passing fair semblance of an unworried smile.

The princess regained her seat with a satisfied sigh. "I have sent Dulcinea. She will return forthwith."

Idala nodded.

Luciana accepted another cup of chocolate and allowed the conversation to lull. As she sipped the hot liquid, she paused at the sound of a distant scream. Her heart leaped to her throat. Something must have happened to the king! She dropped her cup, mindless of the spreading stain over the front of her gown, and rose. "Did you hear that?"

"The king?" Idala asked, turning in her chair.

This time the scream was louder, followed by the sound of people rushing.

Idala rose, her hand to her throat.

The princess set aside her cup. "What are you talking about?"

Another scream, this time louder, pierced the morning, sending the birds to flight.

"Let us find out," Idala said.

Luciana was of the same mind, worried for the king. She followed Idala through her salon into the corridor where the sound of a woman screaming and sobbing became quite clear, as well as the murmur of many voices.

"That sounds like Dulcinea," Princess Bianca said peevishly. "I wonder what's wrong with the little chit?"

Luciana hoped she managed to hide her distaste, if not outright hatred, of the princess as they rounded the corner. How could Bianca be so nonchalant? The king, besides being her liege—no matter what her aspirations were—was her very own cousin.

They found servants pressed into close quarters. The normally wide corridors seemed to shrink to almost nothing when fifty or more people tried to push themselves closer to the screaming woman. Luciana stepped around the queen and forced a path through until, finally, she reached Dulcinea who knelt on the floor alternately sobbing and screaming.

"Stop it! Stop it at once!" Princess Bianca, who followed with the queen in Luciana's wake, snapped.

Luciana bent down beside Dulcinea and put her arm around the girl's heaving shoulders. "Come, child, what is the matter?"

Dulcinea shook her head, unable to speak.

"Send for the chirurgeon," Idala bade one of the servants standing nearby.

"You must calm yourself," Luciana said soothingly. How she managed to remain calm herself when all she could think of was the king, Luciana did not know. Then, she noted that only Dulcinea seemed distressed. There would be other servants grief-stricken if it was Alban. A sudden thought chilled down her spine. She remembered Exilli's quiet approach to Conte Urbano's rooms. Dulcinea had been sent for the conte. She twisted and turned trying to verify where she was in relation to her own and the conte's suites. A new sense of dread began to take hold. Could Exilli have ruined her plans to follow Urbano to Alessandra?

Distracted by her thoughts, Luciana could not move fast enough to prevent the princess from slapping Dulcinea.

"Out with it, *sciocca*!" Bianca commanded, raising her hand again.

Luciana caught her hand and pushed her away, positioning herself between Bianca and her maid. To Dulcinea, she said gently, "Tell us what is the matter." She feared the answer.

"Conte Urbano . . . he is . . . he is . . . ." Dulcinea gulped air.

"Out with it!" Princess Bianca snapped again and reached for her maid once more.

Dulcinea shrank away.

Luciana glared at the princess. If her fears were correct, that the little Italian poisoner had done his business upon the distasteful conte, then he could only have been sent by Bianca, which meant that she knew what she had sent Dulcinea to discover. "That doesn't help, Your Highness. Can't you see the girl is frightened enough?"

"This is nonsense! Where is the conte?" Bianca demanded.

"Dead," Dulcinea said with a gulp of air.

"What did you say?" The princess stiffened imposingly.

Bianca gave an impeccable performance. Rather than risk letting her own emotions show through, Luciana focused on soothing the girl.

"She said he was dead," Idala repeated. Her voice sounded vague. Luciana glanced up at her nervously, hoping that this turn of events would not overly distress the queen.

"Ridiculous! I saw him just last night. He was perfectly healthy!" Princess Bianca said.

"Well, why don't we investigate for ourselves?" Luciana said, motioning to one of the servants to help Dulcinea. The princess continued to play her part well, Luciana thought. Her loathing for the woman made it almost impossible to keep her own council. She could not help but wonder if Bianca knew she had foiled Luciana's plan to reclaim Alessandra's body? Why had she had her confederate murdered? Perhaps his explanations finally exceeded what the princess was willing to allow. In either case, no sign of remorse of any kind touched Bianca's cold demeanor.

"Why *don't* we?" the princess agreed and turned on her heel.

Luciana followed, as did Idala.

At the door to the conte's suite, Bianca paused. It already stood half-open.

Idala turned to the crowd. "Has the Escalade been sent for?" One of the servants ran in the direction of the barracks. She caught Bianca's sleeve as the princess pushed the door open wider. "We should wait until the vigilare arrive."

Bianca ignored her and entered the room, leaving Luciana and Idala on the threshold.

Luciana turned to Idala. She ached to rush past the princess and discover what lay beyond for herself. "Majesty? What will you have us do?"

The queen waved toward the room, but stopped on the threshold and turned. "No one else enters the room until the vigilare arrive."

Together, they entered the room. Bianca stood on the other side of the salon, staring at something on the patio. Luciana and Idala went to her side and looked out.

Conte Urbano had fallen across his papers, a bottle of ink spilled over the table and onto the patio stones. A quill lay in his frozen fingers. An expression of horror and amazement seemed permanently etched on his face. His lips and protruding tongue were dark blue where they were not stained black with ink.

Idala let out a cry and quickly turned away.

"He is most definitely dead," Luciana said quietly, more to herself than anyone in particular.

Try as she might, she could not muster any sympathy for the conte. He had received a just reward. But it also meant that she must come up with another plan to find Alessandra and, more unsettling, the princess or her confederates had anticipated Luciana's plan. Was it intentional or a convenient coincidence? On another worrisome note, clearly they had no qualms over finishing one of their own off. What had Urbano done to displease them? Her stomach turned in knots and what little breakfast she had eaten threatened to revisit her.

Princess Bianca continued to stare at Urbano, her expression one of rapt fascination. Finally, she said, "Most *definitely* dead." Her voice was cool and calm. She stalked across the flagstones and pulled the papers from beneath the conte's head. She looked at them and sneered in disgust. "Poetry."

"At least he passed doing something he loved," Luciana said, swallowing back a hysterical laugh.

The princess looked up, her gaze assessing. "Yes, at least he had that, but he also died unshriven, a most horrible fate."

What more was there to say to Bianca? Luciana turned to the queen who had withdrawn a step or two into the salon. "Will you be well?"

Idala nodded firmly, but looked pale. "I think, however, that I will retire to my rooms."

At the door, Luciana found most of the residential servants waiting for news. She thought, for the barest of moments, that she saw a familiar face amidst the crowd. She blinked and looked again. Had she truly seen Alessandra? Her spirit at least? She recalled with a thrill of fear and relief that Alessandra's *mulló* was no longer tied to the bird. Damned by her existence, at least she could appear when and where *she* wanted.

A contingent of Escalade officers made their way through the crowd. Luciana waved them into the room. As the last of them passed by her, she spotted Exilli in the crowd.

"Lord Exilli? Perhaps you, too, would like to come in?" Luciana said. She longed for an opportunity to still that poisoner's hand, hating him for his expertise.

The little dark man flinched, but edged past her and into the suite.

Luciana watched him, glancing briefly to be sure someone attended to the queen. An Escalade officer escorted Idala away. With Idala gone, Luciana concentrated on the conspirators.

Exilli spent but a brief moment in the salon. He looked about the room, his movements almost birdlike in their quickness, and then fidgeted his way onto the patio.

The princess moved aside for him, but also watched as the little man bent over the conte's body. Exilli's aquiline nose creased as he sniffed the conte's face and then his hands. He reached out with his smallest finger and dabbed at the ink, brought it to his nose, to his lips and then carefully wiped his hands with a crisp linen handkerchief pulled from his sleeve.

"What happened?" the princess asked.

Bianca played to her audience well. She actually managed to sound confused! Maybe even concerned, but Luciana knew better, saw better in the other woman's cold eyes.

Exilli puffed up, gaining perhaps an inch in height. "The Lord Conte has been poisoned, Your Highness."

"Poisoned?" the princess repeated, looking from Exilli to Luciana.

Luciana directed her attention to the little foreigner. "Are you sure, Signore?" She knew for sure, but she, too, must play a part in this little scene.

"*Quite* sure, Your Grace," Exilli said firmly. He studied Luciana for a long moment, but she remained outwardly calm, the picture of unsuspecting innocence. "Yes, well," he said as he folded the kerchief and tucked it into his coat. "I would surmise that the conte, as is common with men of means, has been experimenting in alchemy, perhaps even dabbling with poison, and there has been a most unfortunate . . . accident."

"Accident?" the princess said, looking archly at Luciana and then the vigilare who stood nearby waiting for the nobles to make way. "I will bow to your superior knowledge, Lord Exilli, but what a damnable time for him to die!"

"Come away from here, Your Highness. You must be shocked over the loss of your friend," Luciana urged, taking Bianca by the arm, shocked by the woman's open callousness. Let the vigilare sort things out; she knew what she needed to know.

The princess recoiled. "Thank you, Your Grace, but I can manage sufficiently on my own." To the Escalade officers waiting in the salon, she said, "I leave this matter to you," as though it were her place to do so.

They bowed to the princess who promptly swept from the room.

Luciana turned back, only to discover Exilli watching her with his sharp, bright eyes. He recovered quickly and bowed to her before scurrying from the room. Luciana took her kerchief and pressed it to her mouth. The whole matter sickened her.

"Pray, good Sirs, excuse me, but I think I'd best depart as well," Luciana said to the vigilare as they moved about the scene.

"You look quite pale, Your Grace. Permit me to escort you to your rooms," one of the men said.

Luciana accepted his arm. She did not take a final look at her "cousin," Conte Urbano, but thought, instead, of what she was going to say to Prunella.

Solaja Lendaro handed Stefano the reins to her horses and swung down from her *vardo* with the ease of a woman many years her junior. In the face of the pistolas aimed at her, the Gypsy Queen stalked toward the riders blocking the road.

"What is the meaning of this? Out of the road! Off with you!" she commanded, like a scolding mother to recalcitrant children.

"Out of the way, old woman!" one of the riders said.

Stefano started to get down from the wagon, but stopped when Solaja turned and waved at him to be still, as though she anticipated his reaction. She bristled where she stood. "This is the King's Road and my people have been given free passage on any road held by the White King."

"We only wish to delay you for a moment, Old Mother," the other rider said.

"We stopped only out of courtesy to fellow travelers. If we wished it, we could have continued on whether you moved or no," the *Beluni* said.

"Perhaps, Old Mother, but there are others of us, you see," the rider said. He put fingers to his lips and whistled. From either side of the road, men on horseback broke through the bushes.

The Gypsy Queen snapped her fingers and the menfolk from the *vardos* made their way to the road. Stefano stayed where he was, but pulled a scorpinini from the top of his boot. With most of her menfolk standing behind her, the old woman crossed her arms and looked back at the lead rider. "It seems we are evenly matched, *Gadjé*. But what right do you stop the Free People of Tyrrhia?"

"We seek two men. Noblemen. You might have encountered them on the road," the man said.

The *Beluni* scoffed. "What would we have to do with noblemen?"

The man stared at her, then shrugged and turned his horse off the road.

The old woman said something more and signaled to the caravans. The menfolk returned to their wagons and Solaja clambered back into the front *vardo*. She grinned and winked at Stefano as she took the reins. "Never exactly answer a question, *chavo-pal*, it gives the *gadjé* too much to think about." She whistled to her horses and slapped the reins.

The *vardo* jerked forward and rumbled past the riders. Stefano leaned back in his shadowy corner, his scorpinini ready. The Gypsy Queen only grinned at him and clucked to her horses.

Newly arrived, Prunella blinked rapidly, then sniffed. She looked at Luciana, then to Kisaiya behind her, and, finally, to the queen, in whose very solar she currently sat. "He's what?" she asked, her voice breaking slightly. She put a hand to her throat and swallowed hard.

Luciana pressed a glass of sherry into her hand. "He's quite dead, Prunella. We saw him. I–I'm very sorry . . ." She fell silent, darting a look at the queen.

Prunella took an absentminded sip, blinked, and then swallowed the remainder of the sherry in a single swallow. She blinked again and sat a bit taller, then expelled her breath. "I suppose, then, that it is God's will."

"God's will?" the queen said and sat back in her chair.

Prunella's entire body shuddered with another heartfelt sigh. "Yes, Your Majesty. God's will, and I am but a poor woman. Who am I to question His ways?"

"Yes, well, Pru, would you feel better if I sent for the priest?" Luciana asked, not sure how to gauge Prunella's reaction.

Prunella considered Luciana's offer, then considered her clothes. She patted the dust from her dark brown sleeves. "I will have to speak to the priest, of course, but I think I should change into something darker . . . something black." She shook her head. "I *really* was not prepared for this. I wonder if I have anything appropriate in my trunks?" She rose absently and wandered toward the salon. She stopped abruptly and retraced her steps to stand before the queen and Luciana. She curtsied. "If I may be excused?"

Idala only nodded, apparently unable to speak.

XXXV

"Ill fortune seldome comes alone."

—John Dryden

28 d'Maggio 1684

A LIGHT kiss gently grazed her cheek, waking Luciana.

"I didn't mean to wake you."

He spoke so softly, but it was *him*. "Stefano," she sighed, reaching for him.

Stefano perched on the edge of the bed, meeting her with a kiss as she reached up to him.

She clung to him, fiercely determined to hide her tears of relief. She answered him kiss for kiss.

He caressed her face, discovering the salty trail flowing down her cheeks. Stefano bent and kissed her again, stroking away each of the droplets. "You weep."

Luciana shook her head, denying the obvious.

Stefano tilted her head to see her better by the dimmed lantern. He brushed her hair back from her eyes and stroked her cheek. "Why do you weep?" He dropped another gentle kiss upon her lips.

Luciana wiped her eyes and laid her head against his chest, breathing in the smell of him. "I'd begun to think I would never see you again!"

"I have always returned to you. I could never not," Stefano said.

"But it is the delays that I find so troubling." She

laughed a little, wallowing in the strength of his arms around her.

"And I'm sorry for them . . . for every moment I am away from you. . . ." Stefano shook his head. He took her hands and kissed them, each fingertip, the palms, the wrists. Here he stopped and pushed back the sleeves of her *vestaglia.* "You've been hurt!"

"Never mind that," Luciana said, running her hands up the front of his shirt.

"How did this happen?" Stefano insisted, catching hold of her injured hand.

Luciana sat back with a sigh. "I released my sister's soul by setting a bird free from Conte Urbano's cage. He controlled her *mulló* that way." She reached for him, again, but he sat back.

"Perhaps I should ask you what has happened since I've been away?"

"Conte Urbano returned from his honeymoon—"

"Then they did marry after all?" Stefano asked.

"Give me but a moment, and I will tell you the whole tale," Luciana said. "Upon Urbano's return, I slipped into his rooms and stole the bird from him which he used to control my sister."

"Then that is over now?" Stefano asked, sounding greatly relieved.

"As far as it went. Now he is dead, and I cannot find where my sister is by following him to her body."

Stefano kissed her gently and wrapped her in his arms, "Oh, my *bella,* it is never the easy way with you." He sat back, studying her face briefly. "You did not . . ." He sketched an explicative wave.

"No, Stefano, his death is not done by my hands," Luciana said. "He only returned yesterday, or rather, the day before yesterday."

"So soon? Even for an *arranged* marriage that is unspeakably short," Stefano observed wryly. "So. How did he die? A riding accident? Hunting? Robbers?"

Luciana tugged the lacy cuffs of her *vestaglia* to cover the wounds left by the bird. "It was a small matter of poison."

"Poison?" Stefano repeated. He leaned forward and

tipped Luciana's head up again. "I seem to remember
you know a little something of that art."

She sat back, noticing for the first time his unusual
attire. She reached out and felt the fabric of his shirt.
"Whatever are you doing in these things?"

"Don't change the subject, Lucia."

She smiled. "So Mandero found you, did he?"

"You are clever," Stefano said, kissing her again, "but
you continue to change the subject. How did the conte
come to be poisoned?"

"It's a very long story," Luciana murmured, kissing
him back. She twined her arms around his neck and
pressed close, smiling as she felt his body tremble in
response. Whatever their differences, all she cared about
at this moment was that he was safe and returned to her.

"Shorten the tale for me," Stefano urged, his mouth
dropping to the curve of her neck.

"I have long since lost my innocence," Luciana said,
kissing him, "but I carry no burden of guilt in that affair."

"Which tells me very little . . ." Stefano said, kissing
her shoulder, ". . . which I'm beginning to think . . ."
He kissed the small curve just beneath her earlobe then
took a gentle nip ". . . is very deliberate."

It seemed silly to think about anything else. Now.
With Stefano here. Alive and well and warming to her
touch. But when he pulled away, she tried to concentrate, to say whatever was necessary so that they could
focus on more important things. She kissed him again
and pulled him closer when he started to withdraw. "Exilli put poison in his inkwell."

Stefano grew still. "Exilli? In his inkwell?"

Lucian ran her fingers into his thick, brown hair.
"Hadn't you noticed? His lips were always stained
with ink."

"How very clever," Stefano said, his tone wry. "But
why would Exilli poison Urbano?"

Luciana shrugged, beginning to feel petulant when he
captured her hands, clearly waiting for an answer. "I
can't be sure, but I suspect the conte grew greedier than
even Bianca could tolerate."

"*She* had him murdered?"

"I think so. Why else would Exilli poison the conte?" She reached for him again, but her hands were firmly held.

"Perhaps Conte Pierro—"

"Conte Pierro? He couldn't be threatened by Urbano," Luciana said. Her fingertips traced the lines of his face, dwelled on his lips. She tasted them.

Stefano captured her hands. "Luciana!"

She sighed and dropped her hands to the bed between them. "Conte Pierro's future is assured by his contracts with Bianca and the Church. Why involve himself deeper in the intrigue when he already has such a commitment without risk?"

Stefano lifted the inside of her injured wrist to his lips. "I cannot fault your logic." He brushed featherlight kisses against her sensitive skin.

Passion flared again. Luciana gasped. It had been so long since—

"Forgive me, *Daiya*."

Luciana and Stefano separated. Luciana tried to hide her frustration as she looked to Kisaiya who stood in the doorway to the upper rooms. "What is it?"

"Forgive me, *Daiya,* I wouldn't have woke you except . . . the queen has sent for you. The king is ill," Kisaiya said.

"Ill? Alban? The king? When did this happen?" Stefano asked.

"This morning, Your Grace, during his ride," Kisaiya said.

"His ride? Atropos! What time is it?" Luciana asked. She threw back the coverlets and went to the window. How could she have slept so late?

"Midmorning. I–I didn't want to disturb you," Kisaiya said. "You've been sleeping so poorly of late . . ." She let her words taper off.

"Tell Her Majesty we'll be with her promptly," Stefano said.

Kisaiya hurried away obediently.

Moments later, Stefano and Luciana ran down the

stairs to the salon, Luciana still fighting with a button of her overdress. Kisaiya, who was just returning to the salon, turned back and beckoned them to follow her.

Their footsteps rang on the marble floors, their pace picking up as they neared the royal suites. Lord Strozzini opened the door and motioned them in.

Alban lay on a chaise; Idala wept at his side. Behind them stood several senior nobles, members of the Palantini and riding companions of the fallen regent.

The Royal Physician had already purged the king and, getting little response, now knelt over the king's exposed forearm, lancet and bowl ready for the bloodletting. Luciana went immediately to Idala to comfort her.

"What happened, di Candido?" Stefano asked one of the ducas. He knelt and placed an arm around his sister.

"He said he was not feeling well," di Candido said gruffly. "We turned the horses back to the palazzo, and then His Majesty fell."

"I took him onto my horse and brought him here," Lord Strozzini said, his anxiety plain to see.

"He said he felt unwell *before* he fell?" Stefano asked, watching as the physician made his cut on the king's arm.

Lord Strozzini and other nobles nodded.

Blood ran down the king's arm, trickling along the wrist and flowing into the bowl. Luciana frowned. Something was not right.

Looking from Luciana to her husband, Idala asked, "What is it?"

Luciana shook her head and knelt by the king. She turned his face toward hers. His lips were a faint purplish-blue, but his face was flushed. She bent over him, sniffing his breath.

"What *is* it," Luciana?" Stefano repeated.

She held up her hand, then reached out and touched the blood tracing down the king's arm. The blood was a bright cherry red. She sniffed it, wrinkling her nose at the faint odor.

The members of the Palantini crowded closer, vying for a view. Luciana pushed one man aside and called "Kisaiya! Fetch my bag." She looked up at Lord Strozzini and the king's counselors. "You can be certain the king has been poisoned. I need seawater. You must leave for the Stretto at once!"

"It's nearly an hour's ride to the shore and back again. Isn't there something else we can use?" Duca di Candido protested.

"No, we need the power of the sea in this tonic!"

"This is not medicine," the physician began.

Idala rose. "Do as the duchessa bids. Let us not lose our king because we delayed. Strozzini, you must do this."

"Yes," Majesty," the king's bodyguard said, bowing.

"I'll go with you," Stefano said, following Lord Strozzini.

"Why do you say it's poison? He has had a fall—" the physician began.

Luciana waved him away. "See the lips? The flushed skin? Can't you smell the poison on his breath, in the blood?"

The physician shook his head.

"My *Daiya* told me not everyone can. You must trust me, Signore. The king *has* been poisoned," Luciana said.

"Then I prescribe milk," the old man said. He motioned to one of the servants standing in attendance.

"What say you to that, Duchessa di Drago?" Duca Sebastiani asked.

"I will not argue against it. The milk may help," Luciana said.

All present fell silent, watching the king lying upon the couch. He barely seemed to breathe, no struggles, just a slowly deepening absence of life.

"How was he poisoned?" the queen asked. She sat beside her husband again. "We've been so careful."

"We saw nothing, Majesty," Duca di Candido said, looking to the other ducas for confirmation. "One moment he rode and then, suddenly, he claimed illness and fell from his horse."

Luciana listened to the witnesses, but inspected the king while they spoke. A large bruise had formed on his right temple. A grazing wound covered most of the right side of his face and neck. Looking closely, she noticed a slight but unusual swelling of one of the gravel-embedded grazes. She took the kerchief from her cuff and wiped at the blood and dirt. The swelling remained. She touched the lump and felt a hardness beneath the skin, and, more importantly, noticed a puncture wound.

"My Lord Physician, can you remove this?" Luciana asked, guiding the man's hand to the king's temple.

The physician bent over the king, inspecting the wound, frowning and muttering to himself. He was quick and efficient with the knife. In a matter of seconds, he placed a small, bloody wooden pellet in Luciana's hands.

Idala groaned and turned away. Luciana looked at the bloody thing and took it to the washbasin. She poured water from the pitcher over the bead, and then studied it, holding it up to the light. It might easily be the head of a scorpinini bolt.

"What do you have there?" one of the ducas asked.

Luciana examined the bullet carefully, finding that one side was hollow. Easy for it to carry a measure of poison in the well, and the bolt fragile enough that it broke off easily. It would take a carefully designed scorpinini to shoot such a thing and not have the king notice. She dropped the bullet into her handkerchief and handed the entirety to the king's counselors.

Kisaiya returned, followed by a maid bearing a carafe of milk.

Luciana looked over the tapestry bag Kisaiya brought from her room. From the bag, she took mortar and pestle, a small, oddly made candlestick, and candle.

"Majesty. . . ? Perhaps this is not—" the Royal Physician rubbed his hands, looking exceedingly pained.

"I must protest as well," a member of the council said.

Luciana turned to the physician. "Sir, please do not mistake me. I have in no way any intentions of usurping your expertise. Can you not consider me a peer, a specialist in poisons?"

The physician wiped his balding pate. " 'Tis Gypsy magic you turn to, not medicine, and the king must have—"

"The best," Idala concluded, her voice like stone.

"You will assist Her Grace or be dismissed. If it's magic that can save your king, then so be it."

The Royal Physician bowed and looked at Luciana expectantly.

"Perhaps you might see to the king's comfort and the milk you prescribed," Luciana said.

The Royal Physician seemed happy to be away from her, leaving Luciana to her own work. She dug out a cloth packet, loosed the drawstring and removed a stalk of leaves with a single flower all turned brown with drying. She whispered words of prayer to the Sisters *Fata* before she took it to the king. She touched the frond of mugwort to the king's head and heart, and then laid it upon his temple.

"Simple mugwort, Signores, to draw the poisons out," Luciana explained to her audience.

"Aye, I recognized it," the Royal Physician said.

The members of the Palantini present watched silently now, withholding any criticisms, at least for the time being. As Luciana returned to her table, she found Kisaiya had built a small altar of sorts, laying out the carefully embroidered altar cloth and lighting the appropriate candles.

"Get me fresh Crown for a King, Sweet Woodruff, Cocklebur and Hundred Eyes from the garden, Kisaiya, and have a care in harvesting them," Luciana said softly.

"Yes, *Daiya*." Kisaiya was gone without further word. Luciana noted that she brushed by Nicobar as she left.

Luciana took a widemouthed Venetian glass jar from her bag and selected several prickly leaves. She placed them in her mortar. From another cloth bag, she removed the ever familiar Herb of Grace and smelled it for its potency. Having been collected only a day or so before, the scent was still heady. With gentle fingers, Luciana broke the leaves from the woody stem and dropped them into the mortar as well.

Whispering a blessing over the herbs, Luciana took up the pestle and began to mash the contents. She ground the herbs three times counterclockwise, then three times clockwise and when she was done repeated it twice more. She placed the bruised product upon the small brass dish which fit neatly into her odd little candlestick. From where it sat above the lit candles, the contents of the dish warmed without being set aflame.

Luciana took two white candles from her bag, lit them and placed them in the branches of the candlestick. Immediately, the bruised herbs began to fill the room with a clean, tangy scent.

Luciana poured a bit of oil from a small vial into the dish. It sizzled and the scent increased just as Kisaiya returned with bundles of herbs folded into her apron. Luciana sorted through the herbs even before the girl finished unloading her harvest. She plucked the Hundred Eyes from the bundle and selected the brightest and bluest of the tiny flowering plant. Stem and flower alike she dropped into the mortar along with the flowers and leaves of Sweet Woodruff. She mashed these herbs as she had the previous and added them to the warming dish, stirring the lot with the tip of her stiletto.

At last, satisfied with her concoction, she reached for her kerchief on the table and realized it held the poisonous dart. Someone had apparently returned it. Kisaiya silently offered her own kerchief. Luciana folded it into the shape of a small rectangle, poured the contents of her dish on the kerchief, and carried it to the physician.

"A poultice for the wound. It should draw out the poison, but it must be applied while it is still hot," Luciana said.

The Royal Physician nodded grimly and took it from her, looking unhappy with the course of events. While he applied the poultice, Luciana focused on the king. The purging, bloodletting, and milk seemed to have had little effect. Murmuring yet another prayer, Luciana returned to work.

She took the remaining herbs and mashed them, calling for brandy as she did so. This time, as the herbs warmed in the dish, she poured liquor over it. The scent of warming alcohol and herbs had a dizzying effect, making even Luciana decide to take a seat. Kisaiya quietly opened windows.

Idala sat, white-faced, at her husband's side. The king stirred fitfully and Idala quickly bent over him, talking to him in whispered words. When he could, the physician urged the queen to the side and forced more milk into the king.

Time seemed to slip away. The room grew still except for the sounds of Idala fretting and the Palantini members stalking the otherwise silent chamber. Alban's blood could be heard faintly dripping into the bowl on the floor.

Everyone in the room, save the king, jumped when the door banged open, heralding the return of Lord Strozzini and Stefano. Strozzini brought a leather wineskin to Luciana, who nodded her thanks and took it to the table.

Luciana unstoppered the wineskin and tasted the salt water, then added a liberal dose to the waiting goblet. She added equal parts milk and then poured her syrupy concoction into it. Stirring clockwise with her forefinger, she whispered a prayer and took the goblet to the physician.

The old man looked at the infusion and wrinkled his nose. "What will this do?"

"If I am right, it will further purge the poison and balance His Majesty's humors," Luciana said.

"And if you're wrong?" Idala asked.

"Then I don't know what else I can do," Luciana admitted.

Idala bit her lip, but motioned for the physician to continue.

The old man shook the king's shoulder, but Alban could not be roused. He took a funnel from beside the goblet of milk and placed it between the king's lips.

They all watched the old man at his work, the way his gnarled hands stroked the fluid down the king's throat, the way he tipped Alban's head. Finally, it was done and the physician set aside both goblet and funnel. He turned to Luciana. "How long will it take, Your Grace?"

Luciana shrugged. "It depends upon the poison. All we can do is wait."

So wait they did, sitting around the king, watching his every breath, holding their own at any sign of movement. The room grew stifling as the sun rose higher, shining brightly through the windows. Lord Strozzini took to pacing, his boots making scuffing noises on the floor. The crushing sigh of heavy skirts spoke every time Idala or Luciana shifted. More members of the Palantini arrived, some even left for a time and returned.

Late in the afternoon, Bianca swept into the room with Conte Pierro at her side, breaking the excruciating silence. Standing beside the chaise, she surveyed the king, dispassionately, and pinned the physician with a pointed stare.

"I just heard the news," she announced.

Idala looked up, her face a mask of calm. "I sent for you hours ago. Where have you been?"

The princess drew herself up haughtily. "I've been to the port to welcome my future father-in-law who has just arrived."

"I see," said Idala.

"Will he live?" Bianca asked.

"Only time will tell, Your Highness," said the physician.

Strozzini turned to the conte who stared intently at the grievously ill king. "My Lord Conte," he said, "I wonder if you know the whereabouts of your friend, Lord Exilli?"

"What has that got to do with anything? My cousin may be dying and you concern yourself with the doings of petty men?" the princess demanded, stepping between the conte and the king's bodyguard.

The conte laid a soothing hand on his betrothed's arm. Turning to Lord Strozzini, his expression was disingenuous. "Lord Exilli? Why, the last I saw of him, he was preparing for a morning ride. I did not think it important to look after him before responding to this ill news." He gestured to the king.

"Do you suggest Lord Exilli had a hand in this?" Duca di Candido asked.

"He seemed to know some little bit about poison yesterday at the scene of Conte Urbano's death," Luciana said quietly.

The silence was pointed as the king's counselors

looked expectantly toward the princess and her soon-to-be husband. There was not a kind eye among them.

"If you think it will help, then, of course, I'll send for him immediately," Conte Pierro said, sounding somewhat aggrieved as he snapped his fingers impatiently. A porter stepped forward from the crowd beyond the door, stopping when the bodyguard scowled.

"Don't bother, Conte Pierro. He was departing Tyrrhia when he went for his 'morning ride' as you call it. The Escalade are scouring the countryside for him as we speak," Stephano said.

Conte Pierro looked thunderstruck. At another time, Luciana might have been able to appreciate his acting. "Then I am at a loss as to why you would ask me such a thing!"

"He came as a member of your entourage. It seems only fair that you would know of his comings and goings," Lord Strozzini replied.

"My entourage? Really! He was an amusing little man with friends in Citteauroea—or so I thought."

"As you say then, Conte Pierro," Strozzini said. He bowed and departed, leaving the room once more in utter silence.

The royal family and the members of the Palantini now present stared at one another, waiting, assessing.

"I hope you don't think—" Conte Pierro began suddenly.

Princess Bianca placed a silencing hand on his chest. "Of course not, my dear. You are one of us and we are all dear to one another. Aren't we, Idala?"

The queen met Bianca's steady gaze. "Of course."

The king let out a low moan and his eyes fluttered open.

"Alban?" Idala slipped from the couch to kneel by his side.

The king looked toward his wife. A pallor had gradually replaced the flushed pinkness in his skin, though his lips still looked bluish. "I feel positively ill," he said, his voice no more than a mere whisper. "What happened?"

"You fell from your horse, dearest," the queen said,

gently stroking hair from his face. "Luciana discovered you had been poisoned. It is she who, with the help of Signore Physician, affected your recovery."

"Poisoned?" The king turned his head. He stared thoughtfully at his cousin, but looked abruptly away, his eyes seeking and at last settling upon Luciana. "I have taken every precaution. How could it be that I was poisoned?"

"A most clever device, Majesty," Duca Sebastiani said, taking Luciana's kerchief from the table. He unfolded the bit of cloth and displayed the slug. "Somehow, someone managed to shoot you with this."

Alban wiped a weary hand over his eyes. "But . . . I do not remember being shot . . ."

"I suspect the bullet carried a lethal dose of the poison *Aqua Fina*," Luciana said. "Your memory may be affected, or, in the exhilaration of your ride, you simply did not feel the strike."

"Did she say *Aqua Fina*?" de Candido blustered.

"Everyone knows that's only myth and legend," the young Duca Sebastiani said with a derisive laugh.

"And yet, the treatment for that poison is what worked to save His Majesty," Stefano retorted darkly.

"We are all gratified by your wife's help, di Drago, but how does she come to be so familiar with poisons?" di Candido asked. The question was delivered in a careful, deliberate manner pointedly free of any outright suspicion.

"Yes, that is a question I am eager to hear the answer to as well," Bianca said with a cunning smile. For all of Duca di Candido's care to avoid sounding distrustful, the princess' tone made her words all but a blatant accusation.

The king pinched the bridge of his nose. "I am very tired. Perhaps I could give an audience later?"

"Of course, Majesty," Stefano said, bowing. He placed an arm around Luciana's waist and glared daggers at the princess.

Bianca returned his gaze coldly.

With murmured well-wishes, the ducas filed from the

king's rooms. Luciana waited, thankful for Stefano's re-assuring grip. Apparently, neither she nor Stefano was willing to leave before Bianca and her conte.

At last, Bianca bent and placed a kiss upon the king's brow. "Rest well, Alban."

In the corridor, they found the nobles, servants, and other onlookers dispersed. Bianca, however, hovered outside of the king's salon. "You try my patience, Your Grace! I advise more caution lest you make enemies."

"Sound advice, Your Highness," Stefano replied with a bow.

The princess expelled her breath and stalked away, leaving Conte Pierro to follow in her wake.

"She is normally more composed," Luciana observed sourly.

Stefano grinned grimly. "She was quite remarkable at maintaining her composure until that last, wasn't she?"

"Hmm. What do you think they'll do next?"

Stefano shook his head, contemplating Bianca's departure. "I'm curious to know if the cardinal returned with the Duca deMedici, though. Since the king lived, they will be cautious about their next gambit . . . if they even *have* another."

"Do not underestimate her. It could prove very unwise."

Lord Strozzini joined them in the antechamber, newly returned from his errand. He acknowledged them with a polite nod and reached for the door to the king's rooms.

"What news of Exilli?" Luciana asked.

"None," Strozzini said. "Nothing more than I reported earlier. He's completely quitted his room. No one knows where he might be. I have called out the Escalade and the Corpo d'Armata, but I do not hold much hope. He has, no doubt, been riding steadily since this morning and has already taken one of the ships across the Stretto. He could be anywhere on the mainland now."

XXXVI

•

*"The first wrote, wine is the strongest. The second
wrote, the king is the strongest. The third wrote,
women are strongest, but above all things truth
beareth away the victory."*

—Apocrypha

30 d'Maggio 1684

ALBAN pushed the papers aside and leaned back
against his pillows. He pinched the bridge of his nose
and closed his eyes.

"I'm sorry, Alban, but I didn't think news of this sort
could wait. As it is, we may have already delayed too
long by putting this revelation off for two days while
you recovered," Stefano said. He looked anxiously at
Luciana who stood nearer the king.

Watching both men, Luciana began softly. "If you are
too unwell—"

"No!" the king said sharply. He shook his head
slightly, sounding very tired. "No. We must address this
matter now. It cannot wait even a moment longer."

"What would you have us do?" Luciana asked.

The king looked at Luciana and his expression softened. He took her hand and kissed it. "You, fair Lady,
have served Tyrrhia well, but I fear—now—there is
nothing more that you can do."

"There must be, Majesty," Luciana said, sensing her
imminent dismissal. "Perhaps—"

The king glanced up at Stefano. "I hope you treasure this prize you were so lucky to marry."

"Of course, Majesty," Stefano said, glancing at his wife, "though one never truly or fully appreciates what they have, I think."

"Prettily said, Your Grace." The king grinned lopsidedly. "*Araunya,* would you be so kind as to tell Lord Strozzini I would have an audience with my cousin . . . in an hour . . . in my office."

And there it was, Luciana thought. She curtsied and backed away from the bed. "Of course, Majesty." If she did not argue the point now, perhaps the king might reconsider? Or Stefano would accept her help? She smothered a sigh. She was more the fool if she really thought there was a chance either would happen. So now, close to confronting the lead conspirator, the only one who might know where Alessandra's body had been hidden, she was dismissed. Pride warred with her obligation to Alessandra.

"*Araunya,* if nothing else," the king called as her hand touched the door, "you have a right to know what my cousin has to say for herself. Make yourself available at the appointment."

Surprised, Luciana turned back for a moment. She left before the king changed his mind. Besides delivering the king's message to Strozzini, there were other matters to attend to. Prunella planned to leave for Reggio di Calabria again this afternoon and, no doubt, she still had many preparations to make. Perhaps she could be a little more helpful to Stefano's young cousin now than she had been before the unfortunate marriage. She resolved to do just that, immediately after talking to Nicobar about his continued searches of the garden for the princess' secret passage.

———

A servant let Luciana into Prunella's rooms. She found the object of her errand sitting at a writing desk in her salon.

"Perhaps this is a bad time?" Luciana paused, waiting.

Prunella started, looking up from her writing. "I'm sorry, Your Grace—"

"You are a contessa now, Prunella. I think you may set aside some of the formality without jeopardizing either of our stations, at least in private," Luciana said.

Prunella sniffed, considered the quill in her hand which she set aside. "Very well, then, Cousin. I did not mean to make you wait. I hope you will forgive me?"

"No need for that," Luciana said. "I came to see if I might be of some service to you."

"To *me?*" Prunella said, her voice expressing full measure of her shocked sense of propriety.

Luciana chose to ignore the girl's disapproval. "What is left to be done before you return to your family?"

"I am just about through here. I am writing a letter of apology to Her Highness. Being in mourning, of course it is impossible for me to attend the wedding. Urbano was quite determined to be here, though. Equally determined that I attend as well. My sister, Maria, had to hurry her own wedding so that I could be present. Now it seems I will miss the weddings of my other sisters. I was not prepared to become a widow, at least not so soon." Prunella rose, pressing the flat of her hands against the front of her somber black gown. She smiled ruefully. "Urbano said I was to spend my time in Citteauroea buying a new wardrobe, one that suited a woman of my new station. At least I had not already ordered any gowns. I shall simply dye my old gowns to suit."

Luciana wondered at the thought that Prunella would have any need. The girl's wardrobe was positively dreary, but then, to be fair, hers was not the Romani way. "Where will you go when you leave here? To Reggio di Calabria, I know, but . . . ?"

Her young cousin motioned Luciana to the sofa. "I will go to my own estate." She laughed softly, ironically. "So much has changed in a mere fortnight. I have the farmlands from my dowry to manage now."

Luciana marveled at the change in the girl. While she

had not expected grief, Luciana had expected more than this simple acceptance. "You will do well, I'm sure," she said.

"Of course I will. My father taught me the business of farming, and I was an apt student," Prunella responded. "It seems odd that only a month ago I had no prospects of marriage, and nothing of my own, yet here I am today, a contessa, a widow, and a landowner."

Luciana nodded, considering. "Your father won't be taking over? Managing for you?"

"Well, yes, to a certain degree, but I hope to convince him to let me have a hand in it as well since the land is mine now, after all. As a propertied widow, it is far more seemly to be doing 'man's work' than it was before, when I had nothing."

Strange, Luciana thought, how serendipitous all of this had turned out for Prunella. She had rare advantages not normally afforded *gadjé* women and all while she was still young and resilient enough to make her own fortune. It was ironic that she, a Romani, had so little control over her own affairs.

Prunella sniffed. "I *have* been running on, haven't I? I've been so distracted." She crossed her hands in her lap and stared at them. "It's just that I–I was not prepared. I *hate* not being prepared."

This sounded like the familiar Prunella. Luciana hid a smile. "Have you handled your husband's affairs in Citteauroea?"

"In Citteauroea?" Prunella repeated. She frowned. "You're right, of course, he must have open accounts. I'm so accustomed to being frugal, it didn't occur to me." She groaned. "And I leave today!"

"Allow me to do this for you," Luciana said, taking Prunella's hand. "I'll have Nicobar investigate the conte's accounts. I will be happy to advance the money to his creditors until the rest of his affairs are settled."

"Oh, thank you, Cousin," Prunella said. She sighed heavily as she looked around the salon. "I will miss the palazzo. I had so looked forward to being at court."

"Then you must return when your period of mourning is over," Luciana said.

"Do you think the queen will permit it?"

"Of course! You are her cousin and young enough to be interested in enjoying yourself," Luciana laughed softly.

"Good! That will give me an opportunity to look for another husband. I think this could be a far more pleasant experience the second time," Prunella said.

Shocked, Luciana struggled to maintain her easy countenance. "I wouldn't suggest you mention such a plan in front of the priest, Pru, I don't think he would understand."

Prunella turned at the sound of a scratch on the outer door. "Sage and timely advice, Cousin. I think that will be Padre Gasparino at the door."

"Then I will leave you to your consultations with him," Luciana said, rising.

"You are welcome to stay, Cousin."

"I think not," Luciana said firmly. She had no great desire to meet with a priest. Not now. Not with the cardinal still free to cause trouble. She did not want, however unintentionally, to give the priest something to report to his superior.

───────

Well before the appointed hour, Luciana arrived in the antechamber leading to the king's office. She heard angry voices in Alban's office. Strozzini motioned for her to hurry up the steps. At the top, he leaned close.

"Her Highness was angered by the summons and arrived early. I am instructed to let you in. She's in a foul mood and His Majesty is no better. Have a care."

Luciana nodded and eased her way, as unobtrusively as possible, into the room. Bianca, however, noticed the movement and rounded on her.

"What is *she* doing here? It's bad enough you summon me while I make marriage arrangements and that you even say these things to me, but must you say them in front of these witnesses? And she is only a Gypsy with money! She has no place here."

"She belongs where I welcome her," Alban said sharply. "Won't you be seated, Your Grace?"

Luciana quietly seated herself beside Stefano who sat with arms crossed. Three other senior members of the Palantini—the Ducas di Candido, Mancini, and Correlli—sat at various points around the room. She read her husband's anger in the set of his mouth and his posture. The other ducas were equally pleased with the circumstances, though one of them looked as though he, too, were going to protest Luciana's presence.

The princess glared at Stefano and stamped her foot furiously. "You concern yourself with the cardinal and yet are not distressed by this self-confessed . . . intruder?" the princess protested, waving wildly at Stefano. "I should think you might suspect His Grace of forging these documents. He has already admitted that he willingly violated the sacred ground of an abbey and stole private papers!"

"If he forged them, Bianca, how could he have stolen them?" Alban asked. "Besides, there is the matter of this letter." He took a sheet of vellum from the papers on his desk and handed it to his cousin. Luciana recognized it as the missive from the cardinal.

Princess Bianca perused the letter and appeared shaken. But not for long, she dropped it on the desk with a laugh. "Don't you think the cardinal is capable of better French? Never mind this unspeakable crime against Latin. Some poor semiliterate fool must have created this as a bit of humor, or . . . . How should I know what this is? I've never even seen it—which strikes me as odd since it was addressed to me."

"You worry overmuch about the unspeakable crime against Latin, Your Highness, and too little about the treason you stand accused of," Duca di Candido said, crossing his arms over his imposing girth.

The princess turned her back on him. "This is all stuff and nonsense, Cousin. What *if* the cardinal were taking an interest in the Tyrrhian military? He is a man of God. That he takes an interest in the well-being of the country where he tends his flock should be a matter for celebration, not condemnation. And I do not see why, as a consequence, you make these charges against me. If you are unhappy with the cardinal, why don't you take this to him?"

"That the cardinal wrote such correspondence to *you* is reason enough for suspicion. That everything herein that took place also speaks against you and the cardinal, and because I don't believe the cardinal would take actions such as these without the cooperation of someone who would make his efforts worthwhile, never mind the fact that the cardinal has failed to return from Salerno as planned," Alban responded.

"Majesty," the princess said in a very tired voice, "you have been recently injured and have surely not had enough time to heal. Can we not discuss this when I don't have a wedding to plan and you are wholly of your right mind? The cardinal's failure to return is *certainly* an immediate problem for me, but only because he was to perform the ceremony!"

"You take this matter too lightly, Your Highness," the elderly Duca Mancini said. "People's lives—a kingdom is at stake."

Looking ashen and weak sitting behind the desk, Alban raised his hand in a calming motion and said, "I would resolve this matter peacefully, if I am able."

"I'm insulted by these implications and, what's more, that you do so in front of *them!*" Bianca declared, waving at Stefano and Luciana and then the other members of the Palantini.

"The Palantini has every right to be present," Stefano said. "Our homeland has been threatened and we are here as witnesses for justice."

"Witnesses? You act as if this were a *gabinetto di stella!*" Bianca scoffed.

"You *are* on trial," the king said quietly. "For your sake, I chose not to have this hearing before the entire Palantini. You mistake me, however, if you consider this a mere family squabble. I do not seek to be appeased. I do not seek to be placated. I want answers to these charges against you and your confederates."

Bianca stared at him, her eyes blazing with fury. "You dare do this to *me?* By what right would you try me, the only *true* heir to King Orsinio?"

"Do you forget so easily the prerogative of the Palantini?" Duca di Candido demanded, drawn to his feet.

"The Palantini appoints and approves the Heir. *Your* father, King Orsinio, took part in the Palantini's choice. *He* chose Alban over all the candidates, including yourself, Your Highness."

"So I have been told over these many years. How could I forget the Palantini's preference? You flaunt your selection," Bianca said. "You aren't satisfied with being king, Alban, so you must now humiliate me with the *gabinetto di stella?*"

"I have no intention of humiliating you, Bianca, or any other member of *la famiglia reale,* this is why we use the smallest *gabinetto* instead of putting you *in prova.*"

"Do you truly believe that I would commit treason? Against Tyrrhia? You think that I would jeopardize Tyrrhia?" Bianca asked.

"The Palantini can charge you with treason against the Crown and, thereby, treason against Tyrrhia—" Duca Mancini began.

"Against the Crown? On what grounds?"

"I have not finished, Your Highness. We are ready to charge you with the death of Lady Alessandra Davizzi, and with the attempted murder of Capitano Mandero di Montago," Duca Mancini continued.

"There is also the suspicious matter of Conte Urbano di Vega's death," Duca di Candido said.

"You charge me with murder?" Bianca shook her head, her face reddening with anger. "Why would *I* kill anyone? And why would I ever kill someone as dear to me as Urbano was?"

"I've been presented with considerable evidence of your activities, but it took these papers of the cardinal's and his letter to convince me. I seek only a reasonable explanation so I may pardon you," Alban said, keeping his voice level and clear.

"Pardon me? Pardon me for what? I have done nothing, I tell you! What evidence do you have against me, other than these papers which relate only to the cardinal?"

"You forget the letter addressed to you, and I have heard testimony from Capitano di Montago that you and the cardinal arranged for the marriage contract with

Conte deMedici to demonstrate your commitment to a plan." The king took the papers from Stefano and waved them at her. "*This* plan, Bianca!"

"How could Capitano di Montago *possibly* testify to such a claim?" the princess said with a high-pitched laugh.

Alban smiled. It was not a pretty smile. "You know full well that you were overheard by him in the garden."

The princess shrugged. "I do not know what he could be talking about. He must have misunderstood. Such is the lot of eavesdroppers."

"Bianca, please! Take these charges seriously. You must answer them," Alban said.

"Heed him, Your Highness. By rights the Palantini should have you beheaded," di Candido said urgently.

"You have no confidence that these charges against me will prove false? The evidence against *Araunya* Alessandra proved false. Do you expect these charges will prove no less feeble than those against her? And she was a member of the court, *not* the Princess of Tyrrhia, sole remaining heir to King Orsinio's bloodline!"

"If we were not confident of the evidence, we would not make these charges. Let us also not forget that at no previous time was an attempt on the king made, but this evidence before us suggests you might even be willing to go that far. The council cannot ignore this evidence, not even for you, Your Highness," Duca Correlli said.

"So now you charge me with poisoning you as well? I have scores of people who could testify that I was at the docks welcoming my father-in-law to be!" Bianca said to Alban.

"*I* would not accuse you of the crime directly, but it was through you and your fiancé that the poisoner, Exilli, found his way to Tyrrhia and my court," Alban said.

"Matters are further complicated by this Exilli's sudden and mysterious departure," Duca Mancini said.

"Were we of a mind to, were this the greater council, it might be concluded that with the White King dead, you might consider your path to the throne clearer," Duca di Candido said. "No formal Heir has as yet been named and we are not likely to select a child so young as Dario Gian. We would be forced to select from among our previous choices—the other cousins and yourself. Of these candidates, only you have stayed in court and are readily familiar with politics within and without Tyrrhia."

"And this is reason to condemn me?" Bianca protested. She lowered her voice sweetly, turning to the king. "You are like my brother, Alban. As angry as I am with you, do you *really* believe me capable of murdering you?"

Bianca turned to Stefano. "Your Grace, I confess it. I am not the most agreeable of women, but I am accused of two murders and attempting two more. Do you really think me capable of such a thing?"

"Give us sweet reason, Cousin," Alban said. "What other explanation could there be for the attempt on Capitano di Montago's life when he learned of your conspiracy?"

"He is a soldier, an officer, a peacekeeper. His life is committed to acts that put his life in jeopardy," Bianca said. "I cannot begin to understand the motives of men like Capitano di Montago!"

"Why would the capitano accuse you?" the king said quickly. "And was it not convenient that the 'attempt' came so close to a point when you and the cardinal might have a motive to be done with the capitano?"

"I tell you once more, the cardinal and I have not conspired. I simply thought to save you from making marital arrangements," Bianca insisted.

"Those arrangements themselves were preemptive, an offense against the king and council's prerogative," di Candido pointed out.

The princess crossed her arms over her chest. "Why, then, would I kill Lady Alessandra? And I ask you how I could have murdered her?"

"I do not know, perhaps to convince your comrades you were wholly with them." The king leaned forward intently in his chair.

"But *why* would I do such a thing? Lady Alessandra is—was nothing to me," Bianca said.

"She was nothing to you and, therefore, that much easier to put out of the way. Why? Because the capitano may have told his lover what he suspected and there must be no hint of the collusion between you and the cardinal," Stefano said.

"These things you accuse me of are diabolical!" Bianca protested, suddenly in tears.

"Unfortunately, it also makes so much sense. We have evidence that Conte Urbano meddled in magic, that he used this magic to command Lady Alessandra's spirit to haunt the queen and to influence her mind. What would the conte's or the cardinal's motivation be, unless there was someone to please, someone's bidding they did, in the hope that they would thereby gain standing?" Mancini asked.

Bianca folded her hands and remained silent.

"Have you nothing to say?"

"Why would I do all this?" Bianca demanded. Her head remained bent as she stared at the floor.

"All of it led to the attempt on the king's life. With him dead, you might be considered the most viable candidate for the throne. If you held the throne and were married to another Catholic, well, we know your religious leanings, Your Highness, and none of them, despite your father's teaching, are tolerant, as is the custom of Tyrrhia. The Church would, therefore, have a reason to back you, and to overthrow the balance in Tyrrhia, you would need all the backing you could negotiate," Correlli said, shifting in his chair so that he could watch the princess closely with his hawklike eyes.

"But *I* didn't attempt to poison you. I thought Lord Exilli was accused of that," Bianca said to Alban.

"Ah, but who brought Exilli to Tyrrhia?" Stefano asked.

Bianca shrugged. "He is a friend of Conte Pierro. Why should he not come to Tyrrhia for the wedding?"

"What reason would Exilli have to poison the king if not to secure the throne for you and Conte Pierro?" Alban asked. "Examining these events individually, I, too, believed you innocent, but all these events together are damning."

"If I intended to murder you, why not wait until after the marriage? Why now?" Bianca countered softly.

"The marriage to the conte would be one stabilizing force you could show to the Palantini Court and, if you had the throne within reach at the time of the wedding, all the more reason for the deMedicis to continue on with the plan."

"You're convinced of these charges? There is nothing I can say to dissuade you?" Bianca asked.

"I would gladly hear testimony that I am wrong—that we are wrong—but I will be satisfied if you forswear your involvement by signing this paper for the Palantini Council removing you and all of Orisini's bloodline once and forever from the pool of heirs," the king said. He pushed the paper across the desk to her.

Bianca ignored the paper. "What of my marriage?"

"I am against it politically, but I will demonstrate my leniency by permitting it to go forward if you so wish," Alban responded, his tone gentle.

"You would have me sign away my rights to the throne should something happen?" Bianca was calm, almost affable. "My children's rights?"

'The proof is damning, Bianca. You have little option. Your life is at stake for treason."

Bianca sighed and held out her hand. When Alban stared at her, she snapped her fingers impatiently. "A quill, if you please!"

"You are prepared to sign this, then?" Mancini asked.

"Yes," she said, "if it will convince you all that I have no designs upon the throne and put an end to this. What other steps do you intend to take against me? Exile?"

"I have not decided. I would prefer to forgive you and begin again," Alban said.

"Then have done with it!" she declared, signing the sheet of paper with a flourish and pressing her seal into the wax Alban poured for her. "Am I free to go? I have plans to make."

Alban waved his hand and with that she was gone.

Luciana blinked and looked from Stefano to the king. "Pardon, Majesty, but what justice will there be for my sister?"

"Tyrrhia has been served and that, unfortunately, Your Grace, is to the greater good," the king said tiredly.

"'But what of the greater charge of murder? Does she go completely unaffected by this crime? You believed the charge enough to list it and yet she merely must sign away her claim to the throne? It's paper! She can disavow—"

Stefano rose and pulled Luciana into his arms. She struggled against him, beating angrily against his chest even though she knew further words to the king would not serve her cause. She leaned against him, exhausted, and wept until she could weep no more. When at last she looked up, the king and counselors were gone and they were alone in his office.

"Come. Let us return to our suite," Stefano said softly, wiping hair and tears from her eyes, his arms gently encircling her.

Luciana looked around the king's office and slowly nodded. So this was how it would be. She sighed heavily and allowed Stefano to guide her down the flight of stairs.

XXXVII

"If you prick us, do we not bleed?
If you tickle us, do we not laugh?
If you poison us, do we not die?
And if you wrong us, shall we not revenge?"
—William Shakespeare

1 d'Giugno 1684

"I CAN almost comprehend attending to di Vega's affairs, that being of service to Prunella, of course," Stefano sighed heavily, "but why, when you hate the woman so much, attend Bianca's wedding?"

Luciana glanced back from the carriage window, glad now that Nicobar had discreetly chosen to sit in the driver's seat with Baldo. For once, at last, she believed Stefano tried to understand her. "I must see this to its end. The king seems satisfied that there will be no justice for my sister, but at least let me see Bianca married to the deMedici. When she's done that, then I'll know the Palantini will not have her on the throne. Perhaps when that has been settled, we can feel some assurance that Bianca won't make another attempt upon Alban or your sister . . . or be of further danger to *my* people."

Stefano nodded. "This has nothing to do with your sister's body still being missing, does it?"

Luciana looked away uncomfortably. "I cannot lie to you, Stefano, my obligation to my sister, to find her, free her . . . so that she can go on has not been fulfilled, but I no longer have great hopes that the right thing can be done on her behalf." The words choked out of her. What would she do? What could she say to the *Beluni* if she failed in such an important endeavor? Never mind that Urbano was not killed by her own hand, that Bianca's only punishment was to be a marriage to the bastard son of one of the premier families in all Europe, and that the cardinal would completely escape justice. No justice, no vendetta, not even immortal peace for Alessandra. No *real* assurance even that Bianca or the cardinal would not act against the Romani again.

"Luciana?"

She started at Stefano's voice, wondering how long she had been lost in thought. "Forgive me, Stefan."

He reached across the carriage and took her hand. "You have reason to be distracted. I'll not hold that against you."

"Thank you," Luciana murmured and turned to stare out the window again. She had long missed the balm of her husband's comforting touch.

"Ales— Your sister's body might still be found," Stefano said.

"With Urbano dead?" Luciana shook her head. "Urbano was the *chovahano*. Bianca continues to think of herself as a good Catholic. She, most likely, doesn't even know where my sister is, because she never wanted to know lest she have that on her conscience. But if she does know, my judgment of the woman is that she would take the knowledge to the grave rather than admit she had anything to do with it."

"You could be right," Stefano agreed reluctantly. "But Nicobar might yet find—"

"He has no one to follow and, despite his dedication, nothing to show for these past weeks of searching."

Stefano gave a dissatisfied grunt and sat back in his seat beside her. "At least we will know that Bianca could never marshal the power to take the throne."

Luciana nodded. "At least we know that," she agreed as the carriage came to a halt. She took no comfort in this compromise of justice. She rose, opening the carriage door for herself, looking forward to finding diversion in her errands.

Nicobar met her at the carriage door and folded the step down into place while offering her his hand. Luciana looked back at Stefano. "Are you coming?"

He nodded and followed her from the carriage. He frowned, looking around the marketplace, shielding his eyes from the glare of the early afternoon sun. "Where are we?"

Nicobar gave him a strange look. "Citteauroea, Your Grace."

"You misunderstand me, Nicobar," Stefano said. "Why are we *here*?" He motioned toward the shop Luciana approached.

Luciana paused and came back. She knew the old crone in The Dragon's Hearth had sharp ears and was not immune to irritation for those who neither understood nor appreciated her work. "Have care, husband," she said. "I do not want to lose the shopkeep's goodwill." Especially not, she reminded herself, when the very same shopkeep knew so much about the dark arts and possessed Luciana's freely sacrificed hair and nail clippings. There had been enough bad luck on this adventure, she did not want to bargain for more.

Stefano lowered his voice, but his tone did not change. "I don't like such places, Luciana. Why must we stop here?"

Luciana refrained from making a retort. After all this time, Stefano was as uncomfortable with magic as he'd ever been. Would he ever grow beyond it? And, if he could not, what did that say about their future? Dwelling on such matters would help neither of them at the moment and she felt too raw to battle with him.

"I know that Urbano did business with this merchant. I've come to settle his accounts. Don't come in, if you wish, but I *must!*" she said.

Stefano accompanied her to the door of the shop, but no farther. He stood there, in the doorway, attentive, almost standing guard, but not quite into the shop proper. Luciana wondered at the conflicts he must be suffering over those things his wife embraced. She had no time for such delays and so continued on without him, calling out for the gnomish proprietress.

———————

Nicobar shifted restlessly from foot to foot, trying not to make eye contact with the *Daiya's* husband. In their long years apart, Nicobar had managed to forget what he never thought he would . . . how difficult it was to serve these two when they were at odds with one another. In truth, however, he did not serve these two, he served the *Daiya* and happenstance brought him to serve the duca as well.

In his estimation, the *Araunya* chose true when she married this man. The duca surpassed the merits of most men and came the closest he had ever seen a *gadjé* come to accepting the strange conditions of being married to a Roma. The *Daiya* and her husband were well-matched, silk to thread, fire to steel, if they would ever quit sparring long enough to see it, but it was not his place to speak . . . or, really, to even think about such matters.

Nicobar glanced up at Baldo in the driver's seat atop the carriage. Warmed by the afternoon sun, the coachman had nodded off with the reins wrapped around his fist, his whip laid carelessly across his lap and his coat and hat on the bench beside him.

The duca, on the other hand, leaned against the doorjamb of the apothecary, his right leg drawn up so that the sole of his boot rested against the stonework wall. The *Araunya's* husband was not as well practiced at eavesdropping as the average servant, Nicobar thought. But what drew his attention?

Nicobar shoved away from the carriage steps and crossed the half dozen steps to the door of The Dragon's Hearth. The *Daiya* still leaned over the old *strega's* books. Could the duca be straining to hear them? He listened hard. The women talked of nothing more exciting than money and credit. Nicobar darted another look at the duca.

No longer bothering to hide his interest, the duca

peered over his shoulder as though trying to see some-one without being noticed himself. Were he not so finely dressed, Nicobar might have mistaken him for a footpad.

Nicobar strolled across the cobbled walk, passing the narrow alley which separated the next shop from the apothecary. Two merchant-class women had taken ad-vantage of the shade afforded by the buildings. Through the distance of the byway, Nicobar could see the mer-chant stalls of the first plaza beyond the women.

Adopting a pose similar to that of his employer's hus-band, Nicobar leaned against the neat brick front of the perfumery and listened.

". . . *Sí!* Then this would be a truly Catholic Tyrrhia!" one of the women said, waving a plumed fan.

"My husband says that continental Tyrrhia is much more proper in their dealings with those who are not of the faith!"

The first woman nodded. "I miss Naples. The padre is right. It was better when the princess made it her home."

"*Sí,* and they treat you with proper respect there."

"Don't say that in front of my husband, *Signora,* he'll complain about the Jews and those rogue Gypsies until Cardinal delle Torre himself is tired of the subject!" the first woman protested.

"Mine, too! They are much more . . . assertive here, in the heartland," the other said.

"Assertive?" The merchant woman scoffed. "They certainly do not show due deference, to be certain! And, here, so close to the bosom of the Church! They should be thankful we let them live among us. In the east, they're put to use as slaves."

The other woman made a distasteful expression. "However vile, I cannot say that anyone deserves that fate. But to the princess . . . how soon could she and her consort effect a change? These blackguards have been pandered to for so long . . . even Orsinio was lenient with them. How can we be sure the princess will be any different than her father in that regard?"

Boisterous shouting muffled how either woman re-sponded. When Nicobar and the duca dared risk looking down the alley, the women were gone. The Duca di

Drago's expression could only be described as thunderous. He raised a hand, motioning Nicobar to him.

"This needs pursuing," the duca said. When Nicobar nodded and started to step aside, he found the other man had caught his sleeve. "Not a word of what I have learned to my wife."

"But shouldn't—"

The duca placed a finger to his own lips. "Not a word."

Nicobar nodded. "Not a word of what you have learned."

The *Daiya's* husband clapped his shoulder. "I'll rejoin my wife presently. Where does she plan to go after this?"

"To the Guildhouse, Your Grace."

"In *Terzo* Plaza?"

"Yes, Your Grace."

"Then tell her I will meet her there," the duca said.

"As you say, Your Grace," Nicobar murmured.

The duca nodded once more and ducked into the alley where the merchants' wives had so recently lingered.

Nicobar chewed his lip. He did not care for actively misleading the *Araunya's* husband, but he had no option. The princess, it seemed, remained a threat, not nearly so powerless as his employer believed. The *Araunya* must know about this; he owed it to her and their people to tell. He would not say what, if anything, the duca had learned; he could, however, report what he, himself, overheard.

He turned at the sound of the *Araunya's* voice.

"His Grace has returned to the palazzo?" Luciana asked, frowning when she found only Nicobar and the carriage waiting.

Nicobar hesitated. "No, *Daiya*, he waited until just a moment ago. He had to see to some errand of his own and says that he will rejoin you at the Guildhouse."

Luciana ducked her head, reviewing the contents of her carryall as a ruse to hide her disquiet. Despite the

great steps they had taken to amend their life together,
Luciana still felt the deep pains of his long-term absences, still found it difficult to believe that he loved her
and had not stayed away by choice.

"But, of course, I should have realized," Luciana said.
That her words were a pretty pretense for the sake of
her pride, Nicobar no doubt knew, and he was kind
enough not to contradict her. His behavior seemed
strange nonetheless, and what had drawn Stefano's
attention?

She refused to torture herself with images of pretty
young ladies enamored by her husband's charm. Unfortunately, her imagination refused to cooperate. She took
a deep breath and looked purposefully at her side. "So,
we are to go on to the Guildhouse? Did he give any
indication how long he might be?"

"I'm sorry, *Daiya,* no," Nicobar said. When she
stopped fussing with the contents, he took the carryall
from her. "The Guildhouse is not far, *Daiya,* would you
like to stroll or ride?"

"I'll walk." She watched as her aide rapped on the
coachman's bench, swinging her carryall up. She left
them to their business, they knew what they were doing.
She needed the time to think . . . about Stefano and
herself and their future, if there might even be one for
them and how much she dared risk in her pursuit of
real justice.

Lost in thought, she felt the presence of Nicobar at
her elbow. She glanced back, noting that Baldo drove
the carriage just behind at a lazy ambling pace.

This plaza, *Terzo* Plaza, just beyond the apothecary,
housed the shops serving those customers able to be a
little freer with their coin. Despite the well-known expense of shopping in this quarter, there seemed no lack
of customers.

She wondered if Stefano had come this way. Speculation would serve no purpose. Stefano could be anywhere
by now, let him attend to his own affairs. What affairs
needed tending to she did not want to consider, but even
as she reminded herself of this, she remembered that

there was supposed to be a house in this quarter where unhappy husbands and lonely gentlemen could find comfort. With that thought, Luciana desperately hoped that Stefano was *not* seeking diversions in this plaza.

The Guildhouse stood on the far side of the plaza's neck where one section of the marketplace bled into another. The walkway was barely discernible from the cobbled street. Where the walk was overwhelmed with the throng of hawkers and their clientele, people swarmed into the street, taking the easiest path they found.

Like its neighbors, the Guildhouse rose tall and square above the other buildings in the extended marketplace. Gypsy Silk Guild banners added color to the otherwise dour gray granite edifice. Filled to overflowing with decorative herbs, planters lined the landing, creating the effect of a welcoming bower as one approached the Guildhouse door. Perhaps Stefano had decided he would be more comfortable here and—

"*Daiya,* there is something I must tell you," Nicobar said.

"Can it wait?"

"I'm sorry, *Daiya,* but I think—"

"*Araunya!*"

They both turned at the cry and noticed a flurry of skirts as someone ran from the Guildhouse door into the house proper.

"Mistress Eleni! The *Araunya* comes!"

Luciana smiled ruefully as she turned back to her aide. "I'm sorry, Nicobar, but it seems that whatever you must tell me will have to wait."

Mistress Eleni arrived at the door as Luciana reached the front steps. The Guildmistress, pausing just long enough to shoo away the girls in gray apprentice robes who followed her, quickly closed the distance between herself and the *Araunya* and managed an elegant curtsy.

"*Araunya,* how can we of this House serve you?"

Luciana acknowledged the Guildmistress' salute with a nod and began to make her way up the granite steps. "I've come to settle accounts for . . . a member of the family." She hesitated, repulsed by the thought of Conte Urbano's relation to her—however distant or abbreviated.

Mistress Eleni appeared confused, but motioned her into the house. "You mean for the other *Araunya?* But we discussed—"

"No, I come on behalf of the recently widowed Contessa di Vega. Conte Urbano di Vega *was* your client, was he not?"

The Guildmistress nodded with dawning comprehension. "The conte has passed, did you say?"

A delicate way of putting it, Luciana thought and nodded.

"But he was such a young man . . . well, not so very young, I suppose, but I never would have thought it. Was there an illness . . . or an accident of some sort?" The Guildmistress escorted Luciana into her office and closed the door behind them, leaving Nicobar to the gentle mercies of her apprentices in the foyer.

"Not precisely, no," Luciana said. She took a deep breath. "He was murdered."

"Murdered?" Mistress Eleni paused in her review of a ledger. "Does it have anything to do with the death of your sister?"

"I am without doubt," Luciana replied and chose a chair opposite the desk behind which the Guildmistress stood. "Have you found his records?"

"Oh!" Eleni exclaimed. She pulled her chair closer and sat as she flipped through several more pages. She tapped one and turned the book around for Luciana to see. "Because he was such a good customer—he often referred other clients to us as well as the substantial business that he did here—we allowed him to carry accounts for as much as a month or two. You can see here that no payment has been made since April."

Luciana looked at the figures. Her eyebrows rose at the sum. She had not thought there would be need to bring such a sizable amount with her. "Did his account always run so high?"

Mistress Eleni frowned as she looked at the page again. "This is a larger balance than we generally allow,

but because he was so good to us and there was the
special commission . . ."

"Commission?"

"For the princess' wedding," the Guildmistress said.

"He would order a new suit of clothes, of course,"
Luciana said, drumming her fingers on the desktop. "Did
he perhaps also make an order for his wife?"

"For his . . . The last we spoke, the conte was not
married, *Araunya*, and we received no word. The commission I refer to is a ball gown commissioned by the
conte for Her Highness."

"The princess?" Luciana said, suddenly intrigued. "I'd
like to see this gown."

The Guildmistress nodded and left the room only to
reappear moments later followed by three apprentices.
Between them, the girls carried a cream-colored gown
of Gypsy Silk. Luciana marveled at its quality. Of course,
there was the glamour attached to the fabric which could
only have been enhanced by the seamstresses of this
Gypsy Silk Guildhouse. Only the rarest and finest Gypsy
Silk shone with such luster *before* it was worn.

Drawn by the beauty of the gown, Luciana barely noticed the Guildmistress watching her anxiously. The
creamy folds of the gown spilled out across the arms of
the young girls. Until she stood this close, Luciana had
not seen that the dress was actually made in two layers.
On the base fabric, pearls and dainty glass beads nestled
among the curves and swirls of elaborate embroidery,
giving the otherwise light fabric substance. Delicate
needlework covered every hem, cuff, and tuck. Over the
basic gown lay another, a sheath of the sheerest silk.
The overgown was so thin, so fine, that it seemed almost
invisible, yet, impossibly, it also glistened in the warm
bath of sun filtering through the windows.

"*Araunya?*"

Luciana turned and realized she had been holding her
breath. "The gown is . . . stunning. You must be very
proud." She exhaled slowly and stepped back. This had
been no mere wedding gift. It was meant to seal an alliance—with a contract written in Alessandra's blood. It
seemed a crime all of its own that Bianca would not

honor the contract with Urbano and still get the gown. A gown of Gypsy Silk . . . a gown made by one of Alessandra's own Guilds.

"You are displeased? There is scant time, but tell me what must be done, *Araunya,* and I'll see that it—" The Guildmistress fell silent at Luciana's raised hand.

Backing away, Luciana said, "No, Mistress Eleni, the gown is stunning."

Still frowning, Eleni waved the apprentices away and shut the door again. "I sense that there is more happening here than has been divulged, *Araunya.*"

Luciana smiled distractedly and returned to her chair. "You have missed nothing. The dress appears perfect in every detail. The very essence of magic is there, yet subtle and tasteful. You are quite gifted."

"I may be *pushrat,* but my *gadjé* father was content to let my mother raise me as she saw fit," Mistress Eleni said. "While I'm not gifted with the ability to *dukker,* I am still blessed with a certain insight—I find it quite useful in my work."

Luciana looked up into an equally assessing gaze. "Won't you, Mistress?" She indicated the chair beside her and waited for the Guildmistress to sit down before she began. "I hold the gown's recipient responsible for the *Araunya minore's* death. I couldn't help but see the irony."

The Guildmistress paled. "Are you sure? I—" She paused, staring at her needle-pricked fingertips. "Of course you are, otherwise you would not mention such a suspicion. I know that I am naïve in the ways of the court, but why the *Araunya?* Why would the princess kill her?"

"I believe my sister was sacrificed in the princess' bid for power."

Mistress Eleni closed her eyes, as though fortifying herself. "Since the conte is no longer of this earth, can we not dismiss this obligation . . . of the commission, I mean?"

Luciana considered the Guildmistress' idea. Why give Bianca the "power" of this dress on such an important day for her? She thought of the dress. Bianca would know about the commission. Fittings were a must, so Bianca had tried the gown on, seen it near completion. If the dress were not delivered, she could easily malign the Guild and the Romani. For the Rom, and especially Alessandra as the so-recently-passed overseer of this Guild, it would be tantamount to a sacrilege if the gown was not worn. It could even be made to appear as if even the Rom dismissed their skills and the contributions they made to this adopted homeland, not taking it seriously enough to complete a commission, unable to keep a contract . . . a true lack of dedication and commitment.

Luciana shook her head. "We'll abide by our word or else we cannot expect them to honor their contracts either. Deliver the dress as promised. Let she who dispises us find her crowning moment in a dress made by the Rom, by the very Guild one of her victims once oversaw. We are denied blood vengeance, so we will take what we may."

"Can we not substitute—"

"Can there be any substitute for that gown? I think not, not even if you had a month of days to make another," Luciana said.

"But why permit the princess to have it? By the gown's very design, it is intended to enamor and awe. Wouldn't this give the princess *more* power?"

Luciana shook her head. "With her marriage, the princess compromises any claims she has upon Tyrrhia's throne. Let our dress be a part of that and then, by proxy, my sister will have a hand in her murderer's undoing."

Mistress Eleni bowed her head. "Then it shall be as you say, *Araunya-Daiya.*"

Luciana rose. "I will send my man back this evening with the appropriate funds. I did not anticipate such a sizable debt."

Mistress Eleni also rose and hurried to reach the door before Luciana. "If you are seeing to it, *Araunya-Daiya,* then I have no concern. Send the funds when it is convenient." She opened the door with a curtsy.

In the vestibule, Nicobar jumped readily to his feet, appearing relieved. Two of Eleni's older apprentices also stood, blushing. They curtsied and scurried off in a flurry of skirts with nary a glance back.

The Guildmistress frowned, watching the door to the workroom shut behind the girls. "My deepest apologies to you and your man, *Araunya-Daiya*. Sometimes my girls are overzealous in their duties." To Nicobar, she said, "I hope you are not offended."

Nicobar shook his head, clearing his throat. "They are, as you say, zealous in pursuit of their office, such is often the case with the young." Still, he looked quite flustered as he straightened his coat and tugged at his sleeves.

Luciana turned to Mistress Eleni, "We take our leave of you then and, before the day is done, my man here will return with the funds owed you."

The Guildmistress nodded her consent and stepped aside as Nicobar opened the door for their *Daiya*.

On the front stoop, Luciana took a deep, cleansing breath. Baldo waited at the foot of the stairs with the carriage door open and ready to receive her. She looked up and down the streets for any sign of Stefano.

"Has my husband returned?"

The driver shook his head.

Luciana took another deep breath. She needed to fortify herself, prepare herself to see the princess in a gown made by one of Alessandra's Guilds. It was far easier to talk of a subtle revenge than it was to actually accept it, when everything in her nature called for retribution of the most dramatic and absolute sort.

"*Daiya,* I must speak with you—" Nicobar began as he assisted her into the coach.

Luciana leaned back against the brocade cushions and waved him off. "I must think. Leave me be."

"But—"

"Ho there, driver!"

She turned toward the door of the carriage at the sound of her husband's voice. Nicobar appeared pained as he backed away and held the door for the duca. The door snapped shut behind Stefano and in a moment, the coach started forward.

"Did you find anything to your liking in the market?" Luciana asked her husband as he divested himself of his coat and sank onto the cushioned bench opposite her.

An odd expression of wariness flashed over Stefano's

features, but it was quickly replaced by a smile and a grimace. "No. Unfortunately, I found nothing to my liking."

Relief soothed her fears, if just for the moment. Perhaps she would have a chance at keeping her husband's heart after all.

"Daiya."

Luciana looked up from the flames dancing in the hearth. Stefano attended the king to discuss a private matter, leaving her to her own devices for the evening. "I thought you had already gone, Nicobar."

Her aide shook his head. "Forgive my delay, *Daiya,* but I felt that I must speak with you before I left on that errand."

Forcing a smile, Luciana sat upon the nearby chaise lounge. "Don't tell me that you've let those young girls frighten you."

Again, Nicobar shook his head, but this time in confusion.

"The apprentices."

Comprehension dawned in Nicobar's expression. He nodded absently, which caught Luciana's attention. Something was very wrong. Her man was not the sort to allow for unimportant distractions.

Luciana remembered his attempts to gain her attention earlier in the day and pointed to a nearby chair. "I am reminded that you wished to speak with me . . ."

"Thank you." Nicobar sank into the chair, his expression lightening with relief. "I did not know how to begin. I still do not."

"There is always the beginning."

Nicobar frowned. "But, I fear, the story would be too long in the telling, and you have been central to the plot all the way along."

Luciana leaned forward, her attention caught . . . more by what Nicobar did not say than by what he did. "Is this about the princess?"

Nicobar nodded. "You must understand, *Daiya,* that I have been bid not to speak of this subject with you—"

"And who would do such a thing?"

Her aide looked discomfited. "One who would rightfully have every expectation that the command would be obeyed."

Stefano.

Apparently, sensing her comprehension, Nicobar sighed and continued. "I do not break the literal command, but . . ." He shrugged.

Luciana understood. Stefano intended to hide something Nicobar deemed important, which was true to both men's nature. "The duca is away and I'll not tell him."

"I overheard a conversation between two *gadjé* women. The princess and her associates have not been satisfied with their maneuvers at court. They have a populist movement afoot."

"Populist?" Luciana repeated. Her mouth went dry and her heart quickened. So had begun every other diaspora, and judging by the Inquisition in Spain, there would be no mercy once a popular uprising began. With Bianca as its leader . . . She shuddered.

Luciana rose, chewing her lip. It seemed that the Romani faced more than the loss of one of their *Araunyas,* or even the silk trade. Tyrrhia, because of its tolerance and pragmatic liberalism, had become the Zion of the Romani—and every other race or class of people disenfranchised by the other governments of the continent. The persecutions would begin again. Would that satisfy Bianca and her people? Or would she, like so many other *gadjé* nations, reintroduce Tyrrhian Romani to slavery and the assassination of their culture?

The way was clear. Luciana took a deep breath. She could no longer listen to the counsel of her husband or the king. Bianca must be stopped . . . at whatever cost. Alban would not act against his predecessor's sole living child, and Stefano would side with the king. With this populist movement, the subtle vengeance of seeing the princess' hopes crushed and the woman left to live as a pariah among her class, in a hell of her own making, did not exist. Before, Luciana had been willing to sacrifice herself, now she had no choice, she would sacrifice *anything* for the sake of her people.

"Send for the carriage."

XXXVIII

"God may pardon you, but I never can."
                              —Elizabeth I of England

4 d'Giugno 1684

LUCIANA sat staring at the flickering light cast by the flames of the altar candles. Since Urbano's death, no one had reported visions of Alessandra's *mulló*. Could it possibly mean Alessa's spirit was at peace?

Hope as she might, Luciana knew better. The *mulló* would continue in its own hell until freed. Only fire could cleanse the body and release the spirit. The longer Alessa's soul carried the stain of *marimé*—of its connection to the decaying corpse—the more troubled her soul would become until, one day, she existed as an undead . . . a demon preying upon the living. Nicobar, despite his dedication, provided no definite results on his forays to the gardens and she could hazard no guess when he might meet with success. For all intents and purposes, she saw no further point in searching the grounds for her sister's body. Urbano was dead, and with him went the secret to Alessandra's physical whereabouts. The palazzo and property simply covered too much acreage.

Resignation, however, offered no suitable resolution; that meant magic provided her only options. But could even this justify Luciana calling upon her sister's spirit again? Justify her summoning Alessa in the very way

Urbano had? Necromancy was a foul, black art shunned by even the most debased Romani *chovahani.*

Turning it over and over in her mind would bring no satisfaction either. She knew her choices. There was now more at stake than just her sister. Luciana hoped that her grandmother would forgive her. She glanced over at the bureau table where the letter of explanation to the *Beluni* lay.

She did not hope for the unimaginable—that Stefano could understand or accept what she must do, indeed, what she had already done. Though no one beyond Nicobar, Kisaiya, and Mistress Eleni knew her crime as of yet, it was only a matter of time. She glanced at the ornate clock on the bureau. A matter of twelve or fewer hours before Bianca no longer posed a threat to her people.

Fates forgive me, Luciana thought as she stood. While the Sisters *Fata* might pardon her, could Alessandra?

She rolled back the heavy rug which covered most of her floor and then drew out her *nanta* bag of tools from beneath the altar. There, in the depths of the satchel, lay the bundle of supplies purchased some weeks ago from the crone at The Dragon's Hearth. The goods bought with the intent of breaking Urbano's spells would now be put to use in repeating them instead. Luciana shuddered, feeling dirty even thinking of what she must do.

Rather than delay further, Luciana broke the seal on the muslin wrapping and drew out chalk and salt. Saying prayers at every step, she cast her circle around the altar. With great care to observe the necromantic spells, Luciana worked in every prayer of protection and blessing she knew. She did not want to put Alessandra's soul at more risk than it already was. Her own soul she was prepared to forfeit, but Alessa must be protected at all cost.

She took a sachet from the *nanta* bag and sprinkled lavender to aid in seeing ghosts and bloodroot to prevent possession. Luciana tucked the sachet into the neckline of her simple black gown between the swell of her breasts. Aniseed, for further protection, she sprinkled inside the circle before she took out her tools. She scattered mecca balsam, cat's wort, cankerwort, absinthe, and Dittany of Crete into her smoldering brazier and began to invoke the final stages of the spell.

Whenever she'd used magic before—even the other times Alessandra had come to her—Luciana had felt a draining of her energy. Unprepared for the abrupt surge, Luciana felt a thrill of power well up from the pit of her stomach to her throat, into her words and into her mind akin to a heady, otherworldly wine. Her skin seemed almost to crackle and radiate like lightning ricocheting across the sky.

Luciana tried to stop, startled by the sensations, but the words seemed to come now of their own volition, pouring from her lips in an unhesitating flow. As the final words of the incantation issued from her mouth, power geysered and made her body tingle with an ecstatic pleasure so intense it almost hurt. Her body arched, responding instinctively to the rapture which left her breathless and dazed. She sank to her knees and braced herself, spent.

But there was more! Luciana thought, lifting her head. There was more to this spell! She could not permit the magic to overtake her sensibilities and diffuse!

Collecting her wits about her, Luciana breathed the words of a final spell and rang the silver bell waiting upon the altar. The air grew unexpectedly humid. Pressure in the room seemed to build like a storm waiting to unleash its fury upon the earth. Thunder rumbled and rolled inside her head. She felt like a raft at sea . . . and then the pressure disappeared only to return in an eruption of internal sound and a more subtle, exquisite sensual delight, one that left her fully conscious, full of the power in herself . . . and the magic.

Almost as an afterthought, Luciana recognized the glimmer puddling and taking shape before her. Alessandra! Luciana reached for her, dragging her essence into being.

Luciana felt her sister resist the summons, but it seemed of no more consequence than a moth battering itself against lantern glass. Silken tendrils connected the

sisters over the void of life and death, pulsating leech-
lines which sapped energy from the dead to feed the
living.

"Why do you do this to me?" the *mulló* wept.

Tears of the undead only fed the power washing over
Luciana, leaving her hungry for more.

An unnaturally cool wind blew through the window
opened earlier to expose her circle to the moon. Sea air
buffeted Luciana and enveloped her. The air carried a
thousand formless hands which pinched, pulled, pushed,
and pried at her. Luciana gasped breathlessly at the onslaught and turned within her circle in a frantic attempt
to brush off the attack. Crying out in anger, Luciana
battled. She spun, turning first this way and then that
until, at last, she fell.

Luciana landed in a heap outside of her circle, the
taste of salt in her mouth so strong she gagged. After
the salt, she felt the absence of her magic, of the spells
she had cast. The exultation no longer filled her and she
cursed angrily when she saw that she had also lost control of Alessandra's *mulló*. She rose, a curse forming on
her lips, as she looked over her tools to see if she had
all that she would need to repeat the spell.

"Daiya!"

Luciana turned, her lip curled with the start of a snarl.

Kisaiya stood just inside the bedroom door, her expression one of absolute horror . . . and fear.

Freed from the influence of the dark magic's ecstasy,
Kisaiya's fear seeped into her own consciousness. Luciana felt ill. She had been so close to casting at Kisaiya!
Her legs buckled beneath her, and she sank to the floor.
She put a hand to her head. In the name of all that she
held holy, what had she done! Her mind spun like a
child's top. But even as she became conscious of all that
she had been doing, the dark magic still sang to her,
tempting her to embrace it. Luciana shivered. She felt
violated in so many ways and now she stank of *marimé*,
yet the dark magic continued to be a temptation. The
workings of the dark were so much simpler, so much
more powerful than any magic she had ever before encountered. What if she could find a way to remove the

dark aspects from the magic? Couldn't she help others learn of this true nature of magic? Wouldn't it be a service to—

Repulsed and yet excited, Luciana stopped in midthought. The sea breeze continued to sweep into the room, pooling the salt she had laid out to protect her circle into little swirled mounds. With a sparkle, a new shape formed on the floor between Luciana and Kisaiya.

The shape took a translucent almost human form, glistening like a jewel laid in the sun though only the light of a single lantern and the moon touched her. The woman before Luciana and Kisaiya remained buoyant, resting upon air. Her body stretched into long, almost sharp features. As shining as her body was, it was nothing when compared to the stormy sea coast eyes which bore down on Luciana.

"Lasa!" Luciana whispered and bowed her head. The fairy folk came now to protect Alessandra—from her! But where had they been when Urbano worked *his* spells?

Kisaiya fell to her knees, her hands clenched in beseechment.

"We know you, Luciana di Patrini. Why do you commit this foul treason against your sister . . . she whom we placed in your care?"

"Lasa-Daiya . . ." Luciana began. She stopped, realizing that she could not remember what had drawn her to the point.

Kisaiya rose, her skirts rustling as she approached. *"Lasa-Daiya,* be not harsh with my mistress. Events have made her desperate. Her intent was to help her sister."

Luciana looked up at the girl thankfully. Yes, some of her mind seemed to be returning. Her intentions had been only for the greater good of Alessandra and all Romani. She clambered to her feet and reached toward Kisaiya to catch her balance, but the girl sidestepped and moved outside Luciana's reach.

"Forgive me, *Daiya.* I love you, but you are *marimé* and I will not be touched by it," Kisaiya said.

Luciana fell back, as though physically struck, but it

was true, she must be cleansed. The stink of the *marimé* ate at her soul. She could have been no more unclean if she suffered the ravages of demons. Through the fog left by the dark magic, Luciana tried to gather her wits, to remember why she had taken such a dangerous step.

"I wanted only to save my sister, *Lasa,*" Luciana said, licking her lips. The taste of salt still fouled her mouth.

"Save her? And how would you do that by invoking her as you have done?"

"Your pardon, *Daiya,*" Kisaiya said to Luciana. "We have lost all hope of finding and reclaiming the lady's body through all natural means. The *Araunya* must have been very desperate."

"So very desperate," the fair lady said shaking her head. "You were fortunate that we protected her, Luciana di Patrini, if you meant her no harm."

"No, I would never hurt my sister!" Luciana cried.

"You drank of her essence and she is diminished by the foul magicks you worked this night," the fairy said.

Luciana bent her head. How would she ever forgive herself? Make amends? But even as she thought this, the dark magic still sang in her veins. Her intentions had been good. Wasn't magic judged by the intent? If this was such foul work, then why had the fairy folk not rescued Alessandra when Urbano cast the original spells? Or perhaps the fairy did come in response to Luciana's magic. Did this not mean that the spells worked and, therefore, were worth whatever minor risk?

"That way lies danger, Lady." The fairy avatar reached out with a long-fingered hand and sketched a circle around Luciana.

An incandescent fairy-light bloomed above Luciana's head and fell like a rain of tiny embers; where they touched Luciana they attached themselves until her entire body was covered with the embers. The fairy lady waved her hand before Luciana and uttered a soundless word of the old language. The sparks dimmed, some even blinked out. They felt like tiny deaths and somehow Luciana was moved to grief by the loss of each one.

"There. You see what I see, what your woman sees,

what your sister saw, Luciana di Patrini, only your prayers of blessing and the protection of salt saved you."

Luciana trembled as she looked in the mirror. The dead and dying embers mottled her skin. She looked more the leprous demon than anything else. Kisaiya turned her face away.

"I will take whatever comes for my transgression," Luciana said, "but please, *Lasa-Daiya,* you must help me save my sister. Please! *She* did no wrong." Luciana refrained from reaching out to the fairy lady and she could not even stand to look at Kisaiya and see her rejection.

"When you would save a soul, you must approach as the vindicator, not the victor."

"I see my error, *Lasa-Daiya.*" Luciana rejected the seducing lure of the dark magic and focused on what lay at hand. "How may I make amends? How can I find my sister?"

"When the time is right, she will come to you," the *Lasa* said.

"But—" Before Luciana could finish, the *Lasa* shrank into a ball of light, not so very different from the embers she bathed Luciana in, and flew out the open window.

Luciana followed the witch-light to the window, standing upon the window seat where she could watch should the fairy take mercy on her and speak something more. In an instant the fairy was gone, her speck of light no more than one of the stars overhead. Luciana looked up at the moon and shuddered. How could she have gone so *very* wrong?

She stepped down off the window seat and looked at Kisaiya. The girl's head was bowed, and she avoided meeting Luciana's gaze. Luciana reached out to reassure her, but stopped even before Kisaiya could shrink from her touch. Luciana had been the fool, had played herself into the hands of *Beng,* the devil. With Urbano gone, there was no *chovahano* to despoil Alessa's soul and here she had almost done it herself!

Luciana shuddered at the feel of filth upon her. She was tainted, as was everything she touched. "I must bathe. Will you help me?"

Kisaiya looked up, still not meeting Luciana's eyes. "No mere water basin will serve."

"No, I must have living water and be purified by salt," Luciana said.

"To the sea, then?"

"Aye, to the sea."

———

Luciana slid off the bare back of the brown-and-white mare. She scanned the trail and the ridge beyond, looking to see if Baldo had followed them, in spite of her directions. Kisaiya took the mare's bridle, carefully avoiding Luciana's touch.

"I'll wait here with your clothes, Mistress," Kisaiya said.

"Mistress." The word stung, reminding Luciana of the great risk she had taken, the price she must pay. Not until she was cleansed of the *marimé* would she return to the status of *Daiya* among her people. Despite their long relationship, only her position as *Araunya* earned Kisaiya's goodwill. Among her people, when she chose to embrace—however briefly—the dark arts and assume the *marimé,* she herself rejected their trust.

Luciana took a deep breath and nodded, averting her own gaze from Kisaiya. She did not want to foul—even inadvertently—this girl who served her so well. She gathered her skirts so they would not brush the other woman and made her way toward the Stretto over the uneven rocks, trying not to twist her ankle by slipping or stumbling over the rounded stones.

The night air howled between the ridges, over the strait. Luciana could see across the strait here at this point where the channel was narrowest. A gray fog deepened the gloom of night and let through no hint of dawn.

Luciana undressed, taking no particular care not to be seen. She already bore the greatest of shames, nothing could make that worse. She allowed her clothing to fall where it may and made no attempt to rescue the fortune in Gypsy Silk from the hungry fingers of the Tyrrhian Sea.

The water of the Stretto roiled and smashed against the rocks at her feet. It looked as ominous as the sky above. Luciana longed to throw herself to the waves and let whatever sea creature was near end everything now, but that was a selfish hope and she berated herself for thinking it. While there was no hope for her, there was still some good she might do for her people.

Steeling herself, Luciana walked into the frigid black water, until she stood waist-deep. The numbing cold of the water felt like fists of stone battering her, bruising her flesh, and the saltiness of it stung. Luciana took a breath and sank beneath the surf. She grabbed pebbles from the bottom of the Stretto and used them to scrub at the taint of *marimé*. She felt sick at heart for what she had done this night and scoured her flesh with renewed vigor.

A hand touched Luciana's shoulder. She jumped, her scream choked off by a mouthful of seawater.

Luciana turned, not knowing who she would find behind her. Kisaiya would not have joined her and she had seen no one else. She stared, speechless, at the visage of her sister.

The *mulló* rose above the water. "I know of your sacrifice, Sister."

Luciana bowed her head. "Do not call me that. I'm unworthy."

"I do not know that I would have had the strength to dance with the black magic in the hopes of saving you," Alessa's spirit said.

"It was a fool's choice," Luciana said. She brushed wet hair out of her eyes and glanced up at her sister hovering above the water and then to Kisaiya who had come to the very edge of the shore. "Where have you been?"

"The *fata* came to me. Urbano's spells no longer kept them away. No one could summon me against my will, force me to hurt those I loved and respected in life."

"Then you have gone on?" Luciana asked, the hope which welled within her seemed almost a pain.

"I am given respite from my torment only. I cannot go on, not while my body remains uncleansed."

"Tell me where your body is. Tell me, and I will claim it and do what must be done!"

The *mulló* floated, silent, above the waves.

"No matter the temptation, I will not use the dark arts again. I will not betray your trust!" Luciana promised.

"You must *never* dance with it again, Sister. Only the grace of the *Fata* and their ambassadors saved you this time and even still, if you had not sewn prayers into your spell work, it could not have been done," Alessandra said. "Swear to me . . . no matter what comes, not even to save me! Swear that you will never call upon the black arts again!"

"I swear."

The *mulló* sank lower; her transparent hand reached out and touched Luciana's head. Despite the numbness caused by the cold, Luciana felt her sister's hand and almost wept. Alessandra's hand tipped Luciana's head back and turned it toward the west, away from the first pink-and-gray glimmers of dawn. The spirit pointed up, toward the rough-faced cliffs overlooking the strait. Above the cliffs were the garrisons of the Armato and beyond them the palazzo.

Luciana looked and saw nothing.

Nothing but the cliffs.

Nothing but the cliffs and the wavering light near the top.

"You will find me there."

Luciana blinked and turned back, but she was alone . . . except for Kisaiya beckoning her from the shore. She looked up, marking the spot in the cliff's face where the light shone. She knew, though she could not see, that there would be a cavern there in the cliffs. Did they connect, she wondered, with the catacombs Nicobar had found?

With renewed hope, Luciana waded from the water and gladly accepted the linen Kisaiya offered.

"We must get back to the palazzo—"

"Yes," Kisaiya said, shaking out the folds of a simple woolen dress. "The sun already rises. We have little time to get you back before the duca knows you're gone. We must get you ready for the wedding."

The wedding!

Luciana paused. She dared not curse, not with the black magic still singing to her from somewhere deep inside. She preferred to search for Alessa, but there was no one now who would molest Alessandra's body, so she would be safe for the nonce. For the sake of their people, she must attend the wedding to be sure all went as it should. Luciana gnashed her teeth in frustration.

XXXIX

*". . . And if any mischief follow, then thou shalt
give life for life, eye for eye, tooth for tooth, hand
for hand, foot for foot, burning for burning, wound
for wound, stripe for stripe."*
—Hebrew Bible, Exodus 21:23

NICOBAR greeted them at the patio gate, his demeanor unusually stiff. "Your Grace, the duca has
sent for you."

"Your Grace." Luciana glanced down at herself. The
fairy's spell had faded and there were no other outward
signs of the magic she had done. How did he know?

As though sensing her question, Nicobar said, "I hope
that Her Grace will not be offended by the liberties I
have taken regarding the matter in her private
chambers."

Luciana felt immediate relief that Stefano had not
seen the remnants of her work, but noted, with no small
measure of grief, Nicobar's change in attitude toward
her. She waited for him to close the gate and turn back
to her.

"Where is my husband?" Luciana asked.

"I am here." Stefano came through the large plated-
glass doors. He looked every inch the rich and powerful
noble wearing a coat of Gypsy Silk black brocade over
a dark green satin waistcoat and black breeches. A
sturdy *punto in aria* lace adorned his cuffs and cravat.
His sword hung from the gold satin baldric he wore
across his chest bearing his awards, honors, and rank
within the Escalade. He eschewed the popular periwig
as well as ribbons and lovelocks and wore his hair simply

groomed. Poised as he was by the door, Stefano's brows rose. "It had been my impression, Your Grace, that you planned to attend the wedding festivities in a manner more fitting your station." His voice was devoid of warmth or humor. She could read little in his expression.

Luciana clutched at her loose shawl reflexively, all too aware of her own humble appearance. "I had not thought you to be ready so soon."

"That much is evident," Stefano said. He moved so that the doorway shadowed his face, but she could still read the hurt and anger in his expression. "Would it be too presumptive to ask where you have been, Luciana?"

She sought desperately for something to say. How to explain? In a single night's work she had placed the souls of her sister and herself in jeopardy, lost the respect of her maid and assistant and, now, given her husband apparent reason to suspect infidelity.

"The truth cannot be worse than your silence," Stefano said, his voice breaking.

But it was, Luciana thought.

"I think we have always been honest with one another, even to our own disservice. Tell me you have not betrayed my trust and I will believe you."

She swallowed hard as the previous night's events played out in her mind once more.

"I thought not," Stefano said. He turned away.

"Stefano—" Luciana called. He stopped but did not look at her. She licked her lips, trying to think what to say or how to say what was needed. On top of everything else, she did not want to lose her husband—if she had not lost him already. "I will not lie to you. You have no reason to doubt my fidelity or loyalty."

He turned back and looked her fully in the eye. For a brief moment, Stefano's impassive mask slipped, but then returned. "How, then, *have* you betrayed my trust?"

Luciana looked away. She promised honesty. "In too many ways to tell." She paused and they both remained silent as Kisaiya and Nicobar departed.

This vendetta for Alessandra came at a high price. Throughout this misadventure sacrifices were made, but did she now, knowingly, intentionally sacrifice her marriage? There might yet be some way to save it. But try as she might, she did not see how she could share her burdens with Stefano. No matter how he sympathized, the vendetta was not his, and Stefano was a monarchist after all. He owed fealty to Alban and Idala before anyone else. He would act in their best interest. Somehow, she doubted he would be pleased with her solution, even knowing that Tyrrhia—and thereby her people—would be safer by far once this day passed.

"I presume that you planned to attend the wedding in more appropriate attire?" Stefano finally said, breaking the painful silence between them.

Having no other response, Luciana nodded and slipped past him to her room. Frustration seemed determined to be her constant companion this day, she thought.

"Diaya."

At the landing outside her bedroom, Luciana jumped, startled, and peered up the poorly lit stairs which led to the servants' quarters. Nicobar's bulky frame blanked out the feeble light.

"I have spoken with Kisaiya," he said, coming down the stairs. "She tells me you have cleansed yourself of the *marimé*."

"That which can be," Luciana acknowledged.

Nicobar stood silent a long moment. "You were wrong to cast that magic, *Araunya*."

"I know."

"Kisaiya said the *lasa* came."

Luciana grimaced. "They did."

"If only you could have waited—"

"Waited? For the *lasa*? She said they would help, that they would have shown me the way to—my sister's body, but when? Before the year is out and my sister is a demon? They have no sense of time!"

Nicobar looked down at the toe of his boot, letting silence fall between them. At last he met her gaze again. "I hoped you would trust *me* to find her in the catacombs."

Luciana sighed and shook her head angrily. "You've said yourself a honeycomb would be easier to navigate." She reached out to him. "You did not fail me, Nicobar."

He shrugged. "Kisaiya said that you could see the cavern from the Stretto, I think I know where—"

"Luciana, we must hurry."

She peered down the stairs at her husband who stood watching her. She could see none of his face, but his tone said everything. She glanced back at Nicobar. "We will discuss this later."

"As you wish, *Daiya*."

Nearly an hour later, Luciana descended the stairs to the sala. Stefano stood before the fireplace, turning as she entered. He pushed away from the mantel and approached, obviously surveying her appearance.

Luciana's dress matched his in reverse. The main body of the Gypsy Silk gown was a deep forest green. Its wide skirts were drawn back in the front to expose a black brocade undergown. Lace decorated the off-the-shoulder neckline and cuffs of her puffed sleeves. From the gold satin sash encircling her waist dangled a jeweled gold locket and matching perfume case.

She tried to manage a smile. "I did not expect to find you still here."

"I have no intentions of feeding meat to the gossip mongers," he said, his tone cool. "You are stunning, but you already knew that."

Steeling herself with a deep breath, Luciana captured her husband's sleeve. "Stefano, please . . . don't let's be like this."

Stefano's dark brow rose again. "And how would you have me—" He bit off whatever he had been about to say. His expression cooled again. Silently, he offered her his arm.

Unable to think of anything which might ease the situation, Luciana mutely accepted his arm and permitted him to lead her to the patio and, finally, the walk beyond. They joined other wedding guests as they made their leisurely way toward the front courtyard and the cathedral.

Surrounded as they were by courtiers laughing and calling to one another, Luciana could think of nothing she might say to ease the tension between them. If only this could be easier! She longed for action, to hunt for the cavern where her sister lay and, in that way, do something of use. She shook her head impatiently. Without looking up at him, she said, "Stefano, someone might notice—"

"That we are somber?" he concluded with a shrug. "We are in mourning for your sister, are we not? I intend to give no further consideration to what others might think or say. I advise you do the same."

Luciana searched for some distraction—

A dark-skinned young woman dressed in almost glowing white Gypsy Silk disappeared through the shrubs just ahead. Goose bumps marched up and down Luciana's spine. Had she not known better, she would have sworn the woman was Alessandra. Luciana hurried her step, ignoring Stefano's frown as they reached the turn.

The courtyard lay before them. Foreign aristocrats and ambassadors mixed freely among Tyrrhian nobility. Nowhere among the gaiety could Luciana see the woman who so reminded her of Alessandra.

"Discretion, Your Grace," Stefano said softly.

Luciana continued to search the crowd until Stefano covered her hand on his arm. "I—I thought I saw Alessandra," she said.

"Of course." Her husband's implacable expression seemed frozen in place.

She rubbed her temple, feeling the effects of a sleepless night and the tensions of the past few hours. "I did . . . perhaps it was her *mulló*. I told you what Conte Urbano—"

Stefano sidestepped the path and pulled her into a bower at the edge of the courtyard. "Luciana, I've tried to be patient, to wait for you to trust me, to help you in any way that I can." He glanced over his shoulder to make sure no one stood too close. "I— What the devil?"

Luciana turned, following his gaze. She saw nothing more than the collected nobles.

"I saw her!" Stefano's voice betrayed his disbelief.

"My sister?"

"She was there a moment ago, just there beside the—"

A blare of trumpets cut off his words, and Lord Estensi's voice could be heard by one and all as he announced Tyrrhia's regents.

"It begins," Stefano said. He tucked her hand against him as he looked down at her. "*Tell* me if you see Alessandra again."

Luciana nodded and turned, feigning a smile, but even as she did she felt an unexpected chill. Her fingers tingled. A definite air of *chova* hung over them, nothing of the sort carried by a spirit. Her smile faded as she surveyed the other nobles progressing through the queen's orchards. Someone—she could not tell who—ill-used magic. From the corner of her eye, she saw a movement and twisted. Troubled, Luciana saw no one who stood out.

"What is it?" Stefano guided them into the cathedral.

"Nothing." She took a deep breath and tried to relax. Stefano continued to watch her with sideways looks. She patted his hand. "Nothing! I'm just being silly." Even as she said the words, she knew she did not believe it.

Something was amiss. She scanned the rows of aristocrats and dignitaries filling the pews as Stefano escorted her to their appointed place. No one stood out among the sea of faces. Had she, herself, not seen Urbano's cold, lifeless body, she would have sworn he hid among the attendees. She almost tasted the magic. A *chovahano* was at work.

Common folk lined the back of the cathedral's upper gallery waving streamers with Tyrrhia's colors of white and gold. Flower garlands hung from the arches and filled the main chapel with their heavy scent. No expense had been spared even though, as she remembered, Alban had refused to pay for the wedding.

Despite the early hour and open windows, the temperature in the chapel felt suffocating. Once settled, Luciana made quick use of her fan, which served the additional purpose of letting her continue to observe the crowd.

Her gaze fell upon the deMedici household. No one there lacked for jewels or finery. No *grand dam* who might be mistaken for the Duchessa deMedici appeared in that host, but Luciana had not expected her to be present for the marriage of her husband's heir, a bastard son. The duca, however, was also missing. He, no doubt, waited with his son for the ceremony to begin.

Idala sat alone on her throne along the right wall nearest Padre Gasparino. Luciana realized then that she had expected the cardinal to oversee this marriage he had brokered. Apparently, the cardinal had thought better of making such an appearance after tangling with Stefano. No doubt, he intended now to stay as far away as possible. Her attention returned to the queen. Never had Idala presented a greater contrast. She looked tired and anxious in spite of the enhancing magic of the Gypsy Silk she wore.

Intending to point out his sister's condition, Luciana turned to her husband, but again movement out of the corner of her eye made her twist in her seat. A lone figure stood in the shadows of an alcove. Luciana could not make out her features, but there was something distinctive and familiar about the woman in the iridescent white gown.

She touched Stefano's arm and nodded toward the alcove. Turning, they discovered the woman gone. "I saw her!" Luciana whispered.

Stefano nodded and laid a finger to his lips as the chapel grew suddenly quiet. Hushed excitement filled the air as Conte deMedici and his father left a curtained anteroom and joined Padre Gasparino at the altar. All nature of lace and jeweled frippery adorned Pierro deMedici's cream-colored brocade coat, pants, and lace cravat. The senior deMedici, unlike the rest of his household, wore somber pants and a coat of black, with white shirt and a simple neckcloth.

All eyes turned to the back of the chapel. The choir

began to sing in fluting falsettos. As one, the audience rose.

Preceded by a dozen girls strewing petals of white-and-yellow roses before them, the princess entered the cathedral on the White King's arm. But it was her dress that caught Luciana's immediate attention.

Where was the cream-colored gown? Was all for naught?

Stefano tapped Luciana's hand and leaned close to her ear. "What is it?"

Luciana darted a glance at her husband. Had she been discovered? Did she dare tell Stefano now? No. Not yet. "The gown—it's very lovely."

Her husband frowned. He did not believe her, but the situation prevented him from pursuing the conversation further. Luciana concentrated upon the events playing out before them.

Bianca's gown was beautiful, almost as exquisite as the gown commissioned by Urbano. The fabric was the color of bright green apples, and the cut elegant in its simplicity, tightly boned in the latest fashion, and complemented with a lace mantilla that fell from her flowing red hair over the back of her gown to the floor.

The crowd whispered in surprise when, at the altar, Alban released Bianca and took his place on the throne beside his wife without joining the hands of bride and groom. After that initial breach of protocol, no tradition was left unobserved. The ceremony dragged through the morning which grew steadily less comfortable as the sun rose higher.

At last the wedding concluded. Alban rose and took his wife's hand. With icy nods to the newly married, the king and queen began the promenade from the chapel to the palazzo's banquet hall. Conte deMedici escorted his bride, quite obviously reveling in the moment in spite of the angry glint in her eyes.

The Duca deMedici followed his son and Pierro's new bride, pausing momentarily as he came abreast of Luciana and Stefano. Luciana noticed the stiffness between her husband and Duca deMedici as they greeted one another. As they, in turn, joined the celebrants filing from the cathedral, she asked, "What passed between you and the duca?"

Stefano's expression became guarded. He shrugged. "A matter of business with the bank. I promise to give you the particulars later."

She studied him long and hard as they worked their way through the milling press of people in the courtyard. He seemed as intent as she to avoid making revelations. She let it pass. She could not expect him to be forthcoming when she was not, though Luciana had every intention of changing that, of mending the wounds which tore at their marriage. But first, she reminded herself, she must survive the day.

Moving through the crowd, Luciana once again felt the tingle of magic up and down her spine. She turned sharply, studying the throng. She let out a sudden gasp and started forward, but then the light changed and Alessandra was gone. It almost seemed a trick of the light . . . or an illusion.

"What is it?" Stefano asked. "Alessandra?"

Luciana nodded. "Someone uses magic here today. If this is nothing more than a court game . . ." She shook her head, unwilling to risk even the smallest of curses with the stain of the cast dark magic still singing its siren song in her head. "Perhaps it is only the heat."

"I think not. I saw her, too," he said reasonably. He frowned. "You *are* pale. Let us find some refreshment." He skirted the crush of people adeptly and led her into the palazzo where the nobility gathered for the reception.

While Stefano went in search of edibles, Luciana selected a corner in the atrium which offered her a clear vantage point into the salon, banquet hall, and the rest of the atrium.

Like the chapel, these rooms did not suffer from the hand of anyone concerned about mere expense. Banners, alternately bearing the coat of arms of the princess, the deMedici family, and the Royal House of Tyrrhia, hung from the second-story balconies. Every table—

whether they lined the walls or occupied the center of a room—boasted extravagant statuettes of spun sugar. In the grand salon, a contingent of musicians played and, at the end of the atrium, a troupe of thespians made ready to stage a diversion.

Someone coughed gently to her right. Luciana looked up to discover Capitano di Montago, who promptly bowed with a flourish. "Your Grace," he said.

"Capitano, I had not thought you would attend," Luciana murmured. She made room for Stefano on the settee and gratefully accepted the goblet he offered. "Stefano, you remember—"

"No introductions are necessary. I remember the capitano quite well." Stefano bowed slightly before sitting down. "I hope you are well?"

The capitano nodded. "As well as can be expected."

"Won't you join us?" Luciana asked, motioning to the nearest chair.

The capitano shifted so that he no longer blocked Luciana's view of the rooms, but remained standing. He cut a fine figure in his blue dress uniform and polished boots. Golden braids signifying his rank festooned the coat, and his gold satin baldric looked almost crusted, covered as it was with ribbons and awards of merit.

"I had hoped this day would not come," di Montago said softly as he peered across the room. "The marriage is complete and her contract with the Church is fulfilled." Bitterness edged the capitano's voice.

He referred, of course, to the princess who presently stood in a far corner of the salon attended by the conte and her new father-in-law. Reminded that Nicobar had not been alone when he overheard the women in the marketplace, Luciana glanced at her husband. He seemed no happier about the state of affairs than the capitano. She knew Stefano had reported what he learned to the king, he would do nothing less. But what, she wondered, had Alban and Stefano planned to do and had the capitano been apprised?

Across the expanse of rooms, Bianca excused herself and made her way toward the residential section of the palazzo. Luciana watched her leave. Bianca, she hoped, planned to change into a different ball gown, a further extravagance. It would only be a matter of time now.

A chance to spare Bianca still existed, but there was no undoing what had been done, what *must* be done. Luciana whispered a prayer for forgiveness. It was easier to think of her soul's final judgment than Stefano's reaction.

"You're exceptionally quiet," Stefano said. "Is the wine not to your taste?"

She turned then, recognizing that she held the goblet with a grip that threatened the fragile glassware. He took it from her and rose. "Come. Let us sample the banquet while we wait for the bride to return . . . and then there will be dancing."

Wordlessly, Luciana allowed her husband to draw her to her feet. She had always loved dancing with him, for here, the fire in their relationship came out as passion when they danced. Luciana knew that if her grandmother could see Stefano dance—particularly with her—there would be no more questions about her choice to marry a *gadjé*. The expectation of dancing, of feeling his arms about her, made her breathless.

But she must retain control of her senses. This was not a day when she could allow herself to be swept away. If there were to be repercussions, then they must fall upon her, not Stefano, the regents, or her staff. Or, she reminded herself, the capitano who continued to follow them a pace away.

A rich assortment of foods covered the overladen banquet tables. The first course offered on a table in the atrium featured sculptures of marzipan, Neapolitan spice cakes, wine and plain pastries, grapes and olives, salted pork tongues cooked in wine and a flock of broiled and chilled songbirds.

At another table, the second course offered fried sweetbreads and liver, spit-roasted skylarks with lemon sauce, alternating with baked pigeons or quail, each with its own sauce. Farther along, cooked rabbits and partridges larded and roasted covered in slices of lemon and lime lay in an appetizing array. Pastries filled with minced veal sweetbreads fairly overloaded serving platters. Next came the veal, legs of goat, and a *zuppa* of almond cream and pigeons.

The table beside the kitchen entrance bore the weight of stuffed geese, boiled, and covered with almonds, cheese, and cinnamon sugar, as well as stuffed breast of veal garnished in flowers—yellow and white; the flesh of a new calf smothered in parsley and chopped spinach; stewed pigeons with mortadella and whole onions as well as a stufato of cabbage and sausage followed by poultry pies; boiled calves' feet with cheese and egg.

Beyond this, another table offered sweets in the form and variety of tarts, curds, cakes, wafers, sugared fruits, cheeses and wines, pastries and compotes. Servants swarmed about the room like bees, refreshing platters, refilling wineglasses, setting out new plates.

The overabundance was more than Luciana could stomach. While well-stocked tables were the norm, this sheer, ostentatious depravity unsettled her. She wondered how many of the nobles would keep the chirurgeons busy on the morrow. Or no, she thought watching the blind consumption, perhaps the chirurgeons would be busy sooner than that. But what truly troubled her was the unrelenting feel of magic—dark magic—echoing through those assembled. Like the invited revelers, it consumed, feeding off the greed and desires of those present.

Stefano frowned at her lack of interest in the food, but said nothing as he took a sampling. At last he turned to her and demanded softly, "Will you eat nothing?"

"I'm not hungry. The heat . . ." Luciana shrugged.

The capitano stepped forward. "If His Grace has other obligations, I will be happy to escort his lady-wife outside for a breath of air."

Stefano shook his head, paused, and looked up at the capitano thoughtfully. Again he shook his head and leaned closer to Luciana. "Unless something about the food disagrees with you?"

The question caught Luciana unawares. Would someone take such a risk—poisoning so many? She remembered again that her husband and the king had reason

to believe Bianca still posed a threat to Tyrrhia. She had
elected not to tell him of the precautions she took. She
could not reasonably consider Capitano di Montago. He
would direct his revenge at the princess and, perhaps,
the cardinal. But what if Bianca saw this as a way . . .
poisoning her noble wedding guests to eliminate the Palantini who would object to her claiming the throne?

As the pause became longer, Stefano peered down at
his wife. Hurriedly, he said, "I do not mean to suggest
anything—it is just that you knew when Exilli attempted
to poison us . . ." He fell silent, his lips pinched as he
glanced around the room. Taking her arm, Stefano escorted her to their settee. He knelt beside her, "Luciana,
I meant no offense . . . I just—"

Luciana cut him off with a wave of her hand. "I know
what you meant, but you should know I would not willingly endanger so many innocent lives."

The musicians in the next room began to tune their
instruments, causing, in turn, the revelers to raise their
voices to be heard.

"Ah, but the crux of the matter is there in *your*
words," Stefano said. "You would not *willingly*. And,
truth to tell, I see no innocents here."

Luciana and the capitano followed the wave of his
hand and looked at their party companions.

" 'Tis true none of them did anything to protect my
Al—the *Araunya minore*," the capitano said in a quiet,
choked voice.

Stefano looked as though he were going to take excep-
tion to the capitano's indictment—which included his sister, but Luciana intercepted him with a gentle finger to
his lips. "If you worry for what I have done or will do,
husband, you may set your mind at ease. This vendetta
lies between the princess and my people."

"And what of her husband now?" the capitano asked.

Luciana gazed up at the other man and shrugged. She
looked in the direction where she had last seen the conte
and, sure enough, he had surrounded himself with glittering women and all nature of dandies. "He is
incidental."

"Incidental?" the capitano repeated, his brow arching.

"Do not underestimate the man, *Araunya-Daiya,* no matter what else he is, he *is* a deMedici and a Catholic."

"But neither do we geld unnecessarily," Luciana retorted, making both men wince at her choice of images.

"You have promised an end to this vendetta. Surely, you have done your best. Release yourself from this vow, Luciana," Stefano urged, sitting beside her on the settee.

"*I* was chosen," Luciana said firmly.

Stefano sighed. "There was no uncle? No cousin who could take this vendetta? What of the capitano here?"

The old anger sparked. Luciana stared at him, not trusting herself to speak until she composed herself. "Will you never understand? Romani women need no protection. We are no fools to be coddled like pampered *gadjé mogliettina.*"

Stefano stepped back, visibly shaken by her vehemence. "Is that how you think I see you?"

Luciana looked away, all too aware of the capitano beside them and of his sudden stiffness and attention to their left. She turned, saw Alban, and rose to drop into a deep curtsy. Whatever Stefano might have said was forgotten as he, too, rose to bow before the king.

"You will forgive my interrupting?" Alban said, but it was no request and neither duca nor duchessa nor capitano pretended otherwise.

The capitano gave another bow, stepping back and away, but the king shook his head. "You may stay as well, Capitano di Montago, as this no doubt involves you." The king motioned them to a set of chairs in a sheltered alcove, scowling at the occupants until they understood his intent and scurried out of the way. He motioned for them to be seated while he dropped heavily into the middle chair.

"You look displeased, Majesty," Luciana said.

"I want nothing more than for this day to be over," the king said with a heavy sigh. "Idala has not recovered from the conte's magic, and we wish to put this behind us as quickly as possible." Alban eyed her speculatively. "You seem to fare better than when last I saw you, Your Grace."

Luciana dropped her pretense and met the king's gaze evenly. "I've grown accustomed to injustice since my sister's death."

The capitano's brows rose spectacularly high as he pointedly turned his head away.

Stefano glared at her, but the king raised a hand. "Your Grace, I explained to you . . ." He shook his head and looked back at her, his gaze as appealing as his words. "Your sister—and your adorata, Capitano— was dear to us, but I fear justice, as you see fit, will be left undone."

Luciana glanced over at Stefano. Surely he *had* told Alban about what he had overheard in the marketplace? In any case, it made no difference. "There is a saying, Majesty. 'Justice comes to the just and unjust with equal weight and in its own course.' " Luciana shrugged eloquently and sipped her wine. "I had hoped that justice would come sooner." She turned away from the men, seeking composure.

Even as she turned, Luciana saw her again. Alessandra. Standing amongst the press of nobles, dressed in a gown which glowed like a candle flame, her hair done up in coils of braids, looking as lovely and lively as ever. Their eyes met. A moment, shared by two people, surrounded by many, and then Alessandra looked toward the capitano, she took a step toward them . . . and was gone.

The capitano looked as pale as she felt. Stefano stared at the two of them and leaned close to her ear. "You've seen her again, haven't you?"

"The king—" Luciana began, motioning vacantly.

"Is gone," Stefano said. "He is kind enough to credit your manners to your grief."

"Kind enough—" Luciana began, but stopped and turned away. The king was not just any man, not just any *gadjé*. She did a disservice to her people—as well as her husband—antagonizing him. "I will apologize."

Stefano took her hand. "He credits you with much, Luciana. You have done him remarkable service in this matter and he is indebted to you, but there are greater things . . ." He paused, obviously aware of his misstep.

"I find it interesting," Luciana observed, "that he does

not credit me enough to say these things to me directly nor to keep me informed of new developments."

Stefano looked at her sharply. "New developments? Who said—"

Luciana shook her head and managed a wry smile. "How can there be a wedding *without* family turmoil? The same is true for all families, no matter how humble or elevated."

Stefano nodded, but she could still see his reserve. Luciana mumbled a prayer of thanks for her quick thinking, the very handy excuse.

"Capitano? Will you be well?" Luciana asked. She leaned forward so that she might study his face better.

Di Montago straightened in his chair and lowered his voice, "You saw her, too, *Araunya?*"

"We both have," Stefano said.

"Both?" The capitano appeared pained. "Why did she—"

"She is in no state of grace, Capitano, she cannot be eager to show herself to you. I find it strange that she appears here at all since I was able, at least, to free her spirit."

"Then she is here of . . . her own will?" Stefano asked. Luciana nodded.

"I cannot say that I find it so very strange," di Montago said softly. He motioned across the room as the crowd let out a low murmur.

The princess, escorted by her new husband, made her reappearance. She now wore the cream gown. Its sheen warmed in the soft glow of sunlight filtering into the room to stunning effect.

Conte Pierro motioned to the orchestra and guided his bride onto the dance floor. The conte showed himself to be an agile dancer, well-acquainted with the newest steps.

Lady Ursinia joined them, sitting in the chair beside them while her eyes remained on the royal couple. "Her Highness is pleased that the conte is a good dancer. She grew frustrated with the unimaginative dances we have here," Lady Ursinia said. She winced. "I, of course, mean no criticism of Her Majesty's entertainments."

"Of course," Luciana said smoothly, but her eyes were on the princess.

"Her dress is divine," Stefano said. "I have seen none better." His voice trailed off as his eyes followed the bride around the room, fascinated.

"Isn't it just?" Lady Ursinia agreed breathlessly. "I was there this morning when it was delivered. Conte Urbano ordered it for her as a wedding gift some time ago."

Stefano froze, almost imperceptibly, and looked thoughtfully at his wife. "Did he?" His tone changed, aloof and ironic. "He always had excellent taste in clothes."

Lady Ursinia wrinkled her nose. "I never thought so, but—dear me! Forgive me! I shouldn't speak ill of the dead."

"Have no fear, my lady," Luciana said. "It is forgotten." She pointedly did not meet Stefano's gaze.

The younger woman plucked at her lace fan, ducking her head to hide her embarrassed blush. After a moment, she took courage and tried again.

"How *is* your cousin? I have not heard how she fares now that . . ." She allowed her voice to trail off uncomfortably.

"You mean, Prunella?" Luciana asked. "She retired to her estate in Reggio di Calabria, as you know. I had a letter from her the other day. She reports that she is as well as a new widow might be expected to be."

"I thought of sending her a letter . . . offering to visit her when the initial period of mourning is over," Lady Ursinia said. "But I would not want to impose—"

"I'm sure that she would like that," Luciana said, turning briefly to smile upon the young woman.

The music swelled to a crescendo and ended, drawing Luciana's attention back to the dancers. Bianca and Conte Pierro, moving as though married to the music, concluded their dance with a curtsy and a bow with the last note.

With the princess' dress still swirling, Conte Pierro left his wife's side and instructed the musicians. The next dance, more lively than the first, brought other dancers onto the floor, falteringly attempting to mimic the royal couple's steps.

Luciana's complete attention never wavered from the princess, but she looked to her husband and her sister's *fidanzato*. They, too, watched the princess. The muscles in di Montago's jaw shifted as he clenched his teeth. For him, as well as herself, seeing the princess happy and enjoying her success felt like a dagger to the heart. Alessandra was denied this moment . . . and it had been meant to be spent with di Montago. She could not blame the capitano's bitterness or her husband's unease, but then, they did not know about the Guildmistress' extra lining, of the toxins being absorbed through the princess' skin.

The princess covered her first misstep with blithe confidence. Her face flushed with the exercise, and her eyes looked bright. The conte whirled her around the dance floor, in a challenging series of steps. He frowned and whirled away so that they were hidden behind other dancers for a moment. As they came to the front of the dance floor, Bianca faltered, tripped, and fell.

Someone on the dance floor let out a cry, and all dancing stopped. The musicians faltered to a cacophonous halt.

The king rose from his throne and pushed his way onto the dance floor, disappearing amid the curious onlookers.

Luciana felt more than saw Stefano's eyes upon her. The capitano seemed intent, however, to see for himself what was amiss. She rose and followed in his wake, barely aware of Stefano and Lady Ursinia behind her.

They found Bianca in a near faint. One of the courtiers fanned her as Conte Pierro leaned his new wife against his chest.

"Send for the physician!"

Luciana paused as she saw Alessandra move out of the press of people. Beyond her iridescence, she seemed like anyone else in the room. Luciana heard the hiss of the capitano's sudden intake of breath. It seemed no one else could see or reacted to Alessandra's presence—or so she thought until Stefano gripped her hand.

Bianca, however, stared up at the ghost, gasping for breath, as she scrabbled for her crucifix. With her token of faith held high, the princess swung out at the *mulló*, crying haggardly, "Be gone! Get away from me!" She fell back, shivering and twitching.

The crowd moved back, their voices raised in a rumble of confusion.

Alessandra leaned closer, beckoning. "It's easier than you think. It doesn't hurt."

Convulsions overcame the princess and, when finished, left her gasping and retching in her husband's arms.

The conte, finding his wife taken so violently ill, seemed to want nothing more than to be away from her. Furthermore, it seemed, a chivalrous gesture did not warrant the risk of plague or whatever consumed his wife. He could not, however, quite manage to pull away. No matter how weakened the princess' condition, her grip on his arm was viselike.

"Would that I had had my wedding before death took me," Alessandra said.

Bianca's head jerked spasmodically to the side. Alban knelt beside her, taking her hand in his. The queen stood just behind him. The padre, still not fully changed out of his wedding vestments, pushed into the crowd and hurriedly knelt at Bianca's side.

Alessandra reached inside the princess' chest. Bianca's body went rigid. In Alessandra's hand, a bit of froth, all filmy and transparent, came flailing from the Princess' body. As the translucent thing came clear, both Alessandra and Bianca's spirit disappeared.

Bianca's body went suddenly very relaxed and her groom finally escaped. Someone in the crowd swooned and somewhere someone cried. The king laid his cousin's hand upon her chest and looked back at Luciana and Stefano. They said nothing.

XL

"Death is a shadow that always follows the body."
                                    —English proverb

5 d'Giugno 1684

LUCIANA stepped onto the landing outside of her bedchamber and listened carefully. Nothing. She needed to be about her work soon, dawn would break in little more than an hour. She climbed the steps to the upper rooms and scratched on the left door: Nicobar's. She heard the distinct sounds of rustling bedclothes, the shamble of feet, the lock clicked, and then the door opened to reveal a sleepy-eyed Nicobar. His demeanor changed quickly as he shrugged out of the nightshirt he wore over his clothes and grabbed the lantern from the table by the door.

"You shouldn't have come to my room, *Daiya,*" Nicobar said, following her down the stone steps. "I planned to be—"

Luciana laid a finger to her lips as they reached the second landing. Her chambers lay on the right and Stefano's on the left. Her aide nodded and remained silent. When they were halfway down the stairs to the sala on the ground floor, she turned.

"This couldn't wait any longer. I needed only to give His Grace time enough to go to sleep," she explained and paused, staring down at her husband who leaned against the wall below.

"It gives me great comfort to know what care you take of my needs."

Luciana's heart sank, but, determined to show no shame, she tilted her chin and made her way down the stairs, confident Nicobar followed. She skirted her husband on the last step with a nod and crossed to the glass-paned outer doors. Here, she paused and turned back to stare expectantly at him. It was the best facade she could muster, caught, as she was, unawares.

Stefano returned her stare, measure for measure. The quiet of the night yawned between them. At last, Stefano pushed away from the wall and came toward her, pausing very deliberately, to place his lantern on the table. Standing before her, he folded his arms and fully met her glare with his own.

"I thought you might be going out again tonight . . . or should I say this morning?"

"Oh, please!" Luciana said, throwing her hands up in exasperation. "Surely you can think up better repartee than that!" She swung the patio doors open. "Nicobar, the lamp, if you please!" She stopped and looked at her husband, who seemed shocked by her behavior. "I presume you're coming as well?"

Nicobar hurried ahead to open the gate. "*Daiya,* perhaps—"

Luciana leveled an angry gaze on her aide. "Don't start, Nicobar. You'll only give him the opportunity to try to talk me out of this, and it will waste valuable time!" She turned to go on and stopped.

The capitano rose from his casual repose beside a tree. He dusted his pants and managed a perfunctory bow.

"You, I almost expected," Luciana said. "Are there any more, gentlemen? Perhaps a company of vigilare wait around the corner?"

"I could—" the capitano began.

Luciana saw her husband catch his arm. She smiled grimly to herself. Good! Let them sort this out amongst themselves and all would be done before they thought about contradicting her!

To be fair, di Montago had every right to be part of this foray, but she was not feeling particularly fair or generous at the moment. She intended to make this journey tonight and finish it! Her sister must be put to rest—while Luciana still enjoyed the freedom to see it done. There was no telling what Alban would do about Bianca's murder, though it was clear he suspected her. How could he not under the circumstances? Thankfully, for Stefano's sake at least, the king had made a general inquiry and not focused his attentions on her immediately as he might have done.

She shook her hands, so that the bangles she kept hidden beneath her sleeves fell to her wrists. She wanted the feeling of her wealth and power about her now, as she prepared for what was ahead. She touched the *putsi* at her waist, feeling the dagger of Obeah and Elderwood through the bag's fabric. Even confined by silk and embroidered cotton, the dagger tingled with the promise of power. She had prepared with great care and packed her supplies away so they would be ready in a moment—no fumbling with tangled fabrics or insufficient quantities.

As she followed Nicobar over the familiar path around the palazzo and into the queen's gardens, Luciana unbound her hair from the braids Kisaiya had arranged for her. She rubbed her scalp and combed her hair into place with her fingers, reveling in the freedom and the sensations of unbound power within her. Luciana deliberately ignored the temptations of the darker forces singing in her head, encouraging her and inviting her to revel in *its* power. It would be so easy . . . especially now, tired as she was from two sleepless nights, not to mention the very active days.

Were it not for Alessandra's dire need, Luciana knew she could not have forestalled sleep. Her body protested with exhaustion. All the more reason to use the dark-*chova,* her tainted self whispered. She could do what needed doing and have more power, more energy rather than be drained to the point of death.

Luciana glanced back at her husband two paces behind, side by side with Alessandra's capitano. She was selfish to let Stefano come. It could be dangerous and he did not like her dealings in magic, but the thought

528 ElizaBeth Gilligan

of facing her own death without him beside her . . .
she shuddered.

Despite the odds or, more aptly, because of the odds,
Luciana intended to give neither the capitano nor her
husband the opportunity to suggest she not lead—or
even be a part of—this venture. She would not have
their deaths upon her conscience, too. No matter their
strengths, neither man knew the *chova* and, thus, the
steps necessary to free Alessandra.

Nicobar led them into the maze confidently. He took
each twist and turn with the ease of someone who knew
every inch of the labyrinth. Between the darkness and
the hedges which rose well over her head, Luciana lost
all sense of direction. Trepidation turned her stomach.
Having no sense of where she was, even by the stars,
felt more ominous now than Urbano's meddling with the
darker magicks. She hated being reliant on others and
without resources of her own—even if she only needed
to trust her loyal aide. Luciana did her best to appear
calm.

At a nexus of paths, Nicobar stopped. Luciana, focused upon controlling her emotions, nearly fell into
him. She smothered an exclamation as Nicobar let out
a low whistle.

The responding call from deeper within the maze
sounded like that of a night bird and, yet, not. Only
another Romani—or an expert in birdcalls—would know
the difference.

"Tell me you were expecting that," she whispered.

Nicobar's teeth flashed white in the darkness. "Aye,
Daiya, we have a confederate waiting. I told you about
the lad, Inago."

Luciana tried to remember, but her mind fogged with
exhaustion. No matter how she tried, putting order to
her thoughts defeated her. She failed utterly at recalling
the details of everything Nicobar had told her about his
adventures in the maze. Considering it now, additional
assistance made sense. They must desecrate a dark *chovahano's* altar and Alessandra's profane resting place.
Who knew what protections Urbano created for the site?

"Nicobar? You're armed, aren't you?" Luciana asked.

Her aide stopped, frowning. "I have my scorpinini and my *churi*," he said, patting the dagger at his waist.

"What do you expect to find, *Daiya?*" the capitano asked.

Luciana shook her head. "Nothing. I mean—Nicobar has the experience in the caverns, but I thought . . ."

"The caverns have been empty—" Nicobar said.

"As far as you know." Stefano stroked his chin in that thoughtful way he had when frustrated. Luciana recalled that he hated being unprepared as much as she loathed being lost.

Luciana laid a calming hand on his shoulder. "Nicobar has seen to my safety for some time now. I've no reason to doubt him."

Stefano looked away. Even in the half-light, Luciana could see his facial muscles tighten.

"Neither have I done the job by being careless, *Daiya,*" Nicobar said.

"And you are not careless now," the capitano said softly. "You have rightly chosen weapons you are confident with." He reached inside his coat and withdrew two more scorpininis, and, from the large cuff, he pulled a handful of the small bolts. "Perhaps you might feel more at ease now with support weapons . . . should yours prove overtaxed."

"But won't you need them?" Nicobar asked.

Di Montago gave Nicobar a twisted smile. "I assure you, no one will suffer from any lack."

Someone coughed nearby and all turned toward the depths of the maze. A soft voice called, "*Pral* Nicobar?"

All eyes turned to Luciana's aide.

"Aye, Inago," Nicobar called back.

A lad of about fifteen, all gangly arms and legs, came out from behind a hedge. "All this noise! 'Tis no way to go undetected. We'll be lucky if the Head Gardener doesn't come to see what's about!" He came forward, raising his lantern. His dark features and the tiny glint of an earring confirmed him to be Romani.

"*Daiya,* I present a loyal subject, Inago," Nicobar said,

patting the lad's shoulder. "He comes from a family of *giv-engroes* and is learning what he can of his trade here in the Royal Gardens."

The so-called Inago looked at Nicobar uncertainly. "This is the *Araunya?*" A hint of awe and excitement gleamed in his expression. He turned and managed a clumsy bow. "*Araunya,* I am honored to serve you!" The boy's words were filled with all the heartfelt sincerity peculiar to the very young and uncynical.

At any other time or place, Luciana would have been amused. "I am indebted to you," she said. "I understand from Nicobar that I've much to thank you for." She could feel the heat of the boy's blush more than see it.

The lad bowed again, looking expectant and uncertain. Nicobar stepped into the awkward space by taking her elbow and steering her between two hedges onto a path previously unseen.

"This is no graveyard, *Araunya,*" Nicobar said as he brought them to a fork of paths. For the capitano and duca, he added. "It's treacherous footing in the best of places, and we have not finished our search."

Inago, who strode just ahead of them, turned. "Do you think 'tis a good idea to bring her into the caverns?"

"I think it better that my wife wait—" Stefano began. His tone sent shivers down Luciana's spine. He meant to keep her out of the caverns. She drew herself up to her full height. "Don't speak of me as though I'm not here."

Inago focused upon Luciana, his distress obvious. "I meant no disrespect, *Araunya,* but the caverns—"

"She knows," Nicobar said. To Luciana, he made a small bow. "You will forgive my hesitation soon, I fear." Before anything more could be said, he reached beyond her into the bushes.

A wrought iron gate creaked loudly as it opened.

Luciana winced. "Inago, you mentioned the Head Gardener before. Is he likely to come?"

The youth shook his shaggy head. "No. He's well within his cups, mourning for Her Highness." He maneuvered around Luciana. "If you'll pardon me . . ."

He disappeared through the wall of shrubs and held out his hand.

Luciana surveyed the narrow gate. No one intended ladies of the court with their full skirts to pass through, but then, few people at all were meant to even know of this gate. She gave thanks for her preparation and her experience in the graveyard those many nights ago. When dressing earlier, she had chosen a simple woolen gown and rejected the frumpery which would have been far less practical. In spite of her precautions, though, branches and gate snagged the fabric of her dress and made a tangle of her progress.

Inago's rough hand caught hers. Murmuring *"Permisso!"* with what seemed every breath, he helped her through, tugging at bits of her dress where it caught. Stefano came through easily enough and the larger capitano after him. Nicobar brought up the rear.

She paid the men little attention as she looked over the hidden bower. With barely room for Luciana and Inago to stand without overfamiliarity, she found herself pressed against the tiny stone shed which occupied the greatest portion of the space.

As Nicobar wriggled in among the company, he gave out a grunt and said, "Inago! Open the *bengeskoe* secret door!"

With another "permisso," Inago squeezed in beside Luciana and felt along the mortared wall of the garden shed, prying at the crevices. An odd groan seemed to come from the wall and then, with the sighing sound of rushing wind, it eased open. There came, immediately, the smell of the sea and, with it, a dank mustiness.

Inago picked up his lantern and surveyed the rest of the party. "We need another lantern for the *Araunya.*"

"I'll make do," Luciana said, but already she concentrated upon the gaping mouth of blackness newly revealed.

Nicobar neatly slid between her and the stairs, raising his lantern aloft. "Have care, the ledge below is narrow and others have fallen victim to it." He tucked the additional scorpininis into his belt and drew out his own.

With a nod to Stefano and the capitano, Nicobar loaded both bolts before easing into the narrow stairwell.

Luciana started to follow but was checked by the grip of a firm hand on her shoulder. "I'll go next," Stefano said.

She considered disputing his direction, but decided against it and stepped aside.

Stefano seemed almost surprised that she did not argue, but neither was he willing to forgo the victory. Capitano di Montago moved forward, stopping when Luciana placed her hand firmly on his chest.

"I go next," she said.

Di Montago acquiesced with a courteous bow. "Bring up the rear," he told Inago who shrugged and nodded.

As warned, Luciana found the stairs narrow, like the hidden corridors in the palazzo, except these spiraled downward. The walls and ceiling of rough basalt seemed to close in on their small party. Ahead, Nicobar seemed consigned to navigate the passageway turned sideways.

Moisture filled the air with smells of salt, sea, and the dankness of mold, which accounted for the slippery steps. Stefano reached back and took her hand to steady her at a dangerous dip. Moments later, she caused everyone to stop when she jerked her free hand away from the wall. The rough wall had seemed slick and wet. Luciana felt their eyes upon her as she wiped her hand on her skirts. Stefano and the capitano raised their lanterns helpfully, revealing damp moss growing on the uneven wall.

"It was nothing," she said. To redirect their attention, she motioned forward. "Proceed."

She heard Inago warn the capitano of what lay ahead and took note, not that there was much to be seen, even with the benefit of four men carrying lanterns. Nicobar stopped again, holding out a cautioning hand. Almost reflexively, Stefano tightened his grip and pushed Luciana backward.

The ceiling had got even shorter as they progressed downward, making it impossible for her to peer over her husband's shoulder. Luciana wished Stefano were a little less protective. It bedeviled her already overwhelming impatience and sense of curiosity. "What is it?" she asked.

"We've reached the bottom." Nicobar swung the lantern out wide, all hoods raised.

Luciana craned her neck, trying for a better line of vision. Stefano eased a little to her left so that she might see, but did not release his hold on her. She moved closer for di Montago to see as well.

Nothing but darkness stretched before them. Nicobar knelt and held the lantern out for all to see where their path led them. A great black void.

Nicobar rose to his feet. "It's not a pretty sight what lies below. In other days . . ."

"An oubliette?" Luciana asked softly,

Nicobar squinted into the darkness and nodded. "Perhaps not intended, but just as effective. We could not be sure how many unfortunates lay at the bottom of that pitted well."

"Is there a way beyond?" Stefano asked.

"Not an easy one," Nicobar said and brought the lantern high. Even with all shutters open, the lantern shed a light too weak to touch the cavernous heart of darkness. Distant structures—both natural and man-made—barely hinted at their purpose.

"Keep your hand on my belt," Stefano whispered to her. He took her hand in his as he spoke and tucked it into his wide leather belt.

Luciana made no protest, silently thankful now for the added security he offered.

"Are you ready?" Nicobar asked.

Stefano turned and looked behind Luciana. "Capitano? Boy . . . Inago? Are you ready to continue?"

"Go on," di Montago said from the rear.

Luciana closed her eyes and took a deep breath as Stefano started forward. She wanted to do nothing more than bury her face in her husband's back. But, if all that stood between Luciana and finding Alessa's body was her fear of heights, she was determined to see her way through this.

The ledges over which Nicobar led them twisted north and south, higher and deeper. Sometimes the paths appeared comfortably wide, but usually not. Luciana and the men edged their way carefully along, taking advantage of the walls when fortune provided them. The immense sense of height never eased. Dislodged pebbles skittered off the path and into that great emptiness. The near endless wait before one heard them touch bottom— or perhaps another passing ledge—served to keep Luciana anxious.

Just when she thought she had her trepidation under control, Nicobar stopped again. She looked up. The path ahead appeared to be even more fearsome, the height above seemed just as immense as the depth below. Neither were there walls on either side. Someone had tied a rope around a chunk of basalt. She could not see where or what the other end of the rope connected to.

Luciana gripped the rope with her free hand. Stefano offered the steadier hold. The capitano, just behind her, touched her shoulder. She looked back. He placed his left hand on her shoulder again. Luciana glanced down and saw that he held the guide rope and lantern with his right hand. She felt a gentle squeeze on her shoulder and realized that the capitano offered further support. She nodded gratefully and turned forward again.

The entire party's pace slowed to a crawl as they inched their way along the precarious ledge, lest they make a misstep.

The vastness surrounding Luciana disoriented her. With every step she expected to tumble. And then, as though her fear invoked it, Luciana stepped and felt nothing beneath her. She cried out, grabbing the rope convulsively. Stefano's strong arm circled her waist and the capitano's grip on her shoulder tightened even as he released his own lantern. Stefano pulled her more securely onto the ledge, wrapping both his arms around her.

She allowed herself the luxury of wilting against him as she tried to catch her breath and gather her nerves. For the longest time, he, too, seemed content to hold her.

"You've lost your lantern, Capitano," Inago said. He

leaned out over the rope, holding out his own lantern
with the careless abandon of the young who had no fear
of mortality.

"I did, but let us not lose you as well," di Montago
said, clapping a large hand on the boy's arm and pulling
him back. "We still have three lanterns. We'll manage."

"It's only a little farther now," Nicobar said.

A draft blew beneath Luciana's woolen skirts as
though the immense drop taunted her. Stones kicked
loose by her feet ricocheted off lower ledges, reminding
her just how precarious her position was. Fear threatened to freeze her in place. She took a deep purposeful
breath, securing her hand in Stefano's belt once more.
"Where is this place?" Though she tried to make the
question seem casual, she heard the quaver in her voice.

"We're beneath the castle, *Araunya*," Inago said as
they started forward.

Which, of course, was the answer to her question, but
did not answer what she wanted to know. Stefano took
the hand he held and placed it against a wall. Luciana
breathed a sigh of relief as she felt the presence of earth
surrounding her once more.

"The palazzo is built over the flumes of an old volcano," Nicobar said. "We've explored the caves with
care, but there is only so much one can do in a night."

"Aye, and 'twas here we saw the men that first night,"
Inago said. He swung his lantern high.

Luciana caught reflections of light on cavern walls,
some not so very distant as they seemed.

"Isn't that where we came in?" di Montago asked,
catching Inago's hand to focus the lantern.

"We came from there," Nicobar said, raising his own
lantern higher. Stefano did the same.

Remarkably, they stood on the other side of the oubliette, not much more than a hundred yards across. Luciana could just make out the jutting ledge near the roof
of the cavern. Awed by the contradictions of distance
and openness, she studied what she could of the cavern.
Her sense of immense space did not err so very much.
Like a tangled ball of string pulled this way and that to

find the secrets of its knots, the path of ledges provided a maze of their own. She tried to trace their path to this spot but gave up in confusion.

"You could have been lost in a place like this," Luciana said, turning to her aide.

Nicobar nodded and shrugged. "The duty was an honorable one, *Daiya,* and my life has been yours for years now."

Stefano stirred between them. Luciana tightened her hold on his hand, hoping he would understand. To Nicobar, she said "It is not a gift I would easily part with, so do not treat it so lightly in future."

Nicobar nodded and moved back for the others to take a long look at the chamber they currently occupied. Four passageways—beyond the one they used to reach this point—veered in different directions.

"Which way now?" Stefano asked.

Nicobar frowned, scanning the cavern ahead. "We saw men come from here. It took us three days to get this far."

"We don't have another three days," Stefano said. "We must have resolution tonight."

Luciana appreciated the lack of light. It made hiding her surprise that much easier. It seemed her husband had reached the same conclusion as herself. She hoped it also meant that he planned to stand by her. Would he? Could he, if Alban charged her with murdering the princess?

"I hoped that Her Grace might give us some suggestion of where we might look from here," Nicobar said, drawing Luciana's attention back.

"Barring the extraordinary circumstances of the past few days, what had you planned to do next?" she asked.

"We would have begun searching the passages here," Nicobar said, motioning in their direction.

"Then let us begin," Luciana urged, starting forward.

Stefano caught Luciana's arm. "We need to have a plan. Your man, Nicobar, seems to think you might know where to look first."

"I saw the cavern from the sea," Luciana said.

"Then you know where it is?" di Montago said, excitement in his voice.

Luciana shook her head. "At this point I have very little sense of where I am. Nicobar, am I right that each of these four corridors would lead us in the direction of the Stretto?"

Nicobar nodded.

Sighing, Luciana considered the passages. The silent voice of the dark magic sang to her. How much easier this task would be if she cast a summoning spell. Let Alessandra lead them. Over the temptation, Luciana said, "There's nothing for it, Stefano. We'll have to proceed as Nicobar planned and hope that we meet with early success."

"But it could take weeks for us to find her," di Montago protested.

"Not to mention it's cold and dangerous down here," Inago said.

"Then we must split up," Luciana said. She took control now before Stefano or di Montago leaped into the leadership role. "We have three lanterns and five of us here—"

"True," Stefano interrupted. "That means we can leave someone—Inago, I think—to stay with you while the capitano, Nicobar, and I search three of the corridors." He took Inago's lantern and handed it to di Montago. "We'll have to leave you with darkness for now, but—"

"It makes sense," Luciana replied. She moved out of di Montago's way and found a rock to sit upon.

"You'll wait here?" Stefano asked, hesitating as the other two men headed for the passageways.

"Where would I go? And with what light?" Luciana asked.

Still her husband delayed. At last he gave a gruff nod. "You've experienced the dangers of the cavern. I can rely on your good sense."

Luciana let her husband's statement pass. Arguing with him would serve no purpose and would only delay them.

Inago looked anything but pleased by the turn of events. He hunkered down nearby and folded his arms across his knees to wait.

Darkness did not consume her immediately. Light reflected off the moist walls of the tunnels the men took, but the farther they went, the dimmer the light grew until, rather suddenly, blackness enveloped her like a predator. But darkness itself held no fear for her, it was an old friend. She welcomed it, giving herself up to it as she spread her senses to adjust for loss of sight. She still heard the three men, their booted feet alternately scuffed along hard-packed floors or crunched on smaller rocks. She heard di Montago's soft curses and the banging of Nicobar's lantern against one of the basalt walls.

Luciana continued to focus on the darkness and her other senses. The sea smelled stronger here. She even tasted salt on her lips, and felt soft gusts of wind blowing through the tunnels—stronger first from one tunnel, then the other.

But as she became accustomed to the smell of the sea, she noticed something more. The stinging scent of lantern oil had hidden it at first, but now, a gust of wind brought it to her. She sniffed. Neither sulfurous odors from the long dormant volcano, nor the sea and its effluvium explained it. Drawn, Luciana rose and, ever careful of where she placed her feet, followed it.

Vinegar has a peculiar odor. Cider and wine vinegars were more distinct than any others. Luciana smiled in satisfaction. The scent of red wine vinegar captured her attention. And to what purpose could vinegar be put in a place like this? she asked herself. These caverns certainly did not serve as a storage area for the palazzo.

"*Araunya?* Wait! Where are you going?" Inago called from behind her.

With the boy at her heels, Luciana closed her eyes and focused on the smell of vinegar. She felt her way along the walls. Whether the boy plucked at her dress to get her attention or the rough walls snagged it, she paid no heed. She felt her surroundings narrow as she entered the fourth tunnel.

Luciana paused. She was being a fool and putting

more than just herself at risk. "Inago?" she called as she
carefully backed out. No answer. She took a moment to
review her steps and then cautiously worked her way
back to the main chamber. "Inago?" Still no answer and
nothing but blackness. She cursed herself for the fool
she had been. Where had Inago gone? If he came to
harm because of her—

A flickering light heralded one of the men's return
from the passages. Nicobar exited, grinning with satisfaction. "I've found stairs to the palazzo above. There are
corridors, but I don't know where they lead. We'll discover easily enough and then—" Nicobar raised the lantern. "Where is Inago?"

"I don't know," Luciana admitted. "I went into—"

"Lucia!"

Stefano's voice rang through the vaulted caverns, followed by the sound of running feet. Di Montago responded to Stefano's call with a shout of his own and
then the sound of running increased. Their lanterns
warned of both men's imminent arrival just before they
rejoined them in the chamber. Luciana saw with relief
that Inago stood with her husband.

Stefano closed the distance between them in long
strides and seized her in his arms. He held her for a
moment. It seemed to her that he trembled, then it was
over and he put her away from him. "How could you
have done such an irresponsible thing? Don't you—" He
stopped abruptly, aware at last of their audience. He
straightened his waistcoat and back stepped. "Thank all
that's holy Inago had the sense to find me."

"And that he did not come to misfortune for having
done so," Luciana replied quietly. She turned to the
young man. "I beg your pardon, *pral*." She took a deep
breath and combed her fingers through her hair distractedly. "I believe, however, that I have found Urbano's
cache."

"The last passage?" Nicobar asked. He did not offer
any further comment about her venturing and, thereby,
saved Luciana from having to justify her impetuousness
further. "Let's see what we shall see, then."

Anticipation warred with trepidation, and her stomach

served as the battleground. She almost dared not hope
that this trial neared an end. Luciana took Nicobar's
lantern and returned to the tunnel. Her fingers found
their way to the sachet tucked into the neckline of her
dress. She buried her nose in it, breathing the lavender
and Cat's Wort as she offered a prayer for clear sight.

As expected, Luciana found the passage narrow and
low, forcing even her to stoop in places. The path wound
upon itself like a snake. The smell of vinegar seemed to
permeate the very walls, drawing Luciana ever onward.

"Are you sure you're going the right way?" Stefano
asked just behind her.

Luciana paused and sniffed. She looked back at Stefano, surprised. "Can't you smell it?"

"Smell what?"

She raised the lantern and searched the faces of the
other men. They, too, showed only confusion. Luciana
breathed deeply. The scent of vinegar seemed as strong
as ever. Perhaps the Sisters answered her prayers. Luciana did not care. With lantern aloft, she pressed on.
Shortly, she heard the sea echoing through the tunnel
ahead. The passage took an unexpected dip as it twisted
northeast, toward the sea. Luciana stumbled, caught herself on the wall, and continued. With a sharp turn, the
tunnel ended.

Luciana stopped. She stood on the threshold of a large
chamber open on the right wall to the sea. Steps, just
two, carved into the rock made for a more civilized entrance into the room. But it was what occupied the center of the room that held Luciana's attention.

An enormous altar lay before her. The stubs of two
fat black candles sat on either end. Between the candles
on the altar sat a small cauldron and an offering dish.
Her breath caught in her throat. The altar looked to be
made of solid, polished stone, its top covered with a
cloth. Could it be?

As if in a dream, Luciana covered the distance to the
center of the room. She bent to inspect the rectangle of
stone. Someone had painted symbols of binding and
power neatly around its base. Luciana swept aside the

paraphernalia atop the stone and jerked aside the embroidered silk cloth covering it.

The fringe of the material had covered a crease in the stone. Luciana knelt to look closer. Made of obsidian, the lid felt smooth and sleek. A wedge of green marble, carved with yet another symbol of containment, formed a carefully crafted seal.

Whispering words of power, Luciana pried at the lid, ignoring the pain as a fingernail tore from its bed.

Gently, Stefano took her by the shoulders and moved her aside. Nicobar eased into the space vacated by his mistress. He broke the seal in a single, expert blow with a hammer he had got from she knew not where. Di Montago pressed Nicobar aside and, using the hammer's handle, pried an opening. Stefano's hold on her kept her from leaping in to assist the capitano. Nicobar, however, showed no hesitation in lending a hand. They struggled with the weight of the stone slab lid for a moment before Stefano came to their aid.

Luciana knelt, offering prayers and words of unbinding as the men struggled to break the lid away from the base. With Inago's help, the lid finally tipped and fell.

Fluid lapped over the edges of the sarcophagus. Inago cried out and fell back, burying his face in his sleeve when splashed. Even Nicobar and Stefano stepped away.

Luciana rose to stand beside di Montago, her eyes drawn irresistibly to the contents of the stone box.

Beneath purplish waters, with hair drifting loose of its ornamental braids, lay a mildly bloated Alessandra. Unadorned by her burial gown, only the herbs floating on the surface, and keeping her in a near natural state, covered her.

Luciana ripped the altar cloth free of the top stone and plunged it into the vinegary preserving waters to wrap around her sister's corpse. When suitably covered, di Montago knelt and lifted Alessandra from the depths.

While the capitano held Alessandra's body, Luciana took out the Obeah and Elderwood dagger. Her eyes ached with unshed tears as she moved aside the altar cloth and cut the braided root, aptly named Devil's String, binding Alessandra's hands and feet. She spat upon the pieces and cast them aside.

The capitano rocked gently with Alessandra's body in his arms. His tears flowed freely. Luciana touched her sister's cheek, brushing a straggle of hair back.

"You're free, Alessandra. He no longer possesses you," she whispered.

"Not quite."

The sound of the voice sent chills through Luciana. She recognized it without looking.

"Cardinal delle Torre," Stefano said. His voice betrayed his revulsion. "You've managed to surprise me again."

"So it would seem, Your Grace," the cardinal replied. He stood in the mouth of the cavern where it opened to the Stretto. He stepped to the side so that five men could enter the chamber. "Though this time, I fear, you shall not be so fortunate in your escape."

Luciana looked up at the armed men and then at the cardinal. The dark *chova* sang louder now, but not to her. No, the evil energy coalesced around the priest. There had been two *chovahano* after all. Realizing the depths of the cardinal's depravity, her stomach gave a sickening lurch.

"I must thank you for tending to this problem of mine," the cardinal said, motioning to Alessandra's corpse. To his men, he said, "Take her."

Di Montago pushed Alessandra into her sister's arms and jumped to his feet, a snarl on his lips. "I'll die first!"

"So be it," delle Torre said with a shrug, motioning his men onward.

Luciana cradled Alessandra's body, pulling closer to the sarcophagus and, hopefully, out of the way. Stefano and the capitano stood with swords drawn, facing the cardinal's men. Di Montago lashed out in a preemptive strike. The two lead men withdrew, placing their backs to the wall. As the fight began, more men entered the cavern.

"Cover my wife!" Stefano yelled at Nicobar, who already moved in her direction.

Nicobar dropped to his haunches in front of Luciana, his dagger in one hand and a scorpinini at the ready in his other. He shot off a bolt, before ducking down and helping Luciana move Alessandra's body.

Stefano stood in front of them, his lithe body poised to protect her. Luciana knew better than to call his name when the attack came, three men to his one. None of this was meant to happen. If anyone were meant to be in peril, it was her! *She* had used the dark *chova,* she swore the vendetta!

One of the men lunged while his compatriots clashed swords with Stefano. Bright red stained her husband's sleeve. He spun and struck back. One of the others jumped to the fore. With a viciousness that surprised even her, Luciana drove her ceremonial dagger of Obeah and Elderwood deep and up. If by some grace he lived, she had the satisfaction of knowing he would not be giving morality lessons to a future generation.

"Keep her back!" Stefano shouted and knocked her victim to the ground.

Nicobar may have said something, Luciana could not be sure, but he seized her in an iron grip and wrested her back against the stone altar. With her positioned, Nicobar turned and shot off a second bolt into the melee. A man attacking Stefano crumpled to the ground. Nicobar dropped the used scorpinini and pulled another from his belt. He cocked the weapon and shot in a single motion, taking down yet another man entering the cavern from the Stretto.

Luciana could no longer guess how many of the cardinal's men filled the cavern. Nicobar kept her pressed against the crypt, shouting to the other men in their party. Using his third scorpinini, Nicobar took a man down with a shot to the back of the neck as the *braggadocio* loomed over Inago. The youth saluted and dropped to the ground. Luciana tried to see what happened to the boy, but Nicobar shoved her down unceremoniously while jerking spare ammunition out of his coat.

The scorpinini bolts scattered. Nicobar reached for the nearest, exposing himself to the enemy. Luciana saw only the grim satisfaction on a man's face as he prepared to thrust with his dagger. Without thinking, she lashed out, striking him across the face with her lantern. Oil and flame combusted, becoming a veritable fireball which consumed flesh and cloth alike. The man howled, reeling away. She heard strange men's curses. Someone shoved the man past the cardinal toward di Montago who now fought on the ledge as though hoping to forestall further recruits from the beach below. The capitano shifted and pushed the screaming mass of human flame away from him, down the ledge.

Vinegar splashed over Luciana and Alessandra at the resounding concussion.

"Gunpowder!" Nicobar said as he took aim.

"Behind you!"

Luciana and Nicobar turned as one, alerted by Inago's shout. Before either could react, a loud crack erupted from Inago's corner. The bravo, prepared to strike, fell. Inago looked as surprised as his target when he was left standing, the smoking wheel lock held in both hands. The boy seemed to take heart suddenly and turned his weapon toward the cavern mouth. He waited. Luciana followed his sight line and gasped. Trust the youth to strike at the heart of the predicament! The cardinal turned and the dark *chova* began to sing again.

Luciana rose, shouting to Inago, but she could not move swiftly enough. Inago's scavenged pistola fired. The cardinal waved. The cacophony of the resulting blast brought a temporary stillness—even from Inago who fell, widemouthed in a silent scream.

"You killed the boy!" Luciana screamed. The dark *chova* roiled, a tempting song in her ear.

"He is vermin and I am the Hand of God!" the cardinal declared.

Taking advantage of the distraction, di Montago plunged his blade through the heart of one of his opponents. Almost in unison, the battle rejoined. Luciana stood locked in voiceless combat with the cardinal. She felt the magic welling within him. She felt it pulsing through her, a constant temptation. She tasted the pleasure the cardinal took in his power, smelled his exultation as though it were a physical thing.

Someone grabbed her from behind and pulled her back. Luciana fell into Stefano, his free arm encircling her waist. "Get out of here, Lucia, before he kills you!"

"But I can't leave—"

Stefano shook his head, carrying her with him as he fended off an attacker. In a moment of suicidal passion, Stefano kissed her, then shoved her at Nicobar. "Get her and her sister out of here!"

Falling against the open crypt, Luciana narrowly escaped the lunge of a *braggadocio's* saber. She swept the vinegary solution used to preserve Alessandra up into the man's face. He reeled away, rubbing at his eyes with his sleeves. Nicobar dispatched him with his dagger, then covered Luciana's body with his own. But caught by the chords of the *chova's* dark refrain, Luciana wrestled free to look for the cardinal. She felt him nearby. He came for Alessandra.

Luciana looked around her desperately. There seemed little hope for any of them now. There were just too many, but if Alessandra, at least, could be freed, then perhaps the cost would weigh a little less heavily in the cardinal's favor. She dropped to her knees and seized Alessandra's wrists, pulling her to the end of the crypt.

Cradling her sister's corpse in her arms, Luciana began the words of power which would free her sister's soul from her earthly tether. She pushed aside all conscious awareness of the cardinal, knowing only that her time was limited.

An unnatural wind rose as Luciana spoke the words, driving in off the sea through the cave mouth and into the melee of men. The wind swept in hard and furious, blowing at their clothes and stirring the scattered flames still sizzling from the ignited bravo. Luciana covered her sister's body with her own as debris flew about the room and the wind howled.

Again, the fighting stilled as the wind raged and tore at all of them with unnatural fury.

Calm, sudden and eerie, settled about them quicker

than the wind had risen. The sachet of lavender and Cat's Wort at Luciana's neck tingled and somehow the scent of herbs covered the fumes of the vinegar . . . even the stench of blood, burned flesh, and gunpowder. But did the scent come from her sachet or from elsewhere?

A now silent wind whirled beside the coffin and, as it settled, the figure of a woman—covered in sepulcher silks and a supernatural haze of white—coalesced with hands reaching up as though in some silent prayer of thanksgiving. As her arms dropped, there could be no doubt of the spirit's identity.

"Oh, my beloved sister, I am free! Rejoice!" The spirit twirled, much as the woman had in life when triumphant. Her gaze fell to the sorry corpse in Luciana's arms and the look of joy faded. It was an unsettling thing to watch one's sister stare at her own corpse, but her attention did not last long. Alessandra's *mulló* spun once more, her attention focused on the capitano. "Mandero!" she cried.

Di Montago's sword hand dropped. He stepped forward, his expression disbelieving, his empty hand outstretched.

The spirit approached.

Cardinal delle Torre placed himself between the lovers. He held up an open golden locket. The dark *chova* sang around him, rising to unbearable levels in Luciana's mind. The power staggered her. She fell even as Alessandra screamed.

With every strain of magic Luciana knew, she fought to her feet. The dark *chova* rained down upon her, battering her away from the magician priest. The capitano lay prone; one of the cardinal's bravos stood with his foot on the back of di Montago's neck. Stefano held two men at bay, and Nicobar knelt beside her, also overcome by the dark magicks.

Alessandra's spirit rose. The wind swept in from the sea once more. The *mulló* clawed at the intangible, her voice overwhelmed by the symphonic swells of magical forces compelling her toward the cardinal's locket.

"No!" Luciana screamed She reached deep for the *chova* the *Beluni* raised her with. Baubles and bangles were the stuff of the Romani. Gold held no power over her. She allowed the magic to rise within her, then flung it at the cardinal's locket.

The locket burst like a thousand tiny stars. Bits of gold no more substantial than dust, scattered to the supernatural winds. Alessandra's *mulló* spun free.

"Get away, Alessa!" di Montago yelled, rolling and striking up at his captor.

"Take her!" the cardinal snarled to one of his men.

Stefano flung himself between the braggadocio and Luciana while Nicobar struggled to his feet.

The *mulló* seemed to hesitate. Luciana heard the swells of the dark magic's gathering crescendo. She saw, but could not hear, the cardinal as he began his next spell. Even while the cardinal danced to the dark *chova,* it continued its lover's croon, offering sustenance to Luciana's exhausted body. How easy to succumb and be done with this!

Luciana thought of the *vardo* wheel, the spinning *chakra,* the hub of all Romani life. She called upon it, drowning out the dark song. As her magic took shape, a scintillating swirl formed by the altar. She turned the spinning wheel toward Alessandra, let the wheel gather energy, gather the four winds to its center, pull her sister's spirit into the whirling coil and then, with all the determination she could muster, Luciana flung the wheel out . . . into the Stretto . . . into the next existence . . . as far from the reach of the cardinal as she could manage.

As she released the wheel, she felt the power of the dark *chova* erupt. Luciana looked up, saw the hatred and anger in the cardinal's face, felt death coming for her . . . and then Nicobar rose from beside her, placed himself between the cardinal and Luciana, taking the *chovahano's* spell upon himself. She caught him as he fell and brought him gently to the ground.

Nicobar gasped. Shuddered. "Forgive me, *Daiya*—"

There was nothing to forgive, but she could not tell Nicobar for he was already gone.

Whispering words of prayer to send Nicobar on his way, Luciana lay him on the floor beside her sister's body. Di Montago had his hands on the cardinal's throat, but three of the *chovahano's* men were already dragging him off. Stefano leaped to the capitano's rescue. Luciana felt the deadly swell of *chova,* saw the cardinal directing his attentions toward her husband and flung herself between them.

Music, vile, horrid, and strangely beautiful screamed in her head, ravaging her spirit and devouring her will. In some distant place, she felt Stefano's arms around her, heard him call her name. Luciana strained to open her eyes. The music of the dark *chova* possessed her, her body was not her own. She wrestled for control, felt Stefano's breath against her cheek. She reached up and touched his face one last time before the vendetta's serenade took her.

XLI

"Opré, Roma!"
"Rise up, Roma!"

— —Romani maxim

LUCIANA'S hand fell away from his face. She lay in his arms as lifeless as her sister only feet away. An icy rage, unlike anything he had ever experienced, washed over Stefano as he placed his wife's body on the floor of the cavern. Nothing mattered now. "You've killed her," he said.

"Consider yourself spared from her wicked ways," the cardinal responded casually. He pushed down the sword of the bravo standing next to him, then motioned to Alessandra's body.

"And if I had no wish to be 'spared'?" Stefano replied.

The cardinal made a dismissive noise. "You'll see the sense of it and then you can return to the faith, as your sister has."

"If it is the faith you profess, I'll take damnation," Stefano said. With cold deliberation, he drew the pistola from his belt.

The cardinal's eyes widened, but he held his ground. "I am the Hand of God. I'll bring you to the faith in whatever state it requires."

"Seek absolution for yourself," Stefano said and cocked the gun.

The bravo nearest Alessandra reached for her body. Stefano did not look directly at the man, refusing to take his gaze off the cardinal. "I wouldn't, were I you," he said.

The man froze.

"Go on," the cardinal bid his man, "he won't hurt you. The duca is a civilized man of—" The rest of his words were lost in his rush to avoid Stefano's shot.

The cardinal's howl of rage told Stefano all he wanted to know—he hit his mark, but not well enough. Another of the cardinal's bravos, apparently unhindered by the capitano, edged toward Stefano on the right. Stefano shot point-blank as the man rushed him, snarling in frustration as the man's dead weight took him to the floor. The scoundrel near Alessandra made good his opportunity and struck Stefano in the head with the butt of his wheel lock while Stefano struggled to free himself of his own victim.

A blackness darker and softer than that of the outer caverns rushed over him. He felt like he swam in sheep's wool, distant and removed from the activity and noise around him. How easy it would be to succumb! Stefano fought for awareness, focusing on Luciana who lay so near.

Anger sustained his consciousness. Stefano levered the man atop him off and thrust the body at the man who had struck him. He rolled away from a saber thrust, kicking his legs free of the braggadocio's corpse. The world spun at a sickening pace.

Stefano staggered to his feet and tried to shake off the dizziness, but that only made it worse. He fell, thereby avoiding the greatest part of whatever spell the cardinal threw at him. Even still, Stefano felt horse-kicked in the chest.

Struggling to retain some sense of control, Stefano grabbed Luciana's arms when another of the cardinal's men reached for her. Stefano risked releasing one of her hands long enough to seize the sword he'd dropped earlier. Determination gave him what his body could not. He swung his saber. Nothing so neat as a beheading, but the man released Luciana and grabbed at his throat, gushing blood.

Stefano brought Luciana closer and tried to glean what he could of the battle about him. The cardinal stood in the opening Luciana had led them through not so very long ago. He yelled to his men. They retreated!

A henchman grabbed Alessandra's body. Five more tangled with the capitano, three positioning for escape, two waiting in the wings for an opportunity to strike. Stefano swung his saber at the rogue carrying Alessandra but barely grazed him. Cursing himself for the weakness, Stefano lay Luciana down again and positioned himself over her body so that no one could steal her. Determined to help the besieged di Montago, Stefano pulled the second pistola he carried and cranked the wheel lock.

Jammed! Stefano swore like an infantryman and, rather than waste time with the mechanism, flung the pistola at the man closest. The gun ricocheted off a wall and hit the bravo carrying Alessandra. The men continued on.

"Di Montago! They've got Alessandra!" Stefano bellowed.

The capitano shoved one of the men out of the cavern and turned to Stefano, disregarding the man's scream as he fell to the Stretto below. The other two rogues, seeing the capitano's distraction, took their chance for escape.

"There, where they go!" Stefano yelled.

Di Montago started after the men, but paused. "Will you—"

"Go!" Stefano said and turned his attention on the two remaining men. He stood in their way, preventing either from escaping. Eager to vent his rage and grief, he launched himself at them.

The cavern echoed with the sounds of the men's grunts and the scraping of sabers. Stefano fought a battle of offense, instinct and anger guiding his sword. Disarming an opponent, Stefano drove his blade through the other's poorly positioned wrist. He wheeled around in response to the sword thrust which nicked his arm. In the far reaches of his mind, he knew the wound was not so slight as it seemed just now, but he did not care.

Yet another braggadocio ran into the cavern from the Stretto. "The brown bastarde come! Retreat while you can!" he shouted and chased after the cardinal and other men.

Stefano kept his eyes on the two men pinned against the wall, waiting for either to move first. The wounded and disarmed man panicked. In the process of diving for the exit, he neatly skewered himself on Stefano's sword. As Stephano struggled to free his weapon, the other man made good his escape.

Ripping his sword free, Stefano rounded at the sound of running feet. Covered in blood—not all his own—he turned to face the next onslaught. There could be no way for him to win, but he intended to take as many of the cardinal's bravos with him as he could.

The man in the cavern mouth raised his hands and called, "Peace, *pral!*"

The Romani word acted like a bath of ice water. Stefano lowered his sword. The man—the men—arriving from the Stretto were not the cardinal's. By dress and complexion he recognized them as Rom, his conclusion made all the more certain when Luciana's grandmother pushed her way through the men and into the cavern.

"Ja mander!" the old woman commanded, pointing at the corridor through which all the other men had gone. Her gaze, however, fell to Luciana at Stefano's feet. In a moment, the old woman seemed to age another lifetime. Stefano watched, sick at heart, as his wife's grandmother dropped to her knees and touched Luciana's face.

"I'll kill the man who did this," Stefano swore and turned to leave.

"Stay!"

Stefano stopped. The *Beluni's* expression lightened.

"She was killed by a spell, was she not?" the Romani woman asked.

"I—" he paused. He knew nothing of magic, had always sought to know as little about it as possible.

"Aye, that's what did it. What *benglo* uses such spells?" the old woman asked, cradling Luciana onto her lap.

"The cardinal."

The *Beluni* looked up, her brows disappearing into her hairline. "You mean one of his men, of course."

"No, the cardinal did this," Stefano said. He sheathed his sword and knelt beside his wife. Di Montago had a good number of Rom on his heels in better shape to assist the capitano than himself. He stroked Luciana's still warm cheek. "I cannot believe I've lost her."

"She is not lost . . . not yet," the *Beluni* said softly.

"Not yet?"

The old woman shook her head. She pulled on a satin cord around Luciana's neck, drawing a small pouch from the neckline of her granddaughter's gown. She crouched lower and sniffed. She smiled crookedly. " 'Tis just as well we arrived when we did. Had she grown cold . . ." The *Beluni* shook her head again. "What are you willing to do to get my *chuvi* back?" Her eyes gleamed like daggers.

"What would you have me do?" Stefano asked, trying to hide his reluctance.

He saw the disappointment in the *Beluni's* expression. "There is nothing, then—"

"I'll do what it takes," Stefano said firmly. He took Luciana's hand, the one which so recently stroked his face, and pressed it to his lips. "What do I do?"

The *Beluni's* gaze turned speculative. At last, she nodded. "My granddaughter was *chovahani*. She prepared." As she spoke, the old woman opened the sachet at Luciana's neck and spilled the contents over Luciana's chest. Her dark fingers crumbled the herbs. "Her magic and these helped her . . . still help her."

Stefano watched as the old woman tugged a small horn, carved and gilded, from around her own neck. She unstopped the horn and poured a greenish-gray dust atop the herbs. With a single finger, the *Beluni* began to stir the powders on Luciana's chest and sing. Limited by his inadequate understanding of his wife's language, he waited.

Just when he thought the old woman had forgotten him, she grabbed his hand with a viselike grip and pressed it, palm down, on Luciana's chest. "Will it!" the old woman commanded. "Will it with the might of your love, and *you* can bring her back!"

For the briefest of moments, the *Beluni's* order made

no sense . . . and then, as easily as taking a breath, he understood. Leaving his left hand pressed to Luciana's chest, he cradled her. He thought about the lost years, their separation, their stillborn son, how he loved her from the moment he saw her at court, how she had turned her head just so and the sun flowed over her as she laughed at something his sister said. He thought of their courtship, his passions inspired by any accidental touch, of finally being able to take her into his arms and loving her as he'd craved for so long. He remembered again those cold long years in Peloponnesus and the redwood box which contained his love letters, all unsent, all unread by their intended recipient for so long. If, through some miracle, Luciana lived, he vowed she would fully know the love contained in those letters, *his* love for her . . . even if she scorned him.

With an overpowering scent of lavender and sage filling the air, Luciana breathed a sigh and opened her eyes. She reached up, as she had not so very long before, and stroked Stefano's cheek "My love," she said, then her hand fell away and she went slack in his arms again.

"No!" Stefano cried and shook her. "No, not now, not after—"

"She sleeps, *chavo*. You will not wake her," the *Beluni* said.

"Sleeps? But—"

The old woman shrugged. "Her soul has done battle with death. Were her love for you not as great as yours for her, she could not have overcome it. The battle is done. She is . . . wounded and must rest. You understand?"

Stefano breathed a sigh of relief and pulled Luciana's still form against him once more, but before anything else could be said a deafening boom shuddered through the caverns. Rocks fell. Somewhere men screamed.

A lemon-scented wind buffeted Stefano as he carried Luciana across the courtyard in front of the palazzo. Di Montago bowed and opened the small door to the *vardo* for him. Stefano took her inside and gently laid her upon the tiny bed. She helped him fold the coverlets up over her and did not protest his fussing as she wedged herself into a sitting position.

"You will be well?" Idala asked from the foot of the *vardo* steps. Alban stood behind his wife and appeared to be waiting just as expectantly.

"She'll live," the *Beluni* said gruffly. She waved Kisaiya up onto the driver's seat. "She needs her rest is all."

"But you'll come back soon?" Idala asked.

Alban laid a hand upon his wife's shoulder. "It is for the best that she leaves now. Her excuse of health is a valid one and less can be made of it than any other reason for a sudden departure after the fiasco of Bianca's wedding. Be glad that we can get her away before questions directed at her become too pointed."

One of the *Beluni's* brows rose. She looked up into the *vardo* at Stefano. He saw the reappraisal in her eyes, perhaps he, too, was learning a little of what Luciana called the *dukker*.

"It will be some time . . . perhaps a couple of years before we return to court," Stefano said. He leaned out of the wagon and kissed his sister's cheek.

"All the better to let gossip and suspicions subside," Alban agreed.

"You'll not pursue this further, then?" Luciana asked from the depths of the *vardo*.

The *gadjé* king looked thunderous. "Of course I will continue to pursue the death of a member of the Royal House. There are councils and a new widower to be satisfied." He smiled grimly. "And if I have my way, the blame will be laid upon the head of the true culprit in this game of intrigue."

"The cardinal," di Montago said through gritted teeth.

"There is still no sign of him?" Stefano asked. Knowing how close his own Luciana had come to Alessandra's continued state filled him with rage.

Sunlight only emphasized the deep purple bruises and cuts left on the newly promoted *maggiore's* face by the explosion in the caverns as di Montago shook his head.

"And the prisoner we took is more afraid of what the cardinal will do to him than anything I can threaten him with."

"I would have killed him," Luciana said. Stefano turned and took her hand.

The maggiore nodded. "It took considerable restraint, but if I have any hope of finding Alessandra's body, I need the *bastarde* alive."

One of the Rom from the other *vardos* came jogging back to them. "*Beluni-Daiya,* the boy, Inago, is ready to travel."

"You're taking him with you then?" di Montago asked, rolling his shoulder beneath his uniform glistening with the medals of his new rank.

"He's learned all he will in this *gadjé* place," the *Beluni* said fiercely. "His face and hands will heal proper."

"He could stay here. I could have my very own physician—" Idala began, but faltered under the eagle-eyed glare of the Romani Queen.

Stefano struggled to think of something to say to ease the tension, but Luciana's grandmother surprised him. Her expression softened.

"He's best looked after by his own. No one knows what them *gadjé* physicians will try to do to him," the *Beluni* said. " 'Sides, we can best protect him from any further attacks by that *benglo* priest. We've already lost a cousin's son, I'll not lose another of the *vitsi.*"

"There was nothing to be done for Nicobar, then?" Alban asked.

"Were there anything, have no doubt it would be done," di Montago said. He looked into the *vardo,* past Stefano. "Nicobar died bravely, *Araunya-Daiya,* as he would have wanted. *His* soul has gone on."

No one misunderstood the maggiore's implication. Alessandra's body remained in the possession of a demon-incarnate. The longer she was kept from going on to that other place, the stronger the pull darkness would have over her soul. But everyone also knew that neither the Rom nor di Montago would rest until Alessa had been truly freed, and Cardinal delle Torre had suffered the fate he deserved.

Irene Radford

"A mesmerizing storyteller." —*Romantic Times*

THE DRAGON NIMBUS
THE GLASS DRAGON
0-88677-634-1
THE PERFECT PRINCESS
0-88677-678-3
THE LONELIEST MAGICIAN
0-88677-709-7
THE WIZARD'S TREASURE
0-88677-913-8

THE DRAGON NIMBUS HISTORY
THE DRAGON'S TOUCHSTONE
0-88677-744-5
THE LAST BATTLEMAGE
0-88677-774-7
THE RENEGADE DRAGON
0-88677-855-7

THE STAR GODS
THE HIDDEN DRAGON
0-7564-0051-1

To Order Call: 1-800-788-6262

Kristen Britain

GREEN RIDER

"The gifted Ms. Britain writes with ease and grace as she creates a mesmerizing fantasy ambiance and an appealing heroine quite free of normal clichés."
—*Romantic Times*

Karigan G'ladheon has fled from school following a fight that would surely lead to her expulsion. As she makes her way through the deep forest, a galloping horse plunges out of the brush, its rider impaled by two black arrows. With his dying breath, he tells her he is a Green Rider, one of the legendary messengers of the King. Giving her his green coat with its symbolic brooch of office, he makes Karigan swear to deliver the message he was carrying. Pursued by unknown assassins, following a path only the horse seems to know, she unwittingly finds herself in a world of deadly danger and complex magic, compelled by forces she does not yet understand....

0-88677-858-1

To Order Call: 1-800-788-6262

DAW 7

John Marco

The Eyes of God

"THE EYES OF GOD isn't just about warfare, magic, and monsters, although it's got all of those: it's about the terrible burden of making choices, and the way the seeds of victory are in every failure, and tragedy's beginnings are in every triumph."
—Tad Williams

Akeela, the king of Liiria, determined to bring peace to his kingdom, and Lukien, the Bronze Knight of Liiria, peerless with a sword, and who had earned his reputation the hard way, loved each other as brothers, but no two souls could be more different. And both were in love with the beautiful Queen Cassandra. But unknown to anyone, Cassandra hid a terrible secret: a disease that threatened her life and caused unimaginable strife for all who loved her. For Akeela and Lukien, the quest for Cassandra's salvation would overwhelm every bond of loyalty, every point of honor, because only the magical amulets known as the Eyes of God could halt the progress of Cassandra's illness. But the Eyes could also open the way to a magical stronghold that will tear their world apart and redefine the very nature of their reality.

0-7564-0096-1

To Order Call: 1-800-788-6262

DAW 27